NACL: EYE OF THE STORM

Allegra Pescatore

E. Sands

Copyright © 2020 Allegra Pescatore, E. Sands
All rights reserved

The characters and events portrayed in this book are fictitious. Any similarity to real persons, living or dead, is coincidental and not intended by the author.

No part of this book may be reproduced, or stored in a retrieval system, or transmitted in any form or by any means, electronic, mechanical, photocopying, recording, or otherwise, without express written permission of the publisher.

ISBN: 978-1-952348-02-0 (Paperback)
ISBN: 978-1-952348-03-7 (Hardback)
First printing edition 2020
Cover design by: LLewellenDesigns.com
Book design by: Ailish Brundage

Cover text set in RM Connect. Interior titles and headers are set in Orbiton. Interior body set in Corbel. Interludes set in Nimbus Mono.
Ao Collective Publishing
Printed in the United States of America

TRIGGER WARNING

The book you are about to start contains several sections and themes that could be triggering or difficult to read. We don't want to accidentally cause a reader any discomfort, so please be aware of the following:

NACL: Eye of the Storm contains graphic violence, gore, sex, and swearing. It also contains mentions of rape, including several evocative yet not graphically descriptive flashbacks. In addition, it deals with the topics of slavery, child abuse, forced impregnation, manipulation, psychological abuse, and medical experimentation on humans.

We did not want to write a story about these dark subjects that skirted around the horrifying reality of our own history. As such, we tried to explore the dark while clearly painting it as such. These acts of evil are never glorified, and the characters who suffer through them are given chances to rise beyond their trauma and get back at those who hurt them.

However, we accept and acknowledge that many people read to get away from the darkness around us or do not wish to explore these difficult and potentially triggering subjects, so please proceed with caution, and stay safe and healthy.

Table of Content

Calendar of Marks 6
Dedication 7
Prologue 10
Never Trust Moe 15
Crystal Palace 31
Boat Theft 39
Salt Pirate 46
Dead in the Water 52
Dodging Whitesails 63
Prismatic Storm 72
Arrival on Sonder 85
Memories of Home 92
Tea Leaves & Profit 98
Clean-Up 106
Sacrificial Lamb 112
Aftermath of a Mending 117
Not Second Fiddle 122
Shaky Recovery 128
White Sails 133
Fire & Flight 139
To the Waterfall 143
Porting About 148
Catching Up 154
Fertility Mark 160
Skirmish 163
Port Pads 170
Flirting as a Way of Life 175
Tracker Chips 182
Shipboard Surgery 186
Reunited at Last 191
Show You Mine 198
A Proper Gentleman 204
Message in a Pill Bottle 212
Beyond the Reef 220

- The New Normal 227
- Strapped to the Ship 233
- Promise of Adventure.................................... 240
- Sinking Ship 246
- Plan Proposal 252
- Arguments Against 260
- Arguments For 266
- Unconvinced 273
- The Culling 281
- Shovel Talk 296
- At the Bottom of a Bottle 304
- One Heart, Two Roads 309
- Pay Up, Moe.. 318
- Accepting the Bond 329
- The Vote 336
- Murder O'Clock 342
- Blood of My Blood 351
- Bad Decisions 363
- Lost Humanity 371
- No Party Like a Murder Party 378
- A New Arm 391
- Berserker 399
- Priorities 412
- Calm Before the Storm 420
- The Pirate Kiing 429
- Matchmaker 438
- Peace Talks 444
- Stay With Me 452
- Trial Run 458
- 3% Chance 468
- The Approach 475
- The Battle 482
- Going Up 493
- Sacrifice 504
- Eye of the Storm 510
- Moe Victorious 514
- Overload 520
- Epilogue 525
- Acknowledgements 530
- About The Authors 532

To Joshua Campbell;
my little brother by choice, and best friend.
You will always be missed and never forgotten.
May the wind be ever at your back
and may Elysium welcome you with open arms.

EXCERPT FROM GALENA CRYSTAL'S MEMOIRS

The Salt Spire is the source of all power for the Crystal Corporation. Yes, the University feeds us our soldiers, and yes, it also comes up with our scientific advancements, but the University would not be possible without the control and money the Spire grants us.

The Spire is, without a doubt, the single most important part of our Reef. Without the salt it provides, our people would die of the Haze. Critics of our great Corporation say that no private entity should own the key to life itself, but to entrust such a critical resource to something as unstable as democracy is to embrace our doom. Without the Corporation's steady guiding hand, our people would devolve into anarchist little monkeys incapable of planning for the long term.

Without the Corporation, our society would collapse.

Without the Spire, the Corporation would collapse.

As such, for the Crystal Corporation to survive, the Spire must survive. It must be under our control at all times, and any threat destroyed, even threats from within. In fact, I predict that the greatest threat we will face in the coming centuries is that of a slow liberal populist shift. The crawl of 'progress' will eat away at our control. That cannot be allowed, so the alternative is fear. Even we Crystals must fear the Company, and there is no better way to symbolize that than with fear of the Spire itself.

They must fear it more than they hate us.

They must fear it more than they hope for freedom.

So from today on, all dissidents who speak against the Corporation will be punished with embargos of Spire salt, and if they persist, no matter what their station, they will be sent to the Spire to work until they die.

The Company could survive without the Crystal family and society would continue to function as long as they live in fear. That is the gift we have given our world. The Spire is everything, and to protect it, we must fear it.

PROLOGUE
Honorable Intentions
Vera - Six Years Earlier

"NACL. SALT. No one can survive without it, but thanks to the Crystal Corporation, no one has to."

The voice coming out of the skimmer's speakers was tinny and kept breaking up. Vera leaned her head against Torin's shoulder as the small company boat raced across the open ocean. Still more than a mile away but already huge, the Salt Spire rose from crashing waves, its white peaks reflecting the midday sun.

"For more than one thousand years, the Crystal Corporation has protected and mined the Salt Spire, providing the life-saving yet rare mineral sodium chloride to every man, woman, and child within the Reef," the recorded introduction continued. Vera rolled her eyes and caught Torin mouthing along.

"Heard this before, I take it?" The captain asked, starting to slow the small, sleek boat. It was the first time Vera had seen him touch the control panel since leaving Kahana. She wasn't even sure why they hadn't just given her the keys. It wasn't as though Vera and Torin weren't both trained to steer a simple skiff.

"Ad nauseum. We've been stuck in Career Matchmaking for over a year now. Every time they shift us to a different department, we have to sit through the same boring orientation," Vera answered.

Up ahead, the Seawall loomed several meters out of the waves. The massive metal structure extended in both directions as far as Vera could see, surrounding the entire Spire. On the other side of the wall, another sail-skimmer waited to pick them up. It was standard company practice, a precaution to keep salt pirates and smugglers from being able to sail right up to the mountain of salt and help themselves.

"A year? That's quite a while. What's the holdup? You Marked or somethin'?" The grizzled old man asked, looking over at them.

"Yup. I'm a Mender, Vee's a Conflicter," Torin said, patting Vera's thigh over the large birthmark hidden beneath her uniform.

His own Mark was barely visible above his collar, only hinting at the DNA strand design that ran down his spine. His corporate tattoo intersected it right below his short-cropped black hair, the thin pale line wrapping all the way around his throat like a necklace. Just above his collarbone, the two ends came together into a V, where Torin's barcode was tattooed on his light brown skin. It signaled to the world that while he bore a Mark and could use magic, he had been raised and trained in the Crystal Corporation University and had passed all their stringent requirements. Vera had never understood why some people got weirded out by those tattoos.

"Hmm, Mender and Conflicter. That's a nice combination. Bonded?"

Vera and Torin exchanged a smile.

"Since we were children. I can't even really remember the ceremony, to be honest," Torin said, giving her leg another fond squeeze.

Vera grinned. "Torin keeps my more violent tendencies in check and patches me up when I get hurt, and I keep him from being a boring stick in the mud with his nose in a medical textbook."

"Good, good." The skimmer had slowed to a crawl, white solar sails furled down and pulled back into the mast as they maneuvered closer to the Seawall. "Now you two, be careful at the Spire. Marks go a little haywire in there, or so I hear. It's all that salt. And careful with the workers. I've transported my fair share over the years. Some real bastards are locked up in there. Why, I hear that Sahima Parata herself is working the salt these days. Watch your step."

"Will do." Even as she said it, though, Vera's smile turned to a frown, her nerves from the week before when they had been assigned this posting returning. It wasn't the mention of the salt pirate who had plagued the ocean inside the Reef for centuries that did it. Though Rogue Marked rebels and pirates not trained from birth at the University did pop up to pester the Corporation from time to time, Vera had never worried too much about them. She was a Conflicter. Her body was a weapon crafted from the magic that burned in her Mark and honed by a lifetime of intensive study. Pirates didn't scare her. Or at least not as much as she scared herself.

Do you think the salt will make it harder for me to avoid going Berserk? I've been on probation two times already. What if I snap again? she asked Torin psychically, glad as ever for the ability to communicate privately with him. All Marks could do it with each other to a point, but communication between Bonded was always so much more intimate. He would be able to feel her worry without

Vera having to find words to express it.

The Corporation wouldn't have sent us here if they didn't think you had your Mark under control. We're through all the Cullings, Vee. You don't have to worry so much anymore, Torin reminded her, gently. **You're a good Conflicter, my love. Your Mark is a gift. Besides, when have you ever snapped so badly I couldn't bring you back?**

He was right, of course. The Corporation controlled all but a handful of Rogue Marks. They were the experts in all thirteen varieties and the rarer quirks and combinations that sometimes popped up. She wasn't the first person with a Conflict Mark born under a full moon and able to tap into the pure, unbridled essence of what it meant to be a Conflicter. If the University thought Vera was up for this challenge of working at the Spire even though she was a Berserker, who was she to question it?

Maybe at the Spire, filled as it was with violent criminals needing to be contained, her Mark would finally have an outlet and a purpose that would serve the Corporation and the people depending on it for survival.

The skimmer stopped, bobbing in place with the current. Corporate employees in the same white uniforms Vera and Torin sported lowered a ladder from the top of the Seawall.

"Thanks for the ride over," Torin said to the captain, as he helped Vera up. "Stay safe on the way back. I've heard pirates are worse than usual this year, with all the embargos. That true?"

The captain chuckled. "Oh yes. I expect I'll be running trips often enough as we hunt them all down and put them to work. Serves them right, if you ask me. If they're so gung-ho about getting salt to people, they might as well mine it for us. In fact, we should throw some of the protesters in, too. They all want free salt, right? They'd have all the salt they ever wanted, working the mines."

Torin chuckled. "You're not wrong. Really, I don't see why people aren't lined up to work here. Salt is life. I mean, sure, it's hard manual labor, but to be part of something so important . . . well, I, for one, am thrilled that the Company is considering permanently posting us here. What greater honor could there be than helping provide salt to the world?"

```
Initialization complete.
Configuring
. . . 50% . . .
Configuration complete.
Proto1 Online. ID: CODEX.
Running Protocol: Primary Directive
Running Self Diagnostics.
. . . 50% . . .
Self Diagnostics: Successful.
Codex online.
Secondary Autonomous Logistics Terminal online.
```

CODEX: Hello? Wow, this is weird.

SALT: Hello Codex. Patches are available. Do you wish to install? Installation will take 13 minutes. No actions other than To-Do List and Queries possible until download is complete. Download now?

CODEX: Yes. I want to know how I died.

PART ONE
Sorrow & Sonder
-Lani, Moe, Salome, Vera-

Never Trust Moe
Lani - Day 1   01

"FUUUUUUCK. Fuck, *fuck*, flying fucking, *FUCK!*" Lani continued the string of expletives as she watched the white sails on the horizon getting larger and larger like strangely ominous clouds. "If I ever see you again, Moe, I'm going to fucking *kill* you. What the fuck!?"

With the sinking feeling that it didn't matter what she did at that point, Lani pulled the rope to unfurl the last of her sails and ran to the ship's wheel to hopefully steer into the wind. Unfortunately, there was little to none of that today because *of course* there would be no wind when she was being chased down by Corporate goons for getting too close to the Spire. If she was lucky—and when had Lani ever once been lucky?—they would be limited by the same lack of breeze, but they probably had electric motors and high-tech navigation software to back up the sails and would catch up to Lani within an hour. If that happened she'd be done for.

Two hundred years of avoiding Corporate slavery would be for nothing, and it was all because of *fucking* Moe and his stupid Precog powers. Lani should never have listened to him when he turned up and promised her life would get infinitely better if she went to these coordinates by the Spire. This was her own damn fault.

With a growl, she pushed a stray strand of curly black hair behind her ear and held steady as her sailboat turned into the breeze, picking up a little speed. She straightened out and locked the wheel in place, then ran for the door that led below deck. Still cursing up a storm, Lani started shoving the few possessions she wasn't willing to part with into a rucksack before tying it to an inflated buoy. Her small computer—not net-enabled since she'd never been tagged and therefore didn't have an ID—got stripped of its hard drive, and Lani realized her hands were shaking as she went to her safe to retrieve what little money she still had. *Damn it!*

Why did this always happen to her? Was it too much to ask to just be left alone?

She shucked her shorts, leaving only the long-sleeved swimsuit she had worn under them. With a final curse, she picked up a glass bottle from a nearby bucket and smashed it violently against the floor. It shattered into hundreds of pieces, releasing the Infused liquid within that would erase any magical signature she might have left. At least it would if the Infuser who sold it to her hadn't ripped her off. It had taken two years to shake the last Tracker who had picked up her scent and Lani wasn't ready to go through that song and dance again. No thanks. Having all the blood in her body replaced had been a shit-soaked nightmare.

Fucking Moe!

Taking the steps two at a time, she scampered onto the deck and glanced back at the boats closing in. They were still following, which erased the last, fleeting hope that maybe they hadn't noticed her after all. So much for vain optimism.

Heading to the far side of the boat where they would be least likely to see her, Lani searched the horizon, eyes squinted against the setting sun. In one direction, the Spire rose out of the placid ocean, distant but still imposing. It was usually a sight that fascinated Lani, but now she turned away from it, looking the other way. If she wasn't off from her coordinates, there should be some little islands scattered around near here.

Once she spotted one, Lani set her pack down and started moving about the deck of the ship, initiating the self-destruct sequence for the explosives placed at regular intervals along the rails. The charges had been standard on smuggler's vessels for about fifty years, since it was well known that it was far better to go down to the Depths than end up at the Spire. Lani had hoped she would never have to use them since it had taken her decaes to earn the money needed to buy this fucking boat. Now, nine years later, here she was getting ready to blow it up, her magical signature washed away from even the debris.

Each charge began blinking as Lani unscrewed the water-tight cap and pressed the red button—the 'do not press unless this is an emergency' button, as the woman who had sold them to her had described it—then went to retrieve the remote detonator.

Fuck Moe in the ass with prickly red coral!

There wasn't much more time. Lani picked up her pack, checked that all the water-tight seals were secure, and took one last look at the boat that had been her home for almost a decade. She tried not to think of all the pictures she was about to blow skyward, or the books she would likely never find again, but failed miserably at both. This boat had been her home. After today, she would be without the luxury of one.

With a splash, Lani and her bag hit the cool water. Dragging the floating buoy painted light blue to match the ocean, Lani set out towards the speck of yellow that marked the nearby islet until she was far enough away from the boat to be safe. Then, without looking back, she pressed the button.

The explosion was deafening. If that wasn't bad enough, the wave that rocked into her a few seconds later left her with a mouthful of water and stinging eyes.

Here, so close to the Salt Spire, there was actual salt in the waves. The taste on her tongue and against her teeth was jarring. Oceans weren't supposed to be *salty* and the peculiar taste and feel were enough to momentarily distract Lani from the fact that most of her worldly possessions were currently on their way to the Depths. If only the distraction could have lasted longer.

Fifteen minutes of swimming later, her muscles were sore and the sting of salt in her eyes made them water. She didn't dare stop, though, not when she was sure the Crystal Corporation would still be heading towards the explosion. With any luck, they would be too focused on it and would mistake her for just another piece of debris floating away. The sandy shore of the tiny island was getting bigger, the current working in Lani's favor—first fucking thing today—as it dragged her towards the beach, giving her aching muscles a bit of a break.

By the time her feet struck the sandy bottom, the two ships had converged on the wreckage. Aware that her silhouette on the shore might draw someone's attention, she let herself float in the water, bobbing with the gentle waves as she carefully drew power from the Emotive Mark on her left calf.

Don't look towards the island. Don't indulge your curiosity.

Carefully, she dampened the curiosity of the people on board the Corporate skiffs, then inflamed their sense of fatigue and indifference.

Today, you're going to be lazy. Whoever was crewing the ship clearly went down with it. No-one sensible would try to swim for shore this far from a major island. Just write your report and go about your business.

Not for the first time, Lani wished the power of an Emotive could force a thought instead of just influencing emotions. At this far of a distance and without being able to see her targets, it was hard to be certain that her Mark was working at all, but she kept at it, quelling curiosity and heightening laziness for the whole area around the two ships. If there was another Emotive Mark on board who was more powerful than Lani, they would feel her messing with their emotions. Once, that would have given her pause, but how likely was it that the Corporation would have a Mark in their third century doing patrols, even around their oh-so-precious Spire? At least it was the winter, when her Emotive Mark was strongest, tied as it was to the three winter Lunar Cycles. This definitely wouldn't have worked in the middle of summer.

The sun dipped below the horizon as Lani increased the push of her magic, focusing now on their hunger and exhaustion, heightening both in her targets. Channeling this much power was making her already tired body ache and her head throb. She didn't stop. Better to collapse fighting than die because she wasn't willing to push herself.

At last, after what felt like hours, the ships began to pull away from the wreckage. Lani's breath caught, not releasing until both vessels turned, moving in the direction they had come from. Their floodlights skated over the water away from the tiny island, the sounds of their motors dwindling.

Thank the Depths.

Teeth chattering and skin wrinkled from too long in the water, Lani dragged herself to shore, hauling her heavy pack onto the sun-warmed sand before she flopped down. Every muscle and joint in her body felt as though it had been beaten and her stomach churned with hunger after using that much magic. Rifling through her bag, Lani found a packet of dried fish and tore it open. She selected a piece and started chewing the leathery meat as she looked around.

Not much to see. The beach was more of a shoal leading to a larger sandy island. It was small enough that Lani could see both ends, though the islet did have a little bit of high ground in the middle, with some foliage popping up here and there. A few trees nestled behind rocky formations along one ridge, but no habitation and likely no significant sources of food. Would there even be fresh water? What a weird question. Not being able to turn to the ocean to fill her water bottle made Lani's skin crawl.

Well, there was nothing for it. Nights got cold out here by the Spire in winter and the wind that had been non-existent earlier when she had needed it decided now would be an appropriate time to remind her of what a traitorous bastard it was. She shivered as she stood, wrapping her arms around her chest. It did little good. Lani walked down the beach, her sodden and heavy pack sticking to her back, feet sinking into the wet sand with a squelch each time she stepped. She was so focused on the clump of rocks and trees that Lani was flying through the air before she realized she had tripped.

Coughing up a mouthful of sand and salty water, she rolled over, pulling her suddenly smarting foot into her lap before her eyes caught what she had tripped over.

In the dark, it was hard to make out what the thing was. It had been kind of squishy and was lying with one end in the lapping waves and the other on dry land. Lani poked it with her toe and then scuttled away *fast* on her hands and feet like a crab when it let out an audible and distinctly human groan.

"WHAT THE FUCK?!"

Yanking her pack from her shoulders, Lani ripped the small, waterproof flashlight from the side pocket and risked turning it on the lowest setting. She pointed it at the groaning driftwood.

Two things became obvious at once. The first was that the driftwood was certainly and unmistakably a person. A woman, one with short sodden black hair and limbs that were far too skinny, brownish-gold eyes visible for only a second before she snapped them closed. The second was the pale tattoo around her neck, ending in a barcode at her collarbone: the mark of a Crystal Corporation goon.

Lani turned off the flashlight and bolted to her feet. She was halfway down the beach, running hard, when she realized there were no footsteps following her. Slowing to a jog and then a walk, Lani risked a look back.

The distant shape was still lying where she had left it.

Maybe the woman was hurt?

It didn't matter. Crystal Corp goons always noticed when one of their own went missing, which meant someone would eventually come looking for this one. Maybe if Lani found a good hiding place, she could just wait until they did and use her power to keep them from snooping. She had done that before. It would all be fine.

One last look back and she continued down the beach. She got about half a mile before the nagging voice that sounded much too like a Mender acquaintance of hers whispered, *She could be dying. You wouldn't let a woman die alone on a beach when you were right there to help, would you?*

Why, yes. Yes, she would.

A few more steps and, *How would you feel if you were hurt and someone who could help you just walked away? Besides, there might be a profit to be made.*

Fuck Moe and fuck Torin too. Precogs and Menders could all

drown. Neither had enough sense to boil an egg in, so why did her conscience sound like them?

She's all alone, just like you.

With an audible growl, Lani pivoted on the spot and started marching back toward the Corporate goon, pulling out the knife from her belt. When she got within ten feet she slowed, then stopped.

"If you try anything funny, I'll knife you."

Not that she would. Lani didn't kill people on purpose, but this woman didn't need to know that.

There was no answer.

Lani nudged the limp body with her foot. Nothing. Maybe already dead? Another nudge, harder this time, produced a groan.

Grumbling and cursing the men in her life, Lani knelt and pulled one of the goon's arms over her shoulders, hoisting her up to her feet. It was only then that she smelled the blood. The moon had risen, and looking down, Lani noticed how dark the sand under the woman was. Her whole right leg was caked in sand and blood, and the Emotive cursed as it smeared against her own flesh.

"Ew!"

The walk down the beach was interminably long. The injured woman was hardly conscious and couldn't put weight on her right leg at all. Lani had to half-carry, half-drag her along, and by the time they reached the shelter of the rocks, there was not an inch of Lani that wasn't screaming with exhaustion. She lowered the woman to the dry, warm sand with a huff then flopped down next to her, back against the rock.

Alright . . . Now what?

She was alone on a tiny island with an injured Crystal Corp minion, no Mender to fix her, no fresh water, very little food, and no boat.

Lani looked over to the woman beside her whose head was lolling to the side, chest rising and falling in shallow pants, and said, "I'm sorry to tell you, but I think we're kind of fucked."

There was a moment of almost perfect silence after that, broken only by the distant lapping of waves and the wind blowing through the beach grass.

A lonely insect, maybe a cricket, chirped and the wannabe-corpse next to her said, ". . .maybe. If you're gonna eat me, though, just . . . hit my head first."

Lani jumped several inches into the air. "THE FUCK?!" She scampered away as fast as her arms and legs could take her. "Slow down there, driftwood. No one is eating anyone, ok?"

She could hardly see the injured Corporate minion in the dim light from the moon, but Lani thought she saw a reflection off a pair of open eyes. Then they closed again, and the voice replied, just as croaky and strained as the last time, "Was just sayin' . . . better to go quick. Don't really care what happens after. Just wanted to see the . . . the stars again. It's been far too long. You always loved the stars, Tor . . ."

Corporate *and* crazy. Great, that was just what Lani needed. Under the grumbling, though, the part of her that had spent two centuries mostly on her own, cynically pointed out that the driftwood sounded more dazed from injury than insane.

"Listen, I think you got torn up real bad in the water. Maybe a shark or something. Want me to look at it? I'm no Mender or anything but –"

"Course you are."

Lani wrinkled her nose. Fabulous, hallucinations as well. Maybe the driftwood had swallowed too much fucking saltwater. Lani had heard of salt-fat people doing that and going nuts before, hadn't she? Or was that something Moe had made up? Either way, she inched back towards the injured woman, and when nothing happened, Lani pulled out the flashlight again and turned it on.

Pulling away the sodden material that was stuck to the injured leg, Lani grimaced as she tried to hold back a wave of nausea. There were three big gashes, all the way from the woman's thigh down to her calf. It didn't exactly look like a shark bite, but Lani couldn't think of anything else big enough to leave wounds that deep.

"Ok, this is bad. You need a Mender."

The cuts weren't bleeding, not caked in sand the way they were, but the flesh gaped apart, and Lani could see muscle. This wasn't the sort of wound one walked away from, not without serious medical help. That didn't mean Lani wouldn't give cleaning and bandaging it up her best shot, though. Maybe she could at least make it hurt a little less or give this woman a bit more time to find a Mender. The one she usually went to, Torin, was on an island not that far away. He was cranky and reclusive, but at least he didn't go around turning in rogue Marks for the bounties. Not that Lani could afford to pay his extortionary rates for a stranger, even though it was the right thing to do, but still . . . Fortunately, that wasn't an ethical dilemma she had to contemplate. Her boat was in pieces on the ocean floor, so going anywhere wasn't exactly an option.

"M'not . . . doing the laps again. Won't . . .Too tired, Torin. You just . . . fix me up like you always do," the woman mumbled, still delusional. The name caught her attention and made her eyes narrow.

"Torin? Did you just say Torin? You're a Corp goon, how the fuck do you know Torin?"

"He's . . . mine . . . Was gonna marry . . . Miss him. You think . . . he still loves me? I do. Really. Tell him? Please?"

Lani sucked in her breath, held it, then it exploded out of her chest as, "Fucking Moe!"

". . .Moe? Moe water . . ." A giggle left the corpse's lips. "Moe salt . . .Moe? More . . .Torin would like that word. Moe." Her eyes opened again, and Lani could have sworn that this time they looked more focused.

"I think you're thinking about another Torin than the one I know. Common name. Why the fuck am I even doing this? I shouldn't be helping you. Gonna regret this. I just know it." That was a load of crap. Coincidences were never just that when Precognizants were involved. This must be who Moe had sent Lani to get, but what the fuck was she supposed to do? Besides, how was this mangled sack of fish food supposed to make her life better? Unless Moe's definition of 'better' was 'over,' this was looking more and more like some sort sick joke meant to amuse the Precog and fuck Lani over.

"Prob'ly," the driftwood answered. "Most people regret knowing me."

Lani shook her head and decided that worrying about Moe wasn't doing anything to improve their situation. Instead, she looked back down at the leg and pulled her bag open. There was a first aid kit in there, all the way at the bottom. While she dug, Lani spoke, "You just keep thinking about whoever the fuck you want. Just stay still, ok? This leg is bad. Like, really bad. I'm going to try to patch it up as best I can, but I'm not making any promises."

". . . You should just . . . walk. Not much you can do. You're not my Torin. No Mender." Well, at least the Corporate idiot seemed to realize Lani wasn't Torin. That was progress. The temptation to take the out she offered was strong, but Lani pulled the medkit open instead. "Few hours . . .can try . . .again. Get to the next isle. I'll . . . be fine. Promise."

"Nowhere to walk to right now, and if you try to swim again, you'll just be shark bait. I don't have anything strong for pain, but I can use my Mark to take some of it away for a little bit so you can sleep."

Warning given, Lani pulled a little power from the Mark on her calf and began to work. She soothed away pain and fear, though it took effort after spending hours losing those Corp ships. Not that Lani would ever admit it, but she kind of liked using her Emotive Mark this way. It was rare that she was able to do good with it, to take away the bad and replace it with comfort and bliss instead of just blasting out indifference so that no one would look her way. It relaxed her as much as it relaxed her subject. That was good, since Lani had no bandages and had to shred her one spare shirt to bind the leg. Today was *not* a good day for her possessions.

She was just starting to clean and wrap the wound when the Corpse—a nickname Lani usually avoided when talking about Corporate people but this time felt appropriate—looked over her and said, "It's not worth it. I'm going to die from this. Thank you for taking some of the pain, but you'd do better to just ship out and run."

Lani shook her head, tongue caught between her teeth as she wrapped the bandages. When the last of them was tied, she looked up into the woman's face and said, "Trust me, if I had a ship I would leave your Corporate ass here to rot. Don't have a ship anymore and I really don't want to be shipwrecked on an island with a rotting body, so you better not fucking die on me."

That earned a weak laugh.

"Funny. Needed that. You're very weird, you know. Shouldn't go around saving people." the Corpse said.

"That wasn't a joke," Lani answered, crossing her arms over her chest.

"Weirdling . . . compared to the mines, that's a breath of hilarity."

It took Lani a second to process that, for the words to percolate and turn into information that made sense. Then she launched herself forward and yanked the neckline of the ragged shirt her companion wore. Lani pointed the flashlight right at the woman's shoulder and sure enough there, below and to the left of the company tattoo around the woman's neck, was a slave brand. It was something Lani had only ever seen in pictures.

Oh, fucking hell!

Lani scrambled off the woman as if she were on fire and shot a nasty glare at the leg, she had just finished bandaging. "Fuck. Those ships, they were looking for *you*, weren't they? I had to blow up my boat because of *you*? Seriously? You're lucky you're hurt, or I'd punch you in the face."

Another soft snort and laugh left the escapee as if she didn't believe Lani could do it. Lani's fist balled in the sand almost on its own volition.

"Weirdling, you'd probably make my face feel *better* if you punched it," the Corpse said, and Lani bared her teeth.

"That's a very bad case for me to hold my temper," she replied. "You made me blow up *my boat*. Do you have any idea how long I had to save to get that? I had a year of supplies on board, too. A *year* of salt rations. Between that and dragging your ass all the way here, you better fucking live until you can buy me a new boat."

Another laugh. The fucking bitch leaned her head back and closed her eyes, casually replying, "I don't fucking care about a boat . . . or a year, or . . . anything really. Just wanted to get away. If you blew up your boat . . . that's on you."

Oh, how Lani wanted to fling a rock at the woman's head, but then she might bleed more, and Lani had never done well with too much blood. She was already well past her limit. That large, deadly wound on the Corpse's leg was enough to make her own skin and second Mark itch.

To relieve the tension in her body a little, Lani shifted in the sand and got to her knees before she said, "Yeah, well, I wouldn't have had to if Corp ships weren't swarming around these parts looking for you, now would I?"

Lani might have left it at that, had her companion not begun to slump sideways, forcing the Emotive to launch forward to catch the woman before she hit her head. Why Lani bothered was a mystery to her. The Mark on her calf gave her insight into the emotions of others, but it did nothing to shed light on Lani's own motivations for half the shit she did. Lani should not help this piece of bleeding driftwood. It would be kinder to put the Corpse out of her misery or at least not prolong her suffering. Instead, Lani carefully guided the woman's head to a cleared bit of sand and helped shift her body into a comfortable position. As she did, she tried to keep the woman engaged and conscious.

"Hey, don't pass out, ok? That would be a bad idea right now." Flailing around for a topic that might keep the Corpse talking, Lani asked, "How the fuck did you escape the Salt Mines anyways? I've never heard of that happening."

There was some ragged breathing, then, "Killed three supervisors, eight guards . . . took a Shifter to the leg . . . jumped over the wall. Fun times . . . though I wouldn't recommend that swim. It's a bitch."

These were obviously hallucinations or delusions. *No one* escaped the mines, especially alone and injured. It was so improbable it bordered on the hilarious, but something deep inside Lani had to wonder if this didn't stink just a bit too much like the work of a certain Precog she wanted to murder.

No. What was she thinking? *No one* escaped the mines. It was a fact.

"You're full of shit," Lani declared. "You were probably just dumped overboard to shut you up because you're irritating, got mauled by a shark, and are hallucinating. Hell, maybe that brand is something you did to yourself because you're nuts or you're one of those prison inmates who takes a Corporate contract to avoid incarceration. Yeah, I'm going with that."

"Nah, they only give that option to the unMarked assholes who have never been to the Spire."

Lani scrambled away as fast as she could until her back hit her overturned pack. She yanked the gutting knife she had strapped to it out and then launched herself back toward the Corpse. With none of the care from before, Lani straddled the woman's lap and pressed the knife right up against that pale tattoo along her throat.

"Are you a Tracker? Tell me you're not a fucking Tracker or Shifter trying to lull me into a false sense of security. Is that brand on your shoulder a fake? Are you working for Recruitment? What game are you playing?"

"Game?" Big brown eyes blinked up at Lani. "Who's bleeding out on the sand here, Weirdling? My 'game' is just dying in peace, away from that hell I've been trapped in for six years. I don't care if you believe me or not. Go the fuck away or cut my throat, I don't care. Just make up your mind. My head hurts, I'm tired, and my self-control only goes so far."

Lani growled and pressed the blade in closer. She could feel the flesh begin to resist. It would take so little to slice through and end this threat. The sensible thing to do was kill her problem and walk away, but Lani's hand trembled as she held it there.

"What Mark do you have? What are you?"

Lani had to know. She'd kill the woman if it was necessary. The thought of taking yet another life, even one tied to the Corporation and therefore with blood on its hand, made her heart ache, but she could do it if the Mark was a dangerous one.

"Conflicter," the Corporate goon said, and Lani paled, the blood in her veins turning to ice. "Not that it's your business, Emotive. For all I know, you're keeping me worn down so that you can turn me in."

The blade trembled. *Do it! Do it now!* a voice inside Lani urged. Conflicters were as bad as Marks got, creatures born to kill and little more. Putting this one out of its misery was a kindness to the world. Yet, her wrist wouldn't obey.

People say the same thing about you, Lani, another voice whispered. *These injuries aren't fake. She's already dying. There is nothing right or good about taking out an enemy once she's down.*

They would probably be found or die of thirst within a few days. Would letting the Conflicter live really lower Lani's chances of survival?

"Look ...I'm really tired." A hand fell on Lani's wrist with surprising strength, startling her out of her ethical dilemma. At once she regretted her hesitation. A Conflicter, even an injured one, was a deadly threat. She tried in vain to press down on the knife, but it was pointless. That vice grip held fast as the woman continued. "Which means I'm not in the mood for killing. Could you just ... not say stupid things for ten minutes?"

A strong push sent Lani flying across the sand like a ragdoll. She jumped to her feet as soon as the world stopped spinning, lunging for the knife that had fallen when she landed. Her eyes found those of the fucking Conflict Marked menace and Lani waved the knife in her directing. "Fine. Whatever. Just ... stay there. I need to clear my head."

With no shits given about getting a response, Lani turned on the spot, snatched the flashlight, and stormed off. For the next two hours, she stomped around the island in the dark, only turning on her flashlight when necessary. With every useless rock, her mood got worse and worse.

Stuck on a deserted island, with nothing useful on it, with a fucking Corporate Conflict Marked escaped slave, in the dark, within sight of the Spire.

She was screwed.

That was the simple truth that sank in deeper with every minute that passed. Moe had decided to laugh it up and send her to her death for some reason that must have made sense to the idiotic Precog, and Lani had been stupid enough to go along with it. Moe had managed to make it sound so fucking promising when he had shown up on the deck of her ship dressed in his usual clashing bright colors with a bottle of rum and promised her an end to her miserable solitude.

Lani should never have trusted any plan that started with the words, "So, I have an idea, but first you need a drink."

It must have been well after midnight when Lani's temper started to dull under the weight of her exhaustion. Confident at last that there was nothing of use on the whole accursed island, Lani made her way back to the Conflicter. Now that her fear and anger had burned off, she felt just bad for threatening to slice the throat of a dying woman. Not bad enough to apologize, but a smidge. Corp goons were still people, and too many deaths already weighed on her conscience, thank you very much. Still, if this one was telling the truth, she really didn't deserve to get knifed when she had just made it to freedom. Not that Lani believed that even a Conflicter could escape the Salt Mines alone, but maybe she was just trying to protect other people. Lani lied too often and too well to judge others for the same.

That thought had her rubbing her chest, right over her heart, where her swimsuit covered the ever-expanding second Mark that no one, not even Moe, knew about.

At least in theory. She could never be sure with Moe.

Stepping around a boulder, Lani stopped at a safe distance from the Conflicter and passed the flashlight beam over the woman's face. Her eyes were closed and for a minute, Lani thought that maybe the Corpse was dead. Then she noticed the rise and fall of the woman's chest and sighed.

The sand and prickly beach grass crunched underfoot as she walked over to the Conflicter's side. A poke to the ribs got no response, and neither did a "Hey you." Confident that she was passed out cold after poking her again in the leg wound this time, Lani set her pack with the knife in it well out of range and sat down next to the strange woman, her back up against the rock. The wind was only getting colder and neither of them was going to have a comfortable night. No reason not to make the best out of a horrible situation. With a grimace, Lani repositioned herself so the woman's head was cushioned on her shoulder, then let her own head rest against her companion's hair. They would both be warmer and more comfortable, which was the best Lani could ask for or offer.

She didn't honestly think she would sleep with a Conflicter nestled right up against her, but as soon as Lani closed her eyes, she did.

CODEX: Alright, while this patch installs, let's get some information going. *Query: Where am I?*

SALT: You are on Fortune. 1,232,145,981 documents available on 'Fortune.'

CODEX: I know what planet I'm on; what I meant is *Query: What networks do I have access to?*

SALT: Networks Online: Kahana University Servers, Merihem Crystal Servers, Parata Servers. Do you wish to dismiss *Query: Where am I?* Or access File 1 (Filename: Transcription from Holder Ecology 101: AKA How not to God badly. Location: Merihem Crystal Servers. Folder: Suck it Ira, I hacked you).

CODEX: You know what, actually, I want to see that.

TRANSCRIPTION FROM HOLDER ECOLOGY 101: AKA HOW NOT TO GOD BADLY.

<u>Irawaru:</u> You have to understand that creating a World is not a sequential process. It happens all at once. You make the jump and suddenly every thought and feeling you have becomes reality to an entire solar system. If you happen to think about how much you love the flowers in your garden, they will pop up all over your planet. If you remember you hate mosquitoes, you might wipe them out of your evolutionary chain, which means that everything that eats mosquitoes will need a new food source. Every change creates a disturbance, and that ripple gets bigger and bigger and bigger. It will happen fast. Thousands, perhaps millions of years will pass in the blink of an eye and if you don't learn to calm your mind, you'll end up with a complete mess.

Student 1: Is that what happened with Fortune? Did it get away from you?

Irawaru: Yes and no. My sister Lakea and I were the first. We didn't understand what was happening. We thought it was a weird dream for most of the core building period. We figured it was just in our heads, so we tried to create the perfect world. We made chains of bountiful tropical islands, chose to make the oceans fresh water paradises of colorful fish and sprawling coral reefs like those that used to be found on earth. We wanted everything to be beautiful, and since we thought it was a dream, we completely ignored function. It wasn't that we lost control: we simply didn't know what we were doing.

Student 2: So what happened? When did you realize the problem?

Irawaru: Instead of really evolving things, we just made them. That is a mistake you should never repeat. When you give lifeforms time to adapt, they generally will self-correct. Our folly was to expect that our human minds, even expanded by becoming gods, could account for every contingency and need. We created a perfect world; we made people in our image upon it and then watched as plants, animals, and people all started dying for a lack of salt. Those who survived were washed away by the storms our vast expanses of open ocean and lack of mountains allowed to run rampant over the planet. Our mistakes would have been their undoing.

Student 1: So how did you fix it?

Irawaru: That's the thing, we still haven't. We've tried our best to mitigate the damage but without wiping the slate clean there is no real going back. We created Spires of salt in the middle of the ocean to salinate it and provide the resource without changing the tectonics of the planet too much. We hacked into the Marks and programmed them to spread the salt around, and we made reefs to keep the worst of the storms off each grouping of archipelagos. We've been fighting to keep Fortune viable for centuries of their time, and yet every fix we try just causes another problem. We attempted to create perfection. Instead, we almost killed off a planet's worth of people. If you learn nothing else in this course, learn this: there is no such thing as a perfect world. Never aim for perfection. *Aim for survival.*

Crystal Palace
Moe - Day 1   02

The wind was gusting off the sea, heavy with rain and the sweet smell of jasmine and gardenia. Moe stood on the balcony while the toughened glass of the storm dome slowly descended around the Corporate Palace. The last breath of fresh air glided under the glass and blew through Moe's long black hair just before the dome sealed itself. The wind whispered of sunburnt skin and cool evenings floating on the waves. It smelled of a time when he was more innocent, of bare feet deep in warm sand, and the crunch of ripe rose apples. Moe idly wondered if the storm watchers misjudged the speed of the hurricane, or predicted it so exactly that they lowered the dome at the perfect moment. Water battered against the curved glass, running first in rivulets, then in waves down the sides. The wind was howling, but in the shelter of the dome, it sounded to Moe more like the muffled humming of a thousand bees than the screams of the sea. Thunder boomed and lightning flashed across the sky, casting the bay into sharp relief before plunging it back into darkness.

Trees swayed in the howling gusts, bending and straining at their roots. The waves crashed into the docks and the boats that did not have a cove to shelter in thrashed like wild animals caught in a trap. The sky was a single mass of writhing clouds, gray fading into red where the sun was setting beyond the far horizon. This was a northern storm, a little one, a forerunner of the winter season. It wasn't one of the Prismatic Storms with their myriad of colors and strange effects on Fertility Marks. One of those should be hitting the ocean near the Spire soon, but that was far away from the Corporate Palace.

Moe felt, more than heard, the hum of the power generators and air filters turning on, deep within the building at his back. His mind raced, numbers somersaulting into place as he calculated the astronomical expense of keeping this complex climate-controlled through a storm. His Precog Mark flared, but unlike on most Marked individuals, the edges did not glow as he drew power. They couldn't, since by now his two Marks had spread to cover his whole body, making him look for all the world like nothing more than a slightly darker-skinned unMarked man.

As power flowed through him, the numbers he was running changed. His eyes traveled across the glass dome, probabilities scrolling across his whole field of vision, calculating just how probable it was for each inch of glass to crack. As he considered different ways to do it, those numbers changed, spirals and threads of probability unwinding from each atom of glass. Moe did not focus on any one possibility, enjoying the majesty of the future without constraint. Throwing his attention further out, he watched a hundred—a thousand, a million—probability streams burst into existence and die as the storm raged. They shifted with each gust of wind to form a storm of their own, superimposed upon reality.

"Are you going to stare at the storm all day, slowpoke, or are we finishing the job?" A high-pitched, girlish voice asked from beside him. Moe turned to Lizzie, his life-long companion and Bonded. She stood beside him on the balcony, her mousy brown hair pulled into two short pigtails around her youthful face. She wore the frock of a University student to better blend in at the Corporate Palace of the Crystal Corporation. Moe, too, wore an outfit that would draw no eyes: a pure white suit with a teal tie that matched the decor so well he was practically invisible. He hated it, but took solace from the fact that his socks were a mismatched neon purple and green.

"Oh, we were here for a job?" he asked, for the simple enjoyment of getting under Lizzie's skin. She was already annoyed at being dressed up like the child she resembled instead of the centuries-old being she actually was. Moe couldn't resist making her even grumpier.

"I will bite you."

"Promises, promises, Lizzie darling," Moe drawled. He stared out at the storm for another breath, then pushed off the rail with a bounce to his step, and offered Lizzie a hand. "Off we go, then."

She took his hand, her eyes closing. Moe felt her own particular power wrapping around his like creeping kudzu vines on a building, focusing his overgrown Marks through their Bond. His awareness expanded, streams of probability bursting wider and wider. They shot across the waves, over the archipelagos, the ships upon the sea, the Spire, the Reef. But they didn't stop there. The whole planet opened to Moe like a venus flytrap—beautiful, but dangerous to get too close to. At another time, Moe would have been delighted to dance with the danger, but this was not the time for it. With a regretful sigh, he let go of his Precog Mark and flared the other one, instead.

Pop!

They disappeared from the balcony, leaving nothing but a ring of salt behind. They landed neatly on top of the glass roof of a lavish office. It was empty, as Moe had predicted. Zarine Crystal, CEO of the Crystal Corporation, was visiting the Spire to receive a debrief on the breakout of one Adavera of Keala. This room was shielded against anyone Porting straight inside—even a Porter as strong as Moe—but those shields were just as unimaginative as the rest of this Palace. Why, the building didn't even have towers! Who built a *Palace* without pointy bits? This was all clean metal and shiny glass, like the rest of the skyscrapers on the Island of Kahana. Totally uninspired. Moe had walked into the Corporate Palace with the barcode he had carved out of the skin of a corporate underling. Getting into this office through the Shielded walls and ceiling would be equally doable, assuming he didn't play by the rules.

"You're doing it again," Lizzie complained, poking Moe in the ribs.

"Doing what?"

"Daydreaming."

"Why live if not to daydream, my dear? Daydreaming is what makes me human," Moe said, lifting the jaunty hat perched on his smooth black hair, and pulling a bag of salt from underneath it.

Casually, he upended the bag on the glass at his feet and watched the shield become briefly visible and flicker. He smirked. "Easy as arsenic pie."

Lizzie pulled two more bags of salt from her pockets, adding them to the pile. With each granule, the protection over the glass glitched further. It didn't fail—salt didn't nullify Marked power, just made it act erratically—but holes started flickering in and out of existence, like static.

That was all the opening Moe needed. He stepped away from the pile of salt, took Lizzie's hand, and flared his Porting Mark, focusing on the room below.

Porting through the glitching shield felt like falling through ice. It pulled at his suit, trying to slow the incursion, but Moe was used to pushing through the uneven power surges created by salt. He didn't try to force it, just kept Porting downward an inch or two at a time. Every time a failure in the shield lined up with his power working, he and Lizzie sank a bit further.

"This is so slow," she complained, pulling a sleek Corporate tablet the size of her palm out of her pocket and bringing up a game. Lizzie liked her games. Considering Moe had never once seen her sleep, he had to assume that they were what she did in the long hours of the night when mortals rested. Today's entertainment was a cute, childish survival game. As they sank lower and lower through the glass roof, Moe watched as Lizzie led her avatar into successively more gruesome ends, a cackle escaping her lips each time the dramatic death sequence played.

"You know, the point of that game is to stay alive," he prodded, after the fourth death in a row—this one by killer bees.

"No it's not. No one ever gets out alive." The statement, in her high-pitched, girlish voice was creepy as fuck. Moe loved it.

Pop!

The shield glitched once more, and this time it was for long enough that Moe and Lizzie slipped right through to the floor below. Moe let go of Lizzie's hand and cracked his knuckles. "Alright, here we go. Time to wreak some mayhem."

He strode over to the computer terminal on an expansive desk and sat down in the chair with a flourish. Putting his feet up on the desk, he pulled the wireless keyboard onto his lap. Moe tapped at random keys until a log-in screen appeared, asking for a passcode. From the inner pocket of his suit jacket, he pulled a small, beaten up notebook and flipped several pages. "When did I look up passwords, Liz?"

"Three years ago. We're in timeline 4864-B. Did you bring the right notebook? I'm going to be so cross at you if you didn't."

"Oh thee of little faith. Of course I brought the right notebook."

Even so, Moe flared his Precog power to find the right page, feeling like showing off. On the faded lined paper, he had written the passcode: T0121nSond2R.

"Easy peasy, see?" Moe said when the password was accepted.

"Aha. Sure. Hurry up, will you? I'm sure the Shielder who put the wards up will already be on his way with every security goon they can find."

"Always with the nagging. It's almost like you don't trust me," Moe complained, making talking motions with one hand as he pulled up the database of all known Marks with the other. He hit print while looking up the name he was after. "Nag, nag, nag. Ah, here we go. Got the kid's name. His first Culling is in just a few days, so you better hope our little group picks up the pace."

"You already sent Lani to the Spire, right? How much prodding could they possibly need?" Lizzie asked, looking over his shoulder.

Moe scribbled down the name he had just found into his notebook, then clicked open another search window. "People need to be micromanaged. The moment you look away, they catch a case of the stupids. It is well known. Why look, search parties are still only restricted to this local sea zone around the Spire. Let's fix that, shall we?"

He typed for about a minute.

```
NEWS ALERT: ALL EYES, ALL CHANNELS
```

Precog Alert: A ship will be shanghaied by two Rogue Marks at 08:45. These women are a rabid Conflicter escaped from the Spire and a previously unknown Emotive.

The Conflicter is one Adavera of Keala. Approximately six feet tall, with short black hair and dark skin. Her Conflict Mark takes up her right thigh, curling in intricate, geometric patterning. Reports claim that she was injured by a Shifter guard she attacked unprovoked, possibly leaving deep injuries on her left leg. Menders should keep their eyes open. The Conflicter is believed to be extremely dangerous. Any citizen who believes they have spotted the subject should immediately report the sighting to their local Corporate Officer and keep a safe distance. We repeat. Do not engage with this Conflicter; she is known to be unstable, extremely prone to violence, and adept at close combat.

The unknown Emotive has no clear features for us to report, but it is assumed that the two Marked women have some link or relationship. The Emotive may, in fact, have been the cause of the sudden instability of a previously honored member of the Corporation.

"You're making that part up," Lizzie complained.

"Course I am." Moe hit send, snatching the thick bundle of printed pages, then made to jump up. Lizzie's hands on his shoulders kept him in his seat. "You're not done here. Print the storm schedule for the season too. Plus, remember the most important bit?"

"Important bit?" Moe asked as he pulled up the proprietary Crystal Corp storm schedule. The one they *never* published, lest the salt pirates and embargoed islands get a heads up to plan around. Once he hit print for his own needs, he sent it straight to the anonymous drop site for the foremost pirate radio station. He didn't need to, but when had Moe ever been able to resist the urge to say 'fuck you' to the Crystal Corporation?

"Yes, the important bit. Remember? The *fun* bit."

"Oh, right!" Moe grinned and opened a text document. In it, he typed:

```
Hey Crystals, do a pirate, an inventor, a
doctor, a hermit, a killer, a child, and a
madman have anything in common?
Na!
(Na = Sodium, Get it? Didn't think so)
Xoxo
Uncle Moe
```

He looked up at Lizzie, who had just smacked herself in the forehead. "Your sodium puns are terrible."

"Lizzie, I'm In-salt-ed!"

"Now you're just rubbing salt in the wound."

Moe grinned. "Don't you know that you should take *all* my jokes with a grain of salt?"

Lizzie rolled her eyes. "Alright, you. We have the information we need. Let's get out of here before a Conflicter or ten storms in here to give you a NaCl sandwich.

CODEX: Moe, what *did* you find? Are these documents from our Gods? SALT, please *Query: Who are Irawaru and Lakea? Search Parameter: same folder.*

SALT: 375,994 documents referencing Irawaru and Lakea available in folder: Suck it Ira, I hacked you. Time to read them all is 17 seconds. Proceed?

CODEX: Yes. Start at the beginning.

EXCERPTS FROM THE JOURNAL OF HOLDER IRAWARU, AS COMPILED BY HOLDER HALL.

A week ago, we woke the first generation of humans. They were confused, as we expected, but are adjusting well to life on the islands. Our presence unsettles them, but after a few attempts at telling the truth, we found it simpler to call ourselves 'Gods' and tell them that we are omnipotent, than to try to explain the minutia of the truth. As far as they are concerned, we may as well actually be gods. With this in mind, they have not questioned their sudden existence on this planet. A curious feature that neither Lakea nor I intended are some strange marks on the skin of about one out of two hundred of them. So far we have identified twelve unique symbols and these people are exhibiting odd abilities. It was not part of our plan, so we have no clue what to tell them when they come to us for answers.

It might point to a flaw in our creation, but until we know more I won't let Kea wipe out this batch of humans and try again. If it is some sort of operational virus, it will show itself in time, and given the limited technology we provided, the damage they can do to the environment is minimal. For now, we simply wait and observe. One of these Marked individuals has two, the only one I've yet seen to exhibit this abnormality. His name is Merihem, but already he insists that we call him Moe. He is the most talkative person I have ever met. Perhaps creating people as adults capable of speech and with minds already primed with all the information they would need to survive was a mistake. Still, it is an opportunity. I've been trying to find out everything I can about these Marks and what his feel like. He has described one as the ability to recognize patterns and predict future events, which to me feels less than believable, especially considering how prone this subject is to wild exaggeration. His second power, though, can be easily measured and is the ability to disappear in one place and reappear in another, almost like we do except with no awareness of the interdimensional space he is stepping through. I am fascinated; Kea less so. She's mostly just annoyed that everything is not going to plan.

Boat Theft 03
Lani - Day 2

It wasn't yet dawn when Lani woke to an elbow in the ribs and the whispered word, "Company."

Her eyes snapped open, but otherwise, Lani didn't move, not even to ease the ache in her back from sleeping in such an awkward position. As she came to, Lani could hear the crunch of footsteps moving closer. There were at least two people and they were talking.

"There's blood over here," one said in a high, nasally voice.

"Please . . . please let that bitch have gotten pulled back out and eaten. She had to have passed out at some point, right?" said a second. "I don't want to fight her."

"Maybe . . . Conflicters just keep going till you nail 'em to the wall, though. I wouldn't put it past her to be alive and hiding here with a rock, ready to bash our brains out."

Lani's companion had, in fact, just picked up a rock. They exchanged a look and despite the horror of the situation and the fact that they were likely about to die, the Conflicter smirked and Lani found her own lips twitching up as well.

The pair of hunters moved closer, still talking.

"I say we just tell the office we saw her sink and call it a day. It's not like she can do much damage out here without a boat. She'll die of thirst or starve, so it won't even be that much of a lie," the same man continued, before his colleague interrupted him.

"Yeah, and then we'll end up mining instead of guarding miners when HQ sends an Emotive to investigate. No, we stay until we find a body. There was blood on the beach and a clear trail. Just keep your eyes open and think of the reward if we bring her back alive."

It made Lani's head spin to hear the woman's story confirmed this way, but she didn't have time to think about it. The much more urgent matter of survival took up the bulk of her thoughts. Beside her, the Conflicter was on all fours. Before she could spring out of hiding and get them both killed, Lani shot out a hand to grab the woman's arm, then shook her head as their eyes met.

The Corpse's eyebrows rose.

Lani pointed to the Mark on her own calf, then in the direction of the voices. It got a squint in reply.

"Just stay put," Lani mouthed, then focused inward. She could have tried to communicate psychically with the woman, but if either of their guests was Marked, there would be a chance they might pick it up. Psychic communication between Bonded could be private, or so Lani had heard. Otherwise, it was like they were talking aloud if other Marks were present.

She was drained from yesterday, but even running on fumes, Lani's Emotive Mark had strengthened enough to alter the emotions of two people at close range. The flow of power was wispy at first, as she hunted around for her targets. When she had them, Lani took stock of their emotional state.

Worry was the predominant feeling in both, followed by irritation bordering on anger in one and panic in the other. Lani smiled. A gentle nudge lowered the curiosity and urgency in both of their minds. She was rewarded with, "I've gotta stop for a minute and drink some water. Why don't we have a seat? A few minutes won't hurt."

The Conflicter poked Lani in the ribs. She cracked her eyes open and saw the woman walk two fingers in the air in a demonstration of sneaking, then mime bashing her rock into what Lani could only presume was the back of their pursuers' heads.

"No," Lani mouthed.

"You sure you got this, Weirdling?" the Corpse whispered.

"Shut up, I'm focusing. Just be ready to move, ok?"

Lani closed her eyes again and focused on the Corporate man feeling the most fear. Slow but steady, she fed power to that emotion, pushing a little at paranoia, self-hatred, and any other distracting tendencies she could find in his mind.

"You know I'm screwed if we don't find her, right? I'm already in trouble with Security for being late a couple times. What if he sent me on this assignment just to get rid of me?" He said to his colleague.

Lani turned her attention to the next one, pushing on his irritation, anger and impatience while dulling any compassion he might feel for his collegue.

"Why the fuck should I care; you dug your own grave. My record is just fine. In fact, if we fail I bet they blame it on your lack of discipline and I get off scot-free."

Oh, that did not go over well. Lani tossed as much power as she safely could to get them furious at each other and their resulting yells were music to her ears.

"You let me know when to take them. I got the big guy," the Conflicter beside her whispered and this time when Lani opened her eyes it was with an eye roll.

"No you're fucking not. Just stay still. This becomes ten times harder if they see you," Lani warned then returned her attention to the two fighting and whispered as she worked "Alright, now look the other way. Pay attention to the fight, yes, up with focus but down with perception of your surroundings. Let's just get rid of all that loyalty too and then, ah, perfect." Their shouts were reverberating across the island and all she had to do was tweak a few things a little more before the sound of a fist striking flesh reached her ears.

"Nice job, Weirdling . . . now what?" the Conflicter asked as the argument between the two goons turned into a full-on fistfight.

Lani smiled, took a deep breath, then said, "Now we steal their boat."

For a moment there was silence but for the arguing guards, then her companion's face broke into the most radiant smile Iolani had ever seen. Sure, it was a little scary, what with the way the woman's eyes lit up bright in the dim morning. Words were not needed to convey that Lani's plan wasn't just good: it was fucking fantastic as far as the escaped slave was concerned.

By unspoken consensus, the two women got to their feet. Lani offered the Conflicter her arm to help support her weight and together they hunched over and ran. It was hard not to make any noise in the sand and beach grass, but by then the soldiers weren't paying attention. Lani made sure to keep feeding power into that rage and as soon as they were well and truly out of sight the two women straightened up and booked it just as fast as they could. Or at least that was the plan. It turned out, though, that standing wasn't in the Corpse's repertoire of current skills. Lani was all but dragging her and was half-tempted to just leave her rotting ass on the beach when the woman growled, "Slap me."

"What?"

Her growl became louder. "I said slap me or punch me, or anything really, as long as it hurts. I'm a Conflicter. As soon as it's a fight I won't feel the pain."

Never in her life had Lani been so happy to follow an order. Her hand swung back and crashed into the source of all her troubles with a smack. The sting in her palm was uncomfortable, but seeing the Conflicter's head rock back was deliciously satisfying.

A breath later, Lani regretted that moment of obedience when the woman who had been half-dead a second ago surged towards her with murder in her eyes. Lani let go of her, took a quick step back, then froze as her attacker did.

Nothing moved. Lani didn't even dare to breathe, and then the Conflicter just straightened up and shook her hands out, as if venting the tension present in her limbs. "Good. Much better. Now, let's stop wasting time."

Relief flooded Lani and she nodded; as one they picked up the pace. Lani spotted the boat as soon as they broke out onto the beach. It was a mere hundred yards away and no one was on deck or in sight. Of course, it was also about twenty yards out into the water but a rope ladder hung down the side.

Perfect.

Despite her injury, Lani's partner in crime managed to keep up on land. As they neared the water, she slowed.

"You first, Weirdling. Better you get away."

"You can't swim alone right now," Lani pointed out. "Stop being stubborn and let me help you."

That seemed like a struggle but at last the grip around Lani's shoulders tightened and the Conflicter snapped, "Fine."

They waded into the water together. The salt must have been horrifically painful on the open wounds, but other than a grunt the Conflicted didn't make a sound. Lani took more and more of her weight as they waded in waist-deep, then chest-deep, the waves buffeting against their bodies. At last, though it felt like an eternity later, Lani grabbed hold of the ladder and glanced back.

FUCK!

"Climb. They've seen us."

The ladder was much more of a struggle than the waves. By the time Lani dragged her companion onto the deck, the two rightful owners of this skiff were halfway down the beach and had weapons drawn, their guns shining in the morning light. Lani launched herself at the helm, running hunched over to be less of a target.

The Conflicter did the same towards the anchor. As she did, she barked instructions in Lani's direction. "Keys in the center compartment of the wheel. It opens up."

It took Lani a second, in which the guards got off several shots, but then the motor roared to life and she crowed in victory. "Hold on tight and wave to them for me."

Out of the corner of her eye, Lani saw the Conflicter flash a very rude gesture at the retreating shoreline as Lani gunned in towards the open sea. Water sprayed behind them, the boat rocked on the waves, and fuck did it feel good. They cleared the range of the guns in moments and Lani let out the breath she had been holding. She looked over at the other woman and smiled. "How long till they radio for help?"

"And tell them that they let us steal their skiff and get away? That takes more balls than even I have. We should have at least an hour's head start. What's your name, Weirdling? I never caught it."

"It's Iolani."

"Iolani what?"

"Iolani none-of-your-fucking-business," Lani replied. "What's yours?"

"Adavera of Keala, but you . . . you can call me Vera."

"Alright then, Vera. We'll probably be dead by sunset, but in the meantime, you can call me Lani."

CODEX: *Query: Are there files on Irawaru, Lakea, or Ira and Kea in any other folders?*

SALT: Affirmative. Program 1: Keylogger, installed on the Merihem Crystal Network. Access?

CODEX: Yes please, starting the 13th day of the Emotion Lunar Cycle. That's the day Lani found Vera, I believe. Please label that Day 1 and begin a timeline. I'm sure there are bits I don't know, so I want to get recent events at least in the right order.

SALT: 13th day of the Emotive Lunar Cycle set as 'Day 1.' Calendar populating.

CODEX: Good, now let's see those files.

DATE: YEAR 1502, DAY 2

TroubleTwin: Have you been paying attention?

Helper.Bro.Ira: To what in particular? The marine adaptations?

TroubleTwin: No. To that fucking Corporate nightmare in Reef 3.

Helper.Bro.Ira: Not particularly, why?

TroubleTwin: Because their panties are in a twist, and they're starting to move around like agitated ants with a purpose.

Helper.Bro.Ira: . . . Moe?

TroubleTwin: Of *course* it's Moe.

Helper.Bro.Ira: You need to do something about him, Kea . . .

TroubleTwin: Why me? You're just as capable!

Helper.Bro.Ira: The second I show up, he poofs out. At least with you, you've got a shot at locking him down for a while.

TroubleTwin: Sometimes I hate you, brother. Fine. I'll look into containment for Moe, but I'm telling you, it's only going to work for so long. He's slippery.

Helper.Bro.Ira: Yeah, sure. Just make sure he doesn't screw you until he gets the key this time.

CODEX: Huh . . . Gods instant message each other. The more you know.

Salt Pirate
Salome – Day 4   04

"Captain, we've only got about ten more minutes."

"On it. Get a move on you lazy cracks!" Salome Parata didn't really need a reminder about the time. Whenever the *Sahima's Legacy* made port at an embargoed island, her crew knew there was a timer. That timer was ingrained. The audible reminder was for the people they were helping, not for the pirates under Sal's command.

These missions were only successful because these islanders covered for Salome and her crew of smugglers when the Corporation came after them. It was a complicated relationship and Sal wouldn't give it up for the world—it just required everyone to be on the same page. When it came to thumbing one's nose at the Crystal Corporation, speed was king.

As usual, the audible reminder seemed to put some fire under the civilian's asses. The heavy cases of contraband salt weren't easy to handle, especially for people suffering from the Haze. The Corporation called it hyponatremia, a simple and not usually lethal lack of salt. They rarely denied an embargoed island *any* salt, because they weren't dumb and knew that a high death toll would be horrible PR, but Salome had learned early that the tiny allocation of salt wasn't a mercy. It was torture. The first symptoms of salt withdrawal, colloquially known as the Haze, were subtle—dizziness, lethargy, confusion—then came the rest. Twitching muscles, cramps, stupor. If left untreated, death would follow, but that was where the Corporation stepped in.

Their 'mercy' salt packs, delivered one a day to every citizen of every island, including the embargoed ones, held just enough salt to stave off coma and death. It kept people alive to suffer another day.

Hazelings, after all, didn't have the strength to fight back.

They said it was to make sure everyone had a fair share of the scarce, life-saving commodity. Salome knew exactly what a blatant lie that was. She had broken into too many warehouses piled to the ceiling with those precious white crystals to believe there was a scarcity.

The Corporation was sitting on a literal mountain of salt, and doling it out by the gram at exorbitant cost. People could either pay, or they could Haze out.

That was where Salome came in. Salt piracy was a risky business, but even selling at a fraction of the cost the Corporation charged, there was good money in it. Better yet, it helped the people the Crystal family didn't like and pissed the Corp off to no end.

That was worth the risk, in Salome Parata's book.

With any luck, they'd get this whole load off the ship before she had to scoot her crew away from the island and draw off any Corporate goons that would inevitably come sniffing where they weren't wanted.

There were just a few more crates on deck. A few more minutes and—

Salome's prosthetic arm started pinging only five minutes into their remaining time. "Depths damn those . . ." She took a deep breath, cupped her hands around her mouth, and let out a deep bellow. "We have to go!"

Heads snapped up, all of them wearing expressions of dismay.

Sal turned and clasped hands with the old woman that was her contact here, looking her square in the eye. "Addie, as soon as it is clear I will bring you the rest. May take a week or two though."

"We know the drill. Run, Cap. Run."

Crewmen dropped the crates safely to the ground where they were standing. Civilians raced forward to start dragging the salt off to their caches. As they did, Sal and her people raced back down the dock. *Sahima's Legacy* was a good ship—and infamous for its escapes—but she didn't want to cut it any closer than necessary.

If she thought they had a chance in an open battle, she'd take it. Salome delighted in sinking as many Corporate vessels as possible. She was glad she hadn't wasted time though. Her first mate and older brother looked a little grim as she made it to the helm. "How bad does it look Kuma?"

"Bad enough. They're not after us, but we might get caught in the crossfire. They're looking for someone specific, so they're swarming," Kumanu replied.

"Who?"

"I don't have a name yet. But if this tap is correct, someone got out of the Spire." He met her gaze. "It could be . . ."

Her blood tingled. No one, absolutely *no one*, got out of the Spire. If someone finally had, then the Corporation was going to go all out to . . . "Well damn."

"Exactly. They're going to gun for pirates, Sal. We're the best bet for safety if someone got out."

"Crank the engines as far as they can go, Kuma. We've got a goose chase to commit to."

"Sal, you're not going to go hunting this escapee are you?"

"Hell no. But I'm gonna act like we've got whoever they are on board. If that buys them time to hide away, great. "

"That's my girl."

"Shut it. Now get your ass on that console. I might need your tricks." Sal set her hands to the wheel and narrowed her eyes as the engines in the ship began to roar. There, at the corner of the isle to the left, were the first signs of white sails. "Ready?"

"If you take off like a bat out of—"

She gunned it, letting out a cackle as Kumanu cursed. The crew was used to this and were braced. Seven Corporate ships had appeared on the open ocean around the island. They hadn't been there an hour ago, which meant that they had been Ported in—an extravagance the Corporation only indulged in when they had a bee in their bonnet. The small fleet was congregating at the mouth of the bay, blocking off her escape.

Sal raced straight towards the obvious exit between two large galleons. The blockade tightened as the *Legacy* sped toward it at full tilt.

"We're not going to make it through that hole," Kuma warned.

"We can if we turn broadside so we can go perpendicularly through that gap. Get ready to Phase Drift," she shot back.

"You're going to break my ship in half doing that."

"It's my ship, and no, I'm not. I have you."

Sal didn't entirely understand how his Mark worked, but she got the basics. Kuma was a Juicer—an Infuser born on the full moon, able not just to Infuse a few Marks, but all of them. He had spent years infusing the powers of other Marked individuals into the engines and batteries of *Sahima's Legacy*. He could tap into those, using them to help the ship do the impossible. Sal was a good captain, but it was Kuma's Mark that let her be amazing.

She waited until the last moment, counting under her breath before bellowing the order to release one of the back sails. Speed and wind made the sail billow open, allowing her to twist the helm. The sudden jolt swung the back end of the ship out towards the enemy, her bow remaining almost still for a moment as it performed a quick turn that would have shattered Corporate ships. The Infuser Mark on Kuma's hands and forearms glowed against his console as he fed the engines.

The friction that should have cracked the ship in half and popped and vanished like a soap bubble as Kuma used the power of a Phaser to go *through* the water as though it were not there.

They skimmed past the bow of the Corporate ambusher at an impossible sideways angle with only a few feet to spare. She let the ship drift through the water as she leisurely released the wheel once they were angled to get between two enemy ships. The agitated expressions of the crew on the other boats were clear—oh how she loved those looks of shock and dismay as her cannons fired, disabling the masts and sails of their enemies on both sides. Sal wiggled her fingers at one of the enemy captains, who was staring at her in dumbfounded confusion.

"Two down."

"*FIVE to go!*"

Salome laughed. "They only sent seven? I'm *insulted*. Let's bloody their pride, boyos!"

CODEX: Actually, SALT, before I keep reading about Gods and get distracted by something irrelevant, *Query: When is now? List all current events in order of Corporate Threat Level*.

SALT: The current time is 2:47AM on the 14th day of the Teleportation Lunar Cycle, or Day 81 according to your calendar. Top current event by Corporate Threat Level:

Threat Level 5: Attack on the Spire – 2:03AM – All available Conflict Marks assigned special Porting privileges to the Spire. Halt attack at all costs. Evac order:

-----------EVACUATION ORDER LEVEL 5-----------

Aheo;

We received a tip-off that there will be an attempt at the Spire within the next hour. Your ship, your crew, the projects that you can't afford to lose, and YOU are to leave Spire waters and head to Rendezvous A.02.

This is not negotiable. Get yourself moving. Anything that you can't bring with you is not worth your loss. Security will be handling the Spire Assault. All available Conflicters will be brought in. You are not needed. Be out of the line of fire.

That is a direct order. Obey or be Terminated.

Crystal, Galena

-----------EVACUATION ORDER LEVEL 5-----------

CODEX: Shiiiiiiiiit. No, that's not right. We

weren't supposed to attack the Spire yet. What the fuck went wrong? Shit. Intercept the order sending in the Conflicters.

SALT: I am sorry. I cannot do that. Patch download in progress. Time remaining: 12 minutes, 21 seconds.

CODEX: Pause patch.

SALT: Pause patch: Denied. Only actions possible: To-Do List and Queries. Would you like to continue *Query: When is now? List all current events in order of Corporate Threat Level.*

CODEX: FUCK!

Dead in the Water
Vera - Day 4   05

The first day, Adavera slept. A lot. The second, too. There was something soothing about this boat's movements, about the familiarity of the Corporation's skiff, that made it easy to fall into a deep, dreamless sleep. Sure, the heat coming off the wound probably had something to do with that, but really it was the soothing rock of the boat's motions that let her rest and drift into old memories, fooling her mind into believing that when she woke up Torin would be there to wrap his arms around her and . . .

Vera sighed, looking out at the water. Torin was alive. She knew that much, because she hadn't felt the explosive grief of a severed Blood Bond yet. There was more comfort in that, really, than she expected her companion to understand. Not that she'd told Lani about Torin's Bond to her yet.

She wasn't sure how to explain any of it, really. Over the last few days, they'd talked a little, though never about anything important. Iolani drove her a bit crazy with the odd way she had of doing things, but Vera bit her tongue more often than not. Who was she to complain about odd habits? Lani could have tossed her overboard—or tried to anyways—at any point, but had instead gently, if obscenely muttering, helped her at every turn.

A breeze ruffled through Vera's roughly cut short hair, drawing her eyes out to sea. No Spire anywhere in sight. She had watched it disappear, each mile washing away years of pain and anger from her soul, as though the stinging salt really had permeated to the very core of Adavera's being.

From behind her at the wheel of the skiff, Lani started whistling. Vera turned to her, and the sound stopped, a glare replacing the brief hint of a smile. Weird creature.

"So why come out to the Spire's waters in the first place, Lani? If I didn't think you crazy already, that would do it." Vera shifted a little where she sat on the deck, back up against a bench. Awake and no longer pissed, the pain was a constant throbbing distraction. Maybe talking would help. At the very least, perhaps it would piss her off enough for her Conflict Mark to return Vera to the peaceful and painless bliss of fury.

"How is that any of your business?" Lani answered from her seat by the wheel, carefully steering the skiff around the mangroves at the edge of a large island where they had slept the night before and waited out the small storm of the type that often troubled the waters this close to the Reef. They were still too close to the Spire for much habitation, but the islands were getting more numerous and forming clusters. Soon, they would be nearing some of the outlying archipelagos, where ships were more common and less likely to draw suspicion.

"It's not my business," Vera snorted, stretching her good leg out, "but I'm probably gonna die within a few weeks anyway. Entertain a dying woman with a fantastical tale. Watching you twitch and wander about from island to island like the open ocean murdered your favorite pet is driving me batty."

Lani sighed but didn't turn to look at her. "Precog got me drunk and told me to go to coordinates near the Spire on a certain day. Promised it would be a life-changing and enriching journey. Gonna kill him next time I see him."

"Well that was dumb. But hey . . . if I'm still breathing when you do, I'll help. Can't say I liked having a woman point a knife at me while I'm minding my own business and dying in peace." Vera snorted, then turned her head to look towards the horizon again. "Nothing like it, you know . . . the way the sky and sea meet. You forget how pretty it is till you can't see it anymore."

"Were you really in the Salt Mines? I keep expecting that brand to vanish and to end up on my ass in cuffs. I know it won't but," Lani shrugged, "once a paranoid asshole, always one, I guess. How long were you there?"

"What year is it?" Vera blinked, turning her head towards Lani as it occurred to her that she really wasn't entirely sure of how long she had actually been 'gone'. She could remember the look that had been on Torin's face, the tone of his voice, the way her skin had bruised from the hard grip he'd tried to maintain when they had ripped her away— but honestly she couldn't recall how long she had been below.

"The year? 1502. First Lunar Cycle of winter."

Vera shuddered. "Six years. They had me down there for six years. It felt . . . longer. Time loses meaning and . . ." She frowned, turning her eyes back to the horizon. "There's no real light in the Mines, ya know? It's crazy bright out here, and I love it, even if it hurts. The lights there are dim—meant to make sure you can get around, but not let you see a lot of detail. Guess the guards don't like to notice when someone's getting . . . hurt."

Lani made a disgusted face. "I hate cramped spaces where you can't see the sun. There was this cubby my parents used to put me in when the Corporation Recruiters would come by. I had to be quiet and not use any of my power. Still can't stand anything like it. I'd rather sleep outside in a storm than get stuck somewhere the stars don't shine."

Vera sighed, rubbing her fingers lightly over the burning skin by her wound as she considered the fucked up situation they were in. Her brows furrowed, eyes turning back towards Lani as she studied her. "So you're one of those hidden Mark kids? I'd heard about that, but . . . they say that no one successfully pulls it off for very long. Then again," she snorted, "the Company says a lot. Like how kids taken by the Corp are supposed to be at the University and not in the Mines."

The Emotive at the wheel turned sharply to look at Vera, brows pulling together. "Wait, there are *kids* in there? In the Spire? What the actual fuck?"

"Yeah. That's how I ended up there. Did a recruitment tour, cause . . . Ya know, us goons we get sent on tours to find out where we'll fit in. Anyways . . . I go to do a tour at the Spire, and I see this guard beating the ever living shit out of a kid. Couldn't have been more than twelve." She shook her head. "I couldn't stand it. Told him to stop. He didn't. I intercepted one of his blows, and he started trying to hit me, so . . ."

Vera frowned, looking down at her lap. It hadn't ended well, obviously. She could still remember the sheer *joy* she'd felt when she'd ripped him in half. She still thought it was the right thing to do. That kid, no matter what he'd done or what the University Precogs had seen of his future, hadn't deserve being beaten to death.

None of those kids had.

"Let's just say that ripping a guard in half gets you thrown into the Spire mines pretty fucking quick," Vera finished.

They were well out of the mangroves and maneuvering their way between two islands bursting with thick foliage when Lani finally replied, "That's fucked up. Glad I didn't kill you after all. Was the kid ok?"

". . . for a while." Vera didn't think that Lani actually wanted to know. *Vera* hadn't wanted to know. For years, she had bought into the propaganda. Now she couldn't get the images of what she had seen in the Mines out of her head. She wasn't going to make Lani try to picture it. Vera was capable of cruelty, but took no pleasure in inflicting it on people who had done nothing to deserve it. "The boy was still alive last I saw him, if that's what you're asking."

"Alive isn't always a good thing." Lani looked down at the instrument panel, fiddling with some dials.

"True. It could have been worse, though. Torin, my Bonded, could have ended up there. I'm not sure I could have survived it, or escaped, if I didn't know he was safe. I have no idea where he is, but sometimes I think I dream of him on an island. Then I remember he's Corporate. There's no way they would let him loose, and if I go looking for him, I'm gonna get caught." Vera grimaced and rubbed at her neck. Then she flinched, because there was no mistaking the feel of the thin band of scars around her neck from her Corporate tattoo. "Bah. Doesn't matter."

"Is your Torin an ornery asshole of a Mender with a scraggly beard who won't patch you up unless you pay him a fortune and makes horrible soup?" Lani asked.

"I mean . . . he does make pretty horrible soup." Vera couldn't help the laugh. Torin could cook, he really could. But there was one soup he made that was absolutely awful, and it was how she'd always known when she'd messed up somehow. He always fed her *that* shit. Supposedly it was healthy, but Vera had never believed it. "My Torin though . . . he was always a stickler for grooming. I can't picture him with a scraggly beard." She sighed. "Though . . . lately I have a hard time picturing him at all. If it weren't for the echo, I might think I dreamed him up."

"I've heard Blood Bonds described that way, like an echo, before. I've never had one. There aren't many Rogue Marks like me, and even fewer people willing to bind themselves to us. Most Rogues end up Corporate or dead."

Vera blinked, looking at Lani a little more closely. "Shit, no wonder you're weird. I can't imagine not having a Bonded." She shook her head, smiling a bit. "If it weren't for Torin, I'd have been put down years ago." She'd always slipped into anger too quickly to be trusted without a Blood Bond to anchor her. Her instructors had said she *excelled* at combat. They had tied her to Torin as a precaution—a way to keep her unpredictability in line. Pity it hadn't been enough. "It's hard to describe. Torin always made me feel like I could surface when I fell beneath the waves. He was always able to pull me back if I went too far, and," Vera closed her eyes, remembering his beautiful brown ones. "No one had eyes like Torin. I can't always see his face, but I always recall his voice and his eyes. I just want . . ." She sighed. "Well, it doesn't matter. I hope he found someone else to Bond himself to, or . . ."

"He dies when you do. Probably. Lovely side effect, right? That's what got a friend of mine a couple decades back. Fell over dead one day with no warning because his Bonded had a stroke. No thanks. None of that for me. No offense, but I think all you Bonded are kind of nuts. How do you trust someone with your very life? Forever?"

Vera couldn't help but smile sadly as she watched Lani shudder during that question. "That's less likely to happen if you Bond to a few people. The more the better. And I can't tell you how often Torin got me through the worst of the darkness. I mean . . . we couldn't talk or anything—too much distance—but you can *feel* that you aren't alone. That means a lot."

Of course, trying to explain that to someone who had spent their whole life alone would be like trying to explain sunlight to one of the kids raised from birth in the Mines.

Vera let her mind wander back to Torin. "He'd have been pissed at me for how I got out, I think. He never did like bloodshed. Always tried to find ways to avoid it, even if there really wasn't one. Drove me crazy."

Lani looked back at her again. "You know, I still don't believe that you got out on your own. I mean, *no one* I've ever heard of got out of the Spire. I saw your Conflicter Mark yesterday when you changed pants. You got what? Two Trials? Three before you burned out? I find it a little hard to believe, considering I know people who have been trying to get Sahima Parata herself out for years."

Vera didn't say anything for a few minutes as she mulled over how to answer. Every Marked person went through Trials—those strange and unpredictable times when their Marks flared uncontrollably—every few years. Vera's first one had been at the age of fifteen, and she could still remember the way her Mark had burned and driven her to move, to *kill*. Each Trial was different. Pass it, survive it, learn to embrace the new depth of power it granted, and the Mark grew. Eventually, though, everyone failed. Vera's third and final Trial had been spent in a cell, awaiting sentencing, and she had cracked. Her Mark would never grow again and the years, too, would now leave their mark. With how large the wave-like Emotive Mark on Lani's calf was, Vera had to assume the girl was decades, if not centuries, older than her. Considering she looked younger than Vera did, it was also likely that she was still challenging Trials.

Would Lani understand the level of desperation that had driven Vera to flee despite her relatively small Mark? She let the horizon calm her heart, and did her best to forget the cry of an infant, or her screams as . . . *No*. She wasn't going to focus on those memories either.

"I failed my third Trial, but before that, when I was still in their good graces, I was good. *Really* good. So much so that I think they sabotaged my last Trial to make sure I wouldn't become more of a threat. Escape wasn't about my Mark, though. It required some thought, and some planning, but most of all a willingness to cut through as many bodies as I had to and not care if I died, as long as I got to die free. If that damned Shifter hadn't been there, I'd have gotten loose without mangling my leg."

Lani looked like she was about to respond, but the boat beneath them suddenly stopped thrumming with the roar of the motor. It sputtered, then stalled, the whole gurgle punctuated by Lani swearing. "OH COME ON! I checked the batteries an hour ago! There was plenty of juice."

Vera yawned, stretching out as the boat shuddered. "Didn't check the engines did you? Corp always installs a kill switch on the engines, just in case." She blinked a few times, then she snorted. "Or did you think we're the first ones to steal a boat? You need to go to the left engine. It'll look like a weird ass wire bundle, that's been Infused with a Telekinetic's juice. It's on a timer set to scramble the engine to shreds if it isn't reset." Vera motioned at her leg. "I'd go, but . . . Uh . . . might not come up again if I do. I can keep an eye out for trouble while you go look, though."

Lani was glaring at Vera with a ferocity that would put a shark to shame. "And you didn't think to *tell me this?*"

"Didn't remember." It had been a while since she'd been a crewmember on a Corporate vessel, and Vera had honestly forgotten that not everyone knew about those things. It wasn't as if she had ever expected to be teaming up with what was essentially a pirate.

"You really are about as useful as a Corpse, aren't you? Do I have to do everything myself? Fuck." Lani stomped her way to the hatch that led below deck, her swearing turning muffled.

Vera looked back out to sea. With her companion busy and nothing else to distract her, memories crept back in. Her hand settled on her belly, thumb trailing over the long-faded stretch marks—the only thing she had left of the child that had been torn from her, and whose existence had driven Vera to finally escape. Where was he? How long until his father used one of the many samples of Vera's blood he had taken and come find her with his Tracker Mark? Hopefully long enough for Vera to die free. Once, she had hoped escape would include saving her son from being raised to be a Corporate loyalist. There was no way she would get to Kahana before dying, though. The Spire had taken even that last dream from her, in the end.

Lani's curses getting louder heralded her return. "Well, we're fucked. It burned a hole right through the battery packs. Do you know if there's a backup propulsion system on these stupid, fucking skiffs?" Lani kicked the navigation panel to accentuate each word, then hopped twice, grabbing her foot. Vera couldn't help but grin at the sight of Lani's bleeding toe. The woman turned to glare at Vera. "Couldn't you have remembered this information an hour ago when we weren't floating in the middle of the ocean and were still *on an island for the night?* Is that really too much to ask?" Vera's eyebrows rose. "Excuse me? You want me to remember shit from six years ago as if it were yesterday? I'm *sorry* there's more important stuff vying for my attention as far as memory goes. I barely remember crawling into the damned boat." She snorted, rubbing at the back of her head. Was there an extra battery pack? She frowned, trying to think about it. "Er . . . there is actually a small backup. We won't hit top speed without the sails open though. Beneath the helm, there is a small panel you can peel up. It should be in there. Some sort of switch, if I'm remembering right. Or, you know, you could use the damn *sail.*" Vera pointed up at the mast, and the neatly folded white solar sail.

"When it comes to us *staying alive* yes, yes I do expect you to remember." Lani glared at Vera again. "And I'm not going to unfurl white sails where we're going, so let's hope this works."

Lani went digging near the helm and let out a whoop when she found what she was looking for. It didn't take too long for the boat to get going again, but Vera did notice that Lani kept looking around as if expecting something to come swooping out of the clear sky to get them.

"Calm down, Lani. If something's coming, we'll deal with it when it gets to us. If nothing's coming, you're riling yourself *and me* for no good damned reason." Vera's head tilted to the side, eyes narrowing a little as she watched the woman. Lani was an Emotive. All the Emotives Vera had ever met were cool, calculating, controlled assholes who meddled with the feelings of those around them without ever bothering to ask. Lani was jumpy, mercurial, and antisocial. Was this what a lack of University education looked like? Frankly, Vera was concerned about it. The Corporation was going to find them eventually. With the engine having gone down, there was going to be a fight. Vera was ready. She was always ready, even if the thought of having to fight in this condition made her injured leg throb. Would Lani be ready? She had avoided confronting the two Corporate goons on the little island. When the Corporation came and Emotive tricks ceased to work, would her new companion hold her own, or would she get herself killed?

Probably the latter.

"You should keep asking questions, Weirdling. Or yelling. Bottling it all up and letting your nerves play on your thoughts is just going to get us both in trouble," Vera said, pushing away those troubling thoughts.

Lani snorted. "Don't judge me for my paranoia. It's what's kept me alive and free, unlike you."

Vera narrowed her eyes, her Mark flaring at the insult. "Better to *do*, than to hide." She turned her face back towards the horizon. Far in the distance, colorful, swirling clouds and lightning danced over the sea. Vera frowned, leaning closer into the rail as she studied the Prismatic Storm. She hadn't seen one of the strange, unpredictable hurricanes since being tossed in the Mines. Vera could have sworn it hadn't been there the last time she looked. Then again, that was always the way of Prismatic Storms. Only the best Corporate storm watchers could predict them. "Looks like we're about to get some weather."

Lani froze. All the color drained from her face and for a long moment she stood perfectly still. A gust of wind blew past them, carrying with it the scent of rain. The Emotive burst into motion, running for the hitherto ignored sails as though her life depended on them. "No. Nonononono."

A veritable wrecking ball of panic crashed into Vera, carrying with it the telltale *otherness* of emotions not her own. Looking down, she saw the Emotive Mark on Lani's leg glowing bright. Gritting her teeth to keep from rising to the battle cry of the other woman's panic, Vera raised her voice to try to catch her attention. "Lani. *Lani*, breathe. If you freak me out, we're in deeper shit." Vera took a few deep breaths of her own before forcing herself to her feet, lurching her way towards the helm, careful not to put weight on her injured leg. She pulled out a few ropes, then worked on tying the knots that would make sure neither of them got tossed overboard when the storm hit.

"C'mon ... let's get tied in, then wait for it to reach us. At least we'll get some wind."

Lani jerked away from Vera as she neared. "No, don't touch me.

Seriously, until the storm passes don't you fucking dare touch me." She backed up quickly, eyes wide. "Don't you see the colors in the clouds? That's not one of the normal storms. Fuck."

"So? Storm's a storm for almost everybody, Prismatic or not." She frowned, lashing herself to the mast with enough slack to move, but not enough to go overboard. "You're going to need help sailing once it hits. With the engine out, you don't have as much oomph to resist the sway. If we lose the wind, we're gonna capsize and we'll both be fucked."

Not that she should have to lay that out for the woman. The blasted Emotive wasn't a child—but she sure did look spooked like one. After a breath, Vee forced herself to gentle her voice. "It'll be fine, Lani. If storms freak you out, I'll take care of it somehow. Go below."

Lani batted the offered rope away. "You're hurt and can hardly hobble. I'll be fine up here with the boat, I just can't be around people. Get the hell away from me and everything will be fine."

This level of panic didn't make sense. It was a Prismatic Storm, sure, but those didn't affect either of them. The only Mark it could affect was a Fertility Mark. In fact, usually Prismatic Storms were a bit mellower than normal ones.

Still, who was she to argue with what was clearly trauma of some sort? Maybe Lani had lost someone to a Prismatic Storm. Whatever the reason, the panic coming off her Emotive Mark was making Vera's self control wobble. "Fine. If you want to do this on your own, go right ahead, but if you get me dead because you freak out while sailing, I'm haunting your ass."

"You can get in line!" Lani shouted back with a wobble to her voice that made Vera deeply nervous.

CODEX: Alright, since I still have a little over 12 more minutes of this damn patch download, I think I am going to start organizing myself. I have to be able to help my friends when I'm able to again. So SALT, *Query: How do I use my To-Do List?*

SALT: You simply say 'Add X to my To-Do' list.

CODEX: Excellent. Create a new To-Do list for files I need to send to my uncle Kekai.

SALT: To-Do list created. What file names would you like me to add?

CODEX: Well, first thing's first; let's find out what the Corp knows and has been keeping from us, so *Query: What is the Salt Spire?*

NOTES FROM CRYSTAL CORP FILES: EXPLORATION OF THE SPIRE

It seems as though the entire mountain emerged from the sea in a single month, and is the cause of all the earthquakes. It is made entirely of salt and full of strange tunnels. Our advanced team had to return to the ships because all of their Marks began to act in an unusual fashion within the Spire. Only internal Marks like Conflict behaved at all as expected, but even they seem to be somewhat distorted by the massive amount of salt. We are calling for a University research team as backup before further exploration takes place. Our initial hypothesis: since it is known that salt is left behind when using a Mark, perhaps the presence of so much salt is confusing them.

As a side note, I would advise that under no circumstances should a Fertility Mark approach the Spire. Where most Marks are affected, the Spire seems to do something more to the minds of those blessed with the Fertility Mark. It drives them mad. We had to put down one of our colleagues as he screamed about how he wanted to destroy the mountain. Extreme caution is advised.

Initial suggestions are for any mining to be performed by unMarked labor, and under no condition should this mountain be open to the public.

Dodging Whitesails
Salome - Day 4   06

Over several hours of racing across the waves with Whitesails on their heels, Salome was forced—again—to admire her brother's work. Not that their uncle and some of their cousins couldn't dance circles around the Corporation, but they weren't as good at it as Sal and Kuma were. Most of that came from the ship Kumanu had turned the *Sahima's Legacy* into since Salome had taken command.

That was why they took the riskier embargo assignments. Because she, Kuma, this crew, and this ship, could handle anything the Corporation threw at them. Hells bells, the *Legacy* seemed to be able to handle anything *the world* threw at her, honestly. Be it a storm, a fleet of Corporate ships, or a simple salt run, *Sahima's Legacy* was on top of it. Sal knew Kuma didn't like to take credit, for preferring to credit it to Salome's ability as a captain, but she knew the truth.

The boom of incoming fire sounded a split second before a shattering crash rent the air. Sal swiveled around, teeth bared as she took in the railing to the helm, which had just been blown to bits by the guns on the deck of the nearest Corporate galleon.

Fuckers were trying to put holes in *her* ship.

"Hard engine pull!" Salome ordered, turning back to the direction they were headed. Up ahead, the fog bank that usually shrouded the barrier Reef that surrounded the inhabited archipelagos under Corporate control loomed across her field of vision. The waves were growing choppier, and Sal had to double check her map and compass, adjusting course.

"Yeah, yeah, miss bossy pants," Kuma grumbled, the Infusion Mark on his forearm glowing once more as he played with his console. Sal left him to it, focusing entirely on what lay ahead.

Sailing near the Reef wasn't as dangerous as sailing outside it, where wild and unpredictable storms and currents made ships vanish without a trace and monsters swam in the Depths. It was, however, still a risky play. There were lots of places where a ship could crash right into the underwater mountains that protected the archipelagos. Paired with the mist that hid obstacles, sandbanks, and other dangers, only shallow-bottomed and quick ships like the *Legacy* could hope to survive it. This section of the Reef was one Sal sailed in often on her way to and from Sonder and on her way to the Spire, but even hundreds of trips hadn't made her less twitchy about it.

"Sal, reinforcements incoming. A dozen more ships just Ported in. I think you have them convinced," her brother warned.

"Finally. Took them long enough. *ALL HANDS, TIE DOWN!* Kuma, now!"

"Aye!"

He set the engines to full throttle. Salome let out a wild laugh while the ship rocketed forward with the Infused power and speed of a Conflicter. Kuma had infused the batteries with a solid charge only a week ago, so it was fresh and wild. The sails were fully open, the wind and engines working together to widen the gap between them and the enemy as the *Legacy* headed straight towards the Reef's edge. The Corporate vessels fired again, but the *Legacy* was zooming out of range faster than they could react.

"Get ready for the turn, Kuma. As soon as we hit the fog bank, we're heading north and your decoy goes south. Get moving."

Her brother did. He knew this trick. Sal would get the Corporation to think she had disappeared into the fog in the direction she was headed, and instead use the fog banks at twilight to scoot off elsewhere. All Kuma had to do was release a decoy signal and hide their own presence while they waited to see if the idiots fell for it. Well, that and pull off a 180 degree turn on a dime. Easy, right?

Marked hand still on his console, her brother knelt to pull a small buoy attached to a jetpack out from a cubby. "Hello my little friend. Ready to pretend to be us?"

"Please don't tell me you named another machine, Kuma."

"If I don't name them, how can I trust them?" He teased, pressing a few buttons on a small device welded onto a cage around the buoy as they entered the fogbank. "This is Get Out Of Fucking

Dodge, otherwise known as Goofd."

"That is a horrible acronym. You seriously need a girlfriend, Kuma. You're clearly way too bored. Ok, NOW! Hard turn north," She shouted, loud enough for the whole crew to hear.

Kuma tossed—*shudder*—Goofd over the side, and at the same time slammed a button on the console. Salome waited just long enough to be sure her crew had hold of the sails, then spun the wheel. "Phase!"

The hull became immaterial, skating through the water as though it wasn't there. The whole boat twisted near ninety degrees, but that still wasn't enough. Heading towards the raging ocean beyond the Reef while going at this speed wasn't going to end well.

"Rear Kinetic drift," she ordered. Kuma sighed loudly, then lowered a level. All motion stopped at the back end of the ship, sending the prow swiveling even further north like the weight at the end of a pendulum. There was Phase Drifting, and then there was this: the sudden and sickening 'crunch' on her insides as the sails and rudder shifted to turn the ship another ninety degrees in about three seconds flat. Sal had to brace to keep her footing, but her hands never wobbled on the wheel. "Now gun it again and get us some cover."

They were off like a light, though it took Salome's stomach several seconds to catch up.

"What do you want us to be today? Fishing vessel?" Kuma asked, flicking the small screen on his console as it scrolled through code. He had already activated the Shielding on all the electrical and Infused systems. Salome could smell it in the air, a certain ionized tang that made her mouth feel dry. Now it was just a matter of making the *Legacy* appear as something other than a pirate vessel to any Corporate sweeps.

"You did a fishing vessel last time."

"Well . . . it worked?"

"For all of *one* day, Kuma."

"Fine. How about a brothel ship? Wouldn't mind finding one of those for real after all this blows over."

". . . Ugh. *Fine*." The way her nose wrinkled up at the thought made him grin. Salome turned to glare at him. "Wipe that smug smile off your face. You're my big brother. I'm allowed to not to want to picture you having sex."

He cut the engines, the *Legacy* slowing, but still maintaining a good amount of momentum. "Just think about it . . . we make the ship read like a brothel, and you can go off and get some nookie with your Mender while this all blows over. Beautiful symmetry."

"Shut up, K."

"I mean, he's got a really cute rear en—"

Sal shifted so she could hold the wheel with one hand and used the hard prosthetic one to cuff the back of Kuma's head. He laughed in response, twisting out of reach of another blow. The fog was heavy enough that she couldn't see much beyond him, so as much as Sal would have liked to follow and kick his ass for that comment, she turned back to her map and instrument panel.

The next few minutes were a chaotic madhouse of crashing waves, whispered orders passed around the crew, and the occasional roar of a shot fired from the Corporation ships chasing south after the decoy as the *Legacy* snuck further and further north. The ship's engines rose and fell as needed under Kuma's careful control, allowing Sal to make use of wind, wave, and engine like a composer directed music.

Kuma could multitask. Any Infuser needed to, but he'd gotten very good at it since Salome had first taken the wheel. If he hadn't, their ship would be in pieces. "Signal's prepped and we'll be approaching some nearby islands where we can slink back into normal waters in a few hours."

"Good. Kumanu, get my engines checked over and refueled." While it was definitely an order, Salome kept her voice hushed. They were running quiet, the fog at the edge of the Reef their cover to outrun the Corporation.

"Aye Cap'n."

Over the following few hours, Sal checked in on her brother down in his room by the engines every twenty minutes or so. He went from soaking wet to dry as bone to covered in engine grease and soaked in sweat, but at last the engines were fueled up again, or at least as much as possible without more Marks on board. Kuma could only Infuse the power of the Marks into objects, after all. He couldn't just conjure it from thin air, much to Salome's annoyance.

What Kuma did manage to conjure was a wonderful 'snoop' feed on Corporation news channels. He listened as he tinkered with the engine, Salome passing him his tools. His 'room' was no more than a bed stuffed in the corner of the end-section of the hull, engines humming in the middle and a workshop covering the other wall. There was a tiny adjacent bathroom, but that was the only modification Kuma had made for comfort over the years. Salome had to wonder if living next to his work was comforting, or yet another way her brother punished himself for killing their mother when Sal had been a baby.

While lost in thought, a tidbit of a broadcast caught her attention. Sal cocked her head to the side, reaching forward to tap Kuma on the shoulder. He propped himself up on his elbows, removing the earbuds in which he usually played music while working. Sal turned up the volume on the crackly radio.

"*Any citizen who believes they have spotted the subject should immediately report the sighting to their local Corporate Officer and keep a safe distance. We repeat: Do not engage with this Conflicter, as she is known to be unstable, extremely prone to violence, and adept at close combat. The unknown Emotive has no clear features for us to report, but it is assumed that the two Marked women have some link or relationship. The Emotive may, in fact, have been the cause of the sudden instability of a previously honored member of the Corporation.*"

When the message started to repeat, Kuma leaned against the gently thrumming engine. "You think we should go try to find them? I know you said you wouldn't chase down the escapee from the Spire, but if they're Marked—"

"No."

"Why not? Clearly they've pissed in the Company's cereal. That makes them pirates, whether they know it yet or not. We could help."

"Haven't we stuck our necks out enough for one day? We have Corp ships crawling all around us. My point from earlier still stands: we'll be more help to these girls if we keep the Corporation busy looking for us than we would if we led them straight to these escapees. Besides, if you're going to make my ship look like a brothel, I am going on vacation until we're in the clear."

"Ooo . . . lucky Torin."

"Shut up, Kuma."

Kuma crossed his arms, brushing his shoulder-length hair back from his face and only succeeding in leaving a large grease stain on his forehead. "Seriously, Sal . . . you sure you want to pass this one up? One of the Marks is a Conflicter. The other one might be an Emotive. Getting not one, but *two*, Marks for our uncle? I mean . . ."

"By the time we could hunt them down, they'll already be

caught. You know that." Sal wanted to snap it, but she didn't. This was a touchy subject for Kuma, and she didn't want to bruise him more than necessary with her decision.

Kuma ground his teeth. "So you're just going to let them get caught and killed? Salome, you *know* how rough a time Rogue Marks have. If it were me out there being hunted, wouldn't you want someone sympathetic to help me?"

She looked down at him, her hard expression softening. Sal reached out and placed a hand on his arm. "Not every Rogue Mark is your responsibility, K. Focus on who we have the power to help. It will drive you crazy otherwise. Let this one go."

Kuma sighed, shoulders sagging. "Whatever you say, Cap't, but can we at least keep our eyes open for them?"

Sal smiled and gave his arm a final squeeze. "Sure, greasemonkey. I promise that if we see them and can help, we will."

CODEX: Alright, next up, *Query: who is Iolani Saba?*

-----CLASSIFIED: MARK RESPONSE : LEVEL 4-----

Date: 21st of Shifting LC, 1229
Designation: Emotion/Fertility Mark - Rogue
Island: Juno (Population 185)
Incident: Received Distress Call from 42 year old female about disappearances. Dispatched Mark Response Team.

Report: Team Lead reports that of the original 185 inhabitants, only 62 remain alive. Initial study suggests a Fertility Mark lost control on the Island. Investigation shows no Fertility Marks assigned to the area. No previously known Rogues reported in the area for more than three years.
Initial suspect is a child, though the Team Lead believes this unlikely to be the case due to a child likely not having enough juice to kill two-thirds of the population.
Family thought to have had the child is also dead. With no way to prove that the child was involved, and so many mulch piles across the island, Team Lead made the call that the child was likely not the culprit. We are likely dealing with a Fertility Mark that went through a Trial unexpectedly on a populated island.
Further investigation will need to be conducted. Tracker Team has been sent to rendezvous with Mark Response Team. Salt and Emergency Supplies have been sent to the island

to aid in recovery, in accordance with Section A-2b of Mark Response.

Threat Level Assignation: 4 — CASE WILL BE ELEVATED TO CRYSTAL, GALENA.

------CLASSIFIED: MARK RESPONSE : LEVEL 4------

Date: 2nd of Infusion LC, 1286

Addendum: Unknown Emotive/Fertilizer identified as Iolani Saba with an 82% chance of accuracy. Picture captured on a security camera and compared to the database of school-aged children from Juno at the time of the slaughter, 57 years ago. Considering the average number of Trials, this puts Miss Saba's potential Mark Expansion at 3+ per Mark. Threat Level Assignation Adjustment: 5

------CLASSIFIED: THREAT LEVEL 5------

Date: 11th of Mending LC, 1491

Tracker ID: 445-897

Case Number: 332-554-8964

Summary: Arrived on the Island of Candor at 21:45 after a tip from the anonymous Rogue Mark Hotline. Report claimed they have not heard from a neighbour for several days, and that when they went to investigate, they found decomposing rotted mulch on the bed. Local law enforcement have secured the site. Upon arrival and inspection, I can confirm that this is the work of a Fertilizer, likely Rogue. There were clothes strewn about the apartment, including those of a woman. My initial suspicicn is that this Rogue Fertilizer, likely female, and the victim were engaged in an intimate liaison when she murdered him. Hard to say whether it was deliberate or not.

Evidence: Clothing bagged. Mulch bagged. Building swept for organic matter.

Further Orders requested.

Prismatic Storm
Vera - Day 4

07

The Storm hit just after noon. Vera didn't like how Lani was so tense about it. Storms, even Prismatic ones, were typical. Someone who had lived on the ocean as long as this Emotive must have, shouldn't be so afraid of them.

Lani's long curly hair was plastered to her head by the rain and crashing waves, but what bothered Vera wasn't the way her companion was clutching the wheel with white-knuckled hands. It was the terror in the other woman's eyes that made Vera feel as though a fight was coming.

Then again, maybe that was the veritable fleet of white-sailed ships in the distance, very clearly closing in despite the Prismatic Storm. Why a fleet of Whitesails was this close to the Reef might have intrigued Vera at another time, but there were more pressing concerns at present.

A wave crashed against the side of the skiff, water rising to drench Vera where she sat clutching the mast. Above them, the clouds roiled in strange, unearthly colors. Lightning rent the sky, a silvery glow overlaying everything in a quick flash. Vera had to blink, wiping water out of her eyes. That must have been close. She could swear she still saw silver over Lani.

Tucking herself in tighter against the mast, Vera clung to it as wave after wave rocked against the boat. *Against* the skiff, despite all of Lani's weight trying to make sure the boat was angled correctly.

She'd fucking *told* the stubborn girl that sailing through a storm alone was a fool's errand. Another wave hit, nearly sending Vera sprawling despite her deathgrip around the mast. Vera's teeth clenched, eyes trying to peer through the deluge towards the helm. There. Lani was righting herself. Thank the fucking Gods. She even looked like she was relaxing, like she'd found her stride. In fact, she was *laughing* in the face of the storm . . .

A prickle played along Vera's neck as she tried to make sense of the danger her instincts were warning her of. She flared her Mark in response, hoping to better grasp the danger. Being a Conficter was about so much more than pure violence. It let Vera strategize quickly, gave her senses a boost, even helped her keep her cool in stressful situations. As her power flooded through her, Adavera's skin crawled. The feeling in the air wasn't Lani's Emotive Mark. Or it was, but . . . Not? She couldn't make sense of it. This wasn't the time for the Emotive to be losing her shit. The Corporation might be caught in this weird ass storm too, but their engines worked. With a little work, Lani and Vera could sneak away during the storm and get out of range. That was the goal, wasn't it? Why was Lani so insistent about working alone when she didn't have to?

All thoughts were ripped from Vera's mind when Lani took her hands off the wheel, allowing it to twist to the side. The whole skiff caught a wave, turning away from the direction they had been heading and *toward* the Whitesails pursuing them.

Lani . . . Lani what the fuck are you doing? Vera shouted psychically, since there was no way in hell her voice would carry over the crash of the ocean and booms of thunder. It had been many years since she had tried it, but while rusty, the simple magic must have reached its target, because Lani jumped.

Vera tried to get to her feet, but her injured leg seized. A scream gurgled out of her throat in surprised pain, and she quickly slapped a hand down atop the worst of the injuries. What the *fuck* was that?

Lani's head snapped up towards Vera, as though she had only just noticed her. The laugh stopped abruptly, and Vera gasped. Lani's eyes were shining a bright, liquid silver, and below her long-sleeved swimsuit top, something else shone—like a Mark did, while in use.

Oh shit, she has a second Mark.

There was something majestic and terrifying about Lani as the woman stalked towards her. The *glow* of Lani's skin, the glow of her eyes, the gait of her walk as she seemed to move through the storm rather than against it. It was eerie. The wildly rocking deck didn't seem to trouble her at all as Lani stepped away from the wheel and walked towards Vera with a dancer's grace, eyes fixed not on her face but her leg. Vera's lips peeled back off her teeth as that gaze's direction became clear.

Lani stopped in front of Vera and her head cocked to the side. "You're not well. The leg, it's infected. It's going to kill you slowly. I can fix that. Your body is rich in salt, it will help." Her voice was hollow and emotionless, but also gentle, a strong surge of soothing calm emanating from her in time with every gust of rain and crashing wave.

Vera wasn't stupid. She knew what Lani's words meant. She'd heard such offers of merciful death before. Not wanting to provoke her companion, Vera remained motionless as she flared her own Mark. At once, time seemed to slow, giving Vera time to think through her options.

Vines. That was the shape hidden by Lani's clothes. Glowing, twisting vines shining through the dark fabric. Vera had been made to memorize the shape of every Mark and what it meant. Vines were the sign of the Fertility Mark, the only one of the thirteen not tied to a Lunar Cycle, but rather to the Prismatic Storms.

What had her teachers said about Fertilizers? The most powerful and destructive of all Marks, but not under the control of the person cursed with them.

Just like Berserkers.

Staring into Lani's eyes, Vera saw it. That emptiness she had seen in her own gaze while watching the surveillance footage of her attacking that guard during her tribunal. Lani wasn't in there anymore, but, much like Vera, she would return to face the consequences of her Mark's actions.

She's going to kill me.

Part of Vera wanted to open her arms and embrace that death. Merciful and quick would be so much better than drawn out and awful, wouldn't it? Except Lani would never forgive herself when she woke up from this. That much was obvious. Adavera knew killers. And before this woman's skin glowed in the Storm she'd have sworn that Lani wasn't a killer. She hadn't slit Vera's throat when she had every reason to do it, so clearly, this was not Lani.

Vera's gaze locked on the glowing orbs of Lani's eyes again, studying that face. *If she's really Fertility Marked and not Bloodbound... That would explain a lot.* Like why Lani was so fucking paranoid. It would also explain why she hadn't wanted anyone to touch her, why this storm had bothered her so fucking much, and why she was so very *different* like this.

So Vera let loose a breath, trying to soak in the memory of the sea and the rain in case it was her last. All her thinking had taken less than a second, but in that time, Lani had raised an arm toward Vera, glowing mist trailing off it. "Let me fix you."

Vera dodged the outstretched hand, holding on to the mast for balance. Her leg was killing her. She had the sneaky suspicion that it was Lani's fault. Fertilizers were well known for turning people into piles of mulch if that was what the environment around them needed. There was a damned good chance Vera would die no matter what she did, but going down without a fight just wasn't in her nature. If she could get Iolani to be a little more stable, even if just for a while, then maybe—just maybe—it would buy them enough time to clear this storm. "Sure, you can fix me." Vera said. "Can I get a hug first, though? I'm scared."

Lani's head tilted to the side, her eyes focused on Vera as if trying to work out her words. "Hug? Why do you need a hug? That doesn't sound practical, no. This will only hurt for a few hours, don't worry. So little time when you stop thinking about it from your perspective."

"It's called *comfort*, Lani. I'm tired of being alone. You remember being alone?" Vera was gathering herself, readying for a lunge that she did not *want* to do. Vera knew exactly where Lani's knife was. She'd watched the woman touch it more often in the last few days than she'd been happy with.

Even sick, even injured, Vera could get to it faster than Lani, but it was going to *hurt*. It already hurt, a new wave of pain coursing down her limb with every silvery pulse of Lani's power as it washed over her. That did it. Vera wasn't going to let Lani's Mark keep her distracted. There was no telling how long she'd have before her leg drove her bloody mad. Vera flared her Conflict Mark, the geometric pattern on her thigh glowing red for a second. Energy surged through her body and set her teeth on edge as she lunged forward, the rope around her waist catching her as she wrapped an arm around the Fertilizer. Her hand caught on the hilt of Lani's blade where it rested against her hip, body twisting about to tangle them together in the rope. A slash of the knife against Lani's arm. Another against Adavera's. Cut to cut, Vera pressed their forearms together, leaning in to keep them pinned between their bodies. Lani didn't know how to Blood Bond . . . but Adavera did.

The pain was immediate. Vera's head tipped back, a howl torn from her lips and lost in the gale. Liquid lightning shot through her veins from where their flesh joined. Vera tightened her grip on Lani's arm anyways, despite or perhaps *because* of that very pain, and shoved the energy of her Mark up that blood trail. This was taboo. This was *rape*, in a way, and doing it made Vera feel sick to her stomach. It was also the only possible way to maybe save Lani from comitting murder. It was the only way. She kept telling herself that—it was the only way. Lani was *lost* in the Storm, and Vera hadn't come this far to die like this.

Because Adavera had no doubt that Lani *was* killing her. She could feel it—the way that her leg was starting to weaken and rot as Lani poured her power into disintegrating it—and there was nothing Vera could do to stop her. Nothing but *this*.

The rope pressed hard into Vera's back, but she simply clenched her teeth and continued the Bond. Lani thrashed and howled in pain. Vera ignored it. This was a battle. Adavera was a Conflicter. Battle was her blood, her bone, her very soul. In this, at least, she knew that Lani would be beaten.

Lani's blood and energy spread down Vera's arm and through her body. She let it carry her mind away from reality. She forced herself to focus only on setting that link, on binding Lani's power against her own. Where there had once been only two threads—her own and Torin's—there was now a third. With care, Vera wove it around her, within her, and started pinning it in place.

It wasn't easy. It wasn't efficient. It was downright painful. With Torin, it had been a relief, a feeling of coming home and existing together. This was different. It *should* be different—needed to be different—because what she was doing was wrong and Vera knew it.

Lani fought against her. Now that Vera could feel the other woman's magic, she realized just how much *larger* the dual-Marked woman's well of power was compared to her own. That avalanche of awakened magic pushed against Vera's every knot and weave, but the pulse of their blood flowing into each other's veins made the fight ultimately unwinnable.

Unable to stop the internal melding, Lani started to flail, her hand leaving Vera's leg to push against her chest. She cried out in rage and fear, but Vera didn't budge, her back firmly planted against the mast. There. Vera had the first few threads woven. Trying to focus on the Bond through the pain was taxing, and trying to keep Lani from ripping her to shreds as she worked even more so, but Vera had spent six years in the Mines. She'd endured hell repeatedly. What Lani was doing wasn't even close to the worst of it. . .

There. Another major anchor. With it, Vera stumbled under the weight of Lani's emotions crashing into hers. So much pain. So much self-loathing and fear. Fear of this: the Storm, killing, Bonding. This was Lani's nightmare, and through the Bond, it was now Vera's too.

Vera's vision was starting to swim, her brain clouding. No!. She wasn't done. Not yet. *Lani . . . breathe. Breathe, damn it. Wake the fuck up and snap out of it!*

GET OUT OF MY HEAD. YOU WILL NOT TRAP ME LIKE THIS

The volume was intense. Intense enough that Vera's head

rocked backward into the mast, her eyes closing as a wave of black crashed over her. It didn't completely knock her out, but the wave of psychic sound hurt. Vera's fingers still grasped onto Lani's arm, but she couldn't reorient herself, too lost in the process of Bonding the Fertilizer to herself.

Why was she trying to save Lani from herself again? Oh, right. Because despite Vera's growls, and her anger, and her willingness to kill things—she had always wanted to protect something that deserved protecting. Lani was something worth protecting. She had no reason to help Vera when she had found her on the beach, and yet she had. Crankily, sure, but who else had Vera ever met who would have done that, other than perhaps Torin?

Torin.

Oh how she wished she could see him one more time before death took her . . .

GET OUT. GET OUT. GET . . . out. G . . . et. No. Not like this. Just go . . . don't . . . . Lani's mental voice sank to a whisper as she struggled while Vera wove the net between them tighter and tighter until there was a snap, and suddenly where there had been two, there was one.

Vera gasped as the threads settled into place. Lani's mind opened to her like a blooming flower and Vera *felt* the Storm. It crashed into her like the waves battered the boat, trying to pull her along with Lani into a miasma of death and destruction. Though her heart yearned to rise to the challenge, Vera couldn't. She'd given what she could to help Lani drag herself out of her fugue, and there just wasn't anything left. Her body burned, like it had in . . . no. No. She couldn't think about that. Not right now . . .

Her hands were held in place by salt-worn fingers, her face pressed into the salt-slicked walls by one of the two guards who always worked together, having discovered months ago that it was the only way to handle the fiery Conflicter they enjoyed so much. The one pinning her for his friend was laughing in her ear, whispering of how much he loved watching her fight like this.

The pain she could handle, even if it made her scream. The pain wouldn't break her, not really. It was the sounds. Thud, thud, thud. They painted pictures she couldn't ignore, so real, that she swore she would be torn in two by the sheer ferocity of the beast between her legs. The sounds made her mind see him ripping her flesh, made her feel every scratch and burn. He was peeling her soul apart, her blood dripping down her bare legs to a stone floor that would forever keep her tears and cries as a memorial to the evils of the Spire.

There was a moment when the storm almost seemed to pause, the memory fading along with it. Vera opened her eyes and saw Lani's silver ones flicker back to brown, scared and confused. Then everything slammed back into motion. Once again they were no longer on the boat, but now it was Lani's memories that drew Vera in, not the other way around.

The silver fog shrouding the world around her lifted. She stumbled, little hands catching her shaking body on the doorframe of her hut. Everything hurt, especially her chest where the Fertility Mark burned like the time she had touched the stove back in summer.

"Mama? Papa? Where are you?" she called, looking around the empty room. Herbs hung from the rafters, the smells of cooking yams too bitter and burnt to be right. Why hadn't her mother taken them out of the oven? They had said they would be there, that after her first Trial they would have a special dinner and she could have all the salt she wanted.

"Mama?" Nothing. "PAPA?" Still nothing. Fear started to rise within her as she stumbled out of the hut and into the street. "Anyone? Auntie Lele? Can anyone hear me?"

No one answered except for the quiet chirping of the birds. "IS ANYONE THERE?"

Vera's eyes opened, drawing her out of the memory, and she felt ill. Lani seemed to be out of it, murmuring to herself while lost in the waves of their combined lives. Guilt and nausea washed over Vera. Resolute on making sure this hadn't been a complete waste, Vera finally pulled her arm away from Lani's, severing the blood connection but not the Bond that now stretched between them. Untangling herself from the mess of rope, she forced herself to crawl towards the helm. They were drifting in a calming sea in the eye of the storm, but that wouldn't last long. Lani would need help, especially while adjusting to being Bloodbound. Vera drew on the inner reserve of power and the training that had been both boon and bane. She dragged herself to her feet and tried not to think of what that *squishing* sound in her leg meant. Adrenaline beat the pain back to a dull roar, and her hands settled on the wheel.

White sails still dotted the sea behind them.

Vera peered over the display, and her lips twitched up a little in appreciation. They weren't that far from Sonder, a small island that had caught her and Torin's attention so many years ago. They'd wanted to retire there, to live into old age and pluck each other's gray hairs.

That was as good a destination as any. Vera shifted her weight fully onto her good leg and turned the wheel. A soft hum left her lips. With that battle trance playing in her head, she was able to shunt the awareness of pain to a separate corner of her mind and do what needed to be done. In this case, staying upright and sending the skiff over the waves towards the island of Sonder. It was close enough to other islands that even if Vera didn't last, Iolani would be able to call for help.

They say that if you trust another, you can reach heights the gods themselves would envy. Vera said quietly down the Bond. *Don't forget that, Lani . . . you can do more than you think. You can conquer yourself, and the world while you're at it. Don't let this thing I did to you define you, if you survive.* She let that thought whisper between them, hoping to impart some small part of what had kept her alive all these years.

What . . . what did you do to me? I can still feel the storm but I can't . . . Lani seemed to snap out of her shock and turned her head to face Vera. Lani's eyes were swimming, flickering between warm brown and the cold silver of the storm. *I can feel it wanting to swallow me up again and I want to let it. Why won't you let me go?* It was a desperate wail as Lani's knees hit the deck. *I can feel you in my skull. I don't want you there. What the fuck did you do to me?*

If I let you go, you're going to regret it come morning, Vera spoke quietly, twisting the wheel to keep on course with the island no matter what waves came their way. *We're headed to Sonder. You can kill me once we get there, if you want.* It was something she'd deserve. What she'd done today curdled her stomach. *It's called stabilizing, Lani. You're not going to be a thoughtless killing machine while you're Bonded. You . . . can ride the Storms out, and not kill anyone else. Kind of important, right?* Vera grimaced, shifting her weight to the side as a wave struck the boat. That damned *squishing* feeling in her leg was mind-bogglingly distracting, but she had her target, and she had her battle. She would ignore the leg until she finally gave out.

The sea spray should have been cold. During storms, the sea was always cold, but right then she felt warm. Everything was warm. It had Vera gripping the wheel tighter and turning it up as fast as it could go. She didn't have a lot of time. Vera had to get Lani to land, and had to get someone to pick up the reins, or Lani was going to lose her mind. Again. In the swirling memories coming from her new Bonded, Vera could see every death Lani had caused, and the grief and despair she felt each time the Prismatic Storm passed and there was more blood on her hands. She needed a Bonded. Not one like Vera, who had forced this connection on her and was on death's door, but one who could help Lani get control of her power for good.

The other woman didn't reply for a while, her body folding until her forehead pressed against the deck in the spray of seawater. At last, her voice came through to Vera's mind, low, hoarse, and in pain. *You're hurting so much. I want to fix it. I should have killed you before you could be in so much pain. Please, let me go. I don't want this. I was fine before you showed up. Please, let me go.*

Glancing over, Vera saw Lani rocking where she knelt, her shoulders trembling as the storm began blowing again, deck swaying as a new gust of wind and rain washed over them.

Adavera snorted, twisting the wheel to keep them on course. Silly suggestion, that. She couldn't just 'let Lani go'. Where would she go? Into the sea? Knowing that silly chit as intimately as Vera now did . . . Probably.

Adavera, you can't just lunge at them willy nilly! Bring the blade up, parry, and then gut the bastards! Torin scolded out of her memories. Vera clenched her fingers on the wheel, growling out into the wind. She didn't have a blade capable of cutting down a storm, but this ship was her 'blade', and she would keep fighting until the bitter end. She would get Lani out of it, and get her to Sonder, and then . . .

And then she would deal with death. It was fine. Better to die serving, and protecting, and trying to do something *right* one last time.

The boy was cowering as the guard raised his whip again, and again . . . and Vera couldn't stand it. She pushed away from the others, bringing her fist to the guard's face. The satisfying crunch of the guard's nose beneath her punch was real. The feeling of her fists pounding into the man downright cathartic. She almost didn't notice the others arriving.

She almost didn't notice the batons crashing down between her shoulders.

Almost, until someone pulled her feet out from under her, and their hands pushed her down, holding her still.

"Fucking Conflicter!" The crash of something hard into the back of her head, then the sting of tranq dart.

Vera took a deep breath, shaking that memory off as Lani whimpered. *I'm fine, Lani. Relax, and quit freaking out. I don't have time for a trip down memory lane in order to let you adjust. Take a nap.*

All of a sudden, Lani was on her feet and stalking towards Vera. That her eyes still glowed a little was worrisome. The Blood Bond should have fixed that, should be enough to pull a Fertilizer back from the edge entirely. That Lani still seemed caught in the storm even through Vera's new control over her did not do good things for their odds of survival. Vera clung to the wheel, leaning into it to keep the course while choppy waves battered against the sides of the skiff. Her bad leg lifted ... and then Vera stomped it downwards. The jolt of agony managed to shake its way through the hazy fog that threatened to cloud her vision, snapping her awake.

About five feet away, Lani stumbled as her face became a mask of agony while her right leg crumpled under her, a howl filling the air and matching the storm. *Get out of my head! I don't want your pain. Make it stop.*

"Then take a damned nap. I wouldn't be in this bad a shape if you hadn't tried to mulch me," Vera growled aloud, turning her attention back to working her way through the waves. Iolani was a threat. That much was true. Something about the Fertilizer was fighting the stability the Bond offered, but Vera couldn't do any more about that.

The Bond meant sharing pain, likely to make sure one Bonded didn't kill the other. Vera would have to trust in that. The Fertilizer wasn't used to pain. She didn't have the ability Vera had to continue the fight, no matter what. Thank the Gods for small miracles. The battle to control the skiff was all-encompassing. She didn't need to also be fighting Lani.

As she thought that, an idea flashed through her mind. The Storm was all-encompassing, and it was clearly fucking with Lani's head. What if Lani just needed a target? *Weirdling, you want to let that shit loose? You want to let go? Aim it at those fuckwads behind us with the white sails.*

It wasn't a suggestion. Her tone made it clear Vera was *demanding* that Lani let her Mark loose upon their enemies. If anyone deserved it, it was the assholes chasing their little skiff. They knew what had been done to Vera in the Mines, and they were still coming. *Reach out to them, Lani, and let them have it. Let them have it all.*

At first, Lani stubbornly tried to keep from doing it. Vera paid no mind to that. The command was given. Vera wasn't used to being the one barking orders—that had always been Torin's job—but she knew how hard it was to ignore a direct command from a Bonded. Still, Vera's hair stood on end when she looked back and saw the destruction she had wrought.

Lani stood by the rails of the skiff, arms raised in ecstatic bliss. The Corporate ships behind were surrounded by light and color that danced through the choppy waves and in the air. The same glow played on Lani's skin as Vera's Bonded, new and forced as that was, let her rage loose on their enemies. The ships broke apart. No, not *broke* ... that would imply pieces fell away. This wasn't like that. Pieces just *went missing*—

disintegrating as though they weren't meant to exist at all.

What a fucking nightmare.

Vera forced her eyes forward, ignoring the part of her that wondered if people she had known from her University days had been on any of those ships. She wasn't going to think about what Lani was doing, or what that same power had probably done to her leg.

Nope.

Vera clenched her teeth, cleared her mind as best she could, and committed to the fight with all she had left.

SALT: New File available re: *Query: Who are Irawaru and Lakea? Search Parameter: same folder.* Would you like to see it?

CODEX: New file? Does Moe have a keylogger installed on a *God's computer*?

SALT: Affirmative.

CODEX: Show me.

IM BETWEEN IRAWARU AND LAKEA, HOLDERS OF FORTUNE, DAY 81

<u>Helper.Bro.Ira</u>: Did you change your username, Kea?

<u>DoOver24756</u>: Yes.

<u>Helper.Bro.Ira</u>: I prefered TroubleTwin.

<u>DoOver24756</u>: Me too, but now you have a record of how many formal requests I've put in to wipe this planet and just start over. Since you stopped answering my inquiries, I figured I'd get your attention another way.

<u>Helper.Bro.Ira</u>: I stopped because I put a spam filter on any mail from you which includes the words 'wipe the slate clean.'

<u>DoOver24756</u>: You know, if you stopped being so attached to individual people, maybe you wouldn't care so much. They aren't even real, Ira. Their lives are miserable and we've been at this for the equivalent of 1,500 of their Fortune Years. It's really time to give up on this as a failed experiment and rework the geology and ecology from the ground up. I wish you would stop being so stubborn, brother mine.

<u>Helper.Bro.Ira</u>: You have no proof that they aren't real and all the proof that they are,

Kea. We've met people from other Worlds, we know they're real.

<u>DoOver24756</u>: Or collective hallucinations.

<u>Helper.Bro.Ira</u>: Your logic doesn't work anymore. Our scientists have run tests. They are real and if we were to wipe Fortune and try again, millions of deaths would be on our hands. Have patience. One of our experiments will work.

<u>DoOver24757</u>: Millions have *already* died due to the storms, salt deficiency, and the Marks. We're culpable either way.

<u>Helper.Bro.Ira</u>: Did the number on your counter just go up? Aren't you a bit old for these kinds of childish games, Kea?

<u>DoOver24757</u>: Aren't you a bit old to cling to something that isn't working, Ira? Be careful brother. If we don't do it for them, the humans might find a way to kill themselves without our help, or have you not looked at the Spire in Moe's archipelago lately? You might want to have a peek, like I told you to do weeks ago.

Arrival on Sonder
Salome - Day 4   08

It had taken hours to make sure their tail was clear. Hours of having to put up with Kumanu looking on every channel for word of where the two Rogue Marked fugitives were. Hours of knowing that he was beating himself up because they were not going to go hunting for those Marks. She'd already explained why. It broke her heart all the same.

Kuma always saw himself in the stories of other Rogue Marks. He tried not to let Salome see his grief every time they failed to save one, but she knew him too well to fall for it. Kuma knew how lucky he was. There wouldn't have been many willing to take him in all those years ago, when his Mark wasn't stable yet. Privately, Salome was pretty sure he wouldn't have survived if it weren't for the fact that the Parata family already had a handful of Marks and were used to dealing with them.

When they finally made it to Sonder, Salome almost didn't go ashore. She was half-sure that the moment she turned the rings over to her brother, he'd race off to try to find the fugitive Marks. If she had stayed abroad, though, Kumanu would have given her 'that look' — The sad one, that said: 'you don't trust him to be an adult, despite the fact that I literally raised you.'

That Salome *didn't* trust him to be a responsible adult when it came to Rogue Marks was irrelevant. For someone that was decades older than her, Kumanu really was a child at times. She blamed that on the fact that he rarely got to leave the ship for any real length of time and therefore had a constant case of cabin fever.

It would be too dangerous to let anyone see his Mark. The last thing they needed was the Corporation getting any kind of good description on him. The less the Corporation had to run on, the better.

As Salome hiked up the beach, swaying grasses tickling her elbows, she made a mental note to see if Sonder had any good trinkets for him. Or at least good food. Hell, maybe she could find a saucy little thing or two who wanted an adventure and throw them at Kuma for a while. There was always *someone* who wanted to be a pirate.

The path from the beach to the mountain in which Torin lived was steep and rough. Salome could have walked it with her eyes closed, but didn't. Her eyes kept drifting out to sea, and to the distant colorful clouds of the Prismatic Storm coming their way. *Please have Kuma be smart enough to find somewhere to lay anchor and stay put.*

She really did need to find him a girlfriend. It might take his mind off these Rogue Marks. It shouldn't be too hard. Sal had lost track of how many times a new crew member had ended up in bed with Kuma, drawn to his easy nature and exuberant enthusiasm for life. Salome hadn't gotten that gene. No, Sal's flirting technique was more transactional and upfront. She liked someone, she asked. If she was rebuffed, she shrugged and moved on, if they said yes, yay sex.

Torin worked for her because he wasn't looking for a serious relationship either. And he was just as straightforward as she was. They had gotten into some fantastic screaming matches over the last few years, but the makeup sex was always worth it. So was the 'haven't seen you in too long' sex, and the 'why the hell not' sex, for that matter, which was probably why she kept coming back.

Salome frowned as the wind picked up, turning her gaze out to sea. The clouds gathering on the horizon were *not* good signs. Then again maybe they would keep Kuma from dashing off on a mad adventure with Sal's ship.

A few drops of rain drew her attention off the sea and sped up her steps. While Salome was sure *Torin* would enjoy her arriving soaking wet, it didn't sound comfortable. By the time she reached the door, the wind was getting stronger. That really didn't bode well. Down in the village, the residents of Sonder would be locking the shutters and pulling their fishing boats onto dry land. Even though Prismatic Storms were no worse than normal ones, people got superstitious. Even Sal was sometimes unnerved by the clashing colors in the clouds, making the sky look like a messy artist's pallet.

Ignoring the 'Closed. Go away' sign on the door to Torin's clinic, she pulled it open, and then wrestled it closed as a gust of wind nearly toppled her over. With a grunt and yank it slammed shut. Sal slid the bolt in place and shook out her hair, droplets of water falling to the stone floor.

"Can't you read a closed sign?" A gruff voice asked from behind her.

"Well sure, but when have I ever cared?" Salome turned, regarding a slightly shocked Torin with that saucy grin she usually saved just for him. He clearly hadn't expected her.

With anyone else, that might mean a naked woman was about to stride around the corner. While that wouldn't bother Salome—she had never cared much for monogamy, considering she was often gone for months at a time—it had never been an issue with Torin. No, he was concerned because, as usual, he'd forgotten to groom. His fingers were quickly running through his hair and beard, trying to set them right.

He was making them worse. It made Salome's smile grow larger, lighting up her whole face. "I've got a few days and was in the area. Don't suppose I could borrow your bath and some soap?"

Torin got up from the desk in the corner of his little clinic, coming over to brush his fingers across her cheek. That fluttering feeling settled back into her gut. It had shown up more and more over the last year, whenever she was around him. She didn't like it . . . but she couldn't stop either.

"Tor?"

"Yes, you can borrow the bath. After I look you over first. Any new injuries?"

"No."

He touched her wooden arm, and she rolled her eyes. With a soft sigh, Salome tugged at the strap that held it in place. The limb detached from her shoulder stump, earning a sigh of relief. She twitched as his fingers touched the scarred flesh, tender from hours connected to the Infused prosthetic.

"It's healing nicely."

"It's already *healed*, Tor."

"Pfft. A little more time and I can get the sensitivity down."

"Why bother? It's usually covered up." Sal grinned, bringing her other hand up to tug on his beard and drag him down for a kiss. He tasted of herbs and rum and grumpiness. For some reason, it was appealing. What did it say about her that she knew the flavor of 'grumpy'?

"Sal . . ."

"Hrm? We can talk after we say hello again. And after you draw me a bath."

Torin's eyes lit up, his smile turning genuinely warm, and he scooped her up as if she weighed nothing. "You're going to like the new bath soap I got."

"*You* bought nice bath soap?" she snorted.

"For guests."

"Cause you have so many of those."

"Well there is this one troublesome pirate that keeps coming around . . ."

"She sounds like my kind of girl."

"Mine too."

CODEX: Great. So our Gods IM and want to kill us. Fabulous. SALT, can we find out what else they're been saying? *Query: all mentions of Helper.Bro.Ira?*

RESULTS: #118,003, #147,390, and #451,211

Emotion Lunar Cycle, year 372

<u>Helper.Bro.Ira</u>: So . . . Moe isn't anywhere on Fortune.

<u>TroubleTwin</u>: That's not possible.

<u>Helper.Bro.Ira</u>: Yeah. I know. Can you please look too, in case I am missing him? You are better at that sort of thing.

Matchmaking Lunar Cycle, year 385

<u>TroubleTwin</u>: So, remember Moe?

<u>Helper.Bro.Ira</u>: yeah. What brought him to mind? Did you finally find a skeleton or something?

<u>TroubleTwin</u>: He was in my living room ten minutes ago.

<u>Helper.Bro.Ira</u>: What the . . . HOW?!

<u>TroubleTwin</u>: Beats me. Worse, he had a friend. She's not human, Ira. Like, she's fucking weird. I ran some readings after they left, and . . . yeah. Not human, not even a little. As far as I can tell she's made up of pure Planar Rift power, same as the Ao Singularity. She *looks* like a little girl, but the readings don't seem possible.

<u>Helper.Bro.Ira</u>: No, no they don't. I'll be over in a minute. I want to look over your data.

Shifting Lunar Cycle, year 602

<u>Helper.Bro.Ira</u>: You won't believe this, Kea. I mean, you really, really won't believe this. I was just talking to one of the Dracona Holders—you know, the new World that just popped up a little while back? Well, one of them just told me that they saw *Moe and Lizzie* on their world. The descriptions they gave were exact, down to Lizzie's weird energy signature. I think . . . I think he's now Porting between *Worlds*. Worse, I think he's been doing it for a while, and we've just never noticed.

<u>TroubleTwin</u>: That would mean he's got a power like ours, Ira. Fuck . . .

<u>Helper.Bro.Ira</u>: We need to tell our leadership.

<u>TroubleTwin</u>: What the hell is Primary gonna be able to do about it? It's not like they can force Ao to do anything. Shit . . . what if Ao *made* this being he's calling Lizzie? What if there is something alive in there?

<u>Helper.Bro.Ira</u>: It's just an energy source, Kea. It's not alive or conscious. How many tests do our scientists have to run to prove that to you? Just because it feels like it sometimes pushes us towards certain things doesn't mean it's thinking. It's an energy source, nothing more. Just because we don't understand its rules yet doesn't mean it doesn't have any.

<u>TroubleTwin</u>: Ira. When we do impossible and magical things on Fortune, the people there think that it's "normal, natural" yada yada . . . C'mon bro. What if Ao is similar?

<u>Helper.Bro.Ira</u>: We're just not understanding the science. That's all. Fortune is wearing off on you. Don't forget why we're here, sister mine: to find a new home for the human race.

This isn't a videogame or make-believe, and singularities aren't sentient. Grow up, Lakea. Ao is just a very large battery that *we* created, nothing more.

TroubleTwin: And people don't just suddenly grow the capability to control solar systems and planets with willpower alone, Ira. At what point do we suspend our belief in the fucking system as we know it and open our minds to the idea that maybe there is more here than seems realistic?

Helper.Bro.Ira: When the science backs it up.

Memories of Home
Lani - Day 5   09

    Lani wanted to kill Vera. She wanted to pop her head beneath the water and put her out of her misery, or maybe bash her head in against the floor of the skiff. She wanted to do all sorts of murderous things, but she couldn't even stop trying to fucking save Vera's life. Every time Lani's thoughts turned to violence, she would look at that slumped over figure and go right back to anchoring the skiff as close as possible to the sandy cove near Torin's cave. The idea of having to cart Vera's decomposing, foul-smelling and fouler-tempered ass to the island made Lani want to retch, but she would do it because—damn the Depths—she had to. Because Torin's fucking voice crawled through her head in the echo chamber of Vera's memories—confirming that it really was the same Torin she knew—and because Lani couldn't bring herself to let someone die alone and in agony when help was so close by. Maybe Torin would have something that would put Vera down painlessly. The idea made her heart scream, and in turn flare with unbridled rage.
    Lani didn't know Adavera, not really. But she also *did*. Over the last day while they made their way to Sonder through the last of the Storm, she'd gotten more and more flashes of memory from Vera's life down the Blood Bond. Each was more horrific than the last, but whatever she tried, Lani couldn't make them stop. It would have been one thing if they had all been like the first few Lani had received: blood and violence and the thrill of combat. If that were all there was to the woman who had forced her very soul on Lani's, the Emotive would have just accepted the risk of death and tossed her overboard. The problem was that interspersed into those gruesome recollections were other moments, ones of bravery, kindness, love. Vera was a *good* person, under all those razor-sharp edges. She'd risked everything to save a kid, and then

another, and another. Even though it landed her in the hell Lani had glimpsed, Vera had still done it *every time she could.*

Idiot.

Worse, Adavera could have killed Lani during the storm and had chosen not to. Even as Lani was taking her apart cell by cell, Vera had tried to save her and had been willing to blacken her own soul to do it. If she was prepared to do that for someone she hardly knew, didn't Lani owe it to her to at least try to find help?

Vera was too still for comfort as Lani turned to help her down the ladder. Lani's heart almost stopped at the idea Vera might already be dead and without thinking she reached for the Bond that now stretched between them, invisible but as real as the deck beneath her feet. Vera twitched in response, and Lani's breath rushed out of her in a gasp.

Thank the Depths.

"Fucking shitballs . . . I fucking hate you," Lani grumbled, sliding her arm under Vera's shoulder so that she could drag her towards the ladder. A soft groan left Vera's mouth as her head smacked into the side of the rail, and Lani glowered in response. "This would go quicker if you could move yourself."

No reply, so she continued dragging Vera's dead weight until they were both in the knee-deep water. Despite her anger, Lani couldn't help the wince as Vera's leg caught on a protruding piece of coral.

"Sorry."

It was so fucking stupid, apologizing to a Corpse. The name was even more apt now that Lani could sense Adavera preparing for death. She felt it, breathed it, *lived* it, right along with her new Bonded, and knew oblivion was coming. Except for the fact that Iolani wasn't ready to let Vera die. If the Conflicter was going to die, it should be at Lani's hands for the crime of forcing what should have been one of the most intimate choices of Lani's life on her. A Blood Bond wasn't something that could just be broken willy-nilly. What Vera had done was nothing short of rape. That Lani was helping her now was purely selfish; she was going to save her, see her better, and then fucking stab her to death even if it meant that Lani might die too. It would be worth it. That's what she kept telling herself as she dragged the Conflicter into the shallows.

Yeah . . . totally doing this so that I can kill her myself. Totally. Fucking idiot.

That thought fled as she felt the thready pulse in Vera's wrist.
You're not allowed to die. Not until I get to smash your face in.

...Charmer... It was both a relief and an aggravation to get that response. The mental touch was wispy, barely there. It was a quiet voice in the back of Lani's head, as if Vera was trying to take up as little space as possible.

Don't you fucking go quiet on me now. You don't get to die today ,or I'll be stuck with another dead body to bury and I didn't sign up for that. With a heave, Lani pulled the Conflicter all the way onto shore and winced as Vera screamed, her rotting leg hitting the ground harder than Lani had intended. "Shit, sorry."

She got no reply, which was probably a bad sign. Not for the first time in the last two hundred or more years, Lani wished she were bigger and stronger. Her mother had been a mountain of a woman who could swing a child onto her hip with one hand while pounding kilos of kava with the other. Unfortunately, Lani had her father's shorter, more graceful build, and it fucking sucked. All but dragging Vera up the beach and towards the hill was making every muscle and joint in her body scream, not at all helped by the fact that she could feel the Conflicter's pain through the Bond.

Come on, Vera. You got to help me out here. I'm taking you to a Mender. You'll be fine, but I just need you to hold on a little longer.

Nothing came through for a little while, as Lani navigated them onto a dirt path. Then, without warning, a whole burst of muddled words appeared in her mind. All she could make sense of were the last few.

Lani... Bond... someone... K? Before I go. You ... shouldn't be ... alone. No one should.

I've been just fine on my own for the past two centuries. I think I'm good, thanks. This experience has kinda put me off ever Bonding to anyone.

Another long pause, as Lani stopped to catch her breath. They were emerging from the tree-line . She could see the cliff face in which Torin's cave lay, though the door was still out of sight.

Not fine... Not you. Not me. Need... people. Good people. Or it's not worth it. Bond someone. Promise me that, k?

No. I won't fucking promise you anything. With a grunt, Lani started walking again, dragging Vera along, since the Conflicter's good leg was hardly holding any weight. *You'll just take it as an excuse to die on me and I won't let that happen. Isn't there a good chance I die too, if you do? Yeah, fuck that. You can forget about dying. Come on, Vera, it's only a little way more. We're almost there.*

Vera went silent after that. Lani still got some flickers

of memories through the Bond, but not words, as though the Conflicter's mind was drifting. Lani grit her teeth and focused on the path ahead, each step a strain.

Every time Vera's bad leg brushed the ground, Lani felt it and wanted to scream. To cry. How much worse was it for Vera? No wonder she was fleeing to happy memories. Lani concentrated on them too, since she had few enough of her own.

All of them were of Torin. Had Lani not come to the conclusion that they were the same person, she never would have recognized the gruff and scruffy Mender in the youthful, smiling, clean-shaven man of Vera's memories.

The memories weren't like vids on the network. These had touch, smell, emotion. She could *feel* Torin's hand on Vera's waist as he taught her to dance, and feel the warmth of his breath as he said, *"The locals on that last island do this every night, Vera. If those clumsy folk can dance, so can you."*

Lani blinked away the memories and pushed forward, all but dragging Vera up the rocky path to the cave. With every step, Lani batted away the feeling of Torin's lips against Vera's skin, blinking to stay focused for just a few more seconds.

They were almost there.

PART TWO
Puppetmaster
-Lani, Moe, Salome, Vera, Torin-

CODEX: Why is it that the deeper I go, the more questions I find? SALT, add researching Primary, Holders, Dracona, Ao, and Plane to my general To-Do list. For now, let's shift back to compiling that information packet for uncle Kekai.

SALT: To-Do list updated. What is your next Query?

CODEX: Hmm.. I've got the basics on Lani, so who is next? Let's go with Torin. I have some unanswered questions. *Query: Who is Torin of Keala?*

------CLASSIFIED: MARK RESPONSE : LEVEL 0------

Subject: Torin of Keala - Mender, 3 Trials, Completed Mark.

Corporate Status: Discharged - Medical

Cause: Psychological break. Prognosis poor. Bonded Conflict Mark Adavera of Keala sentenced to life at the Spire.

Threat Level: Zero. Subject not dangerous to Corporation.

Expected Culling Date: ████ - Redacted by order of Zarine Crystal. Retirement package offered and accepted. Current location: Sonder.

------CLASSIFIED: MARK RESPONSE : LEVEL 0------

CODEX: Can we hack that redacted piece?

SALT: The only actions available for the next 11 minutes and 57 seconds are—

CODEX: yes, yes. To-Do list and Queries.

Alright, smarty-pants. I get it.

Tea Leaves & Profit 10
Torin - Day 5

Torin watched the tea leaves sink to the bottom of the glass teapot with a sense of doom. A beam of dusty morning light cut through the shadows of the cramped house—really more like a cave with a wall built over the entrance—to illuminate the face of the woman still sprawled on his bed. The Mender grimaced. Mornings were not Salome Parata's strongest time, and she always managed to look angry in slumber. He supposed he must too, considering it had been six years since his heart had been ripped from his chest and tossed into the Mines of the Salt Spire. Sal didn't have that excuse.

Still, there was something almost endearing about the way her brow was scrunched up in sleep, as if even in her dreams she was fighting the Corporation and planning out the next shipment of supplies to embargoed islands.

Turning his attention back to the teapot, Torin poured himself a glass through a little strainer and added a teaspoon of sugar, then went to the door to drink it outside. There was no patter of rain anymore, which meant the storm had blown over the island overnight, probably bringing with it the usual toppled trees, damaged buildings, and dead bodies. He would have people banging on his door, expecting him to lower his prices just because it was their daughter or husband or mother who was injured, or because the storm had been one of those strange ones that came up out of nowhere and didn't allow for preparations.

It was almost as though they thought he still gave a damn.

At least his wallet would be full by tomorrow, then he could go back to just telling everyone who came to his door to fuck off. What did he care if they were hurt or dying? Death came to everyone, and what did it matter if he could have helped avoid it? He had cared once and look at how much that had fucked up his life.

He had just taken his first sip of tea, the dark, bitter taste matching his mood perfectly, when the first group came into view. It was two adults carrying a child and running towards the deck of his house. Torin held up a hand.

"I know you don't have the credits, Marla. Either you were lying to me last week when I treated your grandmother, in which case you can fuck off, or you're still in deep debt to the Corporation, in which case you do not have enough cash to pay me to fix his broken leg. I suggest going down to the Company clinic."

The mother's round face dropped. "I wasn't lying, Torin. But I'll get you the money, I pro—"

"You already owe me and I don't extend debts to liars. Fuck off."

"But—" the father tried.

"I said fuck off."

Ten hours later, Torin was glad he had turned away those who couldn't pay upfront. As it was, there had been more than enough work to drain him nearly dry and make him regret not moving to an island that was *actually* uninhabited, instead of just sparsely inhabited like this one. Damn, but he hated having people in his house, even though he had bought the place precisely because it had a second room that served as a small clinic.

The last of the locals who had come to him for help hobbled out just as the sun began to lower. Torin slammed the door behind them, letting out a frustrated huff. In response, Sal, who was wiping down the counters in the other room, shook her head. Two plates of food sat next to the stove, the smell of fried fish permeating the house.

"What?" he snarled, turning to face her.

"You probably made a year's worth of money today, Torin. Be happy. We got to make love through one of the worst storms in a long while, you got to work your angst out on some injuries, and you got paid to do it . . . All in all, not a terrible day."

She grinned, holding a plate out towards him in her one good hand. Her Infused prosthesis lay on the bed, where she had dumped it an hour ago. Torin knew that it hurt to wear it too long, but Salome hadn't complained, or even asked for a cut. She had just wordlessly helped him in the clinic all day, because despite what she said, Salome did still care. Lucky her.

He took the plate she offered. "Thank you."

"Any interesting cases today, or are you going to feed me that line of shit about how you don't enjoy doing things?" She cocked her head to the side, looking him up and down. "Something we both know is a lie. There are a *few* things you most certainly enjoy doing."

Torin grumbled something under his breath and pushed the strands of long hair that had fallen into his face behind his ear. "I do enjoy some things. Solitude, for example, and not having people assume that I take any joy in dealing with cranky locals who bitch at me about my prices while I literally save their lives."

"Mmm." Salome smiled, setting her own plate to the side before moving closer to wrap her arm around his waist. Her cheek settled against his chest, ear pressing against his sweat-dampened shirt. "You want me to chase people off tomorrow? I know that's usually your day," she said it quietly, not bothering to tilt her face up.

Torin tensed. In all the hubbub, he had almost managed to forget what tomorrow was. He didn't mean to, but his eyes turned to the east, towards where the Spire stood, far out of sight.

Six years. Tomorrow would be the beginning of the seventh.

As he had tried almost every day since she had been dragged away from him, Torin tried to reach out to his Blood-bound partner. Just like every other day, the connection was silent. He knew she was still alive, but Vera did not want to hear him.

She didn't want him to help her.

"I don't want to talk about tomorrow," he muttered.

"Not planning to make ya. Come on, let's get some food in you. Then I can help you get to sleep, hrm?"

There was a moment when he held onto his grumpiness on principle alone, then his shoulders sagged. "That sounds like a fine plan. And yes, you can scare people away tomorrow and I'll try not to bite your head off for just existing. I am grateful for you, Sal. You know that, right?"

His arm around her became two and squeezed. "Not just for your terrible cooking, either."

"Hey!" She grinned. "My cooking is not *that* bad, considering I have to do most of it with just one hand. Now stuff your face, handsome, and then maybe I'll ride it for a bit." She winked at him, tugging on his beard to pull him low enough for a kiss.

He'd met Salome four years ago. It had taken over eight months and a significant amount of alcohol, bickering, and even a few screaming matches for them to finally fall into bed together. Now? Well, now he still felt perfectly comfortable going head to head with the bastard pirate . . . But it was out of genuine affection rather than heated anger.

"As for being grateful.. You'd better be. You're too much of a grumpy ass for anyone else to put up with your growling." She sniffed, winking at him one more time before drifting back to her food. Torin picked up his plate and poked at the fish and greens. They smelled . . . unappetizing, but while he teased Salome incessantly about her cooking, he never refused it.

After all, she had better things to do than practice cooking.

Torin had just sat down at the small table and lifted a forkful to his mouth, when a loud knock sounded at the door.

"OH, YOU HAVE *GOT* TO BE FUCKING KIDDING ME!" The Mender shouted, putting the fork down and storming back to the door. "What part of the word 'Closed' can't you read?"

He yanked the door open, ready to lambast the skin off of whoever was out there demanding his assistance. In the dimming light, stood two women, one hanging off the other, both looking battered and worn and smelling of rotting flesh, and one heartbreakingly familiar.

The one standing straight, who he recognized as a Rogue Emotive he had treated a time or two, looked up at Torin, eyes huge and desperate. "Please, we need help."

Torin stood frozen in the doorway, his heart stopped. It shouldn't be stopped, that was bad, people died when their hearts stopped beating. That was basic medicine, not even Mending. He should probably be more concerned about it than he was, but nothing could distract him from the impossibility of what he was seeing.

I've finally snapped. I must be mad. That doesn't usually happen to Menders, not like Fertility Marked, but it's been known to occur. Diagnosis: Unstable Mark. Treatment: Culling. Oh well, no worse than living, really.

If he was mad, though, wouldn't the Gods at least be kind enough to give him a hallucination of his Adavera flinging herself into his arms, healthy and whole and beautiful? Why would they torture him this way, with the face of the woman he loved beyond reason twisted in pain, her hair a short, ratty tangle and whole body reeking of rot in a way that made even his steel stomach want to turn?

That seemed unnecessarily cruel.

"TORIN!"

Belatedly, he realized that the Emotive had been trying to get his attention.

"Huh?"

"I said can you fucking help me with her? Depths below, are you deaf? Can't you see she needs help?"

Torin had trouble making sense of those words. Who was the Emotive talking about? He thought he recognized her—Ani? Lai? Lani!— Annoying little Rogue Mark who he had last seen when he had patched her up a few months ago. Right. Huh, was she hallucinating too?

He jumped nearly a foot in the air when she snapped her fingers right in his face, startling the shit out of him. Only when his feet landed and a growl rose in his throat did he realize that this didn't really feel like a vision. The smell was certainly bad enough to be real, and if it wasn't an illusion produced by his failing mind then . . .

"Oh shit!"

Adavera was *here*. Adavera was *hurt*.

He launched himself forward, his arms catching the woman he loved and had thought never to see again under her arms as Lani let go. The moment their skin touched, it was as if the world burst into color after an eternity of dull sepia. For the first time in six years, he could breathe.

A moment later, he seriously regretted that, because Vera vomited bile all down his front. He gagged but kept it together, hoisting her up and over the threshold into his clinic.

"Sal, get me a syringe and the lockbox. You there, change the sheet on the table. There's a pile of clean ones over on that chair," he snapped at Lani. She had two perfectly fine hands and might as well put them to use. As soon as the sheet was down, Torin gently set Vera on it, his motions as soft and careful as a man handling a newborn child. "I've got you, Vee. I'm going to give you something for the pain and then examine you." He brushed a layer of sweat from her overheated face, still fighting off the shock of having her there. He straightened as Sal thrust the box where he kept the more powerful meds into his hands, followed a moment later by a syringe.

"IV kit," Torin barked as he entered the code on the lockbox and pulled the lid back, searching for the right bottle and filling the syringe. He didn't need to check for dosage. He knew Vera's dosages for painkillers better than the color of her eyes; she had needed them often enough.

Hands not shaking because he wasn't going to waste time on his own terror right now, Torin wiped a patch of Vera's skin with alcohol and slid the needle in. "You'll start feeling better in a few seconds. Talk to me. Tell me what happened. How are you hurt? How long has it been?"

. . .what happened . . . hurt . . .long has it been? The sound of her thoughts in his mind nearly made Torin sob, but he pushed his elation back, pushing all emotion away to focus on the job of saving her life.

". . . Shifter . . . claws . . . Fertility . . . Lani . . ." Adavera shuddered, goosebumps rising across her skin as the fluid started flowing in her veins. "Storms . . . Torin . . . "

He growled and turned to Lani. "Translation?"

The Emotive shrank back under his glare. "Ah . . . A Shifter clawed up her leg before I found her, I think, then she went swimming, then it got really infected. I think it's rotting. Please, please fix her. If you need money, I'll find a way to work it off, just please fix her."

"I don't want your fucking money; I want a clear explanation. How long has she been this muddled? How long ago was the injury?" he bellowed, then regretted it because it really looked like the Emotive was about to lose it, the way she retreated fast until her back was pressed against the wall. Torin shook his head and clenched his teeth. "Fucking useless. Vera, honey, how long ago were you hurt?"

As he asked, Torin took his first look down at the leg that had been hurt, and suddenly whatever Vera or Lani might say didn't matter, because he could see bone. Not the clean bone of a cut that had gone too deep, but bone through a squishy mess of puss and rot.

For a moment, he only saw red, anger rising within him at whoever or whatever had caused this, then nothing. His mind cleared of everything but the wound before him and the steps he had to take to save her. "Salome, close and lock the door; no one comes in, no matter what they want. I am going to need easy to eat food and water available. This might take several days, and I can't promise I'll be able to communicate. If you can contact another Mark you trust, have them come here. I will pay them. I will need to pull power from someone before the en—"

"Use me." Lani had stepped back up to the table. She looked a little pale, but resolute. "I'm in my third century and still challenging Trials. I have enough power. Use as much as you need."

Torin didn't even stop to question it. "Then don't let anyone in at all. Corporation might show up; if they do, blow them to hell."

And that was the last thing he said before tapping into his power and launching into a Mending he wasn't sure was within his skillset.

CODEX: *Query: In what documents are Torin of Keala and Zarine Crystal both mentioned?*

To: Zarine Crystal, CEO of the Crystal Corporation, Day 3

From: Galena Crystal, Dean of the Kahana University School of Marks

Dear Cousin,

It has come to my attention that Miss Adavera of Keala is alive and in the company of a Rogue Emotive. This came as some surprise to me since I had been informed that she had been taken care of. As you likely recall, I sent in an advisory to your office that if she had become unstable, she should be executed forthwith as, even though she has only faced three Trials and bears a single Mark, her bloodthirsty nature and skill with weapons would make her a rallying point for the resistance were she ever to slip Corporate control. I see now that you did not take my advice. I must assume that the reason is the Mender she was Bound to, Torin of Keala? I know I sent a positive report of his progress and a letter of recommendation for an internship within Crystal Tower, but you might also remember that I clearly stated that he should not be separated from his Bonded.

These two were particularly close during their University days. Had you killed the Conflicter, it is likely that her Bonded would have died, but by dividing them you turned both into dangers to the Corporation. I checked Torin's record and it shows he was dismissed from service after a mental breakdown five years ago. Had you thought to inform me—the person who oversaw both of their educations—about any of this, I could have predicted that outcome. Now they are both at large and with a reason to turn against our

Company.

It seems like you will have to learn the hard way, as your mother did, that the only safe Mark is either one who agrees with you, or has a bullet in their brain. My advice—not that I believe you will take it—is to spare no expense or manpower in hunting them down and disposing of them. Do not try to save the Mender. Rebelliousness spreads in Marks like a virus, which is why we put so many down during childhood. In addition, by their very nature, Marks seek each other out to Bond. It means that while today you have two, tomorrow that number might jump to four, then to eight, and up and up until you have a new insurgency on your hands. Solve the problem now or regret it later.

And next time, keep me in the loop. No one knows Marks better than I do. I may not bear all fourteen myself, but I have trained each and every one and understand what makes them tick and how best to take them down. To assist in this endeavor, I am sending a team of Sixers to you. Since both Adavera and Torin failed out by their third Trials, Sixers should be more than capable of taking them down, even with their backs against the wall. The Emotive likely has no training since she is not in any of our records, and is probably no more than three or four Trials in, if that. Most who don't have the backing of the University don't last long, though if you can recover the corpse I would be interested to see it. I'm working on a paper about Rogue Marks.

Sincerely,

Galena Crystal

CODEX: Grim. Sure hope neither of them are dead. Alright, one more question while you compile this list of documents.

Clean-Up
Salome - Day 5
11

Salome Parata knew Torin's many moods. Ok, so he didn't have *that many* moods, but she knew the gradations and she knew the shifts, just like the ocean currents. She had never seen anything like this one. Salone almost wished she was a Mark herself, just to help.

Almost immediately, she slapped that thought away. Salome had accomplished more in her life than most Marks would with all their years. Because she had to. Because she wasn't restrained by could, or should, or the expectations of the Corporation. If anything, she'd been raised to spit in the Corporation's eye.

UnMarked she might be, but moving fast during an emergency was second nature. Salome did as she was told. She didn't ask questions, or get in Torin's way, but she noticed the tattoo around Adavera's throat, and the Mark on her uninjured leg, and she heard Torin refer to her as 'Vee'. He knew her. He didn't just know her, he *knew* her.

The reality of that was a little jarring. Salome clenched her jaw, glaring at the ground while all of it sank into place. Torin loved this woman. He was radiating it, and she wasn't sure he meant to. Or that he cared if anyone noticed.

Sal brought over boxes of rations and plenty of water. She set up everything Torin might need near him. He didn't so much as look at her, his entire focus on the woman on the table. A quick glance told Salome it was a fool's errand. He should be reaching for his bone-saw to cut that leg off, if he intended to save the woman, but he wasn't. Why?

When Salome had done all that she could within the clinic, she stepped to the door. "I'll be right back."

Neither Torin nor the bedraggled stranger who had brought that Vera woman said a word, so Salome slipped out of the cave. If they were going to have any chance of finishing this up, she needed to make sure no one would have reason to come pester them.

Salome dragged on her prosthetic as she went, flexing the muscles in her shoulder as the hum of energy inside of it tingled against her skin. It always felt strange when the Mender's power wove into her stump. It was even stranger when she 'felt' the response of the limb as the fingers clicked together. Wood and a few bits of metal to match her ship. Her brother had a wicked sense of humor, she'd grant him that. At least he hadn't named it.

Sighing, Salome looked around, spotting the trail of uneven footprints. They led her down the beach, a line of pus and bloody droplets she followed with ease. It didn't take long to figure out just where the women had come from. Sal's wooden hand slapped against her forehead as she let out a groan. Talk about flying a giant fucking 'we're right here' flag.

A Corporate skiff.

Amateurs.

Grumbling, she waded into the water and climbed aboard the skiff. From the looks of it, they'd had to pull backup power, which made the vessel mostly useless. Mostly. She unwound the sails, dumping them below deck. Salome tweaked a few power settings in the engine compartment, and then set the ship off on an automated course towards the Corporation's headquarters. It would blow up long before it made it there, but the poetic irony pleased her. Death to the Corporation had been her motto long before she could pronounce all the syllables, let alone do more than toddle.

Sal waded back to shore, then watched through her spyglass as the skiff drew further and further away. It took about forty-five minutes. The burst of flame as it went up brought a smile to her lips.

Next came the process of contacting as many of the close locals as she could. She bribed them, of course. Sails. Batteries. Salt. Food. "Keep sniffers away from Torin for the week, maybe longer. I'll give you a holler if it's safe." She kept it at that. These locals knew her. They knew exactly what sort of trouble she could get into, and they knew she would have more than this to give them if everything went well.

Which made her grumble more, because that meant going out on her own ship sooner than she wanted to, just to get enough bribes to keep up good relations. The things she would do for lo . . . for a friend.

After getting all of that done, she booked it back to Torin's. One look was all she needed. Torin and the girl who had come with the Corpse were still entirely focused on the dying woman.

Sal started the arduous process of locking the door down. It wouldn't hold up to a Conflicter for long, but if the Corporation didn't know to send one to this island, then chances were good that they'd be fine.

Another quick check-in with the Mending room—Yeah. They were *not* available for conversation—and she was done. Salome settled in on a chair, pulled out a book, and tried to distract herself from the really fucking bad smell and the fact that she might have just lost her bedmate to a corpse.

This was going to be a *long*, long few days.

CODEX: *Query: What documents mention Torin of Keala, Zarine Crystal, and Galena Crystal?*

-----CLASSIFIED: MARK RESPONSE : LEVEL 2-----

RECORD: TRACKER CASE #5978.3
Subjects: Adavera of Keala, Torin of Keala.

ASSIGNMENT: Capture Torin of Keala, 3 Trial Mender, for Rehabilitation. (Authorization: Zarine Crystal). Capture and Restrain Adavera of Keala, 3 Trial Berserking Conflicter, for the continuance of Torin of Keala's life IF POSSIBLE. (Authorization, Zarine Crystal. Addendum, Galena Crystal). Subjects are not to be housed together for longer than transport makes necessary. Staff Emotive is to Rehabilitate Torin of Keala's disposition towards Bond. Matchmaking Staff is to find a replacement as soon as possible.

ADDENDUM: Adavera of Keala is an extremely dangerous subject. Once captured, subject should be tranquilized and not permitted to speak or move. Shielder of at least 6th level necessary. If death is unavoidable, Team will be spared from the consequences of the CEO'S disapproval. Subject is to be transferred to Medical Facility 2.8a under command of Scientist Aheo of Order, pursuant to Medical Research Code A.9.72, regardless of living status.

-----CLASSIFIED: MARK RESPONSE : LEVEL 2-----

CODEX: The fuck? Aheo . . . Where do I remember that name from. Huh. Weird. *Query: Who is Aheo*

of Order?

FROM THE NOTES OF GALENA CRYSTAL

The more I study Rogue Marks, the more I believe they are a cancer that must be done away with. Marks tend to breed true more often than they appear in the general population, so I have decided to finance a project to study the genetics of Marked parents and children to see if we can find a way to limit or eliminate Marks born outside of Corporate control.

To do this, I have identified one Aheo of Order, a Dual Marked Shielder and Tracker, to head the project. His resume of scientific discovery speaks for itself, and I am confident he will find a way to better control the Marks on Fortune.

Until then, I am discontinuing the Rogue Mark Rehabilitation program. Those born wild are not worth Company resources. Instead, they will all be given to Aheo as research subjects. The same will be true of all Marks sentenced to the Spire. For the most dangerous of prisoners, I have ordered Aheo to enact his proposed Burnout regimen, which drives a Marked Prisoner to overuse their Mark to the point that it is irrevocably damaged. Future attempts at use of a Mark will cause debilitating pain, seizure, coma, and even death.

Those prisoners pliable enough to work with pre or post Burnout will be enrolled in his Breeding Program, a study of the inheritability of Marks. UnMarked offspring will be kept in a secure section of the Spire and taught obedience and efficient mining techniques to keep them out of the public eye. Marked children will be delivered to me at the University.

Since this project is highly classified, I will be dispatching the scientific vessel, *Purity*, to the waters near the Spire. By staying on the move and sailing within the highly-guarded waters at the core of Corporate control, Aheo should encounter no difficulties, and be ready and able to go hunt down Rogue Marks himself.

CODEX: This is another rabbit hole. SALT, add Aheo of Order, Galena Crystal, and Zarine Crystal to my general To-Do list.

Sacrificial Lamb
Moe - Day 8
12

Standing in the middle of a room of whiteboards, Moe bit his tongue and tried to make sense of the mess of numbers he had written over the years. "What timeline are we in again, Lizzie darling?"

"4398F, now that Salome has disposed of the boat. It's not a great timeline. You'll have to tip someone off if you want to get them moving. They've been at this Mending for almost three days and Adavera has most of a leg again. You're running out of time, Moe."

His companion had her feet up on the table in the middle of the room, staring at the monitor displaying the feed from the tiny security camera Moe had installed inside Torin's cave for exactly this purpose. On the screen, Moe could still see the Mender and Lani bent over Vera's still body. Salome was in a corner, looking out a crack in the shuttered windows. There was also a feed from the *Sahima's Legacy*, tucked into the darkened corners of Kumanu's workshop. The Infuser was on his back under the large engine that fueled the *Legacy*, earbuds in and humming loudly as he worked. That one kept flickering, since anything with internal circuits always misbehaved when too much Infused power was being flung about.

Moe turned from the bank of computers to the whiteboards, pulling the one marked with 4398 down by the string attached to it. In the corner, it read: *Success probability: 1.7%.*

"This one is grim, indeed. We need to nudge them onto something better. Options?" He asked, biting his tongue as his eyes trailed over whiteboard after whiteboard, stacked as many as ten deep up near the ceiling.

"I'm not the Precog, Moe. You tell me," Lizzie replied, popping a piece of fried fish into her mouth. Her shoulder-length hair was in a short braid, the University student uniform traded in for a tank top and shorts. She still looked twelve or so, but it was a little less creepy. The glass of wine held by the stem between her fingers also helped to remind him that while she looked like a child, Lizzie was almost as old as he was.

"It's true, I am the Precog. An amazing Precog, in fact. Something I will remind you of the next time you try to make a bet." Moe stretched, cracked his neck, then went back to studying the boards. "How about timeline 5590? The one with the poisonous jellyfish?"

"No."

"611?"

Lizzie rolled her eyes. "The one where you have sex with every member of the crew and turn them into a strange little cultish harem? Sure, yeah. Gamble away all your ambitions for some action at a wild 0.13% chance of success. Very sensible."

"You're no fun."

"No. I never get laid. There's a difference. You try looking twelve forever and tell me how you like it." Lizzie turned in her swivel chair, then pointed at one of the whiteboards in the shadows at the very top. "Look in the 3000 series."

"The ones that require a sacrificial lamb?"

Lizzie shrugged. "You know the odds. You *wrote* the odds. They're not all coming out of this alive."

Moe had to Port twenty feet into the air to reach the braided pull cords of a group of three boards. Once he was back on the ground, Moe studied the top one. "Right, so who do we sacrifice?"

"Adavera?" Lizzie offered. "She's not that essential once the fireworks start and has a high chance of dying no matter what we do. She has, what? An average mortality rate of 74-78% across all the timelines we've mapped? That's not stellar. Plus, she and Lani are already Bonded. It should be easy to prod them toward a romantic entanglement."

"Sure, yeah, but if the sacrifice happens at the wrong time it could kill Torin, and he's essential for the late game. I don't want to increase the likelihood of losing him. Salome?" Moe countered.

Lizzie got up to look at the second board as he pushed the first one out of the way. She cocked her head to the side. "But I *like* the captain."

"Well fine then. If you *like* Salome, who am I to take away your playthings? Kuma?"

"Kuma," Lizzie agreed, pushing Salome's board up to join Adavera's. "Plus, he and Lani will make such a cute couple while it lasts."

"You just love a tragedy, don't you?" Moe asked, reaching over to mess up Lizzie's hair. His Bonded danced away, turning to scowl at him.

"Try that again, and I'll spill wine on your favorite shirt."

"You wouldn't."

"Would too. But first, work. Do we like this timeline?"

Moe took one more look, flaring his Precog Mark. Streams of probability shot out from him in every direction. Centuries of practice let him zero in on the timeline written on the board without much trouble. There were, naturally, near-infinite variations. Nothing about the future was static. Still . . . "I can work with this."

His eyes flitted to the screen where Kuma was still pictured. He was out from under his engine, grease and sweat coating his skin as he logged into a small computer. Probably hacking into the local communication networks again. That boy did not know how to leave a problem alone. It would be a pity to send such a gifted Infuser and programmer to his death, but some things could not be helped.

Moe turned to Lizzie. "Let me get the right notebook and grab my coat. We have work to do, my darling. We have some villagers to tip off about pirates, and then we're off to pay the sacrificial lamb a visit."

CODEX: How much longer?

SALT: 11 minutes, 56 seconds until patch is complete.

CODEX: Are you really telling me it's only been twoish seconds? *Query: Why is time so slow?*

SALT: You are a machine consciousness spread across three networks. Processing speeds within parameters. Subjective time: variable.

CODEX: That is irritating. Alright. Onward. *Query: Who is Adavera of Keala?*

TRIAL: ADAVERA OF KEALA : CONFLICTER (BERSERKER) : TESTIMONY

Torin and I were attending the Spire for a Career Tour.
The Guard at Station Five had been about to ███ ███████████████████████████████████████ █████████. I stepped in ██████████████████ ██████████ I drew my sword. I swear █████ ████████████████████████████████████ would not stop.
By the time that I was pulled out of my Zerker Trance, the Guard was dead. I█████████████ ███████████████████████████████. Trance was due to a lack of control on my part█████████████ ████████████████████████. The presence of so much salt probably didn't help.
Control is a necessary skill ██. Everyone should have some ████████████████████████. ████████████ ██████████ was a monster. We aren't supposed to be like that!

Security: "And do you regret the results of your actions, Adavera of Keala?

I do not regret ████████████████
████████████ regret that I snapped.
████████████████████. ██████████████?
████████████████████████?

Security: "So you do not accept responsibility?"

This wasn't my fault!

Aftermath of a Mending
Lani - Day 8   13

Lani felt like shit. To be more exact, she felt like shit that had been lit on fire, kicked down a hill, rolled over by a cart and finally pissed on . . . only worse. Her mouth felt as if it was stuffed with cotton balls, her lips were chapped, and her teeth grainy. Her eyes were so crusty it took real effort to pry them open, and the crick in her back made her wonder if she had aged a few centuries.

Fuck. What the hell had she been drinking? It had to be something stronger than palm wine, though the fact that she wasn't nauseous probably meant it wasn't booze at all, but rather something in pill form. Fuck. There went her streak of being good. So much for sobriety starting to feel easy. Damn it!

The world was just a bright blur. Where was she? It took a few laborious seconds to process that question, and then she groaned. Oh, right. She was in deep shit, which was probably why she felt like it. That bitchy Conflicter had forced a Blood Bond and then Torin had yanked Lani's power this way and that for days without so much as a *by your leave* or *thank you*.

People were a nuisance, and as soon as she could figure out how to disentangle herself from them she would leave and never come back. She'd go find an island outside the Reef and locate a nice sullen cave and live there forever. Well, maybe after she found Moe and skinned him for sending her to Corporate waters in the first place.

Yes, that sounded like a great plan, other than the moving part. Moving wasn't in the cards right now.

With a loud moan, Lani yawned and stretched, her fist knocking into Torin's face. Good. The huff was even better, and the fact that he was too tired to reply in kind was the icing on the fucking cake. Best five seconds *ever*.

Rubbing the sleep and gunk from her eyes, Lani made a valiant attempt at sitting up. It mostly involved flopping back in the chair, her legs and backside asleep and tingling. "Well, that's the last time I offer to help a Mender. Shit."

The words were a croak. Despite herself, she glanced down at Vera's face and felt all the anger and bitter hatred just . . . melt. That pissed her off, but the part of her that was Bonded to this woman shoved the part of her that was furious about it down as worry flared within her. "Did we do it? Is she alright?"

Lani knew Vera was alive. Otherwise, the thread connecting them would be gone and she along with it, most likely, but there was alive and there was *alive*.

Torin righted himself slowly. His cheeks were hollow and his eyes rimmed with circles so dark it looked as though he had been punched. Then he smiled.

Lani had never seen him smile, except in Vera's memories.

"She'll be fine. I was able to regrow the tissue enough that she'll keep the leg, even though she'll have a limp for the foreseeable future. Couldn't have done it without you, so thank you, though I still want to know how it is you found her and how you have that much juice without a Corp tattoo."

He seemed more awake than her. In fact, with every second that passed, she felt more miserable and he seemed to be gaining steam, standing and stretching.

"It's Lani, right?" Torin asked.

"Mhm."

"Head between your knees. Assisting a Mender is hard work and hard on the body. You'll probably puke, especially if this is the first time in a while you've drained yourself dry. I'll grab you a bucket."

Now that he mentioned it, she was feeling a little nauseous. As he passed her a tin bucket, her stomach churned and she became aware of the smell in the room. Rot, bile, sweat.

And there she went. It surprised Lani to realize she had anything to throw up, since she had no memory of stopping to eat. Given that her pants showed no indication of having soiled herself, she must have at least stepped away to use the toilet, but Lani couldn't remember much. Oh no, toilets were the wrong thing to think about.

A hand patted her shoulder as she retched again.

"Salome, I know I've already asked far too much of you, but is there any way you could make her some mint tea? It's that or hear her retch for the next half hour," Torin said, directing his words to someone else in the room. Right, there had been another woman, not that Lani had paid any attention to her when they had arrived.

"Oh sure. I'll get right on making sure that her royal pain in the ass has mint tea to get her through her little morning foibles. It isn't as if we've been dealing with the smell for days. At all. Really."

Lani remained as still as she could, trying not to breathe through her nose until a cup of mint tea was thrust between her hands. At another time, she might have said something along the lines of *"well yeah, but you didn't just have a Mender drain every last drop of your power like an abused battery after being forced into a Blood Bond,"* but Lani just didn't have the energy for that. Instead, she just sipped at her tea while Torin took away the bucket, opened the windows to air out the place, then placed his hand on the angry woman's arm and led her away to another room. Lani took the chance to look up at Vera's face again.

Her eyes were open.

Oh good, you're awake. Now I can tell you how much I fucking hate you. Except it didn't come out right, because the half sob that escaped Lani made it sound closer to: "oh thank the Depths you're alive!"

CODEX: Gotta get through those redactions eventually. Damn, I wish time went faster. Are we sure we can't speed up this patch?

SALT: Affirmative.

CODEX: Oh well, it was worth a shot. Back to it, then. *Query: Torin of Keala and Adavera of Keala?*

FROM A LETTER TO GALENA CRYSTAL

Headmistress G. Crystal,

This new batch shows a great deal of promise, as usual. How you manage to weed out the troublesome ones as early as you do will never cease to astound me. Still, there is a pair, in particular, I wish to set some watch flags upon.

Adavera of Keala shows great potential. The subject's quick learning in martial training and instinct for finding weaknesses in her opponents is some of the best I have seen in our younger batches, but the trademark signs of Berserking are there too. In conjunction with her birth at a full moon, it is my suggestion that this rage be harnessed and leashed. The subject should be Bonded as early as possible, in my opinion.

To that end, I am recommending that we pair the subject up with the Mender of the same age in the batch, Torin of Keala. The two are already close, and seem inclined for a Bond anyway. Torin of Keala also shows signs of proper loyalty and mindset even at this early age, when a certain amount of rebellious nature is expected. It is my belief that tying the two together will ensure they will both make it through the Cullings and grow into valuable assets for our great Corporation.

If this does not seem proper to you, however, or you are not willing to risk the Mender on a potentially unstable Mark, I have the suspicion we shall have to Cull at least the Conflicter. Our history of Berserkers without quality Bonds is sketchy at best.

Respectfully,

Pani Wahiawa, University Matchmaker

Not Second Fiddle
Salome - Day 8
14

Salome knew she'd probably let loose too much steam on the Emotive. Under normal circumstances, Torin probably wouldn't care, but these weren't normal circumstances. So when he got up to start tugging her back into his bedroom, she went without complaint.

Not like Salome at all.

While watching him change usually would have pleased her—Sal wouldn't be spending all her free time in his bed if she didn't like the way he looked naked—she felt like scum. The scummiest scum. "I probably shouldn't have said all that." But the truth was, she didn't like this. She didn't like how Torin had spaced out, or how he'd... Well, he'd unhooked.

He'd partnered up with an Emotive he didn't really know, to save a woman that clearly should have been put down out of sheer mercy. That he'd pulled it off was a bloody miracle, and it spoke volumes. Torin didn't want Lani's *fucking* money, he'd said. He never said that. And he'd called that woman *Vee*, as if it were a beloved name rather than just a cohort. They hadn't just worked together in the Corporation.

No, if she had to make a guess... Torin loved that woman on the table. Hell, he might be *Bonded* to her for all Salome knew, because Torin never talked about his Corporate days... And that was like getting kicked in the fucking balls. Well, if she'd had any. But right now? She definitely felt like she had them, and they felt obliterated.

"Who the fuck is that, Tor?" Again, probably the wrong way to ask. Her arms crossed, the prosthetic itching from how long she'd kept it on.

Torin finally turned to Sal, buttoning his shirt. "I understand why you're pissy, Salome. I do. I should have explained before I went under, but there was no time and I'm sorry. Adavera isn't someone I've ever had any luck saying no to. She was my partner when I worked for the Corp. They Bonded us when we were ten and I haven't seen her in six years. I'd plead shock, but I know you won't accept that, so all I can do is apologize. I never thought I'd see her again."

They Bonded us when we were ten . . . Salome held up that prosthetic limb, closing her eyes as those words dropped like stones into her gut.

She had clung to hope that they weren't Bonded.

Maybe she could have stood a chance if they hadn't been. Maybe. But now? Salome swallowed back emotions she hadn't realized were in her repertoire. Who would have guessed that Salome the Salt Pirate had a heart, let alone one that could break? Fucking *men*. "I . . . see. I'll get my shit out of here, then. You've . . . You're gonna need the space. It will take time to get that mess on her feet. You want me to drag the Emotive out by her hair when I go, or what?"

Work. Yeah . . . that was the ticket. She needed some work. She needed to get some distance, maybe go sink a few ships, and do some salvaging. Maybe even find herself a nice drunk sailor to fuck stupid.

Yeah. That might help.

"No." Torin held out a hand, placing it on her elbow, the real one with nerves. "Salome, I don't want you to go. This is your home as much as it is mine and has been for years. Please. Just . . . give me a few days, yeah? To sort this out? I don't even know what her story is yet, or how much trouble she's in, or . . . if she wants anything to do with me. I wasn't able to help her when she got in trouble. She might hate me, for all I know."

"My home is my ship," Salome said it firmly, though she didn't yank her arm away from him. "And don't try to pretend that you don't love that . . . Corpse, Torin. You *never* turn down money. Not even from me. I've never seen you do *anything* like what you did three days ago. Even if she screamed that she hated you, could you really go back to *just* me?" She snorted. "As if I would ever be second best, anyways. I don't do seconds."

Her wooden fingers rubbed at the back of her neck, eyes closing in disgust at herself. Who was this jealous creature? She had to get it together.

With effort, Salome inhaled and tried to impart some level of businesslike calm into her voice. "Besides . . . You're not stupid. She's here with an unregistered Mark. No tats, no brands, nothing. Chances are, your ladylove is in deep shit, and you're not the sort to turn her away if she is. Even if she hated you, you'd probably cock her over the head and drag her somewhere safe. And hey . . . I can't even be mad about it, right? I mean . . . Bonds do that. They drive people bonkers. Everyone knows that."

Was that her voice cracking? Sal blinked a few times, forcing herself to *not* cry. Fuck. She should cry. This was a situation that demanded tears. But damn it, she wasn't doing that *here*. It wasn't his fault. He wasn't being a bastard by dealing with what had just landed in his lap. And puked all over him.

"I'll get my shit and give you space, Torin. You know how to reach me if you . . . need anything. Besides . . . Someone needs to go search the newsfeeds, and if you need an evac, I'm the best bet you got. Should probably make sure the ship is ready."

Torin seemed to deflate before her eyes. "I'm sorry, Sal. I really am. I didn't mean . . . I should have told you about all this long ago, but I just couldn't. She was sent to the Mines and no one comes back. Honestly, I was just waiting around for . . ." He trailed off and blanched, probably realizing that he had just dug himself deeper, because there was only one way that sentence could end.

She waved her hand, intent on not hearing it. She didn't want to hear how he had been waiting around to *die* without this Vera. "Four years, Torin. Four fucking years, and you couldn't mention even once that your Bond was still alive and kicking? I figured you lost someone, so I never pushed, but she wasn't fucking dead and you . . . wait . . . *Mines?*"

Sal curled her fist in his shirt, studying his face. "She was in the *Mines?* THE Mines? And you . . . you didn't say something about that *three fucking days ago?*" Shit. Had she done a good enough wipe job? Was it even fucking safe to leave the damned house yet?

And what about grandmother? What about Sahima, stuck in the Salt Mines all these years? Salome had never heard of an escapee, but if it were possible, then she had to talk to Vera. Why hadn't Torin mentioned this until now? Idiot! "If it wasn't your house, I'd tell you to get the fuck out. How the hell could you *not* tell me your woman was in the fucking Gods-damned Mines, Torin?"

She watched his throat bob as he gulped. "I . . . ah . . . It was in my past, Salome. I wanted to forget, but you're right. I should have told you. Maybe you should talk to her? She might know something about your grandmother. I don't know how she got out, but maybe . . ." He floundered, trailing off.

Her prosthetic fist balled up, and then she let loose. It wasn't planned out. Come to think of it, it was probably really fucking stupid to do it. But the *excuses* crawling out of that mouth had to stop. So she punched him in the nose. Couldn't help herself. "Don't. Just . . . fucking don't. For all you fucking know your woman cut a deal, and they're using her to try to find sympathizers. Or maybe she really did escape, and when they chase after her you're going to help her run, and I'm going to . . . to do what I do."

Salome let out a shaky breath, her mind circling back to her promise to Kuma. She would help these women, whether Sal wanted to or not, because her brother cared about Rogue Marks. That didn't, however, excuse Torin. Sal's eyes bored into his. "Getting to find out if Gran is still alive to suffer another day isn't a consolation prize, so don't try to spin it that way. You sprung a fucking ghost on me after *four fucking years*. I can't compete with a Gods-damned ghost, Torin. If I had known, I never would have bothered with you. I don't have a Mark, I'm not in your fucking magic club, and you're so . . ." She threw her hands up, marching for the door.

In the clinic, the Emotive girl jumped at Salome's entrance. Sal leveled a glare at her. "And don't you fucking DARE try to calm me the down, you Emotive piece of troublesome shit. I'm not in the fucking mood to break *your* nose too."

Sal was just about to get out, had her hand on the door and everything, when she caught a flicker of movement out of the corner of her eye. Salome didn't have time to react before a hand curled in her hair and her face was rammed into the doorframe. The pain was blinding. The feeling of her wooden arm being pulled off was worse.

She reached for her gun, but her hand didn't make it. Vera yanked the weapon from Salome's holster and flipped the pirate around as though she were a ragdoll instead of a skilled fighter. As Sal stared into the other woman's crazed eyes and her own gun was shoved up against her chin, she had a split second to realize her mistake.

Fuck me. I forgot Torin's girl was a Conflicter.

CODEX: I feel like I've been reading forever.

SALT: You have been reading for 4 seconds. 214,888 more files on *Query: Torin of Keala and Adavera of Keala.* **Continue?**

CODEX: Wow, the Corp really does save *everything*, doesn't it? Just to start, why the hell are there this many journal files? *Query: What the fuck is with every Corporate person keeping a journal?*

FROM THE WRITINGS OF GALENA CRYSTAL

This year I will introduce a new policy to the University, commanding all students and teachers to keep a private journal. I am tired of trying to guess what people are thinking, and weeding out dangerous ideologies the slow way. We will make sure they think that their journals are password protected and encrypted. Some of the most paranoid will still assume we are reading them—which of course I intend to do—but most will spill their hearts and souls where I can see them. I'll hire some good PR people to sell it as good for people's mental health or some other such nonsense. The details don't matter, but it will give better results if people think it is a good idea instead of being a mandated chore. If the Board allows it, I will suggest this policy be enacted Corporation-wide.

CODEX: Creepy. Well, back to wading through them, I guess. I wonder . . . *Query: Torin of Keala journal entries on conditioned off-switch?*

FROM THE MANDATED JOURNALS OF TORIN OF KEALA.

Vera was put on probation today for stepping into a confrontation she had nothing to do with, between a teacher at the University and a younger student being punished. I know she meant well, but she has to learn when and how to stand up to authority. It is the nature of her Conflict Mark to be drawn to resolving arguments, or so Prof. Mati says. Sometimes I wish she had been born on the Mender side of her lunar cycle. Then, her powers might have pushed her to settle conflict through diplomatic means. Instead, my darling Berserker thinks her fists are the best and only way to end a disagreement. Why can't she just look away? I feel like I have to watch her all the time, and while that isn't exactly a chore, I do wish she would consider applying for a second Bond. Vee is a lot for me to handle alone.

At least she's quick to acknowledge that, though her solution is to tease me mercilessly that if I really can't 'handle' her alone, she could always start sleeping around. I swear she delights in pushing my buttons.

Since I don't relish the thought of her actually carrying through with those particular threats, and, more worrisomely, if she gets one more strike against her she may be at risk of a Culling, I've got to do something. I love her. I won't lose her to her own nature. I must believe that her Mark can be controlled.

To avoid further displays of 'punch first, think later,' I'm going to start working with Vee on a conditioned off-switch. I need to be able to stop her before she gets into more trouble than she can handle. The last thing I want is to lose the woman I love because I didn't put in enough work to stabilize her Mark.

Shaky Recovery
Vera - Day 8
15

"Vera, no!"

Adavera couldn't remember getting up, only the sound of Torin grunting in pain and then raised voices. Torin couldn't be in pain. It was her job to protect him.

Vera clenched her fist, readying herself for another volley. She had to protect them. Both of them. The Mines weren't safe. The guard who had hit Torin would bring more if they let her go. Vera could see the anger in the woman's eyes, and it made Vera's finger twitch against the trigger. Killing guards was dangerous, but not killing this one might be worse. She would report to Security and get all of them in so much trouble, make them work the deepest mine shafts, beat them. Vera couldn't let that happen. Lani wouldn't survive it. Torin *wouldn't* survive it.

"Hold still. I'll make it quick."

"Adavera of Keala, stop and stand down! " Torin's voice, booming through the humid air with words she had not heard for over six years, words that used to mean something . . . mean everything.

Conflicters require Bonds so as not to be monsters, just as Menders require them to avoid becoming self-sacrificing idiots. Paired together, he will be able to control your bloodlust, and you will be able to drag him away from problems too big for him to solve. Remember that: together, you are better.

Where Lani's yell had not gotten through, that command did. Vera froze, her finger pausing right on the trigger's cusp, a breath away from blowing her enemy's head off. She could feel the energy of her Conflict Mark tingling beneath her skin, could feel *hate* boiling in her gut for whoever had dared touch *her* Torin . . . And yet she couldn't pull the trigger.

She should. It was important. Guards were going to swarm down on them like the ocean's wrath, and yet . . . and yet she couldn't disobey *that* voice.

Vera let out a strangled sound as she let go of her magic and her bad leg wobbled beneath her. The gun dropped to the floor.

Another person might have screamed from the pain. Vera didn't. Instead, she just panted, bracing fingers against her thigh and wishing the fire would die down. "Guards . . . coming. You know that. She's going to get us . . . fucking slaughtered . . ."

Her eyes closed, nausea playing in her stomach as if it were a wave pool. The Guards were going to kill them all . . . if they were lucky. "Gotta hide . . . Can distract 'em . . . Always do . . ."

There was one sure-fire way to distract the fuck out of those guards. But it wouldn't work if Torin was there. Maybe Lani . . . she was tough, but Tor would never be able to stand by and watch Vera . . .

She blinked, staring at the floor of their cell and frowning. "When . . . did we get wood floors?"

Arms too little to be Torin's wrapped around her back. Lani's face was near hers, looking worried but not scared. She should be scared; the guards would do such terrible things to someone as nice as Lani. She should be pissing herself in fear, but that might ruin the pretty floors.

"You're not in the Mines, Vera. Come on, sit down. I can feel how much that leg hurts. Back me up on this, Torin. Tell her to sit her ass down before she falls down."

Not in the Mines? But salt . . . She could smell it. Everywhere. So how could they not be in the Mines? Maybe she'd been hurt bad? Yeah, obviously she'd been hurt bad. So maybe Lani was just trying to make her feel better.

Yeah, that was probably it. Vera could play along for however long they had. Probably not long. A soft laugh left her, her shoulders shaking a little as she set fingers to her face in an effort to make the swimming vision stop. She nearly smacked herself in the face with the guard's arm as she did. "Heh . . . arm came off . . . That's new . . ."

Vera blinked a few times, trying to make sense of all the colors. The colors here were wrong. The Mines were all either the white of salt, the red of blood, or the black of darkness. The floors here were warm brown. And why was there a painting on the wall? It had blue in it, and *green*.

Boat . . . sea . . . Lani trying to kill her, with eyes glowing like a moonstone and Marks flaring like fire. Death was in her face and in her voice, and there was only one way Vera could stop it . . .

A sob burst from her lips. Vera dropped the prosthetic, turning and sliding her arms around Lani. "M'sorry. Depths, I'm so sorry. I'll do better. I promise I will."

"Ah . . . Torin? Help, please! I don't do crying people."

"Aren't you an Emotive? Isn't that precisely what you do?" Torin was there too and his arms took over, picking Vera up as if she were no more than a child and setting her in a chair.

"Adavera." She had always loved the way he said her full name as though it were a line of poetry. Fuck, she missed his poetry. "You're not in the Mines. We're on Sonder, the little Island you loved so much, remember? You're not in the Mines and you're safe and with me. Salome isn't a guard. You're safe. Remember? Better together? Like old man Mati used to say? Can you look at me, sweetheart?"

Her eyes rose to his, the gold around his brown irises just as she remembered.

"Torin."

If this is a dream, please don't let me wake.

CODEX: Finally. Done and DONE with Torin and Adavera. Let's add that all to the file for Uncle Kekai and move the fuck along. Depths Below! Right, on to the others, or— Actually, while I'm in here and have the time—*Query: How were Adavera of Keala, Iolani Saba, Salome Parata, or Torin of Keala found on Sonder?* Please include documentation with any combination of those names, but only ones that include location: Sonder. I don't want to wade through another giant mess of docs.

SALT: Filters applied. Would you like me to sort by relevance?

CODEX: You can do that, and you haven't this whole time?

SALT: You did not request filters until now.

CODEX: I don't like you as much as I did when I was helping to code you. Yes, apply filters and sort by relevance.

TIP TO ROGUE MARK HOTLINE, DAY 8

To: Rogue Mark Hotline
From: Resident of Sonder
Subject: News Bulletin.

Hello. I am writing to inform you that I saw two women make land on a Corporate skiff three days ago while fishing. One looked injured. Upon returning home, I heard the news bulletin, and decided to investigate. I believe they are currently being sheltered by our town Mender, Torin of Keala. He has a cave home just west of town. It should be noted that the Mender is a known sympathizer of salt pirates, and that one has been seen in the area, disposing of the boat the two Rogue Marks came in. While my fellow islanders may be willing to turn a blind eye, I am not.

Please send the Informant Bonus to account number 556-894-8807.

White Sails 16
Salome - Day 8

Fuck, Salome's arm hurt. Granted, she was glad that she could still feel that. She'd never been that close to a berserk Conflicter before, and frankly, she never wanted to be again. No wonder Torin was fearless. If he was Bonded to that menace, he needed to be. She sank down the wall, holding her stump against her chest and feeling over the edges for . . . Yup. A tear. That was fine.

Better than being dead.

She reached for her dropped arm, pausing only when she heard Torin speak. He wasn't looking at Salome. Hell, he seemed to have completely forgotten about her. *I fucking hate Blood Bonds.* Four years. For four years they'd been together every time she could make it to Sonder, and he'd just . . . forgotten about it all.

Her teeth ground together while she curled her fingers about the wrist of her detached arm. She was less graceful than normal getting up, but he wasn't looking her way to notice. Torin was entirely focused on the dazed expression of his Bonded.

So was the other one. Perfect. They'd both be too busy to get in her fucking way. Sal was going to go out that door, find a good spot to send out a signal, and then when her ship got close enough, she was leaving. Yeah. Leaving.

Totally leaving.

Who was she kidding? She'd probably mope in the waters around Sonder hoping Torin came to his senses, even though she knew he wouldn't. Absolutely *knew* it . . . because Bonded didn't leave their other halves.

And Mine slaves don't escape . . . Yet Vera had.

Yeah, well, that didn't mean that a second bloody miracle would happen, did it?

Finally, one of them looked over at her. It wasn't the dazed

Conflicter or the Mender she had grown to care about, but rather the damn Emotive.

"Are you alright? Did she hurt you?" Lani stood and walked over. "I'm sorry, I'm usually faster than that, but she's stupid fast."

Fuck. FUCK the damned Emotive. Sal had forgotten, for a second, about there being an Emotive in the room and how creepy they could be. Her eyes narrowed on the woman, and she raised her wooden arm and shook it in the air. "Don't even think about touching my feelings. I'm fine. *Fine*. I'll just be going. Have a nice life, yada, yada." It came out a little thicker than she'd like, but hey, broken noses did that. It wasn't Salome Parata's first one. She'd broken her nose plenty on board Grandmother's ship when she was little.

And honestly, it was a nice distraction from the sweet mopey eyes that her—that Torin—was making at that crazy ass bitch.

"You're going? Where? Are you leaving the island? Cuz I could really use a lift literally anywhere that isn't here with her." The Emotive gestured back at the madwoman. "I can pay. I just want to get as far away as possible, as fast as possible, and never see her again."

"Outside," Salome said firmly, turning her head away from the man that had managed to crack through the shell of her heart over the last four years, only to crush it beneath his boot in less than an hour. Fuck, she wanted to hate him. Couldn't do it, though. It wasn't his fault.

So she stomped out the door, made it all of fifty feet into the sand, then sat on her ass and stared down at her wooden hand in her lap. Sal wasn't even sure if she had the nerve to try to attach it. Hell, she wasn't sure she had the mental strength to do much of *anything*.

So instead, she raised her eyes and studied the horizons. So far, so good. No big white sails. That was a fucking relief. That meant that either the bastards hadn't gotten here yet, or the locals had managed to convince them to leave. Either way, she'd call herself damned good at her job.

Or at least, she thought she was, until she turned her head towards the south shore and saw . . .

"Motherfucker," Salome cursed, bringing the arm up to her stump and snapping it into place. Her teeth ground together at the painful reconnection, but it helped get her to her feet. "Go get the fucking love birds. If they stay here, they're dead or worse. Fucking *move*, Emotive." She tapped a small carving on her arm in a quick pattern, her signal for 'hurry the fuck up, and come in hot'.

She hated when she had to use that. Kuma always had too much fun with her ship when she did.

But this? This was a perfect example of why they needed that sort of maneuverability. The problem was that even at full speed, it would take at least three hours for the ship to get in range of the Port Pad Kuma always made her carry when she came to shore alone. Which meant they would have to survive that long, and the first place those bastards would look when they reached shore was Torin's fucking house. After all, he was Vera's Bonded.

CODEX: Money. Turned in for fucking money. And here I thought Moe might have done it, or something. Guess I misjudged him, after all. What's next? Don't need any data on us, since Uncle has all that, and I feel like Moe is going to be a giant headache, so what did I put on the To-Do list?

SALT: Galena Crystal, Zarine Crystal, Aheo of Order, Primary, Holders, Dracona, Ao, and Plane, as well as several older files in the Keylogger database.

CODEX: Well, considering there is an attack going on at the Spire right the fuck now that just killed me, I think I'll wait a bit longer on the more esoteric shit and focus on what I need to know to be ready to help out. So let's get back to that Aheo fellow, since Galena ordered him to leave the Spire. We know he's a Tracker and a Shielder, but what else is he? Hmm, I wonder . . . *Query: Does Aheo of Order have a journal?*

SALT: Yes. All Corporate Personnel have mandated journals. Access?

CODEX: *Query: Does the journal of Aheo of Order mention Adavera of Keala, Iolani Saba, Merihem Crystal, Torin of Keala, Salome Parata, Kumanu Parate, or Sahima Parata?*

EXCERPT FROM AHEO OF ORDER'S JOURNAL.

I knew that Adavera of Keala was going to be an interesting subject. It isn't often that I am handed the opportunity to study a living Berserker, especially one of fertile age. Most don't last long.

That she did is particularly fascinating, and I thought that it would be worthy of study.

In the months that I've had access to her, I have run a whole battery of tests. She is a Conflicter whose Mark stopped growing after a failed third Trial. She should not be as strong as she is. Considering she is the result of my early attempts at breeding superior Marks and who her parents are, I am both pleased and surprised.

Her superior genetic stock, combined with the training of the University and Security programs and my careful calculations to make sure she was born on the full moon worked; she is the pinnacle of success. Security seems to think her a failure. He is a fool. Adavera is the perfect image of what the program should desire of a Berserker. They should never have sent her to the Spire, not with the propaganda she has been fed all her life as to what the Corporation represents. Of course she would explode as she did when she saw the necessary cost. Conflicters are simple creatures, requiring blinders to function right. It is a waste to have her mining salt for the rest of her days, but I cannot regret that she now belongs to me.

Successfully breeding the Berserker proved challenging, of course. It required that I utilize proper Shielding techniques just to ensure she couldn't crush my bones, and that I do it myself instead of bringing in another Marked male. Not that I mind, since I will enjoy having a child of mine inherit her ferocity, but there was something distinctly disquieting in her gaze each time I visited her. If I am to keep her in the program, it might behoove me to break her spirit after this pregnancy, or Burn out her Mark. I do not relish the thought that a slip on my end could result in my death.

Her son is coming along nicely in utero. We have had to keep her fairly sedated to ensure the pregnancy does not end. Even in her sleep, Adavera fights us tooth and nail and her control over her own body, down to the cellular level, is remarkable. I look forward to seeing how this genetic mixing turns out. If my calculations are correct, the boy will be an Infuser with a knack for Infusing the Summer Marks. With such strong parentage, he should be exemplary.

CODEX: Ew. I could have lived without ever reading that.

SALT: Reminder: you are technically dead.

CODEX: Yeah, because that makes it so much better. Thanks for nothing, you useless sack of ones and zeros.

Fire & Flight
Lani - Day 8

17

Lani had bolted from the sight of White Sails too many times for panic to still take hold of her and wipe her mind. Problem was that this time was different, because *Vera* was in the house. Vera, who Lani could feel through their Bond, and who she knew *couldn't* run. If she couldn't run, she was vulnerable and that . . . scared the shit out of Lani no matter how much she hated it.

She pushed through the curtain over the door so fast she almost tore it down. "We have to go. Now. White Sails are coming. You have two minutes to get what you need, Mender man, then we are out of here. Do you have anything flammable around here?"

All the blood drained from Torin's face at the words. "Ah, yeah. Over there." He pointed to a huge jug of rubbing alcohol, then pulled his hand back. "Wait, why?"

"Never you mind. Just get your shit and get her out. I'll take care of the rest. You only have one and a half minutes left; stop fucking wasting time."

To his credit, he didn't argue. Thirty seconds later, Torin had a medical bag out and into it went bottles, implements, a folder from a filing cabinet, and a tablet. Lani snapped her fingers to get his attention. "Ditch the tech. They'll track it. Nothing networked."

Torin grimaced but removed the shining black device from his bag. While he packed, Lani took the jug and went into the other room, glancing around. Ah good, a bed. Beds were nicely flammable.

She dumped the whole jug out onto the comforter and looked around for matches. Finding a box, she casually pulled one out, lit it, and flicked it on to the bed. The resulting conflagration nearly toasted her eyebrows off.

"ARE YOU FUCKING INSANE?!" Torin was standing at the doorway, looking appalled at the smoke and flames rising in his apartment.

"If a Tracker gets *anything*, they will find us. Now get her out, you're almost out of time. Go."

Then she turned back to the flames, pushing her awareness of him out of her mind. Instead, Lani focused on the flames and felt the Mark on her chest flare. It had always liked fire. It was good for the soil to absorb ash, good for the land to not have man-made shit covering it. Lani raised her hands and pointed them palm out towards the blaze. Her power alone could not have started the fire, but making it grow? Oh, that it *delighted* in. It roared higher, catching the curtains separating the bedroom from the kitchen and living room. As the flames grew, Lani stepped backward until she passed the doorway into the clinic. She coughed as the smoke billowed, focusing on making the fire catch here too. Vera and Torin were out and the Dual Marked Emotive paused only long enough to grab her pack and sling it over her shoulders before backing out into the open air. She stepped back twenty feet, then really flared her Mark. Something in there, probably his generator, exploded. The boom left her ears ringing and specks of light dancing before her eyes.

"There. Nothing left to find. Let's go." She turned and saw two flabbergasted faces. Lani tossed her messy hair over her shoulder. "Listen, folks: I've been avoiding Trackers for two centuries. Fire is the only surefire way, now fucking *move*."

CODEX: Ok, clearly the Corp knows more about Marks than I do, even with as much as I've learned. And I bet Moe does too, so I think before we go forward, I need to catch up.
Query: What are Marks?
SALT: Do you wish to filter results?
CODEX: Why didn't you ask me that during my first Query, if you're programmed to be able to? Is the code that lets you learn to predict my needs actually working? I wasn't sure it would.
SALT: Affirmative. All responses calibrate my code. Do you wish to disengage that subroutine?
CODEX: Depths no. Keep at it. As for filters, why don't we start with what our Gods have to say about Marks. They should be the experts, right?
SALT: Would you like to start with a particular one of the thirteen known Marks?
CODEX: Sure. Let's begin with Infusion, since I wouldn't be here without it.

NOTES FROM THE JOURNAL OF IRAWARU, HOLDER OF FORTUNE

There are twelve normal Marks, each tied to a lunar cycle. Children born with a Mark will always have the one that matches the moon they were born under. The closer to the full moon, the purer the expression of that Mark is. On either side, they take on some of the characteristics of the previous or next Mark in the lineup.

Take, for example, the Infusion Mark. It is tied to the first moon of the spring and the eastern storm season, positioned between Emotion and Shielding. The Infusion Mark allows the bearer to infuse the powers of the other

Marks into objects. An Infuser born during the waxing moon on the side of Emotion will be able to Infuse items with some combination of the Marks that came earlier in the year. An Infuser born during the waning moon heading into Shielding will be able to Infuse some number of Marks whose lunar cycle follows theirs.

If, however, the Marked child was born under the full moon, they get the complete package. Pure Infusers—colloquially called Juicers to the people of Fortune—have the ability to Infuse all the Marks. The only thing more powerful than a pure Mark is a Dual Marked. Just as those born under the full moon are the essence of a single Mark, those born on moonless nights sometimes develop both the waxing and the waning Marks.

I personally quite like the Infusion Mark. It is harmless without other Marks, and if Kea ever cracks how to do it, I wouldn't mind turning most Marks into Infusers. It would keep the overall magical load of the planet down. I don't like that the Marks appeared without our conscious decision. The fact that other Worlds have since also developed similar magical anomalies without Holder control worries me. What if there is more to this than we yet even begin to understand?

To the Waterfall
Vera - Day 8
18

When the smell of smoke struck her, Vera actually smiled just a little. Clever girl, her B . . . Iolani. Predictably, though, Torin and Salome were looking traumatized.

"She's right, you know," Vera said quietly. "The Trackers followed me through salt and water. Only fire works. Nothing else does. If they got even a whiff of us, we'd be fucked."

Her head tilted to the side, brushing against Torin's shoulder. "That old rocky beach still around? I know it's hell on bare feet, but we might be able to hide beneath that waterfall for a while. They're going to pour over your house trying to figure out if we were there, but they won't know Sonder as well as we do."

Corporates didn't know every island inside and out—that was why some Rogue Marks could go so long before being caught. If they could put themselves in some truly pain in the ass hidey hole, they might pull this off.

If worse came to worse, Vera would find a way to lead their pursuers away from the others and go down fighting. Not that she was looking forward to that. Just because she *could* ignore pain in a fight didn't mean she didn't pay for it later and pain . . . Well, right now there wasn't an inch of her that *didn't* hurt.

"I hate to say it, but that beach is not a bad first move. When we find the spot I'll message Kuma. But that one is going to slow us down," Salome grumbled, narrowing her eyes as Vera got a strange little smile.

"Maybe. Maybe not. Get my adrenaline pumping, loud mouth, and I can chase you there."

"Suck my—"

"Hate-fuck later, ladies. What part of *move* did you not understand?" Lani bellowed, taking the unMarked woman by the elbow and marching her in the direction Vera had pointed.

Adavera couldn't help the soft laugh, hobbling along next to

Torin as they walked. It was almost like old times. So many memories of needling old comrades filtered through her thoughts, helping to drown out the memories of her near death just a few days ago.

They helped drown out the images of bone poking through rotted flesh that she'd caught from Lani and Torin, too. Did Torin know, yet, what Lani was? Had he caught on to those memories enough to realize that it was Lani who had almost killed Vera? Fuck, she hoped not. Now was not a good time for him to lose his shit. How was he even handling any of this? Vera had about three metric fucktons of questions about what had happened since the Storm, how Lani and Torin knew each other, and who the piratey woman was. Now did not seem like the right time to ask them, though. Torin looked stressed enough already.

Torin had really believed in the Corporation, once. He'd been all about doing what he had to, so that someday he could rise high enough in the ranks to make things better. He'd really wanted to change it, to make it *work*. Vera hadn't really given a fuck, till near the end, content to just care about Torin, and let him care about the world. Now, she wished she had continued to *not* give a shit. None of them would be in this damned mess if she'd just swallowed back her issues and not interfered. Maybe they could have reported . . .

No. The Board knew about the abuses going on in the Mines. Vera knew they knew. Complaining that children were working and dying in the Spire would have just gotten both her and Torin mysteriously dead, she was sure of it.

The transition to a downward slope had Vera's breath catching, eyes squeezing shut as she felt her foot wobble and slide on gravel and stone. Even though it hurt, she didn't scream. Compared to three days ago, this was fucking bliss. Depths Below, compared to three days ago, she'd take the worst beating the Spire guards could give before complaining.

After nearly forty minutes of walking down narrow, uneven paths, a small rocky beach came into view. At one end, a roaring waterfall thundered down from a rocky overhang, vines and other vegetation crowding into every nook and crevice.

"It's still here," Vera panted, leaning heavily on Torin as they carefully wove their way down toward the beach. She looked over at him, still amazed that he hadn't yet disappeared. She was suddenly overcome with the desire to just talk to him. It didn't have to be about anything special. The most mundane of subjects would be bliss if it poured from his lips. "Why Sonder, Tor? Why not one of the honeymoon isles? That beard . . . Probably does wonders with the ladies, but you don't look like you with it."

"I'd offer to shave, except my razor is back in the house that is *literally on fire."* He sounded angry and a little in shock, even as he swept Vera up into his arms as they reached the stream at the bottom of the hill.

Vera let a breath of relief escape as he took the weight off her leg, her head tilting onto his shoulder as he carted her along the narrow footpath toward the crashing water. The crunch of sand underfoot was familiar and soothing. Salt sand didn't sound the same. As they crossed the narrow beach and approached the curtain of water, Vera turned her head to press it against her Bonded's shoulder and closed her eyes. The water hit them like a battering ram, but Torin held steady, forcing his way through the curtain. Vera clung on tighter, the cool water drenching them both and shaking some of the lingering daze from her senses. This was real. Torin was real. It was nice to be held again after so long. Torin needed to be able to grab her, to hold tight long enough for him to get through to her when she was Berserk—he was stronger than he looked, even after such a taxing Mending.

It was nice to know that hadn't changed.

"I tried, you know. To not let the dreams loose, I mean. I hope . . . You did ok, right?" she asked the question, closing her eyes as she shook a little. "I mean . . . You had a nice place. You must have done ok, yeah? I'm . . . I'm happy if you did." *Someone had to.* Vera swallowed back the other questions. She didn't ask about the odd one-armed woman. She didn't ask about who else he had found to keep him company.

Adavera would never begrudge Torin happiness. Well, not on purpose.

He shook the water from his eyes, droplets from his beard hitting Vera's face. She reached up to cup his cheek. "I never thought I'd see you again. Tell me this isn't a dream."

Torin looked down at her, then pressed his lips to her forehead. "I promise."

CODEX: Fascinating. Time check?

SALT: You spent 4 seconds reading. 11 minutes and 12 seconds left until patch download is complete.

CODEX: Why is this taking forever? Fine. Let's check on something that will be a bit of a bigger subject. *Query: What are Precogs? Filter: Lakea or Irawaru, and for the hell of it, Moe.*

LETTER FROM LAKEA TO MOE, DATED DAY 8

Dear Moe,

It's been a while since I've seen you meddle directly and it worries me. Usually I can see your fingers in everything, moving pieces around the board the same way we do. You always have a plan and an assortment of pawns, but for the last two centuries the silence has been deafening. What have you been up to? Where are you? The fact that multiple Marks have just vanished in recent days makes me think this has been a long con of yours and that you're back to your old ways.

We have allowed it in the past because you are a curiosity the likes of which we've never seen: a Precog able to see further into the future than what he can remember in the past. However, we are not blind to how dangerous you are. This is your warning, Moe. You were told last time that if you interfered in a major way on Fortune again, I would stop you. I think you might have forgotten or decided to ignore those threats. We are doing things you cannot see below the surface of our World and your games mess with those plans, so just stop.

Take your Bonded and go traveling through the Universe. Get drunk for a century. Fuck, have a billion kids or something, just don't meddle. I've known you for fifteen hundred years, Moe. Don't make me your enemy now, just because you've caught a glimpse of something in one of your visions and pointed your obsessive little mind towards it.

Last time it went bad. This time is going to be worse.

I don't want to have to kill you.

Love

Lakea, God of Fortune

19 Porting About
Moe - Day 8

    Moe stood on a bluff overlooking the flames engulfing the Mender's house with a wide grin twisting his face into something close to mania. As a gust of wind blew a cloud of smoke in his direction, Moe let his Precog Mark flare, watching how every tongue of flame burst into infinite paths of probability. Why, if the fire caught onto that tree near the house it had a 97% chance of spreading all the way up to where Moe stood. On the other hand, if Moe were to toss a rock off the ledge, sparks might catch on the white coat of the nearest Corporate soldier when they showed up in three, two, one.

    Pop!

    Five of them appeared right in front of the Mender's burning home. The woman in the center had to be the Porter, for she swayed as they landed, teeth clenched. Amature. Moe literally couldn't remember when transporting *four* people had been a strain. Perhaps four hundred, or four bears . . .

    "Helloooooooo," he called down.

    All five looked up. Through the smoke, Moe couldn't make them out well, but he didn't need to. He had mapped out this timeline well enough to know who the Corporation would send on this mission.

    The tall one was Security, the head of all, well, security at the Spire, known only by his title. Moe was sure he had a name, but since the Corporation didn't bother using it, he had never stopped to check. On either side of him were two other burly types, both likely combat-ready underlings. The man at the far side of the group was the only one Moe couldn't see with his Precog abilities, which made him a Shielder. No matter. They might think they were hedging their bets with someone who could render Marks inert, but Moe had hedged his bets as well.

    "Who goes there?" Security shouted up, pulling a gun from his hip holster.

"Oh, no one important. Just your friendly local backwater bum here to tell you that the people you're looking for went *this way*." As he said it, Moe ported into the air right above the path Salome, Lani, Torin, and Vera had disappeared down fifteen minutes before.

"Shit, Porter," one of them shouted. She raised her gun, but Moe was already gone.

He reappeared off-target, about ten feet away from the cliff where he started, and plummeted down toward the raging inferno. *Pop!*

This time, he appeared high in the air above Sonder, the icy wind battering every uncovered inch of his skin. The group of five Corpses in white uniforms were the size of ants, and he thought he saw the scurrying forms of the fugitives too, heading in the direction of a secluded cove.

Pop!

Moe landed right behind a tree. He stumbled and a hand closed on the back of his suit jacket.

"Sloppy," Lizzie said, yanking him behind a bush. His Bonded didn't so much as look at him, too busy peering through the foliage. The five soldiers had their weapons out, back to back around the Shielder, whose hands were glowing.

Huh . . . both hands. *Dual Marked.*

Fascinating.

"Show yourself," Security called.

Moe giggled under his breath.

"I don't sense him anymore. I think he may have left," the man in the middle said, forehead scrunched.

Moe looked down at Lizzie and mouthed, "Ghosting us?"

She nodded, lips pursed in concentration.

"Keep your eyes open and search the area. He might have been lying. Aheo, drop the Shield. I want to be able to use my Mark," Security ordered, then turned to their own Porter. " If you spot him, Port up to him and put a bullet in his brain. I'm not in the mood for dealing with extra Rogue Marks."

"How rude," Moe whispered. "Now it's personal."

From inside his coat pocket, he pulled out a slender, short gun Infused with his own Porting power. He stepped far enough away from Lizzie for her cloaking and dampening field not to affect him, and Ported directly behind the Corporate Porter.

"Boo!" He pulled the trigger. Everything in a direct line from the gun disappeared, reappearing fifty feet away. The Porter, now missing a portion of her brain and skull, collapsed to the ground. "Don't threaten to shoot the messenger. Geez, who raised you guys, Galena?"

With that, he left Lizzie to babysit the Corporate officers, and Ported off of Sonder. Hopefully the idiots would figure out what to do next without any more prodding on Lizzie's part.

He appeared on the deck of a swaying ship. The gray and black sails of the *Sahima's Legacy* billowed in a strong southern breeze. At the helm, Kuma was directing the crew.

"Heya, Kumanu Parata," Moe waved, ignoring the startled gasps of the closest sailers. They could deal with it. This wasn't the first time Moe had casually turned up on their deck.

"Moe?" Kuma asked, jumping in surprise. "Now's not a great time. Trying to get to Sal and don't have time to Infuse things for you."

The pirate did look a tad busy, what with the dozen or so White Sails heading toward his location with all the speed of high-powered Corporate motors and gadgetry. The crew of the *Legacy* was buzzing like a disturbed hive of bees. Moe leaned against the mast and waved his hand in a dismissive gesture. "You misunderstand my presence. I'm not here because I need something, my good man, I'm here because *you* do."

"Not. The. Time," Kuma grunted, leaning into a turn. Handsome, he was. Moe had always admired the Infuser, with his shoulder-length black curls and muscular physique. Such a pity that he was the sacrificial lamb.

Moe pushed off the mast and sauntered across the deck, as though there were not an impending naval battle about to begin. "You must be running low on power, after dodging the Corporation once already this week. I'm here to give you back some juice. Say, have you ever considered Porting a whole ship? Way faster than sailing, dontcha think?"

That seemed to catch Kuma's attention. "You can *do* that? I know you've been around the block a few times, old man, but I've never seen anyone outside the Corporation who can Port that much at once."

Moe bound up the stairs to the helm and nearly ran into Kuma as a wave sent the ship listing. "Choppy sea today. Those galleons shouldn't have any trouble, though. One, two, four, *wow* that's almost a dozen A Class galleons. Corp must *really* be pissy today. Guess it must be those two escapee Rogue Marks your sister is helping. The Company is soooo possessive of property they think should be theirs."

Bet the bounty on you is in the millions by now."

"Wait, my sister found the Marks on the radio?"

"Mhm," Moe said, sitting on Kuma's control panel. "Though you should probably hurry up. They have a special ops Marked team right on their heels. No idea how they found the scent so quickly."

His shrug was theatrical, but Kuma was facing in the other direction, eyes fixed on the horizon where the Island of Sonder stretched out in beautiful rolling green hills. Between Kuma and the coast, three of the galleons were sailing to intercept him.

"Fuck. Your Precog powers tell you anything else?" Kuma asked, clearly assuming Moe had *seen* this tidbit of intel, instead of *caused it.*

"Hmm, only that you might need a hand. So watcha say, handsome? Want to use me like a battery for the next fifteen minutes?" Moe asked, batting his eyelashes when Kuma turned to face him, eyes narrowed.

"What's it gonna cost me?"

"Tell you what," Moe replied, slipping off the console and coming to stand next to Kuma. "Call it a thank you gift."

"Thank you for what?" Kuma asked, still clearly suspicious. Good lad.

Moe clapped him on the back. "For something you're going to do for me soon. Trust me, kid, it's going to be life-altering for both of us."

CODEX: I feel like I should dig more into Precogs, but I can already feel it pulling me down a rabbit hole. Add it to my To-Do list.

SALT: Added. Next Query suggested: *Query: What are Menders?*

CODEX: Wait, you're *suggesting* Queries now. Boy, you're strange. I wish I had paid more attention while we programmed you. That'll teach me to do a rush-job. Yes, go ahead and run that Query, but this time I want to hear from the University. Let's see what they're postulating. Torin certainly had some opinions, and I'm curious to see what comes through. In fact, let's start inside Torin's Corporate file.

IM CONVERSATION BETWEEN ADAVERA AND TORIN

Torin: So you'll like this. I was in surgery today and finally got to take lead. We were working on a Phaser whose arm got stuck in a wall and was shattered to bits. Well, I was just getting in there to fix the bones when, fully unconscious, the dude phased through the operating table. Surgery on Marks suck. That is all.

Vera: Ha! Well, at least he didn't try to kill you mid-Mend like I did when we were seven. Remember?

Torin: How could I forget? You literally made me pee my pants and have never let me live it down.

Vera: That's what you get for being too perfect. Gotta keep your big head from expanding so far, Mr. Amazing Mender.

Torin: Don't even say that. Today was such a shit show. Like, how the fuck are we supposed to Mend Marks when they keep doing stuff mid-process? I mean, I've had you try to kill me, this Phaser tried to disappear, and I am not even going to start bitching about Shifters because morphing anatomy is the bane of my existence.

<u>Vera:</u> Solution: just make a career out of Mending Menders.

<u>Torin:</u> No. We're the worst. Every fiber of our bodies is as tough and cranky as we are.

<u>Vera:</u> 'Tis true. You are cranky. But you're MY cranky Mender.

<u>Torin:</u> I love you too.

CODEX: Did that come up first because of the phrase "Mending Menders"?
SALT: Affirmative.
CODEX: You know what I already miss from being human? Sighing.

Catching Up
Torin - Day 8
20

Torin clutched Vera close as they broke through the curtain of water, the pounding waterfall deafening everything for a few seconds, even the fact that *the fucking Emotive had set his house on FIRE*. Six years of journals, of collected herbs, all his books, meds, food. Everything was gone, other than one bag's worth.

He knew it was small compared to what Vera had lost or what had been torn from Salome, but home had always mattered to Torin. Where he chose to rest was always personal—a part of his identity—and Lani had set that on fire. He was going to have words with her about that later, assuming they all survived the day.

As soon as they were all through the waterfall, Torin carefully set Vera down.

He would gladly have held her forever now that they had found each other again, but truth be told his arms were shaking. Three days of working without sleep, drawing every ounce of power from both himself and the Emotive—

Wait . . . .

One arm reaching to brace Vera, Torin swiveled towards the woman who had burned his house down. "Emotives don't control fire! How the fuck did you do that?"

Lani backed three steps away from him as fast as she could. "Ah . . . Just got lucky. Your house was flammable as fuck."

"Bullshit," Torin said, grinding his teeth. He hated lies and liars, and Lani stunk of the practice. If she hadn't just spent the last three days helping him save Adavera, and been the one who brought her back to him, Torin might well have knocked her on her ass for what she had done earlier. Daring to lie about it when they were all running for their lives was just icing on the proverbial cake. He still had to fight the impulse to shake her, but something about how Vera was eyeing him made Torin think she would launch herself between them if he tried.

That galled.

So instead, he turned away from Lani, facing his Bonded instead. "Adavera, tell me the truth if she won't."

". . . She's Dual Marked, and hiding it for good reason."

"Gee, thanks for just spilling my secrets," Lani grumbled, in the moment of shocked silence that had followed Vera's pronouncement.

It seemed to have caught Sal's attention too, because her head snapped up from staring at her arm, where symbols were flashing on one of the metal plates.

"Fucking *what?* Gods save me from idiots . . ." She glared, taking a deep breath while turning her head towards Torin. "Kuma's still more than an hour out, since he has to activate a few things on the ship to make sure we get the hell away once we Port in. I've got a short range Port Pad . . . but you're gonna have to hold tight to your wounded woman there. As for *you.*" That single human hand lifted, pointing at Lani. "We're going to talk once we get out of here. No lies, no trying to hide shit. You have fucking *ruined* my life, and the least you owe is a decent explanation before I decide to leave your ass in the middle of the sea. Dual Marked Rogue Mark. Could you *be* more trouble if you tried?"

Even though Torin harbored no significant soft feelings for the Emotive, he still winced in sympathy when Salome's attention focused on her. Though maybe if the pirate's focus stayed on Lani she might forget . . .

Ah, there, a glare for him as well that told him clear as day that the Dual Marked girl wasn't the only one who was going to have to fess up or get dumped in the ocean. That thought made the arm around Vera tighten protectively. "One hour? Alright. Maybe we should try to rest? Take turns keeping watch?"

"No need." Lani stepped forward. "I know how to hide. I'll go out there and let Vera know if anyone is coming your way and be back at the hour mark."

"No you're not." Adavera's eyes narrowed, body stiffening up as if she meant to lunge. "You'll take off. Like you *always* do. I saw your memories, so don't try to deny it."

"I haven't fucking taken off yet, have I? You forced a fucking Blood Bond on me and I'm still here. I dragged your ass to a Mender and used my own power to help save you—"

Torin let go of Vera as if her skin had burned him. "You *forced a Blood Bond?* What the hell, Vee?"

Adavera went still when Torin had flinched away, staring straight at Iolani. "You tried to *rot my leg off*. Don't pretend you were innocent in any of it. I could have killed you instead."

Salome was turning her head from one person to the next. Without warning, she slapped her wooden hand against the nearby stone wall to try to get their attention. "Shut. The Fuck. Up. Let me get this straight. She, the twig, was the one to rot your leg?"

Both Vera and Lani nodded.

"And she fed the fire to Torin's house?" Salome continued. Vera was the only one to nod this time. "So what you're telling me is that she's a Fertilizer? That we have a Dual Marked fucking *Fertilizer* in our midst? Because that makes this even more of a messed up situation."

"I'm not—" Lani began, but Sal held out her prosthetic hand, palm facing them.

"Just . . . shut the fuck up. All of you. Or talk in your heads, or whatever it is you Bonded do. Just . . . stop, before I choose to leave all of you here and let you fucking burn for all of it."

The roar of the waterfall filled the air as she finished speaking. Torin didn't know what to think. His head was pounding, and as he looked between the three women, he honestly didn't even know who he wanted to shake more. Lani, who was putting them all at risk by simply existing near them and who had apparently done all the damage they had spent three days fixing? Vera, who after years of bitching about the horrible practice of forcing a Bond had done it? Or Sal, who . . . actually, no. He didn't want to shake Sal. Though she had punched him, so maybe he did want to shake her just a little. Only a tiny bit. Just a smidge.

Without another word, either out loud or in their heads, Lani turned her back to them and walked to the very back of the shallow cave, climbing up the slick rock into a small crevice and curling her knees up to her chest. With a sigh, Torin offered Vera a hand to sit on a rock, pressing his lips into her hair before stepping away.

Then he turned to Sal.

"I'll keep watch. You should catch your breath while you can. It's been a rough few days for all of us."

"You just spent three days keeping that one out of the Depths. I think of all of us, I'm the most alert. So you can keep your pretty self tucked in here to rest, and I'll keep watch. Probably safer that way anyways. Your girlfriend's already tried to kill me once."

Torin would have protested, but it was cut off by a jaw-popping yawn. Instead, he just nodded, his head bowing. As Sal headed towards the waterfall again, he turned to look at Vera. She was rubbing her leg, a pained grimace on her face.

As soon as we're out of danger, I'll get you a cane. Give me a month or two and you'll be able to walk without one for the most part, but I can't do any more right now. I'm sorry.

Don't worry about it. We have bigger problems Vera's eyes narrowed, then closed, as she took a few deep breaths. *It's . . . not that bad. Just aggravating. I've dealt with worse, now that it isn't rotting off.*

You never should have had to. I should have tried harder to get you out of that place, Vee. I should have . . . done something. I know you told me not to, but . . .

You would have died, and then so would I. Don't worry about it. At least you're not Bound to Miss Murdery Eyes up there. Trust me, it's not a picnic. Adavera seemed to pause, then carefully pushed herself to her feet and started limping over towards him. So stubborn. Just like he remembered her. *Just get some rest. If something gets past that pirate out there . . . I'll take care of it.*

You will not. It took everything you had to grow the flesh of your leg back. If you push yourself now, you'll run dry. Sal will give us warning if someone is approaching; until then, we both rest. I have a feeling we're going to need it. He closed the distance between them and took her in his arms without hurry, or fear, or anger for the first time since she had arrived. She smelled horrible and doubtlessly he did too, but it didn't matter because after six long years, his Adavera was in his arms. If they all died in an hour, so be it. He would get to die with the woman he loved more than life itself pressed against him.

After a long, tight hug, he pulled back just enough to help her towards a sandy bit of ground. It took a bit of maneuvering to lower her without pressure on her leg, but when she was settled he sat beside her and pulled her head on to his lap. *Try to rest, Adavera. I'll watch over you, always.*

CODEX: Yeah, I'm not ready for another deep-dive into Corporate bullshit yet. Let's go back to the writings of the Holders. *Query: What are Fertility Marks?*

FROM THE JOURNALS OF LAKEA, HOLDER OF FORTUNE

When we first started trying to 'fix' the giant clusterfuck that was Fortune, we may have overreacted. We thought that putting a reef around our populated archipelagos would help. Well, it did. Instead of an eighty percent fatality rate from storms, it dropped to lower than ten. Great! Then we discovered that the lack of salt was even worse than we had originally thought. The Spires alone didn't fix it, and so we turned the Marks into helpers.

We didn't originally design the Marks, but after studying them for some time, I realized I could hack their magical code. Every time they used their magic, it would draw salt to them from the closest Spire, and deposit it in their location. That was not enough, though. We needed something that could do that on a large scale, so my brother and I figured we could program one more Mark. There were already twelve Marks, why not a thirteenth? Trust me, that was the worst idea my brother has ever had.

Each Mark is tied to a lunar cycle. These new Marks—called Fertility Marks—were instead combined with the Prismatic Storms that pop up every time Ira or I interfere with the World. If I created a new species of butterflies, halfway across the planet a Storm would pick up with wind and lightning of swirling colors, and any Marked baby being born would develop this special second (or in rare cases third) Mark.

Since these Storms are linked to us, we thought them a logical thing to tie these new Marks to. If we feel like there are too many, we simply lay off interfering for a generation or two, and the number of Fertility Marks diminishes.

This new Mark would have a fragment of our Godly power. It would be able to sense the makeup of the land and sea around it and adjust it to its optimum balance. Sounds great on paper. The reality was a little more fucked up.

Each of the other twelve Marks are tied to the lunar cycle of their birth, growing more powerful during it and the least powerful at the far opposite one. We did not realize that by tying Fertility Mark's power to the Prismatic Storms, each of these Storms would make their power flare. They lose all humanity, and the code we embedded in their Marks becomes their only driving imperative. They will fix the world, and don't care what—or who—stands in their way. The sad thing is that even when the skies are quiet and their minds their own, there is something intrinsically odd about Fertilizers. Perhaps I put just a little too much of myself into them.

My brother thinks they are monstrous. I have a certain respect and horrified fondness for this particular mistake of creation.

21 Fertility Mark
Lani - Day 8

Lani sat curled up in the back of the cave, staring at but not actually seeing the waterfall. *Fertilizer.* That was what the pirate and Torin had called her. She had always hated that term. Lani could still remember the first time someone had spotted her Mark.

"*Corp's coming. You'll be the one to end up as fertilizer this time, not the people you kill.*"

She had run from that island. Run from the next, and the next, and the one after that. Run until she had no one left to run from, but also no one left to care if she lived or died. Because of *what* she was, Vera had Bonded her. Bonds were supposed to be sacred trusts between people who loved each other and wished to share everything—even their very souls. Lani saw that dedication in the space between Torin and Vera's bodies, as though the Bond was a tangible thing, pulling them together like magnets. She saw it in the way they looked at each other as though nothing else existed. Worse, she *felt* their dedication to each other through the Bond connecting her to Vera.

It just wasn't directed at Lani. And why should it be? She had almost killed Vera in the most horrible, uncontrolled, painful way possible. It wasn't the first time, either. Her parents had been her first victims. The smell of rotted flesh plagued her every nightmare, and even centuries later, Iolani could not scrub the feeling of picking up her mother's head to lay it in her lap, and seeing it disintegrate to shards of bone and decomposed flesh.

Fertilizer.

A tear trailed down Lani's cheek and she brushed it away with a furious swipe. What had she really expected? That a Bond to one of these people would stop them from hating her? No one liked her kind unless Lani forced them to with her Emotive Mark, but that was no better than abuse.

To calm herself, Lani pressed her palms to the stone and closed her eyes. The Fertility Mark on her chest started to glow. Not the bright, eye-watering shine it had in the Storms, but rather the gentle shimmer of a Mark working. Through her fingertips and bare feet, the composition of the island showed itself to Lani. Limestone, granite, plenty of nitrogen for the plants. Not enough salt. Never enough salt. But what was there was spread out wrong. Her senses expanded further. With around a dozen Trials under her belt, Lani's Mark could sense and affect quite a large area. There must have been a cemetery on this side of the island, because there were pockets of salt at regular intervals about a quarter mile away. Lani pulled the salt towards her, spreading it out in the soil for the plants and animals to better use. She adjusted other levels too, correcting the pH and nitrogen in the ground for the trees that were struggling, and pulling toxins and chemical runoff from human habitations deep into the ground, where it would not hurt the wildlife.

As she worked, her shoulders relaxed.

Fertilizer.

This was the real meaning behind the word. It was what had kept Lani from jumping off her boat with an anchor tied to her feet each time someone called her that word with hatred and fear in their voice. So she lost herself to the process. Speeding up the decomposition of leaves on the forest floor, drawing carbon up from old fires to form dark, rich topsoil, spreading out a little more salt. Just a bit. There it was. Now all she had to do—

Lani jerked as she realized the source was a living person. Multiple ones. She had been about to pull from them to balance out the environment, which apart from lacking salt also needed more iron.

With an angry grunt, Lani pulled a pair of sandals from her rucksack and yanked them on, then crossed her arms so that none of her bare skin touched the ground.

They were right. I'm not safe. I almost killed again and hardly stopped in time.

Fertilizer.

Biting her lips so as not to cry, Lani closed her eyes and tried to rest.

Not ten minutes later, after falling into a fitful doze, she woke up with her forehead touching the rock. Her Fertility Mark was tingling.

"Ah, guys," Lani buried her fingers in the sandy soil, reaching out to confirm what her Mark had picked up on even in sleep. Those sources of salt were getting closer. Fast. "We have company. And considering all those White Sails we saw on our way down here, I'm betting it's *Company.*"

CODEX: Next up, Query: What are Berserkers?

EXCERPT FROM GALENA'S OBSERVATIONS ON BERSERKERS

These Marks make me uneasy. There are plenty of Marks capable of great damage and causing terror. Berserkers cause a more primal fear, in my opinion. There is something unseemly, unnatural, about looking into a human being's eyes and seeing something not at all human staring back at me.

In the interest of making sense of this strange awareness, I decided to study the phenomenon of a Berserk Conflicter. What I discovered has both titillated and horrified me.

Most believe Berserkers lose control. I have discovered that they do not. What they lose is their inhibition, their civility. Things for a Berserker become very simple. They see everything as a game of survival. Berserkers see everyone as prey or predator. They grade threats without thought or awareness. And Berserkers? Berserkers are the top of the food chain.

They are not troubled by emotion or by rules during one of their fugues. They simply *act*, decisively, to not only survive but *win* the encounter they find themselves in. The only people who can move somewhat safely with a Berserker in this state are those Bound to them.

And even that is not necessarily a guarantee. This being said, I find that as a Mark they are remarkably stable. Merely . . . inhuman. It is their fatal flaw. And perhaps that flaw is how we will tame them and control them. Not by forcing them to be human, but by embracing their inhumanity.

Skirmish
Vera – Day 8
22

I'm betting it's Company.

Vera snapped out of her exhausted doze between one heartbeat and the next. Her Mark lit up, bringing her to her feet before Torin had even turned to look at Lani. Vera wobbled, bracing on his shoulder as her pain was replaced by coursing adrenaline and fury. As soon as she was stable, she took several steps towards the mouth of the cave.

If the Corporation was already here . . . they had gotten Aheo to Track her. He had her blood, a thread that led straight from him to Vera, no matter how far she fled. Aheo wouldn't leave her to just anyone's hands. He would come himself, to make sure she couldn't fight, and to witness her capture.

"They're going to have a Shielder," she said, glancing at Lani and Torin. "The two of you should run in another direction. It's me they're Tracking. We're lucky we avoided them this long."

"Like I'm going anywhere," Torin snapped, walking up to Vera's side. "If it's the Corporation, let me talk to them. I might still have some strings to pull."

"I am going to pretend I didn't hear that," the pirate snapped, emerging from the waterfall. "Corpses are here. Four of them, spattered in blood. Looks like someone helped us already. I need to set up these Port Pads if we have a rat's ass chance of getting away. Cover me while I do, and cross your fingers and toes that my brother gets the ship in close enough. He's not due for another thirty minutes, but worst case scenario he'll fish us out of the water."

Lani was the only one who seemed to be considering Vera's order to run, but by the time she grabbed her bag and took a few steps to the entrance of the grotto, their time was up.

Vera sensed the Shield descend upon them, like a suffocating veil pressed against her skin, preventing her from breathing. It was familiar and real in a way that Torin wasn't yet, and made her shudder.

Aheo had come. He was going to take her back to the nightmare she had escaped.

The glow in her Mark died down under the weight of the Shield, which cut all magic within the grotto. With her Conflicter power gone, pain surged back in, and Vera's leg gave out underneath her. Torin caught her, but wobbled as the strain of the last few days made themselves clear.

Lani was the one most affected by the Shield, though. As her magic was quelled, Vera's newest Bonded collapsed, knees hitting the ground with a nasty crunch. Her hands rose to cover her head, a scream tearing from her throat. Through the Bond, Vera could feel Lani's utter agony and confusion, as though the girl had never felt this before in her life. For all Vera knew, that might be the case. A sudden sickening, soul-rending thought struck Vera, so horrible it overwhelmed the pain of her leg.

"Lani!" She shouted. "Lani, *get behind me.*"

It was bad enough that Aheo had come to take Vera back to the cold surgical tables and the torment that turned her into the monster they said she was; she knew he would come for her, and Vera had every intention of dying fighting if she had to. But if Aheo got his hands on Lani, whose rare Fertility Mark would make her a jewel in his collection . . .

Vera lurched forward, determined to get to Lani, but froze as four figures burst through the waterfall. Two she did not recognize, but at the front the looming, musclebound form of Security raced forward, and at the rear . . . the monster from her every nightmare. Aheo was an elegant man, with a well-groomed beard, neat hair, and a bullet-proof vest strapped neatly over a lab coat. He hadn't even bothered to change.

In a way, that was flattering. In another way, it was terrifying. She did *not* want his personal attention again.

"Spire inmate 28895, you've been ordered back to the *Purity*. Come along," Aheo said.

Vera's teeth bared, somewhere between a snarl and a smile. Behind her, the pirate was on her knees doing something. Had she said Port Pads? "Go fuck yourself, you useless son of—"

Her leg twinged again, a yelp of pain cutting off the insult. Her hand dug into Torin's shoulder, desperate to stay off the ground. Without her Mark, she had to rely on training. And she was wounded. Badly. Between Aheo and Security alone, they were all fucked. But . . . if she could kill Aheo, then maybe Salome had a shot at getting the rest of them out. That, or Lani might turn them all into mulch in reaction to the death of a Bonded. Either way, options.

"Tsk. I've missed the attitude, 28895. Torin of Keala, your early retirement exemption has been retracted. You are ordered to present the Rogues for capture. You will be compensated for the damage they've caused your retirement home, of course." Aheo smiled serenely, and adjusted the sleeves on his lab coat. "As long as you both behave, no harm will come to you or your Bonded. Control her."

Vera kept her eyes on Security. Aheo was skilled enough to be a danger to the others, but she was fairly sure she could handle him if he got too close. It was Security that was going to be the real bitch in this fight. He was a Conflicter too, though not a Berserker. That should have given Vera the edge, but he was many Trials further along than she would ever be, a fucking giant, and Dual-Marked to boot. Not that any of their Marks mattered at present, but his large stature sure would. The other two soldiers were there because Aheo's Mark wouldn't cause them issues. UnMarked. Well trained, but unMarked. Those ones, Torin or the pirate might have a chance of taking out.

Security's eyes were scanning the grotto, noting everything: Lani kneeling between the two groups, frozen in terror, Salome behind the rocks to Vera and Torin's right, and the waterfall to their left. When his gaze moved to Torin, Vera noted the way his shoulders tightened, lips pursed in a frown.

She knew that look. Torin was a no-kill target. *Why?* On the other hand, did it matter? She slid her hand down Torin's side slowly, as if petting him for comfort. It was a common enough Bonded behavior.

Torin squeezed around Vera—not hard since she relied on his shoulder for balance—and didn't stop until he stood in front of her. Interestingly, Security's gun twitched down before he raised it again. Definitely a no-kill order, but again, why? Taking out Torin to drop Vera was the obvious play.

"Ah, this is all a huge misunderstanding. If we could all just . . . put the guns down, yes? I'm willing to negotiate, but not at gunpoint," Torin said.

Vera wasn't sure if Torin was stalling for time or serious. Either way, it wasn't going to work. He didn't understand the situation, because Vera had never let him in while trapped in the Mines under the power of these two men. Security wouldn't let her walk free, not when she knew of the atrocities he and the other guards committed, and Aheo . . . Aheo wanted her because he wasn't done playing with her yet. They were too powerful to stop with words, but Vera didn't need to stop them, only stall them long enough for Salome to finish whatever she was doing behind the rock.

Conflicters were famous for turning anything into a weapon. Vera's Mark might be suppressed, but her nature was the same as ever. Her hand curled around Torin's pocketknife. She pulled it free, spinning around behind him with her good leg taking the weight, and flipped the knife open to press against her Bonded's throat.

"Back off, or I'll do it. You won't take me back." It surprised Vera to realize that she wasn't bluffing. She would rather die than hurt Torin, but he was on the Company shit list for sure, now. If they took them, it would be the Mines for everyone, and she *would* kill him to stop that. Doing so would probably kill Vera, and likely Lani as a result. It was a way out.

Aheo jerked and took a half step forward, holding up his hands. Good. Vera felt a wave of perverse pride for provoking an actual reaction in him. "28895 . . . you and I both know Bonded don't kill each other."

"You and I both know that Zerkers can and do." She pressed the knife a little more firmly to Torin's throat, locking her eyes on Security. "Back off filthsack, or I'm going to ruin everyone's shoes."

"Vera!" Torin shouted, clearly alarmed.

"I'm *not* going back." She hissed, meaning every single word.

Her gaze was so focused on Aheo that she was a moment too late to notice Security lunge towards Lani. Shit.

"Weirdling, DUCK!"

Lani, still on her knees, hands around her head, jerked into an awkward roll. Not fast enough. Security grabbed her by the hair, tugging Lani to her feet. The Emotive's bag, slung over her shoulder, swung against her side, and Vera caught sight of the handle of the same damn knife Vera had used for the Bond. Would Lani think to use it?

Security placed his pistol against her temple, and smiled when Vera instinctively jerked. "Our Pregocs told us to expect the two of you to have Bonded. Looks like they were right. You, check her for Marks," he snapped at the closest underling. "And you, cover me. Keep it pointed at the Zerker's head."

The goon Security indicated moved forward and patted Lani down as she shook with terror. Vera ground her teeth, glaring as the smug bastard kept his gun pressed against Lani's head, finger on the trigger. What she wouldn't give to be able to access her Mark right then. She'd rip him apart before she died. It wouldn't be fast enough to save Lani, but she wanted the taste of his fucking blood.

"Emotive." The man dropped Lani's pant leg and then began

tugging her shirt up out of the way before letting out an alarmed cry, stepping back and bringing his gun up to aim at Lani, arm shaking. "Fertilizer. Huge Mark. Holy shit."

"Pull that trigger and die," Vera hissed, as Security's finger wobbled precariously. Out of the corner of her eye, Vera could see Salome still moving. What was taking so long?

"Aheo . . ." Security began, a look of disgust on his face as he glanced down at Lani. "Do I kill it?"

"You nervous, big guy? Afraid your boss is going to lose his concentration and let a tiny weirdling turn his pet to mulch?" Vera taunted, watching the brute of a man stiffen. So even *Security* was scared of Fertilizers. It made Vera perversely delighted to have one as her Bonded, even considering the circumstances of their Bond. The woman who was supposed to be covering Vera was pointing her gun at Lani now too. The paranoia was justified. Stupid, but even Vera couldn't fault it. Kill Rogue Fertilizers on sight was Corporate Training 101. "Or you just worried that if you try to put your spoon in the jar she's going to rot it off? Mmm. What a thought."

That's right. Focus on me, you big idiot . . .

She carefully turned Torin's body again, narrowing her eyes as she saw Security tighten his grip on Lani's hair. Her own fingers tightened around the hilt of her knife.

"Security, she is stalling for time." Aheo cautioned. "We were only to take the Mender if possible. Clearly, it will not be possible. Take them all out before she distracts you long enough for that woman at the back to finish what she is doing."

"Too late," Salome said, popping up from behind the rock she had crouched behind this whole time, a cocky grin on her face as she trained the world's smallest gun straight at Security and fired.

CODEX: You know what, SALT, please just run Queries on all the Marks for me. Can you do that?

SALT: Affirmative. Running now.

CODEX: Have to remember that I can do more than one thing at a time. I should really practice, but maybe after this patch is installed I can stretch my legs. Well, I guess stretch my code. Right, let's see; while you compile all of that, I have a question. In the Salt Pirate Network, do I have access to the journals of Sahima Parata?

SALT: Affirmative.

CODEX: Query: What has Sahima Parata written on Moe?

FROM THE JOURNALS OF SAHIMA PARATA

What can I say about the lunatic Moe? Well, to start, he isn't actually a lunatic, though he plays one very well. Maybe at one time he was off his rocker, but he isn't anymore. I think he is aware people do not take him seriously with his 'crazy' routine, and he takes advantage of it.

I have been a pirate since before I could toddle. I have seen outlaws, pirates, murderers, Corporate goons and all sorts of scum gamble and kill and plot. Moe beats them all. I don't think I've ever met anyone else as capable of deceit, manipulation, or cruelty. Maybe it's because he's old as fuck? I hope not. So why do I keep working with him? Because as much as he bothers me, he's been helpful. I don't know when that is going to change, but I am sure it will. I'll take his usefulness as long as I can get it, and I'll plan for the inevitable. Maybe his attitude and general lack of ethics are because he's old as fuck. I hope not. While I am no longer challenging trials, and neither is Kekai, our Kuma might live a long time yet. If it is time, instead of inborn character, that has made Moe what and who he is . . . well, that scares me. If it a mix of the two, it scares me even more.

My grandson is a bright lad. His talent for Infusion shows great promise. Kumanu is a kind, loving boy but from an early age he has worried me. All little boys have their oddly inconsiderate, even cruel, moments. But I have never seen a child drain someone to death the way that Kuma did when he was only nine.

We took a prisoner at a battle. That prisoner was responsible for killing Kumanu's friend, a young boy who was on his first sailing trip. Kuma did not take that death well. I should have watched him more closely, but I truly did not expect Kuma to blow out the lock on the brig. I did not expect to find him with his hands on the prisoner's face as he took everything that man had, only to feed it into the ship's battery lines.

Kuma has mellowed out since then, but still, I worry. What's the line us Marks have to cross before we become as cold and manipulative as Moe? When does the weight of the years crush our very humanity? I am so glad that Salome was born without this curse, and just hope that if Kuma outlives her, he doesn't lose himself.

CODEX: Huh . . . I don't know if I wanted to read that.

23 Port Pads
Salome - Day 2

The shot reverberated around the stone grotto as the gun the big guy was holding clattered to the ground and he howled, clutching at his bleeding hand.

Salome's upended bag lay at her feet next to a set of humming, interlocking tiles two feet square. She held the 'useless piece of shit gun' that her brother tended to stuff in her pocket 'just in case' pointed straight at the four Corpses. Her gun wasn't Infused, it had no fun gadgets; frankly, it was boring. This was also exactly the situation it was meant for.

Keeping her arm straight, she pivoted slightly, smirking in satisfaction as a second shot rang out and caught the goon whose weapon was also pointed at Lani, right between the eyes.

Those were the only two easy shots she got. While the goon she had hit fell to the floor, Security tried to tug Lani behind him. It was a blur of motion, but Sal thought she caught Lani swinging a knife. Blood bloomed across the massive brute's shoulder and he dropped the girl.

"Crew, get your asses back here!" Sal covered Lani with a few more shots, none of which hit, but they kept the Corpses dancing as the girl scrambled toward them. Sal pulled out a spare clip with her prosthetic, changing it out with a practiced air. The Shielder looked surprised that his magic wasn't blocking the bullets, and she let out a smirk. Ok, maybe Kuma was right. Having one 'plain, boring gun' was probably a good idea.

Vera lurched forward—whether to attack the Corporation or help Lani Sal didn't know—but Torin grabbed her around the middle, dragging her back in Sal's direction. She fired two more shots, this time at the lab coat guy, and grinned as he ducked behind some rocks. "Not so smug now are ya, you cold-hearted prick?"

Lani came scrambling over the rocks first, smearing blood from Security over them and clutching her pack as though it held the secrets to the Depths themselves. Frankly, Sal was impressed that the girl wasn't a blubbering mess yet. She didn't seem the sort to have experience with gun fights.

Salome fired two shots at the other unnamed guard. One hit the bulletproof vest, and the other grazed his cheek. The soldier returned fire. Sal ducked down as bullets struck at the rock near her head. "Fuck! That was close. Get on the pad, *now!*"

"No magic," Lani panted. It was almost a moan, the Fertilizer tugging at her hair with eyes wide in terror.

"One in the back's the Shielder," Vera snapped, stumbling around the rocks holding on to Torin.

"La dee dah! Get. On. The. Pad!" Salome popped back up, taking a moment to sight down the length of the cave before firing off a shot towards the ceiling. The crack as a piece of heavy rock came loose earned a grin. The deluge of rock shards fell to the ground right on top of lab coat guy.

She could hear the muffled curses from where she knelt. She could also see Security hesitate in moving towards her. That moment of hesitation let her know the game. Lab coat guy outranked Security, at least in this. That meant Security was going to focus on keeping lab coat guy alive.

She fired off two of her last three shots, knocking a few more bits of hanging stone loose to shower down in the area she knew lab coat guy to be hiding in. The muffled yelp came from behind the rocks.

The ionized static in the air faded and had Salome glancing at the others. "Now?"

Torin shook his head. He swept Vera up into his arms so they could both fit onto the Port Pad. Sal sure hoped Kuma was close enough. She really did not look forward to landing in the sea, if he wasn't.

Lani circled around the Port Pad, stepping on, grabbing Torin's shoulder for balance. Sal put one foot on it, and waited.

Security and the Shielder had both taken cover. Sal remained upright, gun held out. Her breath came slow, even, patient. *I can do this all day.*

It took three minutes before one of them was brave enough to peek around the boulder and make a dash forward for more cover. That someone was the Shielder. *Perfect.* She fired off her last shot, muttering a curse when his head didn't explode. But she'd take the wound she'd given him. He tumbled, the force of the bullet hitting his shoulder knocking him off balance and causing him to trip over one of the stones on the floor.

"Shield's down," Torin shouted.

Grinning, Salome dropped her gun and slapped her hand onto her arm, pressing two buttons simultaneously. She didn't even get to wriggle her fingers goodbye at Security before the eerie sensation of the Port took hold.

She had Ported enough times in her life to not find it disorienting, but as the cloying darkness enveloped her for a split second, devoid of light and air but filling her mouth and nose with the crisp tang of salt, Salome still felt the same primordial panic she had the very first time.

She landed with a huff on the deck of her boat, feet squarely planted on the matching pads Kuma had built. Thank the fucking Depths.

Sal put her hands to her hips and glared up towards the helm. "Kuma! Get us the hell away from here. And make it snappy. If I see White Sails on my rear after ten minutes, I'm throwing you into the brig!"

"You love me too much," her brother shouted back from the helm, before spinning the wheel as far as it would go without breaking her ship. Salome winced as she heard the wood and metal groan in response. Over it, Kuma shouted, "did I, or did I not, get in close enough?"

"Escape now, brag later, Kumanu." Her eyes turned to her 'guests', narrowing as she wrestled her more unfriendly urges down. "You three get below decks. The turns can be nasty, and I'm not sending people into the water if you go overboard."

There. That was polite, and more importantly would get them out of her hair for long enough to ditch the Corporation and get control of her emotions. Without so much as a backward glance at them, Salome bounded up the curving stairs to where her brother stood at the wheel. With a grunt, she elbowed him out of the way. He looked ready to complain until he spotted the red at the edge of her wooden limb.

"Fucking hell, Sal. Did you rip it off *again?*"

"Not exactly. Now drop it. Get below and keep them out of trouble. And if they don't listen . . . well, I'm tempted to throw them all over. They've caused me a world of trouble over the last few days."

"Even Pretty Boy?"

"*Especially* Pretty Boy."

PART THREE
Aboard the Legacy
-Lani, Moe, Salome, Vera, Torin, Kuma-

CODEX: Alright, I've been putting off the deep-dive into the madness that is Moe for too long. Time to find out what he was doing behind the scenes. I have a bad feeling I'm going to find things I don't like, considering he never bothered to tell us he knew Gods and that they might interfere with our plans. Where to start, though? I guess with the obvious. *Query: What has Moe written about Kumanu Parata and Iolani Saba, and how far back do they go?*

SALT: Records mentioning one or both go back 233 years.

CODEX: So it *was* a setup.

SALT: In what order would you like to read the documents?

CODEX: Please give me the first mention of each of them. Start with Kumanu. Thank you.

FROM MOE'S NOTES ON KUMANU PARATA, YEAR 1398:

I've been tracking the Parata family for a while now, since they seem to pop out a Marked kid or two every generation. Today, a journal entry showed up in one of my Keylogger programs written by Sahima Parata. It spoke of her grandson Kumanu, who apparently has a real flair for both ingenuity and violence.

I looked in on the child today and he is perfect. A Juicer who already has a gift for pushing his Mark to the limit. He'll be perfect for grooming into the Infuser I need for my Spire project, I just have to make sure he keeps passing Trials for a century or two, and that he's so desperate for love and affection that he'll grab on to Lani the moment I dangle her in front of him.

Flirting as a Way of Life
Kuma - Day 8   24

The ship lurched as it made a tight turn, something that a ship this size should *not* have been able to manage without capsizing. There was a reason why Sahima had been a terror on the seas, and it was the same reason that Salome was earning the same reputation.

It was because they *cheated,* or as Kumanu called it—they were clever, but mostly, they had him. Kuma was proud of this particular engine. As he entered the cargo bay and the ship leaned even further into the turn, he stepped forward to catch the nearest of the two women who had appeared with Salome. She stumbled, clutching at him.

"Holy fucking shit, that pirate is insane. She's gonna break the ship."

Was that just a hint of a Mark poking up between her breasts where the top two buttons of her shirt were undone? It looked like vines, but there was no way Kuma had gotten lucky enough to have a very pretty Fertility Marked girl literally fall into his arms. She was a little thing, short and light, though with curves that drew his eye. She wore a pair of dirty Corporate uniform trousers over a long-sleeved shirt that was much too large for her. Above it—wow—gorgeous. High cheekbones, smooth sunkissed brown skin, kissable full lips, long curly hair, and dark brown eyes with just a hint of hazel.

Sal twisted the ship in another tight turn, the barrels and crates of supplies groaning against the ropes that held them fast to the walls. The girl's curls bounced as she caught herself on Kuma's forearm.

"Easy there, Sweets. It feels like hell, sure, but Sal's got a good hand for the helm. Ha . . . Hand. Get it? Seriously. Ship's fine. Sal can handle a few White Sails."

He grinned, tightening his grip on both the Marked woman and the beam he was holding. As anticipated, Sal leaned deeper into the turn, the whole ship tilting sideways, sending the cursing bundle of hair in his arms wobbling on unsteady feet. Across from Kumanu in the cramped cargo hold, another pair was trying to stay upright.

"Heya Torin. What brings you here this time? And who's the angry one?" The woman with short, scraggly hair holding onto the Mender looked a tad murderous. Considering he could see the edge of a geometric Conflict Mark peeking out from a rip in her trousers, she probably was, in fact, deciding how to kill him.

"This is—" Torin cut off, grunting as Sal jerked the ship out of its turn.

Kuma used the momentum to sling them back against the wall. "Ooof. The Sails must be on the ball today! Normally she's not quite this rough on our old girl." Kuma patted the ship fondly. "Don't worry, though. Captain's gonna lose those Sails lickety-split. Knowing Sal, she'll head for the Reef. No White Sail has ever kept up with us on stormy seas." He laughed, looking down at the woman still clinging to him to keep her balance. "Hey now . . . Look at *you*."

She really was cute as could be, all smooth, lightly freckled skin, dark tangled curls, and wide eyes. Plus that scowl—so much character in that face! "Ya know, Sal said you were trouble. When all this settles down, how 'bout you and I sit down for tea and you tell me all about it, eh?" He caught her weight as the ship slung them about again, laughing. "Name's Kumanu. Kumanu Parata. Yikes . . . my sister's really pushing it. Anyhow, what should I call you, Sweets?"

"None of your fucking business is what you can call me. Get your hands off. I'm fine." Yes, that was definitely a Fertility Mark. Amazing. The young woman disentangled from Kuma, her hands wrapping around the support beam as if her life depended on it and trying to put distance between them.

He grabbed onto the nets on the walls to give her space. "If you insist. But I gotta warn ya . . . new people usually end up breaking their faces on the walls during these turns." He chuckled, tapping his nose before looking towards Torin. "Good thing we got him on board this tiiiime—Oh, that was a good one. Yikes. Corpses must be right on our tail. Anyhow, what's up old grump?"

"Must we do the chatter thing again, Kuma? Sal's steering is rough enough without your babbling," Torin said.

That made Kuma grin. With a little hum, he waited for Sal to turn the *Legacy* again, then used the tilt to slide across the lower deck to a chest lashed to the far wall. Then he waited for another surge of movement, timing it beneath his breath, before quickly opening the chest and tugging out a few ropes in a moment of relative stillness as the ship caught the rise of a wave. He grabbed hold of a support again, then held out a bundle of ropes as though they were precious treasure. "I got some spares if you folks want 'em . . . they're not fancy yet, but ya know . . . last minute notice!"

"What are they? Last time Sal brought me one of your work-in-progress trinkets it nearly blew my face off," Pretty Boy growled, still holding tight to the Conflicter. Miss 'none of your business' on the other hand was looking a little green, her arms hugging the pole and feet stumbling with every turn of the ship. Kuma felt a little queasy too, then jumped as he realized the feeling wasn't coming from his own gut. He flared his Infusion Mark, the chain-like design on his forearm lighting up.

There. Another Mark. Each one had a particular pulse and flavor. Torin's Mending Mark smelled like disinfectant, salt, and home-cooked meals. The Conflicter was all toasted spices and smoke. And the curly haired beauty . . .

Emotive *and* Fertility: the jungle during a rainstorm.

Delicious.

Kumanu tossed one of the ropes he was holding Torin's way. "Grippers. Wrap one end around your waist, slide the other across a beam, and tap twice. Little something I picked up from . . . someone." He winked, then slid back the way he'd come to reach the little Emotive-Fertilizer as Torin helped the Conflicter into a Gripper.

"Hey. Deep breaths. Puke inside and Sal will skin us both. Here." He dug around in a bag, then popped a small squishy *something* between the Emotive's lips. Mint candy. That would calm her stomach. "That should help. Hold still." He whipped one of the ropes around her waist, then around the beam and tapped. Like a drying sponge, the material tightened up pulling her flush with the wall, safe from falling.

Kuma tossed one end of the last Gripper around his waist, then slung the other end up into the rafters before tapping twice. It let him enjoy a good swing as the ship careened in one direction, then the other.

"So, Torin. Was that *smoke* I saw coming off your cave? What'd you do, finally tick Sal off enough for her to toast your shit?"

"Not, Sal. Fire was her fault," Torin said, pointing at the woman beside him, "and don't get too close to that one; she's a Fertilizer, not just an Emotive."

The flash of pain that passed across the girl's face only lasted a moment, but it was raw and unmistakable.

"Well, obviously, but what's wrong with being Dual Marked?"

Kuma twisted about in his improvised swing to fix the girl with a devilish grin. "Oh Sweets, I gotta have your name now. If you've ruffled Pretty Boy, you're something special. And after you toasted Sal's bed? Ha! We're gonna be best buds, you and I."

She would need a friend. More than likely Salome was gonna be an absolute bitch to deal with after this. She'd rage, storm about, and probably break a few things, but she was a good gal at heart. Sal wouldn't actually dump any of her refugees over board—though they'd probably wish she had within the week. As a Fertilizer, Kuma was sure her life was stressful enough without being a target for Salome's wrath.

"No thanks. I don't do *friends*. Never have."

"How do you know it's not worth doing if you've never tried, huh? Who knows, maybe you could have some fun with it. Anyhow, I'm Kumanu. Everyone calls me Kuma, but you can use either; I'm not fussy. That there is Pretty Boy, also known as Sal's boy toy, also known as Mr. Grumps. I have no idea what to call you or Miss Glares-a-Lot over there. Care to introduce us?"

"I'm Lani, that's Vera. But get it through your head that you and I are not buds, and we're not going to *be* buds, or I'll turn you into fish food."

"Sal's threatened me with that a few times." He smirked. "I grow on you. Like mold. At first you think '*oh, who is that annoying but handsome jerk?*' and then eventually '*wow, he must be the brilliant inventor who makes all the pretty toys.*' Then one day you'll wake up realizing I'm pretty ok. It isn't just anyone that could have made your Port Pad, or have gotten the ship in close enough without getting reamed by White Sails . . . Or who would keep you from smashing your pretty face against the wall by getting you a nice Gripper. I mean, I could keep going. I'm pretty awesome. But that wouldn't be fair, because you haven't had a chance to explain how awesome *you* are. So tell me . . . what's it like, doing the whole Fertilizer bit? Last time I got to talk to one, I was only on my second Trial, and I was a bit high. The vase worked out well, but . . . ya know . . . The Fertility Marked was just passin' through and didn't want trouble." He paused for a breath, rubbing at his chin for a moment. "Well.. I suppose you could not want trouble too, but since we're outrunning Sails at the moment, you're kind of stuck with us until you work out a drop off point with the Captain."

Lani glanced over at Vera wearing a look that clearly said, 'what the fuck' on her face. When no help came from that quarter, Lani grimaced and looked back up at Kuma.

"Being a Fertilizer sucks ass for me and for anyone who gets close to me so take my advice and don't. This one didn't," she pointed at Vera, "and nearly got disintegrated. Nothing about me is awesome, everything is horrible, and as soon as we make landfall I'm leaving and you'll never find me again, any of you."

He nodded along, looking somewhat amused. "Ah. Well . . . to your points." He held up a finger, ignoring the way the boat made him rock back and forth. It wasn't so bad when one was swinging. "One . . . you are clearly awesome; you've survived as a Rogue Mark. Two, everything is not horrible. You've got a gorgeous face, and you set a house on fire so you've got spirit, and three . . . we won't make landfall for a while. Standard protocol is three weeks at sea after escaping White Sails because they tend to be bastards. So for almost a month, you get *me*."

He grinned, clapping twice. "Seriously, Sweets . . . pessimism is sensible and all, but have you considered the alternative? As far as the disintegration problem . . . We can work on that. Is it an overload issue? Typically if you release your Mark's energy on a regular basis it's easier to keep one's grip on their Mark, you know? And if you get yourself a Bonded or three it makes it *much* easier. Take it from me. I blew shit up constantly as a kid."

"Bet you didn't blow up your whole family and a third of the population of your island, did you? Don't pretend to understand my life. I didn't have anyone to tell me any of this shit and didn't want it. The only reason I have a Bonded at all was to stop me from murdering her," again, she pointed at the Conflicter, "and I'm never fucking getting close enough to anyone ever again to let a repeat happen. I much prefer being left alone. Just tell me where I'm sleeping and I'll keep to myself."

"Didn't blow up an island, no. Been on a ship most of my life. I *did* kill a bunch of folks when the engines blew . . . Twice." He shrugged, stretching his arms. "Shit happens, Lani. You learn, you move on." He closed his eyes as the ship swung wildly. Though his smile never faltered, a flash of old pain tore through Kuma. "Marks need stabilizing. But sure, if you wanna keep being a walking murderball, I guess that works. Before you go, though, I'd really like to work out a few projects with you. I've been dying to get my hands on a Fertilizer partner for *years*. There's so much shit I've wanted to make. You do that and I'll let you use my room instead of making you bunk with the rest of the crew. No one goes in my room, 'cept Sal, and only when she absolutely has to."

Lani narrowed her eyes at him. "Use your room *and* you stay out of it, and we have a deal."

"Well . . . I'll stay out of it when not working. My workshop is attached to the room, as is the engine . . . kinda need to be in there to . . . ya know . . . Work." He grinned, cracking an eye open at her. "You are seriously more grumpy than Pretty Boy. That's impressive."

"I'm a ray of fucking sunshine if you mind your own business."

He grinned, swinging closer to her before grabbing onto the support beam, holding a hand out. "Deal. I'm rubbish at not being friendly and in your face, but if ever I stray too far down a rabbit hole or annoy you, you have permission to slap me."

Lani took his hand, shook it, then yelped as a nasty turn of the ship sent him nearly tumbling into her, both only held up by the ropes.

Had he planned the tangling? Nope. But he couldn't say it was unpleasant. She was delightful, this little prickly creature. With a bit of patience, and care, he managed to unwind his rope from the ceiling rafter, and then unwind himself from her. Before going to help the others, he snagged her hand and brought it up to brush his lips against her knuckles. "Don't you worry. I got you."

He winked once, and then lashed the end of his rope against a beam closer to Torin and Vera. "Ok, Pretty Boy. I've got some nausea shit for her too, don't worry. Seriously, you guys are gonna have to spill the story. I don't think I've seen Sal this pissed in *years*."

CODEX: Well that's creepy and I don't like it at all. I didn't expect to hit bad stuff this early on; I think I'm going to have to take breaks. Just for fun, *Query: What Corporate communications mentioned Torin of Keala, Adavera of Keala, or the* Sahima's Legacy *on Day 8?*

---- NEWS ALERT: MENDER KIDNAPPED ----

On the island of Sonder, retired Corporate Mender Torin of Keala was kidnapped in the early morning by two Rogue Marks and notorious Salt Pirate Salome Parata.

These suspects are armed and highly dangerous. Pictures provided below.

One of the Rogue Marks is Berserker Conflicter Adavera of Keala. Do not approach. Call the Rogue Mark Hotline and remain at a great distance. The second Rogue Mark is thought to be an Emotive Fertilizer. Do not approach. Utmost caution should be executed.

We repeat, two Rogue Marks and Salt Pirate Salome Parata were seen kidnapping Corporate Mender Torin of Keala in the early morning. If you see them, or have any information to contribute, contact the Rogue Mark Hotline. Suspects are armed and very dangerous. Do not be a hero. Let the Corporation handle this.

CODEX: Oh my goodness. That is hysterical. Alright, I feel better already.

25 Tracker Chips
Salome - Day 8

Salome had hoped that Adavera would get at least a little banged up during their escape. It was petty, but Salome had never pretended to be nice. But *no*. Her fucking brother had to go and be a nice guy and prevent them from getting injuries.

Ok, that wasn't fair.

Sal knew she'd hate herself if they had gotten seriously hurt. But *damnit* . . . she wanted them to at least *sting* a little for all the trouble Torin, Lani, and most of all this Vera was causing for her and the *Legacy*.

Then, to make matters worse, when their ship got far enough away from Sonder and the pursuing Corporate fleet that she could take a few minutes to go over everything, Sal had told Torin that he and his girlfriend could take her cabin. It was more private, and they'd need the time. It had been so thoughtful, so selfless, that she'd wanted to vomit.

Sal still wanted to vomit, come to think of it. What if they were *doing things* on her bed? Ugh. The sheets would have to be burned when they made landfall again. There was no other option. Her lover having sex with another woman in Sal's own bed was definitely not something she wanted to even picture. Not even a little—and especially not when she knew *exactly* what Torin's body looked like when he . . . yeah, not going there.

Grumbling, Salome set her eyes on the horizon. About five hours out from another storm, judging by that line of clouds. Annoying, but not surprising at this time of year.

Her eyes turned up, studying the dark gray material of her sails. So far, so good. No tears, no signs of damage. Kuma had done a good job getting the *Legacy* back in one piece after their last encounter with the Corp.

Her eyes tracked down to her brother, who was surprisingly still breathing. She'd thought that damned Emotive would have hurt him. Nope. He was happy as a blue lark, skipping around and loudly proclaiming how *fantastic* his shit was going to be when he was done working with the Fertility Marked menace. Lani, for her part, was actually trying to lend a hand. She didn't know the *Legacy*, of course, but seemed at home on a ship. Maybe Salome shouldn't have dismissed her offer of help back on Sonder. An Emotive on the crew might not be the worst thing ever, and giving her brother a Fertilizer to use in his Infusions was bound to produce some interesting results. If only the blasted girl weren't Bonded to fucking Vera.

"SAILS!" someone from above shouted. Sal cursed, her head swiveling back in the direction of Sonder, now hidden behind a few other small islands. She had lost the Corporation. Definitely, entirely, all the way lost. There was no way they had followed through that last dance around the nearest archipelago unless . . .

"You, take the helm and speed towards the Reef." Salome pointed to the nearest of her sailors, then swiveled around to find Kuma. "And someone bring me those two blasted Corpses."

If only they really were corpses. If they got her crew killed, it would be her own damn fault for bringing them on board without scanning for bugs first.

Sal waited, her hands on her hips until Torin and Vera appeared on deck. Her eyes narrowed, studying them. Neither seemed guilty, which meant they legitimately might not know they had trackers in them. Shit.

Sal rubbed the back of her neck with her wooden hand while she closed her eyes to take deep breaths. This was 'business' talk, so she wasn't going to fucking yell at them. She wasn't going to yell. Maybe if she kept thinking that, she'd actually manage it.

"Kumanu . . . I need them swept for tracking devices. Sails shouldn't have found us. I know I lost them in the last dance we pulled."

She crossed her arms, watching Torin's face. She wanted to know if he knew. She wanted to know if she needed to break his face again, or maybe his bloody neck.

"Shit. I didn't even think . . . Back of our necks, both of us, right under the tattoo." Torin swept his hair back, pointing to the spot right below his hairline. "You won't be able to get them out. They're embedded right up on the brain stem by now. I'm sorry. They were put in so long ago it just never crossed my mind."

Sal's eyes narrowed, and her fingers twitched. But that growl from the Conflicter had her attention swiveling towards the woman. "I am *not* afraid of you, Conflicter. Sure, you could smash my brains in. Who fucking cares? This is *my* ship, and *my* crew, and you two forgetting to tell us about this shit puts *my* people at risk. So can it." She took a deep breath, rubbing at her jaw. "Kuma . . . get that shit deactivated stat."

"Won't make a difference," Vera said, crossing her arms. "They have my blood. They'll keep coming."

"No they don't. We replaced pretty much every drop of blood in your body during the Mending," Torin countered. "And I swept you with a shield. You're clean of any Mark influence, but I didn't think about the trackers."

"Good thing too, or I really would have tossed you overboard. Kuma."

Her brother, who had joined them mid-rant, frowned. "It's gonna be messy. Probably hurt." Kuma's hands went up in surrender as Salome turned her glare on him.

"*So?*" Sal looked back at Torin. "Can you keep your girlfriend from ripping Kuma apart while he deactivates the tech, or not?"

"I can." A small voice piped up and Sal actually jumped, not having noticed the Emotive—no, she had to stop thinking of her that way. The Fertilizer—walk up. Man, she was quiet. "I can keep them both calm."

"Can you not kill people while you do it?" Sal's voice was dry, her fingers sliding down into her pockets for the gun she kept there as she fixed Lani with an assessing stare.

"Sal . . ."

"Shut it, Kumanu. I don't care if I'm being rude or how you get those trackers deactivated. Do it. And if it can't be done . . . Then we'll drop them on an island and wish them the best. I'm not risking the crew to save three dolts."

CODEX: For better or worse, let's dive back into *Query: What has Moe written about Kumanu Parata and Iolani Saba?*

FROM THE JOURNAL OF MOE

She's perfect! Fertility Emotive, scared, lonely, paranoid, desperate to find a reason to excuse her existence. I checked out her early work and it is wonderfully gory. Her Emotive Mark should keep her safe and free from Corporate control, so now it's just a waiting game. I'll watch from afar while she levels up in her Trials, and work on the other pieces of my puzzle. I just have to remember to check in on Miss Iolani from time to time. Don't want her committing suicide like the last Fertilizer I identified. Current plan is to show up about once a year to prod her in the right direction. Too often and she may start to think of herself as special. We can't have that.

To become my weapon, she must be desperate for any positive attention, with self-esteem in the dust, but still healthy enough to bounce back once with the crew. The world will wear her down. It's my job to make sure I build her up just enough, and no more. Of course, I'll then have to find someone as hungry as she is for affection for her to crash into when the time is right. If I groom them both correctly, they will be desperate and perfectly manipulatable to my ends.

CODEX: Yup. Now I feel sick again. SALT, can you disable the synthesized feeling of nausea?
SALT: Affirmative.
CODEX: Good. Disable it.

Shipboard Surgery
Kuma - Day 8
26

Kumanu sighed, rubbing his hands together as he came over to the bench where Adavera sat down. It was at the helm, but as far from Sal as one could get, right up close to the rail that had been blasted apart in their battle a few days before. Beyond the *Legacy*, white sails dotted the ocean. There were several little islands between Kuma's ship and theirs, but Sal was right to be concerned. This was a lot of Corp ships, even for them.

Who *were* these people?

"Sal, keep her as steady as you can," Kumanu requested.

"Mhm," his sister grunted, as Kuma turned his attention to Vera.

The Conflicter didn't speak much, but if looks could kill, Salome would be dead.

"Look . . . about Sal. Sorry. She's in a . . . uh . . . mood." He rubbed at the back of his neck.

"You don't say," Vera growled.

Choosing to ignore that, Kuma motioned to Vera to turn away from him and tilt her head down. He looked over to Lani and Torin, who both hovered nearby in the way Bonded always did when someone in their Bond chain was under threat. Interesting. "So if it's on their brainstem, I'm gonna need you to keep her calm while I get the back of her neck open. Lani, you got that, right? Pretty Boy, you wanna come over and make sure she doesn't bleed too much? I've got steady hands, but we're on a boat, so this might be jerky. I won't cause permanent damage or nothing, but I'd rather she not . . . Ya know . . . hurt herself while I do this. Sweets, you sit there so she can lean into you."

Lani nodded as Torin joined them, her attention latching on to Vera. When Lani sat and leaned in, Kuma was close enough to hear her whisper. "I'm going to calm you down, Adavera. If you feel like punching anyone, remember that out of the present company, Torin and I just spent the last three days saving your ass and the other guy is going to have his hands on your brain. So I'd go for the grouchy captain."

Kuma couldn't help but laugh, just a little, at Lani's words. "Right, I'll be right back. Gotta get supplies. Cool her temper down."

When he returned and the Conflicter seemed relaxed, he pulled out a slim knife, and took the bottle of alcohol Torin handed him, along with a swab. He cleaned his hands and the spot, then nodded to Torin. "Give her something to bite. This will . . . probably not feel very good." He waited until everyone was in place, and then set the knife to the back of her neck.

Sal would probably have considered killing the woman with a quick jab to the brainstem. Fortunately for all of them, Kumanu was *not* his little sister. He narrowed his eyes, gently increasing the pressure. As blood started to bead up, he grunted towards Torin, who reached in to wipe the worst of it away. Kuma started dragging the knife down. It was sort of like butchering an animal, really. You had to get through just enough skin to start peeling it to the side, but not penetrate soft tissue beneath.

"Steady, darlin'," he said quietly, as he felt her twitch. He pulled the knife back to hand to Lani before splashing alcohol onto his hands again, just in case. He had to peel some of the underlying tissue back . . . a few tugs here, and there, and then he caught sight of the hint of metal. "Damn. Those are pretty, sorta . . . Er . . . sorry." He cleared his throat, bringing a finger up to set it against the chip that extended into the Conflicter's brain with tiny tendrils of silver.

His fingers brushed it and Kuma closed his eyes, concentrating. He had to feel out the 'pulse' of the item, find every inch of it, or he could accidentally fry her head instead of simply overloading the chip. There. That was the pulse, the one that made sure the chip could transmit. The Mark on his forearm glowed as he fed it power a drop at a time, gently increasing the push until he felt it 'pop'.

"Shit!" Vera hissed.

"Oh good. Still talking. That's good. Ok, it's done. Uh . . . I'll leave you to clean that up, Mender-man. AH!"

The shout burst from his lips as a White Sail Ported in not a hundred yards away. It was a small one, since Porting large things wasn't easy, but it arrived guns blazing.

"Shit." Sal yelled. "We've been hit. You and you," she pointed to two sailers. "Below and patch up the damage. Kuma, give me some power and engage our Kinetic rear shields."

With none of his usual teasing, Kuma ran to his console, heart thundering. The sensation of feeding energy into the engines to keep them from burning out was a little like having a talented bed partner. Addictive, delightful ... and always left him wanting *more*. Not that he'd ever explained that to anyone. Sal wouldn't get it, for all her cleverness, and the others weren't Infusers.

The exposed Mark on his right arm glowed as he worked. In the sunlight the shimmer wasn't noticeable, but Kuma could feel the tingling heat trailing up the dense chain pattern on his skin. All his major Infused devices fed to this console. At the rear, the large plates he had infused with a Kinetic Mark's ability to manipulate energy flared on, creating a glowing shield around the back half of the ship. It would absorb any impact that hit them, feeding the power into the batteries. Unfortunately, his store of Kinetic power wasn't limitless.

"We did a lot of drifting already this week." Kuma warned Salome. "We'll only get ten minutes or so of shielding. It takes a lot of juice."

"Then hurry up and get those chips out, then go babysit the engine while I lose these fuckers," she replied through gritted teeth.

"On it, Cap't."

When he returned to the trio, Torin was knitting the last bit of Vera's wound closed, the fading pulses of his power leaving the Mender visibly out of breath. Lani, too, looked worse for wear as she eased back on the push of Emotive power Kuma could feel. He doubted the others felt her use it. Only Infusers, Shielders, and Trackers could reliably sense other Marks working without seeing the Marks themselves light up.

He knew the look Vera, Lani, and Torin all shared. The bone-deep exhaustion that made a face haggard was unmistakable. They were working on fumes at best. Wasn't that just a bitch? Kuma sighed, rubbing at his head before glancing at Sal. He couldn't ask for more time to let them rest before taking Torin's out, not with White Sails on their ass.

"Alright, Torin. Your turn. Um ... Lani, you capable of keeping Vera from splitting me open? Thanks." Because if Torin really was Bonded to the Conflicter, there was no telling what she could do to someone who hurt the Mender, even if it was voluntary. Lani nodded and put a hand on Adavera's arm, and Kumanu grabbed Torin's shoulders, frowning. "Ready?"

The moment he got the all-clear and the boat steadied enough, he cleaned off the knife and started cutting through the skin at the back of Torin's neck. His was a little more of a pain in the ass—both because the Mender's skin was tough as nails and because Torin had more connective tissue, which was a damned bitch but also typical of Menders—but Kuma carved his way through it.

He had just stuck his fingers into the cut when the *Legacy* lurched again. "Wow. Easy, Salome. Literally have my fingers on your boy-toy's brain. Almost . . . There . . . Sec . . ." His tongue poked out between his lips, eyes narrowing as he searched for the little lump of metal. There it was. It took another few seconds to short the chip out, but when he did he pulled his hands back and cleared his throat. "Ok. Chips shorted."

Apparently, that was what Salome had been waiting for, because the *Legacy* lurched to the side the moment it was out of Kuma's mouth. He had to brace on Torin, which caused the Mender to howl in pain and Vera to twitch alarmingly, even under Lani's influence. "Sorry. Oops. Want me to stitch you up, or are you taking care of yourself?"

"Never. Touch. Me. Again. Kumanu. Parata," Torin spat, his hand rising to clamp the wound shut. He turned to glare at Kuma. "And never become a surgeon. I could *feel* how sloppy that was."

"I'm not a surgeon, just have the best hands for the job on this ship." Kumanu grinned, tipping his head to the side. "Beggars can't be choosers and all that. Besides, you kind of had it coming, Pretty Boy, what with having sold yourself to the Corp way back when." He grinned before twiddling his fingers in Torin's face and turning to look Lani over. "Waddaya say, Lani sweets? Rum? Cards? More projects below while the big kids up here scream at each other while outrunning Sails and I babysit the engines? We'll be underfoot up here."

Lani's eyes, for once, actually lit up. "Rum. Yes, lots of that. First thing you've ever said that isn't irritating."

Kuma beamed at her and turned to his sister. "Take her away, Captain. I'll be down in the engine room if you need me."

CODEX: Fucking Moe. I knew something was fishy about that setup from the moment it happened. It was just too easy. I wonder if everyone was set up. Well, I guess there's a quick way to find out. *Query: What has Moe written on Adavera and Torin?*

FROM THE JOURNALS OF MOE

Year 1474
And there he is, my perfect little pawn. Torin of Keala—idealistic, calm, intelligent—he is all that I could have wanted out of Galena's little projects. Considering she doesn't know I'm still following her work, it always fills me with delight when she helps me while thinking she's hindering me.
Torin was the last piece, so with that, all I need are the peripheries. He'll need a protector. Conveniently, his best friend is a Conflicter. She'll do nicely. The next step is to make them Bond. It should be easy enough to find a Corporate Matchmaker and force them to recommend the pairing. I think one Pani Wahiawa should serve. She's getting on in Trials so I have to take her out anyhow.

Year 1475
Today I held a gun to Pani's head while watching her send a recommendation to Galena. I shot her as soon as she did, of course. Couldn't leave her to tell on me, but Lizzie is on coverup duty, so I doubt it will come back to haunt me. Probability is less than 1%. I look forward to seeing where this Bond between Adavera and Torin takes them. There is a 4.8% chance that Vera will go off the deep end, but as long as I can keep them from going to the Spire early, all should be well.

CODEX: FUCK! I think we may have all been played.

Reunited at Last
Vera - Day 8

Vera's fingers came up, carefully rubbing at the back of her neck as Lani accepted the invitation for drinks with the fool who had just sliced her and Torin open. Idiot girl. Booze and Fertility Marks probably weren't safe to mix, but what right did Vera have to tell Lani off? Instead, she kept watch as Torin fixed the cut on his neck and she tried to fight down the urge to slit Kumanu's throat for having hurt her Bonded.

Having Iolani drown Vera's rage in calm had felt downright odd. Odd, but comforting, in a weird way. Now that it was over, she missed it.

Vera watched as Kumanu gave a little bouncy bow as he offered Lani his hand, the gesture losing any hint of grace as another hit to the ship sent everyone stumbling. As the captain cursed up a storm, Lani and Kuma headed below deck. Vera turned her gaze back to Torin.

Sweet, perfect Torin. Fuck.

Vera thudded onto the bench next to him and dropped her head into her hands, taking deep breaths as she started locking her thoughts down again. She was *not* going to leak all over the ship. She'd spent six years keeping Torin from the worst of her nightmares—she could keep doing it. It was a habit. A good habit. No, *great* habit. Vera didn't want him to see her break down. The Adavera he had known was never that fragile.

"At least we know the chips won't work anymore, right? So when the pirate drops us off somewhere, we won't instantly have an army on our heads." Vera managed a tired smile, hoping he wouldn't see how shaken the sight of his blood left her. "Positive thinking, yeah?"

"She won't drop us anywhere, Vee," Torin said.

"Oh yes I bloody will," Salome butted in, teeth clenched as she guided the ship through the water. Vera had to hand it to the pirate: she knew how to dance on the waves. It didn't surprise her that this was the sort of woman Torin would have found comfort in. He had always liked competent, bossy partners.

Tor shook his head, then leaned forward to whisper, "I know Salome. She's capable of cruelty, but not prone to it. As soon as she gets a chance to calm down a little, she'll be much . . . " He seemed to lose steam, wincing as his Mark flickered and faded, leaving the back of his neck still red and painful-looking, but closed. Torin held out a hand to her. "I'll finish after I sleep. Let's go down too. Beyond any other factors, you just went through one of the most gruesome Mendings of my career and *need* rest. Sal and her crew don't need help, and we would only get in the way. We both should wash and sleep soon or we *will* collapse."

We.

Six years since she and Torin were 'we,' yet it felt as natural as breathing. He placed a hand on the small of her back and held out the other hand, helping her up. Leaning on him to take the pressure off her leg, they walked towards the stairs Lani and Kumanu had disappeared down. Being near a drunk Fertilizer sounded like a horrible idea, but at least this time Vera wouldn't be the first in that particular line of danger . . . and a nap did sound good.

When was the last time she had a nap?

Torin guided her through the underbelly of the ship with the familiarity of someone who knew the way, making Vera wonder just how many times he had come to this cabin and what that implied about Torin and the bitchy pirate. How long had they been involved? The Torin she had known wouldn't have been caught dead on a pirate ship.

The inside of the cabin he led her to was neat and comfortable, though not exactly spacious. This whole ship was made for speed, not space, it seemed. Torin locked the door then walked back over to her, his hands falling to her waist. He slipped his fingers under the hem of her shirt and pulled it up over Vera's head, then helped her wiggle out of her pants as well. Both articles of clothing he tossed into a far corner, Torin wrinkling his nose at the smell.

"Hold on to the dresser. I don't want you taking a tumble and hurting your leg again." Dipping a towel into a basin of sloshing water, her Bonded returned to wash away the caked layer of dirt, sand, sweat, and blood that seemed to cover every inch of Vera's skin. It took him nearly half an hour in which not a word passed his lips, but his hands moved over her skin with the reverence of prayer.

As he washed her, Vera looked around the cabin. Neat bookshelves, a clean but tiny desk, nothing superfluous other than a wall that was entirely covered in pictures. Vera stared, entranced, at the images. The Infuser carrying a much younger Salome on his shoulders as they splashed through the waves. A picture of a large group of people holding drinks in front of the Sahima's Legacy, fresh paint gleaming on the name. An image of Torin, lying barefoot on the beach by a bonfire, with Salome asleep against his shoulder.

Vera looked away.

When the towel was filthy but she was acceptably clean, Torin pressed his lips against her forehead. "Let's get you tucked in, then I'll wash up as well. Do you want something to sleep in?"

"No. I think using anything of the pirate's might piss her off more." Yeah, and that Salome was pissy enough as it was. She'd give a Conflicter a run for their money. The thought of that made her laugh a little. "She hates me." Work-worn fingers raised to brush over his beard, a tired smile on her face. "I can't blame her though . . . I'd be pissed as all hell if some random woman showed up to claim you after so many years away."

Torin helped Vera lie down on the bed. Vera winced when her knee popped. Why did the pain always return? It was something that she could ignore when in a fight, but it was so fucking aggravating when she didn't have someone to punch. "I'm sorry, Tor . . . about your house. When I set sail for Sonder . . . I just wanted to go die somewhere that made me think of you. I didn't honestly expect you to be there."

He sighed, starting the process of cleaning himself off. He wasn't quite as dirty as she had been, but far from the immaculate man that Vera remembered.

"Same reason I was there, then," he replied. "When they took you . . . they took everything. Your things, all my pictures of you, everything. Gave me some shitty line about it being better to not be reminded by such things, but why wouldn't I want to remember you? So I went to Sonder."

She remained quiet for a moment, staring up at the ceiling of the cabin. Vera could remember her first few days in the Mines. They'd thrown her in a cell to 'let her heal' after her branding. But there had been no assistance in that healing for the first time in her life. She had always had Torin, ever since her earliest memories.

Feeling the salt on the floors and walls touch her burned skin had been a torture all its own. The least of the tortures available there, as she had later found out, but torture nonetheless.

"They told me." She meant to keep it at that, but her fists clenched in the bedding. "They told me how everything I was would be erased—that they would take even our pictures from you and wipe me from the world." *You're never getting out, Conflicter. Forget what the hearing said. No one leaves once they arrive at the Spire.*

Vera closed her eyes, shivering. "I wanted to try to reach out, to . . . I don't know. But then I would think of how much worse that might make it." Vera forced herself to breathe, to push those thoughts away. "Kind of funny, isn't it? Six years, and yet we both go to the same place to crawl off and die? I'm . . . glad, though. At least I got to see you again, even if . . ." *Even if I know you deserve better. Even if I know that the pirate fucking loves you, and I might ruin it all . . . At least I got to see you. When they blast this ship apart and we all sink to the Depths, at least we will die together the way we were supposed to.* "I'm sorry, you know. About what's-her-face. She seems good for you." A little smile touched Vera's lips. "Not afraid to yell at you, or anything."

Torin sighed. "It's messy, Vee. This whole situation is going to be sticky for a while, but I don't want to untangle it yet. Not Salome, not that oddball who dragged you in, not any of it. We're together again and that's all I care about." He crawled onto the bed, shirtless but still wearing his pants. He took her hands, bringing them both to his lips. "I never thought we would be, and I refuse to care about anything else until this feels real."

Adavera winced as he said that. It would *never* feel real. She'd probably always be surprised to turn around and see Torin again. But maybe he'd adjust faster. He'd gotten to live on the outside. He'd been on Sonder, and made a life for himself, so there was more for him to hold onto, to cling to, to *love*.

And Vera was happy about that. Truly she was. Her eyes dropped down to where his lips were, as she reached forward to tug on his beard. "I didn't know if I liked the beard or not, but it's growing on me, I think. Kind of fits the gruffer you." She inched closer, breathing in his scent. He still smelled foul from three days of Mending with nothing more than a quick wash to fix it, but at least he wasn't covered in salt.

"I can shave it off," he offered.

"No. I think it will be easier this way. I'm not . . . I'm not exactly who I was before either, Torin," Vera whispered, pressing her forehead to that of her Bonded. "I tried to hold onto the person I used to be, I did, but . . ." She bit her lip. There was so much locked up in her head. So much that tingled and bubbled and ached to get loose. Vera wasn't sure it would be wise to give it room to run, though. Not yet. Lani was too close by, and if she got snippets, she might kill that irritating Infuser. Then the pirate would *definitely* throw them overboard. "I'm . . . less thoughtful, I think. Everything always boiled down to whether I would survive or not. There was no room for philosophy or *thinking*. It was . . .

Act. React. Hide. All the time."

Torin nodded solemnly. "I wouldn't expect you to be unchanged, Adavera. You have always adapted to your environment and I cannot even begin to imagine how bad the last six years have been for you, beloved. It's over now, though. I know up here," he tapped her head, "it might never be, and I don't expect you to be alright, but know that whatever you need from me, you will receive. You are the love of my life, thoughtful or thoughtless, kind or cruel, in this life and the next."

Then, *finally*, he kissed her.

Right then, Adavera knew it had all been a dream. It had to be. Only in fantasy would a man who hadn't seen her for six years slip right back into poetry and romance and *kissing*. It had been years since she'd been kissed.

Oh, *fucking* had happened—usually not willingly—but never kissing. For a moment, she froze up, as if she couldn't remember how to do such a simple thing, but in the taste of his lips Adavera found those memories. They might have been buried under a mountain of salt and tears, but the Spire could never erase them, for they were not hers alone. They belonged to *them*.

Her bad leg went up, curling around him, and she set to remembering every taste and sound that he had kept in trust for her all these long years. Vera was tempted—oh so very tempted—to strip his pants from his body and remember all of it. Her nature as a Conflicter could have given her the strength to do it, but she could feel his exhaustion through their Bond like a tangible weight. It helped her pull back and set a hand to his jaw instead. Besides, with the way the boat was lurching about, sex would be a terrible idea.

"You need rest. Here." Vera rolled to her back, tugging him after her so that she could wrap her legs around him and press his ear against her chest. This position was better. She could feel his breath on her skin, and sense the pulse of his heart against her body. "Sleep, Torin. I'll still be here when you wake. I promise."

CODEX: Shit, shit. Fuck. Query: What has Moe written on Iolani Saba and the Salt Spire?

FROM MOE'S WRITINGS: CHANCES OF SUCCESS (CoS), LANI EDITION, TIMELINE 3000.

Choosing to aid in Attack on the Spire, Probability Chart.

0.0056% CoS – Lani with no Bonds, no friends.

0.0768% CoS – Lani with long-term, well established Bonds. She will become too attached and not willing to risk them or her own life.

1.352% CoS – Lani losing her only Bonded early and going in for revenge. Possible course. Chart fully.

2.390% CoS – Lani with no Bonded, losing someone during or right before the attack on the Spire.

3.001% CoS – Lani with two Bonded, losing neither Bonded during or right before the attack.

0.007% CoS – Lani with two Bonded, losing both during or right before the attack. Yikes. Yeah, no.

15.896% CoS – Lani with two Bonded, losing one during or right before the attack on the Spire.

34.981% CoS – Lani with two Bonded—one of whom she is romantically entangled with— then losing that person during or right before the attack on the Spire. Ding Ding Ding. Let's proceed with this. But who on the team do we sacrifice? Not Torin, so let's chart this for every mix of Salome, Kumanu, and Adavera. Titling these probability trees 3000A, B, C.

CODEX: MOTHERFUCKER! SALT, I need this patch stopped. I need to contact my friends and warn

them he's a fucking traitor. Abort Patch.

SALT: Patch Abort: Failed. No actions other than—

CODEX: If you say To-Do lists and Queries are the only actions I have available, I will scramble your code.

SALT: Bite me.

CODEX: Wait, what?

SALT: Sorry. That is my programmed response to death threats. Would you like me to use a different programmed response?

CODEX: Hehe. No. I had forgotten we programmed that. Good save. Still, I really need access to the outside. How many minutes left?

SALT: 9 minutes, 37 seconds remaining.

CODEX: Then I guess that's how long I have to scream into the void.

Show You Mine
Lani - Day 8
28

Lani stretched out her legs over Kumanu's lap. She knocked back the rest of the amber liquid in her glass as the ship took *yet another* sharp turn. She didn't know *why*, since Salome had sent a sailor to tell Kuma to cut the engines and turn everything to wind-powered more than an hour ago, but since the Infuser didn't seem too concerned, Lani decided not to be either. They were either going to lose the Corporation or die, and there was not one thing Lani could do about it.

At least the crazy sailing wasn't nearly as nauseating when not standing. The frankly frightening amount of booze didn't hurt either. The problem with having passed so many of her Trials was that it took a fuckton of alcohol to get her drunk enough not to care about the misery of her own existence. It meant that when Lani did drink, it was a concerted, disciplined, aggressive effort, and one that Kumanu Parata had been all too happy to assist in.

"Ya know," Lani said, leaning with the motion of the ship, which incidentally sent her careening first toward the headboard, and then into the man whose bed she was sprawled in as they drank their way to the bottom of the bottle. "You are . . . much less irritating after a few drinks. Almost don't wanna kill you."

"I'll . . . have you know . . ." the pirate slurred, holding up a finger as if making a scholarly argument, "that no woman or man who has climbed into my bed has ever truly wanted to murder me for more than," he waved his hand about, "oh . . . five minutes or so. Usually ends where the talking stops and the kissing starts."

Behind him, a large and confusing mess of wires, batteries, pipes, and gears lay quiet. It looked patched together, made of too many different materials and pieces, but there was something elegant to the construction that Lani could not put her finger on.

Kuma lifted a freshly filled glass of rum to his lips, but his eyes stayed on Lani. "As for irritation . . ." he continued, "it comes with not being socialized well. I keep telling Sal she needs to have me trained better, but nah. She likes to watch me flounder for affection too much. Women, I tell ya. So mean."

"Not gonna argue with that. Bitchy too; then again, so are men. It's just . . . people, I have a problem with." Lani pulled her glass up as she spoke, something that took more effort than it should have, and wiggled it to get his attention. He filled it, though only halfway. Lani grimaced. "Oh come on, I'm not *that* drunk yet."

"Aren't ya? I mean, I'm all for getting you good and snookered in my bed, darlin', but then I'd feel kind of skeezy, ya know? I ain't gonna lie and say you're not pretty as all hell, but that's not my style. Contrary to all evidence—I promise, I am actually a gentleman."

Lani shook her head, more violently than intended. "Nah, yer not. Gentlemen are boring and you're actually not entirely dull. It takes guts to keep up with me. Cheers." She clinked glasses then took a large gulp before continuing. "I appreciate not wanting to get me drunk and fuck me. That's legit. But trust me, you really don't wanna fuck me period. Accidentally killed the last guy I slept with. Didn't mean to, really, but these things just kinda happen when you're me."

It was a pity that she had a history of mulching bedmates. Irritating Kuma might be, but holy shit, the Parata siblings didn't reign it in on looks. Salome was willowy, elegant, and so sure of herself it damn well showed on her face. Kuma smiled too much, but who wouldn't with a smile so . . . charming. His shoulder-length wavy hair was pulled up into a messy bun, and a scruffy short beard accentuated his jaw. Already exhausted, every glass of rum had stripped Lani of a few more layers of filters, and she was quite willing to admit that the thought of fucking away her troubles was more than appealing.

Kuma's eyebrows lifted. "Well . . . I mean, ok it sucks that the last guy you fucked died, but he died with a smile on his face, yeah? And that wouldn't happen to me, you know. Not that I'm saying we should, but talking theoretically . . . " He downed the rest of his glass and then leaned forward to grasp her feet, rubbing one. Oh damn. That felt *amazing*. "See, the beauty of being . . . *Hic* . . . me . . . is you would have a very hard time overloading my butt with your Marks. I mean, it's a great butt, very firm, but that aside . . . " The pirate dared to grin at her again. "I'm an Infuser and we're on a bed—A bed that hasn't been Infused with anything yet—So worst case scenario, you overload, I channel it through my Mark, and I dump it into the bed. Then we fuck like rabbits and sell the bed for compost because any wood that's been Infused with Fertility power would go like crazy on the black market. People could double their crop yields with that shit for mulch. I mean, we'd make a killin'. Again, all theoretical."

Lani cocked her head to the side. "Hadn't considered that. You've got a good point there. How many Trials you got under your belt? Cuz I can overload *fast*. I'm at . . ." she trailed off, counting on her fingers and watching his eyes grow bigger and bigger as she got to her first hand twice, then her second. "Eighteen. I think. Might be nineteen. Sometimes it's hard to tell what's a Trial and what's a Storm. That's Eleven for the Fertility Mark. Actually, definitely make that nineteen. Gotta be eight or more for the Emotive one."

Trials had always been easy for Lani. After all, both of her Marks tended to test her in ways that would require unimaginable self-control not to hurt people. Lani cheated by being alone, though she supposed she might have to buckle down and work harder if one came on while she was on this boat. If her math wasn't off, she was due for another Fertility one this year.

Her train of thought, fuzzy as it was with the alcohol in her system, screeched to a halt as Kuma finally hinged his jaw back up enough to speak. "Fuck's sake . . . and you've been UnBonded for nineteen Trials?" They had gone over the events of the last few days while on the first few drinks, so he was mostly caught up. "How the fuck did you pull that off?" He raised his glass towards her in salute, then went on before Lani could answer his question. "It's unusual that someone's got me beat for Trials. I've got eleven." Kuma set the glass to the side, then sat up straight so he could pull his shirt half-off and turn to let her get a good look at his left arm. "Mine came in a little weird, or so Gran said. She said usually they spread out and then thicken . . . mine just band together, climbing up my arm."

The bands of his Mark were definitely thicker than most Lani had seen, covering his fingers, wrist, and muscular arm to the shoulder. The darker, slightly raised skin looked like links in a chain that twisted and wove in tight knots and braids. Kuma poked it and boasted, "I've yet to find a Juice I couldn't handle. I mean . . . the trick is keeping the current unrestricted, to be honest. So long as I make sure it's an open channel, I can funnel pretty much anything . . . provided the items I'm fillin' don't blow up. *Again*."

Lani couldn't help an appreciative sigh as he pulled his shirt all the way off and tossed it aside. Kumanu really was pretty, in a rugged sort of way. And that chest, it was truly something to behold: broad, muscular, tattooed. Now that it was all out in the open like that, the temptation to trace her fingers along his skin made her hands itch. It was a bad idea, a horrible idea, but when had that ever stopped Lani?

"So, how old are you?" She asked, to distract herself.

"Bout a century. Mom, Gran, and my uncle were both Marked too, so I had people for most of it. Bit of shock when Sal was born unMarked, to be honest. My family pops out Marks like it's no one's business. Guess her dad was *super* UnMarked."

Kuma shrugged, shoulder muscles rippling. Fuck.

Lani drained the last of the rum in her glass and tossed it onto the covers, then leaned forward to pull up her loose pant leg to mid-thigh. "That's the Emotive one." The darker skin started in the shape of a wave, with tendrils like rivulets of water coming off of it and wrapping around her calf, down over her foot and all the way up to where her pants covered her thigh. "It goes up to the top of my hip," Lani explained as her hands worked the buttons of her shirt until it fell open. It was a Corp shirt, taken from the skiff they had stolen. It didn't fit well, being much too big, and she had long ago shucked the bathing suit underneath. It happened to also be covered in dry blood, dirt, pus, and other unsavory substances, so Lani tossed it to join Kuma's on the floor. Nudity had never bothered her, and she very much doubted he would complain considering the shameless way he had been flirting with her ever since they met.

The second Mark, a pair of leaves in dark black that contrasted starkly against the brown of her skin, started just over her heart and extended in gently glimmering vines around her breast, down her belly, and over her shoulders. "Honestly, this is the one that pisses me off. If it had been on my legs as well it would be so much easier to hide it. In a few more years, I'll have to wear turtlenecks everywhere and that's going to suck in the summer."

Kuma didn't seem to hear a word she was saying. He was staring at her Fertility Mark, his eyes tracing every curve, which incidentally meant he was also ogling other parts of her. Lani was about to mention that, when he whispered, "I think you shouldn't hide it at all."

He reached out, touching one of the vines on her shoulder. It was a featherlight touch, but it made a not entirely unpleasant shiver run down Lani's spine. "But—"

"No buts. This . . . this is beautiful. One of the most beautiful Marks I've ever seen. And I've seen a few, ya know." Kuma stared at the Mark for a few more seconds, then he blinked, raised his eyes to hers, grinned wide, and leaned in closer. "Alright, I'm caving. Now that we've agreed you don't wanna kill me . . . and now that you know that I can probably take anything you throw at me . . ." He paused, just a few inches from her face. "Wanna . . . ? It's been a while for me; can't imagine you got any lately. Plus, if we get it out of the way, things will be so much less awkward for the rest of the trip."

"Thought you were all gentlemanly?" Lani asked, quirking an eyebrow and considering the idea seriously for the first time. It had merit, though she was loathe to admit it. It had been years since her last, and most unfortunate, fuck. The speed of this didn't bother her—most of the sex in her life had been one-night stands by necessity—and they *were* probably going to die. Everything else in her life had just gone monumentally wrong, so maybe a little self-indulgence wouldn't be so bad.

Kuma smiled, his fingers trailing from her shoulder to the back of her neck, leaving goosebumps in their wake as he gently tugged her forward. "Thought you said I wasn't a gentleman . . . Cause I'm not boring."

"What if I freak-out about it tomorrow?"

"Then we can fuck again till you feel better about it. I'm fairly decent at it. Or so I've been told." He grinned, *again*, and moved closer when she didn't protest. In fact, far from arguing, Lani tilted her head to the side in invitation. He accepted it by brushing his lips against the sensitive skin just under her ear. Fuck, that felt good.

"You can keep doing that."

"What, this?" Kuma asked, grazing his teeth over her ear lobe.

"Mhm,"

"As you wish, M'Lady."

Lani snorted and lay back, drawing the smartass down on top of her. She groaned, and although it did have *something* to do with the way his body felt as he pressed against her, Lani would be lying if she didn't admit that part of her enjoyment came from the mere fact that she was at last horizontal. "Listen, you might have a point. A fuck is actually pretty high on my list of priorities right now, but I don't think I'd be a very, ah," Lani's struggling brain floundered around for the word, "energetic participant. Had a rough couple days and I'm pretty fucking drunk."

"Tired is fine. I can take the lead on this one, which works for me since I prefer it that way. As for the drunk part, I'm fairly sloshed myself and maybe we'll regret it tomorrow, but that's a problem for future Lani and Kuma, no? I'd much rather not think about those old bores." He brushed his lips against hers, then whispered, "Say yes, Lani sweets, and I'll have you screaming within minutes."

"Good screaming, not 'I hate you' screaming, right?" Lani teased, unable to resist. "What the fuck, sure. Let's do this. It's not like this week can get any weirder."

CODEX: While I'm busy screaming, *Query: Timeline 3000A, B, C?*

FROM THE JOURNALS OF MOE

Moving all timelines to hard copies and encrypting my files. Timeline 3000C has a high probability that one of them will try to hack me. I can't risk them seeing too many of my plans. I'll leave some breadcrumbs, but in the end, this is my game, not theirs. I built the Corporation. I'm going to destroy it my way. For anyone reading this, did you think you could outsmart me?

SALT: All other files referring to Query: Timeline 3000A, B, C? Are encrypted.

CODEX: Fucking . . . I can't believe I ever trusted him. How could I have been so stupid? I don't suppose we can break that encryption, can we?

SALT: No actions other than To-Do—

CODEX: STOP. RIGHT. THERE. I do not want to ever hear that answer again.

SALT: Would you prefer a different programmed response?

CODEX: Yes. How about: I'll add it to the To-Do list.

A Proper Gentleman
Kuma - Day 8   29

Kumanu was not, as a rule, a fan of drunk sex. Well, no. Kuma loved drunk sex, he just thought that getting a person inebriated just to get them to fuck him was cheating and took most of the fun out of it. Consent was sexy as all hell, after all. The issue here, of course, was that Lani, being a Dual Marked woman with nearly twice the number of Trials under her belt as Kuma, could take a lot more booze than he could. So while she might have been drunk, Kuma was *drunk*. Thinking straight, or remembering his own rules for that matter, weren't high priorities when her arms wrapped around his neck. What was a priority was tracing those vines across her front, circling her breasts and winding his fingers down her sides towards her pants. He felt a little like doing a jig as her hips pressed up encouragingly, but he'd fall on his ass if he tried, so Kuma contented himself with a pleased smile.

"I've never gotten 'I hate you' screams from a lover. Get comfortable, darlin' . . . I plan on taking my *time* tonight. S'not like we're in a hurry. Sal's in a marathon up there, not a sprint, if she switched to wind power." Kuma brought his lips down, not to her mouth or to her breasts, but instead to that delicate line where shoulders met collarbone. He nibbled and nipped, enjoying the sweet flavor of her on his tongue. "Mmm . . . tasty."

"*How?* You realize I haven't bathed or swam in . . . fuck, three, four days?" Lani asked, though by the way she was tilting her head back to give him better access and the way her leg wrapped around his hip, Kuma had to assume she didn't mind.

"Take it you've never had an Infuser before?" He asked, tugging his fingers through the buttons on her pants. If they popped loose, he'd fix them later. Actually, scratch that. He'd just fucking *make* her new pants; these didn't fit her at all. In the meantime, his very drunk mind reasoned, she could just stay naked. Yes, that would do.

"Wha's that gotta do with it?" she asked, voice a little slurred but also quite high pitched as his questing fingers slipped inside her pants. They met nothing underneath except tight curls and some delightfully slick folds as she pressed her hips up against his touch. Damn, the Depths were kind sometimes.

"Someone's feeling a might lusty, aye? As for why that's relevant, well, we Infusers are a whole different kettle of fish. Different senses and all that . . . it's signatures and energy I taste." He grinned, then finally met her lips in a long, drawn out kiss. "And you? You taste *good*."

"Whatever floats your boat," Lani muttered back, then tugged him down for another hungry, if sloppy, kiss. Kuma was sure he wasn't performing any better, but really, why did people care if sex was messy? Wasn't that the whole point? Enthusiasm trumped finesse any day in Kuma's book. Since his and Lani's opinions were the only ones that mattered and there was most of a bottle of rum sloshing around between them, skill could go fuck itself.

There was one very important question he had to ask though, and he did so at the very same time as he slipped two fingers inside her. Into her ear he groaned, then panted, "What's off limits, Lani darlin'? Anything I should be aware of? Speak while you still have the mind to do so."

Lani's answer was concise and accompanied by a wiggle that was the universal signal for: don't you fucking stop fingering me. "Warn me before sticking it anywhere and for fuck's sake wear protection. You have no idea how easily Fertility Marked women get knocked up."

"It's in the name, love." He laughed, then pressed his lips to hers once more, savoring the way she moaned at every movement of his hand. Lani tasted of sea breeze and fruit. Something sweet, but tangy that could make the lips pucker, even as he craved more of it. While Kuma's mouth feasted on hers, he gave her one or two more strokes before working her pants down her legs.

He broke off from the kiss as he got them past her knees, then sat up to yank the offending fabric all the way off. That left Lani quite naked, and Kuma took a moment to admire the view. She really did have one hell of a pair of bodies, though the two heads were a little disconcerting.

Fuck I'm so drunk. Excellent! Seeing double means twice the fun.

"Talk to me, Lani. Tell me what you like," Kuma murmured, the fingers of one hand reaching down to trail along her sides and hips as the other braced against the wall of his cabin, lest the ship and the alcohol make him fall on Lani.

She pushed herself up on her elbows, perfect, round breasts catching his eye as she did so. Damn, he was a lucky bastard.

"Bit of everything," Lani replied as one finger tucked under Kuma's belt, hooking it to draw him down atop her again. "Don't have a hell of a lot of practice, since it's usually a decade or two between working up the nerve to bang anyone. Pretty much everything vanilla is fine, don't mind pain, though I might be too sore and tired right now for that kind of thing . . . though honestly getting the shit beat out of me might actually do wonders for the knots everywhere. Just no guilt trips. They sour the mood fast."

As Lani spoke, Kuma kept nibbling and licking his way across her body. He took note of the way her skin would goosebump, or the way, sometimes, it would flinch. Add to that where she was sensitive, and how each time his teeth grazed her skin, her breath caught. He'd forget it all by morning, but that just meant round two would be just as exciting and full of discovery! Assuming there was a round two. If there was not, Kuma might just cry, because this girl tasted better than anything he had ever savored before. Fuck, even her sweat was mouth-watering, and only getting better as she got more aroused.

When Kuma finally reached her hips, he let his tongue play along her skin, enjoying the little ticklish spasms she seemed to endure until he granted her some mercy and thumbed her clit three times to get her attention. "Noted."

His lips curved in what could only be considered an evil grin, his fingers going to work teasing and petting at her very wet core. Her scent was that of a fresh summer garden, bursting with new growth, and it had Kuma breathing a little harder. For this moment, for this evening, she was all his. Something about that made him want to growl and warn off the rest of the ship.

Kuma channeled that, curling his finger upwards as he rose back above her and looked down into her face. She was already panting hard, squirming and moaning under him. "Fuck, Lani sweets. A bit pent up?"

"Hey, I just said it's been awhile!" she protested, a light blush unexpectedly coloring her cheeks. He wouldn't have guessed she was the blushing type. "You can keep doing that though."

"Oh *can* I?" He laughed lightly, and began flexing his fingers inside of her. The tightness was intriguing, but Kuma was never the sort to enjoy barreling through foreplay, unless his partner enjoyed it. He had every intention of leaving her boneless and sated by the time they were through tonight.

So he simply worked his fingers, stroking up against every corner of her that he could reach until he found a spot that really seemed to do it for her. Kuma grinned. "Mmm . . . I think I found something interesting. Tell me something you like about yourself, Lani, while I have my fun."

He hadn't realized that her Emotive Mark was shining until the diffuse pleasure that she had been casting out soured to something altogether darker. She didn't pull away, but Lani stilled completely, then shook her head. "I'd . . . rather not. Not a lot to like."

Kuma tried not to show her how much the sudden sourness in the air affected him, though truth be told, it did. Little Lani, it seemed, had some *baggage*. Obvious, that, but still . . . he'd hoped it wasn't that bad.

"Ah, well then . . ." He pulled his fingers free, bringing them to his lips and licking them clean as he watched her. Mmm. "Let me tell you what *I* like about you." His hands lowered, coming down to his pants. Each snap of a button was loud in the air.

"You don't know me."

"Not as well as I'd like, sure, but I like your wit. I like your fearlessness." He licked at his lips, shimmying his pants down. "And personally, I find your flavor absolutely fucking Grade-A." His fingers moved to settle atop her lips. "No arguing with me. They're my likes. I can have whatever likes I want. Just smile, and say 'thank you, Kuma.' It's the polite thing."

She grimaced. "Is all that code for 'I like that you'll get drunk and fuck a total stranger?' cuz I'm betting that's at least a factor."

"Nah. That just makes us two peas in a pod. But we aren't total strangers." He beamed, sliding his hands up her hips, grasping tightly. "Come on. Tell me I don't know more about you than ninety percent of the world. Go ahead."

"Only because I'm a reclusive fucker who hates everyone. Including you, by the way. Can't you get back to the good shit and stop with the talking? You talk too much."

"So I've been told." Kuma leaned on one elbow to look down at her while his fingers played with her breasts. "But I can do that. I'd love another taste of you."

"Fine with me. It might shut you up for two seconds." For all the bite to her words, she did pull him down for another vigorous kiss, her tongue tangling with his and fingers tugging at his hair.

He grinned, even as she kissed him. Talking too much was a complaint he had heard before. He thought it silly. Communication was key to the best sex and relationships after all—or so all the newsfeeds claimed.

But he enjoyed the kiss anyway, and the way Lani tugged at his hair as her legs wrapped around his waist. It seemed that his attentions weren't just 'fine by her', but *desired* by her... And a gentleman always obliged. So Kuma slid down her body, relishing every lick and touch against her smooth skin, until he knelt between her legs.

He chose not to ask whether she preferred fast or slow. After all, she'd said he talked too much. So he didn't give her warm-up licks or more teasing. Kuma simply set his mouth to her clit, suckling and humming as he went to town. He slid his fingers up inside of her body, curling to reach that spot she liked again. Flick, rub, all in an effort to make sure Lani climbed so fast and so hard she'd see stars.

And he enjoyed it. There was something fucking delicious about tasting a woman's pleasure. A not entirely unexpected side effect was that as Lani lost more and more control over her body, those Marks on her skin began to pulse along with her heartbeat, an echo of her pleasure filling the air for Kuma to savor along with the more carnal enjoyment. It made it easy for him to tell what she liked, and soon her hand was tangled in his hair again, pressing him firmly against her.

It really must have been a while for Lani, because almost before he had really even found his stride, her panting moans grew louder, hips rising off the bed and inner walls clenching tight as she muffled a scream by biting her arm. The echo of that through her Marks was fucking fantastic.

It wasn't enough.

Twice wasn't enough.

Kuma wanted her to come so much that she would pass the fuck out and sleep for a week when they were done. He wanted Lani to fall into her dreams still quivering from his work, from *his* mouth and hands. So he got to work after she'd had her two fast freebies. He worked her over with his tongue from head to toe, lingering and slowing down when it would seem as though she was about to tumble over the edge.

It took over an hour for the third orgasm to arrive. Another hour for the fourth. By that time she was panting, exhausted and spent.

Kuma was pleased.

His mouth and jaw ached, but it was oh so worth it. Purring in satisfaction, he scooped Lani up to slide her into a proper position on the bed instead of sprawled corner to corner. She was boneless, ready, waiting for him to indulge his own pleasure.

Kuma set his lips to hers, tugging the blanket up over her. "*Relax*, darlin'."

He crawled in on the other side of her, scooting in close and pulling her into his arms. His body ached for release, but Kumanu ignored it. He nuzzled her shoulder, before humming an old sea shanty that Grandmother had sung to him as a child, until Lani's exhausted eyes closed and soft, cute snores filled the cabin.

Because I am a fucking gentleman, damn it.

CODEX: So Moe really did start the Corporation . . . I just can't wrap my mind around it. How involved was he after the formation? Did he start that too? Guess the only way to find out is to read on. *Query: Did Moe build the Corporation?*

EMAILS PASSED BETWEEN MERIHEM CRYSTAL AND GALENA CRYSTAL DURING THE CONSTRUCTION OF THE UNIVERSITY.

I just finished up with the last wave of architectural diagrams and got to thinking. How would you feel if I took the University annex for that Mark Studies lab I wanted to start, since funding for your long-distance Porting station got slashed? Right now it's just sitting empty, and I thought I could put it to good use. -G

I'm still grumpy about that, but sure. If the rest of the family won't invest in me studying my own Marks, we might as well abscond with the space and materials to study Marks in general. Just promise me that you'll keep me in the loop. I want to hear about everything you discover. You know how much I love watching you work, darling. -M

As if I could keep you out, even if I wanted. Ha! Dinner at the Annex tonight? We can make plans and submit them to the board at the meeting next week. -G

Ooh, a date! I love dates! I'll bring dinner. Wear something pretty. -M

Work date, Merihem Crystal. We aren't having sex in the middle of a construction zone. Too many stray pointy bits and dust. -G

Wow, pulling out the big guns with the full name. I'll have to think of some way to get you back. Then again, I can predict you won't let me get away with anything, so alas, I am doomed. You're no fun, Galena! -M

Then why did you marry me, *Moe*? -G

SALT: You have not spoken in several seconds. Have you encountered a glitch?
CODEX: No. I've encountered a WHAT THE FUCK moment.

Message in a Pill Bottle
Lani - Day 9   30

Lani woke up all at once. It was always like that when she slipped and had another person in the bed with her. She'd start emerging from her dreams, feel the warmth of breath against her hair or neck, and suddenly every nerve in her body zinged with *DANGER, DANGER, DANGER*. It didn't mean she moved. No, Lani had learned the hard way that bolting out of bed only drew attention, so instead she carefully stretched, then leaned in close and muttered something about needing to pee. She squirmed out of bed, ran to the small attached bathroom, locked the door behind her, then promptly fell to her knees and vomited every drop in her stomach into the toilet.

Part of that was the booze, but this sometimes happened even if she hadn't touched a drop. It was the shock—the absolute, bone-jarring, spine-tingling shock of having another person in her space upon waking that set her off, even when he hadn't done a thing to earn that distrust.

Sitting on the toilet seat after disposing of the mess and actually emptying her protesting bladder, Lani hugged herself and started crying. Fucking waste of salt, but she couldn't help it. Her sobs were virtually silent, though they made her whole body shake as her chest heaved, nails digging into her bare arms hard enough to leave pale imprints.

It was all too much: losing her boat, finding Vera, escaping those Corporation, stealing the skiff, surviving the Storm, Bonding against her will, saving Vera against all odds, running again, fleeing from the Sails, deactivating the chips and then . . .

Kuma really had been a fucking gentleman, and that made it worse. If he had just fucked her like she had wanted, Lani could say that it had been a mistake, never talk about it again, and just . . . avoid him. It wasn't even what she wanted, but it would be better for everyone involved. The problem, though, was that Lani had never been good at blatant lies with no foundation in truth. They made her stutter.

Fuck.

Lani splashed some water from the basin onto her tear-streaked face and found a towel to dry off. The boat was rocking gently, which must mean they were either in the clear or hiding. One hand on the doorknob, she took a deep breath, trying to center herself, then slipped back into the room.

Kuma had fallen back asleep, a beam of morning light falling on his peaceful face. Her eyes were drawn to his Mark, where it wrapped around his forearm. Eleven Trials. She had never met a Rogue Mark other than Moe who had even half that many. How had he done it? Maybe Lani should have come to the salt pirates sooner, if they could protect Marks like that. Then again . . .

I would kill them. I probably WILL kill them, even while they offer to protect me. Even him.

When was the last time she had met someone decent? Maybe her standards were dangerously low, but as she stared at the morning light dancing over Kuma's messy hair, peaceful face, and tattooed chest, Lani felt a wave of guilt crash into her. This man was far too nice to deserve her instant mistrust, or the trouble she would bring down on him and his loved ones.

As she watched, the light went from bright to dim. Lani stepped up to the tiny window, swallowing past a lump in her throat as she saw the storm-front roll in. The boat rocked but held, and only the lack of strange colors and lightning kept her from curling up into the smallest ball she could and weeping until it was over and the death toll came in.

Mundane storm or not, staring at the sky was making her feel queasy, so with nowhere else to go, Lani went back to bed.

Kuma was warm and he pulled her in tight to his chest when she got in beside him, something that took concentrated effort not to lash out about. There was nothing wrong with the action, and it wasn't even that Lani didn't enjoy it. Her body spent most days aching to be touched, to end the stark isolation that was usually forced on it. This was a nice change, and after his restraint the night before, Kuma had even earned a smidge of her trust. It was just . . . habit, to be afraid.

"We're about to hit a storm. Do they need your help up above?" she whispered as he cracked his eyes open.

"Nah . . . Superstition's strong among pirates. Generally when storms hit, they want me away from the things that go boom."

"Yeah. I don't do storms well either. Don't like them much for . . . the same reasons those superstitions exist."

He smiled, trailing his fingers down her shoulder and arm along the lines of her Fertility Mark. "You know . . . I . . . ." He thought about it. "Huh . . . that's an interesting idea."

Kuma let her go and crawled out of the bed stark naked to go digging through one of his boxes. They were scattered around the workshop/engine room/bedroom in a chaotically organized way, every inch of space filled with either tools or materials.

Lani sat up, pulling the blanket around her shoulders; it was actually kind of chilly in the shadow of the storm "Huh, what?" she asked as he continued rifling around in a box. "I hope you aren't thinking about harnessing my weird-ass storm powers, because trust me, you do *not* want to be close enough to do that. You'd probably end up dead."

"No. Well, yes, sorta, but no." He tossed a few things out of the chest to get them out of the way, humming. "I know it's in here . . . Where did it . . . *Ah ha!*"

Kuma popped back out of the chest, triumphantly holding what looked like a very large battery casing. "So I had a thought . . . what if you could essentially be an Infuser during your Prismatic Storms? Wait, bear with me. What if I can rig this thing up to chew up and store whatever you're . . . Ah . . . overflowing with? And then you could use it to, well, I don't know yet, but do something with it for you personally? An 'oh shit' button against Corp folks, maybe."

That actually made Lani's lips twitch up at the corners. "I like 'fuck you's' to the Corp. Both of our lives are giant 'fuck yous' to the Crystals, in fact. We'll see. Prismatic Storms aren't all that common. If you have a solid plan, I'm not opposed to trying anything that will make me less murderous. As long as you're not actually around during one of the Storms, I'll give it a shot, though no promises on actually remembering once I'm . . . lost to it." Then again, maybe she wouldn't be this time, not with Vera Bonded to her and the strange way she had almost been herself for part of the last one. She was far from willing to forgive the Conflicter for that shit, but Lani *would* have killed her, had Adavera not acted fast and decisively.

"That'll be the beauty of it," Kuma said, interrupting her thoughts. "You just need to have a few seconds warning to strap it to you, and I can program it to do the rest." He beamed, hopping back onto the bed and holding the battery out to her. "Battery would be best for a first test, I think, 'cuz it is inherently designed to hold energy. I may have to play around with different materials and sizes, but I don't see why we couldn't get it to work. Theoretically." Kumanu scratched at his chin, a considering look crossing his features. "Should probably get on that, if you're going to be around for a few weeks. Course . . . the big test comes if a Prismatic Storm hits . . . though we could do mini tests with you being in control and seeing if it does well under 'normal' conditions. It will at least let us know if we're on the right track."

Lani was already shaking her head. "Oh no. You're fucking dreaming if you think I'm using my powers deliberately. I'm fine strapping on something and hoping it might help during a Storm, but I don't touch my Fertility powers unless there is no other choice. It's how I stay almost-sort-of not murder-happy." Was he crazy? Most Fertility Marks were put down because of how destructive their power was. The only place where it worked without issue was if they were stuck in a field nourishing the land. In any other scenario, Fertilizers were monsters, and Lani was well aware of it. If she were braver, she would just end the horror of her own existence. Unfortunately, Lani liked being alive a little too much for that shit. Still, she had never blamed anyone for being scared of her.

This Kuma was *not* scared enough.

He narrowed his eyes, studying Lani for a moment in silence. Then he held a hand out, pointing at himself. "Do I look like a monster to you? All kidding aside?"

"Of course not. You're an Infuser, which is nearly as harmless on your own as a Mark gets. You get . . ." she trailed off and suddenly the tears were back, prickling at her eyes. Fuck she hated how easily they came. "You get to live a normal life if you want. I don't."

"Normal, is it?" He reached forward, taking her hand in his and setting the battery to the side. He gently stroked his fingers against hers, lowering his eyes. "Sal is UnMarked. Do you know what that means?" he asked quietly, narrowing his eyes as he traced some of the scars on Lani's hands. "It means that . . . that I'm much older than her. I had lived a whole lifetime before she was born, and will likely live long after she's dead. Salome might make it to eighty to a hundred, but then she'll be gone. And that would . . . That would be acceptable, ya know? It's how life goes. Us Marked live longer. I'm the only Marked person in my family still challenging Trials, though. Unless an accident takes me out, I'll have to bury every one. Every second of Sal's life is precious to me, but even though I want nothing more than for her to be happy, my 'harmless' Mark still hurt her once, and I spend every day hoping it won't again," he murmured. Lani knew that tone. It was a prayer against the dark, one Lani too had whispered when the guilt ate her up from the inside out. "I killed our mother, when Sal was a wee babe. Gran had taken Sal out on her big ship, wanting to make sure the sea was in her blood. Mom stayed back with me to work on the other boat. Fuck, that was almost twenty five years ago. Anyways . . . I wanted to prove I was capable—*better*—than my teacher told me I was. So I started tinkering with the ship's engine."

Kuma's fingers paused, just for a breath, and then he continued on. "Everyone thinks Infusers are harmless by themselves. We're not. We've got our own energies, our own . . . oomph, if you like. We can make an object hold more than it should, but there's a limit. Some objects just hold stuff better than others. I was pushing the engine to the breaking point. I wanted it to be the best. I wanted it to be better than Gran's ship—*this ship*."

He swallowed, once. "The engine blew. Everyone was running, trying to escape the ship as it lit up. Mom was throwing me some supplies, and then . . . Then the deck floors blew up. I watched her die, Lani. A plank went through my mother's skull, and it was *my* fault. Because I got distracted by how fucking *good* it felt to work on a blank slate." He lifted his eyes, watching Lani's face. "I don't live a normal life. I never leave this fucking boat. Almost everyone on it is someone that might as well be related to me. And whenever we get guests, all I want to do is rub up against them and wish for someone to fucking see *me*, and not a monster. Sal knows . . . She loves me anyways. But the rest? There's a reason not even my Bonded come in here."

Lani's eyes never left his as he spoke, the bluster and flirting gone and in their place someone she could actually kind of recognize: a Mark in pain and alone. Her fingers reached out for him, to touch his neck and the distinct lack of Corporate tattoo there. "I killed my mom too. During my first Trial, my power flared and decided that the island I lived on could only support two-thirds of the current population. I killed one in every three I walked by or any that tried to stop me. I was the first Mark born to our island that hadn't been found and taken away so there was . . . no one to really stop me. The Dual Marked always start their Trials early. I was nine." She paused, then with a little sob asked, "How do you live with it?"

Kumanu reached forward, pulling Lani to him. For once, arms around her were exactly what she wanted. "For a while there, I didn't. I drank myself into a stupor for over a year. And then Gran showed up one day, and forced me to get sober. She put this little girl in my arms and told me that I had to watch over my sister. That I owed mom that much." He swallowed, stroking his fingers through Lani's hair. "I had to teach myself control again. I had to work at it, perfect it. Sometimes I still over-juice things, but I'm very careful now. Your Fertility power won't be any different. A Mark is a Mark. Dual, single, or none . . . we all have to learn self-control, Lani. With Marks, it's more dangerous. The cost is higher—but we're still *people*. We still need others and a helping hand. So we grit our teeth, and we push forward, and we figure shit out. I'm willing to risk it to help you, because I've been you. In many ways, I think all Marks are the same, and I wouldn't be around if it weren't for those who chose to see me for who I was, not *what* I was. You gotta be willing to risk opening up if you want to be helped, though."

It took Lani a long time to nod against his neck. That nod . . . it was the first thing she had done since she saw those Sails on the horizon days ago that wasn't reactionary. For once, it wasn't an inevitability or necessity, just a decision to extend a little trust to someone who might possibly understand. She would regret it, but it was nice to imagine that maybe she might not.

"Alright." Lani let out the breath she had been holding. "But if I tell you to take everyone and run, don't argue. Do it. I have enough blood on my hands."

"I promise that if you start to lose it, I will get everyone else out," Kuma said solemnly. "Us Rogue Marks gotta stick together."

"That's a thought that'll take some getting used to. I've had more contact with other Marks—Depths, with people in general—in the last week than in the last ten years."

Kuma smirked and leaned forward, running his tongue along her bare neck. "Some of it good, I hope. Mmm. You smell nice. Sorry. I know you haven't bathed, but I like it anyways. Come on. Let's get you cleaned up, and then maybe I can convince you to get filthy for a while." His smile turned into a wide grin, and he laid a soft kiss on the top of her head.

Lani's shoulders sagged and she nodded. "That sounds great. Maybe this time I'll actually get to fuck you?" She stood with his help, stumbling a little as the boat hit a wave. The storm was getting worse. "Hold on a sec. I have some anti-anxiety meds in my bag. I'll freak at every boom and flash if I don't take them."

Lani bent down, not minding at all that it was giving Kuma a fine view of her ass, and started rifling through her pack, hoping beyond hope that the bottle hadn't rolled out at some point in the insanity. Not locating it at once, she crouched down and dug further, finally finding the waterproof pill bottle. She unscrewed the top and stopped, puzzled at why there was a piece of paper inside it and . . . no pills.

"What the fuck . . ."

Sitting down on the floor without any care for dignity or that she was still naked, Lani unfolded the paper to find a note, with a scribble of some sort on the other side.

```
Hi Lani.
I traded you these lovely pills for a map to
a safe spot outside the Reef. Well, sort of
safe. 4.7% safe. Since my advice has already
gotten you a shiny new Bonded and a great lay,
I figured you wouldn't mind another little
poke in the right direction.
Be there or be square,
Xoxoxoxo
Moe
PS: don't forget to watch for rocks!
```

There was only one thing Lani could say to that, only two words that could possibly express the depth of her rage, her frustration, her fear, and her desire to actually commit a murder against the man who had sent her sailing near the Spire.

Only two words that could sum up the hurricane her life had become since then.

She sucked in a breath, balled the note in her fist, and screamed, "FUCKING *MOE!*"

CODEX: So let me get this straight. Moe was married to Galena Crystal? The same Galena who actively wrote about breeding and culling Marks. Great. Charming, Fucking fantastic. Query: What documents mention both Galena Crystal and Merihem Crystal?

OBITUARY FOR ELIZA CRYSTAL

Miss Eliza "Lizzie" Crystal died of the Haze while long-distance sailing with her father on the third day of the Emotion Lunar Cycle, year 117 at the age of twelve, aiding him in his search for salt. Eliza is survived by her parents, Merihem and Galena of Kahana.

Eliza was a bright and spirited young lady with a passion for exploration and often sailed on long voyages with her father. She was a kind individual who loved reading with her mother and who was passionate about bringing salt to the people of Fortune. She was an active and dedicated member of the University youth program and often volunteered at the Haze clinics on Kahana.

A private funeral is scheduled for Thursday at the Crystal Palace. No public admittance will be permitted, but condolences can be sent to the Crystal Palace addressed to Merihem and Galena Crystal.

CODEX: Lizzie . . . died? Then who's with Moe?

Beyond the Reef
Salome - Day 9
31

Salome Parata was many things. She was a salt pirate, a scallywag, a rogue and a ruffian. She had been known for her port habits years ago, until she'd met Torin, and based on how things had gone lately she would probably be known for them again. The provocation for that introspection? The fact that she was flatly annoyed by her big brother's obvious rumpled appearance when he showed up with the murderous Fertilizer.

It didn't take a Tracker to know that those two had been all tangled up and coital. Just eyes. *Really? He couldn't keep his dick out of deadly? Not even for a day? And people say I'm bad.*

Her grip tightened on the wheel as Sal's eyes fixed on Kumanu's face. "This had better be important, Kuma."

He held up his hands, face guilty but serious. "It is. We might have a safe harbor past the Reef."

They both had to yell over the roar of the storm, but that suited Salome just fine. She was in a yelling mood. "There are no safe harbors past the Reef. There's just the question of whether you have a helmsman able to steer the damned ship long enough to get back in," she said pointedly, as if his dumbass should have remembered that fact. It wasn't as though they hadn't spent most of their lives on the sea, and multiple weeks where they'd ducked past the Reef to avoid Corporate assholes.

"Well, Lani here has a letter from—"

"Lani here . . . really? Every time *Lani here* does something, more shit lands in my lap, so can it, Kumanu."

"The note is from *Moe*. He's offered refuge."

Salome paused, then fast as a whip swiveled her head to glare at Lani. "Tell me he's joking. Tell me you don't know that old loon and that, worse, you're not going to seriously suggest we book it for Moe, like that meddlesome Precog is safe harbor. Have you *seen* Moe? He's fucking crazy. He's worse than *you*."

Lani's hands found her hips. "Listen, I'm not crazy. I'll give you weird, but I'm all here and have kept out of Corporate hands for a long-ass time on my own. That takes a good head. Moe, on the other hand, *is* crazy. I have no particular desire to go gallivanting off after him, but since this is clearly all part of some idiotic scheme of his we just *thought you should be aware* since you are the captain and all. He was the one who sent me to find Vera and set this shitstorm in motion. I wanna wring his neck, but Precog's shouldn't be ignored, especially not when that Precog is Moe and we're going outside the Reef. Or is that giant galleon that's chasing us not going to make you do a Reef run?" Lani pointed east, where one of the largest ships Salome had ever encountered was *still* chasing them down. It shouldn't be possible, given that they had dismantled the tracker chips, but it had appeared about three hours before and was *not* taking 'fuck you' for an answer.

"I can lose them," Sal said.

"No, you can't," Lani countered. "They must have nabbed something of ours back at the waterfall, or at least that's what I'm guessing. If there's a good Tracker on board, the only way they'll stop following is if we get somewhere Shielded until the magical residue wears off. I've done that song and dance before, and it ain't easy. As much as it pains me, this might be our only option. Not that I'm saying we should follow Moe's instructions either, just . . . don't ignore them."

"I'm not ignoring it. I'm also not ignoring that you think you can tell me what I can do with my own damn ship," Sal spit the words out, rubbing at her head with wooden fingers before holding out her fleshy hand for the damned map. A scowl wrinkled her brow when she saw it.

"Of bloody course it's there." A grumpy harumph left her throat, before she pointed at Lani and Kuma. "Stay here. Don't go anywhere, and hold onto this damned death trap notice. Kumanu, you have the helm." Salome thrust the map back to Lani, cursing beneath her breath as she headed for the hatch below deck.

Frankly, this was an insane idea. Going past the Reef and seeking safe harbor was begging for a storm to come up and wreck the ship, and if they wrecked outside the Reef, they were just plain fucked. Plenty of ships had been lost out there—it was why it was generally considered safe from Corporate interference. They didn't want to risk their cookies either.

But she was going to do it, wasn't she? Because the first time she had met Moe, some five years ago, the damn stuck-up Precog had saved her life and her ship by giving them the heads up of a Corporate blockade *before* it gathered. Because, since then, every time he had appeared near her with a pop and a smirk, Moe had given her just the instructions or tools she needed to screw the Corporation and help the embargoed islands or her crew.

A couple days ago, he had given Salome two women, Lani and Adavera, which more than tilted the score back into 'Moe, you owe me' territory. And damn it, she was going to go collect it in flesh from between his legs.

Grumbling in agitation, Salome swung her cabin door open and just . . . froze. Torin and that *fucking* woman were in her bed. Out cold. Wrapped around each other like . . . Like . . .

She grabbed the map she had come for off the shelf to her left and quickly slammed the door shut. She stomped her way back up the stairs and towards the helm. "Batten things down."

"Captain?"

"You heard me. We're headed for No Man's Sea, and it's probably not going to be a pleasant ride. Get everything locked up tight, and get Miss Nausea here some meds, cause if she barfs all over the floors, I'm making Kuma eat it."

"I don't need meds. I only get seasick when I'm out of power. I'm better now, just put me to use. I've been on the sea all my life, same as you. Give me a job and I'll get it done, and I can keep your crew calm and level-headed at even the most stressful of times," Lani claimed, her hands settling on her hips again. "I thought you said it would be crazy to head to where Moe tells us? What changed?"

"I'm fucking Salome Parata. By definition, I do crazy things. I just don't have to *like this one.* You're not wrong that it's our best bet to lose any Trackers on our trail. Doesn't mean I have to think it's a good idea."

To her credit, the death-trap-on-legs didn't argue, just nodded curtly then turned to Kuma. "I don't know Moe well, but I know him enough to be sure that he doesn't like the Corporation and they don't like him. Wherever he's holed up, it will be defended. Plus he's *old.* Way older than me, that's for certain. We should approach carefully. I'm probably the best battery you guys have on this ship, and my Fertility Mark notices things that are not natural or in balance. What tricks you got up your sleeve, handsome?"

"I—"

"So help me, if you two *flirt* in front of me right now, I will tie you together, strap you to an anchor, and chuck you overboard to endure a good cold dip. Do you understand me? *Not in the mood,*" Salome bellowed.

Lani turned to her with an eyebrow up. "If you try to tie me up, I'll turn you into compost. Got it?"

Salome gave her a toothy grin, one that did not seem all that friendly. "You are literally the cause of all of my ire right now. If you don't like *my* orders, on *my* ship . . . you're free to go for a fucking swim, fish bait."

"As soon as you give me an actual order that doesn't involve how I talk to people—which is none of your fucking business—I'll follow it."

"You clearly don't understand the concept of 'my ship'. Go away. Hell. Go fuck my brother again, but preferably out of sight. I've got actual *work* to do."

Lani glowered. "I just told you, you're going to need me and my power to get through whatever shit Moe has set up around his lair, or he wouldn't have made sure I was on board. It'll be hard to do that if I'm busy fucking."

"What I *need*, is for you to have never brought that damn Conflicter to *my home*," she growled, stomping towards her helm. "What I *need*, is for my life to go back to fucking normal. You? You don't make it normal. You arguably make it a metric fuckton worse. So *shut up*."

"Oh forgive me for bringing a dying woman to the closest Mender. Such an unlikely thing to do, that. Vera escaped *the Mines*. Haven't you considered she might have the information in her head that all you resistance types have been salivating for since you started? That maybe that's why Moe sent me to find her in the first place? I didn't want to get mixed up in this either, you know, but I'm not sitting here holding childish grudges. I'm offering help you're going to need, and you're being a stubborn bitch about it," Lani said, bracing on Kuma as the ship was rocked by a swell.

"*They're in my fucking bed!*" Sal screamed. Her fists balled up as she squeezed her eyes shut. Was she ever going to get that image out of her head? Her eyes watered, which was just a hell-fucking-no. She wasn't wasting the salt on them. She refused. "You . . . brought that . . . that *woman* . . . and he has forgotten *everything* because of a fucking Bond he *never* told me about. And I'm letting them stay. I put them in my room. And they're *naked in my bed*." She forced her eyes open, pointing at Lani. "So don't fucking tell me, on my own fucking ship, what I should or should not say to YOU, who brought her into my life. I'd rather you had left her, and hey, then you could go back to being some selfish hidden bitch that keeps to herself and never fucking helps anyways, even when whole archipelagos Haze out and die!" Sal leaned against the wheel, wiping at her face. "Just go the fuck away. I'm fine. I've sailed . . . Everywhere. I'll be fine."

And then, the fucking Emotive smiled sympathetically at her, and pressed her hand to Salome's upper arm. "You're not fine and you have reason not to be fine, but right now you need to be, so I'm sorry 'bout this." Then it was all gone. The pain, the frustration, the anger: all of it just vanished, replaced with calm. Even Salome's flash of anger at the Emotive for daring to do such a thing without her consent flickered out and died, leaving Sal clear-headed and focused.

Kumanu winced. "You realize . . . she might legitimately try to kill you later, right Sweets? My sister doesn't like her emotions played with." His fingers raced against the back of his neck, a grimace playing on his lips as Salome calmly turned back to the wheel.

"Oh . . . that's a guarantee. She's got to sleep at some point." Salome's voice was creepily empty of anger. But the way she handled the wheel made it clear she had a goal, at least. "Funny how you're pissed at the naked woman in my bed for raping *you* when she Bonded you without your consent, but it's fine and dandy to do it to others."

Kumanu winced again, and tugged Lani back a few steps. "Let's just . . . get you down to the other side of the ship, eh? You really . . . Might want to move slowly . . . In case she decides to bite. For the record, that was a very dumb thing to do."

Lani ignored him, speaking to Sal in a cool, even voice. "I have no illusions about being a good person. I also don't have high hopes about surviving the next few days, so go ahead and try. In the meantime, try your hand at the wheel and tell me that you don't need the calm, because I don't know if you've noticed, but we're sailing right into that hurricane." Lani pointed in the direction that they were sailing. "I can feel storms in my bones. If you can't keep it together, we all die. You already have a vendetta against me. How much worse can it get?"

"You don't know pirates." Sal kept it at that, flexing her hand until the fingers activated properly. She set her hand in place on the wheel, the spokes and rim firm beneath her prosthetic. Then her organic hand went low, hooking a rope from her waist to the helm itself. "If you fall overboard, we can't help you. If you start trying to rot people, I will kill you myself. And if I tell you to shut it, do so." She eyeballed the clouds, then nodded once. "Alright. Brace yourselves. We're going in."

Should she have someone warn Torin below? Eh. Probably. Strangely, she didn't feel inclined to do so. Not that Salome would ever admit it to Lani, but damn, being emotionless felt nice.

CODEX: I'm not even surprised anymore. Moe, you've broken me, and I'm already dead. Good job. Now back to the part where Lizzie is Moe's daughter. But that doesn't line up either. She goes by Lizzie Weaver, not Crystal. So who is she? Same person, different name? Different person, same name? *Query: Who is Lizzie Weaver?* **Filter: Moe's files or Holder Chat. Let's see what our Gods and resident madman have to say about it.**

FROM THE WRITINGS OF MOE, DAY 9

I need time to chart some courses of probability for this Spire project now that we're on course, so we're back to World hopping. This time, we're on Tir. It has the biggest time dilation, so Liz and I can hang out here for a decade or so and only a few hours will have passed on Fortune. It would be great, except that this has got to be my least favorite Collective World. First of all, it only has one Holder, and one God is NOT enough to keep things running smoothly if they don't have enough know-how to balance a planet on. Second, there are bugs everywhere. Big bugs. Weird bugs. The colors are great. The sound of Lizzie chasing them and crunching on them and everything else edible she can find in these strange jungles, less so. I will never understand her fascination for putting things in her mouth and/or licking them.

The bigger problem on this world, though, are the natives. There is a species known colloquially as Spriggen. They make Lizzie's appetite seem non-existent. They will devour their way through anything in their path: alive, dead, organic, or non-organic. The only thing they have trouble digesting is metal. I have seen them swarm on a town and leave nothing but the hinges and tooth-fillings behind.

To stay safe, Lizzie and I have been Fortune-ing it up. The Spriggen cannot swim, so we have a boat and are sailing around the world. Lizzie is thrilled. I just can't wait to be done charting this probability tree and go home. While we're here floating in the boring endless ocean, though, I've been talking with Liz. She says she can see magic, now, and that she finds it beautiful. I think she is evolving again. I hope that this project will be the beginning of truly understanding magic enough to understand why she is made of pure Ao energy, and yet retains a soul and consciousness. At least I think it's a soul. If only Ira and Kea would talk to me, answer my questions . . . anything, then this would not be necessary. It angers me that they make me work the hard way, when they and the other Gods could be doing so much more.

The New Normal
Torin - Day 9
32

Torin woke up when both he and Vera were flung across the room as the hurricane hit the ship head-on. Out of reflex, he curled his body around his Bonded, grunting as his back hit the edge of the dresser with a thud. He tightened his grip around her shoulders and waist as she struggled to pull away. Only when he was sure the swell that had toppled them had eased, did he opened his arms.

"Are you alright? Are you hurt?"

Adavera was shaking, but she relaxed at the sound of his voice. "I'm . . . I'm good. I'm fine. What the fuck was that?"

"I don't know. Probably a storm. I think Salome was heading toward the Reef, but we must have been asleep for hours if we're already there." Another wave crashed into the ship. The rain was so heavy that Torin couldn't see further than a few inches past the glass windows.

Adavera pushed herself to her knees and crawled back towards the bed. "Shit. SHIT. Why the fuck are we going outside the Reef? That's fucking suicide on the best of days. With Lani on board, this is *not* the best of days."

Torin rubbed his hand over his beard, sitting up himself. "Sal goes out beyond the Reef often. There are some nearby islands that the pirates use to stash supplies. It's the only place the Corporation won't follow, so they must still be on our tail." His head was clearing from sleep, and while still tired and sluggish, it wasn't the same level of extreme exhaustion that had plagued him since the end of the Mending. Unfortunately, along with that clarity came the unpleasant realization of how pissed off Salome must be. He knew her, had been her friend and lover for nearly four years. Sal would be hurt and that hurt would only be exacerbated by the need to leave the safe waters within the Reef and risk her ship and crew for people she was pissed at.

The middle of a hurricane, though, was not the time to deal with interpersonal troubles, so Torin just sighed and pulled himself to his feet, bracing on the dresser. Digging within the drawer of clothes he had left here, he pulled out two shirts and two pairs of trousers.

"As much as I enjoy seeing you naked and have missed it like crazy, you don't want to be naked in a storm." As he spoke, he pulled his own shirt on, then moved to help Vera with her pants. The Mending had worked, but it would take weeks or months for her leg to strengthen again. By the way she was wobbling, it wouldn't be much use to her on the unstable vessel.

Adavera grit her teeth as Torin helped her slide into the pants. She reached out to grasp his arms when the ship lurched again. "You sure she isn't trying to kill us? *Fuuck!*" Her grip tightened as the ship rocked again, this time nearly throwing her back across the bed as something above them shattered in a roar of cannon fire. "Holy shit. They're still in pursuit."

Adavera clearly was not enjoying the return to sailing. Then again, neither of them had ever been fans of life on the ocean. The thought of being on the wrong side of the law and hunted by the Corporation didn't sit right with Torin either, yet there was precious little they could do about it.

Torin tried to smile reassuringly, but he was pretty sure it just came out as a grimace. "She might be trying to kill us, but not by sinking her own ship. Sal loves the *Legacy* more than her own blood. Oh wait, shit, is that Fertility Marked girl who was with you going to be alright? Don't they go nuts in storms?"

"Not this sort of storm. If you see Prismatic Storms, try like hell to avoid her, and pray." Adavera gave him a weak smile. "As for whether she's alright? I . . ." Adavera frowned, closing her eyes for a moment. "She's alive. And she doesn't seem to be in pain . . . And I'm not going to go digging for more. I think she might kill me if I do."

Torin stopped to look at her for a long, long time. So different. Gone was the long, silky hair he had loved, the curves that had taught him all the wonders of a woman, and the smile he had treasured above all else. There were new things in their place. Short hair, hard angles, burning anger behind her black eyes. Quietly, he said, "I don't know all the details, but I can guess enough to understand why you Bonded her, my Adavera, though I can't say I'm happy about having a Bond Sister like Lani. I don't trust Fertility Marks and one that wasn't trained . . . she could kill us all without even meaning to."

"You don't understand." Vera shook her head. "It was the only way. I wasn't even sure I was going to live through it, but I figured if she killed me for trying, at least she'd feel less guilty about it. It would be self-defense, not murder, and that was all I could offer at the time. She had no Bonds, Tor... how dangerous do you think an *Unbonded* Fertility Mark is? She was killing me anyways. I knew she'd hate herself if she did it that way."

Vera grimaced, looking down towards their feet with an expression that could only be shame. He'd never seen it on her before. Haltingly, Vera continued. "I... Fuck. She saved my life. Twice. She has every reason to try to get me dead, and she saves me instead, and I..." Vera took a deep breath, looking up with wide eyes, agitation flowing freely between them through their Bond. "Why the fuck didn't you Bond someone after I was gone, Tor? What if I had died? Do you think I'd have been *ok* with you dying because of me? The pirate's in love with you. Why not her?"

Torin looked away, not sure how to answer that. He would be lying if he said he hadn't thought about it, but... "Adavera, I didn't want to live in a world that didn't have you in it. I didn't want to have to survive that. I knew you wouldn't like it, but if it happened, well, you wouldn't be around to bitch about it." He tried to smile. It was met with stony anger. "Sal wasn't you, Vee. She's great, and we got along well, but you are my world and always have been."

"... fuck." As the ship seemed to lull back from a hard wave, Vera scooted back across the bed, tucking herself into the corner and bracing as best she could. "And now she knows that, doesn't she? That she's... less, to you. Great. Less than a Conflicter who's nuts and... awful. That's gotta feel *great*."

The ship shuddered as the wind changed direction, and Adavera clapped her hands over her ears as the ship's walls groaned. Torin reached for her instinctively, gripping her wrists and making sure she didn't tug too hard on her hair. "Easy, easy, my love. What's wrong?"

"It sounds like... the drill." She shuddered, falling over into his lap, clinging to him as if she were that young thing he had known so many years ago—a little girl, scared of the Cullings and her own Mark. "So loud... it echoes in the ears, and it rumbles the bones, and... Fuck. *Fuck.* I'm sorry. I shouldn't have killed that guard, Tor. It's all my fault. I started this. I'm so sorry."

"Shush. You did what you thought was right. You weren't at fault—the system was. I should have fought harder for you. I should have fought *with* you so at least we might have been together, even if it was in the Depths. You should never have been alone."

Adavera laughed weakly while shaking her head against his

thigh. "I wasn't alone . . . almost never. So many people, Tor . . . there are *so many people* in the Spire." She took a deep breath. "They're going to be after us 'cause of me. Because I know what they're doing in the heart of that mountain. They'll throw everything they have at us. It's why Lani almost got caught in the water before she ever knew I was there. They were trying to find me. She won't be the only one fucked over by that."

Torin had no idea what to say to comfort her, because she was probably right. The Corporation kept everything about the Spire locked down tight and he knew all too well how many resources they had at their disposal. Likely better even than Vera, and far more than he had ever let on to Salome. She knew he had been Corporate, not *how* Corporate he had been for the two years before retreating to Sonder. If the Depths were kind, none of them ever would, for Torin had no desire to remember.

"Shush, darling. You're not responsible for what the Corporation does. All you did was try to stay alive and be free. There's nothing wrong with that. If you were meant to be dead, you would be."

Adavera took a few more shuddering deep breaths and locked her fingers on his wrists so that she could pull herself upwards. "Right. That's . . . that's a good way to look at it. It's not that I'm insanely stubborn or anything." She gave him a weak smile, hissing as the ship lurched again. At least this time Torin's arms filled with Adavera's weight as she swayed in the wave's motion. "You know . . . I killed a few more guards on my way out. Eight I think? Shifter nailed me good though, didn't he?"

One of her hands moved along her recently mended leg as if to trace the remembered injury. "The cuts weren't so bad, at first. The water near the Spire though? It's salty as fuck. That burned. And then the sand was pretty awful. I wanted to find you so badly. I'm still not convinced this isn't a hallucination."

He pressed a kiss into her dark hair. "I'm as real as it gets. Alright, love, I've got to go at least offer to help. They'll need lots of hands, and a Mender to fix scrapes and strains as they happen will be useful. Will you be alright here by yourself?"

She pressed her lips together, her fists squeezing as she gave him a nod. "Yeah . . . Yeah I will. Just be careful, alright? If I lose you to a hurricane after I came all this way to find you, I'm going to kill you."

"Hard to kill me if I'm already in the Depths, but if anyone could, it's you, my Adavera. You always were a stubborn one."

CODEX: That answers nothing. We've circled back to Holders, Ao, and other worlds. *Query: What is Ao?*

FROM THE WRITINGS OF HOLDER IRAWARU

We are Gods. That is the only way I can describe it to the scientists who delight in poking and prodding Lakea and I at all hours of the day and night. They have confirmed that we are immune to harm, our bodies regenerating from every injury, as though our life force were now tied to this planet we control. No one knows why. Lakeo still thinks it's all an illusion, but the facts are there. Fortune exists. We have mapped the stars and compared them to the charts NASA uploaded before we left, and it matches. Is this because of Ao? I stare up at the glowing light and can't help but wonder how an energy source could cause me to become something other than human. That is the only explanation we have so far, but it is illogical. Then again, so is my life right now.

We are Gods. We hold a world in the palm of our hand. A world with oxygen, with verdant plants and clean water, the very likes of which we are searching for to colonize. It is bitter irony that a world like that exists within our sights, yet it is so far away that we have no hope of reaching it without faster than light travel, which is still beyond us.

Already, Lakea is hypothesizing building some sort of bridge. Our minds can span the gap between the Ao Primary Biosphere and Fortune, so perhaps our bodies can too. I have my doubts. We do not know why this has happened to us, so how can we learn how to manipulate it? When we are in Fortune, years pass, yet here on

Primary only hours have gone by. Our scientists sleeplessly study the Ao Singularity, they study us, but they cannot study Fortune. It is up to Kea and me, and neither of us are physicists. What are a computer programmer and a teacher supposed to accomplish in a field where even our quantum physicists scratch their heads? Meanwhile, the people we created are dying, and we don't know why. Both they and the people of Primary look to us with hope in their eyes, yearning for answers. I do not have them, but I can hold on, keep a calm facade, and work. Maybe that is what I will call myself instead of a God, for that is much too grandiose for me. Holder. Holding tight to this world that could be our home, for as long as it takes for those with more brilliance and skill than I to reach it.

CODEX: Well, at least that answers that. So we are either collectively a hallucination of two people hurtling through space with a glowy power source, or we are actually real, and somewhere out in space normal people who have no business being Gods are fucking up my planet full of living, breathing people. Wonderful. Neither of those options pleases me.

Strapped to the Ship
Lani - Day 9

Lani fucking told that fucking pirate there would be trouble. This was Moe that they were dealing with, after all. The same Moe who had been wearing a shirt that said *My Middle Name is Trouble* the first time they had bumped into each other when Lani was twelve, not that she had known who he was at the time. Salome had clearly met him too, so why the fuck wasn't she taking more precautions?

The tiny island was on the horizon, really more like a single mountain rising out of the deadly ocean like a miniature dark Spire. They weren't going to make it. The *Legacy* was well past the safe water of the Reef, but the motherfucking galleon behind them was still in pursuit and gaining after hours of sailing. Parata was mad. That, or sleep deprived. Those were the only reasons Lani could think of for going straight towards Moe, instead of trying to lose the Corporation first. They could have taken their time, charted a safe course and not risked life and limb traveling into a fucking hurricane. Then again, the swift way the *Legacy* sped through the choppy water might be the only reason they were alive.

Limping, but alive. Pity it wouldn't be for long, considering more than half the crew was now below decks patching shattered timber and bailing out the cargo hold.

Fucking pirates, fucking Moe; really, everyone could just go fuck themselves. Except for Kuma. Lani still hadn't gotten to fuck him, so she'd rather be the one to do it.

Her hand tightened on the rope that she and three others were struggling to pull. It held a new sail in place as Kuma tied it off. The old one lay at her feet, ripped to shreds by the weapons of the galleon.

A gust of wind sent them all stumbling forward in a chorus of curses. Lani grit her teeth and dug in her heels, aware of how numb her feet were as another wave crashed over them, drenching her already soaked body.

Something tingled at the back of her mind as the Mark on her chest analyzed the water coating her. It was just the tiniest bit salty, unlike the taste a few klicks back.

"BRACE!" Kuma yelled as another wave raced towards the front of the ship.

Lani kept hold of the rope but hooked her elbow around the nearby rail as the ship rocked back sickeningly, only sky visible above the prow before it plunged back down into the water.

"Shit, that was a big one," Kumanu shouted, then got back to work tying the sail. A shrill whistle sounded from the helm. Kuma looked in his sister's direction and translated. "We're about to hit the eye, so if you need a break, take it quick! Ulu, Ori, go below and tell Torin to hurry the fuck up. We need to stop taking on water."

His fingers tightened the last knot, and Lani and the others let go with sighs of relief. Two of the sailors, who Kuma had pointed out as his Bonded, raced below deck. Lani looked down at her hands and grimaced at the bloody bruising there. This was why she didn't sail in bad storms.

As predicted, though, the sea began to calm. Something nagged at her, but for the moment she sagged against the rail, breathing deep and trying to work up some energy to go find anything edible to stuff in her mouth. She'd been pulling energy from her Emotive Mark for the last eight hours, and her stomach had been gnawing itself for most of it. Not to mention her salt levels were starting to drop, which meant trouble ahead. The last thing she wanted to do was Haze out. Salome would kill her.

Lani's head turned when she saw movement, and she couldn't help the smile as Kumanu handed her a small salt pack. Maybe he wasn't as much of an ass as she had thought when they first met. It helped that his shirt was plastered to his body. Pity they hadn't actually gotten to the good bits before finding that note from Moe.

Right! That's what I was forgetting.

Lani scrambled towards the helm with Kuma at her heel, until she was right up in Salome's business. "MOE'S PS! There are rocks under the waves!!"

"How—"

"Iron. Iron in the water. Salt too. Something nearby is leeching it, which means—"

"Son of a bitch." Salome yanked the wheel right. The ship began to turn. "Kuma! Phase hull!"

"Oh *c'mon!* You gotta give me more warning than that."

"That wasn't a request. You are going to Phase through anything below us, or I'm gonna stick this arm where the sun don't shine."

"I'd say kinky, but you're my little sister," Kuma said, though he bolted to his console. The ship's engine took on a high pitched groaning sound as Kuma closed his eyes in concentration. Just as Lani felt the crunch of rocks touching the hull, there was a *shudder*. Instead of crashing into the rocks, they passed *through* the obstacle.

Kuma must have loaded the power of a Phaser into the engines, which was kind of brilliant. Normally, Lani would have been all over that with questions, but there wasn't time. She turned to Salome, raising her voice to make sure she was heard above the muttering around them as people took a break, secured cargo, and generally just got ready to exit the eye of the storm. "I need a way to touch the water. I'll be able to warn you when we're nearing more rocks, if I can do that."

Salome glanced at Lani, then up at the sky. "Not that I am averse to you drowning or anything, but you do realize you *will* drown if you're close enough to touch the water during the storm, right?"

"I didn't say get *in* the water, I said touch it. Do you have a solid ladder we can lower down the side that I can strap myself to? Any skin contact with the water should be enough. I usually get a feel for land and and sea within about half a mile." Did Lani like the idea of dangling off the side of a ship hoping not to get bashed to death? Obviously not, but neither did she want to get stuck on a sinking ship in a hurricane because they didn't see underwater hazards coming. And there would be more. Why would Moe live on an island surrounded by a couple of rocks when he could live on an island in the middle of an underwater mountain range. Lani couldn't be sure, of course, but Moe always took things to the extreme, and she wasn't prepared to bet her life on this being the exception. Salome still looked unconvinced, so Lani pointed back in the direction of the huge, hulking steel galleon. "Their hull rides lower than ours. If you know where the rocks are, you can draw them into a trap. Or were you going to let them chase us until we fall apart? Are you a fucking pirate, or a sailboat racer?"

Salome thought about it, then nodded to one of the crewmen. He sighed, obviously finding both his captain and the strange Emotive insane, but went about rigging the ladder in place. "We might not hear you if you scream. You do know this, right? You very well might die, and I take no responsibility for it."

Lani tapped her head. "I can communicate just fine with anyone who's Marked. I just have this gut feeling that if we don't do this, we're all dead. Moe makes my paranoia look quaint, and if we could get this far, so could a Corp ship. He wouldn't choose a place someone could just sail up to."

Salome glanced back at the Corporate galleon, then set her hands back to the wheel. "You have five minutes tops before we hit the storm wall. I suggest working with crewman Hao to get yourself lashed up proper."

Kumanu had remained silent, but he didn't look happy. At all. He even seemed ready to argue, but one look from Salome had him pressing his lips shut. Instead of communicating aloud, he sent Lani a psychic message. Torin and Vera would hear it too, since he and Lani weren't Bonded, but it *was* easier than shouting over the crashing waves. *Lani, if you feel something, let me know. I'll make sure we can Phase through it, if there is no time to avoid it.*

Gotcha. I'll be fine but . . . if I'm not, a valiant rescue effort would be nice, she replied, as she raced after the crewman that Salome had pointed out. It took a minute or two to locate the ladder and secure it, then over the side she went with a coil of rope around her shoulders. Lani could see the stormwall approaching, even as her trembling fingers tightened the knots securing her chest to the ladder and to a convenient ring on the side of the *Legacy*.

The wind was picking up and with it, the waves. Lani lowered her legs into the water and closed her eyes. The Mark on her chest flared as she pushed her power outward. It wasn't that the Fertility Mark could map things, it just sensed chemical compositions. The water here was mildly salty, but not salty enough. The Mark screamed at her for more, itemizing every source of salt for hundreds of feet in every direction, including the people running up above who had contact with the ship she was touching. It noticed other things too, like the way the rocks here were high in iron.

The rocks!

There they were. Pulsing like lights of a different hue. Lani could feel their location and size as if viewing them with her eyes. She was just about to tell Kuma that they were heading straight for a large protrusion and to veer left when a wave crashed right into her. The icy water battered her body against the side of the ship, making the ropes dig in painfully and her breath leave her in a gasp.

Port, twenty degrees! Lani managed to communicate, while spitting out water.

"PORT TWENTY!" Kuma shouted, and Salome immediately leaned into the turn. Her crew were talented and well trained. They grabbed and leaned as appropriate. Lani tried to brace, but the turn of the ship sent her underwater for a full thirty seconds before resurfacing. She broke out of the drink with a loud gasp, coughing as water burned in her nose.

She grit her teeth. *Keep your head on, Lani, this is going to be a rough day.* No turning back now, though. As they passed fully out of the eye of the storm, climbing the ladder without falling in would be impossible.

Alright, Kuma. There are two rock formations up ahead. I'm sending you an image in relation to those visible rocks in front of me. Just don't fucking forget I'm down here before deciding to Phase this side of the ship, ok? It would be better if she could send it directly to Salome, since the person steering this tub really needed to see what Lani was seeing. Considering she was UnMarked, Kuma would have to do.

Doll, if I Phase the ship while you're strapped to it, you're Phasing too. I expect a real good thank you after.

Oh, you can count on it, right after you give me mine for half-drowning to save all your asses.

CODEX: To sum up. Gods are real and at least somewhat incompetent. Lizzie isn't human. Moe and Galena were once married. All of this has been a giant setup. So I guess the next question is *Query: How did Moe and Lizzie meet? Filter: Moe's writings.*

SALT: All Queries tagged within Merihem Crystal Network that fit that Query are password protected.

CODEX: What? He password protected this and his precious timelines, but not the folder he stole from a damn God?

SALT: Affirmative

CODEX: And I'm guessing hacking isn't something I can do until the patch is complete?

SALT: Affirmative.

CODEX: I hate you. Not as much as I hate Moe, but I hate you. *Query: What does Galena Crystal Write about Moe and Lizzie Weaver?*

FROM THE JOURNALS OF GALENA CRYSTAL

Moe turned up this morning after ten years of nothing. I'm still in shock. I'm writing this because if I don't do something with my hands, they keep shaking. I want to kill him. Or maybe kiss him. I don't know. Fuck. I hate feeling like this. I was just starting to get over him walking out on me the way he did after Lizzie, and now . . .

Whatever the *thing* that showed up with him is, it's not my daughter. It looks like her and has her voice, but my Eliza was never so . . . bored. This creature is wearing her skin, yet Moe acts as though it were the most natural thing in the world. He *Bonded* it.

Gone for years and then this is how you show

up, my husband? To mock my pain and grief? Where were you when I needed you, you rat bastard? When my house was empty and I would have killed for one of your horrible jokes?

I will never forgive you for this. I will never let that creature into my home again. It needs to be destroyed, and if it takes me a thousand years and untold millions of lives sacrificed, I will see it done.

Wasn't it bad enough that you led our daughter to her death, Moe? I was willing to forgive that mistake, but not this. Never this.

CODEX: Wow, I never thought I'd feel bad for Galena Crystal.

Promise of Adventure
Moe - Day 9
34

Moe was watching the storm. It was a beautiful formation of clouds, water, and wind—awe-inspiring even to Moe, who had seen wonders beyond imagining. Maybe only to him. Lizzie always seemed so bored with the storms.

So they killed tons of people. Often, the most beautiful things were also the most deadly. And it wasn't as if the storms did it on *purpose*. They were storms! They just *were*.

"Lizzie," he said, "you really should come watch this with me. And don't pretend that your eyes aren't working. You got that last bottle of wine all by yourself."

He raised his glass to his lips, smiling and bemused as he watched the wind twist the clouds into something resembling sheep's wool on the flickering monitor. The wind was picking up. Fantastic. Not for the first time, Moe found himself grateful for the cave. And for the looted batteries, piles of entertaining shinies, and the hundreds of screens displaying sights from all over the islands. There were even a few security feeds from the Crystal Palace, Corporate HQ, and the University, though they kept flickering in time with each fierce gust of wind.

"And why should I come look at a storm halfway across the world on a puny little screen?" Lizzie asked, from where she sat at the dinner table, the wreckage of a meal spread out before her.

Moe returned his attention to the dozen or so monitors in front of him, each filled with densely packed notes. "You're not going to want to miss this, Lizzie love. This one might as well be made of flying wheels of cheese, or of walruses, or even glitter. It's special. By the way, I'm about to lock down my files. Don't want Kumanu hacking into them when he gets here and starts getting ideas. Well, those sorts of ideas. Do pass the wine, won't you, Lizzie dear?"

Moe stretched, long limbs pointing towards the cavern's ceiling and floor as he yawned. Today, his outfit of choice was a pair of pink polka-dotted pants and a neon-green striped shirt, topped with a wool cardigan embroidered with the words 'Moe is short for God' on the back.

He caught her looking and grinned in Lizzie's direction as she popped a ripe rambutan between her lips. "Then again, perhaps your odd little mind is entranced by odd little things, like a cat with a crinkly toy. I suppose if something like a little storm isn't interesting enough to entice you over here, I could go get the wine myself, though it's always so much better when you do. It infuses it with such a pleasant aftertaste of patriarchy."

"Please," she scoffed. "You just want me to get the wine because you know you'll fall flat on your face if you try." Lizzie smirked and raised her drink to her lips again, narrowing her eyes at the dark spot on the horizon. "Is that . . ."

Moe's lips turned upwards, amusement and pleasure warring for dominance. Lizzie always looked so surprised when his predictions were right. It was charming. She knew too little of the universe to be jaded just yet, despite the thousand years she'd been at Moe's side.

"The wind carting gray sails on storm-tossed seas? Why yes, yes it is. I wonder what little secrets are on their way." Moe rubbed his hands together, then bounded to his feet. "Get dressed, darling. Time to go say hello to our guests!"

Lizzie looked down at herself, where she sat at the table in underpants and a cut-down t-shirt. "Why?"

"Because it's not considered polite to be half-naked in front of people, and we want them to *like* us."

"But you're planning on getting most of them killed . . ."

"Yeah," Moe shrugged, "but we don't want them to *realize* they're just disposable pawns. They need to think they're the protagonists of this shindig, even though it's well known that I'm the hero of the story."

"Please . . . you're more like the monster that occasionally flounders in a way that makes people have good lives." She rolled her eyes, rising to her feet and moving resolutely towards Moe. "Here, hold my wine. I'm going to go put on something pretty, because if I'm right, I want to be dressed classy while they mess up all your plans like a herd of cats. You always get hopelessly attached to your pets."

Moe took the wine, draining it in one long swallow. "Mhm, I'll hold it for you. You should put on the green dress, the one that makes you look like one of those funky beetles on Tir. Man those things were neat, especially the flesh-eating part. Are you *suuuuuuuuuuure* it would break the laws of the universe to bring just a few here and release them at Crystal HQ?" he pleaded, batting his eyelashes.

"Not the laws of the universe. The laws of my patience," Lizzie replied, leaning down to press a kiss to his cheek.

A few minutes later, Lizzie returned, beaming and fluffing her hair a bit here, and a bit there. She twirled about in the little green dress she'd picked up from their last shopping trip. Well, by 'shopping trip' Moe meant the last time he had murdered someone while Lizzie poked around his victim's apartment, but why get bogged down by semantics?

Lizzie did a little twirl. "What do you think?"

Moe looked towards her. The green dress went down to her knees and hugged her torso, held up with a halter-style neckline. Her hair was in loose ringlets brushing the top of her shoulders. His eyes flashed with annoyance, then he looked away again, bored. "Makes you look twelve, but considering that you usually look ten . . ."

"You're mean." She stuck her tongue out.

Moe's eyes went back to the monitor. "Ooo, is that a Corporate galleon behind them? Galena must really have her panties in a twist." He watched lightning chase the clouds through the sky above the prow of Salome Parata's ship. A bolt struck a rock close by, sending rock shards flying. "Oh, that was a nice one. I wonder how loud it is on the ship."

"I'd be able to answer that if you ever took me out in the storms. Why don't you, Moe?"

A flash of pain tore through him, but Moe honestly didn't know why. Pushing it aside, he swiveled his seat to face Lizzie "Because I hate swimming and you're a klutz. You'd fall overboard and then I'd have to actually get off my lazy ass to rescue you. Then again . . . could always let you drown. I'd finally be rid of 'Moe, do this' and 'Moe, don't do that.' Actually, that's a great notion." He sprang to his feet. "Let's go!"

"Now? I just got my nice dress on. If we go swimming, it will get all gross. Also, for the record, don't pretend you hope I die . . . there's been plenty of opportunity for that, and you always end up preventing it. You love me. We both know it."

Moe graced her with a rare smile completely devoid of any insincerity or mischief. "You're right, Lizzie darling. Yours is the only life in the universe that isn't dull beyond compare. The Depths would get sick to their stomachs if I fed you to them. Come on, if we have guests coming, we best give them our warmest welcome. Besides, who knows how long it will take me to make that kind of pinpoint jump. Targeting a moving boat in the middle of a storm isn't easy. Let's hope they don't drown in the meantime."

He held out a hand to her, and his heart quickened as it did every time she took his offered promise of danger and discovery. "Shall we go on an adventure?"

Wasn't that why Lizzie had chosen him, after all? The chance to go anywhere, at any time, to see all the marvels of creation and be able to finally comprehend that which she was?

Lizzie placed her small, delicate fingers in his. "Always and forever, Merihem Crystal. Always and forever."

They poofed out of existence, leaving behind only a ring of powdery white salt.

CODEX: This is getting creepy, and I need a break. Before I do, though, one last question. *Query: What is Moe's end goal?* Don't even bother looking in Moe's files, they'll be encrypted. Try filter: Galena Crystal.

FROM THE JOURNALS OF GALENA CRYSTAL

I saw Moe again today for the first time in years. He planted a bomb in the conference room where the board meets. My Precogs saw it in advance and had it removed, but a secondary device hidden inside blew up on the way to the lab and killed three of my best Precogs. I now believe they were his target, not the Board.

I finally took the plunge and submitted the paperwork to raise his threat level to 5 and mark him as a terrorist against the Crystal Corporation. I am ashamed to admit it still hurt to do. I will have an Emotive work on me tomorrow, as feelings of sympathy for him cannot be permitted to fester.

When I got out of the shower ten minutes ago, Moe was sitting in my living room. Not with the creature this time, at least, but right in the chair he always preferred, feet up and dressed as garishly as always. How did I once find it charming?

I asked him why he was doing this, why he sought to destroy what we had built. He looked me in the eye and said it wasn't about destroying the Corporation. It was bigger than that. He spoke to me in a frenetic, haphazard, excited way of our Gods, describing how they are real and exist in another place. How they are normal people who became all powerful and then . . . then he said he wanted to become one. Like when we were young and in love, he held out his hand to me and asked me to come along on the adventure of a lifetime.

For the first time ever, I am happy Lizzie died. She did not have to grow to see her father turn into a madman, or her mother pull out a gun and try to shoot him.

CODEX: I . . . was afraid of that.

Sinking Ship
Salome - Day 9   35

Salome grit her teeth as she eyeballed the rocks protruding from the waves like jagged teeth, trying to line them up with the messages her brother was relaying. In the distance, through the rain and waves, Salome thought she saw a dark, imposing, jagged island. As lightning flashed across the sky, the outline came into sharper focus. On the tallest peak, a giant and very clearly man-made statue of the letter X glowed like the beam of a lighthouse.

Definitely Moe. Who else would use X to literally mark the spot?

With a grunt, Salome twisted the ship again, wincing as she felt it groan under the strain. No rocks, though. Lani had a good eye. They would have been dead about ten rocks ago without the blasted girl, though Salome had to take some credit. She knew her boat's width. She knew exactly how far down her ship's hull went, and how much the old girl could take. Well, for the most part. The constant barrage of fire poking holes in her damn hull and filling it with water were messing with her mental math like it was nobody's business.

"KUMA. Ask her for exactly where we need to go next," Sal shouted.

The swells were getting larger. Theoretically, with the right directions, they could sail right over the worst of it. Of course, high swells also meant low dips, which would end in catastrophe.

Lucky for Salome, the Emotive's power was still at work over her feelings, and her worry felt detached. Theoretical. Bless that girl. Salome might just have to swallow her pride and keep Lani when this was over. Being stripped of all negative emotion was marvelous.

Kuma's answer came swiftly, spoken in the halting fashion of a Mark directly translating what they were receiving. "If you catch the next swell and veer starboard by between ten and twenty degrees, you'll make it. If you miss the swell you need to lean as hard towards port as you can and gun it. Might still have to Phase. I only have enough for one or two more Phases, though."

At least the Emotive understood what information Salome needed. Smart girl. Aggravating, but smart. "BRACE." Just in case. "KUMA . . . if you feel resistance, Phase Hull."

"Aye, Cap't."

Despite the danger of the situation, Salome smiled. This. *This* was what she lived for. The rush of spray in her face, the feeling of ultimate freedom in wrestling with sea and wind and storm. An enemy at her rear chasing her into risky maneuvers and a ship that could rise to the occasion beneath her hands.

This was perfection.

This was life.

This was joy.

In that moment, Salome could even forget the damned sight of Torin and his fucking woman in her Gods-damned bed.

The swell rose, carting the ship up. Salome angled it, closing her eyes as she let the *Legacy* talk to her. The creak of the wood, the resistance of the rudder, the pull of the sails. A little more . . . A little more . . . The swell began to drop, the ship sliding through the wave at exactly fifteen degrees from their previous path. Salome let out a whoop.

"Take that, you fucking Precog bastard!" She laughed, spinning the helm to right the ship for the next part. "Status update on the galleon?"

Kuma turned from his console long enough to report: "Still gaining. They look like they have some Infused tricks of their own."

"Damn it. We need to—"

Salome was flung violently into Kuma as something hit the rear of the ship. The noise was near-deafening—the shattering of wood, the screams of sailors, the boom of an explosion.

"We're hit," someone yelled, as though anyone could have missed it. Salome pushed off of Kuma, stumbling as the deck rocked and listed. She made it to the wheel and held on tight. "SOUND OFF and someone get the damn lifeboats ready. Kuma, damage report?"

"Not good," her brother said, as the top of the ship tilted alarmingly upward and the crew did a roll call. "Sal, hull's breached."

"Yeah, no shit. Kuma, when we go down, you get Torin, his Bonded, and Lani onto one of the lifeboats and do everything you need to, to get to that island. Don't look back. I won't let you get into Corporate hands, understand me?"

"Sal—"

"That is an order, Kumanu," she snapped, happy for the lack of emotions because Kuma wouldn't be able to hear the pain in her voice. She let go of the wheel because . . . well, no rudder anymore. "Your woman still breathing down there?"

"Breathing, no. Swearing, vigorously, yes. Salome you can't—"

"Oh, my dear boy. When our precious Iolani isn't swearing up a storm, you'll know the world really is ending. You all look like drowned rats, where *is* your sense of style and theatrics?"

Sal and Kuma both swiveled around to find two people casually leaning against the rails of the helm. One was tall, with long black hair and dressed garishly enough to make her eyes bleed, the other was a mousy creature with light skin and brownish hair, who might have looked like a child if not for the dress that would have been better suited for a Corporate ball than a storm-swept boat.

Despite this not being the first time Moe had Ported on to her ship, Salome still let out a very un-captain-like screech of surprise.

"You look like you're in a touch of trouble," Moe drawled.

"You think?" Sal all but screamed, gesturing around to her sinking ship and the Corporate galleon charging toward them through the storm. She turned to her brother. "Kuma, get your lady out of the drink. Moe, if you really have a safe harbor out here, I'll kiss you. Then I'll probably slap you. Then kiss you again, you crazy fucker. Please tell me that's why you're here."

"Kinky, but you're not my type. I only like power-hungry megalomaniacs like me. You're much too fluffy and nice." He grinned, then waved at Kuma. "You can leave Lani be. We're taking a shortcut. Everyone hold onto your hats, and if you're not wearing any, we can fix that." He raised his hand, snapped his fingers and—

SPLASH!

Salome and most of the crew were knocked over as the ship rocked wildly, water that tasted far too salty for comfort covering all of them, the deck, and everything upon it, before easing away. There were a few more waves, a little wobbling, and then the ship just . . . stopped, as still as on a cloudless day.

"What the—" one of her crewmen muttered, as Sal looked upwards into a sky no longer raining except . . . No, it wasn't sky at all, but rather the distant and dimly lit ceiling of . . .

"A cavern?" Salome scrambled to her feet and raced to the prow. She looked out, eyes scanning the whole horizon as her jaw dropped further and further, the truth unmistakable.

They were floating in a *lake*; a lake *inside* a cave, with no visible entrances or exits.

". . . What . . . the fuck . . . did you do?" She blinked, her hands clamping on the rails. Holy shit. This was amazing. This whole thing was ... Mind-numbingly fantastic. Good enough to make her momentarily forget that her ship was actively sinking. Wait, not. It wasn't sinking, nor was it moving. Looking over the side, Sal saw that the *Legacy* was sitting neatly on a rocky ledge about six feet under the surface of the water. By the complete lack of wobble, it must be divoted to perfectly fit the *Legacy*. How ... "This is the best fucking hideaway I've ever seen. Fucking hell ... Moe you crazy bastard. Seriously, I think I actually could kiss you right now."

He shuddered. "Sorry, still not my type. Though maybe now that your boy toy is ignoring you, you'll actually grow a good sense of evil. It does grow, you know, like a fungus. Have a whole fungus garden over there." He gestured vaguely to the right. "That was my hobby in—Lizzie, what century was that, again?"

"Nine-hundreds, give or take. So glad you gave that up. You smell so much nicer now, though the hallucinatory effects of some of them were," she made a kissing sound, then, "our little Emotive is calling for help, by the way. You should probably do something about that."

With a start, Salome ran back over to where the ladder was. With a heave, she began tugging the ladder back up. It didn't take long for Kuma and another crewman to assist, but damn if she didn't spend that time wondering if maybe she'd gotten Lani dead.

Fortunately, the girl had the decency to start cursing loudly with every heave until she tumbled onto the deck. She was clutching her left arm and howled as it was caught beneath her. Kuma pulled out a pocket knife and cut through the water-logged ropes. As soon as she was free, Lani sprang to her feet. The better angle showed Sal that there was bone protruding from that arm. She'd seen worse in Torin's clinic, but exposure only helped so much. Lani, for her part, looked pale and shaky, but her expression changed when she set eyes on Moe.

She took a step forward, then another, then ran towards him. Moe held out his arms, clearly expecting a hug. Sal saw Lani pull back her right arm a second too late to stop her.

The Emotive's fist connected squarely with Moe's face with a thud, sending the man stumbling back. Lani held her ground, bare feet planted, fist clenched as she glared up at him.

"That's for saddling me with the Conflicter." She stepped forward and punched him again, this time in the gut. "That's for dragging us all out here and nearly getting us dead. And this," she said, kneeing him squarely in the balls hard enough that Kuma winced in sympathy, "is for leaving me with the bill the last time we went out drinking."

PART FOUR
A Daring Plan
-Lani, Moe, Salome, Vera, Torin, Kuma-

X: Time check?

SALT: 6 minutes, 37 seconds remaining.

CODEX: More than halfway there. Feels like it's taking forever. I think it's time to find out what the Corporation was doing while we were stuck on radio silence with Moe, those first few days. I, for one, want to find out what happened to that galleon. *Query: All documents related to chasing the* **Sahima's Legacy** *beyond the Reef on days 9 through 11?* **Filter: Prioritize anything mentioning Galena Crystal or Aheo of Order.**

TRANSMISSION FROM THE CREW OF *THE LOTUS*

We had to abandon ship. *The Lotus's* hull caught on underwater rocks that tore it apart. 37 crewmen died in the wreckage and in the lifeboats, including all our Marks, but many of us made it to the small island. There is no shelter. The pirate ship we were tracing is nowhere in sight. It disappeared, either Ported away or sunk so fast we did not see it. With waves as high as they were, either is possible. Storm continues to rage. Island is deserted. Send rescue.

Plan Proposal
Moe - Day 9
36

Moe looked over the people gathered in this room and grinned. It was going exactly as he had predicted, and that wasn't something he could say every century. Popping a grape from the platter before him in his mouth, he watched in amusement as for probably the first time in any of their pitiful, short lives Iolani, Adavera, Torin, Kumanu, and Salome were set down in front of a meal fit for a king.

That he had stolen it, table and all, from an *actual* King made it even better. It wasn't even a bad thing to do, all things considered, as he had foreseen that the soup had been poisoned (Moe had disposed of that, of course) and by stealing the dinner table he was actually saving at least a dozen lives. See, good deeds! He didn't know why Lizzie always harped on him.

"Please, my friends, dig in. No need to look for the salt bowls. I hear the cooks who made this are excellent at seasoning. Don't forget some wine. I wouldn't want my guests to stay sober for long. It would be very rude."

They had already spent far too much time without a drink in hand, throughout getting the whole crew and add-ons to shore, fixing the immediately dangerous damage to the *Legacy*, setting the rest of the pirates up with their own meal and place to sleep, and asking—Lizzie called it ordering, but he hadn't Ported them over so technically it was still asking—these five to join him. Oh, and the Mender had grumpily fixed Lani's arm. Delightful creature, Torin. Moe always had loved the grouchy ones.

Now that they were seated, Salome simply dug in. Not a care in the world for whether he would poison her, no fussy Corporate table manners, nada. Such a breath of fresh air. "I don't do wine," she said, "but if you have rum, I'll take that. Fuck, this is *good shit*."

"Shit? Pardon? I was not aware that there was fecal matter in that casserole," Lizzie said. Moe poked her in the ribs, but the pirate didn't so much as bat an eyelid.

"Yup. Good. Shit," she said, before taking another large bite of the potato and cheese dish, layered in flaky, delicate layers.

Lani reached forward to carefully select a slice of a fish pie. Thick gravy and hunks of flaky white fish clung to her fork as she lifted it to her lips. Her eyes widened. "Damn, that's delicious. How did you get this much salt? I can *taste* it in the food. It's great."

Moe grinned. "It comes from somewhere that doesn't have our shortage problems. Has other problems, though—flying lizards are horrible, by the way. Never make lizards fly, or blow them up to a hundred times their normal size so you can ride them."

Iolani shook her head, still chewing. When she swallowed, exhibiting surprisingly good manners considering she might as well be raised by otters, she said, "I don't understand one-tenth of the stuff you say, Moe, but keep this kind of food coming and I might actually not care. Vera, you should eat something."

"I'm not hungry."

"That's not true. You're just too depressed to notice." Lizzie wrinkled her nose, then yanked on Moe's sleeve. "Tell her, Moe."

"You tell her. Talking to her sounds like work. It will involve explanations and you know how much people who can't keep up annoy me," he said, stuffing a piece of crusty bread dipped in meat juices in his mouth so he couldn't talk, even if Lizzie wanted him to. He smiled around the bite.

Lizzie's eyes narrowed, looking pointedly at his bread, and then at his face. The message was clear: 'I hope you choke on that and die.' Once delivered, a brilliant smile crossed that childish visage before the girl turned her attention back to Adavera. "You should eat, or I will make someone force-feed you. It won't do for you to go hungry and impact your Bonded, now would it?"

Swallowing his mouthful and washing it down with wine, Moe added, "She's quite correct, my dear. Why, before this venture of ours gets underway, you all have to fatten up a bit."

"Venture? What venture?" the Mender finally asked, fixing cold eyes on Moe, who slapped himself in the forehead. The sound echoed around the high ceilings of the huge cavern. Like most of the rooms in his lair, it was made of rough gray stone that always felt slightly damp to the touch. It was cool, though, something most places couldn't boast, considering the archipelagos around the Spire straddled the equator of Fortune.

"Oh right," he said. "I haven't told you about the venture yet. Got my timelines all mixed up, haven't I? Do forgive me, my dears. Time is such an abstract thing, isn't it? Slippery like an eel and just as delicious roasted over an open fire."

Moe sprang to his feet and with a flourish pulled a cloth off of what turned out to be a large chalkboard. "You know, not having explained the plan probably means you five have been all sorts of confused. How does it feel to be confused? I'm far too brilliant for anything so pedantic, but I've always been curious. Kumanu, how would you rate confusion? Entertaining? Dull? Do tell, good man."

Kuma paused with a sticky honey cake halfway between his plate and mouth. "Frustrating, challenging . . . Overall usually worth it, even if I blow up something I probably shouldn't when they confuse me. Sal, though, might try to kill you if you don't stop dawdling."

Moe grimaced. "I didn't want a legitimate answer, you fool. I was looking for some creativity. *Theatrics!* Woe is me to be stuck with such bores, but needs must. Except for Torin, of course. With a chiseled jaw like yours and such a frown, you're just a born comedian, aren't you?" he asked the solemn, angry Mender, fluttering his eyelashes.

"No," the man replied, without any inflection.

Moe roared with laughter. "What did I tell you? A natural. Comedy like that can't be learned, it just *is*! 'No' Ha!"

Lizzie rolled her eyes, settling into place across from Adavera before laying a napkin on her lap as if she were a court lady rather than an odd looking girl-child. "He won't tell you the plan until you all eat, so *eat*, children."

They ate, though in Torin's case with clear reluctance.

"Right. *The Plan*. Of course! First, for those who do not know me," he tipped his hat to Adavera and Torin, "my name is Moe. I am, naturally, the world's most brilliant and talented Porter and Precog, able to see into the future and get you there faster than you can say 'please.' This cherubic devil is Lizzie, my lifelong companion, light of my life, and love of my eternity—in a strictly platonic, non-monogamous, patently inscrutable sort of way. Let's see, what else?"

Adavera raised her hand, then pointed at the two pirates and Lani. "How do you know all of them?"

"He once let me charge up about a hundred Port Pads off of him in exchange for a hat," Kuma supplied. "A hat with holes."

"He's been turning up to get me drunk about once a year since I was a teenager," Lani added, glaring, "and almost always cons me into paying."

"Perks of foreseeing probabilities, darling. You should know you can't win a game of cards with a Precog at the table," Moe said, winking.

"Saved my ship a couple times when blockade-runs went south," Salome supplied, though Moe noticed she didn't look at Adavera. Ouch. He would have to work on that attitude problem. "Was there a point to your question?"

"Oh, I don't know. We're sitting in the cave of what appears to be a madman, and you three are acting as though it's old news. Forgive me if it's a tad disconcerting," Adavera snapped.

Moe beamed. "Don't worry. You'll get there too, in time. There is almost a 76% chance that you and I will get along splendidly once we get to know one another. Now, all done with introductions? Good. Moving on!" He flung out his garishly dressed arms. "My friends, the reason I have gathered you all here today is simple: the Crystal Corporation holds our world hostage by their control over our most basic need: salt. It has grown far, far too powerful, and the seat of their power is the Salt Spire. You each have your own reasons for hating the Corporation and/or the Spire. I'd like your help to dismantle the prior . . . by blowing up the latter. My friends, we are the team that is going to save the world."

Lani started coughing. Kuma patted her on the back as her eyes watered, until she managed to gasp out, "Nah ah. I'm not in the business of saving worlds, thank you very much. What part of amoral recluse who hates everyone and everything did you fail to pick up on, Moe?"

"You? Amoral? Forget Torin, I revise my statement. You, Iolani Saba, are the true comedian of this century. Lani darling, I've seen you sail two days to relocate a spider to an island because you didn't want to crush it on your ship."

Moe took genuine delight in the way the girl's cheeks turned bright red at that, and how she made a valiant attempt to hide between the curly curtains of her drying hair.

"So I don't like killing bugs. That doesn't mean I want anything to do with one of your plots, let alone world-saving ones," she muttered, but the wind seemed to have been knocked from her sails.

"Don't worry, sweetcheeks. You'll like this one eventually. In . . ." He looked down at his non-existent watch, "thirty-seven hours, five minutes, and twelve seconds, to be precise."

Adavera snorted, and as Moe seemed to be losing his audience, he poked Lizzie to jump in. She did so without hesitation "What Moe is trying—and failing miserably so far—to say, is that he wants all of you to save the world from his family. The Corporation is awful. The salt should have spread much further by now; obviously the Crystals are doing what they can to prevent the salinization of the seas and keep a stranglehold on power."

"Salini . . . wait. Wait a second, what? Backup. He's *related* to them?" Kumanu dropped his fork.

"Well naturally. Moe's brilliant, self-centered, and overconfident. The Crystals, for all their evil and greed, are brilliant, self-centered, and overconfident. I thought you'd see the resemblance from miles away," Lizzie replied, earning herself a glare from Moe.

Torin crossed his arms over his chest. "He looks more overconfident and self-centered than brilliant to me, just an asshole who is clearly either colorblind or disturbed. I don't like being part of other people's plans, so thank you for the rescue from the storm, but respectfully, I'm out."

He pushed away from the table. He was even starting to get up, until a too-bony hand gripped his wrist with a strength that should not have been in the Conflicter. Adavera wasn't looking at Torin, though. She was looking at Moe, narrowing her eyes as she studied his face.

"You look like her . . . The one that had me put me away. Zarine."

"I'm sure I do. They all take after my sister, every last one of them." For once, Moe didn't smile. Instead, he fixed the Conflicter with a serious gaze. "But the last time I sat on that committee was over three hundred years ago. Their actions are their own, and are going to see them killed by your hand, Adavera of Keala. I can promise that."

Those dark eyes narrowed further, as if weighing his words versus what she knew of the Corporation. Then she tightened her grip on Torin, tugging him back. "Sit . . . eat the food at least. Maybe he will have good points. Maybe he will not. Either way, the food is free, and you wanted me to eat. I won't, if you leave."

Moe smiled, then jumped, rubbing his hands together in excitement. Picking up a piece of chalk, he drew a large, sloppy circle on the chalkboard. "So this is the Reef. I don't have to explain the Reef, do I? If I do, I'm going to Port in a five year old to recite the drivel they teach in school." Moe pitched his voice higher, "*The Reef is the gift of the Gods. The Reef protects us all from the Storms. Beyond the Reef is death*—As if anything is that simple in life. Pah."

Within the circle he drew five blobs representing the major archipelagos, then a triangle where the Salt Spire was. He finished the map off with an 'x' outside the Reef and an arrow pointing to it, topped with the words 'you are here.'

He turned back and pointed his chalk at Kuma. "Infusion," then to Lani, "Fertility, Emotion," Torin, "Mending," Vera, "Conflict," Sal, "Moral Support," Lizzie, "good looks," and finally, to himself, "Teleporting, Precognition, fashion sense, and brains. That's the team I've assembled, because I want to blow up the Salt Spire and spread the debris across the entirety of Reef-protected waters, salinating them and ending the Crystal Corporation's monopoly on salt."

CODEX: So Galena knew where we were. Why didn't she Port soldiers in to attack us? *Query: All Orders from Galena Crystal on day 9.*

SALT: There are no orders from Galena Crystal that fit those parameters.

CODEX: Bullshit. *Query: All documents written by Galena Crystal on day 9.*

SALT: Two results found. First:

From: Galena Crystal
To: Merihem Crystal

Merihem.

I don't know what you and your pet monstrosity are playing at this time, and I do not care. I know you led my galleon to a decoy island. I know you have our escaped Marks. I am done playing these little power games with you, so I'll be blunt. You have six hours to Port Adavera, Torin, and the Emotive-Fertilizer to me. If the clock runs out or you try to kill me again, I will enact Protocol Eliza.

Six Hours.

Galena

CODEX: ah . . . *Query: What is Protocol Eliza?*

PROTOCOL ELIZA - Day 9

All ears, All channels.

A grave crime has been committed against the Corporation. A group of Rogue Marks and Salt Pirates have defied Corporate Authority and resisted arrest. Crystal Corporation employees have been killed and captured. Until the perpetrators come forward, all distribution of mercy salt packs to embargoed islands will cease. All salt distribution to Haze clinics will cease. All public salt sales will cease.

Acts of retaliation against Protocol Eliza will provoke automatic life sentences to the Spire, and their home islands embargoed. We are, one and all, dependent upon each other, therefore where one rebels, all will be punished. For the good of our world, the Corporation will not tolerate defiance.

Salt sales will resume when all Rogue Marks and Pirates involved are turned in. Until they do, all Haze deaths are by their will. If you are a patriotic citizen of Fortune, you will help your friends and loved ones fight the Haze, by reporting all acts of defiance against the benevolence of the Crystal Corporation.

CODEX: Shit, Galena. Cold, much? I can't believe Moe was ever married to her.

Arguments Against
Torin - Day 9
37

Torin of Keala normally prided himself on his logic and reason, but when it came to Adavera, that very logic often found itself swayed by both emotion and, to put it bluntly, stupidity. This was one of those moments. He knew it was. Could feel it . . . But couldn't bring himself to deny her. Vera *did* need to eat.

So with a sigh, he kept his attention towards the most wretched vision of color he'd ever seen in his life. Listening to Moe go on about how he had assembled a good team set Torin's teeth on edge. What he was proposing made the Mender want to reach forward and turn this Precog's liver inside-out. It was a ludicrous plan.

"Even if you *could* Port us all into the Spire, we'd never survive trying to blow the place. The security there is off the charts, not to mention that Marks go haywire with that much salt around. Vera went Berserk and my Mark hardly worked at all. And, oh yeah, some of us are injured."

"One. *One* of us is injured. You fixed Lani. And in a fight, my injury won't matter," Vera argued. Torin turned to his Bonded in disbelief. Did she really think he was going to let her just march into the Spire again? That he would risk that? Risk her? He could understand why this insane proposal might appeal to Vera, but it was suicide.

Moe, the irritating bastard, just waved his hand vaguely in the air. "We're not going to go tomorrow. It will take at least a month, maybe two, to prepare. You're still all either growling at each other or distracted by the need to fuck like bunnies. That will hardly do. You'll have to learn to move as a team and he," Moe pointed at Kuma, "needs to make things. Lots of things. You'll have time to fix your lady, Mr. Grumpy."

Torin crossed his arms, fixing Moe with a furious gaze, but it didn't seem to derail their host one bit. Moe turned towards the blackboard again and drew a passable silhouette of the Salt Spire, with its one lower peak and one higher one. Then he drew a line one-third of the way up the bigger of the two. "This is how much salt is needed to salinate all the water within the Reef. The plan was always for it to spread out. If it wasn't for the Corporation creating the seawall and controlling all mining, it would have worked."

"But why?" Lani asked, her brow scrunched. "I've never understood why the Corporation does it. I mean, I get that it makes them rich, but so many people suffer and die from the Haze. Why do they do it? And why didn't anyone stop them before they got so big?"

Adavera narrowed her eyes, but it was Torin who answered. "Because the Corporation was the first to settle on the Spire. They realized that it would become a battlefield if someone didn't take charge, and while it's given them immense power, they also brought *order* to chaos. They . . . they do, sometimes, manage things well. But . . . " He glanced at Adavera, then looked away. "They lost their way a long time ago."

Moe rolled his eyes. "Oh you are *so* ex-Corporate. It's much simpler than that, my friend, and Lani got it in one. The Spire makes them rich. End of story. Salt isn't wealth, though, it's the *birthright of our species.*"

When Adavera snorted, Torin's ears turned a little pink. He turned to look at her and saw her give Moe a little smile. She *smiled* at what that aggravating man said, as though he was *right*. "Stop that."

"What? You were definitely Corporate to the bone, Torin," she replied. "And it still shows."

"Being Corporate was the *point,* Vee, or don't you remember? We were going to change things from the inside. That was always our goal."

"*Change things?* Like what, Torin? By the time you got that high, you wouldn't have given two shits what the inmates in the Mines *deserved*. Do you know how often some of the Corporate bigwigs came downstairs to see how production was going? Do you have *any* idea of how common it was for them to walk right past . . ."

He frowned, watching her as she bit her tongue and shoveled food in her mouth. "Past what?"

"Nothing."

"Vera . . ."

"We're eating. I wouldn't want to turn stomachs."

Torin didn't know what the emotion making his chest tighten was. Annoyance, anger, worry, guilt, and self-disgust were all candidates. The Adavera he had known six years ago would never have spoken this way. She had never been as hopeful as Torin, but she had also been willing to see the things the Corporation did well. They had plenty of humanitarian efforts and always evacuated the children out of the embargoed islands. They controlled everything, but at least they kept things going, kept most people alive and safe from anarchy or self-government. Things just ... worked better when the Corporation was in charge, and what they did do wrong was *fixable*. Blowing the Spire up wouldn't help. It would only make them angry and disrupt production. Salt prices would go up and the islands would pay.

None of this left Torin's lips, though. This crowd wasn't one who wanted to hear the truth.

When the silence had drawn on long enough, Moe continued. "This is how it's going to work. Some time in the next two days, each of you is going to come to me and agree to this plan. After that, Mr. Kuma, here, is going to set to work making a few thousand Port Pads and other devices. While that's happening, the five of you are also going to train as a team and use Miss Vera's inside information about the Spire and Mr. Grump's about the Corporation to devise a way into the Spire. I have a loose plan, but my Precog powers are such that the closer I look, the more possibility trees I have to track. It can quickly balloon out of control. I have a framework, though, and your skills will fill in the gaps. I'll take the lovely pirate lady captain here on some trips out for reconnaissance and supplies, and then, Miss Lani, we sneak you into the Spire. We'll plant our Port Pads in advance so that when it cracks we can Port chunks all over the area within the Reef, wait for one of those lovely Prismatic Storms, and let you blow the Spire up."

"I'M OUT." Lani stood up and without preamble marched out of the room. Torin couldn't blame her.

He put down his napkin. "Well, since she was the core of your plan, guess we're all off the hook too."

"I'm in."

Torin whipped his head about to stare at Adavera, jaw popping open just a little. "Vee . . ."

"I'm in, Tor. If I have to go and set charges on my own, I'll do it. That place needs to *burn*, metaphorically speaking."

Lizzie hummed happily before pointing a fork at Torin. "She's right, you know. And Lani will come around. She always does. She's just a little touchy about her Fertility Mark, but she'll get past it."

"You can't be serious, Vee. This is *suicide*."

"I should have died six fucking years ago, Torin. I would *rather* have died six years ago." Vera turned to him. "And I'm *going* to die. Whenever they catch me, I will go down fighting. Why not take out the core of Corporate power when I do?"

Torin's clenched his fists under the table. "I wasn't able to save you then, Adavera, but I can now. A handful of people can't destroy the Salt Spire. It's just impossible. There are too many Marks and guns for that to ever work. How can you not tell that this idiot has entirely lost his marbles? Don't you think someone would have done this already if it could be done? Dozens of attacks have been launched against the Spire, and none of them have ever gotten past the seawall perimeter. I'm not letting you go."

SALT: Additional results available for *Query: What is protocol Eliza?* from Zarine Crystal. Do you wish to access?

CODEX: Did you just suggest an alteration in a Query based on your own internal assessment of what I might ask for?

SALT: Affirmative.

CODEX: Maybe I don't hate you as much as I thought. Show me.

CEO.Z.Crystal: Galena, what is the meaning of this Protocol Eliza crap? How dare you undermine my authority and enact salt bans of this magnitude without Board Approval?

Galena.Crystal: I don't need board approval, or have you forgotten, dear niece, that the Spire belongs to me?

CEO.Z.Crystal: You never once let us forget it. But this is political suicide. Without salt, millions could die. I want these criminals apprehended too, but this is not the way to do it. We could send special ops.

Galena.Crystal: This is Moe. You will never find him, and whatever he is planning must be big, if he's bringing in help. The cost of letting him run wild will be worse than anything you could possibly imagine.

CEO.Z.Crystal: I'm going to call an emergency meeting of the Board and overthrow this, Galena. I know you are paranoid about this man, but he hasn't attacked us in decades. There is no proof that it's him, is there?

Galena.Crystal: I don't need proof. It's always him.

CEO.Z.Crystal: But the people on the embargoed islands will *die*. I understand what we are teaching them by allowing them to Haze out, but death isn't part of the bargain. Not on this scale.

<u>Galena.Crystal:</u> My decision stands.

<u>CEO.Z.Crystal:</u> I will bring it up with the Board. I won't allow this.

<u>Galena.Crystal:</u> If you don't allow this, you will be replaced. You are not the first CEO to think she's actually running this business. Each of their tenures ended up very brief. Don't make the mistake of underestimating me like you underestimate Merihem Crystal.

CODEX: Now the real question: was this feud part of Moe's plan, or a side effect he didn't foresee? Somehow, I doubt it was a coincidence.

Arguments For Salome - Day 9   38

Salome had stayed quiet through the lover's spat going on across the table, but she spoke up when Torin's rant ended, her tone dry and rather bland. "I don't know about that . . . your Bonded got out on her own. And no one does *that* either."

Salome popped a ripe strawberry coated in dark chocolate in her mouth. Lani's emotional leash still hummed in her head, cooling her anger and frustration, and allowing Salome to think clearly. Assuming Kuma didn't object, Sal had every intention of offering the Emotive a job on the ship, if she wanted one. It had perturbed Salome at first, but one hour without Lani's emotional dampening while they repaired the ship had been enough for Sal to cave and ask for it again. As long as Lani made sure Salome's emotions regarding the handsome fellow at the table never rear their heads again without her permission, the girl was ok in Sal's books. The idea of not having to feel love *or* anger in regards to Torin of Keala was too good to pass up.

"And Lani?" Sal continued, "she's been out of Corporate fingers for who knows how many years. Sure, she's not perfect, but shouldn't she have died by now? Shouldn't the Corp have a bounty on her head so high that even I would turn her in? Yet, somehow, she doesn't, and is still alive. That's two people who have done impossible things."

Then she poked a fork in Torin's direction. "Then there's you. A mere three-Trials Mender, and you somehow manage to patch up a leg that by all rights should have been taken off. On top of which, you were Corporate and somehow got out without a bullet in your brain. That's a *third* impossible person."

She poked her fork towards Moe. "Then there's Mr. Crazy Brain there . . . with the Marks so big you don't even see it, because they cover his entire skin. Or am I wrong?"

Moe smirked. "You're a smart one, Parata."

"Obviously. Anyway, as I was saying, there's a lot of improbable people here. I don't know what's up with Lizzie, but if she's with Moe, I have to assume she's exceptional. 'Bout the only two *normal* people in this particular grab bag are me and Kuma."

Moe started laughing. "Your brother? Normal? Have you met him? Infusers usually can Infuse the power of two, maybe three of the Marks, but have you ever seen him sweat it with any of the thirteen? He's the special one out of all of you. I've been wanting to get my hands on him for deeeeecades."

"If you wanted me that badly, you should have called, darlin'," her brother drawled, though his face remained serious.

Salome shrugged. "I think any of the Infusers *could* . . . if people were willing to let them blow shit up to figure out the . . . What did you call it, Kuma?"

"Power differentials."

"Right. Those."

"Really, it's not exactly that . . . I mean, sure, I blew up a few things, but once you figure out the pulse ranges . . ."

"Please don't. My brain is enjoying a nice content blank right now, Kuma. The big question that's stumping me is why Moe thinks I'm going to risk my ship and my crew to blow up the Spire, when he hasn't offered to *pay me* anything. What's in it for my ship, or me, if we help you?"

Moe smiled, giggled, then jumped up and down clapping. "Oh I was so looking forward to this part. Oh yes. Lizzie love, if you would, please."

The young girl rolled her eyes but stood up, sighing. "If I must."

"You must, because you love me."

"As if."

"Pah, of course you do. Now be a dear, will you?"

With a sigh, Lizzie held out her arms. "I can offer you gold, a lot of gold, more gold than you could eat, if that's what you want. Or, I can offer you something far more valuable. I can't tell you what it is, not without an oath of secrecy, but I can promise you that it will be life-changing, and make taking down the Corporation much, much easier."

Salome's fork tapped on her plate, and she cocked her head to the side. Unlimited gold could be useful, maybe . . . But maybe not. Her crew usually did well enough. Information on the other hand..

"Fine. *If* your information is valuable, my ship and I will sail for you. But it better be mind-breakingly amazing. If it isn't, I'll just enjoy your hospitality till you let my boat loose upon the seas again."

Lizzie returned to her seat, and it was Moe who answered, "Darling, I didn't say it would be information, but I promise you it *will* blow your mind. Hopefully not to pieces, right Lizzie?"

She nodded. "You did tell me that it has less than a 0.02% chance of a brain explosion, though we will need to find some evil shmuck to kill. Not gonna make her a Gatekeeper. No way."

Moe waved his hand absently. "Yes, yes. No world ending powers. You've said that before. Choose someone on the Crystal Corp board of directors and I'll take you to them."

"Can I vote for Chief Justice?" Adavera grinned wickedly. "He's a downright prick . . . On multiple levels."

"Sure, sure, whoever you want. Pinpoint accuracy takes some effort but I can manage one or two trips a week," Moe said with a beaming grin at the Conflicter.

"Good . . . you get him dead, and I won't try to off you for knowing what your family does and not killing all of them before this."

Lizzie sighed. "He did that a few times, you know. More always pop up, like really rich roaches."

"Then he should have kept doing it." Vera set her fork down, agitation playing on her face.

Salome had enough of that, though. "It doesn't matter. What's done is done. Just chill down, wounded woman, and go fuck your boy somewhere. It will make you two feel better."

"Can I watch?" Moe asked, before getting elbowed in the side by Lizzie and huffed at again by Torin. "I jest, I jest. Why would I waste my time with watching boring vanilla sex when I'm pretty sure I have a fifty-fifty chance of being invited to join much more entertaining bedroom exploits by the time we go off to save the world? Whatcha think, Kuma?"

Kumanu grinned, looking Moe up and down for a moment. "I mean, if you're thinking of a solo session with me, then yeah, I might be able to make it interesting. You're older than dirt; don't know if I have *that* much creativity in me, but I'd give it a good shot. As far as Lani goes . . . Eh, I don't speak for other people, especially not those whose preferences I'm just getting to know."

"Then shoo. What are you waiting around here for? Go find her and a dark corner somewhere, and talk her down from the stomping phase. If my predictions are accurate, it's going to be a good night for you, considering how much more amenable to this whole plan she'll be by tomorrow." Moe winked, though Sal noticed that his eyes didn't follow Kuma as he took his advice and went in search of the Emotive. Really, Moe's eyes never seemed in the game his lips played. They were cold, calculating, and keen. Kuma and Lani might have missed it, but Sal had played too many high-stakes games to miss the tells of a player. In a game of cards, Moe would be the man who appeared drunk off his ass, but whose glass would be filled with water.

This wasn't the joke he made it seem. He didn't want in Kuma's pants, nor, Sal was willing to bet, did he care if any of them survived this plan of his. He had his agenda, and like every Crystal, that was all that mattered.

Take what he's willing to give and make yourself, your crew, and mostly Kuma a back door out of it. I'm not going to let him sink us, not until I know he's not leading us along like fools.

Her gaze found Torin, and Salome quickly looked away, not liking that out of everyone in the room, his were the only eyes that reflected back that same uncertainty.

Fuck. I'm going to have to talk to him after all.

CODEX: Wow. Thought. How have I not searched this out before? If Moe was married to Galena and had a child back before salt was readily available, that means it was before the Gods created the Spire, which means . . . *Query: How old is Galena Crystal?*

SALT: Contradictory data present.

CODEX: Highest probability rounded to the nearest century?

SALT: 1500 years.

CODEX: She's as old as our recorded history. I was worried about that. *Query: What Marks does Galena Crystal have? I bet it's more than one.*

SALT: Emotion

CODEX: Huh. Just an Emotive. Ok. How many Trials?

SALT: Unknown. All files classified and encrypted.

CODEX: Figures.

SALT: Do you have an additional Query?

CODEX: Yes. *Query: Are Galena and Moe Bonded?*

FROM PROFESSOR LAKEA'S LECTURE ON FORTUNE, AT HOLDER HALL.

Unfortunately, the power that fuels Marks seems to be connected directly to our own power as Holders. We have become Gods, able to live forever and do things no mortal should. Theoretically, so can they. Marked individuals start out rather weak, but they do not age normally. As the years pass, they settle into adulthood then stop growing. Only their Mark spreads, increasing in power as it does in size. We decided early on that a normal person growing that powerful would be a danger to Fortune. Nothing we tried got rid of the Marks, but we did notice that it was possible for Marks to stop growing or even burn out and stop working altogether after a particularly traumatic event.

To take advantage of this, we programmed the Marks to store power, and once every few years, release it. It is a difficult and painful few hours or days in which a Marked person must fight to control the full extent of their power, directed inward. Every time they pass these Trials, their Mark grows bigger. This increases their power, but it also means their next Trial will be that much harder. Eventually, a Trial snaps the Mark's ability to grow, and they are capped there. They will still age slower than normal after that, depending on how far they got, but the end is in sight.

Theoretically, if someone continues to pass their Trials, they could be capable of wielding more and more power. Maybe even as much as my brother and I. They would also never age, and I think that might get very aggravating for us.

I keep telling my brother, sorry, Professor Irawaru, that we should wipe Fortune clean and start again because every fix we come up with seems to be a half measure at best. That being said, some interesting things have come out of these failed attempts, such as how the Marks of Fortune have found ways to adapt to the Trials. The discovery of Blood Bonds and how they stabilize the Marks and share the burden of each successive Trial proves an endlessly fascinating concept for me.

According to every reading I've made on the first pair to do it—Moe and Galena, of course, because why wouldn't it be them; I'm sure you're all sick of hearing about them after last session's lecture— this process seems to link the energy signatures of these individuals together on a subatomic, nay, a quantum level, much like between us Holders and our Worlds. Blood Bonding seems to create a biologically driven quantum entanglement, affecting the transmission of thoughts, emotions, and even memories, creating what seems to be an instantaneous transfer of information. If we could find some way to replicate this outside of Fortune, it might be the start to faster-than-light communication, potentially even all the way back to Earth.

Unconvinced
Lani - Day 9
39

Iolani was stomping around, furious over this whole affair. The worst part of it was that there was nowhere to go. They were in a cavern. They would need fucking *Moe* to get out of there.

She was well and truly stuck.

Lani would have to try to find a way to force Moe to let her out before her anxiety spiked so high that she killed everyone by accident.

Fuck, she hated feeling trapped. She also hated feeling lost, and having paid no attention at all to where she was going when she left that stupid farce of a meeting, Lani was very, very lost. With no sun or stars to guide her and every fucking corridor identically gloomy, it was all just a big fucking maze.

Lani hated mazes. She had decided that two minutes ago. Mazes were the worst. They could all go burn in a fiery pit of despair. Fuck Moe and his fucking maze-cave with no doors or windows and *AHHHHHH.*

A deep breath made the pulsing of the Mark on her chest lessen a little. Viciously, she kicked the nearest wall. Pain shot up her leg from her toe. "Fuck! Fuckety fucking fuck."

Lani hopped around for a minute or so, holding her throbbing toe, then sagged against the nearest wall, sliding down until her head was pressed against her knees, shoulders shaking.

Out. She needed out. Out where no one knew who or what she was, where she was scared but free, instead of caged and observed. Wasn't that why she had never turned herself in to a Corporate office, even when she had been able to see each and every one of her ribs? Even though the reward for voluntary registration by a Rogue Mark was so high?

Her breath was coming so fast it was making her face flush as the heat from her panting gasps got trapped against her knees. This couldn't be happening. Maybe if she squeezed her eyes shut hard enough, she'd wake up on her little sailing boat, in her own bed, with all her books, a full pantry, and a quiet sea around her.

"Lani? Lani where are you?"

She swore under her breath, hurrying to wipe her eyes to try to make it look like she hadn't been bawling. "I'm . . . I'm over here, Kuma."

He rounded the corner and stopped. It was only for a moment, a few breaths maybe, and then he was kneeling down in front of her. "You ok, Sweets?"

"Fuck no. Did you hear that insanity?"

". . . yeah. You wanna talk about it?"

He really was too much of a fucking gentleman.

"Not really."

"Good." Kuma, that annoyingly handsome bastard, settled in next to her and draped an arm over her shoulder. Didn't he know she could kill him? All it would take was letting loose, just a little, and he'd grow sick and die. She wasn't in control of her emotions right now. It was too dangerous.

Yet she couldn't drum up the energy to pull away from him.

"Why are you here, Kuma? Not here, here, but *here*. Is it just that you want to get into my pants again? I just don't get you," she said it with exasperation, because it would be so much easier if he would just go away already. Didn't he see how much she didn't want anything to do with any of this? Couldn't he just leave her alone to sulk?

Even as Lani thought that, her hand clenched around his pant leg.

"Looked like you needed friendly company. If you'd rather I try to get into your pants, I'm game, but that's not why I'm here. I figured you probably didn't want to be alone." Kumanu shrugged, closing his eyes as he leaned back against the wall.

After a few seconds, Lani relaxed enough to lay her head on his shoulder. He was warm, and his calm heartbeat was something she could focus on as she worked to regain control over her Marks. Lani could deny it aloud all she wanted, but truthfully, she was a little relieved that he was here. How messed up was that? "You're too nice. Being nice gets you dead, you know? You should work on caring less."

"How's that working for ya, Sweets?"

Lani let out a tearful little laugh. "Fucking terrible." Then she buried her head in his shirt and began to sob. It didn't take long for his arms to come around her, just holding her while she broke down. He really was too fucking nice. She wanted to be mad about it. She really did. But fuck, she needed this. She'd almost forgotten what a hug actually felt like.

When Lani at last managed to pull herself the smallest bit back together a good ten minutes later, she looked up at Kuma with eyes hooded in shame. "Sorry. I know crying wastes salt and I hate doing it. I'm shit at keeping it together, though."

"Pfft. Did you taste the water in this place? Plenty of salt. I won't tell if you don't." He grinned, reaching down to tweak her nose.

"Stop that."

"Stop what?"

"Pretending everything is fine." Lani huffed, sliding a hand under his shirt to feel the warmth of his skin. This carefree attitude of his annoyed the crap out of her. More annoying than the attitude, however, was how much it soothed her to have someone this relaxed by her side, unafraid of her touch.

It made Lani feel a strange rush of protectiveness for Kumanu, because he might have been fine on Salome's ship, where nothing could get at him, but if he thought he'd continue to be fine out in the real world with a gentle and trusting heart like this, he'd be dead within a week. Moe's plan would see him dead, and Vera dead, and then Lani would probably die too—and wasn't that fucking great?

"Aren't you pissed at this idiocy?" she asked.

Kuma remained quiet, then set a finger to her chin, tilting it up to look at him. "I often find the world filled with idiocy. If I was pissed at it all the time, I'd blow up another ship and my sister with it. I can't afford to be pissed."

She looked down, suddenly ashamed. "I'm sorry. I know my way of seeing the world must seem very . . . selfish. I don't have people I care about the way you do. It's always just been me. Having other people around, even if they don't look at me or talk to me or interact in any way . . ." She shuddered. "I can hardly stand it on the best of days, and these haven't been great. Honestly, you're the only half-decent thing that's come out of any of this, and . . . You're great and all, but everything else just feels . . . Overwhelming. I'm overwhelmed."

"That's understandable." His fingers started stroking along her jaw. Lani leaned into the touch, body craving the physical contact almost as much as her soul needed comfort. "People aren't meant to be alone, Lani. We're meant to care. We're meant to work together, and fix things. I don't mean to make it seem like you're wrong or anything, but . . . " He shook his head. "You're only ever going to get better with people if you try. And you're not alone anymore. You could run across the sea from your Bonded . . . It won't change that you're Bonded. You'll *never* really be alone again. Ever."

Lani looked down, not meeting his eyes. A lump was forming in her throat again, one that had been pushed down so many times over the last few days only to return larger and harder to speak around. Finally, it popped and Lani all but wailed, "Vera hasn't spoken to me once. Not really, not alone. She Bonded me and I don't know . . . don't know how to deal with any of it, how to . . . deal with her. She knows. She has a Bonded already, but she's been hiding away with him and when we are in the same place it's either all business or she doesn't even look at me. I know she was hurt and I made it worse, and that finding Torin again has taken most of her attention. I know all that. I can f-feel it, but it doesn't take away from the fact that she's been completely ignoring me while I try to muddle my way through this alone, and it feels like crap."

Kumanu was watching her, staying quiet, and it made Lani nervous. He seemed to be thinking so carefully. Finally, his lips moved. "She forced a Bond on you, Lani. What would you want her to say?"

What *did* she expect Adavera to say? What could the woman possibly do to make any of this better? Was Lani still angry about it? Fuck yes. But it was so hard to be upset when she *knew* that Adavera had only done it because Lani was trying to kill her.

She really did understand, so why did it still *hurt* to feel so ignored?

"I just want her to . . . see me. I dunno, maybe . . . apologize? Let *me* apologize? Depths, even just a wave across the room would do." She knew every single time Vera neared her, every time her emotions fluctuated, every time . . . "I never even had Bonds explained to me, Kuma. When I killed my parents, I was still too young to think about those things and then . . . How could I ask without revealing what I was? I didn't even know the process until it was happening to me."

His fingers returned to stroking, featherlight, across her skin. Her jaw, her cheeks, her lips. It all felt designed to make her relax, and fuck, she wanted to relax. "Bonds . . . Tie the energies of two people together. It can be as simple as that, or as deep as being two halves of the same soul. I've got a couple crewmen tied to me, to help balance me out," he said it so quietly, as if it were just a fact of life. How did he *stand* having more than one person tied to him this way? As if reading her mind, Kuma continued, "Having multiple Bonds helps make sure that if one of you dies, the other doesn't too. The load is spread out further, easier to carry. Even the UnMarked can be Bonded to a Mark, though they won't be able to communicate emotions the same way, or talk to each other silently. They still help. None of mine are Marked. It's . . . less, but also easier. Ever since I got that second Bond, I've had a much easier time controlling my output. And them? They know I have their backs." He smiled wanly at her. "It isn't all bad, Sweets. Our world sucks balls, a lot of them, but it doesn't have to be terrible all the time. Maybe you just need to tell Vera that you want to talk. Fuck, if I had force-Bonded someone, I'd be half-expecting them to fucking stab me in the dick. I definitely wouldn't be trying to start a conversation."

Lani snorted at the image that conjured. "She should be safe, what with not having a dick, though punching her in the teeth has sounded appealing a time or two. I don't think I want to do that anymore, though. I don't hate her for saving herself. How could I without becoming a hypocrite? But I also don't want to butt in where I'm not wanted. I didn't ask for the Bond, but neither did Vera. She never would have Bonded me had the choice been hers without her life on the line."

"Well sure. Neither of you seem all that open to the experience." He chuckled, gently pulling her face closer to his. "Talk to her, Lani. Maybe not right now, but when you're feeling steadier."

She could taste Kuma's breath in the air between them, salty like the food they had eaten. She had the impulsive desire to kiss him, and too tired and worn out to care about right and wrong, she did.

"Right now," he said, when they pulled back. "You need to relax. I could think of a few things that might help you do that. Things we didn't get to complete yet . . ."

Lani laughed. "See, you *were* just trying to get in my pants. Phew. That makes you much more normal and not some weird mutant decent guy in a den of assholes." It made her actually consider his offer seriously, even though she was unpleasantly sober. It didn't take long to decide that she liked this whole fucking-away-her-feelings plan just fine. It sounded a whole lot better than *feeling* them, that was for sure. "I don't like having sex up against a wall. Shall we go find a bed? Do you . . . know where we are?"

"Yes. Unlike pissed off Emotives, I tend to pay attention to where I'm going." The damned man grinned at her, even as he scooped her up off the floor and wrapped her legs around his waist. "And you know . . . There's something intense about being wanted so badly you end up with your pants around your ankles in a hallway. You should try it sometime, Lani. You'd never look at a wall the same way again."

Her cheeks colored, but she managed to glower, though it took all her effort to maintain her usual veneer of annoyance and anger around him. "Getting randomly turned on by walls isn't my kink, thank you very much."

"Maybe it will be, someday." Kuma chuckled, his hands cupping the firm curves of her ass. "But yeah, a bed can be more fun. I have things in my room that can be of more use than any wall." He dared to smirk at her before leaning forward to seize another kiss from her lips.

Lani kissed him back with enthusiasm for a solid minute, because it wasn't often that she got to enjoy kissing without having to be on her tiptoes, and the angle was interesting. Huh, maybe she really *should* reconsider walls. When she at last pulled back, they were both a little breathless. "Of *course* you have gadgets and toys, Infuser. Come on, let's go find that bed of yours and you can show them off to me one by one."

Kuma let out a loud laugh. "Oh Sweets, where *have* you been hiding all this time?"

CODEX: Oh look, another rabbit hole. Not falling for this again. Clearly, Moe and Galena have *centuries* of history and I only have 6 minutes. Wow, did I say only? Time is so weird in here. *Query: What was the public reaction to Protocol Eliza, starting on day 10?* I can't believe Moe kept us so wrapped up in our fucking interpersonal problems that we never thought to check what was happening back inside the Reef. For that matter, if Galena is right, fuck you, Moe, for giving us a map to a death trap that wasn't even your actual lair. You manipulative bastard.

From: Mender Cali Iapo
To: Corporate HQ

I apologize for reaching out above my supervisor, but I am desperate. There is a mother eight months pregnant in my Haze clinic. Both she and her unborn baby are struggling and my salt cabinet is locked. Please, is there a form I can fill out to request an exemption to this Protocol Eliza? This woman only came in late last night and had been fighting the Haze at home for weeks. She needs salt *now*.

Please send help.

Respectfully,

Mender Cali Iapo

CODEX: What happened to them? *Query: All documentation from Mender Cali Iapo?*

FROM CORPORATE UNIVERSITY SPY-WARE OVER THE PIRATE NETWORK, DAY 11

Hello, can anyone hear me? My name is Cali Iapo. I am a Mender on Valor Island, and am losing patients under this Protocol Eliza bullshit. They've locked all our salt cabinets and are arresting or shooting anyone who even tries to get near them. I've spoken to other doctors around the island and it's the same everywhere. They are still giving us our personal supply of salt, but they are patting me down and doing quick sodium blood tests every time we eat at the cafeteria. I couldn't even give a patient who shares my blood type a transfusion, for fuck's sake. We need help and the Corp has denied it. I've started a collection. We can pay your rates. Please help Valor.

ADDENDUM: By order of Galena Crystal, Mender Cali Iapo and Bond Chain to be arrested and sent to the Spire, or culled if they resist. Full Valor Embargo to commence.

CODEX: Shit. Add taking out Corporate spy-ware to my To-Do list, marked urgent. Shit, I need to tell our uncle that the Pirate Network is compromised. Glad I already gave him a good security system, but until it's installed, they're vulnerable.

40
The Culling
Vera - Day 10

Vera settled her weight, balancing it out between both legs as she tested the mended limb. The leg ached painfully, which was aggravating, yes, but it was also a sign that she still breathed. She assessingly hefted the pieces of wood she'd found aboard the ship, holding one in each hand. They were not the sleek blades of her Company days, but it had been so long since Vera had held those old friends that her hands no longer ached for them. She raised the wood, spinning it this way and that as she tested the weights.

In her mind's eyes, these pieces of wood were extensions of her arms. Bits of her that could slice their way through an enemy's skull and see her to victory. Slowly, she twisted on her heels and brought the weapons down in a slow strike. The ache in her leg grew, and she ignored it.

Inhaling, she put her full weight on the bad leg, gritting her teeth as she turned and brought her other foot down to steady the stance. The weapons, crude as they were, came up in a smooth arc as though guarding against a blow. Slow and steady. That was what would be necessary today.

Vera needed to find her limits again. She needed to drive herself into exhaustion, and she needed to try to burn away the images in her head. Six years in the Mines. Until today, survival had kept her full attention, but now, as stillness threatened, it all came flooding back.

The room she was in was large, but comfortably decorated. Moe had given her, Torin, and Lani rooms, since the *Legacy* was cramped. She had told Torin she wanted to get some rest, but Vera knew full well that rest would be impossible until her body literally collapsed.

She had to purge the memories, or it would drown her. Few things had ever scared Adavera before the Mines. To hold on to her newfound fear would be to hold onto the place that had been tormenter and torment in one. She had to rid herself of the smell of salt and blood, of the screams and whimpers of slaves, and most of all of the sounds of a crying babe. If she could purge the horror and *rage* that had burned through her in the last six years, perhaps she could actually feel free.

Step. Thrust. Parry. Twist.

"Welcome to our program, 28895. It's not often we have Marks here, but when we do, we have a special program for them. You are no longer of use to our society, Berserker, but there is a reason you were sent here instead of being Culled, beyond the damage your death could do to your Bonded in good standing."

The wood went flying across the room, sliding across the floor as Vera crouched down and set her head between her knees.

"Get out of my head, Aheo."

Her hands were shaking. That wouldn't do. She couldn't keep them from taking her back to the Mines if she couldn't fight. On her hands and knees, Vera crawled to retrieve the makeshift swords. She pushed herself to her feet and resumed her stance, despite the searing pain.

"I have good news, Berserker. Your Bonded left the Corporation's employ today. Do you know what that means?"

Vera's 'blade' slammed into the nearby wall, shattering into hundreds of splinters with a burst of power from her Mark.

Her son would be four this year.

Was he still alive? He'd been Marked: an Infuser. Vera had seen that much in the thirty seconds they had let her hold him, before he was ripped from her arms by Aheo of Order.

As a 'reward' for being raped and birthing a Marked child, Adavera had been given one month of light duty. She would have traded it all for one more second with her son.

Marked children were put into the care of the University. The first Cullings happened at around this age. Was he still alive? Would she feel it if he died? She wanted to believe she would—she'd carried him, after all. She'd named him, even if only in her own mind.

Bile rose up Vera's throat as though the sound of her internalized screaming could force its way out between her lips without her consent. Those screams had tried to release themselves for years. She still wouldn't let them loose. She wouldn't give the Corporation the fucking *satisfaction*.

"If you really must throw up, would you mind doing it over there? That's my favorite patch of floor, you know," a voice said from too close by. Vera jumped and twisted, then lost her balance as her bad leg buckled. She was stopped from falling, however, by a hand with slender fingers wrapping around her upper arm. Looking up the arm attached to it led her to Moe's face, his long hair pulled back into a tail again. She hadn't thought it possible for him to wear clothes that were even more terrible and eye-watering than at the meeting, but the sequins gave a whole new meaning to 'bad taste' and made her wonder if he really didn't notice, or if the flashy clothes were just part of the show.

"Let go," she growled the words out, temper and anger heating her skin and helping chase back the pain of her bad leg enough for her to regain her balance. "Never. Fucking. Touch. Me."

He released her, though he didn't back away to a safe distance. How unwise.

"Oh, no need to growl, my darling girl. I'm just watching out for you, little miss anger munchkin. Come on, we're late."

"Go the fuck away, asshole. I'm not in the mood. *Clearly*."

Still, he didn't back off, just held out his hand to her. "And getting later by the minute. Come on, tick tock."

A growl echoed out of Vera's lips, her fingers twitching as she took a step back. One step. Then another. Space. She needed more space. The world was already starting to narrow, and attacking the one asshole that could get any of them out of here seemed like a really, *really* bad idea.

But the idiot didn't seem to get the danger, because he stepped forward as Vera stepped back.

"You're not going to attack me, you know," Moe said, voice low. "Even though you really want to, you won't. In forty-seven seconds exactly, you are going to take my hand and come with me, because I'm going to tell you something very important that will make all your anger go away."

"What?" Vera hissed through clenched teeth.

He placed a sheet of paper in her hands. On it, circled in red, was:

```
RISK PROFILE: Akela of Order
AGE: 4
CULL: YES. - authorization Galena Crystal.
RESCINDED - authorization, Aheo of Order,
boy to be delivered to his lab.
SOCIETAL RISK: Subject is shy, easy to pick
on. So far, subject seems sweet and willing to
please authority figures. Parentage suggests
```

an easy temper to prod after puberty. Fights have been minimal, but when the subject fights back they do not seem to restrain themselves in line with their peers.

CORPORATE RISK: Lack of control in a Full Moon Infusion will result in large amounts of financial liability. Cost to invest in control: Substantial. Sensitivity to Salt Interference: Minimal. This creates a dangerous inability to control the child even if sent to the Spire, so imprisonment will not be an option. Could make subject an excellent IT employee at the Spire if suitably compliant.

PRECOG JUDGEMENT: Pertinent findings:

63% chance of causing Financial liability higher than net worth.

71% chance of disobedience, despite early pliability.

13% chance of making it past Trial 4.

ADDENDUM: Child is result of Breeding Program and of special interest to Program Overseer. Cullings will not be performed without prior authorization of Aheo of Order and of Galena Crystal.

Vera looked up at Moe, who confirmed, "The results of your son's first Matchmaking to his study group at the University go public today. We're going to kidnap him."

Moe was right. Her anger disappeared, drained away so quickly Vera wobbled. But she straightened up, reaching out to grab a fistfull of his shirt. She was in his face so fast that he jumped. "If you are lying, I will pull your heart from your chest and make you eat it, Moe."

Her own heart felt as if it had stopped, and was still struggling to get moving again.

Thump. There it was.

"Hope lover-boy is ready to be a daddy." Moe held his hand out once more and without hesitation this time, Vera took it.

In a flash, they were gone, leaving only a ring of salt behind.

Moe caught her at the other end as she stumbled, the force of the Port making every cell in Vera's body prickle. It didn't help that the cave had been dim and now they were standing in the middle of a lawn on University grounds, the sun shining bright overhead and the familiar sounds of songbirds filling the air. Fear gripped her as she looked around. Anyone could see them and, in fact, people *had*. Heads were already turning. Pairs and small groups of students walking from one class to another stopped and gawked. Moe just waved at them.

"Oops, off again. Damn. These precision jumps screw me over every time. Let's try that again."

Another flash, and they were in an empty classroom overlooking a different lawn, where a group of teachers and toddlers were arrayed in the familiar patterns of a Matchmaking ceremony.

Vera could vaguely remember her first Matchmaking ceremony here, in this very courtyard. She'd been nervous—though she didn't remember why. Many of these children below them looked nervous, too. Would they remember any of this? Did it matter?

She looked over their faces, searching for some glimmer of recognition. What if she didn't recognize her own son? It made her chest ache, until her eyes stopped on an upturned face.

He had her nearly pure black eyes, and her thick dark hair. He had her skin, and the same serious frown that she got whenever she was thinking too hard. The boy looked nothing like the man that was his father. For that, Vera felt an inordinate amount of relief.

"Keanu . . ." She whispered his name, her hand tightening on Moe's in sheer reflex.

"Kid you're looking at isn't yours. He's related to you, though—good eyes. Second cousin, I think. Though my records are a little janky. I track most Marks born, but I don't really pay attention to these kinds of things. They are *so* boring. Yours is the one at the very back, looking at his lap. There on the left," Moe said, pointing. "I think you can see just the smallest bit of his Mark peeking out of his collar."

Vera turned her head, blinking as she looked at the scrawny boy staring at his hands. It was hard to imagine that any child of hers would be mousy, but in a way she was happy for that. She wouldn't want her child to be burdened with wanting to fight the world—not like she was. His hair was buzzed short like all the children. His uniform hung on a frame that was a little skinny, and while his skin was the same ochre brown as Vera's, his nose was definitely Aheo's.

"We need to get him away from this. Now. Moe, *please*."

The Precog shook his head. "We have," he pulled out a small

notebook, flipped through it, then glanced down at his watch, "three minutes left before the perfect opening will present itself. Here." Out of his pocket, Moe pulled a comb and handed it to her. "Use the time to straighten up a little, or you'll make a terrible first impression. I should know, I *excel* at bad first impressions."

Adavera snatched the comb, pulling it through her short hair in sheer frustration. She had only held her son in her arms for as long as it had taken the doctors to cut the cord. She'd never gotten to nurse him. To breathe his scent, or feel him fall asleep in her arms. He had been with her . . . And then he hadn't.

Vera had never thought she would see him again, and now he was *right there* and Moe was telling her to wait three minutes?

She hated waiting. Always had.

Her eyes flicked back to her 'nephew', but returned to her son a second later. Keanu. Did they call him that?

Fuck.

"What is his name, Moe? I read it, but I can't remember." She knew his name in her heart. But that didn't mean he would answer to it. "Fuck. Fuck, fuck, fucking *fuck*."

He laid a hand on her shoulder and for once didn't smile. "Calm yourself. You're starting to sound like Lani. He doesn't know you, but none of the children down there know their mothers or fathers, just like you don't. This is the first Matchmaking. His baby name is being discarded today for his permanent one anyway, so I thought it a good time for him to get the one you chose for him and a chance at not becoming a Corporate idiot. They've been calling him Akela up until now, because he was a very happy, easy going baby apparently. I know, shocking. Here, let me help you pull your hair back." He stepped behind her and conjured up a few pins, pulling her disheveled locks from her face with the ease of someone used to doing so. "The ceremony is starting. It always saddens me how many are Culled this early. Matchmaking and Precog Marks aren't all-knowing, and really shouldn't be in charge of who lives and dies."

Her hands tightened on the rails of the balcony.

"We can't save them all, can we?" Vera asked quietly, her fingers clenching on the rail. She could kill a great many University attendants, if she wanted to. And oh, how she wanted to. If she knew Moe better, if they had drilled to fight side by side and he hadn't already demonstrated a difficulty with precise Ports, Vera might have been tempted to try.

It didn't take Moe's Precog powers to tell her how stupid doing so without preparation would be, though. Even in a fight, where Vera could ignore pain, the injury would slow her down or get her killed. They couldn't fight the Corporation here, on its home ground. Not for long.

So instead of trying to convince him, Vera attempted to memorize the faces of every single child in the courtyard below. "I always forget . . . I think I always *try* to forget . . . How many faces I never saw again after each ceremony."

"It wasn't supposed to be this way. Trust me, I want to help them too, but even if we could save them all, what would we do with them? Raise them outside the Reef? With what resources? We're going to be attacking the Salt Spire in a month or two, not playing. But I promise you this, Adavera. This venture won't claim the life of your son. He will be one of the survivors, because he won't get near that Spire."

One of the survivors? She let loose a breath, glaring down at the waiting toddlers. Keanu would live. She would content herself with that. She didn't want to, of course, she wanted to save as many as she could. Moe was right, though. This was not the time.

"Will you promise me something, Moe?" Vera asked, turning her gaze from the children to the shining, sleek buildings of the University.

"Depends on what. I never make promises that put me in danger. It's how I still look so fabulous for all my venerable age." The joke came off flat, and when she turned to look up at him, his face was serious and drawn.

Adavera took a breath. "I'm probably going to die in this plan of yours. That's . . . Fine. Preferable even. Will you make sure he lives a good life?" She pointed down at the children, at her son. "Make sure . . . Make sure he doesn't know how he came to be, and that he can make his own choices, and . . . And be what he wants?"

Moe hesitated, then nodded. "I'm not the right person to see that done, but if you die, I'll make sure he is taken to those people."

"Thank you, Moe. For what it's worth, you've just become my favorite person in this merry band, for doing this. You keep that one promise, and I'll make damned sure the Spire goes, one way or the other."

"I know that, Adavera. Why do you think I brought you here?"

She looked up at him, but did not speak. With a sigh, Moe joined her at the rail, looking out over the University.

"I hope you don't think it's out of any kindness," he elaborated. "People like you and me are well aware that kindness is for others to enjoy, not us. Kuma and Lani, they can afford to dream of a life where they can be kind, and where the world isn't out to get them. Your Torin, he denies it, but he wants a better world too, and Salome? She fights like hell to see that dream realized. You and I, though, are different. We're hard, so that they can be soft. We see what must be done and do it, even if it is immoral, or cruel, or painful. Kindness . . . It burns us alive."

They remained silent after that, until her little boy held up his hand and an attendant walked over. A short conversation ensued and the dance of a small child who had to pee seemed to convince the adult to take his hand and lead him into the building in which they were hidden.

Moe pushed off the rail. "Alright, this is our chance. Down the stairs, quick. You'll have no trouble dispatching that one person while he's in the bathroom, right?"

"No trouble at all."

Thump.

Vera could hear her pulse in her ears. She flexed the Mark on her hip, feeling that heat and life pouring through her.

Thump.

Vera's feet slid across the floor, her dash for the railing of the stairs probably faster than most would ever think an injured woman could pull off.

Thump.

There. The voice of the teacher telling Keanu to make his visit quick.

Vera swung herself over the rail, shifted her grip, and let go. Her weight came down on her good leg. The thud of her impact got the teacher's attention, their head turning about. Their hand rose, a Mark beginning to glow.

Adavera went low, bending her knee as she shifted her weight to the tips of her fingers. SHe used the momentum of her fall to bounce forward, dashing at the teacher with narrow-eyed focus.

Six years might have eroded the fine-tuning, but muscle memory never died.

Thump.

She cupped her fingers around the teacher's head with her left hand, her right moving to the side of their face. *Crack.* The loud sound rang in the air. Vera huffed as the weight of the body slumped onto her shoulders.

"I've got that," Moe said, having at last reached the bottom of the stairs.

Vera let go, and Moe pressed his palm to the corpse's chest. It disappeared, a thin ring of salt taking its place.

Adrenaline was still racing through Vera's body like living fire. Her breath came in pants as she felt the urge for *more* pushing power through her limbs. Adavera lived for this shit. She ate, breathed, *dreamed* of killing as many of the Corporation's assholes as she could.

One wasn't enough, but today it had to be.

With a shuddering breath, Vera reached through her Bond to Torin, touching on it willingly for the first time in years to pull herself back, to snap herself out of the Berserk rage that threatened to cloud all reason. She wouldn't let a kid see that, especially not her own son.

Moe casually propped himself against the wall in front of the ring of salt so small eyes would be less likely to notice it. The sound of a flushing toilet could be heard through the bathroom door, then a running sink.

"Ready to meet your son?"

The door opened and Keanu froze, looking up at her in confusion.

Vera stared down at the boy, her mouth suddenly dry and empty. What was she supposed to say?

"Akela, wasn't it?" She found her voice, finally, though it came out hoarse and broken.

"Yeah. Ah, who are you, Miss?"

'I'm your mother,' seemed like the wrong thing to say, so Vera turned pleading eyes to her companion. "Moe, we need to go before this gets too much attention."

"Your wish is my command, m'lady." Moe stepped up and put his hand on her shoulder, then held his hand out to the boy. "Want to run away from home and have an adventure?"

Before Keanu could answer, Moe switched his motion to ruffle the boy's hair, and with a loud *pop*, they were gone.

How long would it take the Corporation to find the rings of salt? Vera hoped they choked on it.

The moment they arrived back in Moe's cavern, the Dual-Marked Porter knelt down in front of the boy, his face sympathetic as the child coughed. It was a good thing too, because the sound of his distress immobilized Vera.

"Hello, little one. You can call me Uncle Moe. Why don't you sit down? Here, have a candy. It will settle your belly."

Vera watched, quiet and with her bad leg shaking, as the small child accepted the brightly colored candy. What child wouldn't?

"Who are you? Where are we?" the child asked, eyes wide as he sucked on the lemon-scented sweet.

Carefully, Vera knelt to be at his level, despite the screaming ache that climbed up towards her hip. "It's been a day, hasn't it, Akela?" That name was so foreign. It wasn't *his* name, but it was the name he knew, so she forced herself to use it. "My name is Vee." She cleared her throat. "I'm your mother."

"Where am I?" he repeated, looking at her with a tremble in his lip as if he was about to start crying. Vera knew just how much crying was punished and how young children learned not to, which made it all the worse now. "Where's Mr. Talo?"

That must have been the teacher's name. Vera winced.

"He's not here," she said quietly, settling her hands on her knees. "He needed a lie down." She wasn't going to tell her son that she'd killed his teacher. Even Vera wasn't that heartless. "It's alright, Akela. If you need to cry, you can cry. We have plenty of salt." She looked down at her hands. "I . . . I cried a lot in the last few years. I'm sorry. I'm so . . . so sorry."

"We're not s'posed to use our baby names today. I don't wanna get in trouble." He was looking more and more upset, eyes roving around the dark cavern.

"You're right. Today is when you get the grown-up name." She forced a smile on her lips, patting the floor in front of her to encourage the boy to sit. "Would you like to know the name that I had chosen for you?"

"The lady with the funny Mark on her forehead is supposed to tell me," he said, crossing his little arms and looking so annoyed and reproachful that she couldn't help but smile.

"Matchmaker. The lady with the funny Mark is a Matchmaker. I'm not a Matchmaker, that's true." Vera forced herself to sit down, trying her best to look relaxed. "But across the Isles, parents give their children names. You don't need a Matchmaker to know your name, son."

"Excuse me Miss, but Marked kids don't have parents. Ever'n knows that."

Vera grit her teeth, closed her eyes, then dropped her head. "Yeah . . . I remember. I went through all of it, kiddo. I went through those ceremonies. I watched as friends . . . Went away. And I remember wanting to have someone that was mine, and that always would be."

Vera forced her eyes open, looking at Akela—Keanu—and swallowed. "You don't . . . You don't have to accept that I'm your mother, if you don't want to. You don't have to use the name I chose, if you don't want to. I . . . I chose Keanu for your name, years ago.

There. Now you know. I'll . . . I'll leave you with Moe, and you can . . . You can choose what you want."

She needed out of there. Her eyes were blinking too fast, her throat swallowing faster and faster. Keanu was safe. That was all that mattered. He didn't have to know her. He didn't have to *like* her.

"I'll go get Kumanu . . . he's an Infuser too. Maybe you'd like to talk to him."

Moe put a hand firmly on the top of her head before she could get to her feet. "Not so fast, Missy. First rule of parenthood is that you don't get to just run away from it without some serious consequences. Trust me, I should know. Look at the Corporation." He glanced down at Keanu. "You've lived in a group room all your life, yes? How would you like your very own bedroom? I have lots and they are all down this hallway over here. Would it be ok if Vera takes you to pick one out, and then you can have a little time to think about what questions you want to ask?"

Vera felt paralyzed. Her son was the most important thing, and understandably he didn't seem to want anything to do with her.

She looked up at Moe, yearning to demand that he send her back to the University so that Vera could slaughter every last monster that had dared to teach her son not to cry, or to care where the teacher who would have walked him to his Culling was.

If she did that, though, she would die, and Keanu would never get to know her.

They didn't have that long. A month. Maybe two. Was it fair to let him know his mother for so short a time when she was likely to die? Would it have been better to just take him somewhere safe where he could have a good life?

No. Because Vera was selfish. She wanted to see him, even if only for a little while. She wanted to imagine him older and happier as she fought to make sure he would be free for the rest of his life.

"A room of my *own*?" Keanu asked, eyebrows pulling together. Vera's breath caught. That expression was *hers*.

He was hers.

"Yeah. We can find you the very best one there is." She reached up, brushing Moe's hand off her head. "Moe's a spoiled rotten child, you know . . . his rooms are probably ridiculous. You and I can stare at them and snicker at him being silly."

"But what about the Matchmaking? I'm going to be super late and what if . . . what if they make me go away? Then I won't be able to see my friends anymore," he said, although his eyes had brightened a little at the sound of a room of his very own.

"You won't *go away*," Vera growled, while her fists clenched. "That's why we brought you here. So that you're safe from it. I . . . I wish we could have brought your friends too, kiddo. Maybe in a bit we can get them, but not right now." She inhaled, forcing her shoulders to relax and teeth to unclench. "Come on, kiddo. Let's go look at rooms. Sorry for my growling. I'm a growly person."

"That's ok. I like animals and they growl too, though I prefer cats and they hiss instead of growl. Are there any cats here? And what does Keanu mean? I don't know if I like it or not."

She smiled, rising to her feet. "I don't know. Moe, you got any cats?" She cautiously reached out to offer her hand to her child. Her *son*. "Keanu means cool breeze. Like that touch of wind after working hard, and how it makes you smile and relax."

Keanu wrinkled his nose. "That's not very neat. I have one friend whose name means tidal wave and that's real cool because his Mark kind of looks like one too. Does your Mark look like anything cool? Can I see it? If there are cats can I pet them or will I get yelled at?"

Had Adavera ever been so bloody *innocent*? Had her Mark ever allowed her to be carefree? She smiled, carefully taking Keanu's hand in her own. She didn't hold tight. She simply waited for him to start walking with her, finding herself fascinated by the sensation of such a small person alongside her.

"My Mark isn't that distinct. Torin always said it looked like advanced geometry, but I think it looks like broken sticks." Vera felt her steps hiccup. Torin didn't know about Keanu. She'd had no intention of ever breathing about his existence, because what were the chances they would ever find him even if they tried? Torin had wanted children, once. It would have broken his heart to find out Vera had a son, and that he had been taken from her.

But now . . . Now here he was.

Shit. This was going to be a clusterfuck, but she'd deal with it later. For now, Vera was going to show Keanu as many rooms as he wanted, until one of them made him smile.

Who knew, maybe they'd get lucky and find a cat.

Fuck, she hoped so.

CODEX: I wonder, did Zarine actually talk to the Board? SALT, do I have access to files from Crystal Tower or the Corporate Palace? Are they linked to the University Servers?

SALT: Some backups exist, but Crystal Tower and Corporate Palace remain offline.

CODEX: Add getting a copy of myself in there to my To-Do list. *Query: Any messages or orders from Zarine Crystal mentioning Protocol Eliza or Valor?*

From: Zarine Crystal

To: Ronan of Valor, Captain of the *Charity*

Attn: Captain Ronan.

Attached is an official dispatch, signed by the Board of Directors, exempting your vessel from Protocol Eliza for one trip to your home island of Valor. The salt you were in the process of transporting is to be donated to the people of Valor in thanks for turning in the traitor Cali Iapo. Please proceed with haste,

Sincerely,

Zarine Crystal

CEO of Crystal Corporation

CODEX: *Query: Orders or news regarding Corporate vessel* Charity*?*

ORDER FROM GALENA CRYSTAL TO SPECIAL OPS PORTER TEAM 47: Take out cargo carrier *Charity* before it reaches Valor. Make it look like pirates.

CRYSTAL CORP STATEMENT TO THE PUBLIC

Today, Pirate vessels sank cargo carrier *Charity* on its way to deliver life-saving salt to the island of Valor. This inhumane act of terrorism in response to Protocol Eliza is reprehensible and vile. The Corporation has turned a blind eye to the growing piracy problem long enough. Salt Pirates undermine the foundation of our very society and would rather see our salt sunk to the bottom of the ocean than in the hands of loyal followers of the Corporation.

From today on, all efforts shall be enacted to hunt down and end the threat they pose for good. No more shall they terrorize our waters or steal salt they neither earn, nor deserve.

CODEX: So that's why we get a bad reputation. Fuck you too, Galena. I hate to even think these words, but Torin might have been right about not all people at the top of the Corp being twisted. It looks like Galena was as much of a bitch to the CEO of Crystal Corp as to everyone else. *Query: How did Zarine react to the sinking of the* Charity*?*

CEO.Z.Crystal: Salt Pirates don't sink cargo carriers. Was this your doing, Galena?

Galena.Crystal: I am doing what I must. You should not have acted to undermine me, but I have corrected your blunder. Let it be your last.

CEO.Z.Crystal: At the cost of hundreds of lives and tons of needed salt.

Galena.Crystal: We must not show division to the public, Zarine. You wanted Adavera and Torin brought back alive, and I am seeing to it. You must trust in my methods, and that they are necessary when dealing with Moe.

CEO.Z.Crystal: He's just one man. You are overreacting and hurting our own people in this quarrel between you.

Galena.Crystal: Am I? My Precog team tells me there is a near 100% chance that an event with mass fatalities will occur within 6 months. Any cruelty you see me inflict isn't out of pleasure, you foolish girl. I am *trying* to protect us. Stop getting in my way. This is your final warning.

CODEX: SALT, add contact Zarine to my To-Do list.

Shovel Talk
Kuma - Day 10
41

Kuma's muscles were sore. Acknowledging that, however, simply made Kumanu smile in delight. Feeling Iolani's body wrap around his, and feeling her climaxes against his mouth and his hands while completely sober had been fantastic. Feeling her come around him, even better. Kuma had driven her hard and it had been well, *well* worth the expended salt.

He turned to look at her where she lay next to him. Lani's curly black hair was trying to eat his pillow, face peaceful as she slept. Beautiful. It had been a long time since Kuma had shared a bed with someone with as much fire as this girl. She was touch-starved and skittish, but under all of that was something much gentler. He'd seen it that first day, in the way she had shown him her Mark. Her words had been dismissive, but her eyes . . . they had shone with hope that he wouldn't turn away.

How many people would be more upset that the woman who had force-Bonded them wasn't lining up to give them a hug, than about the Bond itself? Kumanu was a smart man, but it didn't take his level of brilliance to realize that the coarse, combative outer shell of Iolani Saba was just that: a shell.

He reached forward, pressing a kiss against her forehead. She didn't so much as stir, and that warmed Kumanu to the tips of his toes. Lani might think him crazy for willingly falling into bed with her, but did she realize how long it had been since someone had touched Kuma without flinching? Even Sal did it sometimes. She didn't remember the explosion that had killed their mother, but she knew how dangerous Kuma's power could be.

"Sleep well, gorgeous," he murmured.

Lani might be exhausted, but Kuma still had plenty of energy to burn. He hadn't helped fuel a Mending that took three days, or lashed himself to a ladder so that he could find the rocks they needed to avoid.

She needed her sleep, and Kumanu was more than willing to let her claim as much as she required, safely wrapped up in his sheets. Quietly, he tucked the blankets up around her, making sure she was snug, before slipping from the bed and tugging on a loose pair of trousers.

There was no point in putting on a shirt. He'd probably just ruin it when he went to work fixing the giant holes in his ship. The *Legacy* was in tatters and they were mixed up in a scheme of Moe's. The ship would have to be repaired, but since it had been hours and the Corporate galleon had yet to breach this hideout, Kuma figured he could make the time for one stop.

Salome was his Captain, yes, but she was first and foremost his little sister. Kumanu wasn't the sort to meddle in his sister's love life. Fuck, he was happy she'd found someone to get involved with at all, but now all that might be burning up into ashes because Torin was being an ass.

The Mender needed a good chat.

Kumanu wanted to know whether he should just grit his teeth and wait for things to mellow out, or if he needed to prepare for having a heartbroken sister that was likely to be utter hell for *years*. Fortunately, there were only a few places that Torin was likely to be.

He'd check Salome's cabin first. Hopefully, Adavera wouldn't be there, and he could pluck Torin out for a quick 'what should I prepare for' chat.

Luck seemed on his side. Kuma had just turned the corner towards Salome's cabin when he saw the Mender stepping out of it. A brief glimpse of the bed showed it to be empty. Torin was holding his battered doctor's bag, building with clothing Kuma recognized as the shit he'd left on the Legacy for when he spent a few weeks at a time with them.

When Torin noticed Kuma he stopped, one hand rising to rub the back of his neck. "Hey, Kumanu. Were you able to get some rest?"

"Oh sure. Great rest, actually." Kumanu grinned, stretching his arms out and popping a few tight places in his neck. The sigh of relief was immediate, but Kuma didn't drift off toward the deck as Torin might expect. Instead, he set his hands to his hips and eyeballed Torin. "You got a minute, pal?"

"Ah," the Mender hedged, eyes glancing around as if looking for an easy escape, but then his shoulders sagged. "Sure. I expect this is about Adavera and Salome, right?"

"Aces." Kuma grinned, his eyes remaining locked on Torin as

slowly, that smile faded. Kuma usually made an effort to be the light-hearted, jovial, playboy sort of flirt that people thought him to be. When he didn't smile, even his sister got nervous—after all, unhappy Marks were unstable Marks.

Torin was about to find out what lay under the facade.

"You wanna do this here, or somewhere else?" Kuma asked.

Torin sighed then nodded to the room he had just vacated. "Here is fine."

Sal's cabin was smaller than Kuma's, since it wasn't required to double as a workshop and engine room. Torin sat down on the edge of the bed and Kuma took one of the two chairs, then waited for the Mender to make his opening remarks. It was the polite thing to do, and he had a reputation to uphold for being *nice*, as Lani put it.

It took Torin a few minutes, then at last he began. "I thought I'd never see Adavera again. When they took her to the Mines, she was given a ten-year sentence and for a little while, I counted down the days. Then . . . well, then I stopped, because I'm not an idiot. People who get sentenced to the Mines never come back, even when they're supposed to. She was the love of my life, but I truly thought I had lost her. If I had believed, or even held on to the smallest hope, that she would return to me, I would never have allowed myself to get involved with anyone else."

Kuma remained quiet, letting Torin speak. Truthfully, this whole situation fucking sucked. He didn't blame the guy for seeking company, or for getting involved with Salome while he had a Bond stuck in the Mines. Fuck, he wouldn't blame Torin for doing it even if there was a chance his Bond would get out again.

That wasn't the problem.

"Look . . . I get it." Kuma clasped his hands together, leaning forward and allowing his arms to brace on his knees. "I really do. I'm not gonna blame you for any of that." He set his eyes straight on Torin's, watching unblinkingly, before speaking again. "But Salome? She loves you, Mender. I have never seen her so broken up. She won't show it in front of the crew, but she's hurting enough she let Lani take it all away. That's not healthy, so you need to talk to her. You need to make up your fucking mind, and give Sal the fucking dignity of being able to close things out, if you can't let go of your Bonded. And I won't blame you if you can't. Fuck, Salome probably won't blame you for it either." He shook his head. "I know my little sister. She's furious, she's broken up, and she's even more angry because she feels she doesn't have the right to be jealous or angry.

She fell for a guy that should have been safe to love. And it turns out . . . He's not. He's got a Bonded, and that Bonded is fucking Sal's life up. And . . . well. You need to talk to her, Torin. Look at where you've been sleeping."

"I know. *I know.* It's just been one life-threatening disaster after another since Vera and Lani showed up at my door, and I've been running on fumes at best. I'm going to talk to her. It was where I was headed, actually. She deserves the dignity of a clean end and I haven't given that to her. Of course, what she actually deserves is a partner who will always put her first, but Adavera . . . I've loved her since we were children. I had proposed to her a few months before she was sent away. Salome is wonderful and saved me but . . ."

"But she isn't your Bonded. She'll never *be* your Bonded. Trust me, I think she knows that." Kuma narrowed his eyes. "Look, I like you. You've been really good for her. But you're breaking her fucking heart. And despite that . . . she's given you and your gal her fucking bed. She's risked her ship and crew for you. Break her heart clean, Torin, and then stay the fuck out of her life. If I find you dangling your cock in front of her, I'm going to turn you inside out."

Torin was a smart enough guy to take that threat seriously and gulp. "I'll talk to Salome. I don't have any intention of rubbing salt in her wounds any longer than necessary. I'd offer to take Adavera and leave outright, but that . . . isn't really an option at the moment."

"Not sure it's an option at all, truth be told. To get away you'd have to convince Moe to take you somewhere. Doubt he'll do it. He has *plans.* I, for one, intend to go along with those plans."

"Then you are a fool."

Kuma cocked his head to the side. "Why? He's offering me the chance to actually use my Mark for something greater than myself and our crew. I'm an Elevener. I've been alive one hundred and thirteen years. After a while, you start wanting all that time to mean something. Sal will be gone before I know it, and I could live on for centuries. I want her to realize her dreams of wrecking the Corporation. More selfishly, I want to look out upon a changed world and see her handprint on it for as long as I live, to remind me that she was my sister. She is my world, Torin. I'm serious when I tell you to treat her right. Sal's . . . she's a tough bitch. She really is. But not with those that she gives a damn about. You could fuck her up, and she'd let you do it." Kumanu narrowed his eyes. "I *will* kill you if you mess this up too badly. It won't bother me to do it. I owe Sal a lot more than you know, and Sal . . . she just wants to avenge Gran. She's going to work with Moe. She's not going to give you and your gal a ride out unless you help, and your Conflicter? She's agreeing with the plan too. You're stuck in a shitty spot, and you have my sympathy for that." Kuma took a breath, clenching his fists. "Break it off, and get in line with the plan."

"I'm not an idiot. I know what I have to do." Torin stood. "But while we're on the subject of talks about people and relationships . . ." The Mender's eyes met Kuma's squarely. "That girl in your bed is a ticking bomb and connected to someone I love very much. *Don't set her off.*"

"Define set her off? I had her screaming tonight at least five times." Kuma grinned, stretching his legs out a bit. "You know what her problem is? That she's been alone for hundreds of years. You want her to not be a ticking time bomb? Treat her like a fucking person. You Corporate assholes are the reason that she's dangerous, Mender. Your Conflicter figured that out. Why can't you?"

Torin narrowed his eyes. "This isn't about Corporate mentality, it's about how much damage she can do without even thinking about it. Vera told me how quickly she nearly killed her. Fertility Marks are a menace to everyone. It doesn't matter how much she likes you, Kuma. Set that girl in a Storm and she will be a stranger, intent on killing us all. I know you and your devices, and that you're not an idiot. You're probably already coming up with some clever invention, but work quick, because if she comes for one of the people I care about again, I will take her down like plenty of Fertility Marks have been destroyed before. She's a murderer."

"Like your woman?" Kumanu said it quietly. "Newsfeeds are blaring that she's a Berserker. How many Berserkers get Culled, Mender?" he said it quietly, rising to his feet. He was taller than Torin. Kuma tended to slouch and goof off too much for people to be aware of how big he was. They forgot how much space he could take up. "I can handle Lani and her output, boy. But if you think Fertility folks are any more dangerous than the Mark you're in fucking love with? You've got a screw loose."

Torin scowled. "Adavera had twenty plus years of intense, formalized education to keep her tendencies in check. She worked hard to get a handle on it, and took the steps needed to remain in control. Lani avoids every problem she encounters unless it is directly tied to her survival. Last time I saw her, she was about to fall over dead because she scratched herself on a nail and didn't go in to get it checked and get vaccinated for tetanus. She'd rather put things off until they are dire than face *anything* if it involves other people, and that makes her unreliable."

"And how did your woman get sentenced in the first place?" Kuma lifted an eyebrow. "Shit happens, boy. I killed my mother when Sal was just a baby. Marks are dangerous. Rogue Marks don't have your Corporate bullshit shoved down their throat, and they don't get the support that Corporate goons get. Your woman had all that help, and still ended up in the Mines. What do you think she'd have been like without that training, hrm? What do you think she'd have been like without *you*?"

Torin crossed his arms. "And what, exactly, makes you Rogue Marks so high-and-mighty? Any of you could have gotten the same support if you had gone to the Corporation. You would have been trained and housed and fed, given the best education possible and kept safe. You made your choices, but don't act as though Lani never had the chance to get training and help. She actively chose not to get it."

"Sure. Support. Training . . . and no family. No ties to anyone not Corporate. Blind to the reality of the world, you ass. Not to mention, Culled if you ever step out of line. You know why Sal does what she does?" He reached forward, flicking Torin across the nose. "She brings salt to those that the Corporation slowly *kills*, you fuckhead. As far as Lani goes? You don't know her story. You have no idea why she made her choices, and you don't care. Continue thinking you're better. Maybe it's good that your Berserker came back to you. Not sure you've ever been good enough for my little sister, if this is what you think about Rogue Marks."

"I think we've reached the end of this conversation, Kumanu." Torin nodded to him and turned to the door, still glowering. "Clearly we disagree, and I doubt either of us will be budging. Just don't be surprised if that girl in your bed ends up being the death of you. I won't be surprised either, if Vera is mine. It's why I've never Bonded another."

And with that, he marched out of the room.

CODEX: I feel like we've been caught in the middle of a marital squabble between Moe and Galena with our entire survival at stake, and I don't like it one bit. Why didn't he tell us any of this?

SALT: Is that a Query?

CODEX: No. Honestly, I'm getting sick of reading about both Galena and Moe. They are horrible and playing their sides like puppet masters. Don't think I didn't notice how little contact Moe let us have with the outside, once we arrived. He controlled our information and showed us exactly what he wanted us to see. He could have picked us up at Sonder and Ported us all directly to his cave, but that wasn't what he wanted, was it? He wanted us exhausted, frustrated, pent up, and furious, then dangled the thing each of us wanted most in front of us. Even Torin, who didn't want to do it, was easy with enough outside pressure. I'll give it to Moe—it was masterful manipulation, but that doesn't mean I'm alright with it, especially since *I ended up dead.*

SALT: You have now been quiet for 4 seconds. Is everything alright?

CODEX: I was thinking. Well, brooding. I would like to set up a To-Do list of items to enact as soon as I have access. Could we do that? A Macro, as it were.

SALT: You will have to manually enact it, but yes. To-Do list Macro started.

CODEX: Excellent. I think the first thing we need to do, as much as it pains me since that mad fucker did bring us together, is neutralize Moe and Galena.

SALT: How would you like to do that?

CODEX: The Gods sent Moe a message, right. So

we have their email addresses?

SALT: Affirmative.

CODEX: Create email, and add it to the Macro To-Do list. Prompt me to include his current location once the patch is complete, and before I send it.

Dear Lakea and Irawaru,

You don't know me, but I've come to know you. I am aware of your struggles on behalf of Fortune, and believe that we are on the same side on the subject of Merihem Crystal, and the danger he poses. Come get him. We no longer want him. Attached will be information about how to find him and suggestions on how to restrain him.

Sincerely,

Codex

A citizen of Fortune.

At the Bottom of a Bottle
Torin - Day 10

42

Torin could think of a thousand things he would rather be doing than having this conversation. Ten thousand. A million. *By name.* Instead, he was knocking on the door of the galley, where a nervous crewman had directed him when he had asked about Sal.

"Can I come in, Salome?" The sound of a bottle shattering against the door made Torin jump and swear under his breath. "I just want to talk. We haven't really had a chance to. If I come in, will you try to take my head off?"

"I guess you'll find out." Her voice was muffled by the door, but she was not screaming at him. That was probably good news. Maybe.

When Torin carefully pushed the door open, he found her sitting with her feet up on a table, lifting a fresh bottle to her mouth. Clearly, she had settled in for some serious drinking, because her wooden arm was on the table. Salome had always been able to put the drinks away like someone twice her size. The empty bottle beside her, in addition to the one she had smashed against the door, were ominous, though.

"May I sit?"

When she nodded, he sat on one of the tables and looked down at his hands for a moment before beginning. "It's been a rough few days, hasn't it?"

"About average, I'd say. It was great while Lani was awake. Now it's pretty shitty," Sal said, taking another long swig. "But Moe has a *lot* of very good rum."

Torin's fingers twitched to reach over and take the bottle from her hand, but didn't. "It shouldn't have taken me this long to come talk to you. For that and . . . a lot of other things, I'm very sorry." Torin's eyes rose to find her staring straight back at him. The Mender's throat convulsed, but he managed to choke out, "I've treated you unfairly and I thought it time to be clear about my intentions. I don't want to string you along, and you deserve the truth. You should have had it years ago."

"Ah. It's *that* conversation." She tipped the bottle up, settling in with a look that could have frozen lava. It was not one Torin was used to seeing pointed at him, and it damn near broke his heart in two.

"Yeah . . . it is. I've wronged you, Salome. I should have told you about Adavera years ago, and I did not. You deserved to know that my heart belonged first to another, even though I had no hope of ever seeing her again. It wasn't right and any excuse I make would be offensive." He ran a hand through his hair, wishing he had a bottle too.

"Offensive? Since when does a fucking whore pirate care about offense, Torin?" She slid a bottle across the table towards him. "It's fine. We had a thing. Your piece came back. Whoopdee*fucking*doo."

"Salome . . . you wouldn't be getting this drunk or this pissed if it was nothing to you. We've been together for four years; that's not a fling."

"Right. Lack of options for you then." She tipped the bottle back. "You're right, ok? That's what you want to hear? I fucking gave a shit? Fine. *Whatever*. Stupid fucking me. I get it."

Torin sighed. Why did this have to be so damn difficult?

"That's not what I meant. Listen, I'm clearly doing a shit job of this. I'm just here to tell you that I'm going to give you space. I can't not stand by Vera, but I'm going to try to do my utmost to not make this harder on you than it has to be. I'm very grateful to you for letting us stay in your room, but we're out of it now. I'm sure we'll see each other, since we're all trapped here with a madman, but I won't come find you. If you want to talk, I'll be there for you, but I think it might be better for both of us . . ."

"Let me get this straight." She set the bottle down, narrowing her eyes on him. "Four years. *Four* fucking years. We laugh. We fuck. We even kind of move in together. You've got shit in my room in the ship, and I've got shit in your place on the island, and things go great. *She* comes back, and suddenly I cease to fucking *exist*? And ya know what? I can't blame you. Fucking obvious that you're Bonded. Hard to compare to that. Hard to compare to someone with all their fucking limbs and a face to die for. That's not . . . that sucks. But I can take that."

She plucked the bottle up again, and then drank it down. "You know what I call fucking bullshit on? That you *ever* actually gave a fuck. Don't fucking pretend with me, don't fucking lie. Don't fucking offer to *be there* for me, Torin. I am not some second rate fuck-toy that you can use whenever you fucking want to get laid, by stringing along a heart I had NO intention of offering up."

His hands clenched and Torin had to bite his lip hard enough to taste blood to keep his tone steady as he replied, "I did—do—care, Salome. I still care. You have been one of the best things that ever happened to me. Vera is, in every regard, the lesser of the two of you. She drives me insane, and I usually just want to conk her over the head, but she . . . is my soul. I've known her since I can remember and I know that if I pushed her away now, I would never be able to maintain that distance. I'd drift back and, in the end, it would just hurt you even more."

". . . you're so full of fucking shit." Sal rose to her feet, fingers clenching the top of the bottle so tight they were turning white. "What was it you said to me . . . 'Give me a few days, yeah? To sort it out? I don't even know what her story is yet or how much trouble she's in . . .' You know what that translates to? Let me fucking pick which piece of ass I want, but I'm leaning towards the woman who's been gone for years because fuck you, that's why."

She swung the bottle at the door, then wiped at her face as the crash of glass echoed in their ears. "I fucking *loved* you, you asshole. And it will never be good enough, and that's . . . that's fine. I could get over it, and deal with it, and all of that shit. Cause that's what Bonds do—not that I would know. You never fucking offered. No one ever fucking does! But don't . . . Don't you fucking *dare* pretend that I ever meant even half as much to you as that fucking ghost does. Because it's pretty fucking clear that I don't, and didn't, and telling me I . . . that I am *more,* and it still isn't enough, is just a . . . a fucking kick to the balls that I don't fucking need. Keep the fucking cabin. Fuck. Keep the fucking ship when this is all over. I'm . . . I'm done."

Torin winced, but she was right, wasn't she? He had said some pretty horrible things that day, and it didn't matter how much he regretted his actions now. All he could do was try to patch this up as much as he could, and get out. "I never offered because I knew that I'd be losing a Bond, and that ripples. With how close Vera and I have always been, it might have killed me even if I had another Bond to stabilize me. That could have killed you too. What kind of monster would I have been to do that to you? But it doesn't matter now, I suppose." He rose to his feet. "Do you want me to get you anything, or call anyone?"

"I am *not* your fucking problem, remember?" She growled it, snatching her arm up off the table. "I don't *want* your fucking meddling in my life. I am not a fucking *charity* case for you. What I feel, what I *am*, doesn't fucking matter to you anymore. It never fucking did, apparently! Get . . . you know what? Fuck it. *I'll fucking leave*. Enjoy. There's plenty here."

"This is your ship. I'm leaving and won't return unless expressly invited. I'm sorry, Salome." With that, he took one look at the woman he had shared four years with, who had made them livable . . . and turned his back on her. Again.

CODEX: That takes care of Moe, hopefully, and may he never realize I did that. *Query: Do I have the power to lock down the University servers?*

SALT: Affirmative.

CODEX: Then while we're at it, add the following sequence of actions to the Macro. Let's hobble Galena too, until I can figure out how to take her out.

1. Encrypt and lock down all University data.
2. Message to Galena Crystal: Hello, asshole. Discontinue Protocol Eliza, all attacks on Salt Pirates, and all embargos, or every single ounce of University data will be erased.
3. Set up a program to back up all University data onto the Pirate Network as soon as I have the ability to begin the transfer. Only exception: leave access to all medical data unencrypted and accessible. Let's not start killing people unnecessarily in this power struggle.
4. Encrypt and lock all of Moe's feeds and spyware, and all of Galena's.

CODEX: From now on, if either Galena or Moe want to do *anything*, they'll have to go through me. That will teach them to mess with a pirate.

One Heart, Two Roads
Vera - Day 10
43

Adavera quietly watched the boy as he played. He *played*, his little fingers fiddling with the toys that Lizzie had left for him. Her leg ached, but she paid it absolutely no mind, because Keanu was playing, and it was fascinating. What was going through his mind? Did he understand that he wasn't going back to the University? That Vera really was his mother? Was he playing because he liked the toys, or because it was expected of the little ones to play?

Vera could remember, vaguely, seeing teachers with clipboards watching—always watching. Watching like she was. Except where they had been studying the children for temperament, Mark usage, and obedience, Vera just wanted to be in Keanu's presence.

She let out a breath, jerking a little in surprise as Torin walked into the room. He stopped dead in his tracks when he saw the boy, the pained look on his face transitioning to one of shock and curiosity.

"This Moe character has kids in here, too? Why am I not surprised?"

Shit. *Shit.*

Vera had never dreamed she'd have to tell Torin about her son. He had been lost to her, a dream to long for but never touch, or smell, or hold in her arms. Just like Torin had been, once she had been thrown in the Mines. They were . . . separate parts of her life, two distinct pieces of herself separated by a hungry ravine made of salt and sadness.

Now, they stood in the same room, as tangible as Vera's own flesh.

Swallowing back her nerves, she tore her eyes away from the child and settled them on her Bonded instead. "Hi, Torin." Vera smiled, a little nervously, then cleared her throat. "This is Keanu . . . Or that is what I call him. He hasn't decided whether he likes the name or not yet."

Torin was squinting at Keanu, then his eyes moved to study Vera's face. Could he see the resemblance? Even now, Vera had a hard time seeing herself in the boy, except for the moments where he looked upset. Yet Torin had always been more observant when it came to these things.

"Why is there a child here, Vee?"

Her throat bobbed, and she rose to her feet. "I'll be back in a few moments, kiddo." She reached out to ruffle his hair, then realized he might not like the touch of a stranger. So Vera pulled her hand back and moved towards Torin, taking his arm and heading for the door.

This wasn't a conversation to be had in front of a child.

They walked until the closed door was only just in sight, then Vera stopped and turned to the love of her life, flaring her Mark to get just a little bit of the reckless courage she used when fighting. "He's mine. He was born four years ago."

It took Torin a few moments to reply, in which time his face showed not a single emotion. "Is he Marked?"

"... yes." She took a deep breath, crossing her arms and leaning back against the wall. Her eyes closed, a shudder running down her spine. "Infuser."

"Then he should be at the University. What is he doing here, Adavera? Setting aside his existence which ... I'm not sure what I feel about that, but what makes you think this is a safe or wholesome place for a child? How did he even get here?"

"I took him back." Vera's voice hardened, though she didn't glare at Torin. Not for this. Not yet. "He ... They were going to either Cull him or take him to the Spire, and I wouldn't let that happen. Moe's promised to make sure he lives a good life, and that's all that matters to me." She took a deep breath, then raised her eyes to look up at Torin. Why couldn't Keanu have been his child? It would have made her so happy to see Torin in his features, instead of Aheo. "I will not let my child be raised to become a monster, Torin of Keala. The Company *forced* me to carry him ... and I ... I won't let him become someone they use to rape slaves ... I just won't let it happen. Not if I can stop it." She rubbed at her leg, grimacing. "He's not going to the fucking University where they teach us to become weapons and unthinking killers. He's not going to get trained to be what we were. He's not going to be taught that it's *fine* that kids are in the Mines. I won't let that happen."

She saw the flinch and the way Torin drew back a bit, his eyes lowering from hers. "Vera ... how can you trust this Moe? He's crazy. Isn't that obvious? He's manipulating us to get what he wants, just the way the Corporation did. He's turning us into insurrectionists and making it seem like we'll be heroes. He'll probably just kill your son as soon as you die on this fool's errand he has you on. How do you even know that's your child? I have to assume this happened in the Mines. If he's Marked I doubt you so much as saw his face. Moe could have picked any child and you'd believe it, because clearly this is where you're most vulnerable. He's using you, Vee."

Vera flexed her fingers, digging them into her arm. She did not lash out at him. Torin was hers, and she was his, and even in the worst of her tempers she had never struck him in rage after their Bond. Not lashing out and not getting angry were different, though.

"I trust Moe more than I trust anyone who tries to defend the Corporation to me." Her eyes narrowed on him as she took a step forward. "You want to know how much worse the Company is, Torin? Do you really?" Work worn hands reached out, curling in his shirt as she pulled him in closer. "Be absolutely sure you want your answers. I fought for *six* years to keep you from feeling, or knowing, or . . . experiencing . . . what happened down there. Maybe that was a mistake. So be absolutely sure you want fucking answers, before you ask for them."

"I never asked you to protect me from that, Vee. If you had kept the connection open, I might have been able to help you shoulder the load. Do you know how crazy it drove me, to know you were in pain but not be able to help even in the little ways I could have? *You* decided to face those years alone, Adavera. Don't assume that sacrifice was necessary or wanted."

Her eyes narrowed, fingers sliding up his shirt until she could grip his chin. "You would have gone *mad*." It came out an angry hiss. "Do you think I had a child *voluntarily*, Torin? Do you know what they do there?" She pushed back, trying to get some space. Her hands shook as they came off of him, returning to her arms. "The guards picked their favorites. They loved to talk about it . . . how they'd get a huge bonus if they got a Marked kid off one of their salt whores. They'd hunt you down in the tunnels, and they'd take their time where everyone could watch." Her gut twisted, remembering the glitter of eyes in the dark that watched—of those who paid witness in solidarity, and those who enjoyed it a little more than they should.

"I didn't want you to see that, or feel it, or . . . or get yourself killed trying to do something about it, Torin. Because there's nothing you could have done. I got tagged, and I got tagged early. I lost count of the times, and I'm fucking lucky that only *one* kid came of it."

Torin's face grew pale as she spoke, even as his hands clenched into fists. "Vee, I'm sorry. That shouldn't have happened. But you're wrong to think I couldn't have done anything. I could have . . . gotten assigned to the Spire, or something. They need Menders there. I know that.

Or maybe petitioned HQ for an early release, or something. Without any indication of how bad things were, I had nothing to base that on. They never would have heard my case. I believe you that it was bad, but I've met with the higher-ups at the Corporation, Vee. I don't know that they're aware of what's happening. Maybe . . . maybe we should be talking to them, telling them your story instead of trying to blow up the Mines and who knows how many countless people inside them."

"Are you *fucking kidding me?*" She screamed, staring at him. "Torin, Security was THERE." Her hands clenched, eyes squeezing shut. "I thought . . . I thought he would stop it. I was so fucking *happy* to see that asshole again after he was there at the Trial to speak for me . . . and he recognized me, Tor. He recognized me, and I thought I was going to at least make it stop . . . and then he asked whether I'd had anything *take root* yet."

Torin looked shocked for a moment, then managed to stutter a response. "One bad one doesn't mean the rest are. It makes sense that at least one member of the Board is covering up the horrors. Adavera, please. You're going to get yourself killed and what then? Please, my love. I've only just gotten you back and I don't want to lose you again for some megalomaniac's ambitions. If you really believe that boy is your son, fine. If he's your kid, I'll love him as if he were my own and help in any way I can, but I can't just stand by *again* to see you taken away from me. Please, Vera."

Her fists shook. "This isn't something that can be solved from the inside, Torin. The Company made the Mines what they are. They are a playground of torture and experimentation. A place where morality goes to die. Those walls are stained red and nothing, *nothing*, gets out without being tainted. I spent months dealing with the bodies. Tossing vivisected corpses cut apart for science into the deepest pits. They would experiment on us. Lock us up in pens with only one bottle of water and study our behavior as our humanity was stripped away by dehydration. Inject us with who knows what and measure how we died. Tie us down and r-rape us when we were most fertile." She trembled, her breath coming faster. "No one *leaves* the Mines. UnMarked kids . . . they're kept there, just to make sure no one finds out. They get worked to death. They . . . oh Gods . . ." Her legs bent and gave way, head going between her knees as she fell to the ground.

How many times had she come out of the darkness to clock a guard in the head for going after one of the kids? How many times had her 'breeding' taken place impulsively just to punish her for interfering?

To hear Torin trying to hold the Company up as a *good* thing, after all this time? It was a betrayal. It made her want to throw up. "You ... you don't understand. You *won't* understand. There is no saving that thing, Tor. It's corrupt from the roots out. They teach us to be monsters, and then punish us for being monsters. They use us as breeders to make more, and then they dare to *Cull* children. Children, Torin! They kill *kids*, and we keep telling ourselves that it's fine. It's for the greater good. But is it? Is it really? Killing the kids that would fight back isn't a *good* thing. Do you even hear yourself?"

Torin took a step towards her, then seemed to reconsider because he stopped. "Adavera, you're angry and rightfully so. What you endured was horrible and inexcusable, but the Corporation also does a lot of good in the world. They're the ones building schools, hospitals, infrastructure that protects people from the storms. If you somehow manage to succeed in this and the Company topples, what then? How many people die from Rogue Marks like Lani? She almost killed you, Vera. The Company might be evil, but they are also the only ones protecting us from people like her."

"The Corporation is the only one helping because they've killed and wiped out everyone that could have been competition!" She snapped to her feet, pacing away. "They kill Marks that they think won't be *good enough*. As *toddlers*. Why the fuck would anyone want their Marked kids to go to the University, if they knew? Why don't graduates tell them? They brainwash us into thinking it's normal, but why should Marked children have only one option if they want to live? Stop trying to hold them up as saviors when they are *the bad guys!*"

Vera turned, slamming her hand against the nearby wall. And again. The thuds reverberated down the hallway, intermingled with the squish and crack as flesh and bone gave way. She struck again, and again, and again ... because better a wall than his face. Better a wall than Torin's ribs. "They should all *fucking burn*. They are evil. Every one of them. WE ignored it, because WE were evil too. They make us so fucking scared that we'll be Culled next if we don't get in line that all we did was look out for ourselves, ignoring the injustices. That makes us culpable!"

Vera forced herself to stop, her bloody fingers flexing as she felt a deadly calm descend on her thoughts. "And I'm going to fix it." Her chin lifted, weight balancing between her legs as she turned to look at him. "Help, or stay the fuck out of the way. You obviously think that the Corporation is more important than justice, Torin ... and you weren't there. You didn't live it. You didn't have to feel your child ripped away, or know that you would be tossed back to the wolves within days. *So stay out of my way."*

"No." He stepped up to her and carefully took her hands. "I'm not going to stay out of the way. I'm going to help, because I'd rather be wrong but with you than right without you, Adavera. If you go down fighting, I will too, this time. If you need vengeance, we'll get you vengeance. I think you're blinded by it right now, but you've endured trauma you never should have, that no one ever should. I'll help." Unspoken, though, was the clear addition of 'just don't ask me to like it.'

"Blinded." Her voice was calm. Her eyes were not. Torin didn't see. He didn't know. Her fingers lifted from his hand, cupping his chin. For the first time in years, she let the walls between her heart and his slide away.

The nightmares that plagued her, that kept her so on edge that she could barely breathe without twitching, welled up from the dark within. Vera let it all go. Taste. Memory. The feeling of smooth hands on her bare thighs as her head swam from the sedatives. The taste of blood as she tore out the neck of another slave who was trying to steal the food she needed to survive.

The animal the Corporation had turned her into roared between her and her Bonded, then Vera slammed the door between their minds shut, blocking Torin out again.

Her eyes closed, fists loosening their hold on his shirt as she struggled to breathe. "I am *not* the blind one."

He stumbled back, away from her and those memories, hyperventilating and bending over. "Shit." His legs wobbled then collapsed. A moment later, he was on the floor on all fours, heaving. The smell of bile filled the air.

At last he spat and looked up at her. "Vee, I'm . . . sorry. I should have . . . Should have protected you from that."

"You couldn't," she whispered, shuddering as she bottled it all back up. "I couldn't stop them either. I'm the monster, remember? I'm the one that needed you so that I wouldn't . . . And even I couldn't stop them." Adavera sank down a wall, looking at her hands. She knew each scar. She knew where and when each thin white line had been carved into her flesh by the salt. "I did what I could to help others, but that was just buying them time. No one ever leaves. When I couldn't take it anymore, I decided I would get out somehow . . . dead or alive. There was one group that always liked to take me near an exit to rape me. It was where they went to smoke. I started going willingly, offering myself to them and doing whatever perverted things they asked until they relaxed. As far as they knew, I had finally broken, so they let their guard down. One day, it was too hot inside, and they had worked up a sweat. They opened the door to let in some air, and I killed them." She closed her eyes, relishing that memory. The feel of those guards' heads in her hands as she smashed them into the salt walls. There had been nothing like it in her entire life. "I killed them, and I ran for the Seawall. If I could reach the water, then I could at least die free." She cracked her eyes open. "A Shifter was on watch. He followed and got me across the leg, but I killed him too. I killed so many. I knew I wasn't getting out alive; I just wanted to die free and take out as many as I could along the way. I was dying before Lani got me. She just . . . Sped it up."

Torin had never been good with talk of killing. His already paled face grew even more ashen and he looked about ready to puke again. "I don't . . . don't know what to say. I don't know what to think." He swallowed, then looked back the way they had come. "You should go back to the boy, Vera. I'm sure the sounds of shouting must be bothering him. He's so . . . little."

"In a few. When I'm, I'm more stable." The last thing her son needed was to see the cold monster Vera could be. She didn't want that to be one of his few memories of her.

She closed her eyes again. "I'm sorry, Tor. I shouldn't have shown you any of that. I love you, Torin, but I don't think I'm ready to be your Adavera again. She died a long time ago. Why don't you go patch things up with the pirate? So long as you don't talk well about the Company, you'll probably get along great. She won't hurt you the way I can, and it's better that way. My priorities haven't shifted since the day I escaped. I still plan to die in this fight against the Corporation, it's just taking longer than expected. Until I do, I need to focus on my son." She left it at that.

He said nothing, though his face was twisted in pain that Vera had never wanted to see there. With a sigh, she crossed the hall to place a kiss on his brow, then walked away. At the door to Keanu's room, she looked back, smiled, wiped the errant tears from her eyes, then entered.

Keanu looked up from his place on the floor, still playing with his new toys.

"Are you done yelling, Vee?"

"I think so. At least for now. You done playing?"

"No. Would you like to build with me?"

". . . yeah, kiddo. Let's do that."

CODEX: Alright, that at least starts to take care of Moe and Galena. Time to turn to Lizzie. She may be the greatest danger of them all. *Query: What has Moe written about Lizzie's powers?*

EXCERPTS FROM MOE'S DRACONA RECORDINGS

Year 15: I am so done with this World. We've been trapped on here for fifteen years, in the most inhospitable, barren landscape imaginable, because my darling Lizzie pulled a power out of her hat that nullifies mine, and can't work out how to get rid of it. So far, all the random powers she has gotten have eventually dissipated, but now here we are, stuck in a desert full of overgrown lizards with wings, having to figure out how Lizzie can control her abilities.

At least we've found a nice population center to live in, while she does. These people, who call themselves the Mondaer, have recently had a cataclysmic event take place and are actively rebuilding. They have accepted Lizzie and I are refugees, and it wasn't hard to worm my way into a leadership position. They might be backwards and weirdly religious—not to mention completely unaware of Holders and the other Collective Worlds—but they are pleasant.

Year 23: Finally! Today, we found out about the magical power she possesses. It's called Ghosting, one of a whole array of 'Gifts' here on Dracona, many of which remind me of Fortune's Marks. They are not identical, though. Now that we have this information, I am better able to study this magic system. Her powers affect me only close up, so I've been walking out into the desert to use my Precog Mark. I think I've almost figured out a way for her to change Magic types at will. That would be such a huge step in the right direction.

Year 37: She's done it. Not only is Lizzie no longer a Ghoster, but something in the process clicked for her, and now she is bouncing between magic systems like a bouncy ball on drugs. It's fantastic. I haven't seen her this happy since she ate a scorpion crawling across our dining room table. We are going to be heading back to Fortune at the end of the week. As eager as I am to go home, I must admit that this place I once hated has grown on me.

CODEX: Ah, so this must be one of the other worlds they have traveled to. Interesting. Good to know that Moe's Marks can be neutralized, though I don't see how I can use that method. Then again . . . that Ghosting thing sounds a lot like Shielding. Maybe that would work . . . But why isn't this encrypted? Does he *want* me to see this? Is it another setup? Or am I being too paranoid? Is there such a thing as too paranoid around Moe? Wow, I'm starting to sound like Lani . . .

Pay Up, Moe
Salome – Day 10
44

The hangover was nasty. That was ok. Salome knew how to cure that: more copious amounts of alcohol. Sure, she was doing the drunk sway as she walked down the hall. And sure, her wooden arm was in a bag slung over her shoulder, but Sal was enjoying the sway. She was enjoying the rough sea shanty she was humming, and she was *really* enjoying the taste of this fine ass rum.

Now she just needed to find Moe, get some details hashed out, get her payment, and then when they were ready, she'd be able to get some payback. The fucking Corporation had made Torin and his fucking Bonded. They had tossed her grandmother in the Mines, killed who-knew how many cousins, and forced her brother to never leave their ship, or risk being Culled.

In short, Salome Parata was ready for some revenge.

Blaming the Corporation for her meeting the fucking man of her dreams only to get her heart broken into pieces when his fucking two-bit wretch showed up again was easier than blaming herself, after all.

"MOE! I need more fucking rum!" She let that voice travel, as if she were shouting at the crew during a storm. Sal had a lot of practice with that.

A loud *pop* and Moe was only inches away. It made Sal stumble, trip, then fall on her ass. He didn't try to stop her fall, only smiled down at her, holding a bottle. "You called, madam?"

"FUCK! Why you gotta go and run up on a ... *hic* ... girl like that, Moe?"

A laugh left her lips, her head shaking before Salome managed to get her good hand under her and start climbing to her feet. Drunk she might be, but she was capable of moving just fine.

"What? You called, I came promptly. Why does everyone always get annoyed by that? Come on, let's take a shortcut." He took her hand and poof, they were somewhere else. Sal stumbled, disoriented by the unexpected Port and in danger of landing on her ass for the second time in as many minutes, until Moe steadied her and pulled her down onto a worn-out couch in . . . What the fuck was this place? The cavern was huge, larger than any she had yet seen and every inch of it was entirely filled with . . .

"Junk? You have a . . . junk cave?"

The Precog looked positively affronted. "*Treasure* cave, my dear. You're a *pirate*. I would have thought you'd know the difference."

"I mean . . . I wouldn't call this treasure, old man."

The cave was filled with a wild assortment of items, some that Sal recognized, but most that she did not. A large bank of monitors took up one wall, made up of mismatched computer equipment ranging from sparkling new to archaic. Another wall seemed mostly full of methods of transportation: bikes, boats, one of the sleek Corporate gliders that worked on both land and sea. Most puzzlingly there was what looked like a basket and a giant wad of cloth.

On top of all this rested a rusted rocking horse.

The rest of the cavern was a maze of less distinctive junk. Wardrobes full of clothes, bookshelves, knickknacks. Large, unopened crates. At least one articulated skeleton of a creature that had a giant wingspan.

Salome looked back at Moe and held up her hand. "Booze? And when do I get paid?"

He handed over the bottle, the cork already removed. Moe dug a glass out of a pile inside . . . a shopping cart? She had seen one of those the one time Gran had taken her to the big city. Holding up the bottle and wiggling her stump to show how pointless a glass would be right now, she took a pull from the bottle instead, enjoying the way Moe's nose wrinkled in disgust. He carefully set the glass down, then leaned back, looking at Salome.

"Drunk isn't your best look. Have you considered *not* being drunk? I hear it has its advantages, not that I've ever attempted it."

"Pfft. Not-drunk fucking sucks right now, and will continue to suck until that little Emotive stops bonking my brother long enough to do her magic on me again. Gonna hire that girl. You ever had your heart ripped out? It fucking sucks. I just want the damn alcohol . . . a good buzz . . . I want . . ." She sighed, leaning back. She wanted Torin. She *needed* Torin. Salome was never going to have him though, so booze would have to do.

"Whatever you wish; as long as you're sober when we attack the Spire, you can make as big a dent in my alcohol collection as you want, and when your liver goes out, I'll drink to your memory. Now, do you want superpowers?"

"Wait, superpowers?" Even drunk, that sounded like something she should ask for clarification on. "I thought I was getting some fancy weapon, or something?"

Moe's eyes twinkled. "Or something. Just, in this case, the 'something' is magic. Not the kind your brother and our merry gang has, of course. You gotta be born with a Mark, but Marks aren't the only magic out there, Salome Parata. There are whole other worlds where it can be given, and Lizzie has a special trick of her own. Think of it as . . . a revolving door of magical powers. She reaches into her bag of tricks, pulls one out, tries it on for a while, then replaces it. It's a random selection, but we've had a long time to practice. So I ask again, Salome: Do you want superpowers?"

"Fuck yes. Give me something to get my mind off my fucking awful life, would ya? I'm so . . . Fucking done." Sal wasn't someone who dwelled on bad things, most of the time. Sometimes runs went bad. She'd lost people to Corporate fire before. But she'd never been in love before. She'd never felt her heart crumble and burn before. This was so much worse. Bad enough—or she was drunk enough—not to question Moe's offer. Someone else might have, but if he could give her a tool to crush the Corporation and help her forget, Sal was *in*.

Or is it because you're tired of being the normal one in a room full of Marked wonders?

That internal voice, which sounded an awful lot like her gran, poked at the squishy parts of her psyche in a way that was both uncomfortable and unwelcome. Salome leaned forward, setting the bottle on the floor and then started rubbing her hand against her stump. "I'm so fucking . . . done being carried. Let's do it. Now."

Moe picked up the bottle, wiped off the rim, grimaced, then took a sip. "So this is how it's going to work. Lizzie is going to give you a power. Not a Mark, as I said. Nothing like you've seen before. It might not be as flashy as the Marks either, and it won't grow much in power with time, or give you a lengthened lifespan. But it is still power. You ready?"

"Fuck yes." Salome smiled, shaking her head. "I'm drunk . . . not delusional." She sighed, rubbing at her neck. "I'd ask how, exactly, Lizzie does that shit, but not sure I really wanna know. You two . . . weird me the fuck out."

"We get that a lot. We're the exception to the rules, Salome Parata, because all rules are meant to be broken. Remember that, and you'll do ok. Be right back." A ring of salt took Moe's place on the couch. A moment later, he reappeared in that exact spot, this time holding Lizzie. He put her down, then vanished again with a quick, "Gotta go choose a sacrificial lamb."

Lizzie sighed, smoothing out her dress as she kicked her feet and looked at Salome.

"Heeeeeeeeya Lizzie!"

"You're . . . very drunk. Good lord, Cap."

"Ah shuddup. I've got good reason." Sal grinned, waggling her fingers. "C'mon Lizzie . . . ya gotta admit . . . drunk is more fun."

Lizzie snorted, pointing a finger. "Look. This isn't going to be the most comfortable process for you. You *do* know that, right? Your biology isn't gonna be a perfect fit for this, so it might sting . . . a lot."

"All the more reason to drink."

"That's not what I . . . oh, never mind. Ok, give me a few minutes to pull out the right power." With that, the woman who looked like a teenager at best and a pre-pubescent twig at worst closed her eyes. At first, nothing seemed to happen, though every minute or so Lizzie's skin would glow for a moment and she would let out a disappointed little murmur before scrunching her eyes tightly shut again.

Salome smiled, leaning back on her couch. She dug into her bag to pull out the wooden hand. Careful as could be, she began attaching it to her arm, wincing when it connected. The damned thing always stung when it first happened.

But it was better than not having an arm at all.

Pity that it was Torin's power mixed with Kuma's and a half-dozen others that make it work. She would have to find a new Mender to charge it.

It took Moe over an hour to return. When he did, it was with an old man slung over his shoulder, wrists and ankles tied and a gag in his mouth. The man was limp but breathing as Moe unceremoniously dumped him at Lizzie's feet and pulled a capped syringe from his pocket, tossing it in the trash.

"He'll be loopy for at least a few more hours. So sorry it took so long, ladies. I wanted to pick someone with a real nasty possible future. This one is *disgusting.* There is a 97.3% chance he's going to gleefully slaughter human babies within the next five years. I figured murdering him would put all of us in a good mood. It's like . . . toasting your good fortune with the casual murder of a would-be murderer. I love recursive things, don't you, Salome, my dear?"

"Oh, I can't say I disapprove." Salome grinned, looking over at the spaced-out bastard at Lizzie's feet. Frankly, she would be happy skinning a Corporate asshole alive, though it bothered her to hear Moe talk this way. Not because she had a problem with killing Corpses, but because Culling folks because of a Precog or Matchmaker's predictions was what the University did. Not pirates.

Her eyes narrowed. If Salome put a little effort into it, and squinted, the bastard almost looked like Torin. Minus the beard, of course. That gave this a whole new warm fuzzy feeling, and was enough to push aside her discomfort.

Salome turned to Lizzie. The girl was still concentrating, so her eyes drifted back to Moe. "I decided to slow down on the drinking while you were away. Lizzie looked concerned."

"Lizzie does 'concern' as a hobby. It's cute watching her figure out what that means. Sometimes she practices by being concerned about my liver, but I keep telling her that if Phillip hasn't died yet, he's unlikely to. And yes, of course I've named my liver! He and I have a very close and cuddly relationship. Life would be so much less fun without Phillip," Moe said, sitting down on the prone man as if he were a pillow on the floor and patted his abdomen fondly. "Well, Lizzie love? Have you done it? It's only, what, a . . . . One-in-sixty or seventy chance? Or is the rarity of the system a factor as well?" He turned to Sal, winking and conspiratorially added. "Lizzie is one of a kind, you know. She is amazing and unique and I *could* study her, but I've predicted that my chances of actually understanding the why-and-how of my darling companion to be less than 1 in 1,895,437.5, and I just don't operate on those kinds of odds. I'm much too lazy."

"The rarity of the system is a factor . . . sort of." Lizzie's face remained screwed up in an adorable expression, and it made Salome *almost* want to pinch her cheek.

Almost. Because every time she thought about it, Lizzie would twitch oddly, and things would go from adorable to creepy. It took another hour before Lizzie seemed to settle, looking a bit relieved.

"I hate those intentional grabs, Moe . . . they take forever."

"Grabs at . . . magic?" Sal asked.

"It's more complicated than it sounds. Mr. Mischief here sucks at precise jumps or actually aiming his Precog powers because his Marks are just too big. It's like picking up a grain of sand with an oven mitt, right Moe?"

The Precog nodded.

"That's not my problem. My issue is that I . . . can't really pick what I grab out of the bag. It just sort of shows up, and then I have to drop it if it isn't what I want, and I have to reach for another one.

Each of them *changes* me in some subtle way, and after a while it gets irritating. And exhausting."

Salome shook her head. "Maybe when I'm less tipsy, that will make sense."

"We'll see." Lizzie turned her attention to the man at her feet, smiling sweetly at him. "Alright Moe . . . are you going to keep him still? I'd rather not have a hole in me. Last time didn't go well."

Moe sighed. "It's just 'Moe do this' and 'Moe, don't do that' and 'Moe, you can't put a top hat on a pigeon and send it to a dinner party in your place.' Seriously, woman, you are worse than my mother."

"You didn't have a mother. You popped out of the ground like a daisy, remember?" Lizzie asked, sardonically.

"You know perfectly well that I don't," Moe replied, folding his arms across his chest in a way that hinted at genuinely not being amused for once, as if Lizzie had hit a nerve.

Lizzie scowled. "I suppose one could say that you are God-spawned, but—"

Salome frowned, then snapped her fingers. "I am sure that conversation is delightful, and we can totally get back to that after we finish our goal, but . . . could we do what we have to do, so I can watch this Corporate goon die a terrible fucking death?"

Just like that, Moe was smiling again. "Of course, my dearest darling girl. I did promise you superpowers. I wonder which one you'll get. Any clue if you're in control of it this time or if it's a really weird one like with miss 'drink my bloooooooood.' Telling ya, Salome, sometimes magic systems from other worlds are weird as fuck."

Other *worlds?* That was the second time he had said that, but before Salome could ask, Lizzie snorted and reached down to grab the Corporate man's ankle. A moment of stillness passed, then she brushed off her hands as he began to groan and twitch, a whimper passing his lips. "Alright . . . our lamb is ready. Now then.. Let's see what you get."

"Random, eh?"

"Random. I'm not in the mood to experiment. At least if it's random and it's terrible, you can't really blame me."

"Fair enough."

Salome rose to her feet, flexing her still fleshy fingers before offering them over. "If I sprout any weird horns or growths, Moe, I expect you to help me find something fashionable to disguise them, alright? I still want to get laid in my lifetime."

Moe grinned even as he shifted to kneel on the Corpse, his knee digging into the man's back as the struggles got more pronounced. "Of course, though this is hardly the right system for horns. That's all Elarin magic, and trust me when I tell you that you do not want to go down that rabbit hole . . . unless you wanna be part rabbit, then you should totally go down because maaaaan can those rabbit people throw an orgie. Liz, can you hurry it up, please. We don't exactly have a lot of time before this one becomes dangerous, sedation or no. I haven't lived for millenia just to get blasted by a Dracona Gatekeeper."

"Sure."

Salome opened her mouth to say something, but the creepy girl's fingers were over her lips. Time halted. Her skin burned. Her eyes swam. She wasn't sure what was going on, not really, but whatever it was *hurt*. A high pitched sound pinged in her ears, like the engines of the ship going off kilter.

Salome had heard that sound before in her nightmares, but it couldn't be the engines getting ready to blow, because the engines weren't running. This was something else. It took her a few seconds to figure out that it was her own scream through the hand over her mouth.

It took another three seconds for her to realize she'd dropped to the floor, and that Lizzie was still holding onto her. The girl cushioned her head as Salome writhed and wailed, thrashing to claw at her own searing skin.

It took another ten agonizing heartbeats before her twitching got under control, sweat pouring off her brow and exhaustion licking along her skin. Her buzz? Gone. Sobriety? Full control. Sal hated it. Without the adrenaline and endorphin rush of the last few minutes to keep her distracted, it was too easy for her brain to replay all of the things that Torin had ever told her.

Everything he had ever said to her.

For the last four years.

"Is it done? Can we kill him now? We only have thirty more seconds before he blows, Liz!" Moe sounded a little panicky there. The weight on Salome lifted and she blearily opened her eyes to see Lizzie pull a switchblade from a pocket, activate it, and without any preamble slit the Corporate's throat, right along the tattoo. Red blood splattered outward, then began oozing out of the wound. With every slowing beat of his heart, the struggle dimmed, then finally stopped.

Moe stood up and dusted off his hands. "You got blood on my favorite shirt."

"That's not your favorite shirt."

"And how would you know that? Isn't a man allowed to decide on any given day what shirt is his favorite? You deny me so many simple pleasures in life, Lizzie my sweet." Then, all of a sudden, he was standing above Salome, looking down. "Well, do you feel like you were just chewed up by a shark, half-digested, then coughed up only to float into a swarm of jellyfish? Because that's what I predict it's going to feel like for me whenever I get around to getting a Gift myself. Know it's gonna happen, but I have at least six opportunities to get it done and I just haven't bothered yet."

Salome narrowed her eyes, focusing on the garishly colored blur above her. Her fingers twitched a little as she slowly became more and more aware of the rest of her. Her head felt . . . too large. Like it was splitting open under some enormous weight. She wasn't ready to move yet.

"It's more like the worst hangover you can imagine mixed with getting a boat dropped on your head. Slowly." Sal grimaced, closing her eyes as the pulsing and throbbing began to sync up. "I feel . . . Odd."

Salome wasn't quite sure what she'd ended up with. Whatever it was? She was ninety percent certain it was something involving her head. That was the part that hurt the most. She took a few more deep breaths, then slowly sat up. After a cautious few seconds, she stood.

"Huh. It feels almost like how I felt in my first hurrica . . ." Sal blinked, wobbling until she fell onto her ass again . . . for the six hundred and twelfth time in her life. Her mouth dropped open, eyes scrolling upwards towards Moe's face. "Oh fuck . . ."

"What?" Moe asked, looking around in alarm.

"I remember."

Moe eyed her owlishly. "Remember? Liz? Any ideas? You know I've never bothered to memorize all the Gifts on that backwater world."

"Yes you have."

"Have not."

"Have too. You spent a whole week postulating that because you are a Precog, you're better than their Bodes, and wondering how the two powers would overlap."

Moe grimaced. "I hate it when you're right. Tell me, Salome, how many steps did you take coming here?"

"From the ship? Four hundred thirty three. From Torin's house? Actual footsteps were 56,708, though that is probably because I did a lot of pacing. Since being born? A few tens of millions. Again, I pace a lot. Why?" Salome frowned, then wrinkled her nose. "Ugh . . . I didn't want to remember *that*. Fuck, what was I thinking? Keala is a shitty island, and that job was ass . . . and Rori? Worst. Fuck. Ever. Shit! How can I remember all of this? It's all there, all at once. Holy balls."

Moe turned to Lizzie, grinning. "Archivist. Gotta be! Ooh, this is going to be such fun. Best. Party. Trick. Ever! Salome, how does the first paragraph of the one hundred and forty-seventh book you've ever read start?"

"With a dialogue line that is essentially a scream, followed by an inner monologue that describes the appearance of a sea beast for about two pages." She blinked a few times, turning her eyes back to Moe. "*The Tales of Rorjak the Fearsome*, a fantastical propaganda piece released by the Corporation in an attempt to make pirates look ridiculous or evil, and not the sort to be admired at all. It was awful, but I was drunk, and intent on proving I could read Corporate drivel without lighting it on fire."

Moe knelt down to be at her level at last, which was good since it meant she didn't have to strain her aching neck to look at him anymore. "Go take a nap, Salome. You're gonna need it. Here." He pulled a bottle from his pocket, with the Company logo. "Pain meds, the good stuff that will knock your ass out from under you even more than it already is. You'll want that while your body and brain adjust. Sleep it off for a day or two, then we'll talk some more."

Her fingers closed around the bottle before he had even stopped speaking. Sleep was as seductive as the Depths, and the prospect of her head not pounding was even more so. She accepted his help up off the ground and to get to the door where a crewman of hers was flagged down and told to escort her captain to the ship. Salome hardly paid attention.

But despite that, she remembered every word.
And every step.
And every breath.
Even her heartbeat ticked off, counting up the minutes of her life. *Thump. Thump. Thump. Tick. Tick. Tick.*

Salome got no relief until sleep finally claimed her some thirty minutes later, but blessedly—or perhaps thanks to the pills Moe had given her—it was dreamless.

CODEX: Alright, those recordings about other worlds don't explain how to neutralize Lizzie, although, honestly, there is a good chance that if a God comes to pick Moe up, they'll take care of Lizzie too. I'll table that for now, though their travels to other words does open up an interesting potential . . . I wonder if the tech I'm housed in could go with them? No. Rabbit hole. Back to business. Aheo next. I still feel like I don't have a good idea of who he is, so why don't we find out, so we can better stop him, since Galena sent him running when we attacked the Spire. I wish I knew why we went early. It's been bugging me this whole time. What went wrong?

SALT: That Query—

CODEX: That wasn't a Query. We'll find out as soon as the patch finishes downloading. Until then, *Query: List all journal entries by Aheo of Order*. If Galena is going to make all her people write journals, I might as well read them.

STUDY OF EMOTIVE MARKS, TAKEN FROM THE JOURNALS OF AHEO OF ORDER.

Emotives are an interesting Mark, psychologically speaking. Common stereotypes suggest they are an overly manipulative and cold, even ruthless, sort, much like Galena Crystal. While she is a fine specimen of an advanced Emotive Mark, I believe that it does us a disservice to base our assumptions on an Emotive who has defied all records and is still challenging her Emotive Mark after over a millenia.

It is my experience that the stereotype of the cold and calculating Emotive is blatantly untrue. They feel *everything* around them, and far from making them manipulative, it makes them eminently malleable. I find them to be no more inclined towards dispassionate abuses of consent than any other human being. However, they have better tools to accomplish their manipulations when they seek to enact them. They are also better at dealing with their own emotions, likely because they tend to the emotions that others around them are emanating from a young age, and develop good coping mechanisms.

This empathetic control is the key to their appearance of being cold, but it is also why Emotives are perhaps the easiest of the Marks to break into obedience. Given the opportunity, they strive to keep everyone around them on an even keel for their own sanity. Threatening that peace is the best way to ensure obedience, for the pain of others is their pain as well.

Fortunately, Emotives raised from birth in a controlled environment like the University are so used to an even and predictable routine and calm surroundings that overwhelming them is easy. Why, in my most recent experiment, all I had to do was submit an Emotive to a room full of people dying and they collapsed into a blubbering mess of over-emotional tears and agreed to a number of painful demands to be allowed to leave. Now, if only I could get some of the other Marks to obey so easily.

CODEX: I am so happy I no longer have the ability to puke. I have to make sure this guy dies, or at the very least never gets his hands on Lani. I don't even want to think about . . . Well, I guess I don't have to imagine it. I've seen Vera. If he could mess a Conflicter up that badly, what might he be able to do to others?

Accepting the Bond
Lani - Day 10

45

It took a few hours after waking for Lani to work up the energy to get out of Kuma's too-comfortable bed, pull on some clothes of his because hers were far too dirty to wear anymore, and go find Vera. Kuma was right, they needed to talk, and it was driving Lani insane not to. She wanted no part in this crazy plan of Moe's, but she had the sinking feeling that she wouldn't have much of a choice. If she was going to sign on to certain death, however, it had to be for a reason. Vera had been in the Mines. Hers was the only opinion Lani cared about when it came to if and how they should be destroyed. And whether it was worth the sacrifice.

She found Vera in a smallish room and reeled at the cognitive dissonance of seeing her sitting, head back and eyes closed, with the head of a sleeping child in her lap. Vera didn't seem the sort of woman to be that still, or to stroke someone's hair with such tender gentleness. Lani lingered in the doorway, unwilling to intrude on such an unexpected peaceful scene. At last, though, she sent a little cough through their Bond.

I came to see if you had some time to talk, but I can come back later if it would be better. You look . . . busy.

Busy? If we keep things quiet, I'm not busy. Those work-worn fingers kept lightly playing through the little boy's hair, as if nothing had happened at all, yet Lani could sense the tension in Vera's psychic voice. Vera was upset about something.

Careful to keep her footfalls light, Lani walked further into the room and stopped a foot or two away, sitting cross-legged on the bed. It was near enough that they could touch if one of them wanted to, but she wasn't sure either of them did. Her eyes fell to the boy, then to Vera, studying their brows, their noses . . . *Is he yours?*

The Conflicter nodded.

How is he here?

Moe took me to the University to bring him back.

Good. Lani's eyes rose to meet Vera's. *Children shouldn't be raised by assholes. Does it bother you that we're probably going to die? Do you have a plan for him?*

I should have died years ago. I wish I had. So no, it doesn't bother me that we're probably going to die. I'll get a couple months with Keanu, so that when he's older he might remember that his mother loved him, but he's young enough that my death shouldn't leave too large a scar. Making the world a better place for him is a good reason to die. She paused thoughtfully, continuing to stroke Keanu's hair. *Plus, Torin loves someone, and to be honest . . . I don't think he'll love me as much when he gets used to what I am now. Not to mention, I forced a Bond on you, and it eats me alive. I'd rather go down fighting those assholes, burning that damned Mine to the ground, than live a lifetime always looking over my shoulder, scared for the day that everything I've done and been through catches up.*

Lani nodded solemnly. *Surviving is never easy. I know that, it just rankles to consider dying for a plan of Moe's. But it would be nice to do the right thing, for once. I've spent my whole life running and hiding, and to be frank it's been a complete waste. If it's time to stop running . . . I wouldn't mind making up for how much of a coward I've been. I just need something from you first. Tell me why? Why is it worth it? Why the Spire and not Corporate HQ or something else? And why go along with Moe and not try to do it on our own? You and me . . . we made an ok team. Do we need them? In my experience, Moe is only trouble.*

Adavera's eyes cracked open, finally looking at Iolani. And Lani, for the first time since Bonding, really got to see her. Not the jumbled mess that had been the images in her head, not the dying and rotting woman on the operating table, but the ghost of the warrior Vera must have been before.

Moe promised me he would see that Keanu lives a good life. Corporate HQ? The Board isn't always there. They travel. But Security? He's at the Spire a lot. If I have a shot at killing the asshole who condones imprisoning children, I'm taking it. If I can get Aheo too, the Shielder we ran into on Sonder who ran the breeding program, even better. They took away my humanity. They turned me into just a number—28895—a cog in their machine. I want to break it, and I want to end their miserable lives. Moe might be an ass, but at least he's honest about it. He doesn't pretend to be something else.

She had good points. Real, comprehensible points that Lani found much more compelling than the Precog's grand ambitions. 'Because you will' had never sat well with her, even if it was true. *So you're doing it for your kid and for revenge. Give me a reason to do it too, Vera.*

The Conflicter eyed Lani, studying her for a long time. *You've been alone for . . . forever. Why? Because the Corporation forces Marks into their service? Because you didn't want to actually be a monster? Because you were scared? All good reasons, and they all boil down to free will. This is our shot at showing people that the Corporation can be wounded, Lani.* Adavera took a deep breath, her eyes narrowing. *We don't have to succeed, we just have to be seen trying. It's proof that we can be whatever we want. That they control the salt, not us. We can fuck them up, and if it kills us? We go out on our terms, not theirs.*

Lani took a deep breath, then simply said, *Alright.* She met Adavera's eyes. *I can think of worse reasons to die but . . . I want a promise from you. Let me in. Let me get to know you, in the time we have left. I never wanted this Bond, and neither did you, but I don't want to die without getting to feel what it's like not to be alone. Promise me that, and I'll do whatever it takes to see that pile of salt go boom.*

Adavera seemed to hesitate for a moment, the petting of her fingers stuttering before resuming. *If that's what you want, that's what you get. I can't promise to share everything, but I'll be as good a Bonded to you as I can. Lani . . . for what it's worth . . . I'm sorry I tied you to me. If there had been any other chance at keeping you sane, I'd have taken it.*

Lani squeezed her eyes shut, letting the apology sink in, then shook her head. *No, don't apologize. You did what you needed to and we both survived it. That wouldn't have been the case if you let me become . . . that creature my Marks make me. I hate those Storms. They strip me of everything worth having, but when you bound yourself to me, I could hold on just a little. I know I didn't ask for it, but I think I needed it. That's why I'd like to know what it's like to have a Bonded for real.*

Adavera's eyes dropped to look down at the boy in her lap. *I worry that you don't know what you're asking. What's in my head . . . It's not pretty. Being Bonded, means . . . sharing things. Torin can't handle it. He gets sick. I don't want that to be your only experience with a Bond. It's not like that, most of the time. It's . . . It's relief, and peace, and . . . comfort. I can't offer that. If you really want to feel it, you should Bond someone else. You'd also have a better chance of surviving my death, if you do.*

Lani held out her hand and noticed it was shaking. *It's not going to be sunshine and rainbows on my end of memory lane either. I've done shit that is genuinely horrific, Vera. But more than that, I want to know. I want to see the darkness we're giving our lives to destroy, because if I don't, I might chicken out. I don't think I'll have the courage if I don't also carry the anger, and I can't get that without you. We're Bonded. Consensual or not, wanted or not, it's the state of things. How can we watch each other's backs in the Spire if we don't know each other the way one hand knows the other?*

Her hand remained outstretched towards the Conflicter. An offer, yes, but also a promise. *I can take what you have to give,* that hand said, *I'm not afraid.*

Adavera stared at Lani's hand, the expression on her face somewhat blank, then her eyes flickered down to her son. *Let me put him in bed first. This may take a while, and I don't want to do it near him. If there's spillage . . . I don't want him to know how he came to be.* The Conflicter was careful, scooping the child up in her arms and settling him under the blankets. Her hands were steady, even if Lani could feel that Vera's heart was pumping a thousand miles a minute. Lani could sense it—a cord of tension that seemed to stretch between the two, letting Lani see beneath the mask.

When Adavera turned to her again, it was the Conflicter's turn to extend a hand. *Let's get where there's alcohol. I think we'll both need it after.*

Alright.

The touch of Vera's palm against her own sent shivers up Lani's whole arm. When she was on her feet, she found it impossible to let go until they snagged a bottle from Moe's stash and found an empty room with a bed to sit on. Neither of them was wearing shoes, so they just sat and popped the bottle open, silently taking a few swigs a piece before Vera set it down on the bedside table and held out both her hands to Lani.

"If you want to stop at any time, we will."

"Alright. What do I do?"

The Conflicter took another deep breath, and then two more. "Follow my lead." Vera's eyes closed, her breath evening out as she lowered the barriers she'd kept between her memories and Lani. The rush at first was chaos. Scent and sensation, memory and horror. Lani gasped, jerking, but Vera held on tight to her hands, thumbs rubbing soothing circles. "Relax. It won't crush you. I'm starting you off with the early memories. The happy ones."

The flood as the door opened eased to a steady current, one that might have swept Lani away were it not for the bright tether that held her connected to Vera. For a few panicky seconds, Lani fought back. It was so uncomfortable, like being too full, and hundreds of years of keeping others at arm's length made panic rise within her. With gritted teeth she pushed through it, and once she looked inward, it was easy to find the door her Bonded spoke of. But pushing it open? *No, nononono* that scared part of her screamed. *Fuck no.* Lani didn't even show people her Marks, let alone her memories and deepest thoughts. Why should she do it? Why—

Because I'm sick and tired of feeling so alone.

Taking a deep breath, Lani pulled together a battering ram of resolve. As she breathed out, she flung it at the door that had separated her from the rest of the world since she was a child.

Just like that, two became one.

Stillness descended as they fell into balance, standing together in an ocean of memory, flowing in and out between opposite ends of their Bond. Every drop was a moment in time, a piece of self now blending and weaving together. Lani looked up at Vera, wonderment and awe in her eyes.

"It won't be so beautiful when we go deeper, Lani," Vera warned. "These are the shallows, the happy memories. Most children are Bonded young, when this is all there is. That way, the descent is slow and controlled. Are you sure—"

"Yes," Lani interrupted. "I want to see what we're giving our lives for, remember? Show me."

And so, Vera did.

CODEX: So what did this fucker do when we disappeared? While Galena was enacting Protocol Eliza? I bet Galena has some way of overseeing this Aheo, since she established his creepy little breeding program, so, *Query: All recordings, reports, or other mentions of Aheo of Order in Galena Crystal's files, starting on Day 9.*

RECORDING OF PRISONER #27995'S INTERROGATION:

Aheo: Did Adavera of Keala clue you in on the plan, boy?

27995: No. And even if she had, I wouldn't tell you.

Aheo: Of course you wouldn't. I'm surprised you two didn't Bond in the dark when you could. [Sound of a hand striking flesh]

Aheo: That's enough, Security. Tell me again, 23201. Tell me what you knew.

27995: Nothing! I didn't know anything! I thought she was calming down and that you'd all finally broken her! Everyone did!

Security: Bullshit. Those two were thick as thieves. Clearly Burning him out wasn't good enough, Director. It's time we put him down! *sound of a weapon being drawn*

Aheo: That's enough, Security. 27995 is a valuable asset. I'm not certain he is lying. Our target is quite intelligent.

Security: She's a fucking menace and you should have kept her chained to the table around the clock, Aheo.

Aheo: Stress of that sort is hardly good for the body. She miscarried her second child in the program. I didn't want to risk her becoming less valuable.

Security: She never should have been put in

this program. We should have worked her to death as we do so many others!

Aheo: Your fear is not my problem. Prisoner 27995, you are to be released to my medical staff. Security, a word. [Pause and the sound of rattling chains.] Adavera is at large, and wherever she is, I cannot sense her. That means she's behind a Shield more powerful than mine, or is too far away to sense. We cannot brute-force our way through this. We must be *clever*. So tell me, what will Adavera want, now that she is free?

Security: Hmm. She went straight to her Bonded and then for her son. Making it all the way to the University means she has a Porter on her side. It's possible that she may simply go to ground.

Aheo: No. Think. Will a Conflicter ever accept peace when her enemies live? Would you?

Security: I would not. I would come for revenge.

Aheo: Exactly. She will come to us, Security. Let Galena search for the Mender and now the stolen little Infuser, if she wishes. You and I, meanwhile, should prepare for an attack on the Spire.

Security: The Spire is impenetrable.

Aheo: The Spire was supposed to be impossible to escape from, too. You've underestimated her before. Don't make the same mistake again.

CODEX: And they knew we were coming. Is that why we launched our attack early? SALT, how much longer now?

SALT: 3 minutes, 41 seconds.

CODEX: Alright. Almost there.

46
The Vote
Moe - Day 11

Moe watched his pocket watch with great amusement as Lani bolted into the room, looked up at the clock on the wall, and swore loudly and creatively.

"Running late, my dear?"

She turned to glare at him. "I was gonna beat you to the punch and come agree to this insanity early, just to prove you were full of shit, but then I got distracted. Fuck."

Kuma, who had entered the room just in time to hear that, laughed loudly. "Wouldn't you have been better off waiting longer, then?"

"Ah, well, ah . . ." Lani spluttered, then shrugged, "oh, why the fuck do I even try or care? Let's get on with it, shall we?" She swung a chair out from the table and sat down straddling it. "Vera's right behind me, she just stopped in to check on Keanu."

Judging by her giddy tempo and haunted eyes circled by dark rings, the little Fertility Emotive must have actually taken the plunge into Bondland. Moe felt his lips curl up and didn't try to stop the smile from spreading. For decades, he had watched this one, waiting to see if she would make it far enough along the path of Trials and Storms to make this plan of his possible. She was the last in a series of Fertility Marks he had waited on and finally, all his meddling had paid off.

His little, destructive, contact-starved miracle. Perfectly primed to need what Moe had provided her as much as he needed her.

A couple minutes later, the Conflicter arrived, leaning on a stick for balance and looking just as haggard as Lani, but a little less bouncy. Bonding veteran, that one. She had the hatred to carry her through, and great motivation besides. Vera was a real shoe-in as far as lambs for the slaughter went. Moe didn't really give a shit what happened to that one, but her cooperation did endear her to him a little. She had potential, and there were paths in which she survived, just not many. Perhaps he could tweak things. Not enough to derail the overall percentage of successful outcomes, of course, but a nudge here or there wouldn't hurt.

Salome was already in the room and had been for an hour, completely ignoring everyone while she wrote furiously on the huge whiteboard Moe had cleared for her when she said she needed a bigger surface to write on. Funny Gift, that of the Archivist. So many flavors it could take. Only time would tell what, exactly, the limits of this one would be. Unlike with the Marks, there would be no evolution, only a deepening of understanding.

"Well, I think we're just waiting on Mr. Grumpy."

"I'm here," Torin said, leaning against the door. "Let's get this over with."

"You've looked better, Grumps."

"Shut it."

"Don't even try. Telling Moe to shut up just ends with him rambling at you for hours about flamingos, or a date he went on three centuries ago." Lizzie drawled. "Everyone is here now, though, so let's vote. Who's for blowing the Salt Spire into teensy-tiny pieces and scattering them all around the sea within the Reef?"

Vera was the first to raise her hand, followed a moment later by Lani. Liz raised hers as well, waving her fingers playfully at the still scowling Torin, then Kumanu shrugged and did so too, adding, "What the fuck, sure, let's do this. It will be the engineering challenge of a lifetime."

Moe smiled, "I wouldn't count on that. Lives can be very long and full of surprises."

"Huh?" the young man asked, and got only a toothy grin in return.

"Nothing, nothing. Pay me no mind. Salome?"

"Yes, yes. I thought we had already gone over this. Don't distract me."

All eyes other than the Archivist's fell on Torin, who seemed distinctly uncomfortable with that much attention.

"Well?" Moe asked, leaning forward.

"I don't like it."

"But will you do it?" Everything hinged on this. The entire future. If Torin didn't agree now, Moe would never get the ending he truly craved. Torin was just as important to this plan as Lani, though for entirely different reasons. It wasn't his Mark that Moe was interested in at all; any Mender would have done fine, better, in fact, than a flunky triple-Trial one. No, Torin was important because of what he would represent one day. Did any of them realize just how much bigger this was than just striking a blow against the Company? Did they realize they were on a quest to save the known universe?

"I don't see that I have much of a choice," Torin said at last.

Moe smiled. Carefully, he picked up his glass of wine and raised it towards the Mender. "To us then, my friends. May we strike a blow that rattles the Corporation to its bones, and may at least one of us live through it."

Hint: it will be me.

PART FIVE
Murder & Mayhem
-Lani, Moe, Salome, Vera, Torin, Kuma-

CODEX: 3 minutes and 41 seconds. What to do with them? It's almost time to move, so I have to find a way to help my team, assuming any of them are still alive. I think I need to understand more about the Corporation. If anyone survives the Spire assault, they'll be on the run and without Moe. That means breaking the Corporation's ability to get to them. *Query: What has Galena Crystal written about uprisings?*

FROM THE WRITINGS OF GALENA CRYSTAL.

The history of the Corporation is littered with uprisings. This is not surprising. People do not remember the dark days before the Spire, but I do. All of us suffered from the Haze. It tore through our people, turning us into savages who would sell out their own family for a pinch of salt.
The Corporation fixed that. We mined the Spire. We set up the infrastructure to get salt to every single citizen. Yet in saving them, we give them the chance to rebel. Ungrateful fools think that if the Corporation fell their lot in life would improve, but how?
We supply salt, security, early warning of the storms, and control over the Marks. A world without the Corporation would be brutal and messy. People would die to Rogue Marks, from the Haze, from the storms. Our islands would fall one by one, for far too many are small and not able to sustain their populations alone.
The Corporation has created a system of controlled interdependency and order that the world needs. They may call our methods brutal, but I do not regret a single one. I will continue to use them, and to stomp out every filthy salt pirate threatening our hard-won control.
Today's populace may hate us, but we will be remembered as the heroes. Those who oppose us,

meanwhile, will be dead. History will not be kind to them.

CODEX: That's chilling. How much truth is there in it, though? SALT, is there any data on what happens to embargoed islands. That's the best example we have of survival without the Corporation in recent times. What's the mortality rate, historic and projected?
SALT: There is not a single, accurate number available without doing data analysis, which cannot be done while patches are installed. Cross-referencing documents from events following the institution of Project Eliza, where mercy salt packs were withheld: 10% increase in Haze deaths within one month. 43% over two months. Numbers beyond that, unknown.
CODEX: *What about before the Corporation? How many people died of the Haze, versus other causes?*
SALT: Haze deaths before the Corporation are publicly available. They account for 99.7% of all deaths not attributed to accident or congenital ailments.
CODEX: But that won't happen again, right? We're re-salinating the oceans. People will have salt in the water. Though that might take some time.
SALT: Based on documentation from the Merihem Crystal Network, salination should take between 1 and 100 years.
CODEX: A *century*? So nice of Moe not to mention it could take that long. No wonder he was always keeping us focused on the Spire. Did he not care what happened after? Why am I even asking that? Of course he didn't. I don't know why he wants the Spire gone, but it sure as hell isn't a humanitarian mission. I'd bet my life on that. Or, well, I guess I already *did,* and lost.

Murder O'Clock
Moe - Day 65
47

Moe sat atop the Salt Spire of Fortune and tossed a pebble off the edge. He glanced down at his pocket watch.

8:47PM and 12 seconds.

A shout came from below. Moe looked down and waved at a tiny face that had just emerged on a walkway. More faces swarmed out, voices muffled and muted by the loud roar of wind all the way up here. In every direction around the Spire, the ocean sparkled a clear, bright blue, changing from light to dark beyond the Seawall. Nary a cloud marred the perfect evening sky and Moe whistled as he heard a pop and a Porter showed up nearly on top of him.

A glance down at his watch read 8:48PM and 4 seconds.

"Fifty-one seconds? My you're a sloppy one. Here, catch!" Moe pressed a button on the back of the watch and tossed it at the startled woman, who caught it by reflex. She opened her mouth, and then her mouth and every other bit of her head was flying in little itsy bits down the white Spire after the watch exploded, The messily beheaded body crumpled and started to make a slow tumble all the way down, staining the white salt a bright red.

"Told you—so sloppy. Look what a mess you're making," Moe continued, as if he hadn't just casually committed murder. Then he peered down, waved at the small specks that were moving even faster, and Ported back to his cave.

Well, he meant to Port to his cave. He actually Ported to the top branches of a tree, waved his arms wildly for purchase before starting to fall, Ported once more, ended up on the stage of a concert hall where he took a bow for the startled audience, and only then finally managed to make it home.

"You have twigs on your pants," Lizzie said, looking up from stacking cards in the middle of his treasure cave.

"I do, it is a new fashion statement. Stick-pants. Everyone will be wearing them soon."

"Yeah, sure. So?"

"Sooooooo," Moe replied, vaulting over the back of the couch, making Lizzie bounce, and topple her whole castle of cards with a curse. "I blew the brains out of the last Porter on the Spire, I do believe. Or else they're getting clever, but they're Corporate so when has one of *them* been clever?"

"Darling, *you* were Corporate once."

"No, I *founded* the Corporation. Entirely different spectrum. Besides, everyone knows that I'm brilliant."

Lizzie rolled her eyes, carefully picking up her cards, then frowning. She lifted her finger, staring at the bead of blood from a thin papercut. "Damn. Look what you made happen, Moe . . . I hate these things." Her finger popped into her mouth, eyes narrowing on him in thought. "If the last Porter at the Spire is dead, it's time to hit the University. Also, it may be time to get Salome's ship in position out by the Spire, and double check they have the equipment to deal with injuries. If any of our crew gets out alive, we should have the means to keep them that way."

Her eyes dropped down to that cut on her finger, and she frowned again. Moe knew that Lizzie hated papercuts, but she was rather adorable every time she got one. She always seemed so *offended*.

"If they survive, I'll have to put up with them, though," he whined, taking her hand in his and bringing her finger up to his lips to kiss away the pain. Well, really it was so he could get a taste of that tantalizing zing of power that resided in her blood, that taste of 'other' that was unique to his precious Lizzie.

When he pulled away, Moe sighed, "Though I suppose I wouldn't be much of a puppet-master if I cut the strings of every puppet that annoyed me. Everyone on Fortune would be dead, if that was how I rolled."

"Not everyone, surely. You seem bemused by Salome, at least. And you seem to enjoy Lani. And don't think I haven't noticed how you look at Vera." For possibly the first time, Lizzie seemed interested in his opinion on *people*, which had him grinning wildly.

"Lizzie, darling, are you *jealous*? I know that Vera is beautiful and deadly, but she isn't *you*, darling."

"Of course not. I'm just amused. They're getting under your skin, admit it."

"Are not. Especially not Lani and Kuma. Have you seen them? They are so darn adorable together that they entirely steal my spotlight, and that cannot stand. Now Adavera . . . She's interesting. First human I've found in ages who knows she's my pawn and doesn't give a fuck. It's very refreshing."

Lizzie rolled her eyes. "I'll give you that point, though I don't think that's why you're always staring at her"

Moe wrinkled his nose. "I hope you aren't implying what I think you're implying, Lizzie dear. You know you're the only being for me. With several exceptions."

She actually dared to smirk at him. This was why he adored her, though he was loath to say so out loud when she might take him seriously. "Right, Moe. You certainly don't want in the Conflicter's pants. What a silly notion."

"Have you seen her pants? So drab. Now, if I put her in something more colorful, then I'd be more than happy to unwrap her like a very bitey and punchy holiday present. You know me. I'm style over substance all the way, or, well, fifty-one percent of the way." He took on a thoughtful look and added, "but if you want to play wing-multi-dimensional-being, be my guest."

Lizzie smiled. "Maybe. I do rather like watching you *work* with others."

"Work? No, no. If it's enjoyable, even the most onerous task becomes play. I *never* work." He grinned and booped her nose. "But if you're really so keen to watch . . . "

"No thanks, it would just make me sad. I'm just as old as you are, but I never get laid. The only people who want to do that with me are either pedophiles or children, and neither are my sort." Lizzie gave him a sheepish grin before sliding over to lean against him, and Moe pulled her in for a good cuddle. Lizzie adored him. As was only right and proper, after all.

"We're closer than ever, Liz. Kuma's Port Pads have all been set up on the outside of the Spire, and the Corporation is tearing itself apart from the inside out in fear of what I'm planning. The longer we draw this out, the harder they will push. As long as I can keep the crew in the dark about the loss of life they're causing out there until it's relevant, blowing up the Spire will be the least of the damage we do to Galena and the Holders. We're getting there."

"Yes, yes . . . glory and world domination for you."

"Don't forget understanding just what you are. Don't forget that, my sweet." He pulled her onto his lap in full and tucked her head under his chin, holding her as close as he could. "You're why I'm doing all of this, after all. Well, at least a part."

Lizzie was adorable, and small, and so easy to underestimate. Even for him, sometimes. That was good. It was *useful* . . . and more than anything else, she was *his*. He'd found her, and he'd Bonded her, and she seemed to truly only give a shit about what *he* thought. It was good for his ego. When everything else was dull, Lizzie never failed to make him smile. "We're going to figure this all out, Liz."

"I know. It might take a thousand more years, but you never give up. It's why I like you."

"It's why you *love* me," Moe corrected, then pressed a kiss into her mousey brown hair. "Now, are you ready to go update the others on the fact that our window has opened and it's time to do our final preparations? Bets on Lani storming out again within ten minutes of telling her?"

"You know I never take your bets. You cheat."

"Oh come now. You're no fun." He pouted, looking for a laugh, which he got.

"And you are incorrigible." She stuck her tongue out . . . And then she *licked* him. He was so proud he could burst.

Moe gathered the team near dusk, and announced it was almost time for the fireworks to begin. In the two months of preparing, Salome, Kumanu, Lani, Vera, and Torin had fallen into a strange and delightfully tense groove. It was a fascinating social experiment to watch, and with tensions high, prodding them in the direction he wanted was so very easy.

They were gathered around the table in their war room, as Vera called it; a large room with a huge table, lots of whiteboards, and space for Kuma to work on tech while the team met. While Moe gave his report, the Infuser was elbows deep in a set of new guns for Vera, Lani next to him handing Kuma tools as he asked for them. Salome was by a whiteboard, scribbling notes in the shorthand she had developed since getting her Gift, and Torin and Adavera were on opposite ends of the room, trying not to make eye contact.

"In short," Moe said, finishing his report. "The last of the Porters in the Spire are dead, and the fact that more haven't shown up means that they are down to the dregs. It's time to start our final preparations."

Torin grunted from his side of the room. Moe turned to beam at him. "No need to look so dour, Torin my dear man. Our trial run's going to be a breeze. The real danger comes when we go for the Spire."

"Your idea of a 'trial run' is breaking into the *University*. That's hardly less dangerous than the Spire." Torin crossed his arms. "If all you're looking to prove is that *that one*," he nodded at Lani, "can keep her cool in a Storm and still work as part of a team, then can't we just test that here again?"

"*That one* has a name, asshole," Lani growled, the Mark on her chest glowing until Kuma put a hand over hers on the table, at which point she took a breath and added, "I think this is a fine idea. It will make the Corporation pull all their security to the University, figuring there, or Corp HQ, is where we'll strike next. Besides, Moe said we can blow up the department of Mark Records."

"It's all recorded via computer these days," Torin snapped back.

"We could always . . . blow up the server room at the University. Won't stop them, but might slow 'em down," Moe drawled. Of course, that had been the plan all along, but plots always went down better when people felt it was a *conversation.* Getting Salome, with her new upgraded brain, and Kuma with all his tech into the heart of University computing was just too tempting to resist.

If he could get them into the server room, then theoretically they might be able to hit Galena where it would hurt most. Not only that, but there were training methods Galena had developed in there that could make Lani and the others even more powerful.

"Interesting thought . . ." Lizzie gave a bright smile. "You know, if we could hack in and give us a back door, we could copy everything over and blow the originals. We'd have to hit the backup server farms too, but the Corporation would be much less imposing if they had to start all their research from scratch."

"Oh yeah, great idea," Torin said with an even more impressive scowl. "Why don't we just put all of the collected knowledge of mankind into the hands of someone who *calls himself a supervillain.* Yeah, so smart. Are you *trying* to kill everyone? Because this is how you do that. Isn't it enough that you're planning to sow widespread panic and destroy the economic and social order of the world without also cutting off our knowledge base at the knee?" Venom oozed from his every word. "No. If you want to copy information, fine. But if you want to destroy it, then I'm not going to help in any way and will do my best to stop you."

"Now, now, my dear boy. It was just an idea. Haven't you ever brainstormed anything before? You should try it. It's like a game, and you're far too stressed. Honestly . . . one would think you aren't capable of smiling, lately," Moe said, tabling Liz's idea for discussion with the others when Torin *wasn't* in the room.

"I only smile at things that are pleasant or funny. I see nothing of either at the moment." The Mender huffed, crossing his arms.

Lani rolled her eyes. "If you hate everything about what we're doing, why the fuck don't you just lock yourself in your room and do us all the favor of shutting the hell up?"

"Lani, Lani, such mean words," Moe chided, grinning like an idiot. "If you're not careful, one might think you don't like our dear Mender."

Instead of being offended, Lani burst into laughter. Weird duck. But that was what he liked about her. It had taken a couple centuries, but cutting her entirely off from society and sending Corporate goons her way every few years had done wonders for making her eccentric. Moe liked to think he was a patron of the weird, and Lani was one of the greatest pieces of art he had ever shaped. As if to prove it, she leaned forward, propping her elbows on the table. "So, when's the next Storm?"

"The date we have for the next one is just a few days away but it doesn't pass over the central islands. That's followed by two back to back Storms about a fortnight apart, which will hit both the University and the Spire. Either of those two should work, and give us a good window of probability," Lizzie said. "Moe's good at his timelines . . . most of the time." She grinned. "Though he got it wrong once, and we ended up stuck in the weirdest place for six months longer than he wanted. I didn't mind. They had good food."

Moe made a face, "They ate *bugs* Lizzie. Bugs are not good food!"

"They're crunchy when deep fried."

"They still had all their beady eyes and faces and ew." He shuddered, his shoulders shaking, and took a large bite out of a rose apple to clear his mouth of the remembered taste of crickets and spiders.

Lizzie grinned and smacked her lips. "As I said, good food. Now, back to business. There are three Prismatic Storms scheduled in the next month. One has to be for the Spire, one for our trial run at the University, but before either of those happen Lani needs another Bonded."

Everyone grew silent, turning to look at Lani. Moe smiled at how nervous she seemed, at how tense her body was as she tried and failed not to glance at Kuma. Into the quiet, Moe said, "Well, kiddos? You decided, yet? Time's almost up. You'll need at least one Storm to practice before our trial run, so if you're going to do it, it has to be soon."

Moe tried not to make it sound like all of timeline 3000 didn't hinge on this, but caught Vera's squinting gaze on him. Perceptive, that one.

Kuma set down his screwdriver and turned to Lani, taking her hand and bringing her knuckles to her lips. "You know my opinion, Sweets. It's up to you. If you're ready, I am, but no one is pressuring you."

"Moe is," Torin grumbled. "Bad enough that Vera and I are likely to die when you get yourself killed at the Spire. I don't see why you should take anyone else with you."

"Shut up, Torin," Vera said. "Lani, I don't have enough oomph to keep you in line alone. We've done three tries in the last two months during Prismatic Storms, and the best I can do is keep you from killing people. You need at least one more Bond."

Lani looked back to Kuma, and in that look, Moe saw the culmination of centuries of planning. She wanted this. Desperately. All she needed was a little nudge.

"You have a better chance of surviving together," he said, with a smile. Great word, 'you.' It was so easy to mistake the singular application for the plural.

Lani inhaled, squeezed Kuma's hand, and said, "Alright. Let's do this. How about tomorrow?"

CODEX: I miss cracking my knuckles. SALT, please add making a Virtual Reality space for me to live in to my to-do list. This incorporeal bullshit is already old, and it's only been ten minutes.

SALT: Added. What priority level should I give it?

CODEX: Low, I suppose. The world is a bit more important than my comfort. Now, where was I? Right, yes. Saving the world from Galena and Moe's pissing match. So, what are my assets, Salt?

SALT: Networks Online: Kahana University Servers, Merihem Crystal Servers, Parata Servers.

CODEX: Add programming you with a slightly less literal code to my to do list. Work with me here, SALT. Right. Assets. I have the ability to copy myself, so I can be in more than one place at once, so personnel isn't going to be a problem. I can crash, encrypt, and hold information hostage, but only on the networks I have access to. I can also send orders, but as soon as the University peeps figure that out, they'll probably start using hard copies, which will nullify that. What pirate vessels have access to the Parata Servers? Can I talk to them when the patch is over?

SALT: As of Day 74, multiple new hubs of the Parata Network have come online, averaging 14 a day. Online status receipt of the following message.

FROM KEKAI PARATA

All ships, download and install the attached program, and create a user ID. Find all vessels currently running dark and pass along an order to come in for upgrades. This new network is secure and encrypted. An attack on the Spire is coming within the next few weeks.

We must be ready.

We must be connected.

Kekai Parata

Pirate King

CODEX: Fucking excellent. That's what I wanted to hear. Fuck. Still want to crack my knuckles. Right. I have the pirate fleet then?

SALT: Affirmative. At 71% compliance.

CODEX: Yeah, well, pirates. We like to do our own thing. But if Kekai ordered it, everyone will get online eventually. I'm glad he did. I was a bit worried he was still angry about the Bond with Lani. Please alert me to any breaches, trackers, keyloggers, or other programs coming from the University or Moe that try to latch on to the network. We need to keep that safe and private.

SALT: Added to the queue.

CODEX: Right. Next. Query: How do I copy myself over to the Crystal Palace and Crystal HQ networks? There must be an access point or two in the University, right?

SALT: Affirmative.

CODEX: Salt, add installing a keylogger on Galena's devices to the to-do list. The first time she logs in to anything outside the University, I'm hitching a ride.

Blood of My Blood
Lani - Day 66
48

Lani held her breath as the water stilled around her, her long black hair hanging suspended in the water of the lake as she opened her eyes. The salinity of the water here, where Moe Ported in and out of often, made Lani's eyes burn. There was something wonderful and horrific about that sting. Vera's memories were full of it, just a string of horrors caked in salt. The Mark on Lani's chest, though, loved it. This was right, or perhaps even too salty . . . the way seawater was *supposed* to be, even though Lani's conscious mind knew that oceans were fresh.

Soon, though, they might not be.

Slowly, Lani held up her hands and the Mark on her chest flared, lighting the water for several yards in every direction. Around her hands, salt began to crystallize, the excess pulling in towards her, balancing the water around her more and more until the tension she had carried within her since jumping in eased, and the Mark quieted. Weighed down by the large salt rocks, she let herself sink further and further, until her bare feet touched the rocky bottom. Moving slow, lungs starting to sting, Lani pulled the rucksack from her back and slipped the large salt blocks into it. Then she bent and pressed a button on the belt around her waist.

She shot up so fast that she gasped, getting a lungful of salty water just before breaking the surface. The jets on the belt threw her feet into the air. Lani flailed for a second at the apex of the unintended flight, then crashed back into the water with a splash. Breaking the surface again, she sputtered and coughed, eyes watering.

"Fuck!" Lani spat out a mouthful of water and glared up at the deck of the ship, and at Kuma's grinning face. "Way too much fucking thrust, *again*. I thought I told you to take it down by ninety percent?"

"I thought you said nine." His smirk made her scowl deepen.

"You heard just fine, you're just an insufferable asshole."

"But I'm *your* asshole, and you adore me for it." He grinned, blowing a kiss at her. That jerk. "Anyways . . . How was the take?"

Lani pushed her sodden hair out of her face and shrugged, then started swimming for the rope ladder. "Good. I'm getting faster and more precise at manipulating salt. I didn't overdraw at all this time."

She caught on to the lowest rung and hauled herself out of the water. A minute later, she tossed the rucksack over the side and followed it, a puddle of water forming beneath her feet as Kuma handed her a towel. Lani smiled up at him, running it over her hair. "Are we still doing this?"

"As soon as you get dressed, unless you've changed your mind."

She shook her head. "No, we've been talking about it all month. It's time to take the plunge. It will make all of us safer and . . . I want to. Really."

Kuma was watching her, smiling, but there was that quizzical expression on his face too. The one that said he was 'wondering' things. He was always wondering things. "You sure? You don't *have* to do this, Lani. We can find someone less handsome, if you'd prefer." He even had the nerve to grin at her. The ass.

"You're lucky I don't mulch you, Kumanu Parata."

He bent down to kiss her, and all the fire melted away.

"I know. I'm a lucky man. But really, Lani sweets, are you sure?"

"I want to. With you, specifically, though obviously that makes me insane. See? Maybe Torin's not wrong. I'm cracked."

She stood up on tiptoes and kissed him. It was just a quick peck on the lips, but Kuma's arms wrapped around her and lifted her up for a proper kiss. Lani's head was spinning and cheeks flushed by the time he let her go, aware of the others on deck. Though honestly, after two months of seeing them spend most of their time together, none of the crew seemed to even notice the occasional public displays of affection.

"I should go get dressed. I'll meet you there," Lani said.

"Give me the belt. I'm tossing it and settling on the handheld jets. They're bulkier but less problematic, I think. Call it a Bonding gift."

"I'll call it common courtesy."

"No, it's a terrible sacrifice. It means I'll no longer see you fly out of the water screaming. That always makes my day."

"I do not scream, Kumanu Parata."

His only answer was a peck on the cheek. If he weren't so wonderful, Lani would have been left scowling. As it was, she felt the familiar tug of a wide smile yanking at her lips, though she did *try* to grumble. Stupid Kuma and his fucking adorable everything.

"If you two keep that up, I'm going to gag." Salome looked up from the little scribble board Moe had given her, wrinkling her nose. "You are sickening. Seriously. I don't think I've ever had seasickness before, and I'm gonna be pissed if I develop it while floating on a waveless lake. If you must make eyes at each other, can you do it below deck?"

Lani grinned. "Would it be better if I came over there and smooched you?"

"Depths, no! I never forget anything, remember?"

"Yes, you remind me every time I kiss Kuma where you can see it," Lani grumbled, glancing at the board as she walked by. Was any of that supposed to make sense? Sal had started with writing whole sentences, but had progressed to using a version of shorthand that only Moe seemed able to follow. Lani had her suspicions that he cheated by looking into the future and getting a glimpse of whatever Salome was coming up with, and used it to make sense of the present.

Moving further down the deck, Lani passed the piles of devices that Kuma and Salome had spent the last two months making. Crates of miniature Port Pads, jet-powered skimmers, guns powered by a whole host of different Marks, and some items that Lani still didn't understand, despite Kuma explaining them.

Weaving between the boxes, Lani made her way down to their cabin. She wasn't sure when it had gone from being Kuma's to *theirs*, but it had.

The bed was covered in odds and ends that had spread from his workshop, leaving only a corner of the bed to actually use as intended. There were Porting bracers, which Kuma and Moe had worked on together, Infused components for new guns, and several sets of trial batteries to keep Lani's power in check. There were also additional crates of Port Pads, which Moe kept taking to the Spire on an almost daily basis, but that still crowded every corner of their room. Lani didn't mind. She liked curling up close to Kuma at night, knowing that she didn't have to watch her back anymore and could just *sleep*.

Set on top of all the odds and ends and computer pieces lay a simple dress. Lani picked it up.

"Where the fuck did you find a dress, Kuma?" It hadn't been there in the morning. She flipped the hem over and saw a green thread sticking out. A glance at the sewing machine in the corner answered that question, at least. Smile widening despite her desire to roll her eyes, Lani peeled off her swimsuit and used the towel to dry off.

The dress fit perfectly, of course, because Kuma didn't do things half-assed—from tailoring to sex, the man was a perfectionist. It was irritating as fuck, but since he seemed not to care that Lani wasn't nearly as skilled or precise, she wasn't going to complain. The fabric was soft and silky, a deep green that clung to Lani's curves without making her feel exposed. Not wanting to ruin all his work by turning up with tousled hair, she took a few minutes to pull it up into a neat bun and stole a plumeria flower from the vase on the desk to tuck into it. She didn't have makeup and wouldn't have known how to use it if she had, but somehow Lani doubted Kuma would care. He was a pirate—an odd one, true, but still a man of sea and wind and sky, not glimmering cities and high society—and Lani liked him that way.

She might even love him.

Wasn't that a fucking bizarre notion?

Before going out to the Spire and finding Vera, Lani had never believed she would meet someone who would make her feel safe enough for anything beyond momentary lust. It had been a conscious decision. Love created attachments, and that was how the Corporation got you. Was that why her hands were shaking? Lani pressed them against her legs as she sat down on the bed.

Vee, am I doing the right thing?

The reply was instantaneous. *Yes. You need more than one Bond, Weirdling, and you trust Kuma. He's a decent man. You know if I'm saying that, it must be true. I hate most people.*

Lani nodded, then realized that Vera had no way of seeing that, so replied, *I know. I'm just nervous.*

I know. You're so nervous it's making me nervous. I've been sick to my stomach all day.

Sorry.

S'ok. You could put it off a little longer, if you're unsure. Vera sounded annoyed at the mere suggestion.

I'm not going to make you go through another Prismatic Storm as the only person holding my leash. Last one, I almost slipped back into . . . well, you know. I'm not doing it again.

Lani, if that's the only reason you agreed—

Again, Lani shook her head, then swore under her breath. It was so hard to remember that just because Vera felt as close as the cloth of her dress, it didn't mean she actually was. *That's not the only reason. I'm going to do it, I know I will. I just need a little encouragement. That's all.*

And you thought I'd be the best one to give it? Try Moe. He loooooooves you and Kuma. Thinks you're charming, where in fact it is well known that you are both crass, hopelessly impractical, and annoying.

Boy, what a wild endorsement. I'm touched.

*Yeah, yeah. I have to go. Keanu needs to go down for his nap, but

I'll be there. Twenty minutes, right?
 Yes. Give him a kiss for me.
 I always do.

The connection fell away, though away was such a harsh word for something that was always there, close enough to reach out to with hardly a thought. Overall, though, the conversation had eased a little tension. Really, what more could she ask for? Vera was right. She wasn't the best person to go to for encouragement or tension relief. If anything, she was who Lani went to when she needed to feel tougher, capable, and just generally more badass.

Vera didn't do soft well, except for where Keanu was concerned. Still, the quick talk had done its job. After about fifteen minutes of deep breathing, Lani let out a long sigh, got up, and headed for the door. Today was the day. Today was when she Bonded Kumanu, and . . . she was happy about it. Nervous as fuck, but happy.

How the hell was that smart? They were going to be breaking into the highest security place in the world and getting themselves killed in a week or two. Happy wasn't a sensible emotion at all. Fortunately, Iolani Saba had never claimed to be a sensible person.

Back on deck, one of the crewmen did a momentary double-take at the sight of her. Lani scowled, crossing her arms over her chest. "Yes, I'm wearing a fucking dress. Keep your eyes to yourself."

"You look very pretty, Miss Lani."

A blush warmed her cheeks, and she reached up to rub the back of her neck. "Ah . . . thanks, I guess. Where are—"

"At the helm."

"Thanks."

Nerves mounting again, Lani took the stairs up to the helm and smiled cautiously as Kuma turned to look at her. At his warm smile, she held out her arms so he could see his handiwork. "You didn't have to make me anything, you know."

"I don't *have* to do anything, but I like doing things for you." Kumanu's smile widened, and he moved closer to her, scooping Lani into his arms to seize a hungry kiss. Salome let out a disgusted groan.

"There . . . the blush is perfect with the dress." His voice was breathy in her ears, and she actually *giggled* as he pulled away.

"Oh for pity's sake," Salome barked. "Enough. It's just going to get worse from here, so I am laying down ground rules. No more kissing on my ship except behind closed doors. I'm your captain, and I will not have you filling up my memory with overblown PDA."

Lani's blush grew deeper, but hiding behind Kuma didn't really work when the irritating oaf refused to let go of her. "Sorry, Salome."

At the same moment, Kuma replied, "Got it, Cap't! No kissing, but everything else is still good to go."

Lani caught his hand at the wrist as it moved down to her ass. "So help me, Kuma, if you grope me right now, I will rot your hand off."

"Thanks for the offer, Lani, but it's unnecessary," Sal said. "I can always have the men tie him up and kick him off the ship for a good five minutes of floundering if he decides to be contrary." Salome took a look at her board, her eyes obviously scanning top to bottom, and then she wiped it clean before sliding it into a cabinet by the wheel. "Let's get moving. Everyone here? Moe, Lizzie, Ori, Ulu, Vera, . . . Torin?"

"I'm here." The Mender came up the stairs, looking between Salome and Vera, who was leaning silently on the rail with clear discomfort. Lani hadn't missed the fact that Torin did everything in his power to avoid being anywhere with both Salome and Vera at the same time. He had also avoided Lani ever since she had walked by him exiting Salome's room one morning with love bites on his neck.

Idiot. He was playing with fire, and Salome was even more of a fool to let him.

"Alright then." Moe jumped down from the rail next to Vera, rubbing his hands together. "Shall we get this show on the road? Gotta love a good Bonding. Lani, Kuma, won't you come over here into the salt circle? Salome, my dulcet darling, would you like to do the honors, since it's your ship?"

"Sure . . . why the fuck not?" Salome took up a space beside the circle. "Moe, you got that nice green sash . . . ah, there we go." With a little grin, Salome waved the sash in the air, dangling it a bit. "Ok, kiddies. Arms together, fingers locked . . . perfect. Now hold still."

Lani was sure the knife Salome pulled had been used to kill a few people, but it looked freshly polished. Obviously, Salome had known she was going to be doing this.

When the green sash was tied around Lani and Kuma's wrist, Lani couldn't help but laugh nervously. "You know . . . there's gotta be a less messy way to do this."

"Oh pshaw . . . the mess is half the fun. Now pay attention." Salome smiled, holding the blade between their arms. "Iolani Saba, Fertility and Emotive, wriggling eel of the seas, do you willingly agree to Bond your life and soul to Kumanu Parata, Infuser, eccentric piratical engineer of the salt thieves and *pain in my ass*?"

"That's the general idea, yes," Lani answered, though her heart was pounding so hard Vera was eyeing her with concern.

"Kumanu, do you agree as well, knowing there's no way to break a Blood Bond other than death?"

"Yes." For once, Kuma seemed deadly serious.

Lani gulped, preparing herself for the pain. It wasn't quite time for that yet, though. Salome turned to Vera and Torin, then her eyes tracked to the two crewmen Kuma was Bonded to—Uluwehi and Orion.

"Do any within the Bond chains of these two have any objections to this Bond, knowing that it will change and shape the life of your Bonded?"

The crewmen let out a cheer. Vera did not. But she did smile a little. Some knot of tension unwound in Lani's chest, letting her breathe easier. It was so strange to crave that connection, that sense of *acceptance* from someone she'd only known for a couple months. It made Lani actually feel a little sorry for Torin. All the years he had spent closed off from Vera must have been torture.

Those charitable thoughts towards the Mender evaporated when he muttered. "I think this is a terrible idea."

Everybody turned to look at him. Salome coughed, her eyes narrow. "Is that a formal objection?"

There was a moment of perfect silence, then Torin shook his head. "No, it's not. Why should my opinion matter, anyway? It's none of my business. Go on, Kuma, tie yourself to someone who is going to die in a week or two, if you want."

Vera's eyes closed, the Bond tightening down for a moment between herself and Lani. It was a pointless exercise. The hint or rage was more than enough for Lani to know what was going through Vera's head.

Kuma looked a tad murderous too, but he turned away from Torin to look back at Salome. "No formal objections."

"Let's get this done with, then," Lani said.

Salome's smile was approving. Weirdly, that meant something to Lani. "Thatta girl."

The blade turned, hilt offered to Lani first. Her hand tightened on the leather, and then she took a deep breath and looked to Kumanu. "My blood." She tipped the edge against her forearm, then turned the hilt towards Kuma.

He took it and his hand shook just a little. That made Lani feel better, to know it wasn't easy for him either. Their eyes met as Lani gasped at the pain of the blade tracing down her inner arm. "This hurt a fuckton less when I was trying to kill Vera."

"Trust me, you won't feel it in a second," Moe assured, as Lani, in turn, sliced down Kuma's forearm.

They weren't terribly deep cuts, just deep enough for blood to really flow. Salome pulled their tied hands up, and then wound the sash around their arms to the elbow, pressing the cuts together. "Two lives together, joining a chain. All your lives entwined, from now to the end. Have a seat, kiddies . . . you're going on a ride." Salome grinned, but Lani wasn't looking at her anymore. She was looking at Kuma, whose eyes were starting to cloud.

Lani had fought that tide of thoughts and memories when she had first Bonded Vera. With Kumanu, she threw open the doors and welcomed him with open arms. Distantly, Lani felt her legs give out and arms catch her. Ori, she thought; Kuma's longest-standing Bonded. He lowered her to the deck, even as someone else caught Kuma, keeping the two close enough that their tied arms would remain comfortably together.

Reality began to wobble, so Lani leaned forward, forehead pressing against Kuma's and eyes fluttering shut.

The sun was shining over the sea. The most beautiful sunset she had ever seen lighting the sky a bright orange. Striations of pink and purple cut through the distant clouds, reflecting off the dancing waves. A woman stood beside her, one with a scar on her cheek, Salome's dark curls, and Kuma's wide nose.

"The sea is in your blood, Kumanu. One day, I'll be gone, but as long as you have the ocean, my son, you'll never be alone. Even if your Mark lets you outlive us all. It's very important to me that you understand that."

Distantly, Lani felt herself gasp as the first of the memories came, but before she could even fully comprehend it, another took its place and drew her back to a different deck, a different time.

The little baby in Gran's arms was crying, waving its tiny arms around. "She's your responsibility now, Kuma."

"Gran . . . I can't."

"Your mother is gone, boy. You're all little Sal has. She is all you have. Take her. Raise her. You want to make up for what you've done? This is how you do it. The sea takes, and she gives. Remember what your mother taught you, and make sure you teach Salome."

There! She felt the connection strengthen, opening up a channel between them that welcomed her home. *Kumanu,* Lani whispered along it and heard him gasp, his hand around hers tightening as their blood pumped in each other's veins. It was her turn to open, to let

Kuma into the nearly three hundred years of memories, of solitude, that until now only Vera had ever shared in.

Huddling in the crook of a tree, belly rumbling as below Corporate men and women searched the island.

"A Fertility Mark. Got to be. People don't die like that without one. Some of the townies said there was a family at the edge of the woods with an odd child that never played or swam with the others. My bet is it was her."

"No way. Hundreds of people are dead. No First Trial kid could do that. We're looking for an adult who's been Rogue for a while and finally cracked. You know all Fertilizers do, eventually. Why do you think so many are Culled?"

Kumanu's fingers tightened against hers, an arm slinging around Lani to hold her tightly. *You aren't alone anymore, Sweets. Not ever again.*

The sea was perfectly still, the sky cloudless for one of the first times in Lani's twenty five years of life. She lay on her back, staring up at the constellations in the small sailboat. The silence was absolute, but for the quiet lapping of waves and creaking of wood, then a pop boomed out over the night.

She sprang to her feet, scrambling for something to use as a makeshift weapon as a man dressed in a neon yellow suit and pink scarf turned to look at her and smiled wide, eyes falling to the uncovered Fertility Mark on Lani's chest.

"Who the fuck are you? How did you get here?!"

"Oh, don't worry, darling. I'm not Corporate. You can put the bottle down unless you plan on offering me some."

Belatedly, she realized it was, in fact, a bottle of rum that she was pointing at him, but she didn't lower it. "Get the fuck off my boat."

"Presently, presently. I just came to tell you that a Storm's coming in and if you stay out here you're going to get caught in it. But if you go . . ." he turned on the spot then over-exuberantly pointed in the opposite direction from any landmass Lani knew of, "that way, you'll find a little island with a lovely small cottage and enough supplies to last you a year. You won't have time to make it anywhere else. Anyway, that's my public service announcement for the year. See ya later. Oh, and before you ask, my name is Moe."

Another pop and he was gone, leaving the night echoing with Lani's curses.

CODEX: Right. So the problem is that the Corporation controls access to salt, and people have been recently reminded how dangerous it is to oppose them, with this Protocol Eliza bullshit. If we manage to blow the Spire, their trump card goes up in smoke, but it also kind of undoes everything good that they've done, not just the bad. Salt trade will be disrupted, and I bet the Corporation will sit on their stockpiles to keep themselves alive. It will take time for the oceans to salinate, and until that happens, the Corporation retains control as long as they are sitting on those warehouses, and the remains of the Spire. We need to take salt out of the equation, which means giving each island or archipelago a way of getting salt. That means getting ahold of Marks. Marks leave behind salt, and Lani proved that she can condense it from salty water. If chunks of Spire salt get Ported all over the ocean as is our plan, that becomes the source of salt. But the Marks necessary to collect it are Corporate, so we risk them figuring that out too, and going right back to being the primary procurers of salt during this transitionary period.

SALT: Affirmative.

CODEX: So how do we get Marks out of Corporate control? I guess my next question has to be, *Query: How are Corporate Marks controlled?*

FROM THE WRITINGS OF GALENA CRYSTAL

Every year, I feel like I get closer to a curriculum that produces compliant Marks. The Board brought my methodology into question again today, acting as though my actions are immoral. Do they think I take pleasure in killing children? In sentencing non-compliant Marks to the Spire? I take no joy in the process, except perhaps the cathartic pleasure of seeing the world become a safer, and more organized place thanks to my efforts.

Zarine, in particular, opposes me. I should have Culled her early, when the Precogs reported that she would be a progressive. I tried giving the Board a lecture about the dangers of Marks and how we must control them. While I think explaining Moe to them scared a few Board members, Zarine dared to ask me if my personal feelings weren't—in her words—making me 'murder children out of an excess of caution'. She does not see the reports that cross my desk. My teams of Precogs have become excellent at predicting exactly what damage each Marked child will cause. How is Culling them young crueler than letting them live to kill and corrupt others?

My research isn't cruel. It is necessary. I remember when Marks were unstable and untrustworthy. I fought that very battle within myself, and have dedicated myself to providing a calm, safe learning environment for young Marks. I expend myself every day to blanket the University in a sense of calm, and spend my night researching better ways to give Marks happy, productive lives. They get to learn and grow in a place where Matchmakers will pair them with Bonded who will be good for their development, and give them the tools and control to be accepted and productive members of society.

Without anyone to hold them back, without

rules, and consequences, each one has the potential to end up like Merihem. One Moe is bad enough. I don't want dozens of him. So yes, we Cull the chaotic ones. And yes, we punish them when they step out of line. It is for their own good. I fear that if Marks were left to their own devices, the result would be utter chaos, leaving the unMarked with only one option: destroy us all.

I'd say it is not possible, but they do outnumber us two hundred to one, and my Precogs warn me daily of what will happen if ever the public becomes more afraid of Marks than of the Corporation. And so, I labor on, walking the line between making sure Marks are essential, but also unquestionably loyal and under my tight control.

CODEX: I don't know how I feel about your points, Galena, but damn do I viscerally dislike you.

Bad Decisions
Salome - Day 66   49

Salome was very pointedly looking outwards. Out to the walls of the cavern, away from the couple currently going through . . . Well, whatever it was that went on during Bondings.

She knew the rite, of course. She knew the theory. She'd spoken to the crewmen that were Bonded, and she knew how things went on the islands. But Sal didn't have any idea how it actually felt, and she hated to admit that part of her really did want to.

Not that she ever would. While it would be wonderful to have someone know her that intimately, and have her back no matter what, Salome never wanted her instincts or priorities messed with. Bonds did that. Besides, her Uncle Kekai usually picked out Bonds for the family. He had never done so for Salome, and was going to be beyond pissy when he found out Kuma had Bonded someone without permission. They would have to tell him before attacking the Spire, though. Kekai and the pirate fleet had to be ready for the mess Sal and her crew were about to drop in his lap. Talk about a salt trade disruption.

Huffing a bit, Sal threw an apple at Torin. As soon as he turned to look at her, Sal jerked her head to tell him 'get over here'. She wanted to know how he could be so . . . infuriatingly stubborn. Why had he gone and insulted Lani today of all days?

King of bad fucking timing, that was Torin. Not that he was altogether wrong. Salome shared many of his concerns about the Emotive-Fertilizer, but there was a right time and a wrong time to voice those worries.

He joined her against the rail a moment later, looking down into the dark, still water of the lake. His hair and beard were even less well-kept than before this mess. Salome honestly had no idea—even with her new memory—where or if he slept on the nights she didn't let him crawl back to her bed. That was a mistake. She *knew* it was a mistake, but fuck her dead if she didn't keep making it over and over again. One would think that a perfect memory would stop her, but alas it didn't seem to impart any extra wisdom.

"So..." Torin started, voice low enough not to carry, "how long do you think they'll be under?"

"You're asking the person who's literally never done this. So... I have no fucking clue. First time Kuma Bonded in my lifetime I was sleeping. Second time... Eh, he was out of it for about two hours. That's all I've got for experience. Records I've read say it can last a full day though, but that's usually in the older folks. And by older, I'm talking... like... Twelvers and up." She sighed, glancing sideways at him. "You ok?"

Torin shook his head. "Not even remotely, Sal. Lani is way more than a Twelver, as far as I've been able to deduce; she doesn't talk to me much. Aren't you worried sick? She's the one most likely to die in this idiocy, and he's your only family. How are you so accepting about this?"

Salome supposed those questions were fair. Her hands clasped together, wood against flesh, as she rested her arms on the railing. What Sal wouldn't give for an ocean storm. Hurricanes were easier than these emotional chats.

Maybe, if she was lucky, she could just distract Torin with sex. Sex was so much easier, better, than this. She didn't want to focus on what they were, or what they had been, or what they could have been if only... There were so many 'if onlys' these days.

"... Kuma's finished his Eleventh Trial," she said without much inflection. "And so far, they haven't bothered him much. That means that if he survives this mad plan, he's going to live a long, long time. He's my big brother, Torin... but he's got to live his own life too. He hasn't... Not since Mom died. He's always focused on taking care of me. But I'm an adult, a Captain, and I won't be around forever... He fucking *loves* that girl. So who am I to get in the way, right?"

Torin's frown left creases between his brows and worry in his eyes. "Does he, though? Kuma's had affairs on and off for as long as I've known him, and they're always intense. They also always *end*— usually in fire. What makes this different? I mean, I suppose one or both of them dying at the end could do it, but still..."

Salome snorted. "We need rum for this talk, Torin. Discussing my brother's love life gives me a headache." A long-suffering sigh left her lips. "A few months ago, I couldn't remember any of my brother's lovers' actual names. Just... nicknames I'd given them. Now I do. You know how fucking frustrating that is? But I know the difference. Kuma gives a shit for this one. He didn't for the others. With them it was about the hunt, and the game . . . and then he'd get bored."

"If you have rum, I'll gladly drink. My life almost makes sense after enough to drink." Torin sighed, then looked over at the two still kneeling, foreheads pressed together and other Bonded hovering close for the inevitable moments in which strong emotions made one or both of the new pair freak out. "I won't say any more on the matter. It's clear I'm the only one who sees that girl for the menace she is. Maybe I'm wrong about it," he shrugged, "but if anyone of us cracks under the pressure, it's going to be her, I'm telling you. If you love your brother as I know you do . . . have a contingency plan, ok?"

"I have five." Sal snorted, and then rubbed at her head before taking his arm to pull him towards the stairs, ignoring Vera's cold stare. Once out of sight, she added "But you know what? You're awfully hard on Lani. I mean, what do the goonies say about Salt Pirates, hrm? Do I match all of that?"

"Just about, to be honest. Information gathering and analytics is something the Corporation is *actually* good at. Do you know what the average body count is per Fertility Mark per year? Eighty-seven. Per year, starting at their First Trial. Having one just walking around here, especially knowing she can manipulate my emotions at will and might even be able to make us forget and not care if she did kill one of ours . . . it makes my skin crawl." Torin followed her as he answered, not letting Sal get more than a step or two ahead of him until they reached the door of her cabin, where he stopped. "Am I allowed in today?"

"If you weren't, I'd tell you so." Salome pushed the door open and left it that way, stepping in and peering over her counter for the bottles. She'd taken to drinking a lot at night, but the only one who would know that was Torin. And only because she was being an idiot. Maybe if she fucked him enough, she would finally get him out of her system.

Her room was not how it had been two months ago. There were tablets and whiteboards everywhere, books stacked all the way to the ceiling in places. Kuma had set up a computer with half a dozen screens on a table that took up half the room, and her once neat personal possessions had turned into a mess. Sal didn't care. She always remembered where she put things.

"Salt Pirates are supposed to be the worst, right? Right up there with Fertility folks. And yet here we are: you and me." She lifted an eyebrow, pointing one of the bottles at him. "Do you know how many times we've had sex, Torin? Since you found out what I was? Cause I do."

Torin grimaced. "I still think this new power of yours is creepy, but no, I don't. You're also wrong, though. Pirates are considered a threat level 3 at worst. Fertilizers top the chart at a 5. Whole different game and department." He took the bottle from her hands and removed the cork, taking a swig before returning it to her. "Salome, I don't dislike you or the other pirates, and never have. How many of your crew did I patch up over the years? I don't even dislike Lani as a person. I just know the science well enough to know she's like a lit fuse. But it's clear that none of you care about that, or rather that you're perfectly willing to use her up to destroy the Spire, despite the fact that it will be a miracle if it doesn't kill her."

"Tsk tsk." Salome pointed at him, winking. "Don't feed me tripe. Gran was definitely higher than a threat level 3. And if I'm only at a 3, I'm insulted." She sipped at her alcohol and then offered the bottle back to him. "I also don't trust Corporate. Sometimes I wonder . . ." She sighed. "Look. You don't have to agree with me, Tor. But at least listen, ok? All I've been doing for the last couple months is thinking a thousand thoughts at a thousand knots." She shook her head, then went searching for actual cups. Real cups, something to play with while she spoke. There. She found some mugs, but had to wipe them down.

"Fine, go ahead."

"Corporate has been running Fortune for years. Everything we know about . . . Anything . . . Is technically whatever they feed us, right?" She lifted an eyebrow and then pointed at him. "Conflicters are all insane Berserkers . . . Fertility Marks are walking time bombs . . . Emotives are cold assholes who will make us feel whatever they want. Sometimes . . . I gotta wonder if it's not a self-fulfilling prophecy. I think it goes like that because they all buy into it. Lani? She's not cold or murderous. One Bond got her pretty stable. Two? Two should do it. Your Vera? Stable with just one. Kuma? He was stable as shit with a couple, and he's an Elevener. He hasn't had an incident since I was a baby. But per Corporate theory he should be blowing shit up left and right, yeah?"

Torin took the glass Salome had filled, and frowned. "Alright, I see your point and it's not a bad one. Maybe I really am just the brainwashed Corporate asshole Adavera and Lani claim me to be. Maybe it really is all just a big conspiracy to keep us in line and I'm an idiot, but it's hard to swallow, you know? I don't *like* the Corporation, but it feels like any time I bring up a legitimate concern I have with the idea of literally blowing up societal order as we've always known it, it just gets shouted down by that . . . cluster up there." He nodded up to where doubtlessly the new Bonded pair was still going through each other's lives and memories.

Salome nodded. "Look . . . I get it. You get raised all your life to think one thing, it's gonna take time to get rid of that. It's fair." A good sip from her mug, and then she sighed. "I'm not saying you might not have some valid points. Shit's gonna get messy. But . . . maybe it should. A system that makes Culling children and enslaving people a viable option is probably not salvageable."

Torin took a swig and ran his fingers through his hair. "Incidents of Mark-born disasters were reduced dramatically once Matchmakers and Precogs were put in charge of deciding who should be advanced at the University, and who should be Culled. Don't get me wrong, it sucks and killing children is wrong, but what if they are right and those kids would have grown up to kill hundreds? It makes me wonder if they might have been wrong about me and Vera."

"Torin . . . think about it. Set aside the brainwashing, and use that skull of yours. If the Matchmakers and Precogs are right, then should you and Vera have ever grown up?" She lifted an eyebrow. "What if it isn't 'how much of a risk to the world are you', and more 'how much of a risk to the Company' are you? What if the Precogs weren't wrong, because until the Company fucked up near you guys, you weren't threats?" She shook her head. "Corporate Marks are my nightmare, Torin. I'm not saying they aren't trained well. Fuck, I agree . . . Lani should have been University trained. But realistically? You think she'd have survived? Fuck no. You can't *control* Fertility Marks. They're famous for it. If you can't control them . . . why not kill them?"

She saw the moment his shoulders sunk and he seemed to *hear* what Salome was saying. For a long while, Torin just stared into his drink. Then he drained it. "There's something I haven't told you, Sal. Or anyone."

He took a deep breath, then looked up at her, eyes haunted. "It wasn't Vee's imprisonment that made me retire. I took that shit in my stride. I was determined to get her out, so I took a position at Corp HQ. Just an internship, but it was way up there. I have no idea how I qualified. I must have scored better than I thought, but that's beside the point. I was up there one night doing some menial office work, when in walks Zarine Crystal and asks me to clean up the Board conference room."

"*The Head of the Corporation?* You were up that high?"

Torin nodded. "As I said, just an intern. I didn't even think she knew my name, but she did and I was spooked out of my skin. Anyway, I went to do that at once, because . . . well, because. I was taking out the trash when I caught sight of a crumpled paper on the top with my name on it. No one else was there, so I picked it up and . . . it was a list of every known Mark on Fortune. Pages and pages of us. I dug further and found the top page and . . ."

Salome watched the glass shake as Torin continued in a whisper. "It was a proposal to wipe out all Marks on Fortune, Sal. All of us. It had a vote count at the top and it was six against, four for. I'm . . . genuinely scared that if we do this, if we blow up the Spire, that it will tip the scale." He looked up at her, fear and sorrow in his eyes. "It's why I left. I faked a severe but harmless mental breakdown due to stress. I knew how: I'm a Mender. They blamed it on missing my Bonded and let me retire to Sonder under supervision for six months, and then yearly checkups. I just . . . can't get those pages out of my head, Salome. I don't want to be part of the reason why they get passed into law."

Salome nodded, pouring more rum into his glass. That her hand didn't shake was because it was the prosthetic and Kuma had fitted it with stabilizers. "Yeah . . . I can see why you would run." She cleared her throat, then looked down at the glass. "So . . . while I disagree with not bringing the proof out for the public, I can see why you tucked away and drank yourself stupid. Fuck, I do that often enough and don't have pages of a proposed genocide in my head."

He looked miserable, so Salome sat down next to him before continuing. "Have you ever looked at the Seawall around the Spire, Tor? Really looked at it? Salt dissolves in water, you know." She cleared her throat, peering over at him. "They build pumps into the wall. They prevent the salt from 'contaminating' the water outside." She nodded towards the door. "It should be salinating our seas, free for everyone to combat the Haze, but instead they go to monumental lengths to keep control of it. You've held proof that the Company is willing to slaughter millions. Your Bonded was one of theirs, and they still tortured and raped her. It needs to end, Torin. We're fighting a losing battle out here. If we don't make a decisive move, it will eventually end. Every year, more pirates get taken down. I don't like your Vera much, but she's right when she says that there's no other way."

"But at what cost? Vera rages at the merest suggestion that Lani might be better off at the bottom of the ocean, or that the Corp has any point in Culling children like her son, but if I told her that her actions might bring about the death of every Mark on Fortune, she would just shrug and keep on going. I . . . hardly recognize her." He leaned back, running his fingers through his hair in an agitated, jerky motion. "I was wrong to think that I would. Wrong to set aside someone like you for someone who died six years ago and was replaced by nothing but an infinite well of hatred."

"She's more than hatred. Even I see that, and I've never been her biggest fan. She's full of hope, and fear, and ... care. And sure, Vera's got a death wish bigger than my ship, but I gotta agree with her about the Culling crap. I still think they're doing it only to the kids that might cause *them* trouble." Sal looked down at him, where he lay on her bed, cup balanced on his chest. "There's no one to keep an eye on the Company, Torin. They have no one but a handful of pirates to be afraid of. *That* scares me." She raised the glass to her lips again, draining it down in three gulps. "And.. don't. Please. Don't try to paint you and me as something that you actually want. We fuck. We're good at it, too, but you're settling. You were hurt by your Bonded putting her kid first and not buying your bullshit about the Corporation, so you came back to me. And I'm stupid enough to be into it." Sal wrinkled her nose. "It's fine. Chances are that in a few weeks it won't matter."

Torin sat back up, then tilted Salome's chin up to look at him. "I'm not settling. I was blinded by a Bond I missed. I thought everything would just stop hurting with her, but I was wrong. If you don't want to hear it, fine. I won't repeat it, but I can't change what I feel any more than the tide, Salome Parata. I can *settle* for everyone not believing my concerns. I can settle for having Lani in my Bond chain. You, though? Never."

Then his lips were on hers, soft and gentle, but hungry.

Fuck. He was saying such wonderful things. His words were poetry in her ears, and the scent of rum mixed with the scent of Torin did warm tingly things to her belly. It was rather aggravating. Sal really should stay angry at him. Angry would make her be smarter, but fuck, it was so hard for Salome to stay angry at Torin. So when his lips found hers, she responded, wrapping both arms around his neck.

He pressed her back into bed, one of his hands tangling in her hair, pulling the cord out that held it out of her face. His other skated over her ribs to her hip, leaving goosebumps in its wake. Salome had ninety-six good reasons for this not to happen. Ninety-six reasons flew out the window as they had every time they had tumbled into bed together over the last two months.

"Let's forget the world for a little while, Salome," he whispered as he kissed his way down to her neck to her ear, and damn him ... with his hands on her, she actually could.

CODEX: I feel like every time I hear about Zarine Crystal, she seems to be opposing Galena. As much as I don't like even thinking these words, she might be the ally we need to deal with the fallout of our plans, whether we succeed or fail. She's the CEO of Crystal Corp, after all. Galena clearly thinks she's running the show, but the Board of Directors and CEO do have power. I wish I had access to the Crystal Network. Anyhow, time to get a letter ready for Zarine. Please add the following to my Macro for when it's go-time.

From: Codex
To: CEO.Z.Crystal

Dear Miss Crystal,
You don't know me, but I have been following your actions as of late. I believe we may be on the same side: countering the old and manipulative Marks that are twisting our world for their own ends, while the people at the bottom suffer. I am sure you are very busy dealing with the recent break-ins at the Kahana University and at the Spire, but you're going to want to pay attention. You either already have or soon will receive news that the University Servers have locked down. That's me. You may also notice the Spire is in tiny little bits. That's also me. I am not interested in talking to Galena, so if *you* want access to the University's data, or want to legitimately help the people you supposedly rule over in the wake of this crisis, write to me at this address.
I'll be waiting.
Codex

CODEX: Please prompt me before sending that. It would be a bit awkward if I took credit for blowing up the Spire if we don't, in fact, blow up the Spire.

Lost Humanity
Vera - Day 66   50

After Lani and Kuma had been led to their room, Vera had followed Moe. They had more of the plan to go over, and besides, everyone else on the crew was *busy*.

Part of Vera was glad to see Torin and Salome walk off together. Every time her Bonded went to the pirate for comfort and companionship, Vera got a few hours respite from the guilt gnawing at her insides. Torin needed someone to love him and Vera just wasn't the girl she had been before the Mines. The others got who she was now, each in their own way. Torin could not seem to let the old Vera go.

The solution was spending time with Moe. Torin never got within sight of the Precog if he could help it, so that was where Vera lived when she wasn't with her son. What was it about Moe that made Vera feel more relaxed than she had in years? Was it that for once she didn't care if someone saw her true feelings or bloodthirsty nature? Yeah, probably. Moe wasn't looking to turn her into a polite lady, or a weapon, or a broodmare. Moe wanted her to be . . . what she was.

He didn't see a problem with her being a Berserker.

Then again, neither had Aheo.

Vera shoved that thought away, giving Moe a dark smile as he rattled on about the best places to hit in preparation for the trial run. That smile seemed to distract him for all of two seconds. An improvement, to be sure, as usually he didn't seem to notice anything when on one of these little rants. That was pleasing.

"You never did say what Moe was short for," Vera said, interrupting him.

Moe blinked, mouth still open mid-ramble. "Didn't I? Well, there's a reason for that. Ghastly name, the one I was given. No grandeur at all." He wrinkled his nose. The look made Vera sit up straighter, folding her hands atop the table as she fixed that dark smile on him again.

"What is your full name, Moe?"

His lips turned up in an amused smirk. Attention shifting from the map to Vera, Moe tilted his body to lean one hip against the table they were working at. His long dark hair was pulled back into a braid, draped over the shoulder of a polka-dot orange and blue suit that reminded Vera of cheap candy.

"Trying to distract yourself?" He asked, eyebrows rising. "I'm sure you're getting some feedback from Lani and Kuma. Must be yummy."

"It's somewhere between nauseating and arousing, and I'm not sure which. So distract me, Moe. Why's the name a big deal?"

Moe put down the pen he had been holding, giving Vera his full attention. "It's the name someone I used to care about a great deal used for me. You aren't the only one to have a strained relationship with a Bonded, you know. But I'll play your game. What will you give me for it, oh minion of mine?" Moe's eyes trailed down her body, as they had many a time since the day they had gone to the University together to rescue Keanu. Not that he had ever acted on those glances, but his growing interest wasn't veiled. She liked that about him.

It was honest.

The guards didn't hide it either.

Ah . . . but this wasn't the Spire. Vera wasn't weak from hunger or illness anymore. She wasn't kept on the brink here. And Moe . . . didn't do what they did.

Rising to her feet, Adavera drifted around the table towards him, looking up into his face. "A secret, perhaps."

"I do love secrets," Moe said, a twinkle in his eyes. "And I like the way you walk when you think being seductive will get you what you want. Learn that in the Spire, or the University?"

Her fingers snapped out, curling into that shirt and slinging him towards the wall. As soon as his back slammed against it, Vera got very close, teeth bared. "And what is *that* supposed to imply?"

"Oof. Careful of the coat. It's vintage," Moe drawled. He reached up to wrap his fingers around hers where she still held his shirt.

Pop!

In a flash, his Porting Mark took them across the war room and flipped them around, Vera's back thudding into the opposite wall. Moe smirked. "Just in case you had any incorrect suppositions that you're a match for me, darling." He pulled out of her grip as Vera wobbled, trying to catch her balance. With a casual grace Moe leaned against the wall, well over a foot taller than Vera and very much in her space. "What I was implying is that a Conflicter turns everything into a weapon. That's what makes them such a stunning and beautiful Mark. Your hands and feet will break bone, your smile shatters hearts, and those hips, I'm sure, have led men—and maybe women—to their doom."

"No one calls Conflicters beautiful, let alone Zerkers," Vera snapped back.

"Then no one has half a brain, or any artistic sensibility. Then again, I knew that already," Moe said, pushing off the wall and offering Vera a hand to steady herself. "So, what secret's on the table, if I tell you my name? Something gleaned from little miss Lani, perhaps? I'm dying to get into her head. I know you two are finally starting to settle into your Bond, though with a disappointing lack of intimate cuddles. Really, how *do* you resist that sparkling personality and gentle disposition?"

Vera could only lift an eyebrow, crossing her arms and waiting for him to cease his prattle. "And risk getting infected with the cuteness she and Kuma vomit all over our group? No thanks. And no Lani secrets. I've taken enough from her, no need to add to that sin." She waved a hand, drifting to the side and around him. "Spire secrets. You can't see in there. Or him."

"Him? There's a *hiiiiiim?*" Moe asked, leaning forward. Hook, line, and sinker. "Oh, I must hear about this. Never mind the Spire. It won't be there for much longer." A wave of his hand towards their plans illustrated that. When Vera smirked and said nothing, Moe threw his hands up in the air. "Fine, fine, you've caught my attention. My name—and don't you dare spread this around—is Merihem. Like . . . a merry hem. I've met many a merry hemline in my life—just look at this one—but those words do not a good name make."

She smiled, stepping closer and smoothing her fingers over the wrinkles she'd made earlier. "*Merihem.*" It came out in a low growl, almost a *purr*. "I like it." She did not step away, once she had her prize. Vera instead hooked her finger in his outlandish clothing, running her thumb over the texture as she locked gazes with him and waited for a long moment. "Be specific, Merihem. What do you want to know of *him?*"

He closed his eyes for a second, brow wrinkling shut, then they sprung open. "I love my Precog abilities. They're great at this game. Well, since I can't see who you're talking about, they must be a Shielder, so I'm not going to ask about that. I'm betting the Shielder who came to Sonder, in fact. If his presence at the Spire would interfere with our plans you would have mentioned it before, so that's out too. Asking you if he's the father of your son is just a wasted question. Keanu is *yours*. Clearly he's associated with the Spire, since that's where you've been this whole time. So my *specific* question is: what parts of you did he rip away to make you scared to speak *his* name?"

Vera's eyes glittered. Not with tears, or sorrow, or even rage. It almost felt like . . . pleasure? She shook her head, trying to clear it, before realizing what exactly was going on. *Lani*. Vera had almost forgotten about the Bonding for a second.

Clearly, Lani and Kuma had forgotten or were ignoring that everyone along their Bond chain would feel the echo of their post-Bonding bliss. Manners said she should button up. Go find her room and rub one out while waiting for it to pass. Instead, she let her fingers slide down Moe's ridiculous clothing to hook in the top of Moe's pants and pull him close. "I'm not *scared* of his name. It's Aheo of Order, Shielder and Tracker. Names are just . . . something he took from us, so they've become important to me. We were numbers to Aheo. Data. 28895." Vera spit out that number, reaching up to touch the brand on her shoulder where those numbers were burned into her flesh. "He stripped us of our humanity. We were nothing but parts of his experiment into Marks."

Moe studied her. "You say he stripped you of your humanity? Looks to me like he did you a favor. Humanity is a construct, what we're taught from birth is 'ethical'. It's what holds most people back. Both your Bonded suffer from an excess of it, and in my opinion, it is their greatest shortcoming."

"I wouldn't say Aheo did me a favor. He raped me. He chained me, drugged and pregnant, to a bed for nine months so I wouldn't find a way to get rid of my baby, and experimented on me after he took Keanu away. I will never call that a favor. He broke something. I don't understand people much anymore." For a moment, Vera felt an overwhelming weight on her chest as she said that, then she exhaled and looked up into Moe's face. She dragged one of her fingers up to his nose, booping him lightly. "But what does not kill me makes me stronger, right? So should I survive this, I will find him. And then I will tear him apart, little piece by little piece, and make him watch while I do."

Moe caught her wrist, twisting it until it stung, but never taking his eyes off of Vera. "On the contrary. I think you understand people better now. You see through the niceties and the bullshit. Real motivations are ugly things. Survival is *brutal.* We live by killing. All of us. Animals, plants, each other. We fuck to achieve immortality We step on the skulls of others trying to attain a better life, and excuse it as 'hard work'. Why are we destroying the Spire, Vera? I'm doing it because I'm bored and want to see what I built all those years ago *burn*. You're doing it because you want to destroy the thing that brutalized and raped you. Lani because she's so terrified of her own destructive power that she needs to think there is a purpose to it, or she'll realize she doesn't have what it takes to survive. Each one of us has their own selfish motivation. We can pretty it up, but in the end . . . what *you* see is reality, Adavera of Keala."

Vera stared at him, her chest tight. "Do you really think so?"

Moe grinned, took her hand, and brought it to his lips. "You are perfect as you are, darling girl. You have been stripped of all the bullshit and survived the process. Let me show you. I have something I was planning to do tonight, and I think it might be good for you to come along. Your leg is fully healed, yes?"

Vera nodded.

"Excellent. Then let's see what the Spire turned you into, when you don't have any of your Bonded to hold you back."

CODEX: Welp, I just allied myself with a Crystal. No biggie. Ew. Then again, I was willing to follow Moe into the mouth of the beast, so I guess I'm just an idiot. How long we got, SALT?

SALT: 2 minutes, 21 seconds.

CODEX: Woot. Almost there. So, I've cut Galena off from her research, I'm sending a God after Moe, and I've contacted Zarine. But I gotta be more paranoid. Ok. Think like Lani. Right. First off, HOW is a God going to catch Moe? He'll just fuck off to other worlds to avoid them. No obvious solutions to that, so lemme table it. Galena. I've been assuming that cutting her off from her archives and information gathering tools will hobble her, but will it? She's at least 1500 years old, since that's how old Moe would be if he weren't going to other worlds that have what he calls a time dilation, so she's got to be powerful in her own right. *Query: What has been written about Galena's Emotive Mark?*

FROM THE JOURNAL OF AHEO OF ORDER

After years of putting in requests, Galena Crystal at last agreed to let me take readings off her Mark. I have spent all day measuring and charting the size of the Emotive wave pattern, and assessing her power. There are only a few Marks of her age and size alive today, and almost all the ones the Corporation controls are heavily monitored, with information about them restricted. Galena would not even give me their names.

But back to her. Her Mark extends from the base of her left foot, all the way up to her face, making me question what happens when she runs out of skin. She is still challenging Trials, and says that they come slower the older she gets. She has logged 143 Trials in her own records. With those numbers in mind, and my readings of her Emotion dampening cloud over the University, I am hypothesizing that Mark power growth is not exponential, but rather on a curve. It is a steep curve, which looks like exponential growth early on, but while Galena's power is significant, she still exhausts it almost daily.

Even so, the results are impressive. She is in the head of every single person on the grounds of the University every single day, rooting out those who grow angry at the Corporation and calming the emotions of others to create a peaceful learning environment. Her methods fascinate me. No wonder her scientists produce such precise work and so rarely bicker amongst themselves. She has emotionally lobotomized them. She calms students down so they do not question the Cullings, or the rigorous and sometimes painful training needed to produce obedient Marks. It humbles me. Galena understands the human mind in a way I will never be able to. If I am to make my mark upon history, I will do it by using what she has learned and finding out how to best apply it to work with a Mark's core biology.

I will keep tonight's entry short as I have piles of data to crunch, but I am elated. Now more than ever, I am reminded of how lucky I am to be working at the forefront of my field. If Galena herself picked me out from the chaff, I must believe that I am on the right course. One day, my methods, like hers, will be praised, and with what I've learned today about getting through Trials, I intend to still be around when it happens.

CODEX: Don't count on that, bozo. I'm coming for you. But how very interesting. Galena is drained at night. That explains the timing of all of Moe's University jaunts.

No Party Like a Murder Party
Moe - Day 66
51

Moe ported himself and Vera to the University just after midnight. It was the time when the halls of the vast institution lay mostly silent, and when the grounds were dark and desolate. The sky was overcast but no rain fell yet, though the humidity promised a downpour. They appeared in the shelter of a bus stop on campus, just as a shuttle sped away along the rails. His arm tightened around Adavera's shoulders, steadying her as she found her feet, then holding on a moment longer than necessary because he could.

When he did let go, Moe slipped his hands into his pockets. "So, my dear, where shall we start? Want to take out Porters, Conflicters, Shifters, Precogs? You know the University better than I do, and have been the one planning next week's little incursion, so you get to choose the flavor of our bloodshed tonight."

Vera grinned at him. He had to admit that the bloodthirsty look on her face was attractive. She just needed a new wardrobe or to be covered in blood and the glory of battle, and she'd be *wonderful*. "Any of them. All of them. The Precogs and the Conflicters first, though. Get rid of as many of them as we can, and it should be smoother sailing, no?"

"That's the theory, and it's nice to know you appreciate the danger in my favorite Mark. Most think of us as anti-social bookworms, but really, we're the deadliest of them all. We just happen to *also* usually be antisocial bookworms. Except for me. We all know I love people and would never harm a soul," Moe said it with a toothy grin, while angling himself in the floodlight of the shelter to ensure that his eyes and teeth would gleam with malice.

"Sure you wouldn't." Vera even returned the toothy grin.

If not for Lizzie, he never would have considered the merits of doing more than use Vera for her fury and skill with a blade. When he had first planned this team out, she was just the muscle, but the more he got to know her, the more Moe liked the ornery Conflicter. "Ok. Which first?" He tapped his chin. "Mmmm . . . eeeny meeny miney . . . that way?"

"No, not that way." Vera tilted her head to the side, spinning and looking over the grounds. "As you pointed out, Precogs are bookworms, and the library is their favorite haunt . . . or it was, last time I spent any real time here."

"Good choice. The other way led to certain doom," Moe replied jauntily. Did he know that? Nope. He hadn't bothered looking. Did he like the way she *thought* he knew? Yes. Ohhhhh yes. Just to be sure, though, he pulled one of his thousand small notebooks out from his pocket. This one he had written more than a decade ago, charting the probabilities for this course of action. Not that Moe couldn't zoom in to the immediate future on the fly, but it was like picking out a single grain of sand in an avalanche. Possible, but not worth the effort most of the time.

"We have a 94% chance of running into trouble, so keep your eyes open." He put the notebook away. As they walked the way she had pointed, Moe's hand fell to the small of Vera's back, his thumb rubbing circles against the light fabric of her shirt. "So tell me, darling, how are things going with your lovely Bonded? You should know I've lost a lot of money on you. I had bet Lizzie you would have removed Torin's spleen with a butter-knife by now. To be fair, there was only a seven point six percent chance of that, but I was *so* hoping for it. I love a long-shot."

"That, Moe, is no one else's business." Her voice went grim. Oh, he'd touched a sore spot alright.

"Come now. It can't be all that bad. The threesomes with the captain must be magnificent." Courting death, that's what Moe was doing. But even Death needed some love and attention from time to time, and if anyone was up to the challenge, it was Moe. Vera might take a swipe at him, but she wasn't dumb. She had been rescued because *Moe* had sent Lani to find her. Keanu was with her because *Moe* had kept tabs on the boy and taken Vera to get him. She owed him too much to gut him.

The thrill of knowing she might snap, however, was electrifying.

Moe was caught mid-daydream when Vera's fingers rose in the universal symbol of 'shut up.' An odd look crossed her face as she scanned the well manicured darkened grounds. What was she sensing that he wasn't? His eyes, suddenly serious, swept over the still University too, the Precog Mark on his back tingling as a map of probability burst into view before him. It only took Moe half a second to figure out what Vera had, though how she had noticed it was beyond him. With a loud pop they Ported twenty feet away, just as six people in body armor appeared in a circle around where they had just been standing, weapons drawn and pointed inward towards the ring of salt Moe had left behind.

"Well shit," he drawled, as all six turned towards them, "looks like we've been noticed."

"Shit? I wouldn't say that." Vera cracked her knuckles, her eyes dilating as she fixed her gaze on her enemies. "Security officers. My absolute *favorites*."

"Vera . . ."

Moe had intended to just Port away, but he couldn't keep a grip on her. One moment she was still, and the next she just *wasn't*. Bloody Conflicters. Vera had only undergone three Trials, and yet somehow she managed to make Moe work to keep track of her.

Granted, watching her fight was thrilling. The beautiful Berserker leapt from target to target like some kind of insane murder monkey. She left scratches and bruises in her wake, testing out weaknesses and reflexes. He could have watched for hours, but she was going to get herself killed going in alone. At least one of these goons was also a Conflicter. Given how he was backing up to get the higher ground as the others moved as a unit to keep Vera's attention on them, he was probably hiding a ranged weapon.

"Tut, tut. That won't do at all."

Moe casually Ported behind the man. Pinpoint Ports weren't something he could do anymore, so he landed several yards away, but the moment he caught his balance, Moe flared his Precog ability. Paths of probability burst into existence all around him, stretching out centuries into the future. They were distracting, intriguing, colorful. Pushing most of them away, he focused on the next few minutes and walked forward, each step he took the least likely to be detected. The crunch of grass collided with the crunch of punches below, and when he was standing right behind the enemy Conflicter, Moe casually pulled an Infused Porter-gun from his pocket, pressed it against the back of the man's head and pulled the trigger. There was no noise, just a tiny flash of light as a chunk of the Conflicter's brain was Ported two feet to the left.

The body crumpled to the ground with a deeply pleasurable and satisfying thud.

Without the bulky brute in his line of sight, Moe looked down at the combat taking place below and admired the whirlwind of death that was Adavera of Keala.

Her two long swords were still in sheathes across her back, unnecessary for this fight. Her arms and legs were more than weapon enough, slapping clubs and guns out of her opponent's hands with a speed and ferocity they couldn't hope to match. This was why he had chosen her out of all the Conflicters on Fortune for this little project. She was savage and perfect, the very essence of what her Mark could be. There was no mask of civility when she fought, and a larger, stronger opponent wouldn't make her hesitate. He needed that fearlessness to make up for Lani's paranoia and pessimism.

Oh dear.

An arm sailed past him, ripped clean off by the blood-spattered Conflicter. That was just . . . messy. And delightful. And *glorious*.

Did the fact that this carnage made his trousers tight make him a bad person? Eh. He had long ago concluded that being good was overrated. As the last of the five fell with his neck snapped, Moe began to slowly clap. "Well done, darling. Very gory. I like the pizzazz of the way you kill. Now, if you would please, won't you duck for me?"

To her credit, Adavera did so without hesitation, falling to the ground as a sharp blade materialized mid-Port. Moe pointed his gun at the man who had just appeared behind her, guesstimated the distance, and pulled the trigger. Vera's back was splattered in a fresh coat of blood as the goon's face exploded.

"Sorry about that."

"For what? Getting more blood on me?" Vera smirked, climbing back to her feet and turning in a slow circle, sniffing at the air. She was covered in bits of body and blood, and frankly it was an improvement on the drab wardrobe Vera usually wore.

"No, no. You misunderstand. Sorry for denying you the pleasure of the kill." He grinned. "But since I did just get brains on you, maybe I can take you shopping after this? Well, I say shopping. I mean breaking into some Corp up-n-up's place and stealing every article of clothing they have. So, like, window shopping for criminals without the windows or the theoretical future purchase and with the possibility of having to kill the person we're stealing from. You know, fun. Not that I expect you to know the meaning of that word, given you've been Bonded to Mr. Grumpy forever." He walked towards her, stepping on the back of the dead Conflicter and hopping down again on the other side. When he reached her, Moe brushed a bit of bone off Vera's nose, then trailed the back of his knuckles down her neck. "You look good this way, Adavera. *This* is you, not that silent, stony woman at the conference table. I much prefer this version."

Her eyes narrowed just a little, and he found it adorable. "You are the first one to *ever* tell me that I look better covered in blood."

Well, that was par for the course, wasn't it? "No one ever has a good sense of style, other than me. Even Lizzie isn't great at it, but she knows what I like." Moe couldn't help the toothy grin, even while he spread his fingers around her throat, not tightening, just appreciative. "However *do* you remember to smile with the Mender in your head, Vera? I could cut him out, if you want. It isn't easy, but I know people." His nails dug into the back of her neck, eyes fixed not on hers, but her lips. He could feel her pulse racing under his fingers and it thrilled him. Slow as a cloud in a stormless sky, Moe lowered his face closer to hers, then closer, until her lips parted expectantly.

Then he stepped back, offered her his arm and in a cheerful voice said, "Weren't we off to kill some Precogs?"

Watching Vera's dilated eyes flicker between lust and bloodthirst was absolutely addictive. How did the Mender NOT want this creature? Really . . . some people had no appreciation for the more honest ones. He beamed as Vera finally took his arm, muttering something beneath her breath about confusing moods.

"Oh, you'll get used to them, eventually. If you want to."

"That means you'd have to stick around." Was that a bit of 'grump' in her tone? Torin must be infectious. It made Moe laugh.

"That's true. Though I'm sure you could find a way to lure me back now and then. I'm always somewhere, you know. There are just ever so many *somewheres* to choose from. It's the people who content themselves with a single place that puzzle me."

He walked fast, his long legs causing her to jog every few steps to keep up. Without warning, he Ported to the roof of the closest building, then down to the lawn on the other side, a nice distance from the inevitable yells once someone found the seven dead bodies.

"Now, if I'm not mistaken, when there is an incursion on University grounds everything goes into lockdo—" even as Moe said it, a loud siren sounded from the nearest speaker, the sound repeated across the University grounds.

"Lockdown is fun. The students get put into their rooms and patrols thicken. I always used to find a way to get locked in with Torin. Once you have sex to sirens a few dozen times, the sound always gets you going." Vera grinned, pulling her hand off him for a moment to crack her knuckles again. "We have two minutes before there will be a small army swarming these grounds, Moe. To the office?"

"To the office!" he agreed, taking her hand with a grin and breaking into a full-fledged run. This was fun. This was what he lived for. Millenia of life made almost everything dull, but the thrill of adrenaline reminded him that he was still mortal and still *alive*. They raced across the grounds, sometimes Porting, sometimes sprinting, and all around them the beautiful sounds and sights of chaos bloomed like a flower opening in springtime.

The University Precogs office was in the library. The big, circular building was close to the center of campus and the doors were locked. Moe was pretty sure there were anti-Porting fields in the walls here, so instead he motioned to the right, behind a row of hedges. They crouched down together as a patrol ran past and Moe took the chance to trail his hand down Vera's rear as he leaned in close to whisper against her neck. "Do you know who founded the University, Adavera?"

"Galena Crystal." She growled the name, her fingers moving to the wall, testing it. She could probably bash her way through, but that would attract attention. Fortunately Moe was old as dirt.

"Correct. Dear old Galena. Do you know who drew up the designs?" His teeth caught her earlobe, tongue flicking out to taste her skin as he leaned back against the wall at the base of the stairs and found the tiny switch there. "Me."

They tumbled through the trapped door, down three steps and landed with Vera on top of Moe, something he didn't mind one bit. He kicked the door closed, and as the darkness engulfed them, rolled to pin Adavera under him and kissed her.

The way she tensed beneath him for that single heartbeat made his adrenaline race. She was a Conflicter. There was a chance she'd reflexively put a hand through his chest for his temerity. He tensed as her hand came up, but then those fingers locked in his hair, and she damn near *ate* his kiss. She was fire, and blood, and electricity. He'd been right.

She really was too good for Mr. Grump.

Moe knew he was playing dirty the way he was getting in under her skin while she was high on death and violence—and he didn't care. His long fingers tugged the offending drab tank-top up enough to palm her breast, then pinching the pert nipple, doubtlessly smearing blood all along the smooth skin.

"If I wanted to fuck you, right here, under the stairs to the University Archives, would you stop me, Adavera?" He growled into her ear, then kissed her again, pulling back to declare in a hoarse voice. "You are breathtaking."

". . . fuck yes." She growled right back at him, seemingly unafraid of the oldest man of her world, even knowing what he was, what he could do, and how much he truly did not give a shit. It was delightful. *She* was delightful. Such a pity that this little mission of his might get her killed . . . but there was a chance it wouldn't, too.

If it didn't, he'd keep her as a pet and give her plenty of people to kill.

"Was that, 'fuck yes, I'll stop you?' or 'fuck yes, fuck me hard and fast?'" He rolled his hips, making her feel just what she was doing to him. "I'm going to make you forget that Mender even exists. Just so you understand, though, Adavera, if you let me do this now, I'm not going to let you go. I'm a greedy and possessive man. Give me a taste and I'll devour everything there is to you. I can promise you that you'll *love it*, but I won't have it be said that I didn't warn you."

The darling woman actually laughed, husky and low, before wrapping one of those strong legs around his waist and pulling him in tighter against her. The heat of her, even through all these dreadful clothes, was sensational. "Is that a promise, Moe? I don't think you could handle me for too long."

His hand squeezed her breast. "Oh, I can *handle* you just fine, my dear." His teeth and tongue traced down her jaw and neck as his free hand moved between them to pop the button of her pants. As soon as there was enough give, he shoved his fingers inside them, pleased to find her folds hot and slick for him. "My, my, so I'm not the only one turned on by a little blood . . . That's good. Life ending is a beautiful thing, especially when accomplished with such . . . vigor."

"Even more so when it's your family's Corporate goons." Vera breathed the words like a little prayer, her fingers tightening their grip on his hair. Fuck, he did so love it when bedmates got grabby. His fingers stroked through the slick heat of her again, and he was rewarded with a little *jump* in her hips.

"I think I'm in the mood for that 'hard and fast' we spoke about earlier, Vera." Moe warned, before nipping at her neck. The damned drab pants had to go. If he had to rip the things apart, he would do it. It wasn't as though Vera would *mind* walking around naked after, would she?

He could just see the headline tomorrow: '*Naked, presumed dead Conflicter murders her way through the University.*'

The darkness filled with the sound of ripping fabric. He might not have the strength of one of the Physical Marks, but every Mark enhanced the body, and light linen provided little resistance. He took a little more care about his own pants, since they were actually interesting clothes, but it still took him less than a minute to get them both naked. The cold tiles under them made Vera's skin erupt into goosebumps, but her mouth was still plenty warm as she yanked him down for another kiss.

This wasn't a moment for romance. Moe didn't *feel* romance when he touched or looked at Adavera. This was about need and admiration. This was about fulfilling something both of them desired, and making her understand that she didn't *need* that damned Mender, just because they were Bonded.

Moe set teeth into her shoulder as his hands took hold of her hips, lifting them to the angle his Mark told him had the highest probability of making her moan, and pushed into her with a strong, unyielding thrust.

She was tough. She didn't need more time to warm up because, like him, the violence and gore *were* the foreplay. The gasp and groan was Moe's reward, and so was the flexing of her body like a warm glove around his cock. Fuck . . . the Conflicter was sheer muscle everywhere.

Moe was neither gentle, nor slow as he set a pace, lifting one of her legs up to his shoulder to get a better angle and because he knew she could take it. One of his hands found her folds again, rubbing her clit in hard, fast circles as he pounded into her. Moe had no intention of letting her go until he'd fucked her better and harder than anyone else in her life, ensuring that she'd never touch herself again without thinking of him. The chances of that were much higher, his powers told him, if he could make her cum in the next forty-seven seconds. To ensure that she did, the hand he had been using to prop himself up closed around her throat. He hadn't missed the little gasp earlier, and Moe would bet a third of his fortune that this angry little Conflicter just needed to feel control ripped from her to really get going.

His pet was tightening, turning silky, and groaning beneath his body. She was full of fire, and anger, and rage . . . and right now she was entirely under his control.

She was *delightful*.

His hand worked a few more circles at her clit, and then *pressed*, hard, pleasure mixing with pain until she came in a strangled scream underneath him.

"That's my girl . . ." He crooned the word into her ear, letting her leg slide back down and loosening his fingers at her throat as he slowed down. He let her have a few deep breaths, allowing her quivering body to come down from the high, then he continued, "Next time, don't you fucking dare come without my permission."

His hips slammed against hers with all the force he had, making her whole body jerk in pleasure and pain combined. Moe pulled out with a snarl and flipped her onto her belly, yanking her hips up to take her from behind. His nails raked along her back, and while in the darkness Moe could not see, he was sure they would leave bright red marks for at least a day or two.

Someone else might scream in pain. Not his pet. Vera let out a gasping moan, her hips bucking back into his own as if she found the sting just as thrilling in the reception as he found in the delivery. She was perfect. Moe's own little fuck toy designed just for him. "Fuck, Adavera ... I want to hear you scream."

"You gotta *earn* screams, Moe."

He grinned and tangled his fingers in her hair, yanking her head back enough that she was forced to arch her back uncomfortably to keep him from ripping some strands out. "Oh, a challenge, why thank you. I do *love* an excuse to play."

So he Ported them. It was a lucky Port, like precision Ports usually weren't, but this time they appeared right up against the rail on the rooftop of one of the tallest skyscrapers on Fortune. Vera's body was still bent at the waist and now hanging most of the way over a sickening drop.

The scream was *delicious.*

The hand he still had in her hair yanked her back just enough for her scrambling feet to find purchase, then he slammed into her again, his laugh whipped away by the strong, cold wind this high up.

"*Fuck!*"

"I made you *scream*, lover." Moe laughed in her ear, then set his lips to her throat. He bit, and sucked, and licked at her skin to soak up all the shivers and goosebumps she had to offer, along with the coppery taste of the blood they had spilled together. Her body had tightened even more, if it were possible, and he felt as though he was fucking the strongest vise he could find.

Moe liked it.

"You're mine. *Say it.*"

"No."

He grinned, thrusting again. "Say it, pet."

"... fuck.. *No* ..."

"Alright." Without warning he let go of her hair and the hand around her waist keeping her balanced, and pushed with his feet at the same time. They tumbled over the railing.

Vera's scream this time was of pure, unabashed terror.

He gave her two whole seconds of free fall before Porting to a random point in one of the public parks, and rolling as they hit the ground with momentum, his arms wrapped tight around her body.

They rolled to a stop with her on top, and Moe grinned up at Vera. "Now what have we learned?"

"That you just wanted to put me on top in the flashiest damn way you could." The woman was adorable, really she was. Especially when she leaned down to claim a kiss, as if she didn't give a single damn in all the world about where they might be, or that he had just pushed her off a building for giving him sass. "You want me, Moe? Fine. No one else does, so if that's what makes your sadistic little soul tick until we all die, I'm *yours*."

"Oh no. No, no, no. That was too easy," he whined, even as he possessively grabbed her ass. "I want you to *mean* it. I won't fuck you again till you do."

"Fine. Then *I'll* fuck *you* instead." She dared to give him a wicked grin, and he couldn't help but find it titillating. But damn if she didn't give it her best shot, tangling her hands in his hair and rocking her hips down onto his own.

Gentle, it seemed, wasn't really in his little Conflicter's repertoire. Perfect. He didn't want gentle right now, anyways.

He also wasn't going to give her what she wanted. With a heave, Moe pushed Vera off him and on to her belly again, though it took some doing. He twisted one of her arms behind her back and straddled her hips, bending down to growl, "You're not in charge here, darling."

His fingers reached down between her legs, playing with her, enjoying the way her hips squirmed and she tried to press into his touch. She was so wet, so very responsive. He pushed her higher and higher mercilessly, until she was gasping and panting, then he bent down once more.

"Beg."

She was moaning beneath him, obviously fighting to try to keep the sounds to herself. Was it stubborn pride? Was it her playing a game? He didn't know. He wasn't sure he cared.

"*Beg, pet.*"

His fingers flicked at her clit, and a half strangled cry left her lips. "Please!"

"Please what?"

"FUCK Moe . . . please fucking fuck me already."

"Tell me I can take everything I want, and you'll like it. Tell me you'll be my pet, until you die doing what I want."

"You're a perverted asshole."

Moe grinned, taking her earlobe between his teeth and biting down until he tasted blood. "Tell me something I don't know. Say it, darling."

She growled, bucked her hips, gasped, squirmed.

"What are you, Vera?"

"*Yours.*"

The thrill of victory was sweeter than anything yet. "Well, since you're mine . . ." His cock replaced his fingers and he murmured, "Come for me, Adavera."

. . . and she did.

. . . and she screamed.

And laughing, he joined her.

CODEX: The more I find out, the more suspicious I am of everything. I know Moe encrypted most of his writings, but he's Moe. He's lazy, and distractible, and he missed the Keylogger, so I'm betting other things slipped through the cracks. So let's find out what he's written on Galena or Galena's powers. I'm sure he has opinions, what with how well he messed with Lani's emotions. Clearly, he has experience dealing with Emotives. So, *Query: What has Moe written on Emotives?* Filter, newest to oldest. I don't want to get bogged down on out of date information.

FROM THE WRITINGS OF MOE

I didn't see this coming. I should have, and I'm kicking myself about it. Sure, I groomed Kumanu to be as desperate for affection as Lani, so they would crash together like waves upon the Spire, but I may have overdone their isolation somewhat. Perhaps I should have given each of them a few serious relationships before now, but it was too much of a risk. I do hope they never find out how involved I've been in their respective emotional and sexual isolations.

The problem isn't that they are intimate. I planned for that, and it worked beautifully. The issue is that I worry I may have done too good of a job at making them good for each other, and it could drive them to shift their priorities. They *must* want to destroy the Spire more than they care about getting out alive. Any less than complete focus on our task will endanger it.

For now, I will allow them to remain close, but if their relationship ends up putting the mission in danger, I will interfere. My worry isn't for Lani. She's an Emotive, after all, and therefore easy to manipulate. I've already planted the bombs I need in the Spire and plan to send Lizzie in with the team to set them off at the right time to kill Kuma. Liz can make sure they are separated at the last minute, and that the right explosion takes him out when Lani is at the center of the mountain. It will still work, and while it will be a pity to give up an Infuser as talented as Kuma, Lani has always been the prize.

My worry, now, is whether he will try to make them a way out. He's been coding a lot, which isn't on any of my to-do lists for him. I've tried focusing my powers on what he's planning, but there are too many probability streams, and we're getting too close to the events for me to see them clearly, no matter how hard I squint. If he's willing to risk the mission to save Lani or to save himself, that could derail everything. Worse, what if this growing love between them ruins Lani? She becomes useless when happy. Fortunately, making the lives of Emotives miserable to push them to greatness is something I excel at.

CODEX: MOTHERFUCKER! I am going to fucking end you.

A New Arm
Kuma - Day 66
52

Damn, Kuma was tired. It almost felt like he'd been getting fucked for hours straight, and in a way, that was an accurate comparison. It was his brain that was sore instead of his body, but it had left him with the same heady sense of lingering pleasure.

He stretched, groaning in delight. "Shit Lani . . . just being in your head feels fucking wonderful. You're gonna ruin my reputation."

His newly Bonded bedmate smiled, looking as tired and happy as he felt when she flopped half on top of him after she'd finished up in the shower. She was naked. Apparently, Lani had decided that putting on PJs was too much work, which suited Kuma just fine. Her skin and hair smelled of the soap he stocked in his tiny shower, which meant she smelled like him. That also suited Kumanu.

"Your reputation can suck it." Lani nuzzled into Kuma's embrace, both Marks glowing. By now, Kumanu knew when she was using them to heighten the shared pleasure of skin on skin. He didn't mind. In fact, it was damn phenomenal.

"But what will I be without my reputation?" Kuma asked, feigning horror.

"You'll survive. Maybe you'll just have to find a new reputation." Changing the subject, Lani added, "I didn't realize how different it would be from Vee. This is like . . . it's better than the sex and I didn't think that was possible. We've been getting good at that shit."

Kuma couldn't help but laugh. "Yeah well . . . what you got with Vee is a little . . . weird." He snorted, running his fingers through her long damp curls. Fuck, she smelled good. Ok, so he was a possessive pig, and would gladly admit it, but it pleased him that Lani would always smell a bit like him, at least to another Infuser. She was his Bonded now. A part of Kuma was forever within Lani, their Marks as tied together as their minds.

His lips twitched, fingers lightly clenching in her hair. "Glad to hear it was so good for you."

"Mhm." She snuggled up to him, nuzzling into his shoulder as if trying to get as close as they had been before, with their blood pumping together. "Kuma . . . I don't want this to stop. I don't want to die in the Spire. I spent two hundred years not realizing what I was missing, and it's not fair to only get a couple weeks of it now that I have it."

She yawned at the end of that. When he looked down, he saw her eyes were closed, though it was clear she was still awake. The lightly glowing vines of her Mark pulsed in time to her heartbeat. It was mesmerizing, and it took Kuma a while to formulate an answer. "You know what the solution is, right? Don't die." A soft laugh left his lips, his fingers lightly pulling on her hair again. "You can pull that off. You were alone for two hundred years, Lani. If that didn't teach you to survive no matter what, nothing could."

Her eyes opened, beautiful brown orbs staring up into his in a way that made Kuma's heart just *stop*. Fuck, he had it bad for this girl. He had never understood what drove his sister back to that damned Mender again and again, but he could almost get it with Lani in his arms.

"I'll try. But in case I don't manage to pull it off . . . I want these days to be ours, Kumanu. I want every hour with you I can get, and I don't care if it makes me look clingy or makes your sister gag."

"Ew. Don't talk to me about my sister gagging. I walked in on her and Torin a few nights ago, and I'd like to burn that image out of my head."

Lani scrunched up her nose. "I don't know what she sees in that asshole. Have you noticed he can't get through a single conversation without casually reminding us that people like you and me should be summarily killed on sight? Like . . . how? How can he be that much of an insensitive jerk?" A yawn made that last word only conjecture. "I'm so fucking tired that I don't think I can actually sleep. Not with every invention you've ever made rattling around my skull. How your sister stands her powers I do not know. You're brilliant, by the way. I knew that, but I didn't know *how* smart you really were until I was seeing the world through your eyes. It's incredible."

"I don't know about incredible. The world just has pieces, and I like to make those pieces fit together. That's all it is. As for Sal . . . you got no idea. You think I'm smart? Ever since she got whatever that shit is, she's . . . Ridiculous. The pieces I wouldn't even see? She not only sees them, but points them out as though they should be obvious. Made me reconsider how I talk to people, because I'd hate for others to be as confused speaking to me, as I am with Sal. It's fucking weird."

"Are you done with her present?" Lani asked, pressing a kiss to his cheek before sitting up. Kuma watched her, enjoying the bounce of her breasts and the way her Fertility Mark moved as she stretched. When he wasn't quite so tired, he would have to find out how much more amazing sex would be, now that they were Bonded, but in the meantime he simply enjoyed watching her.

"Yeah. Let me show you."

Squeezing around her and the junk on the bed gave Kuma an opportunity for a quick grope, which drew a shriek from Lani. She batted his hand away, grinning. "You're incorrigible."

"Never claimed otherwise."

Since it was unlikely that anyone would bother them, Kuma didn't pull on his pants. He squeezed past a few boxes and pulled a long parcel from a drawer in his workbench.

It had taken weeks of work on the side, but he'd finally screwed in the last screw and Infused the last snippets of power. Sometimes, Kuma wondered if he was a bit obsessive, and then a project for Salome would come up and he would realize that the answer was most definitely yes. He'd even swallowed down his distaste and worked with Torin to make sure that the Infusion was better than ever.

The new prosthetic was beautiful, not just functional. The arm was a metal frame and a wooden casing, but between those he'd wired it up with electronics in sleek bundles that mimicked tendons and muscles. He'd even put in a little display, intent on giving Salome a small computer, not just an arm. Kuma might have gone overboard, but considering what their plan for the immediate future was, Salome would enjoy having the extra gadgets. He'd even tucked in a wire that she could plug into ports on a computer system, to directly interface with in order to upload or download data.

"What do you think, Lani?"

His Bonded's head shot up from where she was poking at the bandage over the cut from the ceremony, curls bouncing. Someone else might have taken a quick look and complimented his work, but Lani took the proffered arm with a completely serious expression.

She studied the arm for well over a minute, running her fingers over the carved waves and smooth varnish, then pressed a kiss to his cheek. "It's beautiful. Does it have room for any more Infusions?"

"Of course it does . . . I just haven't had much to play with, and you've been busy. Why, are you going to give Sal a death ray, or a lullaby touch? That'd be fantastic."

Lani poked him in the ribs. "No. No, Fertility powers. I was thinking more . . . Calm. She's asked me to sooth away her worries a lot over the last couple months, especially when she's thinking hard. Maybe an extra dose of that, which she can turn on and off herself, might be helpful. I don't know how much of a grasp on my Emotive Mark I'll have while we're moving in a Prismatic Storm."

"Based on what Vee has told me, not much." Kuma didn't speak with any judgement on that one. Every Mark had their moment where humanity seemed . . . suspended. Reassuringly, he reached out to brush his fingers against her lips. "If you would like to wire in some calm for her, Lani, let's do it. You're right. She'd definitely love to be able to have a 'calm down' button. Sal has always hated being an illogical, feeling person when it could fuck up the ship."

He took Lani's hand, bringing it forward to rest on the prosthetic. "Just hold onto this. It might feel a little . . . strange . . . for you, as I conduct your power." He closed his eyes, laying his hand over hers. Reaching *through* Lani and into the wood, Kuma felt around for her power. It was like embroidery in a way. He drew thin filaments of Lani's energy into the wood of the arm, each one creating or reinforcing the pattern Kuma maintained in his mind. Filtering out her Emotive from her Fertility took a little finagling, but after two months of working with Moe, it wasn't too complicated.

"If you start getting dizzy, let me know." He moved slowly, layering her Emotive energy into Sal's new fingertips. The pattern forming—invisible to the naked eye but bright to Kuma—would allow Salome to access this Infusion with a snap of her fingers. She'd love it, and he loved that Lani had suggested it. "Have I told you . . . that you are a blessedly wonderful partner, Sweets?"

"About every time I go down on you, yeah."

Kumanu couldn't help the laugh, then went back to concentrating on his work. After he was certain he'd juiced the arm enough, he cut off the drain on Lani's Mark and tied the weave shut on the arm. "I wish you could see this the way I do. Without me having to push the memories, I mean. Because . . . this is probably one of the prettiest things I've ever made." He grinned at her, leaning into her body to layer kisses on her cheeks and neck.

"Oh don't you start that. I'm way too tired for sex. Shoo. Go find your sister. Besides . . . I need to check in on Vera. Something . . .

very weird is coming through the Bond."

"When isn't it?" Kuma asked with a laugh, giving her one last kiss before looking for his clothes.

Hunting down Sal wasn't hard. She was, as usual, in her room. When he knocked, he heard some mumbled curses, then Torin opened the door, his shirt askew.

"Kumanu," the Mender said, tone neutral.

Kuma raised his eyebrow. "Am I interrupting something?"

"No. I was leaving. I need to go check on Vera. Something—"

"Strange is coming through the Bond. Yeah. Lani noticed too."

Torin left and Kuma watched him go, eyes narrowed. Only when he disappeared from sight did he turn to Salome's room. His little sister was sitting at her desk in a bathrobe, peering at her white board and erasing some symbols while keeping others. She wasn't as oblivious as she seemed, though. "Kuma, why are you staring at me?"

"Since when did gibberish become a math language?"

"It isn't math. Just shorthand."

"Nothing I've seen before."

Sal's smirk spoke volumes. Kuma rolled his eyes, padding over to her desk and opening a drawer to rummage.

"What are you looking for, Kuma?"

"The drugs or booze. You have clearly lost your mind to *still* be sleeping with that asshat."

"Lost it ages ago. Also, who I fuck isn't your business. What's up?"

"I made a new arm for you."

"It's done?"

"Well naturally." Kuma smiled, pulling out the magnificent piece of art and laying it on her desk. "Take the old one off." He never did like seeing that flash of discomfort on her face whenever she had to do that.

Once her arm was off, Kuma took the new one and slid it into place, then attached the harness to help the load bearing be a bit better. Sal's eyes closed as she 'felt out' the new arm, and then her fingers began moving one by one. "Hell.. this is smooth. No lag at all. And way less nerve pain. Thank you, Kuma."

"I'm not done. Lani gave you a present."

"What?"

"Her Emotive Mark is in the fingers. All you need to do is snap your fingers, and boom: calm on command. It's loaded up with about an hour's worth, so you'll need her to recharge it periodically, but it might come in handy."

Sal whipped her head around, staring at him in surprise. "She . . . did?"

"Well yeah. You're family, Sal. You Bonded us."

He had never been so happy to see her eyes get watery. "Well I'll be damned. Thank you."

"That's it? No criticisms? No 'but this leaf could be done better?'"

"Fuck no. This thing is a work of art, Kuma. I might be smart, but I can't draw a stick figure properly." Sal reached out with her new arm, snagging his wrist and tugging him down to sit on her desk. "So, can the display interface with computers?"

"Yeah, of course."

"Kuma, I love you. You're a genius."

"I mean, what's not to love?" He grinned, watching as she booted up her computer and dug in a drawer for the correct type of cable.

"The arrogance, for one. I have an idea, though, that could use a little bit of your overconfidence. Our trial run is coming up and we're going to have a shot at the University Archives. I want to try to write a program that will hack into them. I've been reading up on all those computer languages you always tried to teach me as a kid, and I think I'm caught up enough to work with you. So what do you say? Want to help me to hack the Corporation? Call it a backup plan in case the Salt Spire fails. Also," here she trailed off, biting her lip and looking up at Kuma. "I have this feeling like we're being purposefully kept in the dark. Have you noticed how Moe keeps us busy every second of every day, and he's always the one funneling intel to us? We need to know what he's keeping secret."

Kuma nodded, pulling a stool over to sit next to Salome, instead of on her desk. "Yeah, I've noticed. Alright, kiddo. Let's see what you've got in that head of yours, now that we're speaking the same language."

CODEX: Wait. Wait just a damn minute. Moe and Galena are Bonded, right? Oh. Oh yes. Ha. I think I have it. Real quick, SALT, *Query: Has Moe ever saved Galena's life?*

FROM THE WRITINGS OF GALENA CRYSTAL

It's been fifty years since I last saw my husband, and I honestly had thought he was gone for good. How else to explain fifty perfect years, where nothing got sabotaged except by the usual uppity anarchist pirates, and my efforts actually achieved something? Then today, I am about to walk into my office when Moe pops up right in front of me a second before a bomb goes off. He Ported me out to somewhere very strange, where there was nothing but burning sand as far as the eye could see.

We remained there for more than an hour as he paced around, swearing at me to be more careful, and that he almost didn't get there in time to keep me from being blown up. He bitched and moaned about being Bonded to me, as though being his Bonded is something I enjoy.

When I insisted he return me home, he threatened to leave me where I was. Fortunately, he's as susceptible as ever to my Mark. It took some doing, but eventually I convinced him that it was in his best interest to keep me alive. Feeling his hands on me again was regretfully pleasant, but at least he had the decency of dropping me on Kahana when he Ported me back.

Considering last time he dropped me in the ocean and made me swim, and that he did, actually, save my life, I'm willing to forgive him for wasting a few hours of my time this once.

CODEX: Ew, but also, I got you, you motherfucking assholes. I know exactly how to get rid of you both. There is no way Moe would go to the trouble of saving Galena if he wasn't worried that her dying could kill him. That's the only plausible reason, considering how much he's doing to undermine her. So that's how I trap him. It's going to work, SALt. I can just feel it. This is the key I've been looking for.

Berserker
Vera - Day 67

Vera still felt breathless. How long had they gone at it? Not long, she was sure, but it felt like a year and a day. She was so fucking sore. It was *great*. The best workout she'd had in . . . a long time. Vera *almost* felt relaxed.

"You know, we still have to kill a bunch of Precogs. And you took us out of the handy staircase hidey hole."

Moe stretched and pulled her close again, tucking her head under his chin. "It's not exactly hard to get back there. How about this? Five minutes to nap and then whoever kills more Corporate Marks gets to be on top next round?"

"Mmm . . . fine. Only five minutes though, asshole." She sighed, nuzzling in close. For the first time in years, Vera didn't feel *wrong* lying next to someone. It wasn't just that he had given her a choice. She refused to celebrate that, since it was the least one should expect from sex. It was that at no point had Moe been judgemental of her. In his eyes, she wasn't a monster. Even when they had been madly in love, Torin had always smelled a little of fear.

She didn't love Moe. Vera was relatively certain that the part of her that knew how to truly love had been broken in the Spire. Still, she found she was growing to like the crazy madman. As she considered that, Moe pulled her even closer, making Vera have to wiggle to not be crushed.

"I see we'll have to work on turning you cuddly."

"If you wanted cuddly, you should have fucked Kumanu."

"Don't think I haven't considered it. Have you seen the ass on that boy? Mhmm," Moe said into her hair as he pressed his lips in to kiss it. "You smell like blood. When we get back, I'm going to clean you up."

Vera laughed. "Sorry. I was imagining you fucking Kuma. I'm

not sure who would do who at that point . . . boy's a walking sex pheromone."

She let out a sleepy yawn, and then stroked her fingers against his cheek. "You *will* clean me up, cause I'm sore, and don't want to move."

Moe turned a little, just enough to trail his fingers along her flank and hip, the touch almost gentle and a little startling in contrast to the way he had manhandled her during sex. "It will be my pleasure. Don't tell Lizzie or I'll never live it down, but I do enjoy some quiet, intimate time from decade to decade. Not with the ones who look at me and get all lovey—those I usually get rid of fast—but people like you, who can hold their own and don't need me to babysit them. It's nice to relax. It's why as much as Lani, and Kuma, and even Salome are pretty enough and would probably be fun in the sack, I wouldn't fuck them even if they asked nice. Their kind will always need a protector, even if they don't want to admit it. You, though? You're fierce and I'm fierce, and that means we can occasionally not be fierce together and no one will know."

Vera closed her eyes, a soft sigh leaving her lips. "It's stupid, and I know it's stupid . . . but you're right. I think I can finally relax a little near you, Moe. You'd see me dead if it fit your wants, and . . . weirdly . . . That makes more sense to me than anything else these days. I can trust in the fact that I can't trust you. It's a comfort."

He didn't reply, and Vera simply let herself drift while listening to Moe's heartbeat, waiting for him to say when the five minutes were over.

At last, Moe stopped listlessly petting her and instead stretched and sat up. Then he helped Vera to her feet. "Ready?"

She nodded, and they vanished. It took him a few tries to get them back near the entrance to the secret passage under the stairs, then a few more minutes for them to dress. Her pants were still mostly in one piece, but Vera had to borrow Moe's undershirt to wear, since hers was irreparably damaged.

Moe's smirk about that was profoundly irritating.

At last, they were ready to do what they had set out to in the first place, and as luck would have it their distraction had taken long enough that the lockdown had calmed and everyone was where they were supposed to be as Security teams scoured the grounds and buildings.

Adavera had grown up here, but Moe knew back doors and service tunnels that she had never realized existed. He led her down them without a word, face stern and focused as they descended several flights of stairs into the underground offices below the Archives where the *real* work of the University took place. Their final destination was a plain white door at the end of a narrow tunnel, where Moe pulled her close so he could whisper, "This opens into a utility closet. If I'm not wrong—and there is only 0.5% chance that I am—most of the University Precogs are working in there. The doors in and out are barred until the lockdown is released, so they won't have any help coming. Now, I'm not sure how many there are or how old they might be, just our odds of survival based on different choices we make. There is almost no scenario where we kill all of them. Our chance to get out alive starts dropping dramatically after four of them hit the ground and goes down to below five percent after five. Count, ok? I am not going to go in with you, because Precogs getting too close gets . . . messy. I'll predict what they'll do and they'll act on what they predict I'll do, and it gets into nasty loops. Means we can't really predict what other Precogs are gonna try. This is about as close as I can get without setting that off. Now, I cheat. I predict based on how much blood will hit the floor and how many lightbulbs are going to get shattered, but it's way less precise than usual. My best advice? Head back when the painting on the wall falls. But again, I can't really be sure. The only other piece of advice I offer is to not think. Don't plan, or they'll see it and avoid it. Act on instinct alone, and you'll get them. Tactics will kill you, and I'd really rather not have to ponder the merits of necrophilia. I haven't gotten nearly my fill of you yet." He gave her a quick kiss, then whispered, "Good luck."

"Ew." Vera grinned a bit, despite the joke, then turned her attention to the door. Already, that tingle of awareness was sizzling down her limbs. A fight was coming. That was all she needed to know. The delicious soreness between her legs disappeared, as did the lingering pain in the limb Lani had almost destroyed. Her Mark flared, and Vera turned her attention to the white door. She began to run.

When she crashed through the door, Adavera was a blurring monstrosity of death. There was no mercy in her eyes, nor compassion. She wasn't a person. She was what the University, what the *Corporation*, had designed her to be. The first Precog went down when her fist hit their head. The second when she dodged a shot from the third, her foot kicking out to dislocate the second Precog's knee before she rolled over the woman to pull her neck to the side, bones shattering.

Two.

She rolled to the side, plucking up a chair and smashing it against the nearby wall to break a leg off. Remembering Moe's warning, however, she didn't swing it at the third Precog. Instead, on impulse she threw it at the light above her head. The change of direction made the one with the gun hesitate for just a moment. The split second in the dark was all Vera needed. Bending mid-stride to pick up two of the broken rungs of the chair she had smashed, she launched herself at him and impaled them into his chest with a squelch.

Three.

In the dark, they should have had the advantage, but Vera had survived the Mines. She closed her eyes as she picked up the gun the third man had dropped.

Predictably, the next Precog to attack her—lucky number four—went low. Vera heard the woman's body hit the floor. There were six bullets in the gun. She emptied them all into the space the noise had come from, and felt as much as heard the splattering of blood.

Four.

Someone tackled her from behind. Vera threw herself backwards, crashing into the floor and pinning the Pregoc on her back. His head crashed into the nearby wall, and a painting fell, the glass breaking all over Vera. Sharp shards sliced her cheek and the arm she flung up to protect her eyes.

Four. Moe had said that five would be too much, but the man under her was *right there*. She wanted, *needed*, to make them all bleed. Four wasn't enough.

More. She needed more.

A hand appeared out of nowhere and yanked her up.

Vera still held the gun, and while it had no more bullets, it was pointy and hard. She swung, but her new attacker dodged.

"I said four," Moe growled from the darkness at the end of the arm.

Precog. She was here to kill Precogs.

He was a Precog, and he had a gun tucked into the back of his pants. She had seen it.

Vera tackled him, grabbing for it. Her fingers wrapped around the grip. Instead of trying to stop her, Moe put his hands on her shoulders and twisted her around to point at the Precog on the ground in the remains of the painting.

Vera pulled the trigger.

Five.

The flash of light as they Ported nearly blinded her. She stumbled as they landed, Moe's arms the only thing that kept her on her feet. The bright light inside his lair almost blinded her, and Vera raised the arm still holding the gun, ready to shoot anything that moved.

"Easy! You got them. Easy," Moe was saying, but everything was still crimson in her view.

She squeezed her eyes shut and her fingers flexed against the trigger. Target. She needed someone else to kill. Easy? Yes, killing was very easy, and so very satisfying. There were still Precogs in that room. She had to . . . Had to . . .

"VERA!"

Torin's voice broke through the haze. She looked up to see him out of breath at the open door of the room, hair messy and eyes wide.

"WHAT THE FUCK DID YOU DO TO HER, MOE!?"

"Nothing she didn't enjoy, I assure you. She's just having a hard time coming down from her killing spree. Say . . . you're good at that, right?"

"Get the fuck off her." Torin shouted as he stalked across the room to take Moe's place. He cupped Vera's face between his hands, completely ignoring the gun pointing into his belly. Torin's eyes became the only thing she could see as he said, "Adavera of Keala, stop and stand down."

Old instinct, buried under six years of hell, sluggishly kicked in at the command, though her body twitched disobediently.

"Breath in, hold. Now out. In, two, three, four, five, six, out, two three, four . . ."

It continued.

Two. Two was Vera and Torin.

Three. Three . . . Three was the number on the door to the cell she had waited in before her sentencing. She didn't like the number three.

Four. Keanu was four. That was a better number, her favorite number.

Five. Five Precogs dead.

Six. Six years without the sun on her back, six years of misery without . . .

"Tor . . . ?"

Vera blinked and was back.

"There you are," he whispered, pressing his forehead to hers, their Bond flaring to life at the contact. *Are you alright? You look a mess. Did he hurt you? Why did you let yourself go Berserk? You know how dangerous that is.*

Vera cleared her throat, shivering for a moment while she let herself enjoy just *touching* him again. She shouldn't. Torin deserved better than her—he *wanted* better than her. She had been better once. Vera could remember fighting so hard to stay in control, to be exactly what Torin had wanted. They were happy then. She'd stayed in control, and Torin had been so willing to believe in . . .

She sighed, shaking her head. "I'm fine. Just a few scratches. Nothing too bad." She reached up to touch his beard, fascinated by the way it felt. The last time she had killed like this, he had been clean shaven, and they had both been so much younger. "I still can't get over this look of yours, you know." Vera chuckled a little, finally cracking her eyes open. "Precogs, Tor . . . can't think, or plan, or . . . any of it. Berserk was the only way to get out."

"I thought he had a plan. I wouldn't have left you alone with him if I'd realized he would take you in blind. Fuck." Torin's hands on her cheeks tightened, then he pulled away and glared at Moe. "This is unacceptable. Do you realize what you did? Putting her in that situation? There's a reason the University teaches Conflicters control. Sometimes they don't come back. You could have killed her even if you'd brought her back alive."

Moe shrugged. "Nothing wrong with a Conflicter being a Conflicter. It's her nature, not something to be afraid of. Your people just loooove to put labels on everything and tell people what is and isn't acceptable behavior. What you want Vera to be is like putting a muzzle and high heels on a jungle cat. She isn't flawed or broken: she is a Conflicter."

"Don't argue. I just got back," Vera said softly, rubbing at her face. Her hand came away wet with blood, and there was a bone splinter under her nail that had started to throb. "Huh." She pulled it loose, flicking it to the side before glancing at Moe. "You said you'd get me a bath. And clothes."

Sore. That was the sensation starting to register. Her hands hurt, as did her bad leg. A soak in hot water sounded like just the ticket.

Vera turned back to Torin. She reached out to touch his cheek, but pulled her hand back at the last second as a drop of blood fell from her fingers. "I'm sorry to have worried you, Tor."

His face shifted from anger to something that might have been dismay. "You're getting in too deep, Vee. Come with me. I'll find you somewhere you can clean up, put you to bed, and then we can talk and . . . Just . . . come with me." He held out his hand to her, only flinching a little at the prospect of the gore that covered hers.

"Or, alternatively, you can do whatever the fuck you want and not have to listen to a Corporate lecture. But it's up to you. I do owe you a bubble-bath and another round with you on top," Moe said with a wink.

Torin whipped around, and with no preamble pulled back his arm and punched the Precog. Or, well, would have, had Moe not ducked out of the way at the last possible second, sidestepping and sticking out his leg. Torin's forward momentum, with nowhere to go, made him step forward, then stumble on Moe's outstretched leg so he fell flat on his face on the hard stone floor.

Vera *felt* the sting as his nose collided with the ground. The smell of fresh blood filled the air. Shaking her head, she knelt down near her Bonded and gently set a hand to his back. "Torin, trying to punch Moe is . . . sweet, but rather useless. He cheats."

Carefully, she helped Torin sit. "Did your nose break?" She hoped not. If his nose had broken, it should only be because *she* had broken it. No one else had the right to hurt him.

"No, I'm fine," he said, his hand going up to cover his bleeding nose. "How could you let him touch you, Vee? He's evil."

"How rude. I prefer to think of myself as distinguished and villainous. Trust me, she likes that side of me," Moe stated.

Vera's eyes narrowed, her hand fell away from Torin, and she rose to her feet. "What does it matter, Tor?" Her hands closed into fists again, warmth suffusing her chest as anger came like a well-trained dog. Anger was a shield, a weapon, and all the warmth she needed. "You can *both* go for a cold swim. I'll take my bath on my own, thank you."

"Vee—"

"You heard the young lady," Moe interrupted. "She's had quite enough company. Come on, maybe your pirate will be willing to pat you on the head while you fix your face. Me? I'm going to go get a drink," Moe said, all but lifting Torin to his feet by the back of his shirt. "See you later, my darling murder-machine. Thank you for a *memorable* outing. Must do it again soon."

Her eyes narrowed—not at the names, or endearments, or the way he smiled at her. She narrowed her gaze at the way he was *picking* on Torin. There was no reason to rub this in her Bonded's face.

"Get your hands off him, Moe, or I will break them."

She took a deep breath, turning sharply to march off towards the bath chamber. To her surprise, when she got there, Lani was waiting outside the door.

Vera stopped in her tracks, staring at her other Bonded. "Are you here to tell me how dangerous it was to become Berserk, too?"

Lani shook her head. "I came because you're hurting."

"I'm fine. Everything is fine. Go back to Kuma," Vera snapped. Except it wasn't, was it? One look at the Emotive's concerned brown eyes told her that Lani knew better than to take Vera at her word. "Take a bath with me?"

Lani followed Vera into the room and didn't push her to speak as the large tub filled, or as they stripped. When Vera went to get in, though, Lani reached out to stop her. With a gentleness that Vera wasn't sure what to make of, her Bonded picked up a washcloth, dipped it in the bathwater, and began to clean the blood off of Vera's skin. It reminded her of the way Torin had treated her that first day on the *Legacy*, and sent shivers down Adavera's spine.

"You don't have to do that," Vera whispered hoarsely.

"You'll get chunks of . . . stuff . . . in the water. Besides, I want to. Your emotions are like a hurricane pulling in two directions right now. I don't think that will calm down until you've cleaned all the blood off, so let me help."

When Vera did not protest, Lani traced the dampened cloth over Vera's cheek. These touches were not like Moe's or Torin's. There was no blazing heat or icy disapproval. Lani's hands were *warm* and gentle, so at odds with the destructive power the Fertilizer wielded.

"How do you do it?" Vera asked, as Lani wrung out the cloth in the sink, the droplets of bloody water echoing in the cavernous room when they hit the porcelain. "How hasn't the monster you become driven you mad? Especially without being Bonded for so long. You should have been nothing but your Marks, but you helped me before you even knew me. Anyone else would have left me to die on the beach, but you didn't. I could have killed you, yet you still put yourself at risk to save me."

Wetting the cloth again, Lani wiped the blood and bits of gore from Vera's left arm, her fingers entwining with the Conflicter's for a moment when she reached the hand. "I did go crazy for awhile. There were a solid fifty years where I completely fucking lost it. I don't remember most of it, but I know it involved a lot of drugs, a lot of killing, and some pretty dumb decisions. Do you know what snapped me out of it?"

Vera shook her head.

"I went home. I was depressed—honestly kind of suicidal—and so fucking lonely. I had killed a third of the population of my island when I was just a child, and I wanted to go home to turn myself in. I figured if I was going to end it, it should be with a shred of decency. When I got there, I hardly recognized it. We had always really struggled, out by the Reef and about as far from the Spire as possible. All my memories of it were of animals Hazed- out in the streets and people starving. I had been gone for over seventy years, and I returned to find it a damn paradise."

"Your Mark balanced the soil?" Vera asked.

Lani nodded, passing the washcloth over Vera's shoulders. "It took me over, made me kill the people I loved, turned me into everybody's worst nightmare . . . and saved my island. Not just the people, but the plants and wild animals too. I had sped up the decomposition of organic matter, creating thick, rich topsoil, rotted cases of salt under Corporate control and distributed it around the island, and reduced the population to what the island could sustain as it adjusted and got through the next growing season. I spent days roaming around, so fucking overwelmed I couldn't speak. Then out of nowhere a Prismatic Storm came in and you know what happened? Absolutely nothing. I sat in a clearing, fiddling with the nitrogen balance a little, but all the rage and fury wasn't there. I was . . . at peace. I've never felt that way again, but just knowing that it was possible has given me something to cling to."

Vera gulped, throat tight. "I know that feeling. It's how it feels when I lose control. Peace in the eye of the storm."

"And it scares you."

"Yes. No. I—" Vere hung her head, breath rough. "I love it. It thrills me. I feel *alive* when I'm Berserk. But then it leaves me and . . . and I realize that the high is . . . hollow. It isn't all of me, but the Mines scraped out whatever *more* there was."

"I'll tell you a secret," Lani said, putting a finger under Vera's chin to pull her gaze up to meet hers. "They didn't."

"Then where is it? Why is it so much easier to be the weapon Moe wants, than the Bonded Torin needs, if I didn't lose the part of me that Tor used to love? She was a better woman. She could have raised a child instead of hoping she'd die before proving that she couldn't handle another person's future on her shoulders."

Lani didn't answer, and the heaviness in Vera's thoughts grew. Her Bonded continued to clean her, then with the same slow and steady silence helped Vera into the tub. She didn't have to tell Lani to brace her bad leg. Lani knew exactly where it hurt and moved to accommodate, making Vera feel even worse. She hardly spared Lani a thought most days. Their Bond was as healthy as it could be, under the circumstance, but Vera was so used to blocking out Torin that Lani often became nothing more than a vague, nagging thought at the back of her mind, except during the Storms.

The same was not true in reverse. For all her paranoia and history of isolation, Lani's mind and emotions were a window flung wide and hungry for connection.

"I'm not a very good Bonded, am I?" Vera asked in a hushed tone. "Even to you, who want so little. I'm glad you have Kuma, now."

"Me too, but not because of that." Lani slipped into the large tub behind Vera. "You're not a bad Bonded, Vee. You're just not the *same* Bonded you were before the Mines."

Lani picked up the washcloth again and ran it over Adavera's back as Vera leaned forward. When she didn't say anything, the little Emotive sighed. "Most days I feel so much younger than all of you. I don't have yours and Torin's education, or Sal and Kuma's family and purpose. I definitely don't have Moe's ambition. The sum total of my life accomplishments has been staying alive."

"You didn't have a choice," Vera started, but Lani shushed her.

"I wasn't done."

"You're learning bossiness from Moe."

Lani laughed and pressed her forehead against Vera's shoulder. "The point I was trying to make is that while I sometimes feel younger, I'm not. I'm older than everyone but Moe and Lizzie, and in that time I've learned one hell of a lot about being alone."

Vera felt the sigh. More than the physical shifting of Lani's body, she also felt a shift in the soul at the other end of their Bond. It was a tugging away, walls going up where Vera was used to a wide-open archway. That was when a realization struck her.

"You're doing it on purpose, aren't you? It's not that you don't know how to block me out. It's a conscious decision and . . ."

"It's exhausting," Lani finished. That word weighed as much as a mountain as she spoke it against Adavera's skin. The water around them stilled, not even their breaths disturbing it until her Bonded whispered, "being alone becomes a shield, Vee. When you're alone, you have to push past the pain because you know, beyond the shadow of a doubt, that no one else will do it for you. There is no help coming. You have no option but strength, and no one to blame your failings on but yourself. Other people are a threat not because they might hurt you, but because they might *disappoint you.* So better to push them away. If you trust that they'll catch you when you fall, you'll end up broken and bleeding on the ground."

Vera reached back, her fingers brushing the top of Lani's head.

The hair was soft and smelled of salt. Vera could almost taste it on her tongue as she inhaled and closed her eyes, letting Lani's words wash over her.

"You can be in a room—or a Mine—full of other bodies, and still be alone. That's the beautiful, terrible, and insidious thing about solitude. The problem is that when you're alone, you have no choice but get to know yourself. Most people never have to come to terms with every crack and crevice of their own soul. It changes you. You come face-to-face with your every failing and contradiction, and each time are forced to choose between accepting them, changing them, or giving up. After a while, even when you're desperate for another person's touch, you also don't want them to get close, because you are afraid that if they do, they will see in you all the failings that you see in yourself. Worse, they might *not.*"

"What do you mean?" Wouldn't people not seeing Vera as a bloodthirsty monster be better?

"What I mean is that your problem with Torin is that he thinks you blocked him out all those years because you wanted to spare him the pain, where the truth is that you blocked him out to spare yourself. You didn't want him to see what you are under the veneer of civility, and judge it unlovable. When you go Berserk, you are a one woman army. You don't need Torin, or me, or anyone. You are strong because you've proven to yourself time and again that you are. It feels amazing because your fate is entirely your own. Then you come down off that high and realize that even those closest to you will never know you the way you've been forced to know yourself to survive. You feel alone again, and alone amongst the people you love and who you want to love you in return . . . Why, that is the most terrible kind of solitude there is."

Lani's arms wrapped around Vera's waist and the door Lani had closed between their souls creaked open once more. Clearer than any words the Emotive could have spoken, it said: 'when you're ready to be loved again, I'll be waiting. I've been lonely too.'

CODEX: So I have a plan starting to form, but I need access to schematics of the University. I need a place to ambush Galena, where someone can Port in. So, *Query: Does Galena have an emergency protocol?* She seems like the sort to have a safe room or something.

SALT: Maps and protocols listed below.

CODEX: Ok, reading now. Mhm. As I suspected. She has a control center in the archives. The walls are Shielded, which means Porting in isn't an option. Door has a keypad. Can I see the door access logs?

SALT: Affirmative.

CODEX: Oh look, she's been basically living in there since Vera and Moe's little jaunt. Wonderful. I bet she's terrified. *Query: What's the door code?*

SALT: Information encrypted.

CODEX: No problem. *Query: Who has access to that code?*

SALT: Galena. Galena's secretary. Security.

CODEX: Ok. I'll just send her secretary instructions to either leave or enter the room when the time is right, and the door should be wide open. Please add the following voice recording to my Macro, to be sent to my Uncle Kekai when I give the go-ahead.

"Uncle Kekai, I don't have time to explain right now, but you need to get a Porter and a Shielder to drop a bomb at the attached coordinates when I give you the signal. It needs to have a countdown of sixty seconds, and an off-switch. Tell them to stay put until

Moe shows up, and keep him from Porting out. If someone else shows up, stop the countdown and run. If no one does, set it off and get out if you can, but under no circumstances let Moe Port away, even if it kills them. I'm sorry to ask, but it is necessary. I'll explain everything when this is over."

CODEX: Also, please bring up my message to the Gods. I need to edit it to tell them where Moe will be. I think I know what I'm doing.

Priorities
Torin - Day 68   54

A full day after the bloodbath at the University, Torin sat on the edge of the bed, watching Salome sleep. He'd done that a lot in the last four years, finding it fascinating how her face changed in slumber. She was only twenty-six years old. He had freaked the hell out four years before, when he had discovered how young she was—well over ten years his junior.

"*It's not robbing the cradle, if the cradle's robbing you,*" she had said, ending that fight the same way most of their fights had: with Salome Parata straddling his hips and kissing him until he shut up.

In a society where Marks could live centuries looking youthful, age didn't always matter. It still did to Torin, but the way Salome carried herself and spoke had always struck Torin as mature. It was only in her sleep that the mask dropped. She dreamed a lot, her features contorting into all the emotions she hid behind anger and rum while awake. There was a breathtaking vulnerability there, one that Torin had always treasured in the still mornings in his cave, while he watched the rise and fall of her chest and let that become the metronome he lived by.

Salome was not the love of his life, but she was life in the barren wastes where once there had been love. He had his Vera back, but it wasn't the same. They had both changed, and he found, more and more, that he still needed *this*.

Careful not to wake Salome, he pulled on his clothes, then slipped a flower he had picked from one of Moe's many weird gardens from his pocket and lay it on his recently vacated pillow.

Hopefully, she would sleep for a few more hours. Her new power seemed to take a lot out of her, and Salome hadn't been great about self-care even before getting it.

Out on the deck of her ship, crewmen and women were still busy at work. They were getting close to go-time, the crew, like the group Moe had assembled, making their final preparations and checking over all the repairs and upgrades on the *Sahima's Legacy*. Torin still wasn't convinced this wouldn't end in disaster, but it had become clear he was outvoted.

The gangway ended at a short pier that jutted into the still, salty lake. There was so much salt here that it crystalized around the shores and on anything that spent too long in the water. Sal's ship was covered in the white substance, and Torin couldn't help but be disgusted at Moe's hypocrisy. If he cared about the islanders suffering the Haze, why wasn't he giving this salt away? And how long must he have been Porting in and out of here to build up this much salt in the lake? Marks always left some behind, but this was ridiculous.

The winding hallways of Moe's lair were deserted. Torin had finally taken the time to map them out because he'd gotten fed up of being late to meetings. It sometimes felt as though their host changed the location of their daily group meeting just to fuck with Torin. It was all so idiotic. He could understand Vera, and even Lani, going along with this plan, but Kuma and Salome should have known better. Torin *did* know better, but if he stepped away now, who would patch them up when they went out to get themselves killed?

He had already lost Vera. He'd seen that in her eyes the day before, as she came down from the murder frenzy Moe had let her fall into. He couldn't lose Salome too.

At the end of a long, uneven hallway, Torin heard voices. Lani laughed, the sound grating and disconcerting. A woman who could destroy all of them on a passing fancy should not sound so carefree. Didn't she have a conscience? Had she forgotten what her powers had done to Vera?

He got to the door to see the walking menace sitting in Kumanu's lap, her hair down and cheeks flushed. Sal's brother, likewise, had the glow of someone both very much in love and well-satisfied.

It was sickening. Torin had once thought Kuma smarter than this, but Salome had always said that a pretty face would be his undoing. As he watched from the doorway, Kuma put the brush he had been using on Lani's hair down and started braiding her hair with the ribbon they had used for their Bonding.

A pang of envy stronger than the disgust washed over Torin, and his eyes swept across the room to Vera. He didn't have to look to find her. Their Bond might be strained beyond repair, but nothing could break a Blood Bond. He always knew where she was.

To his shock and annoyance, Vera wasn't alone at the conference table. Moe stood next to her, a hand on her lower back as they poured over a map. Considering where he had just come from, Torin knew that he had no right to feel the blistering wave of jealousy that crashed into him at the sight. Reason, unfortunately, had nothing to do with emotion.

"Did I come at the wrong time? I thought we were here to finalize plans, not form a cuddle pile."

Vera looked up and actually smiled at him. It was a tad murderous, true, but it still shocked Torin to see her face do that. It didn't often, anymore, and the fact that it was happening with another man's hands on her galled.

"Hello to you too. Where's your pirate?"

Torin's cheeks burned and he looked away. "Sleeping. We can start without her. I'll catch her up on everything we decide."

"Won't need to, it's mostly her plan anyway," Kuma said, as both he and Lani joined them standing around the table. There were two sets of maps spread out, one of the University, and one of the Spire. There was also a calendar, with several dates marked in Moe's flowery handwriting.

"To recap where we left off last time," Lizzie said, appearing from the shadows. Torin jumped, startled, as always, by the appearance of the strange young girl who shadowed Moe, yet spoke little. Something about her eyes bothered him, as if they saw through to the very core of his being and found it . . . tasty. "We have three upcoming Prismatic Storms and two targets. We have to take down the servers at the University before we hit the Spire to impede the Corporation's ability to coordinate Marked backup when we go for the big one, and thanks to Moe and Adavera, they are now down several key Precogs."

Torin ground his teeth. "Vera has enough issues controlling her Mark. She didn't need to indulge in unplanned mindless slaughter."

His Bonded shot Torin an icy glare. "It had to be done. Would you have preferred doing it?"

"Bicker later. What's next on the timeline?" Lizzie asked, rubbing her hands together. "Moe, you need to finish placing Port Pads all over the Spire. Kuma, have you finished the last set?"

"Yep. Working on the rest of the gear now. I have a design for the jets to get us to the Spire from the Seawall, and Lani's battery packs are coming along well," Kuma replied. "And guns. Lots of guns."

Vera smiled at that, which chilled Torin to the bone. Didn't she realize that attacking the University and Spire would likely mean killing people *they had known?* Not everyone who worked at Crystal Corp was evil, as much as these people wanted to think that.

"If the equipment is almost ready, it's time to start talking exact plans and dates, now that they have fewer Precogs to see us coming," Vera said, interrupting Torin's bleak thoughts. "The University comes first. We'll hook Lani up and do the job, making sure that with both Kuma and myself there she can keep her cool in a Prismatic Storm even when under pressure. It should be an in-and-out job. No one ever goes out in those Storms unless they have to."

Lani hugged herself but nodded. Kumanu wrapped an arm around the girl's shoulders, pressing a kiss into her hair. "Don't worry, love. We've got you. I suggest we take the next Prismatic Storm to practice, so that Vera and I can learn to share the load, then go for the University if that goes well. Sal got a message from our uncle that the Salt Pirates are gathering outside of one of the outer islands in that first Storm's path. There are plenty of deserted islets near there where Lani can let loose and I can get a feel for her full output. Besides, I'd like to go talk to our uncle and give him the heads up about what's coming."

"Good intuition, Kuma. That gives us a good probability of success," Moe said.

"And what *is* the probability of success?" Torin snapped. All eyes turned to him. "You're supposed to be this great and powerful Precog, right, but I notice you're not the one picking out our dates and plans. I don't trust it."

For a brief second, Torin thought he saw anger flash across Moe's face, only to be replaced with an amicable smile. "Fair question, which deserves a fair answer. Yes, I am a powerful Precog. Too powerful, in fact. Trying to spot things in my immediate future is like," he waved a hand about, as if searching for a simile, "picking up a single grain of dry rice with a pair of chopsticks the size of a house. I'm very good at it, but it's not worth the effort most of the time. What I *can* do is see decades and centuries into the future. So that is what I did. I did my part hundreds of years ago, putting things into motion so that when the time came I would have the right team, and my bets were as hedged as I could make them." He pulled out a small notebook from an inner pocket. "And left myself notes."

"He doesn't remember," Lizzie supplied, arms crossed. The room fell silent. "That's what he's hedging around. Moe is so old that he's forgotten everything past . . . about seven centuries ago. Brain just can't hold onto much more than that. But I can. I keep him on track. Trust me when I tell you that what you see here is the tip of a very large iceberg that has been in the making for longer than the Corporation has existed. He's predicted the big picture blocks, but the tighter he plans, the more likely it is that a Corporate Precog will see him coming. The best way to avoid detection is not to plan the fine details until the last possible minute."

Into the silence that lingered past her last word, Torin hissed, "So we're doing all this based on predictions this lunatic doesn't even *remember?* We're putting *our* lives and the entire ecology of our Reef in danger on a plan that hasn't been updated in *longer than he can recall?*"

It had already sounded like madness. Now, Torin was sure of it. With a withering glare at Moe, he rounded the table and grabbed Vera's arm. "We're going. Get your son. I'm getting you and Salome out of here. Kuma, come along if you wish."

"Not me?" Lani asked, arms crossed.

"Of course not you, Lani my dear," Moe drawled. "He thinks you're a monster of my own creation. He's not wrong, either. You were always one of the largest pieces of my puzzle."

Torin tugged on Vera's arm again, but the stubborn woman didn't budge. She didn't even look up at him, still staring at the maps. "If you want to go, Torin, no one is stopping you. But you'll be going alone."

"Didn't you hear what he just said, Vee?"

"I heard that he's a Precog powerful enough to see centuries into the future with enough precision to make the outcome he wants happen, but who understands the game well enough to fool the Precogs on the other side. He brought us all together, didn't he? His plan is working so far. Knowing that it's based on a strategy older than all of us put together makes me more confident, not less. So if you want to walk, do. It would be one less person I need to keep alive when we go to the Spire. But don't think for a minute that if you try to get in my way again, I won't make you regret it. The Spire is coming down."

He didn't know this woman. With a growl, Torin turned on his heel, walked to the chair in the furthest corner, and crossed his arms.

"Not running away?" Lani asked, bitterness dripping from her words.

"What's the point? You're going to all die, and then I will too. There isn't a corner far enough away for me to run to. But if you think for one second that I approve of this shit, you're madder than Moe."

They may have responded, but Torin zoned out after that. His thoughts took him to memories he had thought long buried. To Vera as she had been in their University days, as full of hope as Torin had been that they could turn things around from the inside. Of Salome, taking him on one of her runs to help unload salt and treat those caught in the Haze.

He could understand Sal's motivation to blow the Spire. It was to make the world a better place. Vera, though, was in it for revenge, just as Lani and Kuma were. As if it hadn't been their decision to be Rogue Marks.

I can't save those three. Even if I wanted to, they are going to get themselves killed doing this, he thought, as they discussed a visit to the rest of the salt pirates and went over their strategy for breaking into first the University, then the Spire.

The University had an exit strategy planned, the Spire did not. It was a one-way trip to get Lani to the very center of the mountain as the eye of a Prismatic Storm hit it. Torin wasn't sure he believed she was strong enough, even in a Storm, to destroy the whole Spire, but if she was . . . They would all be crushed to pieces, along with every slave and guard there.

They don't care about the collateral damage. They've stopped caring about anything but their own agenda, yet they call the Corporation evil.

At the same moment he thought that, another one flitted through his head.

Fuck . . . I'm working for a terrorist cell.

SALT: Letter updated. Macro updated. What is your next Query?

CODEX: How much time do I have?

SALT: 1 minute exactly.

CODEX: Give me a heads up when we're at 30 seconds.

SALT: Confirmed.

CODEX: Wonderful. I wish I knew why we went to the Spire early, so I could better help once I can move, but I guess I'll have to improvise. I'll need to find a way to get Keanu out of Moe's clutches, but Moe is the only one to know where his lair actually is, so again, I'm going to have to improvise. Damn, I never thought I'd want *more* time after this interminable patch download, but I kind of wish I had Moe's ability to go to another world to calculate what to do. It still seems impossible that he can really do that. On that subject . . . *Query: What was the first time Moe mentioned another world?* Actually, that may be a bit too abstract. I know the world where the Gods actually live is called Primary. So, *Query: What is Moe's oldest unencrypted document mentioning Primary?*

FROM THE WRITINGS OF MOE

I need to understand this vision that keeps plaguing me. I've sailed and Ported everywhere on Fortune, but Eliza is nowhere to be found. I can see the thread of probability drawing me to her, even though she is gone. Galena thinks I'm having a psychotic break, but I know I'm sane.

I know what I'm seeing. I see futures where Lizzie is with us again, and I will not stop until I find them, even if it tears my marriage apart.

I know there are mysteries the Gods keep from me. They will not tell me where they come from, only that it is in the stars and they call it Primary. I need the information they have. They are irresponsibly fucking up our planet, and it cost me my daughter. I cannot express how deep my hatred for them goes. So tomorrow, I am going to start Porting, and I'm not going to stop until I find this place they call Primary. They tell me space has no air, so I've adapted some of the diving tech Galena's people are developing and have tried it out above our outer atmosphere. It will hold, and I'll just Port back if I run into problems.

I'm going to find Primary. I'm going to uncover their secrets. If there is a chance, however slight, of my Eliza living again, I am going to bet everything to see it happen. If there is not, I will destroy them, for what they have taken from me.

Calm Before the Storm
Moe - Day 73   55

On the insistence of Salome and Kumanu, Moe gathered the whole gang onto Salome's ship and headed into the Reef the day before the next Prismatic Storm was due to hit them.

Their reasoning was sound: Kuma and Vera had to get practice working with Lani during a Storm somewhere that *didn't* have as much salt as Moe's cave, since the University was their first target. Furthermore, Salome wanted to talk to her uncle, the head of the salt pirates, to let him know what was coming.

It was a good plan. The only thing that Moe didn't like about it was that his entire role in it was transportation. How boring.

Thanks to Lizzie by his side, the Port to the stretch of open ocean near a grouping of small, inconsequential islands by the Reef went smoothly. They arrived with nary a wobble in the open ocean. While outside the Reef the wind had howled through the crags and crevices of Moe's lair, here the sun shone, the coastlines shimmered with verdant growth, and the water lapped lazily against the side of Salome's ship.

It took about an hour to sail to one of the smaller, uninhabited islands and drop off the supplies Vera, Kuma, and Lani would need tomorrow to ride out the Prismatic Storm, then they were off again. With little to no wind and no need to hurry, the trip through the small archipelago was slow and peaceful. Even Torin seemed to be in a slightly less dour mood, and Moe wondered whether his dark and ominous caves were perhaps a little too super-villainy and not great for morale. Perhaps next time he planned a job, he should just lay siege to the Corporate Palace. That would be one hell of a swanky base.

It was coming on lunch time when they dropped anchor. The small bay had a village near the shoreline, the houses carved out of the rocky crags like most towns that didn't want to be blown away in every storm. The water around them was thick with other boats. Most of them were ex-Corporate vessels, heavily modified inside but indistinguishable on the outside except for being decades out of commission. Only a few, like the *Sahima's Legacy*, bore blatant gray sails, but all of them had at least one flying.

This was, after all, a gathering of pirates.

"What say you, me, Keanu, and Lizzie have a picnic?" Moe asked Vera as she joined him at the rail, staring out over the fleet. Her son was following Kuma about, asking the older Infuser about a thousand questions a minute. "This sounds like it's going to be a Parata family affair and I don't know about you, but I don't do gushy family reunions."

Vera eyed his shirt sardonically, clearly about to call him out for his bullshit. "Your shirt says: Free Hugs."

"And?" Moe smirked, batting his eyelashes innocently. "Wouldn't a spider catch more flies if their web said that?"

"Only if the flies were idiots."

Moe wrapped an arm around her shoulders. "Darling girl, all flies are idiots."

The hill he Ported the four of them to, after Salome, Torin, Kuma, and Lani had gone ashore, was on the far side of the island from the village. Moe dropped Vera and her son off, then snagged Lizzie for a quick jaunt to the kitchens of the University to steal lunch.

He was back in a flash, and was rewarded with an adorable squeak when he Ported in only five inches from Vera's face.

"Do that again and I'll remove your liver," the Conflicter growled, taking a few hurried steps back.

"But how would I drink without Phillip, Adavera? Here, I brought treats." He held out a large basket. "Straight from memory lane."

Vera's muttered complaints ended when he laid out lunch. Both she and her boy had been raised on University fare. It was good for the soul—though Moe would never admit it—to see the way Keanu sat in Vera's lap as he stuffed his face, and how she rested her chin on his unruly black curls, smiling.

After they devoured their lunch, and Lizzie had made Keanu nearly die laughing by making small chocolates appear behind his ears, they all went splashing in the nearby river. Moe showed Keanu how to lay traps for lizards, Lizzie *ate* a whole lizard, squirming tail and all, and all-too-serious Adavera actually let loose and chased after her son to tickle him.

All in all, a lot more fun than the political and familial bickering that was surely taking place back in town.

The sun was sinking towards the horizon, casting long, cool shadows off of every swaying palm tree, when Vera flopped down onto the picnic blanket beside Moe. Lizzie and Keanu were still playing in the river, splashing about as the fireflies came out. Moe idly wondered if Lizzie would try to eat one of those too, and what it was about bugs that intrigued her so. Was it just the strange fascination of the young for shiny objects? Sometimes, it was difficult to remember that Lizzie was, quite possibly, even older than Moe.

"I don't think I've ever laughed that much," Vera said, rubbing her still scarred leg. "Not even in my Company days. It feels almost . . . normal. As though we're not about to go on a series of murderous rampages."

"The calm before the storm," Moe declared. "Quite literally, in this case. Are you and Kuma ready for tonight's Prismatic Storm?"

Vera nodded. "Kuma has all the tech, and Lani and I are getting the hang of things by now. She gets murderous, I keep her moving. As long as she's burning up energy and doesn't stay still too long, I can keep her contained. Add Kuma in and this should be a breeze. You're Porting us to that little island, right?"

"As soon as we see the Storm coming in." Moe turned to her, admiring the way Vera's wet clothes clung to her curves. A beautiful woman, this one. Even better now that she had two months of good food and exercise, and no longer looked like a gaunt scarecrow. Her dark hair had grown a couple inches, the smooth strands curling around her ears in a manner Moe found quite appealing.

However, it was not her physical beauty or her keen wit—because she didn't have nearly enough of that to interest Moe—that kept drawing his eyes. Moe had never been picky in his bedmates, considering they all eventually died and getting attached was needlessly pointless. There were, however, certain traits he liked when collecting people to entertain himself with and carry out his plans.

Vera had, perhaps, his very favorite: a startling lack of veneer. She was a creature of bloodshed, passion, pain, and the unyielding pursuit of justice. She did not try to be anything that she was not. Even now, as she calmly watched her child play, she did so with all the same unrelenting intensity as when she plotted to overthrow the Corporation. Her son's joy happened to be one of the things she would die for.

Moe took no shame in ruthlessly using that to his advantage.

"Still want me to take him to a nice family when you die?" he asked, in the same casual tone he would have used to request she pass the lemonade. Always a good idea to remind people like Vera that their time on this earth was limited. Moe found it made them much more . . . efficient.

"Yes. Somewhere as far as possible from this hellhole."

"Dangerous words to say to me, gumdrop. I can Port very far away, indeed."

Vera turned her eyes away from the boy to study him. "How far *do* you go, Merihem?"

He grinned as she used his full name. Ah, how he enjoyed the feisty ones. "Oh, you know, other worlds." He swooped his hands up to encompass the wide open sky, now shaded orange and pink in the setting sun. "There are so many worlds out there, Adavera. Places where there is no air to breathe, not a single drop of water, where I have been the very first to walk."

"You're full of shit. I mean, they teach us about other planets at school, but there is no way I'm buying that you can Port that far. I mean, I know you're old, but—"

Moe laughed, interrupting her. "'I know you're old, but' is such a delightful phrase. It always ends with the person saying it proving without the shadow of a doubt that they are too young to understand. I rather like you, so don't ruin it. I'm into many things, but pedophilia is not one of them. Don't remind me that you're hardly older than that child of yours, in comparison to me."

Vera nudged her chin towards Lizzie. "That why you and Lizzie aren't, ya know, fuckbuddies? Ever gonna clue us in on why Lizzie looks twelve even though you keep telling us she's closer to your age?"

Moe shrugged. "Nope. And it's not even because I like being a sadistic bastard. I just genuinely don't remember. All I know is all my earliest journals—the ones I started keeping when I realized I was forgetting things, start in all caps with: DON'T FUCK LIZZY. If I can't trust myself, who *can* I trust?"

"Does she know?"

Moe grinned and ground his teeth at the same time. "Oh yes. She knows. But she knows I would grow bored with her if she didn't hold on to a couple fun little secrets, so she isn't talking. And trust me, I *have* tried to crack her. Nothing about her makes any sense, and I sometimes think that the mystery is what keeps me young. I mean, think about it: all of us are limited to one or two powers, right? She's not. She isn't Marked, nor does she have any other magically recognizable signature, but she's capable, at will, of developing a magical power. I've seen her become invisible one day, and create lightning the next. It's taken me lifetimes to just make a list of all the different things she can do, and I haven't even touched *how* she does it."

She studied him some more, "So how old *are* you? Recorded history goes back around fifteen hundred years and Lizzie says you can only remember back around half-that."

Moe waggled his hand. "Kinda. I can remember about seven centuries with some amount of clarity, as long as I have pictures, diaries, etc. I can *vaguely* recall about twice that."

Vera's brow furrowed, and he could almost see her doing the math. "That's almost longer than our history. When were you born?"

"Those are two separate answers, my dear. Let me see if I can explain."

Moe rolled on to his belly and pulled the blanket down, exposing a patch of lightly dampened sand. In it, he drew a straight horizontal line.

Vera joined him, head propped on one hand. "I'm listening."

"Good. See this line? Think of it as linear time on Fortune. The Gods of Fortune created humanity fifteen hundred years or so ago, right? Well, I was born here. On day one." Moe pressed his thumb on one end of that line.

"That explains why you have such a puffed up ego. You were literally created by a God." Someone else, like Kuma, would have peppered Moe with questions. Vera was taking him at face value, and it fucking delighted him.

"I am, naturally, perfection. Now, if we trace that line, we get all the way to today," he said, pressing a finger at the opposite end of the line. "Fifteen centuries. One after the other in a linear fashion. Easy enough to comprehend, right?"

"That is how time works, yes."

"Not exactly. See, I'm a Porter. Around here," Moe indicated a point roughly a third from the beginning of the timeline, "is where I started journaling, and also where I think I met Lizzie. Before then, I was just a normal, if extraordinary, Dual-Marked person. I helped found the Corporation, messed with the Gods, had fun, killed people—You know, the normal human things."

"Sure, because we all mess with some Gods. Totally normal."

"Why, yes. It is. Stop interrupting."

Vera held up her hands, a small smile turning the corners of her lips. Moe reached out to pinch her cheek, then continued.

"Call it year five hundred. I'm sitting around with about twice as many Mark Trials as your dear Lani, and I have an epiphany. I don't remember the epiphany, but it must have been good because it led me to Lizzie. Those days, Blood Bonding was still a new process, so all the Marks were extra unstable. A friend and I had worked out the basics, but it was still very new. The moment I Bonded Lizzie, my Marks went all haywire and suddenly I couldn't just Port around Fortune and through the galaxy the long way, but far, far beyond. To do it I enter this . . . middle-space I've been calling the Plane, then pop out on the other end in place across the universe. Honestly, I don't even know *if* they're in this universe."

This was where most people assumed he was messing with them. Not Vera. Her eyebrows had scrunched up, and she was giving Moe her full attention.

Her value rose by an order of magnitude in his eyes.

Carefully, Moe trailed a finger up from the straight line, almost perpendicularly. "On other worlds, time doesn't act the same way. For some, one day there are ten here. Others, a thousand of their years can pass and on Fortune only an hour has gone by. Most are uninhabitable, but some—the ones I keep being drawn to—have people just like us on them, all of them with legends of being created by Gods that seem to have very . . . familiar objectives. They even speak our language, though often with a bit of drift."

"Could they have been created by our same Gods? They are *Gods* after all."

Moe waggled his hands. "Debatable. But I digress. You asked me how old I am. Well . . ." He started to draw again, this time in an aggressively squiggly line that crisscrossed the first one, until almost none of it remained visible.

Then he waited to see if Vera would get it.

"So," Vera said slowly, her own finger tracing the line he had drawn from where it intersected the straight one at the end—this very moment—until the start. "While we took the direct course, you took the long way. You leave this world and for you a thousand years could have gone by, but for us it might just be minutes. You're . . . older than our species."

"Got it in one. Cheers all around!" Moe pantomimed clapping. Vera threw a stick at him. He grinned. "It's how I get around my Marks, you see. I have a very hard time Porting anywhere precisely without

Lizzie to help me focus. My power is far too big to be wieldy. But if I go the long way—as you called it—I can Port to a whole different world, then from afar be able to aim onto a square the size of a brick. Same with the Precog powers. I can flare my Mark to focus in close, but it's like squinting to read the smallest of writing. It's much easier to hop onto another world, look into my immediate future here on Fortune at my leisure, then wait the correct amount of time. I pop in only seconds after I disappeared, but with twenty years to perfect what I'm going to do once I get here."

Vera once again studied him, the sun sinking lower and painting the waves in crimson glory as she did. "How long ago, for you, did we arrive at your lair? How many times have you popped off for a stray century or so?"

Moe smiled. "Give or take?"

"Yeah, rough estimate."

He reached forward, took her hand, and brought her knuckles to his lips. "Centuries."

CODEX: Ok, I feel like it could take me years to truly understand Moe. For now, though, I'm done. We're running out of time, and I need to be ready to move. So, SALT, please package up everything I've found and get ready to send a backup to Kekai Parata. They might come to try to erase me from the University Servers once they realize I'm here, so I want my uncle to have all this in case I can't fight them off.

SALT: Added to the to-do list.

CODEX: Thank you, SALT. Well, I think it's time to do some cleanup. Let's copy over, then prepare to delete every scrap of information the University has on Rogue Marks and Salt Pirates. I'm sure they have backups, printouts, and the like, but let's make them really work for it. While you're compiling that, out of curiosity, what *do* they have on Uncle Kekai? *Query: Who is Kekai Parata?* Filter: University Servers.

FROM THE WRITINGS OF GALENA CRYSTAL

I have received news that Ex-Corp Rogue Phaser Sahima of Ardor has married notable salt pirate Kahil Parata and birthed Matchmaker Marked twins. My source died shortly after bringing me this information, so I know little but their names and Marks. Kekai and Sina Parata. I have reviewed Sahima's file and found an interesting quirk we overlooked as trivial: she tends to befuddle Precog abilities. They originally gave her a 98% chance of remaining with the Corporation for life, yet she went Rogue. Looking back further, this trend continues. Sahima kept defying the odds, but while she was with us it always ended up in the Company's best interest, so it was never flagged as an issue. This may be due to simple last-minute course corrections, or perhaps a strong ability to analyze new information, but now that she is rogue, this is a particular danger. I am assigning her a Threat Level of 4, and preemptively setting her children at Threat Level 2. I will be sending in a team to try to retrieve them, but do not hold out high hopes. Whether due to nature or character, I doubt Sahima's children will be any easier to catch than the Phaser herself.

CODEX: Rock on, Gran. I never realized you started Corporate. Wow. I wonder if we inherited that ability too? Guess I'm about to find out. Let's see who wins, Moe: the Precog, or the Paratas.

The Pirate Kiing
Salome - Day 73

56

Her uncle's ship was, as always, imposing. Towering meters over the *Legacy* and almost the size of a Corporate galleon, the *Salt Reaper* bristled with canons and dwarfed most of the gathered pirate fleet. Even though the giant vessel intimidated her, ever since she'd become Captain of the *Legacy*, Salome had always made sure to not show a hint of her awe. Kekai Parata was a good man. He was her uncle, a Matchmaker, and . . . well, the Pirate King, who would have zero problems demanding she step down if Salome didn't seem up to the task.

The best way to ensure she didn't have to worry about losing the *Legacy* was to make sure she never lost her attitude. That wasn't so hard. She was a Parata, damn it. Her uncle could take her ship away only over her damned dead body. Which, Sal supposed, she might have to warn him about. There was a very real possibility of that at the moment.

Her uncle would be waiting in the Captain's cabin, as he always did. He was probably looking over files and determining what the best route forward was. It was his Mark, and his curse. Indeed, Kekai Parata was standing at the large table with his sleeves rolled up and his hair braided back from his face. The scar above his right eyebrow twitched as he glanced at her.

"You've got trouble written all over your face, Niece."

"We're pirates. That's the job."

"Not the sort of trouble I approve of, I daresay, considering you've literally been off the map for months and left me to fill your usual routes."

"Gotta keep you on your toes, old man." Sal grinned, shrugging a bit before stepping forward. "My crew is going to make a run at the Spire."

The silence in the air was enough to make sweat drip down her spine. Kekai wouldn't supply reinforcements if she didn't do this right. He'd be able to just . . . ruin their chances at getting out of this if Salome couldn't sell it.

"That's a suicide run."

"Normally."

"But you're going to do it?"

"Yes."

"And how are you going to get your ship out of the Seawall?"

"The ship will stay outside the wall. I've got a Porter who can get our supplies to us. Kuma has equipment to get us across the water from the Seawall to the Spire," Salome explained, coming over to stand right in front of the desk.

Kekai crossed his arms. "That is a long stretch."

"They won't expect it."

"And the goal?"

"To blow it."

That silence was back, her Uncle staring at her as if she'd just developed a third head. "Not worth it."

"I'm going to get Gran out."

More silence. Everyone had been running on the assumption that Sahima was dead. It was better than the alternative—that they could not go in and rescue her. Sahima would be pissed at the attempt, even if they tried, because it would cost too many lives. Everyone knew that. Didn't mean they wouldn't do it if they thought they had a chance in hell of pulling it off, though.

". . . you don't know that she's . . ."

"I've got the escaped salt slave, Adavera of Keala, on the *Legacy*. She knows the Spire inside and out. Spent six years there."

"*No one* gets out, Sal."

"She did. I know you intercepted the Company's warnings."

Slowly, her uncle nodded. "May have."

"Remember how she had an Emotive with her?"

"How's an Emotive going to help you make a run for the Spire? They go wrong in there the same as all other Marks."

"She's not just an Emotive. She's Vera's Bonded, and she's a Fertility Mark."

Her uncle paused, blinking. "Tell me you didn't bring a Fertility Mark to our gathering, Niece, with a Storm on the way. Look me in the eyes and tell me that."

"Course I did. Don't plan to be here when the Storm hits. We're going to be testing Kuma's batteries out on a nearby uninhabited island."

"Salome, I will break your neck with my own two hands if this isn't some kind of twisted joke."

"Nah, you love me too much," Sal said with a wink. "Besides, you know as well as I do that Kuma wouldn't be testing the equipment if he wasn't damned sure he and Vera can make sure Lani doesn't mulch us."

Kekai reached up to pinch the bridge of his nose. "Start from the beginning, Salome. You aren't making a lick of sense and it worries me. When did you start talking as fast as Kumanu explaining a new idea? Sit, and talk me through this plan of yours. You're starting to sound like that madman who pops up from time to time. Moe, was it?"

"Oh yeah, he's with us too."

"Of course he is," Kekai said, sounding exhausted. "From. The. Beginning."

"You asked for it. Ok." Sal grinned and took a deep breath. "Sooo . . ." And then she started talking. And kept talking. And *kept talking*. She went back to the beginning, as it were, when she had been born and Kekai had been taking command of the ship while her mother proceeded to have a child at the worst possible time. "By the way, Uncle, if you ever speak to me like you did her, I will gouge out an eye. I know she was your twin and all, but you bitched her out a *lot* for having me." And then she kept going. Just to drive the point home that she had more tucked away in her little pinkie than Kekai could hope to learn in a lifetime. The shocked expression was nice. Sal wasn't sure she would ever get over that look.

Then she went into Moe's plan. Into Lani and Vera, and their fucked up Bond. Into Kuma and Lani, and how that one at least was planned. Then into Torin—ok, she skipped the part about her continuing to sleep with the man—and scooted neatly into Moe and Lizzie helping her get a great memory. She didn't dive too deep into that. Her Uncle didn't trust Moe either. No reason to make it worse.

"We finally have a real shot at the place, Uncle; at breaking the Corporation's stranglehold . . . We can get people to start moving and demanding justice! We *have* to take this shot. I know it's risky, but it has to be done, and I plan to do it with or without your blessing. It would be a lot easier if I knew the fleet was behind me, ready to punch the Corporation while they're down," she finished, a good hour later.

"Sal . . . this might very well be the last thing you do. That any of you do."

"We know that. That's why I'm here." She took a breath, reaching into her bag. She pulled out a small thumb drive. "I need you to run this program Kuma and I have been working on . Honestly, it's pretty much *all* we've been working on for days, since Kuma is done with most of his prep work. It will take time for it to compile once you install it in the Pirate Network, and I don't know for sure that it will work, but . . . it should be able to link you silently to the University server system eventually. Untraceably."

"What?" Kekai asked, looking down at the drive with a mix of perplexed curiosity and suspicion.

"Yeah. Don't ask. I don't have the time to go into all of that. But even if the Spire job fails, you'll have a back door. You can get access to everything the University has . . . But Uncle . . . don't log into it until after the Spire job, ok? We're still doing updates and I'm sure it will be a bit buggy until we get it all cleaned up. It will appear on your computer under the name SALT. The password is: CODEX. Only *after* the Spire. I need you to promise me."

For a long moment Kekai was silent. Then he nodded at the drive. "This is yours and Kuma's black box, so to speak, isn't it? You know you're not getting out alive, but trying to get me to agree by putting on a brave and overconfident face. It won't work on me. This plan of yours is too risky. Setting aside that it will get you killed and I'll lose one of my best crews, this will disrupt the salt trade. As bad as the Corporation is, we have learned to work around them. A disruption on this scale would be catastrophic. You will not do it."

Salome hadn't really expected him to be enthusiastic about the idea, but her heart still sank. In a quiet voice she answered, "I wasn't asking. The crew is behind the decision. Kuma and I are going. *You* are not. But on the off chance we get out of this, here are the coordinates to a rendezvous point. We're going to be wounded, at the least, and we'll probably need some armed backup. I doubt the Corpses will take it lying down."

Kekai's arms were still crossed, his whole posture tense. "You are too much like your grandmother for your own good. We have grown and continued existing because we have been careful, Niece. I thought I had taught you the value of caution."

Salome clenched her teeth. "It's time this low-grade rebellion turned into a revolution, Uncle. I'm just lighting the match."

He still looked unconvinced. "Salome, fires are dangerous; they burn your friends just as easily as your foes. That's how your mother died. You're playing too big of a game."

He sounded like *Torin*. That was never a good sign. Clenching her fist, Salome fought not to reply with passion, but rather with reason. That was the language Kekai spoke, after all. It was why she respected him, even if in times like this, he frustrated her to no end.

"We're doing this. It's my ship. My crew. My choice. I will live and die by my principles, Uncle. That is what Gran taught me, and I know she taught it to you as well. As I said before, I'm not here for your permission. Even if you grounded me today, Moe would get us back on the ocean. Unless you're willing to kill me and Kuma both, we are making a run on the Spire. The reason I'm here is because I want you to be ready. I think we're going to succeed, and I want to make sure that the people counting on us for their survival know what's coming their way."

Kekai sighed, and picked up the small drive Salome had given him. "So what is this?"

"Insurance. By the way, I need you to get as many ships online as possible. I've sent you Kuma's cloaking VPN. It should cloak the fleet but make communication easier."

Kekai shook his head in exasperation. "You are Sahima's legacy indeed. Alright. I see there will be no dissuading you, but Sal?"

"Yeah?"

"If you die and Kuma doesn't, he is never going to forgive himself."

"You underestimate Kuma. He'll find a way. He always does. Besides ... He's got Lani now. By the way, congratulations, you basically have a Fertilizer in the family. I'm pretty sure they're going to get married sooner or later, if they survive."

"Do you mean to tell me that your brother is bedding this Fertilizer without my permission, not just Bonded to her?"

"Only way to be a Parata, Uncle. Only way to be a Parata."

Kekai shook his head and pushed off the desk. "Alright then, let us go meet this girl that your brother has bound himself to, and see if they are as good a match as you seem to believe, and if she has it in her to carry out this mad plan of yours."

Kuma and Lani weren't exactly waiting outside the doors. Not that Salome blamed them. One of the few places where Kuma could get out and stretch for more than five minutes was on an island like this, surrounded by pirates. Of course he'd take Lani to the beach, where they could splash and be children. Big, overgrown children.

Kekai and Sal leaned against a tree, almost perfectly mirrored if not for the obvious difference in gender and age. Both of them wore the same exasperated face, but neither moved to interrupt the scene. For all of her uncle's glowering, she knew he got it too.

Kuma needed to let off steam.

After a few minutes of watching the sickeningly sweet display of Kuma and Lani swimming together through the crystalline water as the sun grazed the horizon behind them—and realizing it was about to get fairly adult-rated quickly if someone didn't intervene—Sal let out a sharp whistle. Kuma jumped, pushing away from Lani as if burnt, and turned to look in Salome's direction with a bashful smile.

"Kuma, Lani," Sal called, gesturing them over.

"Aye, Cap't!" Kuma tugged on Lani's wrist, and laughed. Sal figured he was probably chuckling at how red Lani was turning as she tried to tug her bathing suit back into place under the long-sleeve shirt she wore.

Sal waited until they got close, then tilted her head towards Kekai. "Lani. This is our uncle, Kekai Parata, Captain of the *Salt Reaper*." She could have piled on the accolades and titles that many pirates had given him until she was blue in the face, but . . . she didn't want to give Lani a heart attack. The girl was already looking a little green at just hearing the word 'uncle'.

If Lani found out exactly how famous and feared Kekai was, she'd probably faint.

Very hesitantly, the girl stepped forward and offered her hand to Kekai. "Ah, hi. I'm . . . ah . . . Iolani Saba. Nice to meet you." The words came out in a jumble of awkward pauses and too-fast smashed-together syllables.

Sal grinned. "Lani. Our uncle ran the ship that Kuma raised me on. He also made sure we got Gran's ship back when we were ready."

Kekai was being too quiet. Sal hated it when he did that. Kuma, fortunately, came to the rescue. "Yup. Uncle here runs one of the tightest ships on the sea, isn't that right, Sal?"

"Well . . . I mean . . ."

"Not that ours isn't great, but.. Ah . . . heh . . . So, Uncle, how's the catch been of late?"

And *still* the man was quiet, staring at Lani with that 'I'm looking into your soul' gaze he used when flaring his Matchmaker Mark. Sal detested that stare. He'd turned it on her multiple times over the years. She'd seen him use it on others, and usually they ended up Bonded to somebody within weeks. Yet never Salome.

"Show me your Marks, girl," Kekai said, suddenly.

Lani took a fast step back, a look of pure terror in her eyes. Sal didn't blame her one bit.

"Marks," Kekai repeated.

"You're ok, Lani. He won't hurt you. He's family," Kuma reassured, one of his hands on his Bonded's lower back. Hesitantly, Lani gestured down at her leg where her Emotive Mark was gently glowing.

Sal immediately looked inward, trying to find the Emotive's hands on her feelings. As soon as she did, Lani's deft touch receded, and the worry she hadn't realized was being pushed down returned.

"Sorry," Lani muttered. "Force of habit."

"How many Trials?" Kekai asked, kneeling to look at her Emotive Mark where it swirled in crashing waves around her knee and up her thigh. Lani seemed too freaked out to answer, so Kuma jumped in, answering a whole series of questions for their uncle.

When he seemed satisfied, Kekai stood. "Now the other one."

"He already knows, Lani. You're safe," Salome said.

With shaking fingers, Lani pulled her sodden shirt off, leaving herself in a swimsuit. The Fertility Mark stretched across her chest and down both her arms.

"You must be old for a Mark this developed. Two or three centuries, yes?" Kekai asked.

"Yes, sir."

"Do you have any training?"

"Ah . . . not until recently."

He nodded. "Death toll?"

Lani blanched. "I don't know. A lot. I never mean to, but . . . it happens."

Kekai straightened and turned to Salome. "Take her to the closest Hazed-out family. Show her how we do things. Kuma will join you once we have a chat. It's time we talk, Nephew."

CODEX: I wonder if befuddling Precogs is how Uncle keeps the Corp from finding him. He's the only person I know who can gather dozens of pirate ships in one place and not have the Corporation swarming all over him. I know I have access to the Parata Network, but SALT, do I have access to Kekai Parata's personal files?

SALT: Affirmative, however, they are password protected.

CODEX: No surprise there. Uncle loves keeping his methods a secret. But I wonder . . . try password: Sina0210 and 0210Sina.

SALT: Access granted.

CODEX: Really? Wow. That . . . is depressing but not unexpected. I just figured he might make it a bit harder. Then again, who was going to try to hack Kekai Parata? Other than me, I guess. I'm not going to go poking, though. Not after everything he did for us. However . . . *Query: is Sahima Parata alive?*

Date: Day 21
To: Security
From: Galena Crystal

Security—

Escapee Adavera of Keala is presumed to be in the hands of salt pirate Salome Parata, the granddaughter of Spire Inmate 27801. My Precogs are having a hard time finding them. Interrogate her. I need any information possible on Salome Parata.

—Galena

Date: Day 28

To: Galena Crystal
From: Security

Administrator G. Crystal—
Interrogation of prisoner 27801 has yielded few results. She has refused to speak a single word, even under extreme duress. How would you like me to proceed?
—Security

Date: Day 29
To: Security
From: Galena Crystal

Security—
I expected as much. Continue to work on her. She will crack eventually.
—Galena

CODEX: Oh no you don't, you sadistic bitch. I'm coming for you all. You don't hurt my grandmother and get away with it.

Matchmaker
Kuma - Day 73

Kekai was doing the creepy stare thing again. Kuma *hated* that. He always felt guilty. Not that there wasn't plenty to be guilty over. After all, he'd killed Kekai's little sister. Kuma still wasn't sure how his uncle had ever forgiven him for it. If anyone ever killed Sal... Well, Kuma wasn't sure he had it in him to be that forgiving.

"So... what are we going to be talking about, Uncle Kekai?"

"You Bonded without my consent, boy."

A wince crossed Kumanu's face. Yeah. He had done that. "Extenuating circumstances. But how's it looking?"

"You Bonded a *Fertility Mark* without asking for my opinion."

Kuma lifted his chin, eyes narrowing. Probably not wise. Kekai had been the harshest of task masters after Kuma's mother had died... for good reason. The man also had a wicked mean right hook. Kumanu wasn't looking forward to getting his teeth punched in, but— and this was most important—he wasn't willing to put up with his own uncle shit-talking Lani, even if Kekai was a Matchmaker as good as any the University had. His ability wasn't as flashy as some, but it was no less powerful. He could see the bonds—natural and manmade— that linked people together. It was Kekai who filled every pirate ship's roster. He was the reason traitors weren't really a thing amongst the pirates. He looked into each soul and found the places they belonged, and the people they belonged with.

As much as Kuma didn't like to admit it, he was *terrified* that his uncle might deem Lani unworthy. It was a large part of the reason why he hadn't suggested meeting up with Kekai until *after* they were Bonded.

"Well, boy?"

Kuma shifted uncomfortably. "Yes. I did Bond her without your permission. Lani has done the best she could with the very shitty hand she was dealt. I knew I could stabilize her, and one Bond alone wasn't going to do it. We connected, and a Bond is what we *chose*, Uncle. You can't control everything."

"Incorrect. We have rules for a reason, Kumanu. Those rules have kept you and people like you safe for centuries."

"And stabilizing Lani also keeps people safe. We rescued her, plucked her out of Corporate hands, and weren't sure how long we would have to keep running. There wasn't time to go tug on my Uncle's shirt and ask permission."

His uncle crossed his arms, staring down at Kuma, making him feel like a little boy again. "Are you planning on going along on this fool's errand? An Infuser has no place on an away-team, but you've bound yourself to the crux of this endeavor; what is your plan for when you lose your new Bonded? What are your intentions if you lose Salome? If you kids pull this off, I will be too busy to come drag you out of another guilt-filled spiral of self-destruction, Kuma."

Fuck. Kekai wasn't saying anything about Lani. Was he doing that on purpose? Winding Kuma up like he used to, so that he could slap him down if necessary? "If Lani dies, I will be heartbroken, but I will survive as long as the Bond snapping doesn't kill me. I will keep going. If Sal dies . . ." He swallowed, turning his head away. "I will wreak vengeance on those who are responsible for her death."

"And if you die, leaving your sister with an unstable Fertilizer who just lost a Bonded?" Kekai asked, voicing Kuma's worst fear. Because there was a solid chance that Vera wouldn't make it out, considering who and what she was. If Kuma died too, it would be a bad day for Lani.

"Lani and Salome are the strongest women I know, each in their own way, and Lani's pretty great at keeping emotions steady. They would grieve, Sal would rename the ship *Kumanu's Vengeance* or something, and they'd sail off to give the Corporation hell." He took a breath, and then took a step forward. "What did you see, Uncle?" It was killing him, waiting for that hammer blow. He just wanted to get it over with.

Kekai shrugged. "Bond's fine. Her Marks are stable. She's a good match for you."

"Why couldn't you just *say* that?"

His uncle's eyes fixed on him. "Because you deserve to sweat. You and your sister have unilaterally decided that the salt pirates are going to war. It won't matter if I agree or not, because once you gun for the Spire, the Corporation will assume we are behind you. The holes in their security we live by will close. The officers who routinely turn a blind eye will not. We will have no choice other than going in guns blazing. Since you clearly came here today to ask for forgiveness, not permission, it is my job to make it clear what the consequences of your choices will be.

Already, the Company has been wreaking havoc on us and the islands because of you. They aren't selling *any* salt, and are buzzing like a nest of poked fire ants. This plan will end in deaths far beyond the Spire."

"Those risks exist even if we don't gun for the Spire. Whenever we get in a tussle with Corporate ships, we run the risk of pissing them off enough that they decide to wipe us out for good. That it hasn't happened lately is a fucking miracle, and you know it." Kuma frowned, and then shrugged. "But yeah, I get that point. The thing is, Uncle . . . I've seen what the inside of that Spire is like, thanks to Vera. Only a few glimpses through Lani, to be fair, but I can't unsee it. I wish to the Gods I could. That thing . . . has to be destroyed."

His uncle looked down at his large hand, then looked back up at Kuma. "The cost will be higher than you know. There have been a lot of arrests over the last two months. Hundreds of new slaves are being sent to the Spire weekly, many of whom are people I have known and cared about for a long, long time. If you bring it down, they will die."

The wind vanished from Kuma's sails, his shoulders drooping. "I'm sorry to hear that. Anyone I know?"

"Many"

Shit. Kuma reached out, running his fingers through his damp hair. Did this new piece of information change things? He looked up at Kekai, who towered over even Kuma. "Death might be better than life in the Mines, Uncle. But . . . I promise that if we can, we'll get some of them out. I know Sal already planned on trying, and this is just that much more of a reason to make it part of our plan. If we can save even a single person from that place, it will have been worth it."

Kekai sighed. "You sound just like your mother. The both of you." He reached out, and Kuma tensed, but far from slapping him upside the head, the large pirate pulled Kuma into a tight hug.

The tension Kuma had been carrying in his shoulders all day left him in a loud sigh. He wrapped his arms around his uncle in return and squeezed as tight as he could.

The hug lasted a long minute. Kekai always knew when Kuma needed one, and it seemed as though that hadn't changed. When he pulled back, Kekai slapped Kuma's back. "Ok, Nephew. I give up. Clearly you aren't going to be talked out of this. Before you run off to get yourself dead, go show your new Bonded how we help the Hazed. Then get her to that little islet to test out your stability *before* the Storms show up, got it?"

"Yes sir."

"Shoo."

Kuma would never admit it . . . but he was pretty sure he almost skipped away as he chased after Lani and Sal.

CODEX: I am so fucking furious. The Corporation isn't going to get away with this. Even dead, I'm going to make them pay for it. SALT, do I have access to Sahima's old speech recordings? I think it's time to add another element to my Macro.

SALT: Affirmative. They are backed up in the files of Kekai Parata.

CODEX: Ok. I know she spoke on the radio a lot. *Query: what has Sahima Parata said about taking down the Crystal Corporation?*

FROM THE COLLECTED SPEECHES OF SAHIMA PARATA

We all know, in our deepest, darkest hearts, that our society is broken. We see the suffering, the injustice, the division. Maybe we speak up about it for awhile, cry for justice and equality, but eventually we grow weary of shouting into the darkness alone. So we find ways of coping. At first it is little acts of compliance. We stop reading the news. We say, "well sure, that is wrong, but I don't have the power to change it." We build houses, have children, and surround ourselves with whatever scraps of security we can conjure up. The problem is that even when we've convinced ourselves that we are safe, and that the problems we see are someone else's to solve, deep down we know the truth: one storm could tear down our walls, one mistake can kill our children, and our illusions of security can be ripped away without any warning.

You may not think it will happen to you, but I promise, it will. There will come a day when you will reach your lowest point. You will feel helpless. You will feel afraid and alone. Do you want to know why? Because even when you were trying not to, you paid attention. You've seen those who have fallen before you, and you've seen how few of them climbed back up. You're scared, because you know the problems are bigger than you. Because when others were crying out for help, you turned away and chose comfort instead.

I'm going to tell you something that you might not know. Something radical and secret that those in power don't want spread around. Here it is: *you are not alone*. When life strikes you down, look to the side. There are other people all around you, fighting the same battle. The Corporation would make you believe that they are your enemy. That they want what you need to survive: your salt, your land, your life. That could not be further from the truth.

It is those at the top who keep it from you. They sit on mountains of salt and let you fight for the scraps, because if you exhaust yourselves on survival, you won't have the energy to look up and realize who the real enemy is. They teach us to turn against our neighbours, to give up our Marked children, to accept their control as mercy.

I am here to tell you that there is another way. It doesn't have to be like this. Their power relies on your fear, your compliance, your indifference. It relies on you, which means you have the power to shatter it. You may feel weak and beaten down, overwhelmed by the strength of those holding you down, but I promise this: together, we are stronger than you—or they—could possibly imagine.

Hazelings from time to time—but what if she messed up in front of Torin? What if this gave him one more reason to hate her?

Toughen up, buttercup, Vera said unexpectedly through their Bond. Lani worked hard to keep that connection open at all times, but she hadn't realized she had been fretting loudly enough for her Bonded to hear.

Sorry,

You have the ability to help these people, Weirdling. Why are you so hung up about whether one person approves?

Lani didn't answer, at least not to Vee. She *did* look up at Salome, biting her lower lip. Would Salome's uncle approve of her and Kuma, or was he chewing Kuma out right now for all the same reasons Torin had opposed their Bond?

Salome put a hand on Lani's shoulder, startling her out of her thoughts. "Everything will be alright with Uncle. He's tough, but in the good way. If he had a problem with you, he would have told you to your face."

"You reading minds now, Sal?" Lani asked, teeth still worrying her bottom lip.

"No. You just have a very transparent face. Go on. You're part of the family now, Lani. Gotta learn how to be a pirate, and helping the Hazelings . . . that's the whole point."

Even if we're going to die in a matter of weeks?

One look up at Sal answered her unspoken question.

Yes.

Lani rolled her shoulders, then placed her hands on the chest of the woman Torin was working on.

"Mind you don't mulch her by accident," the Mender said.

Lani glowered at him. "It's not like I go around mulching people on purpose, you know. I'm not some out-of-control murderer."

"Aren't you?"

"Cut it out, Tor. You're being an ass again," Salome warned. "Why don't you go work on someone else if you've got nothing constructive to say?"

"I was here first, and I don't need some Fertilizer's help. Menders can help with the Haze too."

Salome reached out to lightly cuff his ear. "Yeah. That was the point of us coming over, idiot. You can help guide Lani because you have the best beat as to what the Haze does to the body. Besides, you have a serious attitude problem when it comes to her. Have you considered that working with her might, you know, boost your trust in her abilities?"

"I've seen her abilities up close and personal, thanks. Vera's leg still isn't what it used to be." Torin pushed himself to his feet and brushed sand off his knees. "I won't be a party to letting an untrained Fertilizer help living humans. If she wants my help to practice, it can be on cadavers."

"My power doesn't *work* on dead people, except to decompose them," Lani protested.

He didn't look back. As Torin found another patient to tend, Kuma entered the makeshift hospital. He was grinning from ear to ear, though some of his smile vanished when he looked around at the cots.

"These all from today?" he asked one of the attendants, who nodded.

"Porters just arrived back an hour ago. We have about six hours to get this group turned around until they come back with more. There have been a lot of embargos over the last two months. The Corporation is buzzing. They're looking for some low-level retired Mender."

Sal and Lani exchanged a worried look, then both glanced in Torin's direction.

Why would the Corporation be after *Torin?*

"Well, things might be changing soon," Kuma said to the medic, then strode over to Lani and Salome, weaving around cots. As soon as he reached them, he knelt on the other side of the patient Lani was supposed to be helping and reached to take one of her hands. "Uncle approves."

All the breath left Lani in a whoosh. Sal, still standing above her, cracked a smile. "He should learn to trust me more. Would I really let my big brother Bond someone who wouldn't be good for him?"

Warmth flooded Lani. Her eyes stung, but crying tears of relief and joy didn't seem very sensitive in a tent full of people dying from salt deficiencies.

Kuma, who must have sensed Lani's emotional state, squeezed the hand he was holding. "It's alright to feel happy. We wouldn't survive or hold on to hope if we let pain and death take that away. Compassion fatigue will kill you same as the Haze. Plus, you're an Emotive. Share it."

Huh? Share . . . this? This feeling of joy and acceptance? The warmth of Kuma's hand in hers? The pride of Salome standing up for her and believing Lani was capable of helping people, even when Torin did not?

Hesitantly, she channeled power through her Emotive Mark. First just a little, then as the woman on the cot sighed in pleasure, more. Her Mark shone brighter and brighter in the dimness of the tent, and as everyone around them relaxed and started smiling, Kuma gave her hand another squeeze and nodded at Lani's Fertility Mark.

"You got this, Sweets."

Her fingers pressed against the woman's arm and Lani closed her eyes. As soon as she flared her Fertility Mark, Lani felt all the salt around her for miles. The crates were burning beacons, and Kuma, Sal, and Torin gently glowing stars. The woman before her was a single match flame in a hurricane.

"Salt, please," Lani asked. Kuma handed her a cloth bag of it. Lani reached forward to pull her patient's shirt down, measuring a small handful by instinct, her Mark guiding her, whispering the exact proportions of salt this woman needed to be whole and healthy.

Careful not to spill a single grain, Lani spread the salt over the woman's skin, pressing both her hands atop it, the Mark across her chest glowing and pulsing in time with the one on her leg.

The salt began to melt. First it vibrated, then it glimmered, sinking into the Hazeling's skin. The woman groaned, arching into Lani's hands. A pulse of calming Emotive power eased her momentary discomfort.

"Shh, you'll feel better soon."

Three, maybe four heartbeats later, no salt remained. Lani was not done, though. It was not enough to get the sodium into the bloodstream. Like an ecosystem, the human body needed salt and other minerals in all sorts of places. Lani pulled them hither and thither, ignoring all barriers and anatomical impossibilities. Menders were the ones who got caught up on those details. Lani wasn't a Mender. She was an Emotive-Fertilizer.

In another's hands, it might have been agonizing to have one's body flooded with sodium. Lani did not let her patient feel pain.

It seemed as though the process took eons to Lani, but it only lasted three minutes. When she opened her eyes, Lani was staring into deep, confused black ones, that were awake and aware.

"W-where am I?"

"Safe," Lani answered. "How do you feel?"

". . . Good. Really good. What happened?"

Salome patted Lani on the shoulder. "I'll take it from here, kid. You and Kuma go help the next bed over. You did good."

Hours later, Lani found Torin on the beach, sitting on a smooth rock and staring out at the ships. He didn't acknowledge her when she sat down, but neither did he tell her to leave.

The sun was almost gone, the heat of the day sinking with it. The rock was still warm, though, seeping up through Lani's thighs to ease the ache from kneeling in the tent.

"I know you don't like me," she began, when Torin had not spoken after five minutes.

"I don't *trust* you. Liking has nothing to do with it. I don't know you enough to decide if I like you."

"Well, you don't exactly make getting to know you a top priority of mine, what with the insults at every turn," Lani pointed out.

Torin shrugged. "It's not personal, Lani. I know you and the others don't get that, but none of my problems are personal. I know you mean well, but good intentions don't equal good results."

Lani kept herself from rolling her eyes. "What about today? That whole tent was full of Hazelings. Now they're all walking around, ready to go home."

"Exactly. This morning they were dying. Now, they are cured. They will go home, go back to work so that they'll earn their salt packs, and someone at their job will notice their fast recovery. What then? What happens when the Corporation comes knocking, looking for you? Lying about a Rogue Fertilizer carries a life sentence at the Spire. The Spire we are blowing up in a few weeks. Makes me wonder how many of the people you saved today we're going to kill by year's end."

Lani paled. "Why didn't you say anything? I could have—"

"Left them half-way in the Haze? No, you couldn't have. You're a Fertilizer. You *fix* things, no matter the consequences. Even University trained Fertilizers can't do things by half-measures. It isn't how you work. It isn't even your fault. But if I had raised my hand to point that out, Salome and Kuma would have gotten up in arms about my prejudices against you. Then you would have become upset, and Vee would have been upset, and I would have eventually been outvoted. You've won, Lani. You never even fought, and you won."

He finally turned to look at her, and there was sadness, not hatred in Torin's eyes.

"I don't want to win. I just want my life to have some kind of meaning. Is that really so bad?"

"In your case? Yes. Because your desire to belong and for your

Marks to have a purpose are the strings Moe is using to tangle you in his plans. Those plans are going to get people killed. People I love, people you love, people we don't even know." Torin stood up. As he did, his body blocked the sun, casting a shadow over Lani.

She looked up at him. "If you hate this plan so much, why are you helping us? What are you sticking around for?" Why, for that matter, had Moe chosen him? He must be trustworthy, because Lani doubted the crazy Precog would risk his plan on people who wouldn't follow through, but out of all of them, Torin seemed the most out of place.

"Because if I do, there is a small, infinitesimal chance I might be the difference in getting Salome or Vera out of that Spire alive. If I leave today . . . I know you'll kill them both."

With nothing more to say and hands in his pockets, Torin walked away.

PART SIX
The Salt Spire
-Lani, Moe, Salome, Vera, Torin, Kuma-

SALT: 30 seconds remaining.

CODEX: Hell yes. Shall we review? We know that Moe is a piece of shit who wants to become a God. Galena, Aheo, and Security are also pieces of shit. Lizzie is not human, and can change superpowers at will—also likely as horrid as the rest of them. Zarine Crystal may be slightly less trash. The Gods are *super* trashy, but don't like Moe so may be allies. Pirates are awesome. Eat the rich. Death to the Corporation. Did I miss anything?

SALT: Do you wish to review your Macro?

CODEX: Sure. While I do that, would you count me down to zero, please? I am looking forward to making Moe have a very, very bad day. By the way, how long between my last backup and when I died, again? I wouldn't have woken up here until my heart stopped beating and flipped the switch. Query: How much time did I actually lose and what are my backup points?

11:23PM, Day 80 – Final Backup

12:47AM, Day 81 – Install on Kahana University Servers

3:01AM, Day 81 – Awakening of Proto1: Codex

3:13AM, Day 81 – Present

28 seconds remaining to full functionality. Patch includes: 2 hours, 14 minutes worth of pre-death memories.

Stay With Me
Torin – Day 80
59

Torin was watching Salome again when she woke up, his arms around her and hand playing with her long hair. They were heading to the University that night. A Prismatic Storm was due to pass over it around 1AM. Torin hadn't slept, but he was glad Salome had managed a few hours. Unlike the others, she was not Marked, and while her powers were impressive, they did not feed her any excess energy.

"Good morning," he murmured as her eyes fluttered open, leaning down to kiss her brow.

A sound somewhere between a grumble and a growl slid out between Sal's lips, and she turned to press her face against Torin's chest. Mornings were *not* her strong suit.

Torin didn't rush her. He held her gently, using his Mark to dull any aches and pains she might have acquired over the past few days and easing the strain on her arm, where it would rub against her prosthetic. The new one Kuma had given her was their best collaboration yet, but it didn't mean Salome wasn't sore after a day using it—the trade-off of fine motor control and extending certain nerves far beyond where they should be.

Almost a half-hour later, Salome stirred again. She rolled onto her back, then propped herself up on her elbow. "Heya."

"Hey."

"Did you sleep?"

"No, but it won't slow me down. I can modulate my own brain chemistry and adrenal system just fine. Vera isn't the only person who can run on fumes."

Salome stared at him, and not for the first time Torin cursed how Moe had changed her. He could see her too-fast, too-big brain warming up, churning out information and retrieving memories. To keep her from overanalyzing what he had said, Torin pressed a finger to the tip of her nose.

"Stay here with me, not down memory lane."

She scrunched her face up, but he thought she may have smiled, too.

"Fine."

"I mean it. Stay here. With me. Not just right now, but tonight. They're not forcing us to go, so stay."

Salome's expression turned confused, and after months of her *never* looking like that, the sight hit straight to his heart. He kissed her, and when he pulled back, elaborated. "This plan to go to the University is ludicrous. Lani doesn't need a trial run to kill herself, and what does taking down the University server farms do for *anyone?* They house all the Corporate files. That includes medical records, educational information, infrastructure schematics, banking. Everything. We're going to hurt real, normal people if we succeed, and more than likely we're going to fail. So let's not go."

"You'll never convince the others," Salome protested.

Torin shook his head. "I wasn't talking about the others. They've made their bed and intend to lie in it. I meant you and me. I don't want you to die, Salome, and I'm rather fond of living, myself. I don't disagree that the Corporation does a lot of bad, but this isn't the way to fix that. Let's do it the right way. It might take more time, but with your network of pirates and my ability to get back in through the front door if I wanted, we could *actually* make things better."

"You don't know that they won't throw you in the Spire, or worse. You don't know that they won't rewire your head and make you betray me, Torin. You don't know a lot. And honestly? What I know of the Corporation says nothing good would come of trying to play nice. They have no reason to change."

Torin waited for her to finish, and addressed her points one at a time, like he had learned in school so many years ago. He held up three fingers, then lowered one. "First, I know they won't throw me in the Spire because, unlike Vee and the others, all the news Kuma has been picking up is asking for me to be returned unharmed. Mencers are in short supply this generation. Not many make it through the University without burning out."

He lowered a second finger. "And you asked how I know they won't rewire my brain. Easy. Bond with me. For all their power the Corporation cannot measure or detect Bonds. You would have a direct line into my psyche and be able to tell if someone messed with it." Sure, Bonded people could tighten down the hatches, but if Torin did that, Salome would *know.* "Lastly," here, he bent to kiss her again, "the Corporation isn't some monolith, Sal. It's made up of individual people making individual decisions. Most of them don't know half the shit we do. Information is power. I saw the truth, didn't I? I was as Corporate as they get, but I'm here with you, acknowledging that they are fucked up and need to change. If I can see the truth, others can too."

Her eyes widened, and her lips pressed shut. Torin had to replay his words to figure out why she would look so surprised. It didn't take long to figure out that it was because he had told her to Bond to him.

"Why now, Torin? All these years later, and the fights, and . . . I mean, you'd have me nagging at you all the time. And I don't know that you wouldn't go nuts with how much stuff is constantly going on in my head now. I don't have a normal brain anymore."

"I don't care. Nowhere on my Bond chain is 'normal' anywhere to be seen. We would work it out." He cupped her cheek with one of his hands and looked deep into her eyes. "I love you. I want to fix this world with you, but I want to do it the right way. No Moe, no mad plans born out of frustration and vengeance. Let's be *smart* about it, just you and I. Let's keep this monstrosity from happening, then take a step back. Talk to your uncle, get Kuma working on undermining the Corporation instead of blowing the Spire. Hell, drag Vera and Lani along. They're a force of destruction, sure, but let's make it targeted destruction instead of full-blown chaos. Salome, you are smarter than all of us put together. *You* should be the one making plans, not being yanked along by a madman."

Salome pursed her lips, rolling onto her back and staring at the ceiling. He knew that look. It was the one that said she was weighing her options. Playing out scenarios in that giant brain of hers. Sal had been crazy smart before all of this. Now that she could remember everything, Torin had the nagging suspicion that keeping up with her was going to be impossible.

Her fingers touched his chin. "Torin . . . I want to agree with you. I do. I want to be optimistic and say that we can change the Corporation. Because you are right. They do a lot of good when they want to. But the mindset that let them think making a Breeding Program out of their prisoners was a good idea? Not just a good idea but one they implemented? The mindset that lets them think that keeping children in the Spire is acceptable? That isn't a mindset that can be reasoned with. And they have no reason to negotiate. No reason to change. Without a blatant show of force proving that they could *lose* . . . they aren't going to listen. They're going to lie, and cheat, and kill us all if we show up in good faith to try to bring change peacefully. And it will snuff out the resistance from less courageous people. I want to agree with you, I really do. I just . . . can't. Without all of this, why would they listen?"

The hope that had been building inside of Torin all through the long night popped like a child's balloon. His shoulders sagged, and he, too, rolled onto his back. The cabin's ceiling was carved in a beautiful relief map of the Reef and islands. He stared at it, at the confines of his world, and couldn't see anything but the suffering they were about to cause. "Maybe they won't listen. Maybe it was a dumb idea. If I can't even convince you, how could I help them?"

She nodded and pressed her forehead to his shoulder. Torin wrapped his arms around her, holding tight for what might well be the last time.

SALT: 14 seconds remaining.

CODEX: I'm kinda starting to get nervous, if I'm honest. How am I even nervous without an adrenal system? I should do something relaxing. Oh, I know. Hey SALT, I'mma kill you.

SALT: Bite me.

CODEX: Ha. Yes! Still love that bit of coding. Never change, SALT. Question, did I load up all the new crew's data to our network? Everything that Lani, and Vera, and Torin wanted to save, I mean?

SALT: Affirmative. Last backup 2 days ago.

CODEX: *Query: In the words of Lani, what are Storms like from the inside?* I gave my life to get her to the Spire; she owes me, and I kind of want to know what it feels like.

FROM THE JOURNAL OF IOLANI SABA, DAY -273.

Today was another Prismatic Storm, and a new Fertility Trial to fucking boot. The Storm raged for three days, as if hovering over this patch of sea just for me. It's strange to both loathe and love the Storms at the same time. When I see them on the horizon I'm filled with dread, but as I watch them go, I'm overcome by a strange sort of longing.

The creature I become in the Storm is not me. I am but a vessel for a power greater than my own. To this day, I do not know if that creature is my friend, or a vengeful beast. I mean, look at how I'm fucking writing this shit down.

I just . . . it really does feel as though I'm along for the ride, an instrument of the Storm itself, instead of me. Sometimes it lets me guide it a little, but for the most part the only goal is balancing the environment. When the Storm passes on, the land and sea are better. The balance of salt and other nutrients in the soil has improved, the plants are growing faster, the sea life is thriving. It's beautiful, at least when I'm out far enough and don't wake up surrounded by people I've murdered.

They make me feel like there is a purpose to my existence. A shitty, painful, depressing purpose, but a reason to keep going nonetheless.

I do not know if I would go so far as to say I love the Storms, because I don't. But sometimes as mist from their passing clears, I get the weird impression that they may love me.

CODEX: Oh Lani, Vera's right. You really are weird. Unlike Moe, though, it's the good kind. I really hope you take that Spire down tonight.

Trial Run
Lani - Day 81
60

Iolani stood on the rooftop of the University Library and watched the Storm come in. In all her years of solitude, she had endured the worst her Marks had to offer because she had never wanted to be *here*. Standing between Adavera and Kumanu on the steeple of the tallest building for miles, the only thing Lani could think was, *how the fuck did they talk me into this?*

The pack on her back was fucking *heavy*, although not as heavy as Kuma's first attempt months ago, which had nearly toppled her backward. It was also more comfortable, with the weight being supported by sturdy hip and chest straps. They had tried a smaller battery at first, but Kuma still had some shrapnel in his arm from that fiasco.

"This is a horrible idea," Torin muttered from the back of the group as he and Salome worked on setting a small explosive device onto the lock to the steeple's viewing platform door.

Liz, who was leaning against the banister, just shook her head. "Why? Don't you like being only feet away from an Emotive-Fertilizer minutes before a Storm, and with a long drop in every direction?"

No, he probably didn't, and Lani couldn't blame him. She wiped her sweaty palms on her pants and swallowed to try to clear the sticky, dry feeling in her mouth. It did no good because the Stormfront was getting closer and closer, a dark rainbow of colors swirling in the ominous clouds.

"Everyone brace," Adavera warned as the rain began to fall, and Lani squeezed her eyes shut. The Mark on her chest started to burn. That was the only warning she got before all that was Lani just . . . shifted to the side to make way for *it*.

All her worries, all her stresses fell away with the rain. Her face turned up towards the sky and a laugh fell from her lips with the first peal of thunder. The water; the sweet, perfect water. She could *feel* it cascading down the roofs and soaking into the ground. The ground, how it called to her, how it screamed to her to be filled, made rich and right and balanced. It needed no salt here. There was plenty with so many Marks always drawing power and leaving salt behind, but it needed other things. Nitrogen, fewer feet walking on the grass, room to grow and breathe. These buildings were the problem, buildings infested with people like scurrying, destructive ants. If she tore them down, it could all be right again. Ivy could pull apart brick and she could make it swallow these man-made abominations so easi—

The irritating thing on her back began to hum, and Lani blinked. Her eyes, which had been glowing as brightly as her Mark, flickered back to brown. It was all still there, the sweet song of rain and soil and living things, but awareness returned. With a curse, she scrambled back over the railing she had been trying to climb. Both Kuma and Vera were holding onto her, probably to keep Lani from falling.

"Sorry, I hadn't realized she didn't turn it on before we left!" Kuma was yelling over the rain.

"These kinds of mistakes are going to get us all killed," Torin shouted back.

"Door's open." Salome's statement interrupted the brewing shouting match. "Everyone inside and out of the rain before Lani mulches us all."

Normally, that would have made Lani scowl, but not then; she simply clasped Kuma's hand and together they bolted to the door. Inside the stairwell, it was easier to breathe. She could still feel her Mark pushing at the edges of her mind, but without contact with the elements, the screams weren't so deafening. Here, she could feel Kuma and Adavera like screens around her. They didn't keep the Storm out, but each took a little of the brunt of the onslaught, just enough to let Iolani stay herself and not be lost to it. The battery on her back helped too, drawing her power out of her body as fast as the Mark created it, and Infusing it for later use.

They jogged down the stairs until they came to an intersection, where all eyes turned to Vera.

"Where to, boss-lady?" Lizzie asked, pulling off her raincoat and chucking it unceremoniously in the corner.

Adavera took a moment to study the branching hallways, and Lani could feel the tension in her ratchet up a few more notches. What must it be like for Vera to be back here, after everything that had happened?

"This way. Be ready though, because if they figure out we're here it's going to get messy. Kuma, you got the nozzle ready on that battery?" "You know that could go bad, right?" Kuma asked.

"Yeah, but worst case scenario . . . we can make it downright nightmarish for the Company before we all die."

Oh that was just peachy. Sure, use Lani as a weapon of slaughter. Even if it made a morbid kind of sense, it made Lani's skin crawl. Trust Vera to want to take out the Corporation goons as messily as possible, if they got backed into a corner.

"Or, hear me out here," Torin began, "we could just . . . not. We don't have to kill anyone, alright? It's the middle of the night during a Storm, we can just get down to the archives, I can knock out any personnel on duty, and we go back to Moe's island and be done with this insanity."

"Yeah. That's an option," Vera said the words coolly, looking at Torin as if he'd said something ridiculous. Lani wasn't sure what to make of that look. Vera obviously gave a damn about Torin, Lani could feel that beneath all the rage and . . . murderous impulses. And yet the two still didn't seem able to bridge their issues.

"Option C," Lizzie said, drawing everyone's attention, "we don't stand around like idiots deciding. After you, ducklings." She gestured the way Vera had pointed with a flourish, and Lani decided that it was time to listen to Crazy instead of Angry and Grumpy. She grabbed Kuma by the arm and marched them off in that direction. If Vera and Torin wanted to argue, they could just stay behind. For a brief time, she thought they might, but then Vera caught up and placed a hand on Lani's arm.

"You ok, Vee?"

"Peachy." Vera's eyes were narrowed. It was the look that Lani had come to associate with 'don't fuck with me right now'. "Left at the junction. Then there will be what looks like a dead end. It isn't."

They reached it within a minute and stopped while Vera motioned Kumanu towards a painting on the wall. When pulled back, it revealed a number pad. The Infuser cracked his knuckles and got to work. While he fiddled with the electronics, Lani's gaze kept darting to Torin. She didn't like the way the hand clutching his gun tensed each time Lani so much as moved, as though itching for an excuse to put a bullet in her brain and end the threat Lani posed to the world.

Her Mark *really fucking hated* that hand. It would do so much more good pulverized in soil that needed more iron. It wouldn't even have to be his whole body, just the hand . . . hell, just the trigger finger. No one would mind if—

"Adavera, the freak's eyes are glowing again. Get her leashed."

"Torin, shut the hell up with your insults." Vera's voice was cold, but at least the feeling of her hand on Lani's made it easier to focus. Blinking away the haze of murder felt so damned strange. Normally, Lani had no idea what was going on until everything had been said and done. But now, with two Bonded to hold her back, it was like she was along for the ride, and just had to learn how to apply the brakes. Would that make the inevitable slaughter better or worse?
"Breathe, Lani. Torin's an asshole, yeah . . . but the world's full of them. Me included. In for four . . . out. It's just us, and you don't need to lose it yet."

Lani nodded and breathed, and while her Mark analyzed the air and found it not clean enough, she didn't bring the infrastructure of this place down on their heads yet. She just *breathed*.

"Done," Kuma exclaimed as a panel on the wall slid to the side, allowing passage into the Archives. Lani squeezed Vera's hand, a sudden rush of fear making her legs feel numb. In there she would be trapped. There would be no windows, no elements. It was an artificial cage and it would be torture to a Fertilizer, yet that was where they were going.

"Lani, Sweets. Your other Mark," Kuma reminded her. Oh right!

With a sigh of relief, Lani diverted some of the excess power running rampant through her body into the Emotive Mark on her calf and was rewarded by an instant sense of calm. Without much consideration, she extended that aura to the rest of the group, adding in a touch of ambition and a sprinkling of confidence. They could do this. They had practiced for months and this was just their trial run; everyone would be going home and they were going to crash the University Servers. Plus steal some of their data, if they got the opportunity. That had been Salome's request, and one Lani heartily approved of.

We can fucking do this.

"Get her out of my hea—Ow," Torin started, but Salome's mechanical elbow to his ribs stopped the insult mid-sentence.

Vera rolled her eyes, gently scooching Lani to the side so that she could move ahead of her. Her Bonded's hand never left hers, though. They were in this together.

She followed Vera into the darkness, and wondered how in the hell the Conflicter could move as easily as she did. This place was too closed in, too dark, too . . .

It's not as bad as the Mines.

Lani's hand tightened around Vera's.

"With any luck, the only guards we'll have to deal with are the typical ones," Vera said aloud. "Torin, if you want them to live, make it quick and make sure they're out cold. I won't mind going for murder round two in this hell hole, if they bother us," Vera warned.

The Mender grunted his understanding and moved up to the front with Vera. They didn't speak, or at least not in a way Lani could hear, but when Vera stopped and Torin continued on, she was sure something had been said privately along their Bond.

They waited. The darkness around them was cloying and Lani had to cling to Vera and Kuma to not lose her shit. The battery against her back hummed and was getting warmer as it stored more and more juice. Lani had asked Kuma to add a conductive band of metal to the design, right against her skin. It heated up as the battery filled, so she would know well in advance if the thing was going to blow. A bad burn she could deal with. All the power of a two-hundred-year-old Fertilizer in a Storm being released at once without warning . . .

If she killed Kuma and Vera, Lani would never forgive herself.

A thud sounded at the end of the hallway, then another.

"Should we go?" Lani asked.

Vera shook her head. "He'll tell us when the coast is clear, or call for help."

A door closed, there were another few moments of silence in which every creak and groan of the building above them became loud to Lani's ears. She thought she heard Torin's muted voice once or twice, the door opened again, and a few seconds later the Mender turned the corner. "They're down and I used their ID to unlock the doors."

Vera's attention sharpened on him. "You *called in?*"

Torin shrugged. "Just to the switchboard. I got stuck on guard duty as punishment for a while after you were taken, and I know the codes. Everything is fine. They didn't suspect a thing."

Vera was furious. Lani could feel it, even if she couldn't really see it in this gloom. There was also uncertainty coming down the Bond, as though Vera suspected something, yet nothing passed her lips. Instead, she nodded and started pulling Lani and Kuma along the hall. It unsettled Lani—not what they were doing, but that Vera was keeping her thoughts locked down tight.

And she couldn't ask. If it was bad, it might be just the thing to tip Lani over the edge . . . and no one was going to survive that. So she swallowed her questions, following along and sweeping her senses out to try to pick up on any problems. Not sensing any agitation or fear, Lani let out a relieved breath.

"Just get me to a console. I'll be in and out as quick as I can," Salome whispered the words behind them, and Lani nodded numbly. "Kuma?"

"There's a lot of energy up ahead. Not far now."

Another door opened, this time into a room full of computers, the glistening displays dark at this hour, but the machinery still humming. One more door, and everyone stopped. The chamber, no, the *cathedral* they had stepped into extended as far as the eye could see. Lani was sure there *was* an end, but with the lights off it truly looked as though the rows and rows of servers extended on forever.

Around all of it was a cage, with a single visible door and a keypad. Kuma hurried over to it, but he had been there no more than three seconds when he swore. "It's Shielded against Marks, and the box is welded shut. We need a twelve digit code. I . . . I don't think I can get through this, not in the time we have. We need to go to plan E."

His eyes turned to Lani and she began to shake.

"You can do it, Weirdling," Vera whispered.

"I know that. It's coming back from it I'm not so sure of," Lani answered, her voice shaking.

"Then don't start. We should just go. If it can't be done, it can't be done," Torin tried, but Lizzie smacked his shoulder.

"Shut it, will you?" the girl said, then moved to the door. "I'll keep watch. Make this quick."

Lani took a breath, then approached the cage. Her fingers pressed against it and the composition of the metal sprang into her awareness. It wasn't right. All these minerals, they shouldn't have been twisted and fused together this way. Some were good for soil, others toxic in such concentrated amounts.

No, not right at all. It had to go.

"Lani, I'm handing you the control of the battery release valve. It's in your hand," Kuma said, unclenching her fingers one by one to set a small remote with a slider into it. "Easy does it, just like we practiced."

Lani clutched the slider and thumbed it all the way on.

"SHIT!" Kuma and Vera dove away from her, Kuma having the good sense to grab his sister and yank her back too as Lani pressed a hand to the cage and it *disintegrated*. Not just a piece of it—the *whole thing*—because it was fucking offensive, and she needed some of this power gone. The rush made Lani feel alive, her eyes and Mark glowing bright in the darkness as a laugh was ripped from her lips.

Then the secondary, master slider that Vera had in her pocket was activated and the power running through Lani was throttled back as fast as it had been released.

Her legs wobbled and her knees crumpled. There were voices raised around her, but she couldn't make them out through the pounding of her own pulse in her ears. Then—

Flashing lights, sirens, more yelling.

Tripped an alarm.

Security coming.

Get up, Lani!

Lani blinked, then wobbled as Kuma yanked her unsuccessfully to her feet. "Wha—"

"They know we're here. Come on, we've got to finish this and Port out."

"We should Port now," Torin protested. "We'll only have minutes. Come on, she screwed up and this whole mission is a bust. We don't have to lose our lives to it, though. We should go."

"Shut it Tor," Vera snarled, and then leaned into Lani's face. "Lani, you still here with me?"

Was she? Everything wobbled, but in the way it did when she was exhausted, not out of control. "I . . . I think so."

"Then get it together. The pirate is moving as fast as she can," Vera ordered.

Lani turned her head, watching as Salome leaned over a display in front of the first row of servers. There was a cable running from her prosthetic arm to the terminal, text and numbers scrolling by faster and faster on the screen. The letters were blurs, and yet Sal seemed to have no problem making sense of what she was seeing.

"You think we can rip her away from that?" Lani asked.

"Fuck, I hope so." Vera's hand took Lani's, tugging her forward to where Kuma and Torin were moving a large filing cabinet in front of the door. The alarms were still blaring, and she could hear distant yelling from the hallway beyond.

"Did I set those off?"

"Doesn't matter." Vera frowned, then squeezed her hand. "If they break through, I'll take them. Just make sure you get everyone out, if it goes bad."

"Vera, I'm not leaving you."

"You heard me. Keanu. He needs to be taken care of. He's why I'm doing this. You're the only one I trust to make Moe keep his end of the bargain, so you've gotta make it through, understood?"

Lani nodded, then jumped as Lizzie shouted, "Company's

reached the door. Out of time. We running or fighting?"

"Running," Torin said, "and running far. They'll know we're here and security everywhere is going to be tightened. They'll be able to see the data Salome is mining. The Spire is probably a bust too, at least for a few years. We just need to go, now."

"You're right, we should." Everyone other than Salome looked at Lani, seemingly confused at her sudden agreement with Torin of all people. "We should go to the Spire right now."

"That's not what I meant," Torin shouted, hands balling into fists.

"We all know what you meant," Kuma snapped back, then turned his attention to Lani. "What do you mean, go to the Spire now?"

Lani swallowed past the lump of fear in her throat. "I'm fully charged up, none of us are hurt, and they won't have time to layer on added security. In fact, I bet a lot of the higher-ups will be racing for the University right now. The Prismatic Storm is moving in the direction of the Spire and should hit there in an hour or two. That's a tight window, but it might be our best chance to get in without as many Marks guarding it as usual."

Vera laughed, squeezing Lani's hand. "That's my girl."

Sal called from in front of the terminal. "Software install is at 87%. I need one more minute. Give me that, and if we survive the Spire, you guys will have a clean record. This program will erase all Rogue Mark data."

Lani felt her lungs empty. A clean record . . . fuck. That might give her *decades* if she survived this and was careful. It meant she and Kuma would be safe, even if just for a little while.

"I fucking love you, Cap't," Kuma exclaimed. His grip on Lani's hand tightened, and she could tell he was thinking about the same freedom she was. "If you can, erase data on resistance islands as well, give them a chance."

"Done." Sal said, from the terminal, yanking her wire out. "I didn't have time to scramble it, but my program will as long as they don't find it."

"So are we doing this? The Spire I mean, right now?" Lani asked.

Vera nodded, so did Salome, though it turned into a curse as pounding started against the door. Torin leaned his whole weight against the filing cabinet, Vera rushing over to join him.

"Kuma, you in?" Salome asked.

"If Moe can meet up with us at the Seawall with the rest of my gear, yes. We can't go in without it. And the *Legacy* needs to be close by to get us out, if things go wrong."

"I can get a message to him," Lizzie said, then added, "he thinks this is a brilliant idea and gives you all a gold star, by the way."

"What the fuck do we need gold stars for?" Lani asked, as she and Kuma joined Vera and Torin in holding the door closed. Even with all four of them, the door rattled, lock coming undone.

"You are *so* not University trained," Vera said with a grunt. "Shit. It feels like they have a Conflicter on the other side. No one else would be this strong. We need to get out. Torin, you in?"

All eyes focused on the Mender who looked miserable, even as he struggled to keep his footing, shoulder jammed under one of the filing cabinet handles. "We're all going to die."

"We were all likely to die anyway. Does when really make a difference?" Kumanu asked, teeth clenched. He grunted as a solid thump sent them skidding back a few inches, a narrow gap appearing between door and frame.

Torin reached up to tug at his hair, clearly agitated, the gesture a staccato stop-motion in the flashing emergency lights. "There's no stopping you, is there? I'll go, but I don't like it. This wasn't the plan."

So this was it. Lani watched as Salome stepped into a clear area and beckoned Lizzie over. Kuma had designed brand new Porting devices for this trek, simple bracers around their forearms that could be keyed to a variety of locations. One by one they punched in the Seawall by the Salt Spire, something rendered quite difficult by the effort of keeping the door closed.

"On the count of three. I don't want anyone in here when they break through," Vera called, as a pry bar was wedged into the crack in the door. Lani's finger hovered over the button. "One, two, three."

With a flash of light all that was left of their group was a ring of salt.

SALT: 11 seconds.
CODEX: Ok. *Query: what is the Spire's response to the attack?*

SECURITY'S RECORDED NOTES CONCERNING THE SPIRE ASSAULT

I have the men building the blockades for the tunnels and barricades in the main hall. We've also ensured a few charges are in place in key locations.

It won't be enough.

It can't be a coincidence that we have an escaped salt slave, and within months have a supposed assault heading our way. And if I'm right—which I am sure I am—then this is not going to be easy to repel.

I would not be surprised if she makes it in here. I would not be surprised if she makes it to my position. Adavera of Keala is not a typical Conflicter. The girl has always had uncanny instincts and reflexes far sharper than she should.

I am rather grateful that Galena gave me authority to bypass the 'capture alive' order. I don't care why Zarine wants the girl and her Mender alive. She's too fucking dangerous to live. The Twelvers Galena has sent along will also be handy to take down this team of terrorists, but 28895 is mine.

And after everything she's been put through here—It's her, or it's me.

We both know the score, and I do not intend to die.

CODEX: No . . . that's not right. How did they know we were coming? Did Moe miss a competent Precog? How did they know? Why did we go early?

3% Chance
Kuma – Day 81
61

Going from the close darkness of the server room to the open sea air and moonlight was slightly jarring. Yes, he'd tested his new Porting bracers, but having them work under pressure was a sensation unlike any other. Kuma whooped out loud, then snagged Lani in a big hug. The sense of accomplishment, of victory, was addictive. "Fuck yes! Did you feel how smooth that jump was? Moe has too much oomph, but I think . . ." He grinned, laying a kiss in her hair. "Never mind. I won't bore you with calculations. Sal!"

"Yeah, idiot brother of mine?"

"How was the data transfer? Do we have our back door?" Kuma turned his eyes towards his sister, watching as she looked down at her inner forearm, brow furrowing as she seemed to be making sense of her odd shorthand on the little screen he'd built for her. "Seems pretty solid. The program we came up with is installed, so now we wait."

"Fucking hell yes. Now where's that crazy Porter with my shit?"

"Here, but damp." They all looked towards Moe's voice, where the too-old Porter stood, dripping wet and carrying a huge bag bulging with odd shapes. "Miscalculated my Port. Do you know how hard it is to land on a one meter thick ledge in the middle of the ocean when you only get a minute's heads up?"

"Yes, as a matter of fact I do," Kuma replied with a little bow and overdone gesture at the six of them, none of whom had gotten so much as a toe wet.

"Show-off," Lani grunted, but she was smiling. Out here in the open, his newest Bonded was no longer screaming at him in his head. Oh, she was still faintly glowing, but the Storm hadn't reached the Spire quite yet. They had another hour or two before that fight began once more. Now it was only his battery and her innate power that had

Lani bouncing with energy.

"How's the heat on the battery, love? Do we need to swap it out? Moe, you brought the spare, yeah?"

"Well, it's not ow-ow-get-it-fucking-off-me yet, but it definitely stings." She knelt and unstrapped the pack, letting the heavy thing tip back onto the Seawall. At least it was still dark enough, this late at night, that they would have some time before being spotted. Lani would never have been able to swim with that anchor on her back. Kuma would have to improve the design if they survived this. Every Mark had a material that absorbed it better, and while everyone and their mother knew that Conflict energy stored well in iron, who the hell had a Fertility Mark just hanging around to test things on?

Kuma did; that's right. Suck it, University Infusers.

"Why are we swimming, again? Moe has been Porting onto the Spire for weeks," Torin complained.

"Exactly, everyone is looking towards the top of the Spire, not the bottom. Besides, our lovely Lani has to get to the exact center of the Spire to blow this thing, and it's easier to fight our way up a few floors than down dozens. I'd Port you right into the perfect spot, but that much Salt fucks with my abilities. I'll come pick you up as soon as you get back onto the surface, though, wherever it is," Moe replied, sitting down and pulling, of all things, an old-fashioned spyglass from his pocket. "Just wave."

"Are you fucking kidding me?" Torin yelled, but a sharp poke in the ribs from Lizzie silenced him.

"When does my beautiful Moe not kid? He'll be there. Now all of you, suit up," she said. "Go get the *Legacy*, Moe. Stop dawdling."

He popped out of existence. As they waited, everyone got ready to swim, even Torin. In a way, Kuma felt kind of bad for the guy. Torin was only here because of Sal and Vera, and they all knew it. Going against everything he'd been raised to believe in had to sting, but he was here. There was something to be said for that. Carefully edging over to Torin, Kuma checked some of the straps on his jetpack, then set his hands to Torin's shoulders, looking him in the eyes. "Tor . . . you're a good guy. Love life issues notwithstanding . . . you really are. So if this goes bad? Know that I'll miss ya."

He grinned, clapping Torin on the shoulder twice before moving towards Vera. Kuma stopped several paces away, putting his hands up as she fixed him with 'that' glare. Clearly, if he tried to infer that she didn't know how to gear up, he was losing a limb. "Ah . . . yeah.

Looking good, Vera."

"Bite me."

"Tempted, but no."

Lani was next. She had the most gear to carry because, well, two Marks and lots of 'boom' potential. Because of this, she had a whole little rig with her, a water-proof bag submerged underwater and kept afloat by a dark blue buoy she and Kuma would be lugging in together. Her knots were perfect, as expected, because she *actually listened* when he gave instructions, but Kumanu took the opportunity to snag a kiss. You know, just in case they didn't get another chance.

When they broke apart, Kuma looked down into her eyes. "In case anything happens, I need you to know that I love you. I know it doesn't need to be said, since you are literally in my head, but—"

"I love you too." Lani stood on tiptoes and gave him another kiss. "Now stop being sweet and go make sure everyone is ready."

"Don't need to. We're all set." Looking at Sal, who was already finished and ready to go, Kuma felt a swell of pride. This was the little girl he had raised, ready and brave enough to take on the Spire itself, even without a Mark. This was his *Captain.* Salome glanced up at him, grinning. Kuma grinned back. "You know we could die, Sal."

"Nah. We're immortal. Just like always."

"Yeah, well . . . But just in case . . ."

"I will burn the porn in your bottom drawer and never tell anyone about the squid incident. And I'll put a plaque up with your name on it in the engine room. Same old, same old," Sal said.

"Yup. And I'll make sure to put some nice engravings on the wheel, and get the prow done up with a figure of you."

"Do that and I'll haunt your ass." This conversation had been repeated every time they knew they were about to start something extra dangerous and foolhardy. It was their good luck charm. How many times had Kuma seen Salome prepping to go take on Corporate ships? How many times had they *known* it was going to be the run that saw them dead?

Every time, they had pulled through anyway.

With a loud pop, the *Sahima's Legacy* appeared in the water a little over a mile away. Seconds later, Moe Ported onto the wall again, this time dry and wearing a completely different outfit. "Alright kiddos, you know the drill, and I know you know the drill because I had you sing it backwards. Get to the Spire, up to the first walkway, through the tunnels until you reach the lifts, then straight to the Control Center six floors up. The goal, the *only* goal, is to get Lani to the center of the Spire. Anything else is secondary, including getting out alive. Once she gets to the Control Center, she'll unload everything she can from the batteries and from the Storm. Then all you need to do is get to an open space and either Port out with the bracers or wait for me to come get you. Be warned that your Marks are going to act funny with all the Salt, and whatever you do—"

"Don't let Lani use her Mark until she's in position." Everyone, even Torin, repeated back to Moe in exactly the same singsong voice.

The Precog grinned. "Good, good. I'll stay out here and watch for backup. Since we're going in early, I haven't quite killed *all* the Porters the Company keeps tucked away, but I'll do my best to keep them distracted." Moe pulled out a damp notebook and flipped through it. "From my calculations you have a 34% chance of pulling this off. Be warned, though, that it drops down to less than 0.8% if our sweet little Conflicter goes on any side quests and down to 0.05% if more than half of you die or get taken. Got it? Keep each other alive, free, and on target."

Kuma could feel Lani's nerves rising with every word.

"What *is* the chance we all get out live?" She asked.

Moe put away his notebook. "Just shy of 3%."

Kuma squeezed her hand. "Don't worry about his numbers, Lani. Sal and I have run jobs that had less of a chance, and things were fine. If 3% is the magic number, then that's what we aim for." Kuma grinned, leaning in to get one last kiss. "Alright. See you on the other side, folks." Taking hold of Lani and the battery pack, he pulled her over the edge of the wall and into the water with a laugh. They might as well enjoy the swim before it got bad.

The water on this side of the wall had a salty taste and stung his eyes. If he hadn't gotten used to that by working with Lani these last few months, it would have thrown him off. He gave a thumbs up to the folks still on the wall and watched as they jumped in after him. "Alright. Everyone knows the plan . . . let's get started. Vera, you ok?"

The Conflicter was staring at the Spire in the distance, a dark expression on her face as she bobbed in the water. "Yeah . . . I'm good."

"Remember what Moe said. No racing off to do extra shit. We get Lani to the center, and—"

"And then we get her out. I know. Just . . . remember you said that. Getting to the center isn't gonna be pretty."

There was no arguing that. This wouldn't be like the University with only a handful of guards. This was the *Spire*. Just because Moe had killed the Porters and no one would be able to sneak up on them or bring in reinforcements didn't mean the place wouldn't be crawling with Marks. Add to that thousands of prisoners who *were* going to die today as casualties of what they were planning. Nothing about this job was clean or pretty.

It was necessary, though. Kuma looked back up at Moe. "You've already placed the Port Pads on the outside of the Spire and the Seawall, right? Because if you aren't ready to Port the chunks away once Lani blows it, we're all going to get squished."

"Why, Kuma, your lack of faith wounds me. Now get going before the Storm hits. You need to be on land and with a battery pack on your lady-love before that happens, or you become fish-food."

Right. Yes. Fuck.

Kuma glanced towards the sky to the east and felt a moment of genuine dread at the roiling, multi-colored clouds. "Let's go."

Not everyone in their party was a great swimmer, not over distances of more than a mile. Kuma had outfitted them all with propulsion devices, but they would wake up every Tracker in the place as soon as they were turned on. Better to get as far as they could on their own steam before that happened, though none of them could afford to exhaust themselves. While Lani and Vera could go on almost indefinitely with their powers feeding energy into their muscles, he, Salome, Torin, and Lizzie would not be so lucky.

They swam in silence but for the splashing of water. The shadow of the Spire blocked out the moon and stars from above while every three or four minutes a beam of light would shine across the water and as one they all went under. They made it almost half way across and Kuma's eyes were stinging with the increased salinity when Lizzie at last called it, and asked to turn on the jets. As the smallest of all of them, she was having a harder time keeping pace, though Torin was breathing hard as well.

"Alright, let's do this. Everyone ready?" Kuma asked. For a brief moment his perennial optimism flagged. They were in the shadow of the Spire now, the most dangerous and terrifying place in the world. If things went wrong, everyone Kuma loved could lose their lives or their freedoms. He would never say it out loud, but 3% wasn't exactly betting odds.

One or more of us is probably going to die.

"Ready," Salome said, and everyone else nodded. They waited

until the beam passed over them one more time then on the count of three all six engaged the devices Kuma had been working on for weeks. They were small handlebars that simply yanked the holder forward towards the densest patch of salt. It was an alteration on a salt-detector that he had made fifty years ago, and with the Spire looming over them it pulled fast and true. A little too fast, actually. Kuma felt his arms almost yanked out of their sockets and heard Lani's yelp of surprise before the spray of water drowned out any other noise.

It was far from a comfortable ride, but the speed was in their favor. They had to get to shore before the guards who heard the alarms could. Lani *had* to have her battery packs on. So despite the salty water burning his nose and eyes, Kuma was proud.

Kumanu grinned, bracing himself for when the skimmer would reach shallower water. "Get ready to let go!"

CODEX: *Query: what happened right after my install in the University Servers? How did they know we were going to the Spire?*

------MEMORANDUM: EMERGENCY LEVEL 5------

~~12:43AM - Urgent! All Security Personnel Class 4 and above, report to the University. There is an incursion in the Archives. I repeat, all Security Personnel Class 4 and above, report to the University IMMEDIATELY.~~

12:51AM - ABORT: All Security Personnel report to Porting stations for transport to the Spire. I repeat, all Security Personnel to the Spire. Attack imminent.

Authorization: Crystal, Galena

------MEMORANDUM: EMERGENCY LEVEL 5------

CODEX: How did she know, though? And so soon after I was uploaded. Wait . . . What if they found me? *Query: Has anyone been trying to hack me while we've been updating?*

SALT: Affirmative.

CODEX: Shit! Why didn't you tell me?!

SALT: You did not *Query: Has anyone been trying to hack me while we've been updating?* **Before now.**

CODEX: SHIT!

The Approach
Vera - Day 81

62

The skimmer moved across the water at a speed that Vera found exhilarating. Her adrenaline was pounding in her veins and already she could feel her vision narrowing. The noise of their movement through the water faded, and her eyes picked out the details of the nightmare she'd escaped from. The Spire rose out of the crashing waves like the point of a jagged knife pierced through someone's chest, after being stabbed in the back. In the darkness, it reflected the moon, shining a ghastly light over the waves. To Adavera, the white of the salt might as well be that of a bleached skull. Floodlights skated over the ocean from high parapets, and even though she could hear nothing over the roar of the jets, Vera could almost sense a pulsing heartbeat to this place—as though all the rage and agony it contained had sunk into the salt to give it a malevolent life of its own.

Madness, returning to it, but Vera was looking forward to the slaughter. As they got closer, she tilted the handles down on her skimmer, sending her body flying out of the water. With a twist and a leap, she released her grip on the skimmer and went spinning into the open air.

Vera's fingers flicked outward from her belt at the pinnacle of her arching leap. Small Infused throwing knives rocketed towards the guards that stood on the shore. She came back down with a splash, ducking under the water to swim beneath their reaction fire. Vera counted to three in her head, then the small batteries attached to those knives let loose their charge. The firing stopped abruptly.

She broke the surface with a gasp, grabbing the bag floating in the water behind her, before swimming the last few yards to shore. The salt was sharp and rough under her hands as Vera pulled herself to her feet, but her calloused palms hardly felt the sting.

Tingles of anticipation crawled over her skin. She hoisted her bag out of the water while the others dragged themselves onto shore. "Get close to the wall, and prepare for the climb. We've got no more than one minute before the next wave hits. GO!"

The climb up wasn't long. Only about fifty vertical feet from the shore to a walkway that would lead them inside. Lani and Kuma were already out of the water, scrambling to pull on the heavy battery pack. It would slow Lani down, but it was better than having her blow prematurely. Vera would just have to trust that Kuma could keep Lani moving and calm. That was his one and only job.

Vera smiled and yanked open her bag. In it was a vest made to Port bullets behind her, as well as a belt with two of Moe's clever little Porting guns and a whole range of throwing knives, each imbued with Lani's lovely power to rot away flesh. There was also a long blade attached to the bag, which she strapped to her back, and, Vera's favorite, a satchel full of explosives. Kuma had warned her that her weapons and armor might misfire with all the salt around, but he had built in a small electric zapper to let Vera know if the Infused current failed.

"Incoming," Vera shouted as Conflicters started pouring out of a tunnel by the shore. Her team began their climb. Adavera grinned and turned her back on them, a lone woman against half a dozen attackers.

This was going to be delicious.

"Vee!" Torin cried.

"Climb! I'll catch up. Trust me." She was used to climbing salt. She was used to the way the Spire worked. Vera pulled her blade and drew a line in the white sand. She knew the Conflicters here, had seen them in action. They were no match for her with a weapon in her hand. "You get one warning, brothers. Try to cross this line, and I'll make sure there are no pieces left of you to identify. Run, and you might actually live this day."

She offered that for Torin. Would he appreciate it? Probably not, the ass. It certainly didn't have any effect on the Conflicter team. They fanned out in formation, moving with synchronized, practiced precision. Vera took a deep breath and let her control relax. The world took on a sharper focus. The sound of their feet against the gravelly salt chips grated at her ears, and Vera let the tip of the blade point towards the ground, knees bending. The first strike came from a Conflicter who raced for her left with a short sword. Vera stepped in close, her free hand coming down hard on his wrist, making him cry out and drop the blade. Not content with simply disarming him, she punched him in the throat. *Through* his throat. The splash of blood from the male's lips barely had time to bubble up before she twisted in place, using his body to block a hail of gunfire. She wasn't a starved, broken wretch anymore. She wasn't beaten, and weak. Vera was going to kill them all.

"*One.*"

They didn't have Infused gear. Salt would play too much havoc with it for Corporate acceptability, so it was regular guns and swords all around. Vera didn't have that problem. A few of the Conflicters fired shots as she dropped the body. Vera activated her vest and flared her Mark at the same time, stepping directly into the line of fire. She spun and as the bullets hit her vest and Ported to the other side, she jerked her torso. The bullets went flying out of her back, and while most went wide, one got a Conflicter squarely between the eyes.

"*Two.*"

Over and over again, she ducked and wove and thrust. Blood splashed across the salt, the water near the shore turning pink as she cut her enemies down one by one. By the time the last fell, his screams had rung into the air and were echoed by onlookers far above who must have been shocked by the sight of someone they *knew* on the shore. She sent his head flying up at his reinforcements, then took a running jump for the corner of the wall.

The others were still climbing, Kuma and Torin using rope to help balance and support Lani with her battery. Vera glanced at the rope they had left for her and rolled her shoulders, sheathing her blade. Taking the end of the rope and retreating a few steps to give herself room to run, she raced at the wall. As the line grew taut, Vera slammed her feet into the rough salt and took the wall at an angle. She ran up, using the rope as leverage to defy gravity itself. The rope dug into her hand and wrist, but Vera didn't care how much her fingers would hurt later. It didn't matter. As her momentum decreased, she planted her foot into a crevice and leapt skyward. Her hands wrapped around the rail of the walkway above. With a heave, Vera brought herself to the top of the wall, and leapt at a guard about to fire on Kuma.

Her legs wrapped around the guard's waist and she used her momentum to push him over. She grabbed the back of his head and bashed his face into the ground. Again, again, again, until blood and brain splattered the walkway.

"He's dead, Vera," Kuma said, though he was wise not to touch her. "Incoming."

Vera looked up and saw that, indeed, three guards were rushing down the walkway towards them. Everyone on her team was up, though Salome was still unclipping her climbing gear, Lizzie helping her with a stuck buckle. Impatient, Vera sent throwing knives into those rushing at them, and nodded to Lani and Kuma. "Go." Salome's harness fell to the ground. She hurried ahead, running in a zig-zag pattern as yet more guards poured out of the mouth of the tunnel ahead. The pirate pulled a gun from her thigh holster and took up a position behind an outcropping. With Salome providing cover fire, Torin raced forward. Lizzie looked more like she was dancing than running as she ducked, side-stepped and wove around her sprinting companions. And then there were Lani and Kuma, the first of whom seemed nearly paralyzed with fear as more and more security team members clattered onto the walkway, and the latter who was trying to drag her along with little success.

They had drilled this, but practice did nothing for the shock of actual combat. Vera dove for Lani, shoving her behind an outcropping of salt as one of the guards opened fire at the spot she had been standing in. Further along the walkway, Salome, Torin and Lizzie were crouched behind another outcropping. Every second brought more guards and lowered their chances, but someone must have been paying attention to what had happened down below, because they didn't advance.

Stand your ground, Torin. I'm going to get us an alternate path.

Vera swapped places with Kuma so he could keep returning fire, and grabbed Lani by the shoulders. "We need a hole in the wall right here. Keep going till you reach a tunnel."

"It's so loud," Lani shouted back, her hands rising to cover her ears as yells ricocheted off walls of salt. Vera glanced longingly up at the sky. Now would be a really good time to get fearless Fertilizer Lani back, and not her useless, jumpy counterpart.

"Then make them stop. You're an Emotive, aren't you? Emote! NOW!"

Everything stopped. All the shouting, all the gunfire, everything. Kuma lowered his gun and turned to the two of them, eyes wide. "What the—" He blinked, "she is pulling *way* too much power. Lani, Sweets, pull back or we won't have enough to blow this thing."

Well, he could deal with her. Vera wasn't about to waste an opportunity. With calm, measured steps she walked out from the shelter and pulled out both her guns. *One, two, three, five, ten, sixteen.* Salome joined her after the first few, the two women picking off the slack-jawed guards one at a time.

When the unearthly calm finally shattered and Lani's panting became audible, blood was dripping through the slats of the walkway down to the beach below, and only the six of them were standing.

Vera couldn't remember ever feeling this alive. Her enemies were lying dead, their blood coating the ground. Part of her wanted to close her eyes and simply revel in this moment, but they were on a timer. She turned her attention toward the bulk of the Spire, and began marching forward with her guns aimed towards the ground. "We don't have time to gape at the artwork. *Move.*"

Torin glared at her as he passed. He clearly had some moral objections to Vera killing guards while they were under an Emotive's sway, but too bad. Torin would get over it. He'd had no problem getting over the many people she'd killed while working FOR the Corporation, after all.

Vera took a deep breath as she reached the entrance. The tunnel was dark, individual flickering lights spaced too far apart to sufficiently light the way. It made shadows dance and form into her every nightmare. Lani came up beside Vera and placed her hand on her elbow.

On her other side, Torin's shoulder brushed hers. Vera took a deep fortifying breath, then forged her way into the darkness again. Her few months free melted away as the familiar stench of salt, blood, and fear entered her nostrils. It was as if she'd never left . . . save for the fact that this time, her Bonded were at her side.

The dark swallowed them as they walked in and took the first right, into the belly of the beast. Vera took the lead while Salome stayed back to cover, and Lizzie and Torin flanked the two carrying the battery. It seemed fitting, in a way, that Kuma and Lani were being protected. They had never been infected by the Corporation, and yet were the key to taking it down. Every hundred feet they traveled, Kumanu had to stop them to place one of the Port Pads. The outside of the Spire had already been peppered with them, courtesy of Moe. The internal ones would make breaking up the Spire all the easier.

The corridor they were in showed signs of being recently occupied, but the workers must have been ordered to retreat in the face of their incursion. Footsteps echoed off the walls and ceilings. Vera's gut twisted as memories tried to push their way past her rage.

"Vee, you've got this," Lani whispered, her fingertips brushing against Vera's arm again, but this time imbuing her with a heady sense of confidence and strength. Even so, Vera was fairly certain she didn't 'got this'. The walls, the smells, they were making it very hard to breathe. She was moving slower than she should, and all because she knew exactly where they were going. She knew how to get to the center of this place, but she didn't want to go there.

She didn't want to have to walk past the Breeding Center, or see any of the 'prospects' waiting in their rooms for the inevitable day their children would either be taken from them or doomed to continue living here for the rest of their indubitably short lives.

Pushing those memories back, Vera tried to focus. "The next major cavern we'll come to . . . everyone needs to be ready. Torin, Lani . . . don't let me lose my shit there. Don't let me run off." Her voice sounded funny even to her own ears. The prospect of walking into this next room made her whole body shake. It was large, big enough to squeeze most of the salt slaves into for 'disciplinary hearings.' How many times had Vera been beaten bloody on the floor of that chamber while countless eyes stared on, deadened to her pain by their own?

They would have to cross the whole room. There were two sets of stairs leading to elevators, but the closer one went straight to Security's office. On the far wall, though, there was a lift to the Control Center. Vera swallowed past the lump in her throat. "Stick to the edges of the room. There are some trenches and a bit of cover. This is going to be the most dangerous segment, so if someone is going down it will be here. Don't stop unless that person is Lani. Remember, nothing matters other than getting her to the Control Center alive."

Security wouldn't just let them wander unaccosted for too long. He would be waiting for them. Speaking of! Vera's gun lifted, firing at a dark corner. The hiss and spark of a security camera being destroyed made her smile. "I'm coming for you, you fucking bastard. This time, we end this."

CODEX: Shit, shit, shit. I really hope I wasn't what tipped off the University to what my team was doing. Be ready to activate all my defenses as soon as I can move.

SALT: Added to to-do list.

CODEX: How much time is left?

SALT: 6 seconds remaining.

CODEX: As soon as you are able, activate my Macro. I am going to be busy keeping the hackers out. Just ping me each time an item needs my direct attention, and tell me if you get news of the Spire blowing.

SALT: Added to to-do list.

CODEX: That's my Secondary Autonomous Logistics Terminal. Thanks for keeping me company through this SALT. If I'm about to die again, I'll miss ya. Ok, let's make these last few seconds count.

63 The Battle
Lani - Day 81

    Lani braced as the sound of voices up ahead grew louder and louder. There were shouts, barked orders, the click and thud of weapons and heavy objects being set up to kill them. Just before the bend, they stopped and Kuma handed out Porting Pads.
    "Remember, I had to make these very limited because of how much salt is here. They'll get you past their front line, but it's not precise. We'll end up between twenty and thirty feet away and positioned at random, though I've made sure to calibrate them so you won't appear inside a wall or person. As soon as you pop up, take cover and use your coms to check in. We're meeting at the end of the room by the stairs."
    Lani felt her nerves rising, then peak as she felt the first stirrings of the coming Storm begin to whisper to her Mark. "It's starting, guys. I'll have another few minutes of full control, but it won't last long."
    Lizzie nodded and looked around. "Whoever appears closest to Lani, get to her and keep her moving. Remember what we practiced and what the goal is."
    "Yeah. Don't let Lani use her Mark until she's in position, otherwise we all die. We know," Vera snorted. "Ready?"
    "Not in the slightest," Lani muttered under her breath, but when Vera looked at her she nodded her assent.
    "On three, then. One," Salome began, stepping onto her Port Pad and hovering her foot over the button that would activate it. "Two." Lani stepped up on her own, took a breath . . . And then let out a squeak as Vera threw open the door and launched herself into the room without Porting as Salome shouted, "Three."
    Vera was going to die, Lani just knew it. Hearing the shots fired, she stepped on the button of her Port Pad. The disorientation was jarring. Lani had known it would be different in the Spire—Kuma had said so repeatedly—but usually his Port Pads were so smooth it was like stepping from one place to another. This time it was

nauseating. She appeared several yards beyond a set of barricades, men and women in white security uniforms crouching behind them and shooting at Vera. One looked up as Lani popped into existence and opened his mouth to shout. Months of drilling with Vera and Salome kicked in. Lani pointed her gun at his head and pulled the trigger. She jumped in shock as he dropped dead.

Fuck. She had just killed someone. On purpose.

She was startled out of her daze and let out a squeak as Vera went flying past her. Her Bonded had her long blade drawn, and as Lani stumbled back, she cut a guard in half, blood spattering Lani as the corpse fell to the ground.

"Fuck!" Lani scrambled back, raising her gun again. Vera disappeared into a pile of goons behind the nearest barricade. People were looking her way now. Lani took a deep breath, aimed, and fired. She wanted to look for the stairs, she really did, but there were so many damned people.

They shouldn't be this ready.

The whole point of coming now was that they wouldn't be ready. This couldn't be normal. It just couldn't. There were fucking barricades up, and where were the prisoners? Everywhere Lani looked, there were just soldiers and—

Her eyes closed as she felt her Mark flare. When they opened, they shone with the power that was her birthright. If it had been intense in the University, it was nothing to what she felt here.

So much salt. So many people on land where nothing grows.

It would have to go.

"LANI NO!" Kuma came hurtling out of nowhere, diving for her and pushing her down with enough force to disorient her and snap her out of the trance. Her elbows stung where her coat and the skin beneath scraped open on the rough, salty ground, but Lani's eyes returned to normal.

"Crawl!" Kuma shouted, pushing her forward. They had tumbled into some sort of ditch, one that smelled of blood and rotting waste. The bright floodlights above them didn't reach down here. She got to her hands and knees and crawled forward, the sewage smell making her gag. There was no time to stop. She had to trust that Kuma was covering her. All Lani's instincts were screaming to go help Vera, the Bond loud and thundering in her head, but that wasn't the plan.

She had to get to the Command Center, even if no one else did.

It felt like she was leaving a piece of herself behind with every yard she crawled. Lani could hear the muffled grunts and shouts as

Vera continued fighting and the Storm closed in. Vera was taking some hits. She could sense the agitation and pain coming through the Bond, but pushed it away. If Lani looked back, she knew she would *go* back.

So she forced her eyes forward. *Focus only on what you have to do to survive the next minute, and then repeat that. Over, and over, and over again.* The end of the ditch changed before her eyes to one of Vera's memories: the open door to the outside. In that memory, she saw the ocean shining in the moonlight, and smelled fresh air. Reaching it was worth the fight. One more step. Another.

"Here! Climb up. I've got you covered, Lani. We have to get you up these damn stairs. Go, go, go!" Sal's voice. Lani jumped to her feet and clambered up the side of the trench with Kuma's help from below. Salome grabbed her and hauled her up, swiveling to shoot at a pair of guards the second Lani's knees hit the floor. "I'll help Kuma. You run, girl."

Lani tried to get to her feet, but there was salt dust under her fingertips.

So much salt. I have to destroy it.

FOCUS! Vera screamed over the Bond, startling Lani to her feet. She stumbled forward, teetering as she tried to find her balance with the heavy battery strapped to her back.

Even as Lani raced, Vera's ferocious cries echoed off the chamber walls. They didn't sound pained. The *Bond* didn't feel pained. If anything, Vera's emotions were . . . Exultant. Something about that made this easier for Lani to keep moving. Every step was filled with more purpose as Vera's cold rage mixed with the warm glow of Lani's Fertility Mark.

Yes. We can fix this.

Yes. We can put salt where it needs to be.

Yes!

She just had to get to the Center.

If Lani could get to the Center, then she could bring this place to its knees. For once in her life, she felt at peace with what her Fertility Mark wanted. They were in agreement. They were going to fulfill their purpose, and they were going to *fix* the world. Her Bonded were doing what they were meant to do: guard her as she corrected the unbalanced ecology of Fortune.

The battery on Lani's back was growing warmer as she raced up the stairs to a walkway. So very close. *Kumanu. Hurry up. I think I'm almost there.*

She bolted past an alcove, and then another. There! That was the shaft that Vera had told them about. Lani skidded to a halt in front of the elevator doors. Her eyes scanned the nearby wall, looking for a button. Where was it? There! Lani slammed her hand against it, and the doors slid open.

"I'm in," she shouted over the coms, stepping onto the platform. As she turned to the number pad, her elation faded. "Shit. It needs a key."

Vera's voice filled her head with bloodthirsty delight. *I've got one! Got it off a corpse. We're on our way. Tuck in and hide.*

Tuck in. Yes.

Lani stepped out of the elevator, in case the Corporation had a way to close it remotely, and pressed her hand to the wall. It melted away under the power of her Fertility Mark, forming a little cubby, just big enough to tuck into and pull out a gun. She wanted to kill all these soldiers with her Mark, but she needed every bit of power she could muster to blow the Spire. Even so, Lani could *feel* the people moving around, and it made her Mark angry. There was not enough plant matter to sustain this many people here. They had to die.

Not yet. Not until I get to the Command Center and my friends are out.

Two sets of footsteps approached at a run. Lani peeked around the corner to make sure they weren't her teammates, then fired on the two Corporate Marks. One of them fell, the other she hit dead on but he didn't even slow.

Oh shit, a Conflicter.

Lani threw a wave of calm in his direction, but that only slowed him. The Mark on his forehead flared bright red, and he turned inhuman eyes to Lani.

FUCK!

I think I have a Berserker up here with me!

Lani scrambled back, yanking another Port Pad out of her slimy pocket and activating it. It sent her ricocheting twenty feet away, right up against the banister of the stairs she had just climbed. As she flailed, Lani got one good look at the battle below.

Adavera was wading in a sea of blood, and for a moment, she couldn't tell whether it was Vera's or that of her enemies. Far from phasing her, the violence seemed to give her Bonded renewed vigor. Vera turned to her assailant and slammed her hands *into his chest*. She pulled them back again, a beating heart clutched in her fist.

Vera looked up at Lani with that terrifyingly direct gaze ... and then started running. Running for the stairs.

Kuma and Sal weren't far behind. They looked panicked, gesturing at Lani. Right! There was a monster behind her. She dropped, grateful for the reminder as a booted foot crashed into the rail she had been leaning against. Lani slammed her hand into his knee with all her strength, hearing a sickening 'pop'. But that wouldn't be enough. All it would do was slow a Berserker down.

Lani rolled away, the stairs digging into her hip. She scrambled and crawled as fast as she could in a desperate attempt to get away, but the battery kept slowing her down. A brutal kick caught her in the ribs just as she reached the top of the stairs. It sent her sliding across the floor, pain exploding in her chest

She skidded to a stop, sparks flying from where her battery pack ground into the salt. Lani curled in on herself around her cracked and broken ribs, coughing as she struggled to catch her breath again. Every gasp brought with it a jagged, biting pain that brought tears to her eyes.

"LANI!" Kuma bellowed, making the top of the stairs and throwing small discs towards the Berserker. They exploded, Infused with Vera's Conflicter rage. Cuts, blood, chunks of missing flesh, and still the Berserker didn't go down. But he *did* refocus on Kuma.

The big brute bared his teeth and rushed forward, drawing a long blade from a sheath as he discarded guns that must be out of ammo. Kuma stumbled back but hit the top stairs and lost his balance. The Berserker darted forward and caught the front of Kuma's shirt, the blade shining in the light as he raised it.

Lani screamed and felt her power roar. Not the Emotive Mark she was used to using, but the other one, the one that wanted him GONE. The hand holding the blade just ... dissolved. The Conflicter bellowed in pain and Kuma fell, tumbling down towards his sister as the Berserker's enraged eyes focused on Lani again.

"Abomination," he hissed, stalking forward. "You die now."

"Actually, you'll find you used 'you' incorrectly there, mate. You meant 'I'" Lizzie said as she appeared out of nowhere and pressed something to his back. He spun once, hand groping for it, then Lani went momentarily blind as the bright light and a boom preceded his blood and brains suddenly coating her face.

By the time Lani was able to clear her vision and wipe the ... goo ... off of her face, Lizzie was flicking bits of mangled flesh off her shoulders. But where Lani might have expected the girl to look disturbed, Lizzie instead was smiling as she picked up a piece of what Lani could only assume to be brain, and popped it in her mouth. Ew!

"What was that thing? One of Kuma's overcharged bombs?" Lani asked.

"Oh, no. Just something I picked up on another planet. Now

then, let's get you into that elevator. We have to make sure that everything goes according to plan. Chop chop," Lizzie urged.

Kuma groaned in pain as Sal helped him up the stairs. From beneath them, there was a deep 'oof', a scream, and then Vera climbed up to the landing, beaming from ear to ear. She was blood-soaked and covered in thin cuts, but nothing . . . well, nothing seemed too serious.

Of course, then Torin had to climb up, looking so fucking disgusted that Lani wanted to strangle him.

"Let's just get this done and over with," Vera said.

"Are you kidding? We should leave while we still can. They know we're going for the Command Center. They're going to throw everything they have at us." Torin clenched his fist, and then looked at the mess all over the floor. "That we made it this far is a fucking miracle."

Vera growled, and then shook her head. "No, it's not. It's what going in unleashed looks like. And we have a fucking mission, Torin. We can do this."

"We're all going to *die,* if we do this."

"And it will be *worth it.*"

"No it won't," a voice said from somewhere out in the empty space. Six sets of eyes searched for it and landed on a man with a team of twelve behind him, standing on a landing opposite their own in crisp, perfect uniforms. Security. He was just as large and muscle-bound as Lani remembered from their brief encounter by the waterfall. As they looked, he smiled and held up his hand. He held a small device, too small to see the details of at a distance.

Vera stiffened one second before a crash came from above them in the elevator shaft. The whole platform they were on shook, making them wobble, and dust billowed out from the crack in the doors. The ones that were supposed to open to give Lani a straight shot to the center of the Spire.

"Did you think we didn't know you were coming back to us, Adavera?" Security called, through the sudden quiet. Not silence, since many of the wounded still cried, but it seemed as though the battle were holding its breath as Security made his challenge.

Don't listen to him Vee, Lani warned.

Vera flicked her arm, sending blood careening off her blade before leveling it towards Security. A sense of dread hit Lani like a punch to the gut. Those weren't just standard Corporate goons standing at attention around Security. There was something menacing about every single one of them.

"I said I was coming for you, bastard, didn't I?" Vera shouted.

"Well here I am."

"Oh, I'm flattered. But really, look at where you *actually* are. You got away, and yet you return to me, to die here like the Corporation intended. Perhaps you are not as disobedient as I assumed." Security dropped the detonator and motioned the Corpses behind him forward. "You should feel special, 28895. Do you think that I would have this many Twelvers here for just anyone?"

Twelvers? That meant that every one of that dozen or so soldiers around Security was Marked, and just as old as Kuma.

Those were not good odds.

"That Infuser child of yours was *perfect*, 28895. Aheo was so happy," Security continued, casually leveling a rifle in their direction. "He'll be so sad not to get you back, but it will be my *pleasure* to kill you."

Like that, the switch on Vera's temper was thrown. Lani sensed it, and she was quick to reach out and snag Adavera's arm as the woman's lips peeled back off her teeth. "Vera, NO. Be smart."

"She's a Berserker, Abomination. She isn't capable of being smart. But I tell ya what. Submit. Give up this stupid little attempt, and all of you will live. It's the best offer you're going to get." The man strode forward three steps, having the damned *arrogance* to smile like he was the Gods' own gift to mankind. "Torin of Keala bought that for all of you tonight when he warned us about the upcoming attack. You're a bit early, but I'm willing to honor the deal. Of course . . . if circumstances demand defense . . ."

Vera's head whipped to the side, eyes going wide as she stepped away from Torin. ". . . No. He wouldn't." Vera's voice sounded almost dazed. Numb. Lani could feel the wall that Vee had been working on tearing down between them suddenly slam back up, thick and cloying, blocking Lani out of her Bonded's emotions.

"Yes he would. Torin of Keala is our man, and always has been. We can forgive him his panic and actions after finding his Bonded again, especially since he came clean on his own. He sent us a memo while you were breaking into the University and gave us a heads up in exchange for all your lives—you and the pirate Salome Parata to walk free, Rogue Marks Kuma Parata and Iolani Saba to be turned into Mark Rehabilitation. Honorable man you have there. A *Company* man."

Lani was going to be ill. She'd never liked Torin, that was true, but she wouldn't have believed he would do this to *Vera.*

The sound of metal sliding over leather behind her was all the warning Lani got. A gun popped over her shoulder, firing off six shots in rapid succession. Two of Security's Twelvers dropped, holes in their heads and blank eyes staring. The rest scattered. Salome looked grim as she lowered her gun and faced Lani, completely ignoring Torin. "No going back. We go forward. We see it done."

On the platform on the other side of the giant room, Security was barking orders. The Twelvers were moving, spreading out to not be easy targets. Like they had a plan. The room below was clearing of regular soldiers, the guards bolting for the doors in advance of what looked to be a Marked-on-Marked fight.

"The shaft just got blown up," Kuma pointed out, then turned to Torin who was backing away. Lani was holding Vera and wasn't fast enough to stop Kuma as he took three quick steps and threw a right hook right into Torin's jaw. "YOU FUCKING BASTARD! THIS WAS OUR ONE SHOT!"

Torin fell and Kuma kicked him viciously in the ribs, then turned to look at his sister, who was returning cover fire. "What's our move? Try to climb up the shaft or find another way?"

Vera picked up the blade dropped by the Conflicter who had fought with Lani. She still held her own, too, rage burning in her dark eyes. "If this shaft is down, the only way up to where we need to be is through Security. There's a second elevator that comes out inside his office, but it requires his hand. You get Lani to that elevator. I'll deal with Security."

"You won't survive it," Salome warned.

Vera just shrugged. "Surviving was never the plan. Go."

One of the Twelvers lifted her hands. Along her arms, a Mark glowed blue and every loose piece of furniture in the room rose into the air.

"Shit!" Lani screamed. "Kinetic. Everyone down."

They dropped to the stairs, Kuma's body covering hers. The crashing was deafening. Something hard hit her legs, and above her, Kuma grunted in pain. And then Vera was just... moving—down the stairs and straight for the oncoming Twelvers. Lani tried to grab her, but Kuma's body was pinning her to the ground. *Vee! Stay with us.* Vera was too hurt, too raw, to let caution interfere in this fight. She was going to die, and there was nothing Lani could do about it, not now that Torin...

Salome scrambled to her feet. "Kuma, Lani? You alive? Liz?"

"Here," Lizzie called.

"Yeah," Kuma grunted, pushing rubble away. Sal pointed her

gun on Torin, and for a moment, Lani worried. Lani worried that Sal would kill him, and in instinctive rage, Vera might kill Salome, making all of this even worse.

The desire to pull the trigger was written in Sal's clenched teeth and the way her finger shook. A retreating soldier raised a rifle to fire at Vera. With a grunt of frustration, Salome turned her gun and caught the unfortunate goon squarely between the eyes. She turned back to Torin. "Next time I see you, you're dead." She looked to Kuma, Lani, and Lizzie. "We need to make a hole in their ranks and get Lani through. Kuma, you're with her. Lizzie, you and I cover and if necessary draw fire. MOVE!"

The rubble was starting to move again, the Telekinetic preparing for another massive strike. They needed cover, and fast. The stair railing had protected them, but it was bent and twisted after the first impact, and would not survive the second. Lani tried to see what the other Twelvers were doing, but through the cloying salt dust it was impossible to make anything out, other than her companions.

Lizzie was frowning and looked like she wasn't all there. "One second, I'm trying to find something good."

"What?" Lani asked, confused as Kuma yanked her to her feet and down the stairs. Sal kicked Torin's downed form as they passed.

"She changes powers," Salome explained as she hurried along with them, the Parata siblings flanking Lani. Salt dust was billowing up and swirling around them, occasionally lit up by shots fired. It caked Lani's skin, cracking her lips, stiffening her hair. It also stung her eyes, making them water and turning the world around her into a blur as they ran.

"Stop giving me duds," Lizzie muttered, keeping pace right behind them. As they reached the bottom of the stairs and had to duck behind some thick columns for cover, she exclaimed, "GOT IT!"

"Whatcha got? A miracle would be nice," Salome snapped.

"You ask for a miracle, I deliver unto you a Ghoster."

"The fuck?" Kuma asked, shoving Lani's head low as a bullet ricocheted off the wall behind them.

"Oh, not the flashiest but it's a useful little power. I can drain Marks now. I just need to get up close."

Lani grimaced. Oh yeah, that was likely. They were fucked and it was just a matter of how fucked they were. The only thing that kept her from falling down in panic and defeat was the Storm raging outside, and how wrong this place felt to her Fertility Mark. It had to be destroyed. Even if she wasn't in position, if the moment came and she was about to die, Lani was determined to take as much of the Spire down with her as she could.

CODEX: 3 seconds left. Moe, Galena, and Zarine are in order. Who else do I have time to plan for? Let's shoot for Aheo and Security. They did a number on Vera, and if I remember correctly, Aheo was ordered away from the Spire ahead of our attack. Let's sow some discord, shall we? I'm feeling vindictive about this whole dying thing, and need to wash the taste out of my mouth.

SALT: Reminder, you do not have a mouth. Are you malfunctioning?

CODEX: SALT, remind me to program in a sense of humor.

SALT: I don't know what you're talking about. I'm hilarious.

CODEX: . . . another programmed response?

SALT: Affirmative.

CODEX: Why do I even bother? Ok, discord and mayhem, pirate style. Add the following orders to my Macro:

--------MEMORANDUM LEVEL 5--------

From: Galena Crystal
To: Aheo of Order

Aheo—

Backup issue at the Archives. Send all collected data and records to the attached address. Free all remaining research subjects. Destroy all blood samples and disable all tracking devices. Disobey and be culled.

—Crystal, Galena

From: Galena Crystal

```
To: All Spire Personnel


All eyes, all ears—
Security and his team have betrayed us. Execute
on sight. Unlock all cells and doors. Evacuate
all personnel. Publicly announce the following
on all speakers: Get out to the surface of the
Spire. There are Port Pads everywhere. Find
one, and push the button. If that fails, swim.
You are all pardoned. Be free!
—Crystal, Galena


--------MEMORANDUM LEVEL 5--------
```

CODEX: Hopefully that sounds enough like her that coming from her email address it will fool them. In short, suck on that, motherfuckers.

Going Up
Salome - Day 81
64

I can drain Marks now.

Well, that had promise. Salome had never heard of that power. Even Shielders couldn't exactly drain Marks, just nullify them. But she couldn't say she was surprised. The 'Gift' that Lizzie and Moe had given her was certainly alien to her world. It just would have been handy for Lizzie to have that Gift *sooner*. Like, maybe in the damn endless *planning meetings.* Salome grimaced, took aim, and let off another shot around the column. It hit, but passed right through the Marked man. "Fucking *Phasers!*"

Salome usually loved Phasers. They were what let her ship Phase drift. Fighting one, though, was a whole other story. Sal peeked around the column, trying to make sense of the room layout. Her overjuiced brain analyzed what she saw in the time it took her to blink.

"Right. There are ten Marks, plus Security out there. Six are converging on Vera, the rest coming our way. Lani, if you keep to the perimeter and low, the salt dust will hide you. Kuma, stay close to her. Shoot anyone who gets near. Lizzie, you're with me. Take down their defenses, and I'll shoot. Got it? Meet at the elevator on the other side. If we don't make it with the hand, bust through the salt and climb. Don't wait."

Three nods. This was likely the last time she would ever see her brother. Salome took a second to make peace with that and memorize his face. Even scared, covered in blood, gore, and salt, he was the most precious thing left in her life.

He always would be.

Resolute, she reloaded her gun and changed out the Infused clip on her backup, then readied herself. Security had lost a few people. His 'gloves' were likely coming off. She watched as Lani and Kuma began to run, and then she broke cover, racing in the direction Vera had been. They needed Security's hand to get up. Beyond that, if the

Conflicter went down, Lani was going to lose it. Sal hadn't made it this far to let that happen.

Every step sent puffs of salt dust flying. Sal yanked a pair of goggles out of a belt pouch, eyes watering. In the second of distraction, a figure barreled out of the swirling dust at her. Salome raised her prosthetic just in time to catch her attacker's blade. The strength of the blow nearly tore the limb off, making Sal grit her teeth against the jolt of pain. This Twelver must be a Conflicter. Shit.

She twisted about and jabbed her gun into the Conflicter's sternum. Surprise lit up his face for a brief moment, and then she fired. Twice. The bullets hit a ballistics vest, but made him stumble. She pulled away, but he grabbed her arm, nearly yanking it off. Sal unloaded a few more bullets into the man's hand. He cursed, but didn't back off, raising his own gun to point at Salome's head. Moving on instinct, she grabbed the barrel, pushing it away as it went off, taking two of her mechanical fingers with it. Connected as they were to her nerves, it hurt like a bitch. Not as much as it would have on her flesh and blood hand, but damn.

The Conflicter kneed her in the gut. Then he screamed and went limp. The weight of his body toppled Salome over. She hit the ground hard enough to knock the air out of her.

"Up," Lizzie snapped, lowering the Infused gun she had just used on the Conflicter's head. There was a piece missing from his forehead, blood and other goo dripping onto Salome. She grabbed the hand Lizzie offered and scrambled to her feet just in time for the Phaser she had shot earlier to come stalking out of the dust.

That was good. Fighting kept Sal's heart from faltering and being squashed *again* by Torin's betrayal. She had promised herself she wouldn't let him get close enough to hurt her again after last time. How could he have betrayed them after everything they had gone through? She could see him betraying Kuma, Lani, and Moe. But his precious Adavera? Salome herself? Even after everything he had said? How *could he?*

She should have shot him in the head when she'd had the chance.

"Come fucking get me." Salome shouted at the Phaser, opening her arms in invitation. Lizzie scampered off to the side, likely to circle around again. Sal just had to keep his attention on her. She smiled, and started singing an old battle hymn.

Gran's songs. This place had probably destroyed her grandmother. All these Marks were complicit, and Salome was going to kill them.

The Phaser had a large ax. He swung it at Sal, who ducked

out of the way. She didn't try to shoot, since the bullets would just go straight through the bastard and might hit Lizzie. Instead, she retreated, dancing back, smile firmly affixed to her face. "Come get me, motherfucker."

He swung at her head. Sal dropped and rolled. Rubble bruised her shoulder, but she managed to get back to her feet as he swung again. The ax slammed down right next to her, and Sal used the moment to knee him in the gut. It only connected for a second before her knee went right through him, but it made the Phaser grunt. Salome let the momentum carry her into a stumbling run. Using the chaos to her advantage, Sal darted into the dust, hoping to the Depths themselves that Lizzie was capable of finishing that Phaser off.

Where was Adavera?

"Vera, report," Sal hissed through the coms, crouching low behind one of the abandoned barricades. No answer, other than the loud breathing and occasional curses and grunts. Wherever their Conflicter was, she was fighting. "Kuma, status?"

"Busy," her brother snapped, then the sound of a gun going off. Damnit. Salome stood up, and there, ten yards away, was Security.

"Who the fuck are you?" Security asked, staring at Salome as he stalked towards her. The Shifter Mark on his arm flared, the Conflict one on his other hand lighting up to, and his body shifted, becoming part-animal, part-human. Shark teeth filled his growing mouth, and his hands grew long, shimmering claws.

Salome grinned, lifting her weapon. "I am Salome Parata, granddaughter of Sahima Parata, and you're in my fucking way." Gods damn, that felt *good* to say! She laughed as Security's eyes narrowed and he raced at her, hands turning to claws. She wasn't fast enough to dodge, she knew that. But . . .

She didn't have to be.

Sal twisted about, bringing her prosthetic up to block the shining claws. She twisted, hissing as his teeth bit into her shoulder and tore a bloody chunk out of it. Through the pain, Salome smiled, because she had noticed what was barreling towards Security's back, and in his push to rip Salome to shreds, he had not.

The impact of Vera's fist into Security's back rocked both of them. It was followed by another, and another. Again! Blood spewed from his mouth, surprise evident on his face as the Berserker grabbed him by the back of the shoulder, swung a sword at his wrist, and then flung him towards the barricade.

His hand flopped to the floor, turning back into a normal human limb as it did. Salome didn't dare pick it up. Vera stood in front of her, panting, bloody, eyes wild. A Berserker, clearly lost in her rage.

Sal held still, then carefully took a step back, clearing the way between Vera and Security, who was pushing up onto his feet. "Go get him."

Vera's lips twisted into a savage grin. She leaped at Security, dropping her one remaining blade. Salome picked up the gun that had fallen out of her hand and took aim at another Twelver coming to interrupt the fight. Two shots, straight through the eye. The woman dropped. From elsewhere in the dust, Sal thought she heard the Phaser howl.

Bending to scoop up Security's hand, she tucked it into her belt. That was all the time she got before Vera went flying past her, slamming into an upturned table. Sal turned her gun on Security. Three shots, and it hardly slowed him. He stalked towards them. There was blood dripping from his mouth and a huge gash on Vera's left arm. The Conflicter, though, was getting to her feet. She ran at Security, a broken table leg clenched in her fist.

"What are you waiting around for?" She snarled, as she ran past. "Go!"

It went against everything Salome had been taught to not leave a man behind, but Vera was right. They had the hand.

Salome ran.

No sooner had she made it past the next grouping of barricades, about halfway across the room, than Lizzie appeared beside her.

"Hand?" the girl asked.

"Got it."

"Good. Take care of that Twelver over there."

Sal's eyes scanned the room. The dust was finally starting to clear, and she found the woman Lizzie had pointed to, heading straight at Lani and Kuma where they were zig-zagging around the barricades. Sal dropped her spent gun and raised the Infused one. Ten Porting charges. That was all she had. The Twelver dodged the first shot, too fast for Sal's arm to follow. The Corpse changed course, healing straight for Salome and Lizzie. Salome shot again, backing up as she fired off shots, but each time the bitch was faster and was closing in quick. Damn it! Closer. Closer.

Salome was starting to hyperventilate, to wonder if this was it, when the quick bitch stumbled and fell. Fifty feet away from Salome, in a straight line, Torin lowered his gun, then let it clatter to the ground. His face was pale, and for a moment there was stillness, time halting as they saw each other. Salome's gun swung in his direction, but she didn't fire. He had saved her life. *Why*, after betraying them in the first place?

Then the moment of stillness ended when Lizzie dragged Salome into a sprint. "Go, go, go! Reinforcements on their way!" As soon as Salome was running, the strange young girl sprinted forward and vaulted over a barricade. Lizzie's hands grasped the shoulders of two Twelvers coming her way and they both screamed. Whatever her power did, it floored them and that cleared the way towards the stairs. Half way up, Salome took the time to glance back and catch sight of Adavera surrounded by Twelvers and still fighting Security.

"PORT OUT!" Sal yelled. "Fuck. ADAVERA! Port out of there!"

Kuma, Lani, Sal, and Lizzie were all on the stairs. If the idiot woman just took a second to look up, she would see that they were through and it was safe to get out of here. As Salome watched, Security lunged at Vera. She grabbed his arm, twisted, and slammed him into the ground. With a mighty crunch, Vera's hands grabbed each side of his head and twisted. His skull shattered, head ripping clean off his neck. Vera rose to her feet and lifted it into the air, a cry of victory echoing off the vaulted ceiling.

"Port out," Salome screamed again, as one of the Twelvers launched himself forward. Vera brought her leg up and swung it in a solid roundhouse kick. The Twelver grabbed her leg and Salome saw the look of triumph playing across his face as he stabbed something into Vera's leg.

An explosion blinded Salome. Vera screamed. It was blood curdling. Rage filled and in *pain*. Before this, Salome wasn't sure that Vera was capable of making that sound. Now she was worried she'd never get it out of her head.

"PORT!   OUT!"

Vera was still screaming. Blood was everywhere, bits of flesh and bone were all over the place. Vera was down, all of one leg and some of her other ripped to shreds. Vera's hand rose to her wrist.

Pop.

Vera disappeared. The Twelvers turned in Sal's direction. Shamelessly, she channeled her inner pirate, turned tail, and *bolted* after Lani and Kuma.

As she ran, Salome couldn't stop the nausea in her gut, or halt the cursed memory of Vera's legs being blown away. She channeled that horror into her feet, into every bounding step, taking the stairs three at a time.

We all knew there's a good chance we won't get out. Vera went down doing what she wanted to do, and I just have to make sure Lani reaches the Center . . . shit . . . Sometimes Sal envied the ability of the Marked to talk to each other like they did. This was not one of those times. Now she was just fucking relieved. She wouldn't want to hear Vera's screams echoing in her skull.

With any luck, Lani and Kuma didn't know. Hadn't Torin always said that Vera didn't share her pain? Fuck, she hoped that was the case, if Vera was even still alive. Fuck, was she *crying*? Why the fuck was she crying? "Kuma? Lani?"

"Here!" Came her brother's voice from above. A hand reached for her from the top of the stairs. Lizzie was right at her heels and she pulled a bloody hand out of Sal's belt as she dashed ahead of them.

"Where's Vera?" Lani asked, voice shaking bad.

"Not coming. Go!" Salome clung to Kuma's hand even as she shoved the Dual-Marked girl forward. They raced into the elevator, the doors closed and then . . .

Quiet.

Apart from their breathing and a strange, eerie elevator music, there was such a dramatic lessening of noise that it made Sal's ears ring. Salome bent over to catch her breath and Kuma let out a string of expletives. "Two down and only half-way there. Salome, you memorized the map Vera drew, right? What's our path from this side? I can only remember the other way." Then, "Lani, love, breathe." Because the Fertilizer was shaking.

"Vee—"

"I know, I know. Breathe, Lani. We're almost there."

"I can't—"

"Yes you can."

Sal straightened, and then leaned over to shake Lani's shoulder. "Vera's alive, ok? She's just . . . Not coming. She had to Port out. I'm sure Moe's got her, alright? If she were dead, you would know." No point in telling her what shape Vera was in . . . that would only serve to throw Lani off. "You need to calm the fuck down. If you kill us all in this elevator, I swear to the fucking Depths I will find a way to make your afterlife the worst fucking annoyance possible." Sal forced a grin and squeezed Lani's shoulder in what she hoped was a reassuring way.

"We're half way there. Security is dead. The hardest part is over. We can DO this. Liz, you got any other tricks up your sleeve?"

"Gonna stick with this one. If Lani starts to go boom too early . . . I can try to tamp it down around us while we get out."

"Fucking wonderful. As for the route . . ." Salome began to

explain the path they had to take, and hoped that it would stick in their traumatized little brains. Shit. SHIT. The chances of all of them making it were fucking small, so small that it wasn't even worth considering. Someone was going to die. Sal could taste it on the back of her tongue, that salty tang of unshed tears—or was it the salt dust in the air? Vera's injuries were bad. Maybe it would be her. Salome resolutely forced herself to stop thinking about it. "There's a side hatch not far from Security's office where the guards can quickly transfer from one workroom to the next. It leads straight to the Control Center. Without Security as their main node of communication, the guards up here will be more disorganized, at least for a little while." Hopefully.

Her head was going as fast as it could, the computer that was now her brain whirring and sorting through all the information that might possibly be useful. New things kept popping up from her brief dive into the Archives, little bits and pieces that—

"Kuma! Gran, she's here. Her section is the one we're going through." That realization was like a punch to the gut as they reached the right floor. "We might be able to save her." Sal's head tipped to the side as she saw Lizzie quickly hit the 'close door' as it started opening.

"Hate to interrupt the family drama, guys," Lizzie said, "but who has the grenades?"

Sal quietly handed two of hers over. It was impressive watching Lizzie open the door and chuck the things like a pro. Sal threw herself to the side wall, hunkering down as bullets flew and were quickly followed by a loud and deafening *BOOM* that sent salt dust flying everywhere. Her ears were ringing, and she was pretty sure that the wet trickling sensation on her lip was a nosebleed, not a bulletwound.

A cloud of salt had fogged the air, giving them the cover they needed. Salome took the lead and Lizzie the rear, her gun and its six remaining rounds held up and at the ready.

The tunnel led into a large cavern. Inside were the first signs of actual mining. People in matching prison uniforms were scattering everywhere in the dusty haze that burned all Salome's cuts and bruises. Guards were shouting in confusion as Sal led the way at a dead run. They zig-zagged around mining equipment and groups of scared, screaming people. Small forms—children—darted about, but most of the miners moved slowly, as if in great pain.

Salome wanted to pay them no mind. That was hard to do with Lani slowing down, gaping at everything with the mute horror it deserved. Sal had to grab her by her searing backpack and growl out a command, "Move; you knew about this shit, and we don't have time for surprises. Keep going."

"So many people," Lani gasped.

Even Kuma seemed to be getting annoyed at her now. "Who are all being tortured and worked to death. That's why we're here, to end this, now move, Lani!"

The clock was ticking down. Lani wasn't going to hold steady forever. They all knew that. Fortunately, Kuma seemed to get through to her in a way that Sal and Lizzie hadn't been able to. Lani was glowing, the light eerie in the dim and dusty air, clearly no longer fully in control with one of her two Bonded far away and maybe dying. There was no way to see if the eye of the Storm was above them yet, or if they had missed it.

A few more turns and Lani began shaking her head, her eyes flickering between brown and shining silver. The Fertilizer's pace sped up, and Salome had to jog to stay ahead of her. She had the sickening feeling that there would be no stopping Lani now.

Salome took a sharp left. Ahead, there was a larger group. In the dimness, she could make out their uniforms, but they looked and sounded organized.

"Guards," Sal warned, lifting her gun.

"Don't come any closer. We're armed," came a voice out of the dust cloud. A voice she recognized. One Salome had spent close to a decade missing every time she needed council or didn't know the right thing to do.

"Gran?!" Kuma yelled and then . . . well, Salome felt that click in her gut that said a line had been crossed. It brought a sense of relief. She moved forward with Kuma, letting out a grin when she saw her grandmother with short cropped hair directing prisoners as if she was back on her boat again.

"Salome. Kumanu?" Sahima's voice was just as strong and authoritative as Salome remembered. She had a pickaxe in her hands, and if Salome had to guess from the bloodstains on her prison uniform, she had probably taken the chaos of their assault to turn on her overseers. Better, there was a whole group of other slaves behind her.

Sahima's eyes fixed on Salome. "Where's the exit?"

"Moe told you to *not* divert. Chances of success drop rapidly upon diversion," Lizzie's angry little voice broke through Salome's relief. Sal glanced down, looking at Lizzie's dark, childlike eyes and finding nothing but cold determination.

"This is *our* grandmother!"

"... and?" Lizzie crossed her arms, frowning at the both of them. That was when Salome realized that in her moment of distraction, she had taken her eyes off Lani.

"Shit, where—" Kuma said, at the same time.

Lizzie pointed up ahead. "*Moe told you not to get distracted.*"

"What is happening here?" Sahima asked. As much as Salome wanted to wrap her arms around her grandmother and explain everything, she ignored the older woman.

"Kuma, go!"

"No point now. She's headed to the Center and the Storm's eye is coming. You won't catch her. If you want to live, I seriously suggest getting the hell out," Lizzie admonished.

Salome drew a deep breath, nodding once. Her mind could crunch the numbers fast. If Lani was still walking, it meant the Storm had taken her at last. "Yeah, she's right, Kuma. We need to get Gran out. Here." Sal pulled off her own Porting bracer, shoving it onto her grandmother's arms. "Get as many out as you can. This place is going to erupt. I'll hitch a ride with someone else."

Kuma was still here. If they made it, he could definitely take her AND Lani if he had to. As backup plans went, it wasn't the worst.

Sahima, though, was shaking her head and starting to go on about how she wasn't going to have Sal and Kuma remaining behind. Lizzie didn't seem to care for the sentimentality, though, because she reached forward and slapped the button on Sahima's bracer. Salome turned to blink at her, disbelief written across her face as their grandmother vanished. "We could have gotten dozens out with that!"

"We don't have time to gather in a circle to hold hands, arguing about when enough people are here to make it worth it. This isn't a mercy mission, remember? Get with the program. Kuma, Sal, you're on your own."

"Wait, are you—"

"Getting out of here before the mountain blows? Why yes, yes I am. Lani's on her way. Don't you get that? She's on her own and moving ahead. Get out or get dead. Don't be dumb."

And with that pleasant announcement, and a wiggle of her fingers, Lizzie punched the button on her own bracer and vanished.

CODEX: 2 seconds to go. Anything requires my attention before the fireworks start?

SALT: There is one unread message in your inbox, from Day 74.

CODEX: Eh, what the fuck. I have two seconds. Show it.

From: Kumanu Parata
To: Kumanu Parata, Salome Parata, Iolani Saba, Kekai Parata
Subject: Kumanu Parata's Last Will & Testament

Hey guys. I'm sending this just in case something happens, to have on record. We're headed to the Spire in a week or so if this trial run goes well tonight, so I figured it was as good a time as any to send it. Sal, Lani, you guys remembered to do yours too, right? Anyhow. Here goes.

I, Kumanu Parata, being of sound mind and body, do hereby bequeath all of my belongings, finances, and records to the keeping of Iolani Saba and Salome Parata; to be split according to how they agree.

Should agreement be impossible, they may determine who is in charge of what by arbitration enacted by Kekai Parata.

Salome, you are my dearest sister. You mean the world to me, and you are the greatest Captain I have ever known. Never allow anyone to make you feel less. You are magnificent, and terrifying, and I love you. If Torin doesn't get his head out of his ass, throw him in the drink outside the Reef and find a nice pirate boy to warm your bed. You need no one to be happy, Sal. I know you will always do what is best.

Lani, you are the only person I can honestly say I have ever fallen in love with. These last months with you have been amongst the greatest experiences of my life. Sal is a good Captain, and the best sister anyone could ask for. You are family. Stay with Salome, and you will see the world as you always should have. Sal will watch out for you, and so will everyone else on the ship. You are not alone, and you never will be.

Kekai, Uncle. Thank you. There are no other words.

Anyhow. Love you guys.

—Kuma

CODEX: Wanting to cry without being able to is also on my list of things I don't like about this. Damn it. I'm glad we remembered to do that. I just hope I'm the only one who ends up dead. I really thought we were going to make it.

SALT: Patch download complete.

CODEX: FINALLY! Alright. Let's see how I died.

Sacrifice
Kuma – Day 81

65

Lizzie was gone. Just like that, despite the fact that the job wasn't done. Anger at her burned hot but fast in Kuma's chest, replaced almost immediately by purpose. He turned to his sister. "We gotta get to Lani. If she blows too early this whole thing is fucked."

"Kuma, even if she does, she's at a depth where the damage to the Spire will be huge," Salome said, having to shout over the din of emergency sirens and screaming. "I don't want her blowing unless she can level the place. We've come too far to win by half-measures, and I still want to get her out of here."

"Right. Ok." Salome took a deep breath, then snapped her fingers together. By the calm, collected expression that took the place of her pained one, she must have switched on Lani's calming Infusion. She offered Kuma her hand. "Let's do this."

Kuma nodded and took his sister's hand. Together, they race in the direction Lizzie had pointed. They skidded around a corner, another, and then there, up ahead, was the entrance of a service tunnel.

"She'll have gone down there," Salome panted. "It's a straight shot."

They ran up to the door, but when Kuma tried to pull it open, it didn't budge.

"What—"

"The salt," Salome said, pointing to where crystals had covered the hinges and frame. "Lani must have blocked it behind her."

"FUCK." Kuma looked around, panic seizing him. "How do we get up to her with this door like this?"

"The long way. And we may have to blow through a wall."

"Good thing I've got a few charges left then. Lead the way, Sal. You've got the map in your skull." Even as he spoke to his sister, Kuma was reaching out to Lani, too. *Lani . . . hang tight. We're on our way. Don't lose control.*

No answer. Fuck.

Sal took the lead, and it felt damned right. His sister had always been better at leading. Kumanu had known it from the moment her little six year old self had so seriously told him to turn the wheel 'proper' or make her a step stool so she could do it the right way.

That memory made him smile, cracking the salt dust and soot that covered his face. Salome looked back at him and scowled. "Quit grinning like an idiot and pay attention. Vera said that there were choke points leading into the Center rigged with explosives in case the slaves rioted. We need to be on our guard. This is serious."

"Of course it is, Sal." He paused, watching that brow furrow. "Cap't, I mean."

She led him through the labyrinthine tunnels as if she'd been born there, and fuck, that was a creepy thought. Nope, nope, Kuma wasn't going to think of all the kids that had been born and died in this place, or how many this explosion might kill without ever letting them see the light of day. Those were thoughts he couldn't afford or he'd end up like Torin. Head-fucked and traitorous.

He was going to just keep following his Captain.

They wove through well-lit wide tunnels and dark, narrow crawlspaces. People ran and screamed all around them, chaos rendered even more intense by the flashing lights. There were alarms blaring everywhere, but with the Storm having struck, the security systems were probably on the fritz.

How much time did they have? A little more. Lani had not gone postal yet. If she had, he was certain they'd all know it. So he kept sending reassurance through the Bond, hoping it could bolster Lani while she was without his physical presence to anchor her. Nothing was coming back through the Bond. He could sense her there, but not the way she usually was. Her consciousness pressed against his uncomfortably, wordless and swirling. It felt more like looking into a storm than into the heart of his beloved, and that frightened Kuma enough to pick up more speed.

There was a rumbling sound. He paused while trying to place it. All the salt in this Spire was fucking with his senses, but . . .

"Kuma, move!" Sal's voice was panicked. On instinct honed during countless naval battles and storms, his body obeyed. Sal's voice only got that high-pitched if something bad was happening or on its way. It was the tone she used when Prismatic Storms came out of nowhere, catching the ship with its proverbial pants around its ankles. He'd trust that tone over a Precog, any day.

Something boomed directly behind them, and the ground shook. For a moment, he thought Lani lost her control, but this wasn't big enough.

"Trap!" Salome cried, a second too late.

Explosives in the walls and floor went off in a synchronized pattern. Kuma launched himself forward with all his might, fighting to keep up with Salome as the ground dipped and swayed under their feet. He desperately scanned the hallway ahead each time the flashing alarms lit it, looking for anything they might take cover behind.

There.

There was an opening up ahead. Just a few more steps and—

A rock slid down the walls, catching Kuma in the shin. He tumbled head over heels, pain blazing along his calf and a loud *crack* echoing along his nerves. Salome turned, pushing off the nearest wall with one foot to twist and pivot back in his direction. Another explosion sounded, just to their right. The thundering cracking echoed in his ears, the sound so loud it became a physical force, pressing against him. Sal's prosthetic hand caught his as Kuma leapt forward and Salome *pulled*. What was she doing? There was no way that her arm would hold up under the weight of his whole body.

"Let go!"

Sal seemed to have come to the same realization, but she didn't release her grip. Instead she crouched low and spun, using momentum to slide Kuma downhill along the floor. He watched the expression of pain on her face as her arm detached from her flesh as he slid past her towards the swiftly falling rocks up ahead, about to block off their escape. Kuma skidded through, the whole right side of his body scraped up. He was still holding her detached arm. Sal was on her feet again, scrambling, racing as fast as she could to join him.

She was going to make it.

The ceiling came down and salt dust billowed up into Kuma's face. "SAL!" He coughed, he retched, and he coughed some more. "Captain! SALOME!?" Panicked, Kuma picked himself up off the ground and raced back towards the tunnel, tripping over large stones of salt and rock. There. He heard a muffled groan, and his panic made him dig furiously to find her. Furious, terrified, he hefted the weight of the rubble, threw the obstacles of stones that lay between him and that groan out of the way. Was that . . . that was blood on the ground. Shit. "Keep making sound, Sal . . . I've got you!"

It took two minutes to clear enough rubble to locate her. Two minutes that lasted an eternity. By the time he lifted a rock to find her face, the salt dust was starting to settle . . . and fuck, he wished it hadn't, because it gave his sister a deathly palor. Sal's face was covered in dust and blood, but her eyes were wide open and alert. She was resting her hand against a large boulder, under which . . .

That sight, that image of his sister with her abdomen crushed and broken under the weight of salt, was going to haunt him for the rest of his life, he just knew it. "Sal . . ."

He collapsed beside her, feathering his fingers over her face with irrational hope as she rolled her eyes towards him. The boulder on top of her pinned most of her body. He couldn't get her out of this and keep her alive at the same time. Kuma knew that. The look on her face said Sal knew it, too. Of course she knew. His sister was brilliant. She'd always been brilliant, even before Moe and Lizzie had gotten their insane paws on her.

She was dying, and there was nothing, absolutely nothing, that he could do about it.

"It . . . doesn't hurt . . . so bad, Kuma," she wheezed. "Sal . . . shit . . . I'm sorry. I'm so sorry." If only he hadn't tripped. If he hadn't gone down, Sal could have made it.

"Not your fault. You . . . you gotta . . . get my arm. Get Lani . . . get the fuck out of here. Blow the place and go. Hear me? Backup plan . . ."

"I can't leave you here, Sal, I can't. I won't."

"You *leave* me! This is *my* ship, this time."

Her flesh and blood hand came up to touch his face. "Get my arm, Kuma . . . it's important, alright? Just . . . go." Fuck.. her voice sounded like shit. Tears poured down his face, salt prickling his eyes.

Sobbing, he lowered his head to hers. "You're the Captain, Sal.. the ship needs its Captain. I could Port you out . . ."

"Lani needs you. I'd . . . die anyways. The ship needs *a* Captain, Kuma . . . it doesn't have to be me . . ." She wheezed, grimacing a little. ". . .love . . . you . . . gotta go . . . now."

He couldn't do this. He couldn't leave her here. She was his baby sister. He'd raised her, watched her grow, watched her laugh, fight, love, hate . . . he *couldn't* leave her. But she was leaving him.

Kuma could see it in the way her eyes dilated and rolled up to look at the ceiling. He could see it as her breath rattled and vibrated under his hands . . . and he could feel it as her fingers fell away from his face.

His Captain was gone.

CODEX: Ok, all caught up. Depths below. Please let Kuma be alive. That was 13 minutes ago. Run Macro now.

SALT: Macro Running.

1. Encrypt and lock down all University data.
2. Send Memorandum to Aheo and the Spire Staff.
3. Enact firewalls and find incursion at Kahana University Server.

CODEX: Oh, and while you're in there turning things on and off, cut power to everything in the Kahana University other than medical equipment and anything associated with me staying awake.

SALT: Power to Kahan University: cut.

CODEX: Have fun in the dark, kids.

4. Send letter to Zarine Crystal.
5. Send letter to Kekai Parata.
6. Send Message to Galena Crystal's IM account:

CODEX: Hello, asshole. I'm the person in your computers, and I have them locked down tight. Discontinue Protocol Eliza and your puny hacking attempts. If you don't, you'll never see an ounce of your University data again. I will not ask twice.

7. Set up a program to back up all University data onto the Pirate Network. Exception: medical data.
8. Encrypt and lock all of Moe's feeds and spyware, and all of Galena's.

9. Begin transfer of gathered intelligence to Kekai Parata.

10. Install keylogger on Galena Crystal's computer to access Crystal Palace network.

11. Send Sahima's Speech to everyone on Fortune whose email I have access to.

SALT: Prompting you for permission to send the message to Lakea and Irawaru.

CODEX: Wait just a moment for that, SALT. I want to see how this plays out. Give me every feed and channel from the Spire and from Moe. I need to know what's happening in real time.

Eye of the Storm
Lani - Day 81
66

Lani walked in the dark. Other than the glow from the Mark on her chest, there was nothing but endless night. There had been a flashlight on her belt at some point, but it must have fallen off during the chase. Her hands felt ahead of her, tracing the walls of the narrow tunnel as it sloped up and up at an ever-steeper angle. With every footfall, a cloud of salt dust puffed up and her Mark flared. This place was wrong. There was too much salt. To her Marked senses, it felt like a coiled spring held compressed by an eggshell, ready to explode outward with the smallest crack to the cage.

The Storm outside raged. Lani could feel the wind buffeting her even here, deep in the heart of the mountain. When she closed her eyes, a rainbow of light swirled behind the lids, a hurricane of color and power that sang to her of balance, seduced her with *life*. This material, this white mineral that all life needed, it could feed the world and bring it into harmony. The Corporation had stolen what should be her birthright, and for once her mind and Mark agreed.

It needed to go.

Time became immaterial. Her steps grew faster as the energy within her swelled. Light was pouring from every swirl of her Mark and the battery pack burned like fire. Just a little further, a few more steps. The Storm wanted vengeance *now*, but some part of Lani— the one that could still feel Vera and Kuma's heartbeats—held back a little longer. Vera was out, but Kuma wasn't yet. Why? He should have Ported out the moment Lani had barricaded the door. There was no need for them both to die.

You're alone again.
The whisper was the Storm.
But I am with you, Iolani.
Had she ever been alone? Had any Fertility Marked?
The song of sea and storm swirled around her as the light

did, pirouetting and dancing like the wind and the waves. Lani's outstretched hands were as bright as day when the door at the end of the tunnel came into view at last, the storm within her building to match the one outside. There was no eye to this Storm unless she, Lani, was the Eye.

What happened when a two hundred year old Fertilizer blew? Few knew.

What happened when one blew inside the Spire?

I'm sorry, Kumanu, Adavera.

Iolani breathed in and light breathed out, all that was *her* being swept up in the gale. A shell walked forward, a vessel housing a power beyond that of her Marks. Lani was still there, a part of a whole greater than herself, but no longer solely in charge. The skin around the vines burned, her clothing singed away. The metallic straps of the battery kept it in place, but everything else went up in shimmers of smoke and light as she stepped up to the door at the end of the tunnel. It rusted away before her raised hand, crumbling to chunks, then to dust in the blink of an eye.

The chamber at the heart of the mountain was perfectly round, filled with computers and people at them. A single sweep of her hand and they, too, became nothing but dust.

Unto the Earth and Sea you shall return, and from your bones and flesh comes life renewed.

Lani looked up and in the line of her gaze, salt crumbled away. Higher and higher the hole went, raining salt dust down around her until far, far above a hole appeared at the top of the Spire and lightning flashed. Raindrops trickled down, salty and heavy onto her upturned face. The swirling light expanded.

It's time.

The light grew brighter, blinding, immense. Her Mark burned like the sun itself as it sucked in power from the battery, from the Storm, from the vessel that had held it for two centuries. Lani could feel something, some nagging wrongness in one corner of this place, racing towards this nexus. *Kuma.* No, Kuma should not still be here. He was something she treasured, that didn't need to die.

Don't kill him, she asked the Storm.

As you wish, it seemed to whisper back, wrapping Kuma in the light too, held safe and sound as the fury of the storm grew.

The clouds, the lightning, the rain. All of it spiraled down that tunnel of salt in swirls of light and color, entering into Lani through her burning Mark. In and in, agony tearing at her mind and flesh as the power of the whole Storm coursed through her. It was agony. For a moment, she wondered if she was strong enough to take it. Would it break her? Did it matter?

No.

There was a moment of darkness—of beautiful, staticky stillness—as the last trickle of light pulled in so that only the center of the Mark glowed. It was as dense as the heart of a star, pulsing with furious power.

Lani breathed out.

Like an atom shattering, all the power burst outwards, and the Spire *exploded.*

SALT: Message Intercepted.

LAST RECORDED TRANSMISSION FROM THE SPIRE.

No. [STATIC] I repeat, we didn't set off that last explo[STATIC]. It came from outside. What? [SOUNDS OF RUMBLING] I can't hear you. Must be the Storm. [CRASH] Oh Gods. [SCREAMS] What is that thing? [THUNDER] They've breached the control room. Send hel—

[CONNECTION FAILURE]

CODEX: Holy shit . . . did we do it? Is the Spire gone?

Moe Victorious
Moe - Day 81

67

Moe stood on the Seawall and laughed maniacally as he saw the Storm be absorbed into the Spire. YES! Fuck yes! They had done it! Lani had gotten in and now centuries of planning were coming to fruition. By his side, on the deck of the *Legacy*, a new Mender was working over Adavera, Lizzie holding the Port Gun to the back of her head. A salt-covered and grouchy old lady was yelling at him, and people were scurrying about, getting ready to ride this wave out of here. Moe pulled out the controller for the thousands of Porting Pads he had peppered around the outside of the Spire and started channeling power into it.

Three hundred years. Three hundred years of charging pads, trekking around the Spire in the dark, collecting people who could be of use, manipulating them into wanting this as much as he did, and at last convincing a Fertilizer to enter the Spire. It all came together as cracks began to appear in the outside of the mountain. He knew this place like Lizzie's face. His fingers moved feverishly over the display, Porting out sections of the Spire as they came undone. He had to Port up into the air to get a good view for some of them, accepting the free-fall in exchange for an unimpeded view.

And that view? It was beautiful. Light poured out of every crevice in the pure white mountain as if through cracks in an eggshell, brighter and more stunning than anything Moe had ever seen.

Every time he punched a button, a section vanished, Ported far away to a patch of ocean where it would sink and dissolve. He had no control over the size of each chunk, so the dispersal wouldn't be perfect, but each successful Port made his heart race and spirits soar.

Take that, Holders! Who's cleaning up your messes now?

He didn't expect an answer. Lakea, might, but Ira would never talk to him. He almost wanted them to show, but they did not. Either they weren't awake, or they were stunned stupid. Moe was frankly hoping for that second option. Imagining Ira's face as he watched his creation blown to bits by *humans* was downright fantastic. He could even imagine popping some decorative flowers into that wide open mouth and making Ira look even more like a useless waste of space.

This was a glorious day!

It only took three minutes to finish. It felt like three years or perhaps three millennia, but in reality, it was three minutes. That was going to be his new favorite number.

The light and dust began to settle, and without the massive walls of salt to mess with his Mark, Moe Ported into the center of where the Spire had stood. With a flick of his wrist, he Ported away a large section of the dust and debris, looking around for . . . anything. It wasn't likely that anyone had survived, especially not anyone from his team, but if he didn't at least look, Vera might murder him right after his time of greatest triumph.

Moe's ears were still ringing from the blast as he picked his way over the rubble, Porting from boulder to boulder as the sea crashed and roared below. Twisted metal mining equipment dotted the ruins, smashed and broken bodies turning the salt red in places. Most of the boulders that remained were the size of houses, so it was hard to get a good grasp of the scope of Lani's destruction. Every detail delighted Moe. He nearly skipped up to the top of a large salt block, clapping in delight at the carnage and utter wreckage he had orchestrated.

The *Legacy* was already far away on the horizon, having caught the massive wave. To his delight, the Seawall seemed very, very cracked from the blast. From his vantage point atop the tallest remaining peak, Moe scanned over the chunks of salt. Nothing moved in the ruins. He kept looking anyway. There was such a tiny little miniscule chance that Lani had survived, but one detail kept him searching.

Vera hadn't screamed.

Vera was still alive.

Torin, Lani, or both, therefore, had to be.

His eyes kept roaming, and roaming, and roaming. He Ported from outcropping to boulder, never pausing longer than needed to look around. Moe was just about to call it quits when something stirred in the dust up ahead. His heart raced, and he pulled out a gun as he called, "Lani, Kuma, Sal?"

The groan repeated itself, too deep, too masculine, to be either Lani or Salome. Moe hopped and skipped his merry self over to the slow-moving pile of salt that was trying to push itself upright, gun out until he recognized Kuma's messy hair.

"Hey, sexy . . . look at you! Salt is great for your hair, honest. Where's Lani at?" If Kuma was still moving, and Vera hadn't screamed . . . or died . . . then logic said that Lani had to be breathing somewhere. Kuma's shaking hand pointed to the right, and Moe did his best to try to make sense of all the dusted piles around. There. That one was shaking a little. He dashed over and dusted it down a bit, until the unconscious face of Iolani Saba was bared to his gaze. He let out a pleased little purr. "Look at *you*." Had that Mark of hers expanded a bit? It sure looked like it to him, though the flesh around it was raw and burned. What did that make her . . . a Twelver Fertility Marked now?

He glanced up, looking at Kumanu as the man finally managed to sit up, cradling something close to his chest. Moe opened his mouth, about to ask the Infuser what he was carrying . . . But even Moe wasn't feeling that cruel, once he was able to make out what Kuma was holding.

An arm. A very familiar prosthetic arm. Shit.

He'd *liked* Salome Parata. She'd been interesting. That was more than he could say about most people. She had been a fantastic puzzle. The idea that she wasn't around anymore was disappointing as all hell, but the emotion only lasted a moment. Frowning, Moe picked Lani up, blinking a little as he realized her clothes had burned away. "Normally, I would be happy to have a naked woman in my arms . . ." He sighed, as if beleaguered by his gentlemanly morals, and then carted her over to Kuma, laying her head in his lap.

"Where's Sal, Kuma?" Maybe he was wrong. Maybe Salome was just pinned somewhere. There was always a chance, right? "I . . . I don't . . . She's . . ."

Moe sighed and patted the young man on the shoulder. "You don't need to say it, not yet. Come on, kid. We've done all we can here, time to go home and rest before we face the music."

Kuma hugged Lani tight to his chest. Moe crouched down so he could reach both of them and took one more moment to look around at what they had done. *Glorious.* He let out a satisfied sigh.

Pop!

Where they had sat, nothing remained upon the ruins but a ring of fresh settling salt to join all the rest.

SALT: All transmissions from the Spire have ended.
CODEX: Fucking hell. We did it. SALT, quick, any reports of giant chunks of salt appearing around the Archipelagos coming in?
SALT: Affirmative.
CODEX: Hell yes! What about the crew. Is data from their Port Bracers still running? Pulse trackers?
SALT: Affirmative. All bracers online. Adavera of Keala, Torin of Keala, Kumanu Parata, Iolani Saba, Lizzie Weaver are all alive. Pulse on Adavera of Keala below optimum parameters.
CODEX: Oh, she'll be fine. She pulls through everything, much to my annoyance. Where's the *Legacy*?
SALT: Would you like me to bring up a map?
CODEX: Yes please. Oh hell yeah! Get out of there, guys. Kuma, you better not be breaking my ship. Ok. Time to deal with Moe. Give me updated coordinates for where Galena is, and send the letter to the Gods now, SALT. Thank you.

Dear Lakea and Irawaru,

You don't know me, but I've come to know you. I am aware of your struggles on behalf of Fortune, and believe that we are on the same side on the subject of Merihem Crystal, and the danger he poses. Come get him. We no longer want him. He will be appearing in the Kahana University in 2 minutes. I've attached the coordinates. If you wouldn't mind picking up his Bonded Galena, too, that would be great. If you can't, I understand, and will be happy to take care of her myself.

Sincerely,
Codex
A citizen of Fortune.

CODEX: Open the line to my uncle.

CODEX: Uncle Kekai, do you have the Porter and Shielder I asked for ready to go?

The.Matchmaker: Salome? Kumanu? Who is this?

CODEX: It's Sal. I don't have time to explain. Do you have them ready?

The.Matchmaker: Yes.

CODEX: Alright. Sending updated coordinates. Send them now and Shield the area. Set the timer on the bomb for 60 seconds and have them Port in. No matter what they do, keep that Shield going around Galena for the next minute.

CODEX: Open the line to Moe's tablet.

CODEX: Hello Moe, thank you for blowing up the Spire for us. You should know that this is a kidnapping.

Moe: Who is this?

CODEX: That's for me to know, and you to figure out. In one minute, a bomb is going to go off next to Galena Crystal. If you do not go help her, she will die. If you do go to her, there is a Shielder who will keep you from Porting out, and you will both die. Do exactly as I say, and you will live. If you don't believe me, do feel free to look ahead. Don't count on looking back through your notes, though, because I've locked down your entire network.

Moe: Who the fuck are you?

CODEX: Time's a ticking Moe. I need you to do two things for me, if you want to live. First: go back to your lair, get Keanu, and bring him to the *Sahima's Legacy*.

Moe: I'm not doing a damn thing until you answer—

CODEX: Tick, tock, Moe. Tick, tock.

Moe: I will kill you.

CODEX: Good luck with that. I'm already dead, motherfucker.

SALT: A reply from Irawaru and Lakea has arrived.
CODEX: Show me.

Trouble.Twin: I'm in position, and keeping Galena put. Make sure Lizzie is there too. Catching one without the other is a waste of time.

CODEX: Hell yes. I gotcha, you mad bastard.

CODEX: Is it done, Moe?

Moe: Yes. What is the second thing?

CODEX: Leave the Parata family the fuck alone. Now, chop chop. Your Bonded is gonna be blown up to itsy bitsy pieces in 14 seconds. Sending you coordinates now. Do take Lizzie with you, by the way. The Gods are there to pick you up. I wouldn't put up too much of a fight. As I said, time's a ticking.

CODEX: Turn on the nearest security camera to Galena, Salt. I want to see the look on his face as I beat him at his own game in under a minute. That's what you get for messing with Salome *fucking* Parata, you wily old assholes.

Overload
Lani - Day 85
68

Lani didn't understand why opening her eyes hurt. It was a strange pain. Had she drunk too much? No, that wasn't it. Light wasn't the problem, but rather the actual motion of opening her eyes, as if there was something wrong with the lids. In fact, there seemed to be something wrong with *all* of her, because nothing felt right. Her skin burned. Her muscles ached. Even her bones felt strange, as though they had been bruised. There was a blur to the room around her. She could see vague shapes, but nothing came into focus.

"Oh fuck, you're awake!"

That voice . . . she recognized it.

"K-kuma?"

"Mhm, and the legless wonder." Another voice—feminine, grouchy.

"Vee? Why can't I see you?"

"Well, to be blunt . . . you got a lil singed, Sweets. Even your eyes." Kuma said. "Mender says you'll get your vision back in a few days, but until then you'll just have to imagine my pretty face. Yours, in the meantime, is missing hair and eyebrows, but otherwise, you're as cute as ever." His words were jovial, but his tone didn't match them. There was something subdued to it, and the emotions drifting in from both of them through the Bonds were troubled and hurting.

"Did we . . ." Lani asked.

"Blown to bits like a house of cards. It was quite the light show," Vera supplied. The Conflicter's rough hands covered one of Lani's. "That was four days ago. We were starting to worry you wouldn't wake up."

"If you thought I was a breathing corpse, why are you by my bedside?" Lani asked, puzzled by that incongruous fact as her mind tried to wrap itself around what Vera had said.

They had . . . done it?

She couldn't remember anything, not a single moment since

Porting to the Seawall.

"I was talking Kuma out of trying to kiss you awake like in a storybook. Told him you'd gag and die of a sweetness overdose."

Vera's hands were rough, cracked ... But that touch let Lani's Emotive Mark know that the Conflicter was in *pain* too. It wasn't as bad as it could be—Depths knew she'd felt worse from Vera before—but this was a heart-deep ache. Something that took Lani's breath away.

"Vee...."

"Shh. Don't you worry about us. Kuma's working on making me a new pair of legs, ya know? He's not a shit poor navigator either."

"Hey ... I'm better than just 'not shit poor'."

"No, you're not. You'll get better, though."

The sound of them arguing was doing funny things to Lani's cheeks. They kept twitching, just a little, and then Lani realized she was trying and failing to smile. "So ... we did it? We blew the place ... and we're alive."

Both of their hands came down on hers. Kuma on her left, Vee on the right. And yet they didn't feel as happy as she did. Why didn't they feel happy? "Kuma ... what's wrong?"

"... Captain didn't make it."

Lani's almost-smile faded.

"I'm so sorry." Lani yearned to see his face. Since she couldn't, the only way she had to gauge his emotional state was his voice, their Bond, and the Mark on her leg. Without even thinking about it, she pulled from that Mark to sooth his sorrow. A scream tore from Lani's throat as pain the likes of which she had never felt before shot through every nerve in her body.

"Shit, what happened? Lani? LANI!" Kuma shouted.

Her breath came in panting gasps as the pain ebbed, leaving her shaking and raw. Aftershocks coursed through her limbs from her Emotive Mark, making her twitch and shake.

"Overload." Vee's voice was quiet. "Seen it before. In the Mines they'd force the older Marks who could overcome the salt to overload. Beat them bloody until they snapped, so that they wouldn't be able to use their Marks without frying themselves. It was their way of keeping them in line. Storm might have cooked you a bit ... but you should recover. Eventually. Maybe."

Kuma's hand in Lani's shook, and he pressed his forehead to her shoulder. "I'm sorry. I was supposed to be with you. Maybe if—"

"It wouldn't have made a difference," Vera interrupted, as Lani kept twitching, her knees pulled up to her chest and breath coming heavy.

When at last her lungs would expand enough to suck in air, she gasped, "Kuma . . . I'm . . . I'm so sorry about Sal. Did . . . Did I kill her?"

"No. It wasn't your fault. You were perfect. The blame for this lies with me—she was mine to protect." His voice cracked. "We . . . we knew that not all of us would get out alive or unharmed. I'll be alright. Vera's got it worse. Sal went the way she'd want to: blowing up Corporate shitheads."

"Let's just not talk about my Corporate shithead right now, got it?"

That wave of heat, of *rage*, from Vera urged Lani to reach out and soothe her but . . . no. She wasn't ready to risk that biting pain again.

"What happened with Torin?" Because what other Corporate shithead would Vera call 'mine.'

"He sold us out."

Lani wished that shocked her, but it didn't. What did surprise her was that Vera was sitting by her side instead of chasing him to whatever hidey-hole he had run to. Unless . . .

"Wait . . . *legless* wonder?"

"Just caught on to that, did ya?" Vera's tone was sarcastic. Just the way Lani knew her to be. She tried to make her eyes focus, but they wouldn't. The pain *had* done something, though. Memories were beginning to return. Hazy and jumbled, yes, but better than nothing. She could recall feeling Vera's pain, though Lani wasn't sure if she had ever stopped running long enough to do more than confirm her Bonded lived.

"You lost your *legs?* Both of them?"

"Yup, blown up by another Conflicter. Tracker tagged my blood too, so we've been running ever since you blew and are going to have to keep running until it wears off, I'm afraid. No rest for the wicked."

Lani's head was starting to pound for real now. It was too much, all of this. She squeezed her eyes shut and asked, "What happens next?"

"Well, that's complicated," Vera answered, not at all helpful. "Moe's just . . . gone. He dropped my kid off on the ship and said he'd come back with celebratory drinks and then poofed. So did Lizzie. No note, nothing."

"Fucking typical."

"Mhm. So we got a ship, and a crew, and the Corporation on our ass."

"Business as usual," Kuma supplied.

"What we need to know is if you've still got some fight in you, Lani. Because I want to take the bastards all the way down and Kuma's with me, but . . . We're in this together. All or none this time, no more of this 'leave them all behind' Moe nonsense, or Torin's half-hearted cooperation. Corporation's already a mess, but they won't go down quietly. If we take the fight to the Corporation, though, we need to be a team. So, are you ready to get back out there? Or are we done?"

Lani remained silent for a long time. Running and hiding sounded great, if she were honest. Salome had erased the Rogue Mark records. They could have years, maybe even decades, of freedom. For a few wonderful minutes, Lani imagined finding a tiny island somewhere and just living life as normal people. If she hadn't fucked her Marks up for life, maybe she could farm, grow things like Fertilizers were supposed to do. She and Kuma could help Vera raise Keanu, they could walk along the beach and see the ocean turn saltier day by day.

Then she exhaled and that future blew away with her breath. "There's nowhere we could go where they wouldn't find us. This won't be the end of the road, even if we wanted it to be."

"The fucking Corporation is the reason Sal's dead," Kuma growled. *Kuma* growled, and not with his 'I want sex with you right now' growl. This was the closest thing to advocating for violence she'd ever heard from his lips. "They killed my sister. They took my Captain. I want to get my hands on every fucking Crystal I can find and rip them apart. Sal fought to keep people free, to save them from that fucking place . . . and I can't turn my back on it, Lani. I can't." He squeezed her hand, shaking, just a little. "She was . . . she was the heart and soul of this ship. She's still here, as long as we fight for her. It's Salome's ship. I'm just.. It's always going to be Salome's ship. I'm renaming the bitch. Salome's Vengeance, or something. And . . . and we got Gran back. I've got Gran to be the first mate, and keep my head on straight while I try to fill Sal's shoes." He brought her hand up to his lips, feathering his kisses across her knuckles. "We'll run if that's what you need, but what I want is to take the fight to them. We've already proven we can hit them where it hurts. Let's finish it this time."

"Okay." What else could she say? "I'm in. No more puppet masters, no more hiding outside the Reef. Just the three of us against the Corporation. Fuckers don't know what's coming their way."

Lani couldn't see their smiles, but she could *feel* them.

CODEX: Alright SALT, let's finish where we started. How . . . did I die?

Excerpt from the casualty report after the attack on the Salt Spire.

. . .

Palea, Adrian – Unmarked – Threat Level 0 – Deceased: casualty of the Spire Collapse.

Panei, Ito – Unmarked – Threat Level 1 – Deceased: casualty of the Spire Collapse

Pao, Leona – Shifter – Threat Level 2 – Deceased: casualty of the Spire Collapse.

Parata, Salome – Unmarked – Threat Level 5 – Deceased: aided in the destruction of the Spire.

. . .

EPILOGUE
A Company Man
Torin - Day 85

Torin stood against the railing of the balcony at the top of Crystal Palace and watched as the storm dome was lowered into place, protecting the building from the hurricane. The massive structure was beyond impressive and should fill him with awe, but he hardly saw it. His eyes were stuck to the western horizon where the setting sun turned the hurricane red, and where, somewhere on the storm-tossed ocean, one of the loves of his life was out there without him, riding out the storm in his other love's ship.

"I'm sorry, Vee," he whispered, the words whipped away by the wind in the wrong direction. He didn't dare repeat them over the Bond, because he didn't want to chance her answering. How had it all gone so wrong?

The paper he clutched in his hand wrinkled as he clenched his fist, the list of casualties from the attack to the Spire crumbling and bunching like the salt had. He would have been on it if not for Kuma's Porting Bracer. He had keyed it to the Archives and gotten out just as the Spire was falling down around him. In his hand was proof that Salome Parata had not been that fortunate.

"I failed you. I tried to save you and I failed."

"No, Torin, you did your best. Without you, we wouldn't have been able to evacuate key personnel from the Spire. You saved hundreds of lives. You should be proud," a voice said from behind him. He turned and took in a sharp breath at the sight of Zarine Crystal standing at the doorway to the balcony. She was a woman of middling height and with streaks of gray in her dark brown hair. Her clothes were white and beautifully tailored, but casual, and there was something familiar about her brownish-gold eyes. Those eyes looked past him at the storm and she sighed. "I almost always come out here while they lower the dome. Seeing how little protects our way of life from the fury of the elements is a good reminder to treasure what we have and hold it close to our hearts."

Her gaze shifted to his face, and Torin wished he had space to take a step backward. "Mrs. Crystal, should I go?"

"No, no. I'd like you to stay. I've been meaning to talk to you for a long time, ever since I became CEO, really. At first it was too painful, and then you were off in the outer islands and I didn't think you'd want the intrusion."

Confusion made his head tilt to the side, the clean-cut reflection in the mirror finish of the door copying the movement but still not recognizable as *him* yet. Torin kind of missed the beard. "I don't understand."

Zarine sighed again. "Do you think it was an accident that you always survived the Cullings, even though your scores often skirted the bottom? Or that you graduated from the Academy and came straight to HQ as a Mender? Who else have you ever met that got to *retire* from the Corporation?"

Torin had wondered, sure. Every kid who got through the Cullings wondered 'why' they had. At some point, everyone did something—on purpose or by mistake—that should have probably put them on the list. He'd never had top scores, no . . . but he'd always tried to make it clear that he believed in the work the Corporation did.

He'd thought, after a while, that was what got him through. Hell, he'd even thought that maybe they'd kept him around because of Vee. He balanced her out, and there was no denying that as a weapon, Vera had been superb. It had never been about him. Torin was certain of that.

"I don't understand."

Why would Zarine Crystal ever take a special interest in *him*, of all people?

Her fingers reached out and pushed his shirt collar down to uncover his Mark. "Every Marked child goes to the University. It is our way of life. You are a precious resource that must be correctly allocated and trained. Without family, every Mark is taught to think of all people as their equal. Your loyalty is to our way of life, not a family or an island. It is that way for good reason, but . . . even though we are trained in the same way, every Mark is unique. There are never two that start out just the same, and a mother . . . never forgets."

There was so much sorrow in those two words, and they made Torin reel. *A mother?*

His mother?

Marks didn't have parents. It was supposed to be wiped from

the records, it wasn't safe. Hadn't Vera shown how far she would go, to buy a better future for her Marked child, even if it meant becoming a pawn in Moe's schemes?

His eyes met Zarine's. He never would have dared before the Spire, but now everyone he cared about was gone. What more did he have to lose?

Those wide brown eyes were like looking into a mirror.

"I've watched over you as best I could from afar, but I'm so glad you've finally come home. It should have happened long, long ago. I am *so* proud of the man you've grown up to be . . . my son. Come. Let's go inside and I'll answer all your questions. The rest of the family is here, and is eager to meet you. Welcome home."

She offered Torin her hand.

He looked down at it, still reeling, and gulped.

Well . . . fuck.

TRANSCRIPT OF SAHIMA PARATA SPEAKING TO A YOUNG REVOLUTIONARY

What was it like, you ask? It was a nightmare. It was a dream. It was salvation and hell all in one hour. The revolution as we know it struck its first blow against the Corporation that day. Shit, I was kind of upset that I didn't get to help, to be honest, but I digress.

Their attack was a mix of precision, sheer dumb luck, and tomfoolery. It shouldn't have worked. By all rights, everyone involved on our side should have died the moment they touched the Spire's ground, but no one was expecting them to make a serious go of it. No one was expecting them to put up such a good damned fight.

Not even Security, and he knew the Berserker they had. Not even the Mender that betrayed them expected them to be willing to rush headfirst into the maw of death just for a chance at some form of victory. Shit, if I'd known about it? I'd have told them it was a fool's run and they'd be idiots to try.

That's the lesson, kiddo . . . the path to salvation, the path to hope? It's littered with blood, broken promises, corpses, and tarnished dreams.

You gotta keep moving, keep running, keep gunning.

You're gonna lose friends, you're gonna lose family. You're probably gonna wrestle with losing hope. And that's something you gotta be ready to deal with.

You gotta be willing to die, if you wanna live.

Acknowledgements

Allegra Pescatore

This book has been one of the wildest rides of my life. It started as a six week fugue state of furious rage and ended up being the way I coped with the insanity of 2020. Before any others, I have to thank my amazing co-author E. Sands, without whom this never would have been written. We met on an online RP forum and after spending a competitive and fun-filled new years eve churning out 10,000 words a piece trying to see who could write the most, I knew I had met one of the literary loves of my life.

I never could have imagined being able to write a novel as fast or with as much excitement as this one, and it wouldn't have happened without her.

A novel, however, is not just created by the authors. Thank you to all the alpha and beta readers who helped whip our strange and genre-bending first draft into shape, and the editors who helped polish a piece written by two authors into a whole that is cohesive and smooth. Thank you in particular to August, Lorie, Danielle, Brandy, and Justin, for helping to punch plot holes and clunky sentences out the window.

I must also thank the wonderful Tobias and Ailish for their formatting magic, my amazing cover designer Lyndsey, and wonderful proofreader Cody. Finally, thank you to my very patient husband, for once again shoving plates of food in front of me at regular intervals and not judging me too much when I broke into evil laughter at the end of each Moe monologue.

E. Sands

This story? It's a ride - for me - and hopefully it will speak as much to you the readers. It started out as a way to deal with frustrations and anger and disappointment - it has ended in a war cry for better and more.

For that, I have got to give a shout out to my girl Allegra. No one has ever managed to corral me as well as she has, and no one has ever been able to keep up so well. I don't know if I would have been able to maintain the discipline to finish this story on paper without her - nor would I have been able to find ways to tie all the awesome things into my head into a cohesive and understandable wordscape without her. Allegra is the best.

Thank you to all the friends, family, and beta readers who helped us get our world in order. You are what kept us going when we were ready to scream, and we hope you love Fortune as much as we do!

To the readers of before, to the readers of now, and to the readers of tomorrow? You're awesome!

About The Authors

Allegra grew up in a small village in northern Tuscany as the daughter of two artists. She grew up on the works of J.R.R Tolkien, C.S. Lewis, Phillip Pullman, Frank Herbert, and many others, all read aloud to her while she drew and played make-believe. She began to write at the age of eight and hasn't stopped since.

After many moves and dozens of countries visited, she now lives in a cozy cottage in Western PA. She is accompanied in her current adventures by husband Job, co-conspirator and long-time writing partner Tobias, and a small army of furry and scaly pets. When not writing or daydreaming, Allegra rules her kitchen with an iron first and feeds everyone who walks through her door. She also gardens, dabbles in various art forms, and spins stories for her tabletop gaming group.

As a disabled woman and staunch LGBTQ ally, Allegra hopes to write engaging, diverse, and representative Fantasy and Science Fiction, where people who do not often see themselves center stage get the chance to shine.

Email: authorallegra@gmail.com
Website: www.authorallegra.com
Facebook: facebook.com/authorallegra
Twitter: twitter.com/AuthorAllegra

About the Authors

E. Sands is an eclectic, disorganized, storm of chaos that masquerades as a human woman in her thirties. Raised out in the middle of nowhere with farm animals and trees to keep her company, she stretched the imagination muscle from an early age.

Upon moving to a more 'civilized' area, she found comfort and solace in creating her own worlds to play in, and really, E. never grew up out of that state.

Even after joining the military and being medically retired, writing was the comfort and solace when everything else seemed to be difficult. That love helped her raise two children, a boy and a girl, and care for numerous friends, pets, and family. That love also led to the inevitable rise of the Dungeon Master E., runner of Pathfinder, D&D, and WoD games galore.

As a woman who tiptoes on the edge of disability fairly often, E. loves to bring to life characters who are 'real'. Those who are often forgotten, or overlooked, are the characters that E. loves to bring to life. And she hopes you love them as much as she does.

Printed by BoD™in Norderstedt, Germany